ALASKAN FIRE

GUARDIANS OF THE FIRST REALM:

ALASKAN FIRE

SARA KING

Published by
Parasite Publications

ISBN: 1942929021
ISBN-13: 9781942929024

TITLES FROM SARA KING

Guardians of the First Realm: Alaskan Fire
Guardians of the First Realm: Alaskan Fury

Millennium Potion: Wings of Retribution

Outer Bounds: Fortune's Rising

Terms of Mercy: To the Princess Bound

The Legend of ZERO: Forging Zero
The Legend of ZERO: Zero Recall
The Legend of ZERO: Zero's Return

UPCOMING TITLES

Guardians of the First Realm: Alaskan Fate
Guardians of the First Realm: Alaskan Fang
Guardians of the First Realm: Alaskan Fiend

Terms of Mercy: Slave of the Dragon Lord

Outer Bounds: Fortune's Folly
Outer Bounds: Children of Fortune

The Legend of ZERO: Zero's Legacy
The Legend of ZERO: Forgotten

DISCLAIMER

All events and characters described in this book are fictional representations of one kinky author's imagination, and any resemblance to real people or events is purely happenstance. While Alaska is a really big place, it's also a *real* place, and the author has real experience with it. The locations herein were kept as vague as possible, and in some cases, names have been changed. While there is a Yentna River, an Anchorage, a Wasilla, and a Willow, there is no Lake Ebony, no Ebony Creek, and no Sleeping Lady Lodge on the Yentna River. So yeah. If you're looking for werewolves, good luck finding them.

DEDICATION

For my sister, who pestered, cajoled, whined, and threatened me for years to write an Alaskan Paranormal.

For Renae, arguably my oldest, biggest fan. May you someday get your Sleeping Lady.

And for Stephen, because your epic enthusiasm and exacting, nit-picky standards matched even my own.

TABLE OF CONTENTS

ONE

Meet Jack

"So I guess Candy told you my brother called in a favor 'cause he's blowing chunks?" Blaze's 'replacement' pilot was striding over to her from the brand new Mercedes he had parked with a gravel-slinging spin into the Bruce Rogers' Flying Service driveway not a minute before.

Blaze, who hadn't really thought about what a Bush pilot *should* look like, was now finding herself very concerned. The skinny kid approaching her was dressed in ragged cut-off shorts, a skateboarding Bart Simpson T-shirt, sandals, and sunglasses. He looked for all the world like an out-of-state transfer student Blaze might have shared a class with in Business 101, not at all like the plaid-and-jeans-clad Bush pilot, Bruce Rogers, who was *supposed* to be flying her and the rest of her worldly possessions out to her new life in the Sleeping Lady Lodge.

"You're Lance?" she asked, trying not to wince as she attempted to calculate how old the kid was. He barely looked past eighteen. And, now that she got a good look, his hair was still wet from a shower.

"Yep." He spun the keys of his Mercedes on a finger and stuffed them into the pocket of his pants. Holding out his hand and peering up at her, he said, "You Blaze?"

"Yeah, Blaze," she said, taking it.

"You're tall, Blaze," he said, still peering up at her. "You got a little Viking in your family, then?" As if she hadn't heard *that* a million times already in her life.

"Six-four," she agreed, forcing a smile. "You know how to fly one of these things?" She gestured at the floatplane that was secured to the dock beside her.

"Oh sure," Lance Rogers said, peeling off his sunglasses and glancing at the Cessna 206, which was approximately the size of a sardine can. "Been in those things since I was a kid. Did my first solo at twelve, much to the consternation of my dad." He grinned at her, showing a perfect white smile, even further removing him from the 'Experienced Bush Pilot' column in Blaze's head. "Didn't fly again until I was sixteen, after that. Dad started locking the keys in his safe." Rubbing the little blue airplane beside him like an old friend, Lance said with a note of wistful regret, "Never did figure out how to hotwire 'em."

"Uhhh," Blaze said, glancing quickly back at the weather-worn wooden sign of Bruce Rogers' Flying Service, and the little hut beside the aircraft hangar where Candy, Bruce's wife, was working on paperwork. "I don't know, I can probably wait for Bruce to get better…"

"Bah!" Lance said. "I fly STOL Cubs and shit for air shows and do a little crop-dusting when I'm bored, which is basically whenever I'm not behind the wheel of a 747." He shrugged at her widening eyes. "Copilot. Haven't given me my own bird, yet. The chicken-shits won't come out and say it, but I'm not bald enough." At Blaze's flinch, Lance grinned at her. "It's okay. I get it a lot. Probably like you and being tall." He looked up at her expectantly.

"I do get it a lot," Blaze admitted.

"I'm sure." What he left unsaid—but what dangled uncomfortably in the air between them—was, *When you look like you just crawled out of a spaceship from Planet Orangutan.* After an awkward moment, Lance cleared his throat and patted the little blue airplane again. "But yeah. Don't worry, I won't crash us. Brucey would kill me if I dinged up his baby. Besides, I hear you just bought a nice place out on the Yentna. Candy said ya had to wait through Breakup to get out there. Bet you're dyin' ta see what ya got, right?"

"Yeah," Blaze said, breaking into a nervous smile. "Fishing lodge. The Sleeping Lady."

Lance made a sound of appreciation as he started unwrapping the two ropes holding the Cessna's float to the dock cleats. "Nice place. Landed on the lake for coffee a couple times." He gestured at his brother's airplane. "Candy got ya all loaded up?"

"Yeah," Blaze said, still a little stunned by the fact she was standing beside a commercial airlines pilot. "You fly 747s? Really?" He just didn't look…*stuffy* enough.

Lance shrugged. "I fly anything with wings." He yanked open the door of the Cessna for her and motioned at the blue leather seat beside that of the pilot. "Climb on in. Try not to bump your head. Gonna be a tight fit for you, but nothing I can really do about that. Just be glad it's not a SuperCub. Man, you'd have trouble getting *inside*."

Oh, thanks, Blaze thought, once more reminded of just how far from the Law of Averages that Mother Nature had decided to throw her. She stepped on the convenient little foot-rest, grabbed the inside of the door, and tried not to wince at how much her body made the little plane sink on its floats as she heaved herself into the cockpit.

"How much you weigh, Blaze?" Lance asked almost thoughtfully. Then, when Blaze cast an irritated look back at him, his eyes widened and he held up both hands and quickly said, "Just tryin' ta judge how close we are to payload." He gestured at the back of the plane, which was completely packed full of groceries, luggage, and furniture, so much that it was completely blocking out the back windows. "Candy packed you in there pretty good. Everything but the kitchen sink, huh?"

And this was only the *first* load. Blaze had many more scheduled, to bring in groceries, lumber, and other supplies.

"I'm one-eighty," Blaze muttered, estimating about twenty pounds low, just because the only people who needed to know that information were her and God. She delicately climbed past the pilot's console, careful not to touch any of the controls, and sat down in the tiny passenger seat allotted to her.

"Call it two hundred, then," Lance said, in consideration. "Hmm. I think we can do this thing."

Blaze hesitated in buckling herself in. "Wait…you *think*?"

But Lance was already lunging into the pilot's seat and pulling the door shut behind him. "Headset's right there," he said, gesturing to the dash as he buckled himself in and tugged his own headset on. "You ever been in a small plane before, Blaze?"

Blaze, who was still staring at the exit, considering whether it was worth trying to crawl over a commercial airlines pilot to get out of the little sardine Can 'O Death before it exploded into a ball of fire on the far end of the lake, didn't really hear him. *Anyone* who had lived in Alaska for any amount of time heard of the dozens of planes that went down every year. Most because they were overloaded, or because the pilots got cocky.

"Jesus, you're sheet-ass white," Lance laughed. "Come on, I already told ya I been in these things since I was a toddler. Okay, look. See this little case behind my seat? That's the emergency survival kit. We go down, there's flares, fire-making gear, some rations, all that good stuff in there."

The casual way he said 'go down' made Blaze's stomach clench.

"But if we *do* go down," Lance said, "you'll survive it a hell of a lot better than me. I mean, hell, look at me. Brucey didn't give me much warning. I'm wearing shorts and a T-shirt. Didn't even get a chance to dose myself with DEET. Mosquitoes will eat my ass alive." He flashed her a big white smile. "That should make you feel better, right?"

It didn't. But then Lance was firing up the engine, and the entire Cessna shook as the prop rumbled to life.

"*Headset*!" Lance shouted to her over the roar of the prop.

Oh my God, Blaze thought, reluctantly grabbing the headset and tugging it over her head, *I am so totally going to die.*

"So I got to talking with Brucey on the way here," Lance said conversationally as he increased the throttle and the little plane lurched forward, out towards the open water. "In between shitting himself and puking all over the phone, he was kind beatin' around the bush about tryin' to con me into talking some sense into you."

"Come to think of it," Blaze said, already feeling ill as the overloaded plane started idling towards the middle of the lake, "I could probably stand another day or two in town."

"*But,*" Lance said, as if he hadn't heard her, "I think it's awesome you bought the place. You just have to watch out for crazies, and make sure you have a baseball bat behind every door."

"Baseball bat?" Blaze asked, swallowing hard. Very tentatively, because she couldn't think of why she would possibly need a baseball bat in the woods, she ventured, "Bears?"

"Nah," Lance said, "To beat all the lonely guys off of you, when they come knocking. There's a *lot* of single guys out there. Now shut up for a second. Gotta make a call to the tower." Then Blaze listened to him babble off a ritual-sounding string of words to 'Willow traffic' about 'north-northwest departure' and 'no traffic in sight' and waited until Lance had tucked the radio away again before she asked, "Bruce wanted you to warn me about lonely guys?"

Lance laughed, "And other things. Mostly the crazies. Now hold on, 'cause here we go."

And then the little plane's engine roared and Blaze was clinging to her seat in a panic as it started rumbling across the lake like a locomotive.

"Huh," Lance said, as the spruce on the end of the lake loomed near, "looks like we're a bit overloaded." And kept them barreling towards the line of trees. Then, just as Blaze was about to scream "For God's sake, shut it down!" and wrench the controls from him, the plane came out of the water and they were soaring.

"So," Lance said, once their floats cleared the tree line and they were gaining altitude over the highway and aiming out towards the mostly-uninhabited Lake Ebony on the Yentna River, "you planning on running the Sleeping Lady as a fishing lodge? Got a guiding license?"

But Blaze was *stunned* at how wonderful it felt to fly. She had squished her face to the window and was peering outward at the stands of birch and cottonwood below. "Oh wow," she said, watching the plane's shadow slide across the ground below them. "This is so *cool*!"

"Bah!" Lance snorted. "This ain't nothin. Should come check out the air show this summer. *That's* cool. Oh, and you're smearing up Brucey's glass. He hates that."

"Sorry," Blaze said, quickly tearing herself away.

"It's no prob. Here." Then Lance ducked the right wingtip down, giving Blaze a better view of the ground.

Shrieking in glee, she plastered herself to the window again.

When Lance put the aircraft back onto a level plane, he was grinning at her. "You remind me of me, when I was a kid. You ever wanna learn to fly? I also teach classes when I'm bored."

"I would *love* to," Blaze blurted, ecstatic. Then winced as reality kicked in. "Well, I've gotta get things at the Sleeping Lady under control first, but yeah. Maybe next year?"

"Sure, sure." Lance glanced out at the twisted array of silty gray rivers and hundreds upon thousands of lakes and ponds that made up the Matanuska-Susitna Valley. "So my brother made me promise to tell you about the kinds of guys that live out here. Most of 'em are out here for a reason, you know what I mean?"

Blaze tried not to groan. She had heard this rant before, from Candy, from her mom, her Econ professor, and just about every other woman who'd ever spent any amount of time out in the Bush. "I'll be fine," she said. "Hell, any idiot decides to get frisky, I could probably just bench-press him and he'll back off." Not exactly the happiest truth of her existence, but by sheer luck of the draw, Blaze was more 'manly' than most of the nerdy men she'd shared her Business classes with.

Lance chuckled. "Okay, sure. But just watch out for the crazies."

"What kind of crazies?" Blaze asked, frowning.

Lance shrugged. "I dunno. Bruce wanted me to say that. Made me promise to say, 'Just watch out for the crazies.' I think he was on NyQuil or something." He yawned and checked his watch. "Man, you never really appreciate how much sunlight Alaska's got in the summer 'til you gotta fly to the Lower 48 a few times a week. Really puts things into perspective."

"Crazies?" Blaze insisted. "Have there been burglaries or something?"

Lance laughed. "In the *Bush*? Hell, they all leave their keys in their 4-wheelers out there. Most places don't even have locks. Who's gonna burgle them? The *moose*?" he chuckled, shaking his head. "Nah, I think he was talking more about one guy in particular, but I'm not gonna name names."

"Who is it?" Blaze demanded.

"Jack Thornton," Lance said. "But I heard you hired the guy as your handyman, so you're kinda screwed."

Blaze felt a spasm of panic, since most of her long-term goals depended on Jack Thornton *not* being crazy. "What's wrong with Jack?"

Lance laughed again. "Oh, well, you mean aside from a really bad attitude?" He turned and grinned at her, paying absolutely no attention to the air in front of him. "Well, on one of those stops for coffee at the Sleeping Lady, Jack swam out to our plane, grabbed Brucey by the back of the head and dunked him under the lake a few times. Called him a 'prissy flyboy' or something like that. Bruce kinda still remembers it. Brucey's big, but he said the guy's got gorilla-strength."

Blaze's mouth fell open. All she could say was, "What?"

Lance shrugged. "You want my opinion, this was back when Bruce had just got his wings and was still being a cocky asshole to everyone. Jack was out fishing and Bruce parked on his hole. On purpose. Then demanded to know what Jack was gonna do about it. So yeah. I think Brucey had it coming."

"How long ago was that?" Blaze demanded, pretty sure that her guests would take umbrage to being dunked in a lake.

"Oh, at least ten years," Lance said. "It was before I had my license. Brucey was flying me out for a fishing trip, all proud of himself. You ask me, I think that dunking did a hell of a lot for Brucey's attitude. He used to be such a prick. Mellowed him out something fierce."

"That is not acceptable adult behavior," Blaze managed.

Lance only laughed. "Oh yeah? Try telling Thornton that."

"You bet your ass I will. It's my lodge, my rules." In fact, with just that little morsel of information as a guide, Blaze would have a *long* discussion with her handyman about the proper rules of decorum when potential clientele, paying guests, and lawyers were concerned.

She and Lance chatted for a few more minutes about some of the eye-opening things that her only employee had done in the last ten years he'd done business with the Rogers' family, and then Lance sat up in his chair to peer over the dash and said, "There we go. Lake Ebony. There's your baby, up on the hill."

Blaze, whose mind had been shocked into stunned overdrive somewhere between 'assault' and 'destruction of personal property' nevertheless had all her worries vanish in a wash of bliss the moment she saw the huge green roof of the Sleeping Lady slide into view between the spruce trees on the crest above the lake. Immediately, she found herself having trouble breathing.

Her dream. Everything she'd ever wanted in her entire life was wrapped up in that big green roof and its half-dozen outbuildings. Bought and paid for, sight unseen. Six hundred thousand dollars for ten thousand square feet, thirty acres, and all the machinery and equipment to run it as a fishing lodge. Every penny of her inheritance, gone, and then some.

Then Lance pulled the flaps and the pitch of the engine changed as the small aircraft began its descent, aiming for the deep black waters of Lake Ebony.

I'm here. Oh God, I'm here... Blaze's heart was pounding, somewhere between elation and absolute Oh-My-Shit-What-Have-I-Done *terror* as she watched the last of the spring-budding treetops slip under the plane's big floats. Hers. The Sleeping Lady was *hers*. It was her dream come true, and it was only a lake's-length away.

The landing was surprisingly gentle, and once they had come to a relative stop in the middle of the lake, Lance revved the engine again and got them moving towards shore.

He idled them over to the far bank of the lake, beneath the crest where the Sleeping Lady sat like a mistress of its domain, surveying the lands around it. As they neared the shore, Blaze lost sight of the lodge through the hillside of birch and spruce trees.

When the Cessna's floats slid into the gravelly mud of the narrow beach, Blaze was close to hyperventilating. She was *here*. She was either going to sink or swim, and had nobody to blame for it except herself.

...And she was already in debt up to her eyeballs, just *getting* here. She'd been wanting a lodge her whole life, but now she *had* it, and was in *debt* for it, and she already almost felt like puking with nerves. Her hands were shaking as Lance unstrapped himself and crawled out onto the plane's left float. "Well," he said, "here we are. Lake Ebony." He pushed the pilot's seat out of the way and gestured for Blaze, who was still staring at the woods in front of the propeller in shock, to climb out after him. "You got a ride up to the shop, or should I just pile the stuff on the beach?"

Jerked out of her stunned silence, Blaze climbed down onto the float and stood there, gripping the wing strut with white knuckles, as she stared up at the woods shielding her new home from view, trying frantically to tell herself she was not making the biggest mistake of her life.

Lance gave her an empathetic grin. "Excited?"

Swallowing, Blaze nodded down at him. This close, sharing space on the float, there really wasn't any way for Blaze to back up and give him space—and thereby the illusion of a lesser disparity in height. Even now, she could see the little gears turning in Lance's head as he realized just *how* big she was. At six-foot, Lance really shouldn't have had to look up at her. Unfortunately, Blaze was about twelve inches and eighty pounds off of average, and every checkout cashier and bank teller in the world had let her know it. Some gigantic Amazon somewhere had birthed Blaze, and, once Blaze had passed between her massive thighs, the woman had left her in an alder thicket on the mountain behind her father's house. And, having just lost their baby due to a miscarriage, her parents had taken her in, quietly raised her on their own, and could probably be sent to jail for life for not turning her over to the authorities, if they weren't both already dead.

That was one of the many unhappy surprises that Blaze had discovered in the lawyer's office four months ago. Adopted. It still hit like a freight train, every time she thought of it.

Then she realized Lance was still looking up at her, waiting for her answer.

"So excited I think I'm gonna puke," Blaze managed, still trying to focus all of her attention on the textured aluminum plating between her men's Size 11 hiking boots, attempting to force her stomach into submission.

"Well," Lance said, "If you wanna go sit down, I'll unload for you."

Blaze automatically felt herself prickling at how quickly he offered to do her work for her. "I'll be fine," she said. She ducked her head through the door and grabbed a load of groceries from behind the pilot's seat, not waiting for Lance to unlatch the back compartment. She normally tried not to make a big deal of it, but she wasn't stupid—she knew that the Alaskan Bush was a man's world, and that if she didn't want to start a precedent of Let's All Take Care Of The Poor Helpless Woman, she needed to start proving her competence the moment she stepped off of the plane. First impressions, her mother had taught her, were everything. If Blaze showed every man she met on the river that she was smart, capable, and willing to work, they wouldn't patronize her, and those that did, she could simply tell them to get screwed.

Blaze had been raised by the epitome of an Independent Woman—her mother, who had made her millions in real estate, had insisted on keeping separate finances despite her father's greater wealth—and after earning her way through her Business degree, Blaze was *not* going to allow a bunch of scruffy, rugged, largely-unemployed men to treat her like a second-class citizen because she had a couple of A-cups and internal plumbing. Groceries retrieved, Blaze gingerly started towards the shore, picking her way across the wet aluminum float. Out in the woods, she heard the sound of an engine and looked up.

A stout-looking man was driving a blue 4-wheeler down a winding dirt track, pulling a flatbed trailer behind him. It rattled and bounced as it jumped over roots and stones, making a ruckus as it worked its way down the hill to her. Blaze watched it approach as Lance worked his way around to the other float and began opening the back compartment of the airplane to access her luggage.

When he came fully into view, the man driving the 4-wheeler looked *nothing* like what Blaze had envisioned over the phone. Instead of the hairy, dirty, graying, plaid-covered Bushrat she had been expecting after exchanging instructions with his gruff voice over the phone, he was clean-shaven, with jet-black hair, relatively tidy, and wearing tight blue jeans and green flannel shirt. A well-worn Carhartt jacket was slung over his shoulders, zipper open, exposing a broad chest beneath. And he looked *young*, which was completely at odds with how long she'd heard he'd been skulking around this part of the Yentna.

Hell, from the way *some* people told it, he'd been living in the same damned cabin since the Gold Rush, so Blaze had hired him fully expecting a wrinkled old fart who had to grab his reading glasses to figure out which nut went on which bolt.

But to her shock, even from this distance, Blaze could see that Jack Thornton was built like a Greek god. Pecs that strained against his shirt. Shoulders that made divots in his jacket. Legs that looked like they could crush the 4-wheeler like a used soda can. When Jack slowed the vehicle and the deepest green eyes that Blaze had ever seen met hers, however, Blaze felt her heart give an extra thud. Then she watched his muscular ass stretch against the jeans as he dismounted…

…and her elephantine foot slipped out from under her, and she went crashing backwards into the frigid waters of Lake Ebony.

Cold and humiliation washed over her like a wet blanket from God, putting out her idle fantasies as quickly as if she'd been dunked in liquid nitrogen. Blaze sputtered to the surface, gasping, blinking up at the horrified face of the pilot, who was kneeling on a float, offering a hand to help her, and then her very first employee, who was smirking.

…smirking?

"Damn," Jack said, wading out to meet her. He was wearing rubber boots that hugged his hips, secured to his waist by loops snapped to his belt. He offered his big hand, grinning. "You dye your hair to get it that orange? Like fucking carrot soup." No 'Sorry, miss, gotta watch your step,' or 'Don't worry, it happens to the best of us…' He just smirked down at her and commented on the prison-orange hair that had been plaguing her since childhood. Hair that, despite her ongoing attempts to dye it, *would not* retain any other color.

Blaze's jaw fell open in her horror, gaining her a nice mouthful of lakewater as it drained through her soggy scalp. Her first two minutes in this place that was to be her new home—hopefully for the rest of her life—and Blaze had made herself look like that helpless woman she was trying desperately not to portray, in front of the very man she had hired to help her maintain the lodge. She could see the amusement in his green eyes, knew that whatever respect for her brilliant mind and sharp business sense that she had managed to earn in their quick, crass phone conversations had just exploded in a wash of cold water and lake weeds.

The water where she had fallen was little over two and a half feet deep, so Blaze easily got to her feet on her own, red-faced and shamed to her core. Jack's face darkened a bit when she refused his help, but he shrugged and started helping Lance unload the plane, wading to the trailer and back with each load of luggage and groceries. When Blaze hurriedly slapped together an armful of soggy groceries and sloshed past him, a traumatized corner of her brain noticed he was only about five-nine, giving her a full seven inches of headspace over him, leaving Blaze with the horrible realization that she towered over her mechanic like an A-cupped beanpole.

As she walked by, Jack's neck craned back so he could look at her, his mouth fell open, and he dropped the box of bread he'd been carrying into the lake.

What was left of her ill-conceived fantasies were utterly shattered as she watched the muscular little man scrabble to pluck loaves of bread from the water. Men, Blaze had learned from hundreds of lonely nights at the bar, did not like their women taller than them, and anyone who said otherwise had never been a six-foot-four-inch behemoth thundering through the college dating scene.

After the four years she'd spent at the University of Alaska to get her degree, Blaze had long since given up. Those men who on the off-chance happened to be taller than her often had some genetic species-survival switch tripped in their brain that made them crave women on the opposite end of the height spectrum, to balance out the gene pool. As of yet, she'd only found two men who showed any interest, and both had been skinny computer geeks she had met in college, some perverted part of their nerdy brains somehow turned on by the whole Amazon thing. Both had tried to get her to wear leather armor and wield a broadsword sometime during bed-play. Neither had stayed long.

Fighting despair, Blaze went to the trailer and sat on the back, sloshing a flood of water from her clothes as she went. She sat down and pulled off her boots, emptying small rivers from their insides.

On one of his trips from the plane, her luggage over his shoulder, Jack paused and glanced at her shoes. "Jesus," he said, "Those are even bigger than mine. Where you get feet like that? A Clydesdale?" Then, chuckling, he went back to carrying groceries as if he hadn't just made Blaze's stomach clench with shame.

Blaze almost fired him on the spot. She was so humiliated that it was all she could do to keep the words locked behind clenched teeth. The only thing that saved him was that Blaze knew she couldn't make the Sleeping Lady run without Jack's help. She was a Business major with secret fantasies of one day running a self-sufficient homestead-slash-fishing-lodge in the Alaskan Bush. He was a mechanic, handyman, and carpenter who had spent his entire life actually living her dream...and knowing what it took to make it happen.

When the Cessna was fully unloaded, Blaze watched as Jack pushed the plane off the beach and waded out into the lake as he got it turned around and pointed in the opposite direction, then gave it a big push. As Jack was wading back to shore, Lance started the engine and began idling the airplane out across the lake, toward a little channel that Blaze had noticed on the flight in.

"Where's he going?" she asked, as Jack rejoined her at the 4-wheeler.

Jack raised an eyebrow in a manner that suggested she had just asked a stupid question. "He's gotta go take off on the river. Not enough space to take off on the lake." He gestured at the 4-wheeler. "Wanna drive?"

Blaze, soaked and still feeling sick with humiliation, shook her head. All she wanted to do was get home and get changed.

Jack chuckled, green eyes twinkling. "Wanna get rid of the evidence, huh?"

Blaze peered at him. "What?"

He gestured at her soggy clothes. "Evidence." When she just stared at him, he offered, "That you're a dumbshit city-slicker." The way he said it, it was the most obvious thing in the world.

Blaze's mouth fell open, and again the words, "You're fired, asshole," tried to tumble forth. Instead, in her horror, she managed to clamp her throat shut and only a strangled garble came out.

If Jack noticed or cared, he didn't show it. Chuckling, he threw a leg over the 4-wheeler, once again exposing her to his tightly-muscled posterior, started the engine, and did a tight U-turn on the muddy gravel lakebed and started them back up the hill, Blaze clinging to the back end of the trailer as the bounces and jolts tried to throw her off into the dirt.

When they crested the hill, Jack slowed and glanced behind him. "Still back there, Boss?"

"My name's Blaze," she gritted, still fighting the urge to say something unkind.

He grinned, and she saw that sparkle in his green eyes again. "Okay, Boss." He turned back to the trail and gunned the 4-wheeler again, weaving them back and forth on a long, yet much more gradual, upward climb. Birch, spruce, alder, and willow trees blocked her view of the lodge through the woods, and she got only glimpses here and there of a log structure before it disappeared again.

Even on the back of the trailer, the bugs were bad. Blaze had to cough and swat them away, despite being drenched with bug dope. Completely unfazed, a swarm of mosquitoes and tiny black, stripe-legged flies landed on her skin and started biting her arms and legs, sometimes even drilling her through the cloth of her shirt.

Jack glanced back at her as Blaze killed half a dozen on an OFF-soaked forearm. He grinned. "Around here," he called over the engine, "We wear layers." He grabbed the brim of his green boonie-cap between gloved fingers. "And hats. Keeps the bugs off." He slowed down to give her a quick perusal. "You might wanna find a long-sleeved shirt and some workpants…loose-fitting. Lots of city-slickers come out here without good pants. Bugs bite right through tight shit."

Blaze felt another stab of shame worming through her stomach. She was dressed in fancy jeans and a T-shirt, no hat, no gloves, and—because it had been such a beautiful day on takeoff—her jacket was stuffed in her duffel bags.

Jack apparently mistook her shame for admission to being a city-slicker. He nodded. "Gal next door, Jennie Mae, should have something that fits. Her husband's about your size. Real big guy. Built like a brick shithouse."

Blaze narrowed her eyes. "Brick *shithouse*?" But Jack was already turning back to the overgrown dirt track leading to the lodge, and either didn't hear her over the rattle of the trailer, or didn't care. Glaring at his broad back, Blaze began to plot out exactly how she was going to bring up Jack's obvious lack of people skills without getting herself re-introduced to Lake Ebony a few times for being a snooty city-slicker. Some of Lance's stories had been…eye-opening.

When they finally broke through the trees, however, Blaze's breath caught and she forgot about uncouth cads and brick shithouses. The ten-thousand-square-foot fishing lodge was *not* what she had been expecting. The grounds were unkempt and overgrown, its paneling was much more weathered and gray than she had noticed in the pictures, and the big windows were boarded up, rather than open and inviting as she had been led to believe.

"What *happened* to it?" she blurted, when Jack drove them around back of the massive structure, exposing more ancient buildings in bad need of love and new paint. The driveway to the back was completely overgrown with yarrow and grass, the lawn speckled with baby cottonwood trees.

"Owners abandoned it four years ago," Jack said, once again presenting her with an extremely interesting view as he dismounted. He reached into the flatbed beside her to grab a couple of her duffel bags. Hefting them each over a broad shoulder, he eyed the massive building and shrugged. "Just boarded it up and left."

The realtor had told her something about the aging husband having a heart attack, and the couple having to pack up and move back to town. With the economy as bad as it had been, they'd been looking unsuccessfully for a buyer for many years—part of the reason why Blaze had managed to get a ten-thousand-square-foot lodge, six outbuildings, thirty acres, and all the machinery to run the place for only six hundred thousand dollars.

Blaze jumped off the trailer and took one of her bags—he'd left her the lightest, she realized, with irritation—and struggled to lift it out of the bed. Her eyes narrowed as she watched Jack's broad back swagger away, a bag slung easily over each shoulder.

All the height, none of the brawn, she thought, disgusted. Viking warrior-woman she might look, Amazon she was not.

Gritting her teeth against that irritation, she grabbed her duffel with both hands and lugged it to the back porch, where Jack had set the bags down and was digging in his pocket. "You wanna do the honors?" he asked, dragging out a keychain and holding it up to her.

Blaze's heart gave a flutter when she realized, for the first time in her life, she was standing on her own property, about to enter her very own home. A place that would, hopefully, become her primary source of income until her death.

Tentatively, Blaze lowered the bag to the creaky wooden porch and held her breath as she reached out to take the keys to her dream-home.

Jack dropped the keys away and held out his hand. "I'm Jack Thornton."

Blaze's eyes were fixed on the keys that now dangled at his side. "Blaze MacKenzie," she growled, ignoring his proffered palm.

"Blaze, huh?" Jack said, peering up at her like an interested ferret. "Why you called that?" What he didn't add, but Blaze could feel hanging in the air between them, was,…*when you're the size of a gorilla?*

"I don't get cold," Blaze growled.

"Oh yeah?" He kind of sniffed the air, at that, like a dog sniffing out a new scent. He frowned, his green eyes watching with a thoughtful expression. "Huh. All that mass helps keep the heat in, then, eh?" He chuckled as if he thought that was somehow funny. "What's your real name, Boss?"

She felt like snatching the keys from where they hung against his leg and stuffing them down his throat, but years of training on how to deal with difficult people made her force a smile. "Technically, it's Beatrice MacKenzie, but if I hear you use it, you're a dead man."

He grinned. "Sure Boss. You gonna shake my hand?" He was still holding his palm out.

"You gonna give me my keys?" Blaze snapped.

Jack's voice was calm but firm when he said, "I like to shake the hands of those people I'm going to be working with." His smile remained, but there was a wary calculation there that Blaze found irritating.

She didn't feel like shaking his hand, but, realizing that she probably wasn't going to get her keys otherwise, she did it.

And, it might have been her imagination, but the moment Blaze's hand came into contact with Jack's, the handyman stiffened, his green eyes going just a bit wide. His nostrils flared again, and this time he bent and blatantly sniffed at her knuckles before jerking his head away like a startled fox. His green eyes lifted to her face again, and this time, there was no mistaking the wariness there.

"What..." Blaze gritted, when he just stood there, staring at her, holding her hand, "...are you staring at?"

That seemed to break whatever stupor that Jack had fallen into. He shook himself and released his grip, looking, for all the world, like a weasel that had just encountered something new and dangerous. She could almost *see* him brushing down his hackles as he scratched at the back of his neck.

"Well, uh, Boss, here ya go." He tossed her the keys, instead of simply handing them over. Then he took a big step backwards, out of arm's-reach.

That made Blaze scowl. Because she had been chronically affronted by the uncouth ass since the moment she had gotten off the plane, Blaze couldn't keep her mouth shut. "What," she growled, gesturing at him, "You afraid whatever disease I've got is gonna rub off, you'll drop your testicles and grow tits?"

For the first time, Jack flushed, looking extremely embarrassed. He glanced at the 4-wheeler as if he wished he could hop aboard and speed away. "Uh, no, Ma'am."

"I'm a girl," Blaze growled. "You don't believe it, I'll fucking drop my pants and prove it to you."

"No," Jack said quickly, his face reddening to a refreshing shade of crimson, "I know you're a girl. I can *smell*—" He stopped suddenly, hesitating, his green eyes flickering across her face before quickly looking away.

"*Smell*?" Blaze raised an eyebrow, quietly wondering if Lance had been right and all those years alone in the Alaskan Bush had been a bit too much for the poor bastard. "Smell what?"

"Perfume," Jack said, wrinkling his nose in the very picture of disgust. "City-slicker perfume."

Blaze narrowed her eyes. "I don't wear perfume."

His mask of disgust cracked a little, leaving what looked like nervousness and indecision in its place. Jack glanced again at the 4-wheeler like a man wanting to make a high-speed getaway. "Must be your detergent."

Blaze crossed her arms, reveling in his discomfort. "I use non-scented hypoallergenic. Better for the environment."

"Expensive shampoo, then," Jack muttered, using a scuffed work-boot to pry at a splinter in the porch. "You got your hair wet."

...Which was true enough. Even then, she could smell the scent of Biolage mingling with the stale dirt-stink of lakewater.

Still, Blaze scowled at him. Something was telling her that he wasn't divulging the whole truth, and that bothered her.

"So, uh," Jack said, motioning at the door, "You gonna open it?" He was giving off the nervous energy of a wolf that was just hungry enough to come sniffing at a human doorstep for its next meal ticket, but was also ready to drop anything and bolt at the slightest provocation. She was pretty sure that, had Jack not needed the job, he would've already been gone.

And he *had* needed the job. Judging by his worn clothes and the scuffed and scrapped-together look of his four-wheeler, she was pretty sure the poor bastard was living on food stamps. After all, employment in the Bush was fairly limited. This was probably the first real job he'd had in years.

Blaze eyed him a moment longer before turning her attention to the keys in her hand. As soon as she started sorting through them, Jack too-quickly ducked to grab the duffels—*all* of them, this time—and threw them easily over his big shoulders. He then waited anxiously on the deck just out of reach, looking at anything but her. Blaze hesitated in picking through her keys, instinctively wanting to get to the root of the matter, but her gut was telling her if she pushed the subject any further, her handyman was going to disappear and never come back.

And she needed him.

Blaze may have known the proper way to tally up a Balance Sheet and deliver a Quarterly Earnings Statement, but she didn't have the first clue how to unclog a pipe that didn't succumb to Drāno.

Blaze found the right key and inserted it into the lock. She could almost feel the sigh of relief behind her as she turned the knob and shoved the door open, revealing a darkened interior beyond.

"I'll start taking the plywood off the windows tonight," Jack said, following her inside. The place smelled of old smoke, wood, and dust. "Get some light in this place." He set the duffels down inside the foyer, then started digging in his jacket pocket. "Until then…" He fished out an LED flashlight and handed it to her.

Blaze reached for it, grateful.

Instead of handing it to her, however, Jack flipped it on suddenly and shone it in her eyes.

"What the *hell*?!" Blaze cried, holding up a hand against the blue glare.

Jack lowered the light, frowning. He started sniffing the air again, short, brief little whuffs, like a confused bear. "You ain't a vampire," he said, sounding stunned. Just when she was starting to blink the red dots out of her vision, he shone the light into her eyes again. "And you ain't a fairy."

Blaze snagged the LED flashlight from his grip and yanked it away from him. Growling, she switched it off. "Look, Jack," she said, "I know you've been out here in the sticks a long time on your own, buddy, thumb squarely up your hairy little ass, but you're gonna learn some people skills or you're not working for me." She frowned when Jack simply stared at the flashlight in her hand, seemingly caught between the urge to bolt and the urge to snatch it back. She switched it back on and shone it on his face, making him start. "You listening?"

Jack blinked up at her and shielded his face, and she almost thought she heard a low growl rising in his chest.

"Good," Blaze snapped. She waggled the light at him. "First rule. I don't care if she looks like she belongs in steel and boiled leather, manning the helm of a Norse battleship—you don't call your boss a blood-sucker, and you *don't* ask her if she's gay."

Jack lowered his hand, looking confused. "Huh?"

"Second," Blaze said, turning the light on the room, "If you're going to have any contact at all with the guests, you're going to stop making rude comments. Period."

"Rude comments?" Jack asked, sounding perplexed.

She switched the light back to his face. "Suggesting I have a bit of draft horse in my ancestry? Or that I'm a 'dumbass city-slicker?'"

"Well," Jack said gruffly, "You got big-ass feet and you fell in the lake. Now do you mind? I've got sensitive eyes."

Blaze stared at him, stunned by his hypocrisy, and left the light on his face another few seconds. Finally, she turned it again to the inside of the lodge. "So what do you think?"

Jack lowered his arm from his face suspiciously. "Think you got a hell of a deal on the place."

"It's a lot of work," Blaze said, shining the light around the basement floor, the light catching the reflection of windows that were still boarded from the outside.

"Yeah," Jack said. He gave her a long, guarded look. "What are you?"

"Business major," Blaze said, distracted. "Ditched everything to come out here, though, so I can't afford to screw up." She crossed the room to shine her light on a pile of grass and black deposits on the floor beside the wall. "What is that?"

"Looks like a squirrel found its way in here," Jack said. "They'll probably be all over. Stuff'll be chewed, too, so you'll probably have to replace some walls and flooring." He paused, seeming to hesitate. "I mean really, what are you?"

Blaze flashed him again, irritated. "Remember what I said about rude comments?"

She almost *saw* his hackles go up again. "I'm gonna go get the rest of the groceries." He turned on heel and left.

Blaze sighed. As they'd loaded the Cessna 206 while waiting for Bruce's brother to arrive, Candy had warned her that people in the Bush were…different. Most of them, the energetic little woman had told her, had retreated to the Bush because they couldn't deal with their problems in town. Unfortunately, that meant most of them were eccentric, egotistical, hard-ass recluses who wanted to be left alone. Between Lance's brief recountings of Thornton's past misdeeds and her first twenty minutes with Jack in the flesh, Blaze got the general idea that her new mechanic fell into that category, and that it was desperation—and a dearth of paying jobs in the area—that had finally made him come out of his shell.

Jack dropped her remaining luggage and foodstuffs unceremoniously at her feet, all in a single massive load, and Blaze was pretty sure she heard some stuff crunch that shouldn't have. "I'll see if I can find some firewood," he said, ignoring the sound of breaking glass. Then he was gone again, his broad back disappearing as he made his way to the largest of the outbuildings.

Because she *refused* to dig through her luggage to figure out which prized artifact of her life had succumbed to the brute, Blaze started searching the basement for a good spot to stow her stuff and take shelter for the night. Near the back, she found a small room with a tiny cot, dusty and stale-smelling. Blaze's feet would be hanging off the end, but she decided it would work for now.

"I'm taking this one for the night," Blaze said, as Jack stepped inside, muscles straining under a big armload of firewood.

Jack grunted and dumped the logs beside the stove, then gave the tiny room a curious look. "Owner's suite is upstairs, top floor."

"I don't feel like dragging duffels all the way up there," Blaze said. "Now if you don't mind, I'm gonna change." She gestured at the room. "You want proof, here's your chance."

Jack flushed. "Don't need proof." Then he turned and retreated again. After a few minutes, she heard something creaking against the nearby window, and a piece of plywood began to pry free, allowing a blast of light into the dark basement. Ignoring it, Blaze dragged her belongings into the room she'd picked out and, by the bluish glow of the LED flashlight, closed the door and sorted through her duffels for a new set of clothes.

She found it—camouflaged cargo-pants, a T-shirt, and a long-sleeved, button-up flannel shirt—and quickly doffed her wet clothes to exchange for fresh. She replaced her hiking boots with the brand-new pair of work boots she had bought at the army surplus store right before hopping on her flight, then topped the ensemble off with a pale green boonie cap she had purchased at the same establishment.

When she stepped back out of the room, the basement was well-lit from the three pieces of plywood that Jack had pulled from the windows. Her handyman was currently on his knees in front of the fireplace, his grease-stained jacket thrown over a rough-hewn wooden chair, his muscular shoulders bunching as he gently laid kindling into the fancy box-shaped woodstove.

When she stepped into the basement with him, Jack looked up. She saw both eyebrows go up as he took in her new style of dress.

"Better?" Blaze demanded.

"Miss GI Jane," Jack said. "You in the army, Miss Jane?"

Blaze scowled. "The name is Blaze."

Jack grinned at her, green eyes dancing. "That like a nickname you got from the military, Miss Jane?"

Blaze stared at him for so long that Jack went back to making a fire. Finally, Blaze blurted, "Are you *trying* to piss me off?"

"Nope," Jack said, "Trying to figure out what sort of critter landed on my doorstep, that's all."

Blaze choked. "*Your* doorstep." She waved a hand at the lodge around them. "I'm sorry, did you just spend six hundred *thousand* of your hard-earned dollars on this place?"

"From what I hear," Jack said, still working with the fire, "It was an inheritance." He pulled back and got a little cut-open pop-can full of clear liquid and sloshed it on the wood inside. Then he yanked a book of matches from his back pocket and struck a flame, then touched it to the kindling. The fire spread fast—not as fast as gasoline, Blaze realized—but he had definitely used some sort of accelerant.

An inheritance. Blaze found herself so infuriated that it was all she could do not to tell him to get his tight, Greek-godly ass packed up and out of her lodge. *Now.*

"And when I say my doorstep," Jack said, turning to her, "I mean my neck of woods. I've claimed this place. Everything for about ten square miles. Tied myself to the land, keep it nice. Kind of makes me anxious to see just what sort of critter is holing up right smack in the middle of it." He peered up at her expectantly, then, like he was waiting for her to tell him she was a Martian, and oh, by the way, here's my raygun and the keys to my spaceship.

Blaze sighed, looking at the dusty drywall of the ceiling. "Damn it. Are there any *other* people that can turn a wrench around here, or are you it?"

"You haven't answered my question, missy," Jack said. "I woulda said you got some snake in you, but smell's not right. Kinda bitter. Like burned metal. Kinda like those flame-throwing gorillas in Africa."

"Get out," Blaze said.

Jack stood up, but he leaned against the wall and crossed his arms over his big chest. Over the crackle of the fire, he gave her a flat stare and said, "Are we gonna have to tussle, then?"

Blaze stared at him, completely unbelieving that he was not listening to instructions. "I told you to get out of my house."

"'Your' house," he growled, "Is on *my* land. I've kept it free of all sorts of nuisances and vermin for over a hundred years, and I'd hate to let it down now."

Blaze's mouth fell open. "You're insane."

"Maybe," he growled. "And you're trespassing, tootz." And his growl sounded almost feral, animalistic, like a warning rattle that was coming from deep in his chest.

Impossible, Blaze thought, listening to the odd sound.

"So, sweetie," Jack said, still leaning stubbornly against the wall, "Dispense with the bullshit. Who are you, and why the fuck didn't you pay attention to the warning signs I posted all over the place?"

He's completely off his rocker, Blaze thought, staring at him. She began to think of the gun she had stashed in her duffel, in case of bears. She glanced behind her.

"Wouldn't try it, if I were you," Jack said. "I've been shot about fifteen-hundred times in my life, and stabbed a time or two before that." He flexed a bicep, then looked at her. "Ain't seein' much effect... You?" He grinned, and in the firelight, Blaze could have *sworn* she saw long, sharp canines.

"Uh, look," Blaze said, deciding that she really didn't want to get into a brawl with a coke-snorting Bushrat dopehead. "I don't know what you're talking about. I was told the deed was for thirty acres. If you think some of that belongs to you, I'm sure we can work it out in the courts."

His mouth fell open and he frowned at her. "Are you smoking crack?"

"I could say the same for you!" Blaze cried. "I've told you twice, now, to get out of my house, and you're still standing there. You know, people go to *jail* for trespassing."

That got his hackles up. She could *feel* the energy in the room jump as he tensed his muscular body and pushed off of the wall.

"Maybe you didn't hear me, sweetheart," he snarled, pointing a finger at the floor, "But this is *my* home territory, and anyone with any brains knows to check out who's claimed what before putting six hundred thousand of their 'hard-earned' dollars into a few acres right in the middle of someone's home range."

Blaze just stared at him. "What are you *talking* about?" she finally managed. "This is America. Nobody can 'claim' ten square miles of land."

He grinned fiercely, and Blaze once again thought she saw the flash of teeth. "That's where you're wrong, sugar." He took a step towards her, and Blaze suddenly realized why it seemed like she had been seeing his hackles raise every time he got angry. His back, unlike his face, was *hairy*. Almost inhumanly hairy. And the hair was standing on end, so that it pushed up over the shoulders and up his neck, puffing up his shirt. "So," Jack growled—and this time, the growl was definitely not human, "Tell me what you are and stop fucking around." It was his eyes, though, that finally made Blaze take a nervous step backwards. As she watched, they started to glow. The black pupil elongated, becoming a narrow slit.

"Listen," Blaze whispered, "Whatever you're on, I'm sure it's wonderful, but I really have no idea what you're talking about." She took another step backwards, into the bedroom. She glanced down at the doorknob, saw the lock.

"Don't even try it," Jack growled. In the flickering light of the fire, she thought she saw his teeth lengthening to points.

Blaze ducked out of the way and slammed the door shut. An instant later, she twisted the lock and dove for her duffel bags.

Which one's got the gun? she thought, panic clawing at her brain. She had an insane woodsman in her home, and he was obviously on some pretty expensive medication. Blaze found the duffel and had just knelt beside it when the door exploded off of its hinges, the shattered bits of wood and paint so tiny that they drifted around her like feathers. Seeing that, Blaze's body locked up all at once, her frantic mind thinking that the door had somehow been hit by a shotgun—or a small thermonuclear device. She looked up, half-expecting to see the black barrel of a gun pointed at her.

What stood on the other side, however, was much worse. Over six feet tall, it seemed to be a mixture of man and beast—bearlike, but with more delicate features. It stood hunched on hind legs and was snarling, its compact body covered in four-inch-long brown and blonde fur.

Those places, of course, that weren't still sporting ripped jeans and a shredded flannel shirt.

Blaze screamed and scrambled backwards, away from her duffels.

The creature followed her into the room, easily tossing aside the seventy-pound duffels as if they were made of Styrofoam. The eerie rumble was still coming from its chest, magnified now, its snarl bearing long, saliva-soaked ivory fangs, its glowing green eyes fixed on her with deadly purpose.

Blaze's back hit the far wall before she realized she'd left herself trapped. She cringed as the thing rushed her, then screamed as it pounded a taloned fist into the brickwork beside her head, powdering it to dust.

"Answer me!" the creature snarled, hellish green eyes only inches from her own. "What the *fuck* are you?!"

"I don't know," Blaze whimpered, hiding her head with her arms. "Please. I don't know what you're talking about."

The creature grabbed her arm and pulled it from her face as easily as if she had been a reluctant toddler. It peered at her, searching her face with its slitted eyes. When Blaze tried to protect herself from its gaze with the other arm, it, too, was removed with a powerful, clawed hand and held above her head. Blaze cringed, utter terror leaving her struggling for breath. She felt her lungs locking up, terror clamping down on her chest like a vice.

The creature leaned close, its nightmarishly fanged face dropping until its whiskers brushed her neck. Blaze trembled and tried to pull away, struggling to breathe, but the beast easily held her in place. She felt a cold draft near her jugular as it took a deep breath near her neck, nostrils flaring.

Feeling the warm tongue slide out and lick her throat, however, Blaze lost it. She screamed and kicked out, catching the thing between the legs with all the strength of her terror.

The slitted green eyes went wide, then the creature kind of crumpled sideways, releasing her.

Blaze got up and ran.

She didn't slow down for the gun, didn't stop for her coat or gear, and, once she realized she didn't know how to start the 4-wheeler, kept right on running, making a panicked bee-line for the trees.

Behind her, she heard a crash within the lodge, then she was hurtling through the woods, diving over fallen trees, running as fast as her freakishly long legs could go.

"Wait!" she heard, behind her. Too close. Blaze screamed and ran faster, trying to make the lake. She could see the water in the distance. Just a little further…

A rotten birch caught her ankle, sending Blaze tumbling face-first into the brush. Behind her, she heard the sound of footsteps crashing through the undergrowth, catching up. She let out a panicked cry and struggled to get to her feet.

"Now just hold on!" a very human-sounding voice cried, within kicking-range. Something grabbed her shoulder and held it. In an instinctive panic, now, Blaze rolled onto her back and started slamming her boots into anything that moved.

"Jesus!" Jack cried, stumbling backwards, hands up. "I'm not going to hurt you, okay?" He peered at her as if she were some sort of dangerous insect, keeping his distance. His clothes were tattered. "I just want you to calm down so we can talk." His green eyes were anxious. But not, her mind babbled, glowing anymore. "Let's just talk, okay?" He started easing towards her, one hand out.

Blaze got up and bolted. She had gone maybe thirty feet before Jack tackled her, bringing her solidly to the ground with all the authority of a ton of bricks. She screamed into the undergrowth as he crawled up her body and sat down on top of her, then flipped her over. At five-nine, Jack had to weigh something like four hundred pounds. She was finding it hard to breathe from the weight on her stomach.

"Listen, Blaze," he panted, leaning over her and holding down her arms against the mossy forest floor, "I think we got off to a bad start." Brilliant green eyes that had been slitted like a goddamn snake's not a moment before were now filled with concern.

She saw his tattered plaid shirt, remembered the huge beast that had assaulted her, and sucked in a huge lungful of air.

Jack clapped a hand over her face, glancing nervously at the lake. "Okay, sweetie," he said, over her muffled screams, "We can do this the easy way or the hard way. The easy way is you stop screaming, follow me back to the lodge, and we have a nice long chat. The hard way is I use this shirt, here, to gag you, tie your hands behind your back, throw you over my shoulder, and take you back anyway."

Blaze bit his hand. Then, as he cursed and yanked his palm away to examine it, she bucked and kicked underneath him, trying to dislodge his body. He remained as solidly in place as the Great Pyramids of Egypt. She screamed again, this time making full use of her lungs.

Jack had a piece of his shirt stuffed in her mouth and secured before she could repeat the performance. Making nervous glances at the lake, he flipped her over, easily dragging her hands behind her back as she thrashed. Blaze heard the sound of cloth ripping and cursed into the gag as she felt him wrap strips of fabric around her wrists, securing them in place.

Oh God, Blaze thought, her gut twisting in horror. *He's tying me up*...She knew what happened to women who got tied up in the woods, a hundred miles from the nearest road.

Jack released her wrists, fully-bound, and started on her ankles. Blaze twisted and strained against the cloth strips, but whatever else he was, he'd probably been a Boy Scout—he tied a damn good knot.

"You are going to *jail,* asshole!" Blaze cried into the shirt, in desperation, as she felt him finish with her ankles.

Jack flipped her over again, his face strained with anxiousness. "I'm not gonna hurt you," he said again, almost a babble. "Just wanna talk, okay? Iron some things out. Nothin more than that." Then, as if her six-foot-four, two-hundred-pound frame weighed no more than a carryon backpack, he flipped her over a muscular shoulder and started carrying her back to the lodge. Blaze flailed and kicked as best as she could, but she might as well have been batting at a bear with a feather for all the affect it had on him.

Jack took her up the porch steps, stepped inside the threshold, and, after scanning the woods beyond the yard nervously, yanked the door shut behind them. As soon as they were alone in the gloomy basement, Blaze felt a lump of dread forming in her gut. She stopped kicking, knowing she was probably going to need her strength.

He walked over to the wall beside the woodstove—across the room, she noticed, from a roughly beastie-sized hole in the drywall—and set her down on the floor with surprising gentleness. Then he stood up and scratched at the back of his neck, swallowing hard. "Jesus," he muttered, "but that gives me the willies." He seemed to shake himself, then peered out the window nervously.

This is where he rapes me, takes my valuables, and buries me in the hill, Blaze thought, realizing for the first time where Bill and Susan Olson had most likely disappeared off to. The elderly couple who had owned the Sleeping Lady before her were probably even then buried out in the woods somewhere, rotting in their nice, neat little graves.

Instead of ripping off her clothes, however, Jack squatted in front of her almost carefully, his green eyes cautious. He cleared his throat. "You…uh…really didn't have any idea what I was talking about, did you?"

She glared at him over the gag.

"I'm gonna pull the shirt out of your mouth," Jack said, "But don't scream, all right? You're all right. Nobody's hurt. I haven't assaulted you and buried you in a hill. Let's just talk about this like reasonable adults, all right?"

Blaze's heart thundered at his last comment and she felt her nostrils flare as she tried to get enough air.

For a moment, Jack looked to have second thoughts. Then, reluctantly, he leaned forward and freed the gag from her mouth.

"You are *so* dead," Blaze blurted.

Jack froze, looking somewhat unnerved. "Oh? Why's that?"

"When the police find out about this," Blaze began, "you're going to go to prison for the next thirty years. Kidnapping, assault—"

"The police." Jack scoffed, and the complete *disdain* with which he did so shut her up. Blaze hesitated, the wind thoroughly swept from her sails with the realization that he absolutely *did not care* what the Alaska State Troopers had to say about his little misdeeds…probably because he planned on going down in a blazing shotgun-battle on his back porch.

Jack leaned closer and tilted his head to the side as he peered at her, like a wild animal giving her a closer inspection. He made a couple gentle sniffs of the air between them, then frowned. "You've got no one else coming for you, do you?"

The certainty with which he said it made Blaze go utterly stiff. "Bruce Rogers and his wife know exactly where I am. My *realtor* knows I bought this place, and if I turn up missing—"

He waved a dismissive hand. "No. I mean friends. Family. *Kin*." He was watching her again, giving her the feel she was blessed with the full attention of a wary predator. Yep. *Definitely* a serial killer.

"I have tons of friends and family," Blaze lied, "And they're all scheduled to show up next week."

He eyed her a moment. "You're alone."

Stated like that, so blatantly, Blaze felt her prepared lies shrivel up and die. She turned her head and scrutinized the wood stove, trying to hold back tears. Crying, she had learned *long* ago, only made things worse.

Jack sat down, just out of kicking range, and drew his knees up. Throwing his bulky arms across his knees, he leaned his chin on his forearms and studied her. For long moments, neither of them spoke.

Blaze eventually began to get creeped out by the stalker-like stare he was giving her, and to hide her bone-crunching terror, snarled, "What are you looking at?"

Jack flinched. Then, softly, he said, "You ain't got *no* family? Nobody who knows you're up here?"

"Just kill me already," Blaze muttered to the stove.

Just at the edge of her vision, Jack seemed to flinch. "Now hold on a second, love. Nobody's gonna go killin' nobody. I'm just trying to figure out…" He hesitated. "Well, I'm just trying to figure out what's going on, is all."

Blaze's jaw dropped open and she turned to frown at him. "*You're* trying to figure out what's going on?"

"Uh, yeah," Jack said. "What *are* you doing out here, anyway?"

She stared at him until he started to fidget with a hole in his jeans. Finally, she found the ability to say, "I'm trying to start a fishing lodge. Something you obviously took offense to." She looked him up and down, trying to decide if she could convince him to let her call Lance and fly back to town. She decided probably not. He may look rugged and dirt-poor, but his eyes didn't hold that dullness of an idiot.

"Look," she managed, "I really think we can work this out. I won't press charges, I swear. Just let me go, *please*."

Jack blinked at her, his green eyes startled. "You really have no idea what's going on here, do you?"

"You're on some pretty wicked drugs," Blaze said.

Jack raised an eyebrow at her. He winced, then swallowed, glancing again at the floor. Then, clearing his throat, he looked back up at her and said, "Okay, how about we try this another way. You saw what happened a few minutes ago." He gestured at the shattered door, the gaping hole in the drywall. "Just what do you think you're dealing with, here?" He sounded, for all the world, like a friend engaging in a pleasant debate with her.

"Cocaine, most like," Blaze said. "Though I never heard of it making your eyes go funky, so I'm thinking probably a combo drug."

Jack scratched the back of his neck again, sweat breaking out on his forehead. "Shit."

Blaze laughed. "What, I pegged you?"

"No," he muttered, "I just made a total ass out of myself."

"Was it the crack or the LSD?" Blaze asked sweetly.

"Honey," Jack growled, "I'm a wereverine."

Blaze's confusion must have shown, because he quickly added, "A wereverine that's managed to keep his head low for a century and a half, and then *this* happens." He gave her a worried frown. "I dunno why, but you just set off about every alarm trigger I've got, and my instincts are pretty damn good."

"Alarm trigger?" Blaze asked. "I didn't think this place had an alarm system."

He slapped his forehead into a hand, dragged his fingers down his face. Then, peering at her through his fingers, he said, "I'm not human. Do you need another demonstration?"

Blaze remembered the wet fangs as his tongue had slid across her throat and she laughed nervously. "No thanks." Whatever he thought he was, she wasn't surprised. She'd heard of plenty of guys who thought they were *birds* when they jumped out the windows of skyscrapers, high on some new wonder-drug.

He raised a brow. "You sure? 'Cause I'm getting the general idea you don't believe me."

Blaze glanced at the shattered door and the hole in the drywall, then thought of how fast he would have had to run to catch up with her long legs. She swallowed and shook her head.

"Okay," Jack said, watching her. "I'm not human. You okay with that part so far?"

She nodded quickly, wondering what kind of drug could make *teeth* grow. Or maybe that was just some residual hallucinogenic smoke that she had picked up off of him…Hell, maybe the prior residents had been some sort of diehard druggies that had thoughtfully left the smell of twenty years of narcotics embedded in the very walls of the place.

"All right," Jack said, taking a deep breath. Then he swore, seeming to deflate. "I never thought…" He groaned and slapped his forehead back into his hand. "Shit."

Blaze waited, not quite sure what to make of the crazy woodsman on crack. He didn't really sound mentally impaired, and, if anything, sounded *anxious* about his latest blunder. Maybe there was hope for him. She was pretty sure that most of his swan-diving buddies were still convinced of their own avian ancestry a split-second before impact.

"I've never told somebody that wasn't one of the People," Jack said. "You're, uh, the first mortal I've entrusted—" he chuckled nervously, "—well, been stupid enough to tell—in about four hundred years."

"You know," Blaze said softly, "I can get you some help."

Jack narrowed his green eyes at her.

"They have centers for this sort of thing," Blaze insisted. "Really, there's one downtown."

"Okay," Jack said, seemingly coming up with a new line of attack, "We both agree I'm not human, and that I can prove it to you again, if you need another look?"

Blaze snorted. "No, I'm fine."

He peered at her, seemingly coming to a decision. "Actually, I don't think so. I'm gonna get right up close, give you another good look. Don't get scared or scream—it'll only piss me off, all right?"

Blaze made a nervous laugh. "I don't need another loo—"

But he was already changing shape, his body becoming larger, hairier, more hunched. She watched brown and gold fur push through his skin as his face elongated and sprouted fangs like something out of a horror movie. He crawled toward her on all fours like a mutated bear, and she heard the sound of talons on the concrete as he moved.

Then he was *right there*, the light of the window above her head illuminating the rabid features, the slitted eyes, the carnivorous teeth, the long, silky fur. Whatever it was, it wasn't drugs.

"Oh my God," she whispered, her head slamming into the wall behind her as she tried to work her spine through the masonry. "Please..."

The beast opened its mouth and pointed a long brown talon at its teeth, "See the fangs?" it demanded, its words an otherworldly snarl. Then it pointed out its slitted eyes, clawed fingers, and slicked a hand down its fur and yanked on a patch of whiskers like some tour-guide giving a demonstration to a class of eighth-graders. "Okay," the *thing* said, "Now watch this." He jabbed a hairy finger back at his mouth.

As she watched, two more layers of teeth sank down through the gumline in both the top and bottom jaw, pointed backwards toward its throat. Crimson started dripping from the teeth from where they had punctured flesh as more teeth-rows built up behind them, leaving its mouth with the general likeness of a shark's multi-layered jaws.

"Oh my *God*!" Blaze screamed, once again feeling her chest locking up with terror. She squeezed her eyes shut, trembling against the bindings that held her in place, so frightened she couldn't breathe.

She felt the creature move backwards, heard Jack clear his throat. His normal, somewhat gruff, yet *human* voice said, "All right. You satisfied I'm not on drugs yet?"

When she looked, he was wiping his mouth with the back of his arm. His hand came away bloody. As she watched, he indifferently wiped it on his shredded pants, then pulled his legs into a cross-legged position across from her, and waited.

It took Blaze several minutes to get her breathing and her heart rate back under control. "You're not on drugs?" she finally whispered, her eyes fixed to the dark red stain on his jeans.

"Nope," Jack said. "Don't touch the stuff. Less control, which is deadly for someone like me." Then he winced. "Well, deadly for other people."

Blaze got a cold chill. "Please let me go."

He frowned at her. "I told you I'm not gonna kill you. I don't make a habit of hurting women, okay?"

"I won't tell anyone," Blaze babbled, eyes still on the stain. "I promise. I'll just pack up everything and leave, no questions asked."

Jack was beginning to get agitated. "No one's telling you to leave, sweetie. I just thought you were horning in on my territory, but looks like I was, uh, wrong." The way he frowned at her, though, made Blaze wonder if he wasn't so sure.

After a moment, Jack delicately offered, "Is there anything...special...about yourself that you wanna tell me, considering what I've shown you?"

Blaze stiffened, thinking of the feather her father had willed to her. *For you, Blaze. May you someday discover its true value.* A hundred different *priceless* artifacts in her father's house, and he had given her a damn feather.

Jack tensed, his big shoulders tightening in muscular knots as his knuckles whitened on his knees. "What is it?"

Blaze bit her lip and glanced at the stove again.

"Lady," Jack warned, "I got all damn week."

In a desperate, sarcastic sneer, Blaze said, "Well, gee, let's see. I'm six feet four inches tall, I generally don't need a bra because I've got A-cup tits, my hair's the color of carrot-filled babyshit, and my feet are somewhere between a Size Fourteen and a Size Seventy-Two, as you so thoughtfully pointed out this afternoon." She laughed, a wretched cackle of despair that tore at her chest, and then looked away. Staring at the wall, because staring at *him* was scaring the shit out of her, she whispered, "What do you want?"

Jack's chuckle sounded just as miserable and full of despair as her own. "Truthfully? To be able to take back the last hour and pretend it never happened."

"I can do that," Blaze said, quickly swiveling to face him. "Just let me go, I'll go get on a plane, and you'll never see me again."

Jack gave her a flat look. "Do I look stupid to you?"

Blaze looked him up and down. "You look like you could use a few thousand dollars to buy groceries. Let's say...ten?"

Jack hesitated, still out of kicking range.

"I can make it fifteen," Blaze whispered. "That's as much as I can afford." She had already dumped massive quantities of her capital into the state-of-the-art sprinkler system that the bank financing her pretty new fishing-lodge had made as part of the requirement to signing the loan. If she dumped any more than fifteen thousand on this bastard, she wouldn't have enough to get the lodge running.

"How old are you?" Jack asked, completely ignoring her question.

Blaze frowned. "Twenty-five. Why?"

He winced. "Around the same time as that last Mount Redoubt eruption, right?"

"How the hell would I know?"

Jack took a deep breath, then sighed and tilted his head back against the wall. "Shit."

"Shit what?" Blaze growled. "And are you gonna untie me or keep me here all damn night?"

He lifted his head to look at her suspiciously. "You gonna run?"

"You gonna *rape* me?" Blaze snapped back.

Jack jerked as if she'd hit him. "Fuck that shit."

…As if she'd asked him if he were going to fornicate with a Clydesdale. *Well*, Blaze decided, *Sometimes being as sexually attractive as a mastodon has its bennies…*

"So what do we do now?" Blaze growled. "You're obviously not bent on assault, and I'm pretty well stuck here until Bruce drops off his next load tomorrow." That wasn't *quite* true, since she had this handy-dandy little thing called a 'cell-phone' tucked into her front pocket, but the rabid little creepy-crawly certainly didn't need to know that.

Jack seemed to consider that for a long moment. "No hard feelings, then?" he asked, tentatively. He gestured at the way he'd trussed her up like a turkey. And in case she hadn't fully understood his meaning, he considerately added, "For tying up your hippo ass?"

"The only hard feelings," Blaze bit out, "are gonna be the ones directly preceding the chunks of lead going through your brainpan if you call me a 'hippo' again." She may be tied up and helpless, and roughly the size of Paul Bunyan, but as her mother had often insisted, there were some things that a woman simply did not tolerate said to her. By the anger suddenly coursing through Blaze's veins in hot, fiery waves, giving her the sudden desire to wrap her manly hands around the creep's neck and choke the life out of him, 'hippopotamus,' it seemed, was one of them.

Jack gave her a long look, then got up, turned his back to her, and went through the beastie-sized hole in the wall into her room. A moment later, she heard thumps and rustling as he went through her things.

"What are you doing?!" Blaze shouted.

She heard a metal *snap*, then Jack came back carrying two pieces of her revolver. He dropped them on the floor beside her feet. Gesturing at the ruined weapon, he said, "We don't have a problem with bears in the area—they stay outta my territory—and I don't really feel like being shot." He bared his teeth at her when he added, "It hurts, and I'm often like to return the favor."

Blaze's mouth was hanging open. The metal hadn't snapped at a weak point. He had broken it in half in the very middle of the gun, cylinder and all. She could still see the finger impressions left in the steel.

All she could think to say was, "That was a Colt." Her father had assured her that nothing—not even getting kicked around in the woods—would hurt a Colt.

"Good gun," Jack agreed. "But like I said. I don't like getting shot. I'll buy you another one when I'm sure you're not gonna point it at my head and pull the trigger."

"Oh, don't worry about that," Blaze muttered, staring at the fingerprints in her gun. "I was really looking forward to living in the Bush. Dreamed all my life of being self-sufficient, went into Business, had pretty big hopes. But you convinced me, okay? I'm getting the hell out of here just as soon as you let me up. I'll have the realtor put this back up for sale and move on. There's plenty of other places in the woods. I'll just find a spot that doesn't have something…" her eyes locked at his bloody pant leg, "…nasty in it."

"Good luck finding one of those," Jack said. "Alaska's one of the only wild places left. Our kind have started gathering around here, and you're just as likely to run into someone else like me at the next place, but a guy who's got a few less scruples, if you know what I mean."

Blaze didn't like the way he said 'our' kind. "Gathering how?" she growled

Jack gestured to the woods. "To the south, we've got a young wolf pack. Really full of itself. Always trying to grab a bit more territory, expand to the north. They're currently claiming about eight miles. To the west, there's an ursine couple. Don't really want to be disturbed. Nobody messes with them, not even the upstart wolves. They've got about four miles. To our east is a group of fawns. They're holding down a tween zone, gathering fares from passing fey and guarding it against human invasion. Sixteen miles, there, and I wouldn't touch them with a ten foot pole. Likely as not they'll witch your tail afire, or leave you barking like a seal the rest of your life. Ornery little bastards. To the north there's Thunderbird. Real uppity snot—"

"A Thunderbird?" Blaze interrupted. It was the first thing he'd said that made any sense to her.

Jack shrugged. "That's what the natives called him. You ask me, just a glorified raven with a few bennies."

"Bennies?" Blaze felt like she'd stepped into the Twilight Zone.

"Weather-witching, that sort of thing."

Blaze nodded, having absolutely no idea what he was talking about.

"North of *him*, we're not really sure, 'cause the arrogant shit won't let anyone cross his territory, and it covers like fifty square miles." He frowned. "As far as I know, though, the south is claimed all the way to Anchorage, and the east and west is spoken for all the way to the ocean in either direction. I know the land in and around the Brooks Range is taken, too. Mostly dragons up there, though. They like to stay away from humans as much as possible, and caribou tastes real nice roasted."

"Dragons." Blaze wondered if she'd swallowed some bad lakewater. Could she have gotten sick that quickly? Alaskan water *did* have some nasties in it to put Mexico to shame. Beaver-fever, baby...She wriggled, trying to judge just how bad off she was. She didn't *feel* like she had a temperature, but then again, she couldn't really check with her arms tied behind her goddamn back. She ended her struggles irritatedly, settling on glaring at him, instead.

Jack peered at her, looking thoughtful. "You said you didn't get cold?"

"Don't change the subject," Blaze snapped. "You said *dragons*? And untie me, damn it. My wrists hurt."

He shrugged, completely ignoring her complaints. "Of course there are dragons. Where you think the myths come from?"

Blaze laughed, but she really didn't find it funny. "I think I need a drink."

"Can't help you there," Jack said, glancing at the staircase to the next level, "But I could go take a look-see upstairs, see if the last owners left any booze. Weren't big drinkers, though. The husband had heart problems."

Blaze peered at her gigantic feet. For a long, long time, neither of them talked. Then, finally, she whispered, "You're serious, aren't you?"

"Serious as a heart-attack," Jack replied. "You probably picked one of the only non-urban areas where you wouldn't be killed on sight."

She jerked her head up and squinted at him. "*Why* would I be killed on sight?"

Jack sniffed at the air between them again, then just shook his head and frowned. "Never mind. Must be wrong."

"Wrong about *what*?" Blaze cried. "*Please* let me up."

He squatted back beside her and peered directly into her face, his green eyes penetrating. "Blue eyes," he muttered.

Blaze felt a little heart-stab when she realized he was seeing the color of the Johnson & Johnson eyewear products hiding her freakishly-colored irises from view of the general populace.

"That is *so* weird," Jack growled, pulling back and rubbing goosebumps from his arms. "I could've *sworn*…"

Blaze was about to blurt out that her mom had helped her hide the color of her eyes back in grade school, when kids started calling her 'Carrotbrain,' when Jack grinned and said, "Well, I guess I don't have to eat you, at least."

A cold sweat washed over her and Blaze clamped her mouth shut. *Now might not be such a good idea to tell the lycanthropic woodsman you're wearing contacts,* Blaze thought, cringing back against the wall behind her.

She flinched when he rubbed his hairy arms again, *sure* he was going to figure it out, revert back to that *thing*, and eat her. Still peering her like a guy in the park puzzling over a chess board, Jack growled, "But shit. A smell like *that*...You *sure* there ain't nothing 'bout you that I need to know about, sister?"

Blaze thought again of the feather. Delivered in a heavy, locked metal case that could have withstood a nuclear bomb detonating on top of it, it had been like nothing she had ever seen before. Definitely avian, but with no air-catching capabilities whatsoever, the red-orange-yellow tendrils had seemed to float on the wind, much like an ostrich's. And the color...it almost shimmered. A dye-job, maybe?

Blaze hadn't even gotten the courage to pull the damn thing out of its custom-fitted case. She'd just gotten all excited at the thick metal box, inserted the little metal key the lawyer had given her, all expectant and hopeful, lifted the lid, seen her father had given her a *feather* and willed the rest of his millions to charity, and then shut the lid to go contemplate Life. She hadn't opened it again after that, though it had certainly occupied a nagging corner of her mind ever since. Almost like the damn thing had *wanted* her to pick it up.

But that was stupid.

"Anything...strange...about you?" Jack prodded gently. The nosy little shit. "Somethin you haven't told anyone else, maybe?"

For a breathtaking moment, meeting his sincere green eyes, Blaze almost told him. Then that refreshing wave of self-preservation snapped back into place and she scrambled to come up with something that would throw him off of the scent. "You mean *beyond* the obvious?" Blaze growled. "Sorry, let me think. Oh, okay. Here's one. 'Cause I'm so damn huge, I need to use extra-large maxi pads. Don't believe me? I brought a half a dozen boxes with me. They're tucked away in my stuff, but if you want, help yourself. I'm sure there's enough to share."

Jack narrowed his eyes at her. "All right, sugar," Jack said, "You said you're a businesswoman. So let's talk business."

She lifted her head to glare at him. "It would be easier for me to talk business if I wasn't sitting on the floor, bound at the wrists and ankles, being intimidated by a hairy little man with an attitude problem."

"Sarcasm," Jack growled, "is not going to make this go any smoother, sweetling."

"You have me *tied up* in the basement of my *own house*!" Blaze cried. "*Please* tell me how that's supposed to make things go 'smoothly' you asshole!"

"You ran away," Jack snapped.

"You tried to *eat* me!" Blaze retorted.

"You kicked me in the *jewels*!" Jack growled.

"You *slobbered* on my *neck*!"

That actually seemed to make the grumpy little man look somewhat abashed. "I was just getting a little taste," Jack muttered, picking at the floorboards between his feet. "Tryin ta figure out…" He jerked his head up and peered at her again, then shook it. "Never mind. Frankly, tootz, I need your assurance you're not gonna run off and blow this thing way outta proportion if I let you go."

"And the alternative?" Blaze gritted.

Jack's green eyes narrowed. "I don't let you go."

"Then gee," Blaze said, "Give me a few months to think about that."

Jack shrugged. "You figure it out, I'll be upstairs sweeping up squirrel shit."

And, good as his word, he stood up, wandered over to a dusty closet, pulled out a *broom*, and proceeded to climb the stairs. Blaze heard his heavy footsteps creaking around on the floorboards above her. Blaze waited until she was pretty sure he was well into the groove of things, then lifted her butt, hunched over, and pushed her long, gangly arms over her ass. Drawing her legs through her arms, she pulled her wrists out in front of her.

Listening to the bastard start to whistle upstairs, she began yanking knots loose with her teeth. Hands free, she reached out, quickly unbound the cloth strips from her ankles, and carefully got to her feet.

Above her, the footsteps paused. Blaze froze, her heart afire as she crouched there, listening to the silence that seemed to pound in her ears like a blacksmith's hammer.

"You figure it out yet, sister?" the wereverine bellowed through the flooring.

"Go suck on an exhaust system!" Blaze screamed up at him.

She heard the wereverine chuckle and go back to sweeping.

With the utter surety that her mechanic probably had the ears of a German Shepherd, Blaze began to make the agonizingly slow creep across the basement to the back door. The *only* door, she knew, that wasn't boarded up from the outside.

"I told ya I got all week!" the wereverine shouted, in between whistling. "The moon-kissed live a *long* time, honey. You decide to stop being unreasonable, you just let me know."

After what seemed like an eternity, Blaze reached the back door, but stood beside it, frozen in terror, staring at the latch. Some deep, inborn prey-instinct was telling her the moment she made the latch click open, the wereverine was gonna come barreling down the stairs in a bundle of saliva, talon, and fang, ready to rip her into little, bite-sized pieces. She stared at it for long, heart-pounding minutes, considering her alternatives.

She heard Jack continue his progress through the house, then heard big feet on a creaky staircase and guessed he had moved to the third story. Holding her breath, Blaze touched the door and carefully twisted the knob.

Upstairs, Jack resumed his whistling, much more muted, now.

There was a tiny, insignificant click that almost left Blaze in a seizure, then the door swung ever-so-slightly inward. Biting her lip, Blaze glanced up the stairs, then slowly inched the door open until she could fit her unwieldy body through it. Pulling it shut until it latched again behind her, she hesitated to look at her latest obstacle. The rough-hewn lumber of the back porch was like something straight out of an

1800's saloon, and it had creaked and groaned with their every step, an hour ago. Heart shooting blasts of fire through her chest, Blaze took five agonizing minutes crossing the back porch to a place where she could step off onto solid ground.

Once she was on the grass, though, she bolted, as softly and quietly as she could go.

TWO

Your Friendly, Neighborhood Wereverine

Jack puttered around aimlessly, heart still hammering from sheer *proximity* to the sleek, fire-haired beauty he had trussed up in the basement. Like some long-legged Aphrodite clipped straight out of the pages of a damn swimsuit magazine, except she came with a complimentary wave of goosebumps that crawled up his limbs whenever he made contact. Goosebumps that gave his heart tremors…and made the predator in him start panting.

Touching her hand in that first handshake, Jack had felt that insane rebel side of him—that usually-hibernating side with a built-in death-wish that got turned-on by near and imminent danger—start awake and take *notice*. It had only gotten that revved-up a grand total of four times in the past, and each time, it had been the start of a long, tumultuous, utterly breathtaking, sizzlingly exciting love-affair…

…that had ended in four deaths. Four horrible, pain-ridden murders at the hands of strangers. Alone, and afraid, when he should have protected them.

He was *not* letting it happen again. Especially not with a completely clueless, nerve-wrackingly smart, absolutely *gorgeous* redhead. He'd rather *die* than see that happen to another woman.

Hell, Jack realized, idly dragging the broom across the floor, at this point, he really did just want to rewind the last three hours and start over. If she decided not to cooperate, maybe the fey could concoct something for him that would erase a couple days for her. *Just tilt your head back and drink this, sweetie, and all your problems will go away…*

He didn't want trouble. And the way she made his hair stand on end and his heart thunder in his chest, hell, he'd be happy to wash his hands of the whole mess and head back to his house and forget she even existed. But how do you explain that to a girl whose biggest concern was that you'd just sprouted fangs and slitty eyes? She was probably going to sing to the tabloids the first chance she got.

Dammit. Fighting the lingering tingles in his chest, Jack paced with the broom in his hand, trying desperately to think of what he was gonna do if his new neighbor decided not to cooperate. He hated using fey-magics on people. It felt…dirty. Besides, the buggering little bastards always exacted an exorbitant price for their services, and he could just *see* himself losing another sword over the matter. Jack sighed. He wasn't gonna kill her, much as that would simplify his life, but if she went singing to the authorities, he was gonna have to pack up and find some other territory to call home.

And, after living in the same place since 1893, the longest he'd managed to live in one place since he'd been created, he was rather reluctant to just pack up his stuff and leave.

Damn it. He once again cursed himself for being a rash, impatient fool. He could've gone weeks, hell, *years* watching the elegant little bird from a distance, trying to scope out the situation, before revealing himself to her. If he had to at all.

To all appearances, she had absolutely no idea what she'd been getting into when she stepped onto his land.

And here I thought she was trying to pick a fight. Jack cursed himself again, then, pausing to listen to the basement, sighed again at the ringing silence of the lodge. "Look, Boss," he called, "this ain't really gonna change nothin' between us. I mean, hell, I'll still work for ya and all that. I just want you to promise you're not gonna run off and tell the world you got a wereverine living in your backyard, that's all."

Her silence that followed made Jack's eyes narrow. He started sweeping again. Just about any other moon-kissed out there would have ripped her head off and got it over with, but Jack kinda felt sorry for the girl. He figured he at least oughtta give her a chance. Maybe they could come to some sort of understanding…

Another hour passed without another peep from down below, and Jack bent to sweep up another pile of squirrel droppings, then dumped them into the cardboard box he was using as a trash bin. Straightening out a crick in his back, he raised his voice in a peace offering. "All right, say I come down there and let ya loose. All I *really* want, right now, is to make sure you aren't gonna run off and get us both in trouble."

Absolute silence answered him.

Jack sighed. "All right, sugar, look. I'm *sorry* I ran you down in the woods, okay? I really didn't want to, but you didn't give me a damn choice!"

He heard a rafter creak as the house settled.

"I know I probably scared you," he offered to the floorboards beneath him, "but I said I wasn't gonna hurt you and I meant it. Give me the word and I'll come down there, untie you, and we can talk about this like civilized adults."

Several more minutes left him listening to his own heartbeat.

He needed to come up with something to ease her mind, he knew. She was probably terrified, thinking he was some creepy-crawly asshole in the woods.

Well, some *other* creepy-crawly asshole in the woods. He was not gonna hurt her, damn it. But how to *say* that? He'd always been *horrible* with words. He struggled to think of the samurai and the other warrior-poets he had rubbed elbows with in the past. *They* wouldn't be having this problem. *They* would have her clinging to him in gratitude for saving her from the big bad world and giving her a safe place to live.

Jack wrinkled his nose, trying to think. What would a samurai say?

What happened was unfortunate, but it has enriched us both. Never before have I met a woman so utterly breathtaking in every way, whose body is art in motion, whose mere smile is like the rising of the sun. That I made your fears a reality is only a necessary evil for me to introduce you to a great new world, the magnificence of which you could never dream. My sword to protect you, if you will only continue to grace my worldly domain…

Yeah, that was good. Jack listened for a moment, collecting his thoughts. Then he awkwardly cleared his throat "Uh," he started. "What happened was…"

What happened was but the first step in a long path towards surrender, our souls to become one, our worlds mingled to face this new day…

"What happened was…" Jack grimaced as it all vanished on him again.

What happened was a turning of the wheel of Fate, a great dune in the sands of Time…

"Stop being a damned unreasonable little broad and *agree* already!" Jack blurted. "I don't like this any more than you do!"

She taunted him with her silence.

Jack bristled. "Fine! You just stay down there. Maybe I'll go home and drink a couple beers while I decide what I'm gonna do with you!"

She said nothing. The uppity city snot.

Growling, Jack started dragging the broom across the floor again. The whole building smelled of squirrel piss, and the little tree-rats had done a damn good job of ripping through every bag of flour, oats, sugar, and every other non-perishable box of food that the Olsons had left behind. It was probably going to take a week just to get the place smelling like something other than rat shit. His spoiled, primpy, rich, pampered new boss might not mind, but he had a *very* sensitive nose, and he'd always found the smell of rodent particularly unattractive.

Then a part of him demanded, *Why do you care? It's not like you're gonna be living here.*

He wrinkled his nose. He supposed he could be doing more productive things with his time than cleaning up his new neighbor's squirrel-shit.

He *really* didn't want to go back downstairs, though. Hell, if she didn't answer him, he was probably gonna curl up on one of the dusty mattresses and spend the night staring at the ceiling, wondering just how he was going to unfuck this particular disaster.

"It ain't gettin any lighter outside, sweet-cheeks," Jack called, dumping another load of droppings into the cardboard box. "You might as well stop wasting both our time and start listening to reason, 'cause you ain't goin *nowhere* 'til I've said my piece."

She didn't reply.

Growling, Jack finished sweeping the kitchen pantry and, slapping the broom down against the wall, went off down the side-hall to start checking the plumbing situation.

Thankfully after a quick inspection, he found that the Olsons had apparently drained their system rather efficiently before taking off for town. None of the porcelain had been cracked, and all the faucets had been run dry. After he'd checked every bathroom in all twelve rooms, Jack went to the big, windowed prow on the top floor of the lodge and started yanking dust-covers off of the furniture and wadding them into a big pile in his frustration.

He knew he was avoiding the basement and the gigantic problem that it contained, but he was too old to really give a crap.

Finally, once Jack couldn't think of anything else to do without a toolbelt, and he was well and truly tired of sweeping up squirrel shit, he marched back down to the top of the stairs and shouted into the basement, "What the hell are you trying to accomplish with the damn silent treatment, you ham-fisted *hippo*?" That seemed to have worked rather well to get her attention last time, so he thought he could expect a similar response.

Instead, the lodge all but hummed with silence.

Narrowing his eyes, Jack decided it was time to go make sure his new neighbor hadn't asphyxiated herself on that pretty orange hair of hers. He got to the bottom of the stairs, turned the corner, and said, "All right, tootz, you've just about pissed me—"

Aside from a few strips of cloth laying abandoned on the spark-guard beside the woodstove, the basement was empty.

Cursing, Jack was sprouting fur and fang before he even reached the back door.

THREE

On the Lam

Blaze made it a good mile straight through the woods, staying *well* off the trails, getting as far away from the Sleeping Lady and her attacker as possible before she stopped, panting, and pulled out her cell phone.

Except her cell phone, she discovered, with growing horror, had been tucked inside the front pocket of the soggy wet shirt that now lay on the floor in her abandoned bedroom, conveniently protected from 'accidental submersion' by a handy little hundred-and-fifty dollar case.

I am so totally dead, Blaze thought, staring at the woods around her in horror. It being early May, the snow had mostly melted and there were buds on the trees, but there wasn't even *grass* yet. Temperatures still had the nasty habit of dropping below freezing at night, and she hadn't even brought a coat.

Or, gee, a pack of matches and a cooler of hotdogs.

She was on the run, stumbling through God Knew Where in the first week of May, and she didn't even have a way to build a fire.

Hell, she wasn't even entirely sure exactly which direction she was headed in. Once she'd been walking long enough, all the fallen birch trees, the scraggly white spruce, the twisted willow, the alder thickets, and the towering cottonwoods looked the same.

Damn it, Blaze thought, briefly considering backtracking to retrieve her phone, but deciding that she would simply tough it out, instead, and hope she made her way to a river or some other waterway that she could follow to its confluence with something bigger. People, she knew, congregated on flowing water. The more water, the more people.

She had stumbled through the woods for at least four or five hours before Blaze happened into a small clearing, seemingly in the middle of nowhere. A squat little cabin sat in its middle, and beyond, she could see the open area of a lakeside. Thinking maybe she had taken some crazy and convoluted path back to Lake Ebony, Blaze stumbled out into the clearing and down towards the lake.

Looking over the shallow, mud-bottomed lake, however, it was pretty obvious to Blaze that she'd found one of the thousands of other lakes, ponds, and swamps dotting the wilderness in all directions from the Sleeping Lady. Tentatively, knowing that she probably wasn't going to find a better place to spend the night, Blaze went up the steps of the quiet little cabin and knocked on the door.

When no grungy old fart with a six-foot beard yanked the door open and shoved a shotgun up her nostril, she gently twisted the knob and pushed the door inward. "Hello?" she called, softly.

No answer. Of course not. Most of the cabins in the area were recreational quarters for wealthy doctors, lawyers, and businessmen in the Lower 48, only used during a couple weeks for fishing in king season, then again when the silvers were running. Sometimes, the real diehard outdoorsmen came out in late fall to fish the streams for trout and dolly varden, and a few went canoeing through all the lakes, looking for that fifty-inch pike.

Somehow, however, by the abandoned look of the dilapidated structure, she doubted it had seen an occupant in at least a couple years. She stepped inside and shut the door. The place smelled of mosquito coils and woodsmoke, and she was pretty sure that whoever owned the building had a penchant for tobacco. She was also pretty sure he hadn't visited in something nearing a decade.

A quick inspection of the dusty interior told her that the cabin had no phone, which wasn't very surprising, considering that it was mostly only the lodges and full-time residents who could afford the cost, upkeep, and long-term maintenance of a full-fledged satellite phone system. The only thing the little cabin *did* have, she discovered, was a pretty complicated radio. The cabin's owner, it appeared, liked his music.

After discovering the pantry and its meager supply of expired canned goods, Blaze slumped into the main couch with a can of tuna and, after cracking the lid with the temperamental old-school can-opener that she had found hanging from a nail nearby, ate fish from the can with her fingers, reveling in how wonderful it tasted after such a long, chilly hike through the woods.

Can demolished, she sat there trying to figure out what to do next.

She had a…*thing*…occupying her lodge, convinced it was a werewolf. Or a wereverine. Or something. Something really big and ugly and with lots of teeth. God, she needed the authorities. That, and about six different guns each with a thousand rounds of ammunition, all strapped to her chest in her best impression of Rambo. Let the little twit fuck with her then.

Blaze leaned back, feeling the first warm tingles of exhaustion dragging at her chest. It was *hard* to walk through the woods. Like trying to keep your balance on an ever-changing, never-level earthquake reproduction machine with built-in tripping mechanisms.

God, she was tired. Until now, she'd never really liked tuna, but as it had been the only choice aside from canned Great Northern beans and baby onions, the little pack of fish had tasted better than anything she'd ever eaten before. Blaze knew that was probably just the exhaustion speaking, but at the moment, she was too tired to critique culinary merit in the middle of the damn woods, on the lam from a guy who thought he was a medieval monster, born again to terrorize some really tall chick on her own property in the wilderness.

I really have to find a way back to town, Blaze thought, as she started drifting off. She had seen other cabins from the lakeside, when she had gone down to figure out where she was. Tomorrow, she would spend the day circling the lake, hoping to find a permanent resident with a telephone.

Blaze had only been asleep an hour, maybe an hour and a half, before the door slammed inward, imbedding itself in the little stove that marked the beginning of the cabin's tiny kitchenette. Blaze screamed and tried to scramble to her feet.

"All right," the fanged, taloned, *drooling* monster in the doorway roared, "since you seem to be intent on doing things the hard way, wench, I'm thinking I should just bury you in the damn hill and be done with it!" He stepped inside and slammed the door behind him, making the windows rattle in their frames, trapping Blaze in the tiny room with the wereverine.

Blaze cried out and backed up until her spine was pressed up against the back wall.

Growling, the wereverine strode towards her—

—and yanked a chair off the middle of the floor, dragged it back until it was positioned directly in front of the only exit, and sat down hard enough to make the wood squeak.

"You," the wereverine growled at her, pointing a taloned hand at the window over the lake, "almost made it off my territory, you long-legged pain in the ass." As he spoke, his form shifted back to something more human, until the only bit of monster showing was the way his canines extended past his lips in a snarl. "Do you *know* what would've happened to you if the fauns caught you on their land?"

"Accost me, tie me up, fling me over their shoulder, *lick* me, and try to convince me not to tell the police?" Blaze snapped.

He gave her a flat green stare. "They would've eaten you."

Her mouth formed a little O as she tried to think of some way he could be joking.

"Probably with mushrooms and wine sauce," he added. "The creepy bastards are all about fungi."

I'm in a stranger's cabin, having a chat about fairy-tale culinary preferences with a man who's claiming to be a wereverine, Blaze thought.

"So," Jack growled, "You use the CB?"

"The what?" Blaze demanded.

"The CB. The *radio*?" He gestured at the black monstrosity taking up an honored spot beside the woodstove.

Blaze just stared at him. "Why would I use the radio?"

Jack narrowed his pretty green eyes at her. "You're trying to tell me you just spent five hours running from me through the woods, but you didn't even try to use the CB?"

This has to be some sort of nightmare, Blaze thought. "I wasn't really in the mood for music, thank you," Blaze gritted, showing teeth. "Getting *kidnapped* kinda put me out of the mood. Now if you would just *get out of my head* and let me wake up, I'd be much obliged."

He cocked his head at her, making his black curls twitch against his scalp. "I can't fucking believe this. You *still* don't believe me, do you?"

Blaze gave the wereverine a long glare. "All right," she gritted finally, when he didn't vanish in a puff of mental exhaust. "Let's say your argument has some merit. What now?"

"That's what I was gonna ask you," the man bristled. "*You're* the one who seemed to be getting butt-hurt about the whole thing."

Blaze considered repeating the fact that he had *kidnapped* and *assaulted* her, but then decided not to waste her breath on a creature that obviously had less mental acuity than a vole. "You," she said carefully, "have obviously got some misconceptions about me, and—thanks to you—I now have some less-than-welcome revelations about you." She took a deep breath, using all of her tact in an attempt to punch through this man's thick skull. "It seems to me that we need to come to an understanding before one of us gets hurt."

Jack laughed. "Let's hear it, tootz."

"You're fired, for one."

He raised a brow. "Who said I was letting you fire me?"

"...letting you..." Blaze stammered, shocked. "Look, you *cretin*, just because you're *starving*, I don't have any obligation to pay you for trying to eat me."

"Already told you," Jack growled, "if I'd tried to eat you, I'd be shitting a really big Yeti turd right now, instead of sprawled over a chair, listening to her bitch."

Blaze's mouth dropped open. She stared at him in silence for a long, horrible minute, then glanced at the nearest window, wondering if she could wriggle through it and make it to the lake before the wer-everine caught her.

Immediately, Jack lazily unwound himself from the chair and got to his feet. "All right, girlie, seein' as how you're still not going to be reasonable, I'm just gonna take your ass back home and give you a couple days to think about it."

Blaze hastily backed away from him, stumbling into the far corner of the cabin, rapping her head on an iron frying pan that had obviously been hung there out of head-reach by the previous occupant. Immediately, she yanked it off of the wall and held it up between them. "Back off," she growled, swinging it back and forth. "I will bash your brains all over the goddamn walls, I swear it."

Jack's eyes darkened. "Put that down."

Blaze gave him her best impression of a confident laugh. "Not a chance, buster. I know six different forms of judo, and I could kick your teeth out through the back of your skull with just my big toe."

He crossed his huge arms over his burly chest. "That so."

"Uh-huh," Blaze said, grinning in her best impression of a crazy martial artist on the edge. "Just try me, asshole."

"You know judo, huh?" he said, eying her dubiously.

"Sure do," Blaze growled. "Been doin' it since I was old enough to walk. Eight different black belts."

"Eight, huh?" Jack said. "Just a minute ago it was six."

"Uh…" Blaze said, scrambling for an excuse, her face flushing. "I double-majored."

A grin actually twitched the corner of the bastard's mouth. "Double-majored, huh?" He gestured at the frying pan. "And what's that? A form of kendo?"

Blaze didn't have the first idea what 'kendo' was, but she went with it, "Sure as fuck is, asshole, now back the hell off before I kendo your skull into the next lifetime."

Jack sighed and stepped forward, completely indifferent to the iron skillet. Gasping in panic, Blaze put as much upper body strength into her swing as she could, aiming for his left ear.

Jack reached up and caught the handle of the skillet with one hand, without even looking, and held it there as if there were a cement statue suddenly fused to the frying pan. "Kendo," Jack said, as he stood there, only an arm's-length from her, looking up into her eyes, "is a relic of the time of the shoguns, and is based off of the kenjutsu of the samurai, a form with which I am intimately familiar. It means Way of the Sword. Not," he twisted the skillet suddenly, making her lose her grip in a spasm of pain, "Way of the Frying-Pan." He blithely dropped the pan at his feet, looking utterly unconcerned that she might bend and retrieve it.

For a long moment, they stood like that, with Jack much too close and Blaze backed up against the wall, her heart a pounding inferno in her chest.

"So," Jack said, as he peered up at her, "I think maybe we got off to the wrong start."

When Blaze glanced down at the frying-pan, she saw divots in the handle where he'd held it. Finger-prints in the *cast iron*. Realizing then that the man in front of her could simply reach out, take her face in his big hand, and squeeze her brains out through her eye-sockets, Blaze swallowed and lifted her chin, fighting down sheer animal terror. "I'd say," she managed, "you're probably right."

Jack grunted and held out his skillet-crushing palm. "My name is Jack Thornton. I'll be working for you as your mechanic while you're running the Sleeping Lady."

Blaze swallowed, fighting a sudden, gut-wrenching terror that her hand was about to become a crunched fleshy puree in the man's callused fist. She didn't want to be within the same *room* as that hand, much less put her *palm* in it. If she could have backed further into the wall, she would have, her heart ratcheting up to minor white-hot explosions in her ribcage.

Jack seemed to sense her reason for hesitation. "I already told ya, Miss Blaze," he said, his green eyes softening. "I'm not gonna hurt you. Now fucking shake my hand and introduce yourself 'fore I just throw you back over my shoulder and dispense with the bullshit." The gentle way he said it, Blaze realized that was this man's version of compassion.

Biting her lip against the sickening dread in her stomach, Blaze squeezed her eyes shut and tentatively reached out until her fingers made contact with something warm.

Jack's hand suddenly engulfed hers, and he held it gently, waiting.

"I'm Blaze," she whispered, cringing as far into the wall as she could get. She'd never been so scared in her *life*. Half of her wanted to dribble to the floor in terror, and the other half wanted to just puke all over him and pee down her leg.

"All right, Miss Blaze," Jack said, still lightly-yet-firmly holding her palm in his, "I'm a good guy. Know it don't look like it, when I change, but I really am. I don't hurt people, if I can get away with it. I'm pretty much like every other guy you ever met. I like to drink beer and tinker with shit 'til it runs good. We clear so far?"

"Crystal," Blaze managed, through the knot of fear in her throat.

"Okay," Jack grunted. He still was holding her hand, encasing it in a fist the size of a grizzly bear's paw. "We can help each other. Our goals are basically the same. You want to get a lodge up and running, and I wanna earn enough so I can buy steaks regular. You get me?"

Blaze flinched at the mention of 'steaks', but seeing how he wasn't releasing her hand and the cabin wall wasn't yielding at her advances, she could only swallow.

"So tell me about yourself," Jack continued. "What are your goals for the Sleeping Lady? And open your damn eyes, woman," he snapped. "Am I hurting you?"

Every part of her trembling, Blaze forced her eyes back open.

Jack peered up at her a moment before he grunted. "Okay, tootz. Let's hear it. What made you run out into the Bush and land in this ol' wereverine's backyard?"

"Why are you still holding my hand?" Blaze whispered.

"'Cause I'm trying to prove a damn point," he said gruffly.

Blaze glanced down, saw her hand where it disappeared into his, realized just how easy it would be for him to break it off at the wrist and toss it through the window, and looked back into his eyes nervously.

"You gettin the picture yet, sweetie?" he asked softly.

She bit her lip and swallowed, her heart thundering against her ribcage, every part of her wanting to squirm backwards through the rough boards of the cabin wall to get away from him, but between him and the wall, she was unable to move. "I think so," she managed.

"Okay," Jack said. "Talk to me. Where you from, what you doin, why'd you pick my neck of the woods?"

It took all of her control to manage, "I'm from Anchorage. Trying to build a fishing lodge. And because it was cheap."

There was kindness in the man's face when he said, "Six hundred large ain't really all that cheap."

"It's what I could afford," Blaze said. "Most lodges are a million and up."

"So, what," Jack said, still keeping her palm wrapped in his warm, callused grip. "You just wanna get it back up and running as a fishing lodge?"

Blaze swallowed nervously. "Uh. No."

His gaze sharpened. "No?"

"I wanted a farm," Blaze squeaked, suddenly seeing fingers flying across the room when the hammer that was his grip came down on the anvil that was his palm. She tugged back slightly, but there was absolutely no give in his arm, and she had to swallow down her terror or simply devolve into a whimpering puddle on the floor. Babbling, now, she added, "But I don't need one, if it bothers you. Really, I don't."

"A farm is a lot of work," Jack offered. "Especially around here." There was no derision, no disgust, no humiliating disdain. Just a statement of fact. And...curiosity?

Blaze held her breath. Then, tentatively, said, "I did a lot of research."

"Yeah?" Jack asked. He shifted his stance idly, which moved her hand ever-so-slightly away from her. Immediately, Blaze had to fight down the insane fear that she was about to lose her entire *arm*, not just a few digits.

"What kind of research?" Jack urged softly, when she didn't respond.

"How long are you gonna hold my hand?" Blaze managed, eyes riveted to their joined grip.

"'Til the damn conversation is over," Jack barked. "Like I said. Tryin' to prove a damn point. Probably falling flat on my face, judging by the way you keep acting like I'm gonna rip your arm off, but I'm trying."

"Sorry," Blaze managed, biting her lip. "You're scaring the crap outta me."

Jack groaned and slapped his other hand over his forehead and dragged it down his face. Peering at her from between his fingers, he said, "You're missing the point."

"Sorry," Blaze babbled, cringing.

"Don't apologize, dammit," Jack growled. "Listen. See this? See how I'm *not* breaking your arm or twisting off fingers or anything like that? I'm doing my damndest to calm you down, okay? I feel somewhat guilty for being a shit earlier and I'm trying to remedy this whole situation by showing you I'm not the boogeyman. That said," he gave her a flat stare, "I'm not letting go of your hand until you've convinced me you're O.K. with having a wereverine as a neighbor. Whether that takes the next couple minutes or the next three days, I won't be leaving you alone again until you do."

He's serious, Blaze thought, instinctively trying to inch away.

Jack held her easily in place. With his other hand, he gestured at the woods in general. "Tell me what kind of research. I know a bit about farming, myself. You talkin' pigs and chickens, or you talkin fields of potatoes, or just a greenhouse, or what?"

Blaze actually felt a flutter of excitement at the question. "All of it," she managed.

He raised a heavy black brow. "All of it?" No contempt. Just curiosity.

The lack of mockery in his voice—something that Blaze had dealt with from the very first day, sitting in her father's *lawyer's* office, when the stuffy old prick had scoffed at her casual mention of how she could now start a farm out in the Bush—gave her the courage to continue. "I want to raise heritage animals," she said slowly. "Rare livestock. Stuff that our grandparents used to raise."

He snorted. "I doubt *that's* possible, but keep going. Why rare stuff?"

"'Cause the older breeds are more independent," Blaze said. "They haven't had their survival skills bred out of 'em. They don't wander out and die in a blizzard 'cause they're too stupid to step inside the barn that's twenty feet away."

"And the plants?" Jack asked.

"Non-GMO stuff," Blaze said immediately. Then, before he could ask, she said, "GMO—it means Genetically Modified Organism. Something that somebody grew in a test-tube, by tinkering with its genetic code. Animals that glow in the dark. Plants that have been given the genes to produce their own *insecticides*."

Jack's eyes widened a bit. "They're *doing* that?"

She nodded. "GMOs represent about ninety percent of all corn, soybean, and cotton grown in the US. It's such a huge part of our food supply that just about everyone in America has it on their shelves and doesn't even know it."

He squinted and wrinkled his nose. "That's not good."

"No," Blaze said, getting excited, now, "And the big GMO companies, they plant their crops right next to the heritage farmers so it contaminates their crops, and then take them to court saying they 'stole' their genetics, because the heirloom farmers use the same seed as the stuff they grew to plant the next year, which is gonna contain any DNA that was introduced from the neighboring crop. They have basically copyrighted certain sequences of DNA, and then they sic their nasty, overpaid lawyers on the little guys to run off the competition."

"The asswipes," Jack commented.

"Yeah," Blaze said, "The old stuff is dying off, and we're losing those genetics forever. Stuff that took farmers *hundreds* of years to develop, *poof*, it's just gone. I read an article about a fava bean researcher that found a gal that had seventeen fava bean seeds—seventeen—from a species he'd thought had been completely extinct. He actually managed to bring it back."

"Fava beans," Jack said.

"*Yeah*!" she cried, gesturing. "They're real good for cold, wet weather, but most people have never heard of 'em because they're *controlling* our *food supply*."

"The pricks."

"No kidding," Blaze agreed. "Like most of America really only eats a single breed of each type of vegetable, when there used to be hundreds. Did you know there are *thousands* of varieties of heirloom tomatoes?! And you see, what, four types in the store? If you're lucky?"

"Never been to a store," Jack said.

"See, that's *cool*," Blaze cried. "That's what *I* want to do!" She waved a hand at the window in the general direction of the woods. "So I wanna find some varieties that are good up here in Alaska—did some research on that, but I've gotta test some theories, first—and then basically grow enough stuff to feed myself, my employees, and my guests."

"Cut yourself out of the system," Jack agreed.

"We're *already* off the grid out here," Blaze said, excitedly wiping her hair out of her face when it fell into her eyes. "Why not wean ourselves from the huge agricultural conglomerates, while we're at it? They barge all that stuff up from the Lower 48 and it takes two damn weeks to get here, anyway. Ends up all tasteless and mushy by the time it actually makes it into the grocery stores. And hell, we're just sending our money out of state, unless you go into Fred Meyers and buy Alaskan stuff like carrots and potatoes."

Jack was nodding, looking fully enthralled, which only made her more excited. *Finally*, someone who *understood*. Thank you, Jesus!

"So I figure, I get the farm started this summer," Blaze went on, gesticulating emphatically, "fix up the lodge this winter, and have the place all ready for guests by next spring. I'll start small, maybe only a few heritage breeds, something like chickens and goats, maybe rabbits, and try to feed them as much as possible on the surrounding acreage, and supplement that with a few bargeloads of grain and hay from the farmers in Palmer—"

"You like to talk about farming, don't you?" Jack said.

Blinking, Blaze realized Jack was looking up at her with a calculating expression. Getting nervous again, she said, "Uh, yeah. Why?"

He shrugged and crossed his arms. "Just an observation."

"Well, yeah," Blaze said. "It just seems so *wrong* what they're doing. I mean, people are eating *crap*. Stuff that isn't even *real food*. I mean, think about this." She lifted a hand and started counting off fingers with the other. "They're turning animals into machines. They're breeding them stupider and lazier and screwing with their genetics. They're giving us hybrid fruits and vegetables that are bred for their abilities to *withstand travel*, not for their taste. They're bleeding all the nutrients out of the soil, so much so that people now have the crazy idea that homegrown chicken *tastes funny*. You know why that is?!"

"No clue," Jack said.

"It's cause they've got *vitamins and minerals* in the flesh, instead of being raised in a cage, so damn fat they can't get up from the food dish. You know that's what chicken nowadays is, right? It's all the same crossbred Frankenchicken. Cornish-Rock. They finally hit upon the magic combo that switched their little muscle genes into such high gear that they grow so huge so fast that most can't even walk by the time they get to slaughter at *five weeks*. Tons of them die of heart attacks, just 'cause their tiny little hearts can't pump blood through all that muscle."

"So what if I built you a farm?" Jack said. "From the ground up. Whatever you wanted—barns, stalls, hutches, greenhouse, fields to plant—we'd make it happen."

Blaze felt her heart *melt* at the idea. "Oh gawd," she giggled. "That would be so *cool*! I mean, I know *about* it, but I don't have the technical skills to build a barn or hell, even a chicken-coop. I got all the plans, but really no way to implement them."

He was peering at her like she had grown tentacles from her ears. "You *really* like to talk about farming."

Blaze frowned at him, breathlessly wiping more hair out of her eyes. "How do you figure?"

He shrugged. "I let go of your hand about five minutes ago." Indeed, he was standing in front of her, arms crossed over his brawny chest, eying her with obvious interest.

Blaze froze and glanced down at her hand. She'd been using it to gesture ever since her diatribe on the agricultural conglomerates. "Uh."

"So," Jack said, "Seein' how I got the technical knowhow, I *didn't* rip your arm off, and you really *really* seem to want to have a nice little ranch in the woods, what say you we go back home and draw up some plans?"

Blaze bit her lip, once more realizing what the man claimed to be, and just how freakin' scary that was.

"Hey, now," Jack growled, unfolding his arms from his chest in warning. "Do we gotta repeat the last twenty minutes?"

"No," Blaze said quickly. Then she gave him a considering look. "You'll help me build a farm?"

"On the side," Jack said. "You'll be paying me to get the lodge up and running. Don't really wanna take the wind outta your sails, but farming don't pay near as well as gettin a bunch of rich fucks in a boat and takin' em out to thrash the water for a few hours."

"I know," Blaze muttered. She took a deep breath, then let it out with a sigh. "Just seems like I should be able to *do* something about all this, you know?"

He gave her a long, analyzing look. Then, shrugging, he said, "You will." He turned back to the front of the cabin and yanked the chair out from in front of the door. "Come on. Let's get home before it gets dark."

This far into spring, it was already almost twenty-four hours of daylight, but Blaze wasn't about to argue the point. When he opened the door for her, she stepped through it and out onto the tiny, rickety porch.

"Just so you know," Jack said, behind her, "I can track something by scent."

Though his words clawed at her insides, Blaze gave him a sweet smile over her shoulder. "I'll have to remember to stock up on ammonia." Then she turned, stepped confidently, out onto the weather-worn boards...

...and fell to her knees, vomiting over the edge of the porch, into the grass.

Jack immediately squatted beside her, giving her a worried look. "You okay?"

"I'm having minor digestion issues," Blaze whimpered, ashamed at the fact she'd been unable to hold it down. "Must have been the flight."

Jack watched her, his pretty green eyes telling her he knew exactly why she was feeling ill, and that he was sorry. "Was pretty windy up there today," he agreed.

"Absolutely," Blaze said, once again feeling a pang of queasy fear looking into his deep green eyes. Inhumanly green, now that she thought about it. Her stomach heaved again and she retched up the rest of her breakfast into the meager pile beside the porch.

A big hand touched her shoulder. "Hey, sorry."

"You're an asshole," Blaze whimpered, but she didn't shrug off his grip.

Surprisingly, Jack chuckled and rubbed her back. "I'm a wereverine. We're not exactly a friendly bunch."

Blaze swallowed, hard, and met his gaze. His pants were still shredded, leaving him mostly naked as he squatted beside her. "So," she managed, "You bite me and I get sick and…?"

Jack wrinkled his nose and snorted. "No. My kind aren't into that shit. The wolves, on the other hand…" He sighed. "They've got dominance issues. Gotta have a pack. So they make themselves one, usually from whatever mortals strike their fancy, whether they're interested or not. It's *them* you gotta avoid. Nah, if a wereverine gets hold of you and don't like what he sees, he'll just sputch you and get it over with."

…*sputch?* "But you *could* turn me?" Blaze insisted.

Jack made a dismissive sound, but his shoulders stiffened, the subject obviously making him uncomfortable.

"How?" Blaze demanded, wiping her mouth with a sleeve.

Jack scowled at her. "I'm not gonna turn you into a—"

"Tell me," Blaze snapped. "For Christ's sake, what am I gonna do? *Force* you to bite me?" She scoffed, though her whole body was trembling. "Just ease my mind a little bit, okay?"

"I'm *trying* to ease your mind, girl," Jack growled. "I stopped turning people four thousand years ago, once the intrigue wore off."

Blaze waited, watching him.

Jack sighed, throwing up his big hands in surrender. "Fine. You saw those little teeth in the back? The ones that punched through?"

"They weren't little," Blaze managed.

"Those are them," Jack grunted. "They've got venom-tubes, basically. Something gets bit with those, they're in trouble. Either they're lunch—which is mostly the case—or sometimes they escape long enough for the poison to take hold. Then it's a really long, really *painful* process of figuring out just what the hell is happening to them." He winced, his gaze growing distant. "*Really* painful." Then he shook himself. "Nowadays, most of us older ones see an accident, we sputch it. There's enough of us as it is, and the way humans are moving outwards, we're only getting more crowded."

"An…accident." Blaze swallowed, hard. "I'm sorry. I think I should head back to Anchorage." She stood up, intent on marching straight back to the lodge, grabbing her things and using her cell phone to call Candy Rogers to schedule the next flight out.

Jack stood with her and caught her by the shoulder. "Hey," he said softly, "My mistake, all right? You're obviously not one of us, so it won't hurt to have you on my land." He gave her a wolfish grin. "Besides. You said you wanted a farm."

Blaze's irritation rose, despite herself, at mention of 'his' land. Nonetheless, she hesitated, remembering how the lodge had felt looming around her. She had been *standing* in her childhood dream, and it had easily been one of the greatest moments of her life—until it had been shattered by a monster dragging his tongue across her neck.

Then again, she knew she wasn't going to have another opportunity like this. Besides, who really *cared* if the area seemed to be inhabited by a shape-shifting lycanthrope? He seemed to be friendly enough…

"Come on," Jack said. "I'll lead you home." He started off into the woods, hesitating just long enough to see that she would follow.

Reluctantly, Blaze did. They chatted awkwardly about little things—how Jack had to hook up the battery system and show her how it worked, how the generator would probably need some tinkering before it would fire up, how the four-wheelers had all been put away in storage—until Blaze was simply too tired to make conversation. While she had maintained a gym membership back in Anchorage, trudging through the woods used a whole different set of muscles, and it wasn't long until she just wanted to sit down and die.

Eventually, Jack sighed. "All right, sweetie. Come here." He half-squatted in front of her, showing her a large stretch of his muscular back.

"What are you doing?" Blaze asked suspiciously.

"I'm getting this show on the road," Jack said. "We keep going like this, it's gonna take hours."

"It took me hours to get out here," Blaze said.

Jack winced. "Uh, yeah, hmmm." His green eyes caught hers and she saw indecision there. "Well, see, tootz, that whole little jog took me about ten minutes. Maybe. Once I stopped being Captain Oblivious upstairs."

Oh shit, was all Blaze could think.

"So, uh, yeah," Jack said. "Please climb on?" By the nervous way he was biting his lip, Blaze was pretty sure he wouldn't force the issue, if she didn't cooperate. She opened her mouth to say she'd rather walk.

Jack sighed and straightened. "All right." He resumed picking his way back through the woods.

Blaze, who hadn't yet spoken, said, "Just don't brain me on a branch or something."

The wereverine gave her a surprised look over his shoulder, then obligingly squatted again and held position while she awkwardly climbed onto his back, like a Zulu mounting a midget.

"Here goes," Jack said. "Hold on. This is probably gonna scare the crap outta you, but it'll be over quick."

And then he was growing *fur* underneath her hands, and Blaze was clamping her cheek to his hairy shoulder, just to keep from having her head snapped off at the neck from the sheer *speed* at which they bounded through the woods. She squeezed her eyes shut, feeling sick again, and fervently began praying she didn't vomit down the wereverine's fuzzy spine.

"There we go," Jack said, sliding to a gravel-crunching halt in the back yard of the Sleeping Lady. He lowered Blaze gently to the ground, but she fell on her ass anyway, staring up at him in horror.

"What *was* that," she blurted. "Mach 2?"

He grinned at her as his fangs started sucking back into his face. "Never really had a way to measure it." He cocked his head. "Faster than a horse-and-buggy, though."

"You *think*?!" Blaze cried. Her world was still moving around her in a wild, twisty chaos in her inner ear, and she carefully puked into a pile beside her forearm. Then, shakily, she got to her feet and stumbled towards the lodge and her cell phone.

"I'm really sorry I scared you, Miss Blaze."

Blaze froze on the back steps, hearing genuine regret in the wereverine's voice. She turned slowly and peered at him.

He was standing in the middle of the yard, still dressed in his shredded remnants of jeans, wincing, looking like he wanted to say more.

She looked down into his sincere green eyes, considered going back to her apartment in Anchorage—which only had another six days left on the lease—laughed in despair, then slumped against the doorframe of the lodge, using it to slide down onto her ass. All of her plans had just come tumbling down around her shoulders. She needed to decide if she was going to stay or go. Then stick with it.

She glanced out at the decrepit outbuildings, the ancient, meager woodpile, the graying, weathered siding, the weed-strewn lawn. It was her childhood dream, staring her right in the face. Unfortunately, so was Flash the Wereverine. "So how's this gonna work?" she managed. "I mean, you *seem* nice enough, but do you eat people who piss you off? I intend to run a *fishing* lodge. With *guests*. Anyone who works in customer service knows that guests can be dicks."

Jack gave her a pained smile. "I don't eat the other white meat. Too stringy. Tastes like chemicals."

That he would *know* something like that was enough for Blaze to put another checkmark next to Return To Anchorage. She dropped her face into her hands. The Sleeping Lady had spent four *years* on the market—possibly more—until some really tall rube in Anchorage dropped all six hundred grand of her inheritance in it in an insane scheme to make her dreams of self-sufficiency come true. It might spend another *ten* on the market until she could find someone to buy it from her, and she wasn't going to be able to pay off the loan—currently on a one-year deferral to allow her business to get up and running—if she didn't operate the lodge.

"I am so screwed," she whispered to the rickety wood panels between her knees. She had just gotten so *exuberant* and *excited*. Like a goddamn three-year-old. Four years of Business classes and three years of accounting work, completely tossed out the damn window the moment she had a chunk of change actually *worth* anything sitting in her bank account. She was a disgrace to her family name. And it wasn't even her *family*. She'd been freakin' *adopted*. The rat fucks should have *told* her. Not let her find out when they *died*.

Blaze quickly re-routed that thought, knowing it would lead to tears, and the *last* thing she wanted to do right now was become a sobbing wreck and deal with the consequences that followed.

"I always wanted a farm," she confessed to the porch. "A place of my own out in the woods, you know? Ever since I was a little kid."

Jack, a total stranger until she had called him a week ago in search of a maintenance man, gingerly climbed the stairs and lowered himself against the opposite frame, listening.

"I've always had a good head on my shoulders," Blaze continued. "Only really get worked up about the way the agricultural conglomerates have been taking the *life* out of foods, but that's just crazy, right? I mean, who cares about that shit?"

"It's not crazy," Jack said softly.

Without lifting her head, Blaze snorted. "You don't have to patronize me." Shaking her head at the porch, she said, "No, I'm usually not this knee-jerk. I just got that check, six hundred thousand after taxes, and I just kind of dropped everything and headed for the Bush. Thought I'd found a way to make my dreams come true."

"Who says you haven't?" Jack asked. He was picking at a splinter in the weathered wood.

Blaze gave a mirthless laugh and gestured at him.

Jack glanced up at her quickly with a frown. "I'm not runnin' you off."

Blaze snorted miserably.

"I'm *not*," Jack insisted. "And frankly, I'd rather you stayed."

He'd rather she *stayed*? Blaze blinked at him, suspicion rising within her at the way his words almost sounded like a plea. *Gee*, her logical mind said, *what* would *a lonely little man all alone out in the woods want from an all-too-available female?*

"I mean," Jack said hastily, "I can protect you. You obviously can't take care of yourself, so I'd do you a favor and keep you safe."

Yep, that answered it. He was going to do her the *favor* of screwing her. Blaze felt her hackles raise. "I can take care of myself."

"Uh," Jack said, "No offense, Blaze, but you start walking in any direction from here and you're gonna run into something that would sputch you 'soon as look at you."

Blaze didn't know what 'sputch' meant, but from the context, she was relatively sure that it wouldn't be pretty. Looking wistfully at the lodge's outbuildings, she said, "Maybe I could sell it and buy a new place in Canada or somewhere."

"I told you," Jack growled, "I'm not warning you off."

"Then what *are* you doing?" she cried, exasperated. "You attack me, scare the *crap* outta me, run me down, lick me, run me down *again*—"

"I'm asking you to stay," Jack interrupted. "Under my protection."

"I don't need your 'protection,'" Blaze said, bristling.

"Believe me," Jack said, holding her eyes for a long moment, "You *do*." He sounded utterly serious.

And, considering that he seemed to have the ability to shape-shift into a monster at will, a tiny little self-preserving part of Blaze suggested that maybe she ought to listen to the little man that sprouted hypodermic fangs when he got angry. Deciding to change the subject, she said, "So what do you…you know…want from *me*? I mean, aside from a paycheck."

"I want you to stay," Jack said. He shrugged. "After that, who knows?"

Blaze glared at him. "I'm not screwing my employees."

Jack gave her a startled, half-cocked stare, then blurted, "Lady, did I *ask* you to screw me?" The way he said it, she might as well have asked him to go screw a rhino.

Well, question answered. The headline was written all over his face. Greek God Not Interested In Screwing Yeti. Cheeks heating, once more fully aware of his beautiful, perfectly-chiseled body, and just how awkward and ungainly her own six-foot-four form really was, Blaze said, "So, uh, what do you know about farming?"

"Farming?" Jack twitched, like his brain was still fully occupied with trying to picture the nasty mechanics of elephantine sex, then said, "A lot. Anything you decide to grow is gonna do well."

Blaze felt somewhat irritated at his ego. "I was asking for *facts*, not boasting about your farming skills."

He frowned at her. "I wasn't—" Then, cutting off, he muttered, "What you wanna know? Raised a lot of rabbits in Russia. Had goats in Arabia. Chickens in Japan. Pigs and cows in the colonies. Geese and ducks anywhere there was water. Hell, sometimes just trapped some wild ones and started breeding my own."

Wow, Blaze thought. *This dude's well-traveled.* Hiding her surprise, she said, "How about potatoes? You know anything about those?"

He snorted. "More than I care to. You clear a spot of land, dig a trench, drop a few spuds in the bottom of it, and in a few months you're gonna have 'em comin out your ears. So many you gotta hand 'em out to the neighbors. Hell, *more*, if you find your..." He suddenly bit off his words and gave her a wary look.

"More if I find my what?" Blaze asked, curious.

"More if you use fertilizer," Jack said, quickly lowering his head in a manner that told her he had been about to say something else. He started picking at the porch again, and now that Blaze was looking, she saw the point of a black talon extending from the tip of his finger. He was using it to idly scrape at the wood, drawing up more splinters.

"Stop that," Blaze ordered.

Jack frowned up at her. "Why? I'm just gonna be replacing it when I rip out the porch."

"I find it annoying," Blaze said, "Especially when I'm trying to think."

"Really?" He pried up more splinters, raking his finger across the deck. "I find it *helps* me think."

As she sat there, listening to the *scratch-snap* of wood, thinking about how her day had completely devolved around her, only feet from a man who had made a very convincing case that he wasn't human, Blaze began to wonder if this was what losing her mind felt like.

"You are close to pissing me off," Blaze finally said.

"Honey," Jack said. *Scratch-snap.* "I've had a long day."

"*You've* had a long day," she sputtered. "Who *kidnapped* you and went rabid kangaroo and *licked* you while drooling all over your shirt?"

He lifted his head and gave her a flat look. Then he returned to drawing designs in the wood with his talon.

Blaze took a deep breath and glanced again at the yard. She let it out between her teeth, forcing a smile. "All right. So we've agreed that you'll *let* me stay on *your* land, and you'll protect me from…" She gestured at his finger where it was digging into the wood. "…things like you."

Jack grunted. "Sorry to tell you this, honey, but there *ain't* nothin' like me. Not anymore." He looked up at her and grinned, but it was fierce and filled with pain. "Wolves got the last one 'bout six years ago. Part of how them assholes got themselves that land. Killed the gal that was sniffing around, seein' if I'd make a decent enough mate." He gestured to the south. "Pretty sure she sputched a few of them, and there's more than one who's got a good limp, now, but I haven't seen her since they moved in."

"Maybe they drove her off?" Blaze suggested, a bit horrified.

He shrugged. "Maybe." *Scratch-snap.* "But I doubt it. We, uh, kinda have trouble backing down, once we're worked up." He gave her a sheepish look before returning to the porch.

"Wereverines," Blaze said, just to make sure. "Like were*wolves*."

Jack snorted. "Nothin' like those droolin' pussies."

To distract herself from the way he was demolishing her porch, Blaze started picking dead grass and loose twigs from her hair, deposited there from her tumble in the woods, hours before. "So we agree you're gonna *let* me stay." It still grated her to say that, considering she had spent over six hundred thousand dollars for that right.

"Sure," Jack said, as if she had been asking. "I'll let you stay." He kept prying at the wood. By the way he wouldn't look at her, she felt like he was hiding something.

"I'm staying," Blaze bit out. "I don't have anywhere else to go."

He gave her another quick look, startled. "You ain't got houses in town?"

The casual way he said 'houses' made her feel sick. Obviously, he had the wrong idea just how much money he was dealing with, here. "Jack," she said slowly, "Let me clarify something for you. Before I got the six hundred thousand from my dad, I was eking out a living on ramen and corn, working an accounting job during the day, taking classes at night, and sometimes I couldn't afford the *corn*, when it came time to buy textbooks."

"Huh," he said. She could see his prospects for that steak-buying money fade from his face so quickly it hurt. Poor guy. She wondered what his last good meal had been. It was pretty common knowledge that a good number of the Bushrats out here were just barely eking by on the Permanent Fund Dividend and food stamps. She actually felt bad for getting his hopes up.

"But hey," Blaze offered, "All that could change if I actually get this lodge running. Then there would be enough money to throw around, you know what I mean?"

He stiffened with a healthy case of Poor Man's Pride. "I don't need your money."

Sighing, Blaze said. "Okay. Sure. So tell me about this farm you're gonna build me."

Jack snapped off a large shard of wood, then disgustingly picked it up and started using it to dig between his teeth. "Guess it all depends on what you want, tootz. I'm here for the next few centuries or so, so whatever ya want, I can build it." He pulled out whatever had been stuck between his teeth and held it out, frowning as he examined it.

Blaze slapped at a group of mosquitoes clustered on the back of her hand. "Something self-sustaining, if that's possible," she said.

"Sure," was all he said. "What kind of materials and budget are we looking at?"

This time, Blaze winced. "I've already scheduled some barge loads of lumber to be delivered in the next couple weeks. I can add some fencing to the mix."

Jack sniffed the air between them, wrinkled his nose, then gave her a considering look. "You got a green thumb, don't ya?"

"It's why I want a farm," Blaze admitted.

Jack nodded. "You get some Plexiglas and I can build you a greenhouse. Big one. You like any particular fruit trees? Oranges? Pears?"

"Mangoes," Blaze said, laughing, "But nobody can get a mango to grow this far north."

"We'll get you some mango trees, then," Jack said. "And whatever else you want."

Blaze eyed him suspiciously, distrustful of his sudden willingness to please. "You make it sound like you're wanting me to settle in."

Jack's fingers stopped working the splinter between his teeth. Blaze wasn't sure, but she thought she saw him blush. He coughed. "Girl, I been around awhile. A male's got a few important duties in life, and a wise man knows it, and he does his job, quickly, without complaint."

Blaze raised a brow, her hackles already bristling. She knew where the conversation was headed and she'd heard such chauvinist crap before. "I already told you, I don't need you taking care of—"

"—cause if they don't, they get bitched at 'til they do." He flicked the splinter across the yard. He crossed his beefy arms over his big, relatively hairless chest. "So, one-story greenhouse or two?"

Blaze stared at him, caught between laughing and crying. "You can make it two?" she finally managed.

"Two it is, then," he grunted. "You got any idea what kind of critters you want on the place to start? Rabbits? Chickens?"

Reluctantly, Blaze told him her complete plan for the place.

Jack raised his eyebrows, but he didn't say it couldn't be done. On the other hand, for some time, he didn't say anything at all. Then,

"*Yaks*, you say?" He sounded dubious. "Don't those live up in the Himalayas?"

"They're more feed-efficient than cows," Blaze said, her spine straightening under his scrutiny, "And their milk is richer."

"But you said you wanted cows, too," he said, frowning at her.

"Highlands and Galloways," Blaze agreed. "They're heritage breeds. Really hairy. Raised in Scotland. Hardy as hell. Can eat brush as well as grass."

He gave her a long look, then, slowly, nodded. "And you eventually want to turn this place into a renaissance faire?"

"Only during a couple weeks in the summer," Blaze said. "I'm hoping to get four to five hundred people to show up. Offer free flights out and everything. Give 'em all a taste of what life is *really* supposed to be like. Good food, no internet, no TV…But that's *years* from now."

Jack looked ill. "Uh, no offense, Boss, but I kinda like my privacy."

"They won't leave the grounds," Blaze promised. "We'll be roasting our own pigs, butchering our own chickens…Nobody will need to go off hunting in your territory or anything."

He gave her an irritated look. "This *is* my territory."

"It's only thirty acres, Mr. I've Got Ten Square Miles," Blaze snapped. "And if I can get five hundred people to show up in the summer and get some cabin rentals and campsites built, we're looking at almost two hundred thousand dollars a year, pure profit."

That got his attention. She could *see* his stomach calculating out just how many good steak dinners that would be for him that winter. "For two weeks a year?" he asked, sounding incredulous.

"That's it," Blaze said. "And if we get the client base for an agritourism group going, then we could earn more money that way."

"Agritourism." He sounded like she was talking nuclear physics.

"It's basically people who live in the city who get tired of the traffic and the stress and want to hire out a cabin out on a farm for a week or two, just to get out of the fast lane for a bit. We'd totally have the setup, too."

"We," Jack said, looking cautious.

Blaze shrugged. "No way I could do it alone. You help out, I'll cut you in on the profits."

Jack grunted, then wrinkled his nose. Tentatively, he said, "Do you have any idea how much *work* you're talking about here, sister? That's like full-time jobs for ten people. Just the fishing lodge itself...Hell, that's gonna take you, me, and a couple more guys as it is."

Blaze deflated even as her pride prickled. "Then I'll hire people."

Jack snorted. "You and what inheritance?"

Oh, the *bastard.* Another check mark went up beside Return to Anchorage. Shields down, Captain. Engines at twelve percent...Wasn't looking good, Jim.

Blithely unaware of her scowl, he went on, "I get the pigs and the cows—they're good eatin. I get the birds, 'cause they're easy to keep. I even get the goats, the buggering little bastards. But *yaks*?"

Blaze shrugged. "I dunno. I've just got this feeling like maybe the world won't be around here much longer, and I'm gonna do what I can to save a piece of it."

Jack stiffened, his green eyes squinting at her. "What do you mean?"

Blaze laughed. She never told anyone of her fears of an impending apocalypse, knowing they would laugh her out onto the street. Somehow, though, faced with this man-beast-*thing*, she felt confident enough to tell him.

After listening to her explanation, Jack grunted. He started picking at the deck again in silence. *Scratch-snap. Scratch-snap.* Just when Blaze thought she was going to lose her mind, he said, "So you want to save some heritage breeds, grow some heirloom veggies, and maybe see us through the end of the world, is that it?"

The blunt way he put it made Blaze's spine stiffen. He thought she was crazy. *He*, a goddamn slitty-eyed *freak* thought that *she* was crazy.

But his voice was low and serious when he said, "You got any particular reason why you feel like the end is coming?" He looked at her, and when his eyes met hers, they were utterly alert, waiting.

Blaze let out a nervous laugh under his acute stare, caught completely off guard by his solemnity. "Uh. Just my gut. Like the Earth was never meant to hold all these people, and Mother Nature's gonna end up fixing the problem." When his gaze sharpened, she anxiously picked a few pieces of dried grass from her shirt. Quickly, she added, "Probably just all the books and movies out there. Kind of rubbed off, I guess."

He grunted, his brow wrinkling in thought. Then he shrugged. "Sounds doable." As if that were the end of the conversation, he pushed himself to his feet and held out a hand to assist her. "Let's get inside and get the door shut. We're letting the bugs in."

Warily, Blaze took his hand. Jack heaved her to her feet like a lead statue, then released her hand like it was infested with lice, staring down at his forearm.

Following his gaze, even Blaze noticed the goosebumps that crawled up his skin at her touch, like he'd dunked his arm in icewater.

"Still ain't gotten used to that," he grumbled, opening and closing his big fist like he'd just slammed it into a brick.

"Used to what?" Blaze demanded, more than a little unnerved to see that kind of reaction on a guy who spent half his time running around sprouting fangs.

Jack glanced up at her, and for a moment, it looked like he was going to say something really important. Then he let out the breath he'd been holding and shrugged. "Nothin." Then, to her consternation, he turned his back and went into the basement. Beside the woodstove, however, he paused and glanced over his shoulder. "How long would you say we've got?"

"I need to start running guests through this place by next summer," Blaze said. "The renaissance fair is gonna have to wait until I can get the cabins and the livestock around. Probably like ten years. Who knows."

"I mean 'til Mother Nature gives us the boot."

Blaze hesitated, caught off-guard. "Uh. Maybe ten to fifteen years?"

He grunted. "The fey have been sayin' five." Then he brought out a second flashlight, flipped it on, and started up the stairs, leaving Blaze staring after him.

FOUR

Tongue-Twisted

Jack helped the Sleeping Lady's new proprietor get settled in for the night, then retreated to the woods to sit and watch the place, thinking. He was actually rather shocked when the leggy redhead didn't try to sneak off again. He would have bet a sword she would've tried to rabbit on him the first night. It was, after all, an awful lot for somebody to digest for the first time, and it was a really *long* night to spend alone, staring at the ceiling in the dark.

And yet, he heard the unmistakable sounds of sleep coming from the room she had requisitioned for herself. He sat down under a spruce, listening to the rhythmic sounds drifting from the basement, wondering what the hell he was going to do with this fancy new critter that had landed on his doorstep. She was *way* outta his league. He had known that the moment she put her big-ass foot on his land. It was pretty much the same feeling a lumberjack got when a grizzly snuck up behind him and tapped him on the back with a big, hairy claw. That whole Hey Buddy, Hope You're Packing Fresh Shorts, 'Cause You're Gonna Need 'Em moment.

Yet, Jack had always had a sort of death-wish, and he'd spent his life flirting with danger like most guys flirted with women. And after spending centuries with a *dragon*, Blaze's particular breed of nasty wasn't as terrifying as it should have been. Just...interesting.

Way *too* interesting. Gods, she was like a freakin' alabaster-skinned *goddess*. An Aphrodite that made his breath catch every time he got too close. Just her *proximity* gave him those deliciously wicked goose-bumps, and it had been everything Jack could do to keep her from seeing the way she made him pop wood, every time she moved. 'Pretty' didn't even *begin* to describe her long, coppery hair, or her fine, elegant lines, or her slender fingers...

Jack quickly derailed that train of thought before it could go any further. He would *not* do that to another woman again. Never again. The world was just too dangerous to fall in love with a wereverine. Especially for some drop-dead gorgeous, painfully innocent chick from the city who seemed to have absolutely no freakin' clue what was going on...

...or what she was doing to him.

Damn it, Jack thought, again crushing that thought. *Not gonna happen, chump. She's a princess to your dickcheese. Some dragon's gonna come down and whisk her away, so don't even bother getting your hopes up.*

Then he realized he was thinking about saying fuck the dragons and trying to make the bond anyway, even after losing Tavva to an iron maiden, and Jack started pounding his head into the nearest birch tree to clear it. He didn't need another mate. His mates died. Because of him. Because he couldn't protect them. Because they trusted him and he *failed*. This cute little bird didn't need that.

What she *did* need was for him to keep his damned distance. The less Jack's enemies saw the two of them together, the less chance there was that one of them was gonna sputch her out of spite.

Still, the *tingles* he got when she got close...Like freakin' Heaven had decided to part its clouds and shine its light down on his skin. Jack groaned, just thinking about it. Heaven. Freakin' heaven. It had been all he could do to leave her alone in her busted little room and walk out the back door 'to go back home.' In all reality, he didn't even want to wander off what he now considered, in growing bewilderment, 'her land.' He could feel her energy in it already, spreading outward from the Sleeping Lady, mingling with his, invigorating it, giving it *life*…

"*Way* outta your league," he muttered, slapping his forehead against the birch again. "Stop it, you dumbass, before you get another one hurt."

Once he'd managed to get his reckless side back in check, he went back to his original plan of watching for intruders. And there *would* be intruders. With something like *that* settling down on his property, he would be lucky if he could fend them off with a freakin' Howitzer.

The rhythmic sounds from the basement continued, and Jack was just starting to drift into a light doze when he heard a soft *click* from the front of the house. Inside, he heard Blaze continue to snore. Jack sat up quickly, summoning the beast in a liquid surge, and hurried around to the front of the Sleeping Lady.

Immediately, however, his snarl cut short.

Blaze was slipping out an open window. As he watched, she gave furtive looks in either direction, picked up a backpack that she must have thrown out the window ahead of her, and began tiptoeing across the weed-choked yard, fully dressed. Behind her, something continued to snore.

Crafty little bird, aren't ya? Jack thought, his heart beginning to pound with the thrill of the hunt. This could be *fun*.

As he watched, Blaze passed the shop and headed for Lake Ebony. No doubt because she didn't realize the neighbors were just a quarter mile down the opposite trail, with satellite phones and battery systems and full contact with the outside world.

Fun, Jack amended, watching her go, but why bother? Was he just going to keep her hostage for a few months, until he *grew* on her gangly ass? How was he going to keep her from singing to the authorities about her hairy little kidnapper, the moment she found a phone? Or keep her from telling Bruce everything, the moment the pilot returned with their next load of supplies?

Jack almost let her go. After all, his life would be a *lot* easier without something from the Fourth Realm gracing his doorstep, and he could always find new territory if he had to.

Then that stubborn, death-wishy part of him that had always loved a good hunt kicked in and he was loping off after her.

Instead of simply running her down and dispensing with the bullshit as he would have with any other girl that happened to accidentally complicate his life, however, Jack decided he needed to take another tack with this particular woman. Not only did he want her to hang around and be his business partner, but there was a deep, instinctive part of him that didn't want her to be afraid of him. He'd always had a soft spot for the womenfolk, and no matter how old he got, when they screamed and ran from him, it hurt.

Gotta be polite, he thought, as he snuck through the woods to circle around and head her off on the trail to the lake. She was obviously a smart kid. He just needed to appeal to her logic. He *thought* he'd done a good job of that, letting her talk about farming and greenhouses and GMOs until she was blue in the face, but apparently, she needed a bit more persuasion.

I'm rich, Jack thought, deciding that would be a good opener. *Honey, you stay with me and I can buy you all the fancy chickens you could ever want.*

Even as he slid through the alders, Jack winced. Even to him, that didn't sound all that great. *I'm rich*, he amended, *Stay with me and we'll make you right at home.*

No, that was fucktarded.

I'm rich, he tried again, *I can help you build whatever operation you want at the Sleeping Lady. Just* please *don't go squealing off to the authorities that I sprout fangs. I've really started to like it here.*

No, that was just begging.

I'm rich, he thought, creeping through the underbrush, dodging under low-hanging branches, *what more could you ask for, honey?*

Nah, that was just inviting her to say something nasty. Like, "Oh, I dunno, less of a midget?"

Jack decided to strike that chain of thought and try something else.

I'm a badass, he thought. *You keep pissing me off and I could rip off your head and—*

No, that probably wasn't the right way to get her to cooperate.

I'm a badass, Jack revised, *I can protect you. All you've gotta do is stop being stupid and trust me to take care of you.*

No, that hadn't worked the first time, and losing Henrietta still hurt bad enough that he didn't really want to promise that to another woman.

I'm a badass, he thought. *Of course you'd want to stay with me.*

No, that sounded too much like a damned dragon. In desperation, Jack ditched that train of thought, too, and tried to come up with some other reason why she would want to stay with him. Rich, and a badass. Two things women loved. Right?

Somehow, though, he got the distinct idea that *this* woman, the lanky pain in the ass that she was, probably wasn't gonna fall for his two most obvious assets.

Then he had another startling thought. *You're* still *thinking you're gonna try and keep her, aren't you, Jackie-boy? Wake the fuck up, asshole, she's made it perfectly clear she's not gonna be hanging around for long...*

Then, stubbornly, he decided that she wasn't going to get to make that decision. After all, *she* had made the mistake of putting *her* big foot on *his* land, so that made her *his* problem. And he was good at problem-solving. All he had to do was figure out what she wanted.

Jack settled himself into the center of the path, watching her dark shape move tentatively down the trail, towards him.

A farm, obviously. And she probably wasn't too keen on the hairy little wereverine that had made an ass out of himself, but there *had* to be something he could offer her to keep things from getting out of hand.

I'm a rich badass, Jack thought, as she approached, a deeper shadow tentatively picking its way along the trail in the dark. *Man of your dreams, baby.*

No, no, *no,* he thought, with increasing frustration. He needed to say something eloquent, something that would ease her fears, make her trust that he really wasn't out to rip off her head. Not for the first time, he wished he had a dragon's command of the spoken word. He just wasn't *good* at these sorts of things. He considered that. What would a *dragon* say?

While neither of us asked for this, Blaze, I swear upon the blood of my ancestors that I will never harm you, nor will you ever have anything to fear from me, as long as you live. Please accept my oath that you will be safe upon my lands, and that I will endeavor to help you to achieve your dreams and make this place your home.

Blaze was almost on top of him as Jack frantically started working that over in his head, trying to figure out the best way to end it.

Please, as I kneel down before you here this moonlit night, promise me that you will accept my honest service...

"Where the fuck do you think you're going?" he blurted.

Blaze gasped and dropped her backpack, hastily backing away from him, looking ready to bolt.

Seeing the fear in her eyes, when Jack had done nothing but be nice to her all day, really pissed him off. He started growing fur and fang, despite himself. "Okay, tootz," he growled. "I guess that understandin' we came to earlier didn't really do the trick and I gotta go find a fuckton of rope, 'cause you ain't gettin' out of the lodge again until you can promise me you ain't pullin' any more of *this* shit." *Damn*, he thought, as soon as he'd said it. *What happened to the fucking poetry, you goddamned idiot?*

But it was too late, and Blaze was stumbling away from him, eyes about as big as dinner plates. Jack sighed and stepped towards her, deciding it was, at long last, time to dispense with the bullshit. He'd learned awhile ago that it was a lot easier on everybody involved to tie up the babes first, then explain yourself later. She was actually lucky she was a babe. If she'd been a guy, Jack would have gutted her by now.

"Wait!" Blaze cried, holding out a panicked hand between them as he started towards her. "Please don't."

Jack grimaced. She'd said 'please.' He hated it when the girls said please. Wrinkling his nose at her, he muttered, "So you *weren't* just trying to boogie out of here, after we had an agreement, sister?"

She glanced at her feet and scuffed at the dirt with the toe of her boot. He could smell the fear rolling off of her, and it made him grimace.

"I told you ya got nothin' ta fear from me, girlie," Jack muttered.

"I *know*," she blurted, lifting her head quickly, actually looking embarrassed. "I just…um…" She swallowed hard. "Had a bad dream. Just…Thought maybe I should go."

She wasn't off to sing like a canary, Jack realized, a little stunned. Jack folded his arms over his chest, peering up at her. "Why? You already told me you ain't got nowhere to go."

"Honestly?" she whispered.

"No, I want you to lie through your teeth," Jack retorted.

"Because you're an asshole," she said. "I don't think you'd get along with guests, and you already made it clear I can't tell you to leave."

Jack's mouth fell open. *Well, she's gotcha there, Wonder Boy.* "I can fix stuff," he blurted. "All sorts of stuff. Trucks, toilets, chainsaws, you name it. And I'm good with wood. Saws and hammers and shit. Anything you want to build, we can build it. Please don't run off."

Good with wood*?* his mind babbled in a panic. *Oh*, *now* that *was smooth.*

She peered at him warily, and he saw all the intricate little gears turning in her head as she watched him with all the alertness of a fox. "Why are you so interested in having me stay?"

Oh shit, Jack thought, windmilling to recuperate from such a blunder. "Uh, 'cause it's been awhile since I had a decent neighbor that wasn't a loudmouth gossip who spread rumors I been livin' here since the gold rush." The *last* thing he wanted her to know was just how decadent her presence was making the ground he was standing on, and how if *he* could feel it, *other* woodland creatures were going to feel it, and pretty soon his territory would be crawling with all sorts of edible furry friends.

Blaze lifted an eyebrow at him. "But you said you *have* been living here since the gold rush."

"Yeah," Jack muttered, "but she don't need to go tellin' everybody." He *hated* the way it sounded like he was sulking. He wasn't sulking. He was in charge here. He needed to put his foot down, tell her she was way outta line and he was gonna go tie her ass to the—

"So are you gonna stop being an asshole?" she asked.

"Yeah," he said.

Blaze crossed her arms, and her elbows came to rest about at his nose-level. "Somehow, I find that hard to believe."

Immediately, his hackles shoved through his skin and he snarled, "Oh yeah?! You'll find it easier to believe when I shove your *head* up your—" He cut himself off abruptly, a growl rattling in his chest. Biting out every word, he said, "I'll see what I can do."

She raised an eyebrow.

Narrowing his eyes at her, Jack said, "It might take some…work. Don't get your hopes up too quick, all right? Gimme some time."

"You've got a year," Blaze agreed.

"A year," Jack said, relieved. He could do that. One year to learn how to not be an asshole. Yeah, piece of cake. No sweat. Easy-peasey. Just a few minutes a day…Then he frowned, wondering how the hell *him* running *her* down in the woods had left *him* promising to be nice to people. He peered up at her with increasing wariness, trying to piece together how this leggy little vixen had warped the conversation to this new low. "So…you done trying to run off?" he asked slowly, trying to recover some of his control of the conversation. Except it came out like a goddamned Mexican standoff, one where she had all the guns. Yeah, he *really* needed to find a way to put his foot down…

Blaze shrugged. "You done being a dick?"

"I could rip off your arms and *bury you in the hill*!" Jack roared, growing to eye-level with her and sprouting fang.

Blaze peered back at him flatly, looking utterly unconcerned. "You done?"

Jack's jaw fell open, utterly taken aback by her lack of fear. "Uh…"

"Good," she said. "I'll be back at the lodge. The battery on my phone's probably just about dead from looping that recording, and I still gotta call Bruce in the morning." Without another word, she bent down, picked up her backpack, and headed back up the trail, leaving Jack staring after her, mouth agape.

Way *outta your league, buddy…*

FIVE

To Be Sputched...

Over the next few days, Blaze worked out an uneasy truce with her new business partner. Though she was technically the boss, she had absolutely no idea what it took to get the place on its feet again, and they both knew it. Thus, she ended up following him around like a very large lost puppy as he started fixing up the grounds, doing her best to keep up, getting frustrated when he made it look so easy.

The boards came off the windows, first. Then Jack began the complicated process of getting the generator running again, after four years of sitting idle. Between taking it apart, changing the oil, cleaning rust and corrosion off of parts, griping about 'cobbled-together pieces of shit,' and putting it all back together again, that took almost an entire day on its own. In the end, Jack had to jump it with the battery off of his 4-wheeler. Though Blaze had assumed the machine and trailer he'd used to pick her up at the lake had been part of the lodge package, Jack took her to an old shed and showed her the three dusty 4-wheelers sitting on flat tires in the back of the jumble of mechanical junk.

Which, Jack less-than-politely informed her, wasn't 'junk.'

"It's all got its uses," he growled, sounding offended. Now that the generator was running, he had pulled an air compressor off of the shelf in the big shop and had dragged it out to the shed. He was hooking a hose to the flat tires of one of the 4-wheelers, glaring at her over the handlebars. "Everything in here is something you're gonna need me to use for you someday, sweetheart."

Blaze bristled at 'sweetheart,' but by then, she had learned that mentioning it only made the bastard repeat the offense about a half trillion times. "Is there anything I can do to help?" she growled, watching him work.

"Yeah," Jack said, wrestling with the tire.

Blaze's heart skipped. Being both a gifted klutz and mechanically incompetent, she had been feeling like a fifth wheel all morning. "What?" she asked, hopeful that it would be something other than fetching a tool for him this time.

"Get out of my light." He gestured at the open doorway and the sun beyond.

Blaze stared at him for some time before she narrowed her eyes. "I'm going to go pull weeds."

"Don't waste your time," Jack said, distracted with the tire. "I can mow them down later."

"I'm going to go *pull* them," Blaze said sweetly. "It should be relaxing to have the company of a few noxious garden pests over a glorified wall-ornament."

His head snapped up and frowned. "So what crawled up *your* asshole?"

But Blaze had already turned and was walking back to the shop. She snagged a pair of men's work-gloves off of the wall—Blaze, embarrassingly, had neglected to bring her own, not realizing just how rough-and-dirty much of the reconstruction work would be—and yanked them onto her hands. The gloves were too tight, riding the tips of her fingers, but Blaze left them there anyway and headed out to the yard, mentally adding it to the list of things she would be buying on the next town run.

She pulled weeds until she got blisters through the gloves, and kept pulling. She had gotten a full twenty-foot-wide swath of lawn finished when she heard Jack start up an engine inside the 4-wheeler shed. Expecting a 4-wheeler, Blaze was shocked when, a few moments later, Jack rode a lawnmower around the edge of the shop. He saluted, then kicked the blades into gear, sending a gust of chopped grass and pulverized tree shoots in her direction. In thirty seconds, he had covered more lawn than Blaze had tended in four hours.

Blaze jumped up and stormed into the lodge, listening to the whine of the mower at her back. She slammed the door and dragged a chair in front of the woodstove, staring at the orange tongues flickering behind the tiny glass portal in the door as she fumed.

Flames had always calmed her, which was a *good* thing, considering that the next step after fuming was starting to cry. And, Blaze viciously assured herself, she would rather stick the barrel of a twelve-gauge down her throat than cry again. It was so…inconvenient, unpleasant, *embarrassing*. And she was *not* going to do it in front of a four hundred and fifty pound weasel.

Blaze stared into the flames for long minutes, listening to the mower as it circled the big yard. Then, once she had calmed down, she got up, went outside, slamming the door behind her again, and stalked right out into Jack's path and stopped.

For a moment, it looked like Jack wouldn't slow, and she was playing chicken with a lawn-mower.

Then, reluctantly, he kicked the blades out of gear and turned off the machine, rolling to a halt a few inches from her big boots.

Blaze slammed a fist down on the lawn-mower's front. "I *hate* feeling so useless!" she snapped.

Both of Jack's brows went up. "You just dented the hood."

"I don't *care*," Blaze said, denting it again. "It's *my* hood. Find me something *useful* to do before I lose my *mind*."

The wereverine grunted. He peered up at her like a fox analyzing just how long the Yeti would make a nuisance of herself before she got bored and trundled off.

"It's not up for debate," Blaze growled. "You want a check? I want something to do."

The wereverine heaved a huge sigh and climbed off the mower, the muscles in his arms and shoulders flexing as he dropped to the grass.

"Okay," he said. He gave her a dubious look. "You know how to run a bulldozer?"

Blaze flinched inside, but she forced herself to remain stoic. "I'm sure you could teach me."

He looked her up and down, then grunted. "Maybe." Without another word, he turned and walked off, leaving Blaze standing with her fist still resting in the brand new pucker of the lawnmower's hood. Frowning, with him giving her little else to do, she straightened and followed him.

He took her around the back of the last outbuilding, to a forlorn-looking parking-lot of heavy machinery. Old fireweed stalks had grown up and died around the six rusted metal monstrosities, which were for all the world looking as if they were slowly returning to the Earth.

Jack stopped at the biggest one and climbed up onto a long metal track so he could peer into the leaf-strewn driver's compartment. He cursed and jumped down, without another word stalking back over to the shop. He came back out with a key, which failed to get the machine started when he inserted it in the ignition and turned it.

It took another two hours for Jack to add the various fluids, charge the battery, check the gas tank for water, clean *out* said water, and otherwise get the engine sounding like something other than a dying weed-whacker.

Blaze was actually rather impressed when he fired it up the fourteenth time, to the sound of a low, healthy rumble. She didn't say as much, of course. The prideful bastard already needed about a seven-peg attitude adjustment.

"There," Jack said, making a satisfied grunt. He gestured for her to get in the driver's seat. "I'll show you how this baby works, then you can go play in the woods for awhile."

Blaze narrowed her eyes. "I told you I want something important to do."

"You want yaks, right?" Jack demanded.

She stared at him in confusion, her mind unable to follow the convoluted twist that had brought the wereverine from bulldozers to yaks.

"What does that have to do with an angry yellow machine?" she finally demanded.

He groaned and dropped his head into his hand again. "Just get in the seat," he growled. "You're gonna go make some pasture for your damn farm animals."

Blaze froze, realizing he meant for her to push down trees. She glanced up at the towering birch and spruce all around them, suddenly not feeling so confident. "Uh…"

"Well?" he snapped, gesturing at the seat. "Or ya gonna chicken out and make me do it?"

When Blaze only stared at the rumbling machine in horror, Jack sighed. "Better be some good hot food waitin' for me when I get back," he said. "I'm tired of this cold sandwiches and fruit shit." He started crawling into the cab.

Snarling that he could make his own damn food from whatever meager supplies he could scrounge from the pathetic contents of his *own* pantry, Blaze shoved him out of the way and climbed into the seat herself.

"Okay," Jack said quickly, "Now don't touch anything until I've given you an explanation." He then spent the next twenty minutes detailing just how deadly the machine she was sitting in could be, and just how many ways she could tip it over, dig her own grave, plow into something important, or otherwise get herself killed. Here and there, he would intersperse his warnings with a hint or two about how the machine worked—right before he launched right back into how easily she could 'sputch' herself.

'Sputching,' Jack informed her, when she asked, was a wereverine term for the sound of blood and gore exiting the body as one's soon-to-be corpse contacted something brutally hard, sharp, or otherwise destructive. Generally, it applied only to non-weres—a.k.a. 'mudborn'—when attacked by a were, dragon, titan, vampire, or other critter with the power to squish, stab, flatten, dismember, or otherwise brutally and liberally spread gore across at least fifty feet with 'a good kill'. In other words, to be sputched, Captain, was to become gore.

And Jack had a *word* for it.

The Return To Anchorage column got quite a few more checkmarks during *that* particular lecture.

Blaze found, however, to her amazement, that the gruesome scenarios he painted in her mind somehow fixed the meanings of the controls into her brain. Under Jack's direction, she was able to raise the blade, move the machine forward in halting jumps, and even turn it slightly.

After a few minutes of watching her, Jack gave her a thumbs-up and walked back toward the 4-wheeler shed.

"Wait!" Blaze cried, above the roar of the engine. "Where am I supposed to put a pasture?"

Jack grunted and made a dismissive gesture at the trees. "Wherever you want it." Then his broad back was disappearing into the dim interior of the shed, his tight T-shirt giving her yet another excellent view of his chiseled torso before the shadows swallowed him.

Blaze scowled after him a moment, but when she realized that he wasn't going to come back out and offer any more assistance, she reluctantly turned the dozer towards the woods and started forward.

Three hours later, Blaze had a twenty-foot-square patch of churned earth, and she had just pushed down her first tree. She felt an exhilarated thrill as it groaned and came down, and automatically turned to see if anyone had been paying attention.

Jack had been standing ten yards off, tool-filled workbelt clinging to the sexy bulk of his thigh, watching her. Seeing her look, he grinned and gave her another thumbs-up, then headed back to the shop.

It got easier after that. Once she had the hang of it, Blaze managed to push over a good dozen trees, clearing a forty-foot swath through the woods. When Blaze finally shut the bulldozer off, it was the hazy half-dark of an Alaskan summer, indicating it was probably sometime after midnight, and she was all but giggling in glee.

She had slid out of the driver's chair and was climbing down off the tracks when she saw the man watching her in the forest.

He was tall and lithe, his lean form dressed in a pale robe that seemed to shimmer like a cloud in the dusky haze of the Midnight Sun. His hair was *long*—the braid having enough thickness and length to be flipped over his shoulder and wrapped several times around his waist, then tied like a belt. It was his eyes, though, that had left her feeling cold. They were flame-blue, and they shone like twin lightning-bolts in the dim light.

When he saw her looking, he turned and unconcernedly walked away, seeming to disappear in the very forest itself.

Blaze slowly lowered herself the rest of the way to the forest floor, then, when she was sure the man was gone, turned and bolted for the lodge.

The wereverine, at least, was a familiar evil.

"I saw a wolf!" she cried, lunging inside and slamming the door behind her. She had to shield her eyes from the orange light of the gas-lamps that Jack had found in the attic, and realized looking out the blackened windows that it was later than she had thought.

Jack looked up from a book he had been reading. It was one of hers, a smutty action-adventure she was still looking forward to devouring, once she had the time. Seeing it, Blaze bristled, knowing that the last time she had seen it, it had been safely buried in the bottom of her underwear duffle.

"Thought you were gonna be out there all night," Jack said, closing the book. He yawned, and she saw pointed teeth. "How many trees you get down?"

"I saw a *wolf*," Blaze repeated, pointing in the general direction of where the guy had disappeared.

Jack raised a brow. "So?"

"Glowing blue eyes. He just stood there, watching me. Big long braid. Robes like he's the second coming of Jesus or something."

"Wait," Jack said, frowning. "Hold on. Back up a sec. You said you saw a *wolf*? In a *robe*?"

"Well, it was a guy," Blaze said. "But you told me about the were-wolves, and he had evil glowy eyes and I'm pretty sure he wanted to eat me."

Jack threw down the book in a snarl and got to his feet, a deadly look constricting his features. "You stay right here." He was already changing, his body growing in size and hairiness. Blaze flinched and got out of his way, which was just as well, because the way he brushed past her, he probably would have knocked her down if she hadn't.

He slammed the door open—probably broke off a hinge, considering the metallic snap she heard—and then was out into the night, moving too fast for her eyes to catch up.

The hinge was, indeed, broken. As she tried to drag the door shut against the bugs, Blaze made a mental note that, next time a ghostly visitor appeared in the woods, watching her, to take Jack *outside* before telling him about it.

Blaze settled for propping the door up against the jamb, then went back to the chair to pick up her book.

She didn't see the man standing in the shadows behind her until he moved. His pale, shimmery robes blended with the walls as he stepped closer, something dark in his hands. When he stepped into the light of the gas lamps, his eyes sizzled with their own eerie blue light-source, and every hair on Blaze's body suddenly lifted with a major case of static electricity.

The man was looking at her over the open case of her father's feather.

Blaze went absolutely still. She had hid the case in the bottom of the freezer, on the other side of the house.

Still watching her, the man shut the case and handed it to her. He seemed to regard her thoughtfully a moment, then turned and walked deeper into the shadows of the basement.

"Hey!" Blaze cried, the heavy case like a lead weight in her hands. "Stop!"

When she went after him, however, the slender form simply vanished into the shadows.

Heart hammering, Blaze yanked the case open.

Her father's feather, a glowing mass of flickering golden fire-tendrils as long as her forearm, was still tucked safely inside. Blaze swallowed and clicked the lid shut again, the sight still giving her the unholy willies.

"Hello?" she called.

The house was empty.

Grabbing the case and tucking it under an arm, she hurriedly went upstairs, climbed into the loft, and set the case against a rafter in the attic, packing insulation around it as she tried not to hyperventilate glass dust. The *last* thing she wanted was the damned wereverine finding it, deciding she was somehow safe to eat, and then ending her dreams of a pretty little fishing camp in the woods when he chomped on her head.

Still trembling, Blaze went back downstairs to sit with her back against the wall, the gas-lamps illuminating the room all around her, and tried not to panic. This *dude* with *glowing eyes* had just plucked her feather out of *cold storage* and given her a quizzical look, like 'Why do *you* have this?' and then vanished into thin air. *Dad*, Blaze thought, *what the Hell did you give me?*

As the night wore on and Blaze found herself alone but for the crackle of the woodstove, she realized just how creepy the woods could be at night, when one was alone. She drew her legs up to her chest and settled her chin on her knees and tried not to think about how quiet the place was.

Jack came bursting through the door sometime much later, ripping it completely from its hinges in a feral snarl of teeth and talons. "That effeminate bastard led me on a merry fucking *goose* chase," he roared, throwing a chair aside. It embedded itself into the wall even as his form began to shift to something a bit more human. "I oughtta go up north and wring his damn *neck*."

He stopped in front of the fire, he clothes once again torn and tattered, his ribbed torso visible under shreds of his shirt. Then he hesitated, sniffing the air. Fur started to sprout again as he said, "He was *here*, wasn't he?" He slammed a fist into the top of the woodstove, leaving a dent. "The *arrogant prick*!" He peered at her cautiously. "He hurt you?"

Biting her lip, Blaze shook her head.

"Offered to marry you?" The way he said it, Jack almost sounded serious.

The hilarity of that was enough to drag Blaze out of her shock. Chuckling, she said, "Not likely."

"Well, what *did* the feathered twit want?" Jack growled. As if marriage had seemed the most likely scenario.

Blaze thought of the feather, then thought of the huge fangs sprouting from Jack's mouth, and what they would look like from the inside. "Uh, I'm not sure," she lied.

Jack sniffed at the air, then scowled. "You're hiding something."

"He didn't *say* anything!" Blaze cried.

Jack gave her a long, hard look, then grunted. "Well, the little lightning-tossing dweeb shows up on my doorstep again, I'm gonna pluck me a turkey and roast it for dinner."

"That was Thunderbird?" Blaze whispered, cold chills suddenly working down her spine.

"You smell the rain?" Jack demanded, gesturing at the busted door.

Blaze glanced outside and heard the soft patter on the porch roof through the gaping maw he had left behind. "You know," she said looking at the ruined door, "Drywall and lumber are expensive."

Jack winced. "Uh, yeah." He scratched the back of his neck and gave a nervous chuckle, eying the new hole in the wall. "I'll work on that."

"So what did he want?" Blaze asked, looking out at the sudden thunderstorm, feeling a bit numb.

"Whatever he wanted, I'm sure he got it," Jack muttered. "That elitist prick operates under the assumption that the world is his oyster…and he's the pearl."

"Maybe he was afraid of taking anything," Blaze ventured, remembering the way the man had given her the feather almost thoughtfully.

"Afraid?" Jack said, frowning. "Why?"

She gestured at his ripped clothing.

Jack threw back his head and laughed. "Well, uh, I'll take that as a compliment, there, princess, and while it's true I can generally hold my own in a fight, the hard truth is that my furry ass wouldn't be the one crawling back out, if the two of us got in the thick of things." He gestured out at the rain. "You saw how easily he waltzed into the center of my territory without so much as a by-your-leave, and I didn't even sense the prick was nearby until you opened your mouth about wolves."

"Should we go talk to him?" Blaze asked.

Jack snorted. "If the conceited ass had wanted to talk, he would've stayed. He probably just wanted to see what kind of interesting new critter had shown up next door."

What kind of interesting new critter…"What do you mean?" Blaze asked, nervously.

Flinching slightly, Jack gestured at her body. "Well, uh, you ain't exactly Miss America, there, if you know what I'm saying. He was probably just…curious."

He's saying I'm the latest addition to the freak show, Blaze thought, miserable. She looked down at her gangly body, her manly feet, her flat chest. "Well," she said, *refusing* to cry, "I guess he got a good look."

He misjudged the agony in her face. "Oh, don't worry, sister. He wouldn't have hurt you."

Like I'm a helpless woman whose very existence depends on the charity of others. So much for first impressions. "So," Blaze said, changing the subject from the one that was about to leave her running to her room bawling, "that Thunderbird guy wasn't dangerous?" The native-looking guy had just looked…curious.

"Oh," Jack said, chuckling, "I didn't say *that*, sugar. Nonono." He shook his head. "He's just so goddamned stuck-up that he probably didn't think carting you off was worth his time. After all, he's supposed to be God's Gift to America. Spiritual being from the heavens, and all that. If he had wanted you, he would've just taken you. If you had tried to stop him, you'd be dead. Simple as that."

"Oh," Blaze whispered, once again wondering just how intelligent a decision it had been to stay in the Bush with the wereverine, "kaaay. So we're back to Neanderthals with clubs out here, is that what I'm hearing? You just grab a girl when you get horny and drag her back to your cave?" Another check-mark next to Return To Anchorage.

"On a happy note," Jack said, "He didn't take you and you're not dead. That means he's not gonna take you, and he's not gonna sputch you, at least for now. Two very positive developments that I've been dreading ever since I figured out what—" He choked off the rest, his green eyes flickering in her direction warily.

"You figured out *what*?" Blaze demanded, her attention sharpening.

As if he hadn't heard her, Jack picked up some firewood and started feeding the stove. "We'll pick out a spot for your greenhouse tomorrow. And we need to plow out some area for a garden. Traditionally, folk 'round here wait to get stuff in the ground 'til the first of June. Much earlier than that and frost might kill it."

Blaze laughed at him. "You were telling me you wanted to grow *mango* trees up here."

He gave her an awkward look that said there was more accumulated in his tiny brain that he wasn't telling her. "Yeah. Probably in a greenhouse."

"*Probably*?" Blaze scoffed. "We aren't wasting my greenhouse space on a mango tree."

"You like mangoes?" Jack demanded.

"Sure I do," Blaze said, "But there's some things that just can't—"

"Then I'll have Bruce ship one out," Jack said. He left her sitting there, gritting her teeth, as he started pulling ragged strips of cloth from his body and left to get changed.

SIX

Feathers and Firepits

The glorified turkey *knew*. Jack stalked around the Sleeping Lady all night, on the off-chance that he would come back and Jack could work out some of his frustrations on his pretty-boy face.

The worst part was he didn't know why it should bother him so much. If the feather-headed asshole wanted to come claim himself some pretty young wife, why should Jack care? More power to him, right? After all, she'd been nothing but goosebumps, sass, and heart-hammering *panic* since she got off the plane.

Yet Jack paced through the woods with every intention of ripping the avian little asshole rim from limb if he caught him snooping around his territory again. And, he realized with a wince, he now firmly considered the leggy little bird to be 'his' territory.

Never mind the fact that she was so damn gorgeous he kept catching himself staring at her like a dipshit. Or that she set all his hairs on end if she got too close. Or that every fiber of his being was demanding to make her his. Permanently. Before anyone else could do it.

Jack paced, trying *not* to think of how much he wanted to cinch that bond and make her his. Between just casually walking past him while he was relaxing in the basement and leaning over to see what he was working on out in the shop, Jack was pretty sure he had a permanent case of the most delicious heebie-jeebies he'd ever felt. It had taken all of his control not to just seal the link that first night and deal with the consequences later. The oldest, feral part of him was *demanding* it, the sensation so strong it was *pulling* at him, tugging him around like a puppet on a string, and it was all Jack could do to ignore it. Hell, he'd already accidentally barked at the poor girl several times, when she idly got close enough she was setting his hairs on end.

Damn it. Growling deep in his chest, Jack made another loop around the Sleeping Lady in the dark, already beginning to carve a circular path through the woods where his feet had plastered the moss and cranberry bushes to the ground. This was *not* how he'd wanted to spend his summer. He liked to relax. He liked to be alone. He liked to chop firewood and watch the sunset. He did *not* like feeling like his chest was being wrenched apart by this beautiful Scottish temptress.

Too close. He was getting too damn close. He'd only known her a few *days* and he was already feeling that gut-clenching pang whenever he thought of her. This was not good. Not good at all. Hell, he might as well light his ass on fire, roast it good and tender, and hand it to her on a silver platter.

Jack made another loop, listening to her sleep inside her cozy little basement, completely oblivious to the contortions she was putting him through. She didn't even seem to *notice* how damned sexy she was when she moved, which of course made it worse. All long leg and sinuous curves…

Stop it, you fool, he growled, disgusted with himself. *You got a strange little bird that showed up on your doorstep and you're already trying to pounce. You've been lonely* way *too long, buddy. She's outta your* league. *She's dragon-bait, babe. Thunderbutt dropping by proved that. Soon or later, something else is gonna catch a whiff, and when it does, she's gonna be spirited off to some damn cave up in the mountains where you'll never see her again.*

But that wasn't helping the hammering in his chest, or the ache in his gut knowing that her silky-pale body slept stretched out only a few insignificant feet away. Naked. He'd heard her undress.

Damn it! Jack threw his head into his hands and pressed his palms to his ears, trying to force the images from his skull. This was wrong.

This could *not* be happening. Not again. He wouldn't let it. She was just too innocent. She had no *idea* of the kind of crap out there, the monsters that would be happy to tear her apart, or worse, just because she lived in the same square mile as Jack. He would not do that to another woman. Never.

Please, Aphrodite, Ishtar, Innana, Venus, Ashtart, Freya, whatever the fuck you want to be called, Jack prayed. *Don't let this get out of hand.*

If the Goddess of Love heard his prayer, she casually gave him the cold finger.

• • •

Blaze didn't sleep well that night, and had only gotten an hour or two when she heard Jack moving around upstairs near dawn, tinkering with the pipes. She crawled out of bed and went upstairs to figure out what he was doing, and why he didn't keep to normal workday hours.

She found him on his hands and knees in the main upstairs bathroom, and the first thing she noticed upon tentatively pushing the door aside was the way his jeans were stretched deliciously tight against the hard round curves of his buttocks. She swallowed, hard, but found herself unable to look away.

"Should have the water turned back on by the end of the day," Jack said. He hadn't even looked over his shoulder. He was bent over the toilet, *shirtless*, peering down the back, muscular arms flexing as he fiddled with something inside. "Damn," he said. He leaned back on his knees and wiped sweat from his brow as he turned to her. His fingers were black with grease. "They literally disassembled this place. Drained every pipe, emptied every toilet, broke it all down."

"Why?" Blaze asked, trying not to stare at the way his naked shoulders were rippling as he lowered his arm.

The flat Oh-My-God-I'm-Working-For-A-Stupid-Ass-City-Slicker look that he gave her, however, was enough to drag her out of any potential fantasies in a hurry. Thank you, Jack.

"Gets about forty-five below zero around here in the winter, Boss," Jack said. He always used 'Boss,' she had noticed, when he felt she had done something particularly stupid. Like he was reminding himself where his next meal was coming from.

Blaze frowned. "I know that." She'd researched the weather extremes when she'd been deciding which crops to try and grow.

When she added nothing further, Jack sighed. "Stuff explodes when water freezes." He tapped the toilet bowl with a knuckle, making the ceramic ring.

Blaze felt her face redden furiously when she realized the obvious. "Oh," she muttered, utterly humiliated yet again by the crass, utterly-capable handyman shit.

"But," Jack said, getting up, making the muscles in his abdomen ripple, "I can finish that later. Now that you're up, let's go get you caught up on the inverters. You tried to leave the generator running all night. You have a *battery system* here. If you don't shut it off once the inverters are done charging, you're just burning gas you could've used for winter."

"Oh," Blaze muttered, feeling like someone had scalded her face in a pressure cooker.

"No biggie. Now you know." Standing, Jack peered up at her as he shrugged back into his plaid long-sleeved shirt. After dropping the bomb that Thunderbird had paid her a visit, the wretched bastard had proceeded to tell her, oh, by the way, I'm headed home, now, have fun all alone in the dark. As if this kind of crap happened to him on a daily basis. Return To Anchorage had gotten quite a few checks that night, while staring at the ceiling in the darkness of the creepy, too-big house, a broken Colt arranged beside her bed.

"You know," Jack said conversationally, as he buttoned his shirt, "You don't have to know everything."

Blaze blinked and stiffened. "What?"

He gestured at the toilet. "So you didn't know the pipes would explode if they weren't drained. So what?" He cocked his head at her. "I'm sure you learned some stuff back in the city that I don't know."

Blaze snorted. "Nothing important."

He gave her an uncertain, wary look, seemingly trying to decide something as he scanned her face. "What about math?" he finally suggested.

She frowned at him. "What, like Calculus?"

He cleared his throat and then looked away again. "Any math."

Blaze stared at him. "You can't do *math*?" She hadn't meant it to come out as a sneer, but it did.

Jack stiffened as if she'd hit him. "So that's what it feels like," he said softly. He grabbed his hat off the floor and yanked it over his head, then moved to push past her.

Blaze caught his shoulder. "Hey," she said softly. "Sorry."

He gave her an irritated look. "Was just trying to make you feel better." Narrowing his eyes, he added, "You know? Like I promised?"

Meaning he was still taking his oath seriously and trying not to be an asshole. She frowned down at him. "Then you really *can* do math?"

"Lady," he said in a growl, "I can't do math any more than I can read a book."

Blaze snorted. "I saw you reading one last night."

For the first time, she saw genuine longing in his eyes before it was quickly masked again by his callous snort. "Of course I can read. What dumbass can't read? It was a stupid book, anyway." He gave an indifferent shrug. "Hell, as old as I am…It's not like I haven't read every book there is out there already, twice. All the time I been around…hell, there were a thousand places for me to learn something stupid like that. Every town had a school, and every church had a pastor. Not too hard to learn." He shoved past her and started toward the stairs.

"Wait a minute," Blaze called after him, her mind tumbling over his words. "You told me you stayed *away* from the cities."

She saw his shoulders stiffen.

He can't read, Blaze realized, her heart suddenly going out to him. All the brusque comments, all the cruel jabs were starting to make sense. Her heart started to pound as she realized he wanted what she had. Badly. So badly it hurt.

"Want me to teach you?" Blaze asked, as he started to walk off.

His broad back hesitated again. For a moment, it looked like he would turn. Then, softly, he said, "I gotta show you the battery system." He ducked down the stairs, leaving her staring after him.

Over the next brain-wracking hour, Jack described the battery system, how it worked, how to charge it, and how to make it explode. Blaze could have done without the last part, but he seemingly took great relish in explaining to her what battery acid did to the wallpaper and human flesh.

Then, once he was done with his heart-pounding lecture that left her somewhere between afraid to touch the generator and absolutely terrified of the car-sized nuclear device embedded in her basement, he said, "All right. Let's go put in that garden 'fore your pretty head implodes."

She narrowed her eyes at the back of his head as he made his way out across the yard.

Over the course of the next few days, Blaze once again fell into the role of Jack's errand-monkey. He even took the bulldozer back from her, when she didn't have the skills and finesse necessary to drag nice, even furrows through the dirt for her garden. Then, once garden and crop-rows were complete, Jack stood around and started to tell her how to plant her seeds.

"Let me do *one* thing by myself, all right?" Blaze snapped, unable to take his macho, utterly-capable handyman bullshit anymore. Standing in the soft, newly-exposed virgin earth that she was still tugging roots and grass-clumps out of, she jammed a finger back towards the shop. "I pay you to get the lodge running. So go get the lodge running. I can handle this."

Jack opened his mouth, looking like he wanted to say something, then shrugged and went on with his business. She saw him puttering around the shop and grounds several times after that, a pile of lumber over his shoulder or a power-tool in his hand.

Working out her frustrations in the earth, Blaze spent a few days yanking out roots, shaking out sod clumps, and delicately arranging the garden rows into something usable. She planted about a hundred different types of heritage seeds in small, well-marked test-plots, and then spent a few more days planting heirloom red, purple, and fingerling potatoes in the open, muddy field she'd uncovered with the bulldozer's massive blade.

Potatoes, in Alaska, were a sure bet. Kind of like cabbage, carrots, and peas. She planted those, too, though she didn't have much hope for the cabbage. Those, she knew, pretty much needed to be started four to six weeks early, in a nice, warm, sunny window.

Blaze poured every ounce of her love and care into her new garden, even going so far as to endure the embarrassment of asking Jack to show her how to hook up the hose so she could water her rows. Instead of showing her, however, he just *did* it, and dragged the hose out of the shop and hooked it up to a little faucet she hadn't even seen set into the side of the Sleeping Lady, then switched it on and handed her the business end. Like she was a total moron.

"Don't use it too much," he said. "Might run the well dry." And then, with *that* startling little revelation, he went on with his merry business, leaving Blaze staring at the edge of a quarter-acre of crops and wondering just how she was going to keep it all wet enough for the seeds to germinate. Aside from the brief visit by Thunderbird, the sun had been burning down on them every day, all day, and as far as she'd heard, there was no sign of rain.

This, she realized, was the first of her mistakes in the planning stage of her little farm in the woods. Back in Anchorage, hooked into the city main, she'd never even *considered* that someone could run out of water.

And, as the scorchingly hot, sunny days went on and the moist, fluffy earth she'd exposed began to dry up into dust, water quickly became Blaze's primary focus in life. She would use the hose until the grinding sound from the pump told her she'd run out of water, then she'd started dragging it up from the lake. Totally illegal, she knew, but she was desperate, now. She'd poured *thousands* into seeds, and she *needed* those plants to help feed guests, because she'd never calculated on having to buy *potatoes* at the grocery store, when it came time to feed fishermen.

And yet, as many trips up the hill she made with water-buckets, wasting fuel and time painstakingly pouring gallon after gallon into the parched soil, most of her field simply didn't sprout.

"You know," Jack said one day, having stopped in his daily tasks to watch her for a minute as she moved along the rows, hunched over, five-gallon bucket in hand, "You might as well give up on the field and save what you can. It's late June." He jabbed a thumb at the sky. "It ain't cooperating wit' ya."

Indeed, with all the time she was putting into the field, her garden was bone-dry, and most of the tiny seedlings had shriveled.

Interior Alaska. Gotta love it. Blaze dropped the bucket and slumped to her ass in a row, staring in despair at several weeks of wasted effort....And hundreds of dollars of rare, heirloom seeds that would never sprout.

"Hey, at least you tried, right?" Jack said. By the commiserating look on his face, that seemed to be his way of trying not to be an asshole. At least he was still trying. "Maybe livestock would be a better idea."

Blaze lowered her head between her knees, shaking it in despair. "Part of the reason I needed the crops was to feed the livestock. If oats won't grow, we can't really have chickens without barging in several tons of grain at thirty cents a pound."

Jack grunted. "Well, ya kinda got a point there." He grunted, then scratched his nose, leaving a grease-smear.

The whole garden was suffering from lack of water, and no matter how many gallons she emptied onto the soil, walking through the rows was like padding through a desert, leaving two-inch-deep footprints in the powdered dust.

Her eyes caught on the scraggly little mango tree that Jack had insisted on planting at the end of one bed, then she gave a depressed laugh. "I don't think I'm as cut out for this as I thought I was."

Jack gave her an odd look. "Well, honey," he admitted reluctantly, "I *did* kinda think you'd do a bit better than this."

Oh, great, Blaze thought, humiliated. He sounded like a disappointed parent. She flopped backwards into the non-germinating row to stare at the sun as it made its way across the deep blue sky. She supposed it wasn't the end of the world. So she'd have to buy groceries at Costco. Big deal. Everyone in the Bush did that. At least the air was clean, and she didn't have to deal with traffic.

She could *hear* Jack shrug when he said, "But I coulda just been wrong about you from the start. And hell, if it was easy, more people would have done it." He turned to wander back off to one of his projects.

"Wait." Blaze twitched and lifted her head to peer at him. "Wrong about me how?"

Jack stopped, and she could have sworn he flinched.

"Oh, come on," Blaze cried in despair. "What'd I do wrong? Not enough work ethic to be a farmer? Should've been out here *sixteen* hours a day, instead of fourteen? Planted at the wrong time of the day? The *moon* wasn't right? Too *tall*? Too much distance between me and the seeds? Just tell me now, so I can go inside and die."

Jack turned to face her, slowly, his face a mixture of reluctance and unhappiness. "Uh, well, I *thought* I'd pegged you, but stuff just ain't adding up. So, uh, yeah. Sorry I got your hopes up." He gestured at the withered rows. "But I'll still build ya a barn, if ya want."

"*What's* not adding up?" Blaze demanded, sitting up onto her elbows to get a better look at him.

Jack seemed to want to say something, then just shook his head. "You're just a rich brat from the city with some expensive perfume or somethin. I hear they add hormones to that stuff nowadays." He shrugged. "Probably what got me."

Remembering the goosebumps that had climbed up his arm when she reached out to shake his hand, Blaze said, "Hold on a sec. I don't wear perfume. I told you that." Then she frowned. "And what's that got to do with my garden?"

"Probably nothin," Jack said, shrugging his big shoulders. "Felt like maybe you carried somethin…special…with ya. But it was probably just wishful thinkin'."

Blaze bit her lip, thinking of the feather neatly stashed between the rafters. "And this…special…you felt. It had to do with growing things?"

Jack laughed. "Sweetie, you have *no* idea."

"What, like fairy dust or something?" she growled. She picked up a handful of powdered earth and dropped it pointedly, letting him see it puff and blow away.

Giving her an irritated look, he wiped sweat off his brow, then glanced up at the sun. "Okay, look. While you're out here taking a dirt-nap, I really gotta get back to work on the chainsaw. The forty-year-old piece of shit snapped its cord again." Conversation over, he turned and wandered back towards the shop.

He thinks the feather would help. Blaze turned her head, looked at the desiccated rows, watched a lone ant crawl across the desert that was her garden, then rolled her head to look up at the sun again.

Drier than Texas for months, then rains that make the Yentna flood its banks and take boats, gear, and even *houses* with it. What the hell had she been thinking?

Blaze pushed herself out of the dirt, struggled to her feet, and, without even bothering to dust herself off, strode towards the back door of the lodge. She passed Jack as she went, her longer stride carrying her across the back yard in ground-eating steps that quickly left him behind.

"Hey, now," Jack called after her, "you aren't about to go do something stupid, are you?"

Blaze yanked the newly-repaired back door of the lodge open, then slammed it shut behind her, entering the wonderfully cool basement. She took an immediate right, climbing the staircase into the kitchen, not even bothering to take off her muddy boots.

She heard Jack crack the door behind her, then groan when he saw the clods of dirt she'd left caking the steps. The weasel was, she had discovered, almost OCD in his desire for cleanliness. "Oh, *that's* helpful!" he cried up the stairs at her, before slamming the door again and disappearing back into the shop.

Blaze ignored him, trodding across the fancy carpet, right up the stairs to the third story, then storming up the ladder into the attic like an elephant in a china store. The ladder swayed beneath her in rickety complaint as Blaze yanked the layer of insulation off of her father's present, stuffed it under her arm, and jumped back down to the rug, leaving a double-footprint where she landed. Ignoring it, she stomped back down the first set of stairs, through the kitchen, down the second set of stairs, and ripped open the basement door again.

Sending it crashing into the jamb behind her, she stomped across the weathered floorboards of the back porch, jumped over the steps, and headed for the shop.

Inside, Jack was bent over a side-table, back to her, fiddling with a lump of unidentifiable clutter in front of him, country-music radio blasting in his ear as he worked. He was tapping his foot on the cement floor of the shop, whistling in tune with the song, when Blaze slammed the metal box down on his workbench, scattering parts everywhere. The wereverine shrieked and dropped his screwdriver, stumbling backwards, eyes going slitty on her.

"Tell me what that is," Blaze snapped, pointing to the box.

Jack stared at her like she was some sort of poisonous snake and didn't even look at the box. "I have no idea what that is. Never seen it in my life." Looking irritated as his startlement faded, he growled, "You know, you just made it so we gotta buy a new chainsaw, right? I'm *not* going hunting for all that shit." He gestured at the floor of the shop, which was even then scattered with tiny parts.

"I don't care about the chainsaw," Blaze growled. "You said it was a forty-year-old piece of crap anyway."

"It is," Jack said, "But that don't mean it don't still get the job done."

"Tell me," Blaze gritted, "What that thing is." She jabbed her finger at the box.

For the first time, Jack looked down at the metal case, but made no effort to touch it. He sniffed the air, then wrinkled his nose. "Uh. Well, it ain't got a dead body in it, if that's what you're worried about. Where'd you find it?"

"*That*," Blaze said, "Is what my father *willed* to me when he died."

Jack seemed to relax. "Oh, all right," he said, reaching for it. "What'd the old fart leave you?" he asked, as he opened the latch, "Some mummified monkey's peni—*Oh my shit!*" He jumped backwards, hitting the far wall of the shop, making tools rattle off of their hooks and clatter to the floor.

His reaction left Blaze feeling both vindicated and utterly terrified she'd just made the biggest mistake of her life. "So you know what it is?" she demanded, biting down her fear that he was about to rip her head off and use her neck like a popsicle stick.

The wereverine tore his gaze from the feather and looked at her, his mouth hanging open.

When he offered up nothing else, Blaze urged, "You *do* know, right?"

The wereverine swallowed, glanced at the doors of the shop, then returned his eyes to the feather and swallowed again. Very carefully, he said, "Honey, you said your father is *dead*?"

Blaze squinted at him. "I put flowers on his casket."

"But he's *dead*?" Jack demanded. "You're *sure*?"

She remembered seeing her father's dead body, stretched out in a nice black suit. A few days later, she'd been called in to the lawyer's office and gotten that sweet little story of the poor, abandoned babe in the woods and how, oh, by the way, you're adopted and *that's* why you were always ugly. Her face hardening, she said, "I kissed his cheek and cried over his corpse." *And put myself in the hospital again…*

Jack blinked at her, looking a little surprised. "Oh." A tiny knot formed in his forehead. "So that wasn't his feather?"

"Of course it was," Blaze said.

"But he's *dead*?" Jack demanded.

"Well, that's a stupid question," Blaze snapped. "Of course he's dead. What the hell does that have to do with anything?"

Jack seemed to be having some sort of aneurysm. "So…your dad… where did *he* get it?"

"How the Hell should I know?" Blaze demanded. "He collected old, weird shit all the time. Had a whole basement full of junk when he died. What is it?"

Jack was still pressed up against the far wall like he thought the feather was gonna bite him. "Uh. Just really special, that's what."

"So that's what you were feeling when I showed up?" Blaze demanded. "And don't try to lie, I saw you sniffin at me whenever you thought I wasn't looking."

"Yeah," Jack said, almost in a pant. He was sweating, his face glinting in the shop light, "That's probably part of it."

"Okay," Blaze said, "So what is it, and what are we gonna do with it?" She cocked her head at him. "You said it could make stuff *grow*?"

Still backed up against the far wall, the wereverine made a nervous sound. "You, uh, mind taking it out of the box, then, there Boss? I gotta get a good look at it, and those things don't, uh, *like* the moon-kissed..."

Blaze narrowed her eyes at him. "So basically, if it explodes, it'll turn *me* into a puddle of blood and gore, while you watch safely from afar?"

Jack jerked to peer at her. "You mean you ain't touched it yet?"

"Of course not!" Blaze cried, gesturing to the tendrils floating out of the case. "*Look* at that thing. It looks *alive*." She glanced back to the feather and shuddered. "Hell, the damn thing's basically *whispering* to me." Even then, there was a nagging sensation that she should reach out, should pick it up, should *do* something with it...

Jack's eyes suddenly narrowed with some sort of recognition. "Whispering, huh?"

Blaze gave him a long, hard look, waiting for the wereverine to divulge some more information. When he didn't, she growled, "Fine. I'll just go throw it in the river." She slapped the case shut and tucked it under her arm.

"No!" Jack cried, leaping forward to catch the case in one hand, her shoulder in the other. Very carefully, he twisted her back around and made her set the case back on the workbench. "All right, tootz," he said. "That..." he took a deep breath, scanning her eyes, then, as solemnly as a man pronouncing an entire city's doom, looked up at her and said, "...is a magic feather."

"Oh, for chrissakes!" Blaze snapped, disgusted. She reached for the case again.

In a flash, Jack grabbed her hand and held it against the workbench, pinned. "Listen, honey," Jack said evenly. "Maybe it *is* yours, but you *ain't* throwin that in a river. *Wars* have been fought over feathers like that."

"Wars, huh?" Blaze asked, peering down at him.

"Yeah," Jack said, utterly serious. "Wars."

Blaze frowned. "That why Thunderbird looked at it?"

Jack froze, and she watched fur slide out the pores of his face. "What?"

"He dug it out of the freezer," Blaze said, shrugging.

"And you forced him to put it *down*?" Jack cried, in disbelief.

"He handed it to me," Blaze said. "Then walked away."

Jack frowned. For a long moment, he just stared at her. Then, gruffly, he said, "Okay, sweetheart, you got some sort of high-grade rocket-propelled nuclear warhead I don't know about?"

She blinked at him.

He waved a disgusted arm in the general direction of the forest. "Then how the hell you get the glorified turkey to put the damn thing down?" he demanded. "I can think of a dozen ways he could've used it. Not that he needs any of them. Hell, probably would've braided it into his hair, the arrogant prick."

"That's why he visited, then?" Blaze demanded. "Just to see it?"

Jack made a disgusted grunt. "The nosy bastard probably wanted to know the source of the magic seeping into his neighbor's land."

Blaze glanced down at the feather's case, impressed. "So it *is* magic."

"It is," Jack said. "We're gonna bury it, *soon*, before it attracts something more dangerous...like the fey. The ground will help mute the power a bit, spread it out more evenly, instead of letting it sink into the ley-lines and hit the whole damn network."

"Okay," Blaze said, "this magic feather...what's it *do*?"

Jack gave a nervous laugh and glanced at the door. "Keep your voice down, sister."

"What's it do?" she hissed. "Can it help my plants?"

"Can it help..." he stared at her as if she'd asked one of the most retarded questions he'd ever heard. "You *really* don't know what it is, do you?"

"Would I be here asking you, if I did?" Blaze growled.

Jack released her hand and, giving her a nervous look, pushed the lid of the case open. "You said you ain't picked it up?"

"Would *you*?"

He gestured at her. "Go ahead. It's not gonna bite." The pale, sweaty look on his face, however, told her that the wereverine was lying through his teeth.

"You pick it up first," Blaze growled.

Jack's eyes widened at her and he licked his lips, then glanced down at the feather. Instead of arguing, though, he tenderly reached down, and as if he were picking up spun glass, lifted the mass of red, orange, and gold filaments from its nest. It didn't turn him to a frog, as Blaze half-expected.

"Here," he said, offering it to her. "It's your garden. You're gonna need to work the magic."

"Hey now," Blaze said, holding up her palms warily. "I don't know the first thing about ma—" But Jack grabbed her hand, flipped it over, palm-up, and settled the feather into it.

Instantly, the thing flared to life, the iridescent filaments suddenly *blazing* in glowy strands of red, orange, and gold.

"Jaaaack…" Blaze managed through clenched teeth as the feather lit up the room like a glow-stick. "What the *fuck* did you just do?"

But the wereverine was staring at her, a slack look on his face. "You're…"

"Let," Blaze gritted, biting out every word, "Go. Of. My. Hand." She could feel the feather *crawling* on her, caressing her skin like it was some sort of little gremlin made of goose down. When Jack didn't let go, and she could almost *feel* the tendrils digging into her skin, heating up her blood, making her heart suddenly start throbbing as embers began tracing their way through her veins, she screamed, "*Now*!"

Jack released her suddenly, stepping back so quickly that he tripped over a can of used oil and set it sloshing over the pristine floor of 'his' shop. He landed on his ass nearby, staring up at her in perfect horror.

Blaze quickly detached the thing from her palm and set it back into the box it had come in, then gave it a wide berth. She stood there, watching it, for several moments before she said, "It's still glowing."

"Yeah, uh," Jack said. "I'm pretty sure you just activated it."

"Oh, that's nice," Blaze said. "Is that like, what, arming the detonator on a wad of C-4?"

"Uh," Jack said. He swallowed, hard. "How many kids did your parents have?"

Blaze made a bitter sound. "My mom was found to have a protein deficiency that made her body abort. She had three miscarriages before the doctors pronounced her infertile."

"But she had *you*," Jack said.

Blaze laughed bitterly. "They found *my* Amazon ass in a firepit in the woods." Even four months after her father's lawyer had so thoughtfully handed her the envelope describing her parents' misdeeds, it still hurt to talk about it. "Took me home and raised me as their own, used their money to fudge a few records, let me live my whole life thinking they were my real parents. Dad's lawyer dropped the bomb I was adopted when he gave me the feather." She glared at him, her words poison-tipped when she growled, "Now that you've rubbed salt into an open wound, would you mind telling me what I'm dealing with? My dad obviously thought it was special. It's the only thing he gave me when he died, aside from the cash. Donated the rest to charity."

Jack's hands were shaking, and he got to his feet blindly, the ass of his jeans having soaked up spilled oil. Instead of clearing up all the mysteries of Life for her, however, he carefully crossed to the far wall again, then slowly slid down the edge of the workbench to a seating position, a good twelve feet away, watching her like she'd just grown slitted eyes and sixteen rows of teeth.

"He said they found you in a *firepit*?" Jack asked in a quiet voice.

"Some sort of human sacrifice, they were guessing," Blaze said, shrugging. "Whatever it was, my parents were pretty sure that the people who put me there weren't really the type of people who needed me back."

For a long time, he said nothing, simply giving the case on the workbench a wary look. Finally, he said, "If I were you, I'd bury that feather. Plant an apple tree over it."

"Apple trees don't grow in this climate zone," Blaze said automatically. In her planning stage, she had done thorough research into different types of foodstuffs that she could grow on her new property. She had already considered the option of having an orchard, but between the moose and the bitterly cold winters, apple trees didn't survive this far north.

"That one will," Jack said.

She hesitated, considering his expression warily. "What are you saying?"

"I'm saying," Jack said, "That feather in there's about the equivalent of putting whatever you plant around it right on top of a feylord's life-stone. Whatever you put around it, they'll probably still be fruiting in December."

Blaze snorted.

Then she realized he was completely serious.

"Uh," she said, when he just raised a brow at her, "How do you know that?"

Jack sighed. "'Cause I've seen nations fall over a feather like that. The fey would kill to get their hands on it, without even thinking twice. I can think of a dozen critters within an eighty mile radius who would slit their own brother's throat to have it in their possession. And a *dragon*..." He shuddered and cleared his throat. "Don't let a dragon know you've got it. Just...Don't." He grimaced. "Last time I saw a slaughter like that, they were in a clan war. I think four hundred of them died before the survivors on both sides crawled away to lick their wounds."

"For a *feather*?" Blaze cried. "That grows *apples*?"

Jack licked his lips, seemed to debate. Then, almost reluctantly, he nodded his head toward the lake. "You know Lake Ebony?"

Blaze frowned. "Are you changing the subject again?"

"You take that feather down to the shore and dip it in the water and anyone who decides to go swimming in that lake for the next ten years is gonna come out healed of whatever ailed him. Fountain-of-Youth style."

Blaze's mouth dropped open. "Oh."

"You can see how that might be trouble."

She swallowed and nodded.

"So yeah," Jack said, "Stick it in the ground, give the wildlife around here a boost, and when people ask why you've got apple trees blooming in December, tell them you've got a really, really green thumb and you spend a small fortune on Miracle-Gro."

Possibilities began to filter through Blaze's brain.

Sitting across from her, Jack scowled. "I know what you're thinking…" he began, a low warning in his tone. "You're thinking about *using* it…"

"I'm thinking what I can plant around it," Blaze snapped, bristling. "Just bugger off and let me concentrate a minute." She leaned her head back and considered. A good portion of her long-term plan *relied* on growing her own fruits and vegetables for her meals. Eventually, she wanted multiple greenhouses, gardens, and animal pastures…

She frowned, looking back at him. "Would it help livestock?"

Jack wrinkled his nose, looking agitated. "I thought we decided you'd bury it."

"I didn't say *anything* about what I would do with *my* feather," Blaze retorted.

Jack gave her a long, cold look. "You do anything stupid with it and it's gonna disappear."

She narrowed her eyes at him. "Define stupid."

"Anything other than burying it," he growled back.

She met his gaze, challenging. "What would happen if I put it in their water-trough?"

The wereverine bristled. "No."

"Why not?" She snapped. "It's *mine*."

"Too many things could go wrong," Jack growled.

"Like what?"

The wereverine looked uncomfortable. His hackles had started to bristle again, puffing out against his back, before he seemed to slump in defeat. "Who am I kidding? You can do whatever you want with the damn thing." He gestured disgustedly at the yard. "Go put it on display, for all I care."

Blaze felt a bit of her guard drop with his admission. Curious, now, she offered, "I told you I always wanted a nice farm."

"Yeah," Jack said, "But in the *water*?" He scoffed. "Believe me, honey, you don't want it *that* nice." He gestured at the yard. "Put it in the ground, pen your animals nearby, and anything within ten acres is gonna grow twice as big and breed like rabbits."

Blaze glanced back at the glowing filaments. "Let's bury it where we're gonna put the greenhouse."

Jack was on his feet in an instant, hastily grabbing for a shovel nearby. "You got it, sweetcheeks."

Inwardly realizing that the wereverine was just a bit too eager to get the feather in the ground, but willing to do just about *anything* to get her plants to start growing, Blaze picked up the case and followed him.

By the time she got to the garden, Jack had already started digging a pit at one edge. His eyes caught on the metal case in her arms and he gave a nervous laugh, then way-too-quickly fell into a one-sided chatter about all the different things he was going to have to do to the lodge before winter, to keep the place from freezing on her when the snows hit, and oh, by the way, he was going to be moving in with her downstairs.

Blaze's mental reel came to a screeching halt and she floundered, backtracking, replaying the wereverine's words in her head. "No you aren't," she blurted, when she realized she had heard him correctly.

"I'll have to go get my stuff," Jack continued. "So I can be moved in by the end of the night."

"I said 'no,' Blaze repeated, for his clarification.

Jack stopped digging long enough to give her a flat look. "Honey. About ninety percent of the world would sputch you in a heartbeat to have what you've got in your hands right now."

That got her heart pounding little waves of molten metal through her chest.

Grunting, Jack started digging again

"Okay," Blaze said, "but if you're gonna stay here, you're gonna start teaching me how to make the stuff around here work."

He glared at her over the hole. "I showed you how to run the bulldozer."

"That's *one thing*!" she cried. "And then you *took* it from me because I wasn't doing it fast enough."

"I'll take care of the rest," Jack said. "You don't need to worry about stuff like that. Just fiddle with your garden and make the place look pretty. I'll take care of the important stuff."

Just fiddle with your garden…Blaze found herself having trouble speaking through her rising fury. "Contrary to your belief, *Jack*," Blaze growled, "I'm not a helpless bimbo. I *want* to learn that stuff, and I'm *paying* you to *teach* me. I will *not* be dependent on a man for the rest of my life. That's the whole *self-sufficient* thing, got it?"

He gave her a look an irritated look. "Every woman's gotta depend on a guy sometime in her life. Right now, I'm that guy. Just deal with it, tootz."

Narrowing her eyes at the surge of rage that made her want to wrap her fingers around his bovine neck, Blaze watched him dig for some time, just to keep from screaming. "All right," she finally gritted. "I'm a businesswoman. You wanna stay? We both have something the other wants. You know about engines and stuff. I know how to read."

Jack lost his grip on the shovel and it went sailing across the yard with his last load of dirt. He stared at it for a long time, a flush creeping across his neck and face. "Musta got oil on my hands from the shop," he said.

"I can teach you," Blaze insisted. "Fair trade."

Jack twisted to glare at her, his green eyes dark. "I wasn't askin' for your help, honey. I been doin stuff just fine on my own." Still scowling at her, he went over to the shovel, yanked it off of the ground, and returned to the hole.

Blaze shrugged. "I was offering to teach you, but I guess if you *like* being illiterate…"

She heard a deep-chested growl, but the wereverine said nothing and started to dig again. It was almost as if he were pretending she didn't exist.

"Or maybe you're just a total chickenshit," Blaze sighed. "Been stuck in a rut so long…Maybe you're too afraid to try?"

Jack slammed the shovel into the dirt and glared up at her. "We need to get that feather out of sight, Boss, 'fore the fey get a whiff of it. Unless you've got something *important* to say, you're kind of breaking my train of thought. Okay?"

"By all means, carry on," Blaze said, gesturing at the hole with her free hand. "Manual labor must really be an intense experience for you, if I'm breaking your train of thought." Then, after a moment, added, "Chicken."

"I just wanna get the feather out of sight without listening to your stupid—" Jack tensed at her last. Then, slowly, he turned to look at her, and she saw hair sprouting from his back, teeth sliding from between his lips. "You," Jack growled, shovel handle gripped in a taloned fist, "are about *this close* to getting a shovel through your brainpan." It was the feral sound, the rattling deep in his chest.

"Okay, chicken," Blaze said. She waved at the upturned earth. "Go dig me a hole, then."

"I'll dig your *grave*!" Jack snarled. She heard a snap as the shovel handle splintered in his grip. Then the wereverine was stepping forward, shoving his muzzle into her face. "I didn't tell you so you could *rub it in*, goddamn it."

Even fully transformed, he was still only eye-to-eye with Blaze. "You're right," she said into his mouthful of fangs, "I'll just go read a book. Leave you out here to your manual labor." She turned to go.

Jack grabbed her by the back of her shirt and yanked her around so hard she would've fallen had his grip not been like iron, holding her in place. His glowing green eyes were fully slitted, now, and blood was dripping from the inner rows of teeth. Blaze just peered back at him, long ago having learned he was harmless.

"You're gonna teach me," the wereverine said, his breath scalding her face, "Starting tonight."

"You asking or telling?" Blaze said, utterly calm.

"*Telling*!" Jack roared.

"Then I'm telling you," Blaze said, "You're gonna stop screwing around and start teaching me how to run this place. No more of this, 'You're just a city-slicker who doesn't know any better,' crap. Stop blowing me off. Start teaching me mechanicking, carpentry, plumbing, stuff like that. I'll teach you to read and write, and we'll call it a fair bargain."

The wereverine's unholy slitted green eyes scanned her eyes over its bared fangs, and for a moment, she thought he would simply bite off her face. Then, almost reluctantly, he seemed to shift back to his human form.

"Fine," he said, releasing her. He handed her the splintered end of the shovel. "Your education starts now."

Blaze frowned down at the broken spade. "You're gonna teach me to *dig*?"

"Basics of Manual Labor 101," Jack said, crossing his big arms over his rippling chest, an amused smirk on his face. He nodded at the ground with his head. "I'd say we're gonna need something about six to eight feet deep."

Blaze balked. "Eight *feet*?"

"Yep," Jack said, gesturing to the dirt. "Get started." He reached out and took the feather case from her. "The shovels are in the shop."

Blaze scowled down at him for several moments. Then, furious, she stomped back across the yard, yanked an un-crushed shovel from inside the shop, stalked back, and slammed the shovel into the dirt and pried up a clod of dirt. She tossed it aside, glaring at him. "How was *that*, smartass?"

"You could work on your technique," Jack suggested. "Your arm didn't quite get the loft I was looking for."

Blaze narrowed her eyes at him and shoved the point of the shovel against his chest. "You think this is funny?"

Jack glanced at the sun. "I'm guessing it'll probably take you five to six hours. If you start now." He dropped the feather's box into the dirt at her feet, then turned and walked off toward the shop. Over his shoulder, he called, "Oh, and you're gonna want gloves, to keep your soft, city-slicker hands from getting blisters."

Blaze threw the shovel at him, but it fell humiliatingly short. Jack laughed without even turning.

Scowling at his broad back, thinking about how much she'd like to see it peppered with birdshot, she returned her attention to the shovel. Snarling, she picked it up and started digging again. She ignored his warnings about blisters—she hadn't seen *him* use gloves—and put all of her concentration into prying out the next clod so she *wasn't* thinking about how much she wanted to pound the shovel into his fat head.

She had gotten about four feet down in two hours when she heard another big engine from the heavy machinery lot start up, putter, then die. She chuckled to herself and kept digging.

She heard him try a dozen more times, and each time it died, she cackled inwardly. "Some mechanic!" she shouted into one of the quiet moments in between cranks of the engine.

If Jack heard, he didn't respond, but the pause in between starts was longer this time. When he finally turned the engine over again, it roared to life and fell into a low, healthy putter.

Asshole, Blaze thought.

The engine revved and she heard something big move forward, slowly coming out from behind the shed and the shop, making the trees themselves rattle.

Blaze ignored him. Her hole was halfway done, and when it was finished, and she'd stuffed the feather down there and covered it up, she was going to go back, sit down in front of the fire, and spend the rest of the day reading in front of him.

The sound of the engine increased, however, until it grew so loud that Blaze *had* to look, to make sure that it wasn't running her over.

Her jaw dropped when she saw the enormous John Deere backhoe slide into position beside her. Over the roar of the engine, Jack shouted, "Manual Labor 101—Never Do Any More Work Than You Have To." He then hit the hydraulics and the bucket scooped out in a single load what Blaze had struggled to accomplish in almost three hours.

As Blaze started to shake with fury, he dug out four more scoops, dropped them aside, then swung the bucket out of the way and switched off the engine.

Hopping down, he cheerfully said, "All right, tootz. Let's see that feather of yours."

Blaze hurled a clod of dirt into his face, paused just long enough to watch it explode upon his brow, spun on her heel, and stormed back to the lodge, so angry she couldn't even speak.

She was dragging her duffels down the porch steps, heading toward the trailer of the 4-wheeler, when Jack finished with the backhoe and returned it to the lot. He came walking around the shop frowning at her.

When he got close, he tossed the empty metal case onto the trailer in front of her. "Where you think you're going?" he growled. He still had a smear of dirt in the hairline of his right temple.

"Away," Blaze said, dropping the last duffel onto the trailer. She reached into her pocket and yanked out her cell phone. She started dialing Bruce Rogers' charter service, but before she could punch out the full number, Jack snatched the phone from her and snapped it in half. Then in quarters. Then he tossed it into the lawn.

"Get back in the house," he growled. Like he was talking to a hormonal teenager.

Blaze stared at him, then stared at her broken phone. "That's *assault*," she finally snapped.

Jack snorted and continued past her, stopping to pluck the key out of the 4-wheeler's ignition on the way by.

"You *asshole*!" Blaze screamed, watching him tuck it nonchalantly into his pocket.

When he only laughed and disappeared inside the hastily-patched back door, Blaze had to grab the trailer to steady her rage. She had never been so angry in her entire life, and had he not already broken her gun in half, she would have yanked it from her pack and shot him. In the knee. Then the foot. Then the head.

Instead, gunless, phoneless, Blaze slumped onto the trailer and stared at the broken remnants of her lifeline to the rest of civilization.

Some time must have passed, because Jack came out onto the porch to lean against the doorway. "I boiled some eggs," he called, biting into one. "You hungry yet?"

"Go suck on a revolver!" Blaze snapped.

She heard his chuckle as he ducked back into the lodge.

She hated him. She hated every perfect inch of his sculpted body, wanted nothing more than to punch his pretty teeth in. Blaze looked down at her hand. It was huge, for a woman. For a man of her size, though, it was tiny. Smaller than Jack's.

The worst of both worlds, Blaze thought, disgusted. She closed her fingers, made a fist.

The trailer rattled as Jack sat down beside her, his body almost touching hers. After a moment of silence, he set something heavy in her lap. Blaze looked down, saw the strange red wrench, and fought the urge to throw it to the ground.

"That's a monkey wrench," he said. "It's used for tightening pipe." He set another one in her lap, this one silver. "That's a channel-lock. Good for getting a grip on something to give it a good twist. See the head there? See how you can adjust it?" He pointed.

Blaze's vision blurred as she looked down at the two tools. She quickly wiped an arm across her face and buried her cheeks in her shirt, feeling the first wave of exhaustion hit her like a hammer to the brain. *I will* not *cry*, she told herself, breathing slow, deep breaths through the flannel, horrified at the idea of Jack seeing her in that state. Once she'd gotten herself under control again, she lowered her arm. "Just go fuck off, all right?" she whispered.

But he settled a tiny, knobby hammer onto her lap. "That's a ball-peen hammer. Good for pounding out dents and little things like that. Good with an anvil." He added another silvery tool onto the pile. "That's a socket wrench. See this here?" As she watched, he removed the round head and, plucking a smaller one from the pile beside him, exchanged it. "You can change the sockets to fit any size nut or bolt. Good for getting into tight spaces where you don't have much room to maneuver."

The wave of despair came back, burning her eyes like wet coals. Blaze sniffled, barely able to see the tools through her tears. *Dammit*, she thought, as the soul-deep fatigue started to sink in. Aside from a brief cry for her father, she hadn't shed a tear in *years*, and here this sonofabitch had her weeping like a school-girl. And there was no helping it, now. She'd felt it already reach that tipping point inside. In half an hour, she was either going to be in bed, asleep, or collapsed on the damn trailer, utterly helpless.

Oblivious, Jack cleared the tools off her lap, then held up another. "Vice grips," he said, working the handles so that the toothed mouth worked like a hungry puppet. "Good for getting a hold on something and not letting go." When she didn't respond, he gently lowered it into her open palm and wrapped her fingers around it. "Adjustable. Little screw in the bottom raises or lowers the teeth. Go ahead and try."

Blaze looked up from the tool, meeting his gaze. She felt her tears overflow from the motion of her head, making it run down her cheeks.

He looked up at her, his green eyes wide, his mouth open. He seemed caught by her stare for several moments before he cleared his throat embarrassedly and looked back at the little stack of tools he'd lowered to the trailer beside him. "There's more," he said, running his big hands over the pile beside him. "I'll give you a few more each day." He was silent for a long minute. Then, "I really am an asshole, aren't I?"

Blaze wiped her face again and looked away. Her gaze fell on the bulldozer, still parked where she'd left it, forty feet into her new pasture. She'd abandoned that project around the same time she realized the sun had wrested her dreams away from her.

"Blaze?" Jack said softly. When she couldn't find the words to answer him, he swallowed hard. "I'm trying. I really am. Every night, I think about it before I go to bed. I still got 'til next June. I'll figure it out."

She set the vice-grips onto the trailer beside him and got to her feet. "I have to go to bed now," she whispered. "I'll see you in the morning, Jack." She didn't wait for his response. She crossed the yard, went inside, got undressed, and slipped into bed even as she felt herself slide into another coma.

SEVEN

Catchin' Some Rays

He'd made her *cry*. Jesus, he wasn't trying to make her cry. He'd just been trying to do…what? Prove that she wasn't as smart as she thought she was? Prove to her he wasn't stupid? So what if he never went to school? He had plenty of smarts in other stuff. It wasn't like books were what was important in life, anyway.

And Hell, she *had* tried to make him feel stupid, and after he'd tried to break the ice by letting her in on his horrible little secret. That was *her* fault. So he couldn't read. Big deal. There were plenty of people who couldn't read. She shouldn't have rubbed it in like that. She'd been *asking* for an attitude-adjustment.

Yet, despite all that, as Jack watched Blaze go, he still felt like an utter shitheel. She'd given him a chance to shape up his act and he'd screwed the pooch even worse than before, all because he couldn't get his damn tongue to work the way he wanted it to. Once she disappeared inside the lodge, he glanced down at his little pile of tools, miserable. *Way to go, Jackie-Baby*, Jack thought, disgusted. *She's gonna be on the next flight outta here.* Maybe she wasn't gonna sing like a canary, but he doubted she was gonna hang around much longer.

Sighing, Jack put the wrenches aside and got back to his feet. If there was one thing he'd learned about women, it was that it was best to apologize first, then figure out *if* you were wrong later. Well, it was even *better* if you just assumed you were wrong in the first place, but Jack wasn't about to belly up to the sexy giantess. He'd already handed over thirty acres of his land and spent a good portion of the summer putting her place back together for her, and like hell he was gonna start crawling around on his hands and knees asking forgiveness for *her* trying to make him feel stupid. Jack Thornton didn't beg.

Muttering, Jack went back inside and walked to the door of her room, which was locked. Sighing as he twisted the knob, Jack said, "Come on, Blaze. You know this fucking door won't do shit. Let me in."

She answered him with silence.

Jack narrowed his eyes and dropped his hand from the knob. *Do* not *be an asshole*...It had become a private mantra for him for the last couple months. *Don't be an asshole. Don't be an asshole.* About one out of ten times, it worked.

This time happened to be one of them. Instead of putting his fist through the drywall and unlocking the door from the inside, Jack cleared his throat and muttered, "Sorry."

Silence on the other side.

Immediately, Jack bristled. "What, you're gonna give me the silent treatment? Make me beg?"

She said nothing.

Remembering what happened *last* time he got the silent treatment, Jack stuck his ear to the door and listened.

He could hear her breathing.

"Okay, tootz," Jack growled. "You and I are gonna come to an understanding. You might own this place, but I'm living here with you from now on, and seein' how I'm the one doing all the repairs, I've got no problems busting down a goddamn door so I don't have to speak through a fucking wall because you're having a pity-fest on the other side."

Nothing.

"I'm serious," Jack warned. "Open the door."

She was still *in* there, but she was completely ignoring him.

He narrowed his eyes a long moment, then grated, "Please?"

She didn't even shift on the bed, didn't even make any indication she'd heard him. Jack had a moment of panic, wondering if she'd set up her phone with another recording, but when he got on his knees and sniffed under the door, he could smell her in there.

Her and…fire? Jack wrinkled his nose and sniffed again. Yes, he was pretty sure he smelled smoke.

"Okay, sweetheart," he growled, "I'm getting fucking sick of the silent treatment. What are you burning in there?"

She continued to ignore him.

"*Please* let me in," Jack muttered, when the acrid smell under the door continued to get stronger. He tried to think of what she could be setting on fire. The bed, her underwear, books…

His eyes widened slightly as he remembered the book she'd brought out with her. "Oh, no, please, honey, no, don't burn it. I really wanna learn, I swear. Please don't do that."

The stench continued, and this time, he saw lines of smoke pass under the door. Seeing that, Jack narrowed his eyes. "Okay. I'm trying *really* hard not to be an asshole, sweetcheeks, but you're being a real pain in the ass. So I hurt your fucking feelings. *I'm sorry.* Just don't burn the damn book, okay? I'll teach you anything you wanna know. Just cut the fucking bullshit and open the door so we can talk or I'll *bust it down.*" At her continued silence, he tapped politely on the door again. "Last chance. Let me in and talk to me. *Please.*"

She still wasn't listening to him.

Okay, so maybe he needed to class it up a bit. She was a rich brat. High-society. She probably didn't appreciate the crude little cluster-fuck of a wereverine cursing at her through a door. Jack took several steadying breaths. What would a feylord say?

It pains me to see you in such distress at my hand. Please, end this silence and allow me to make amends for my past misdeeds…

"I…uh…am pained…that you are upset…"

Listening to her continue to mock him with silence, Jack found himself getting more and more irritated, and it was becoming difficult to think straight. All he *wanted* to do was put his fist through the door.

Don't be an asshole, he thought, taking a deep breath. *Don't be an asshole.* Think *about this, you dumbass. You can do this. You've got time. No pressure.* He concentrated, trying hard to work out exactly what he could say that would make her stop being a stuck-up, pity-partying drama-queen. He thought again of the arrogant, prissy feylords he had known in his time, remembered how eloquently they had wooed the ladies right out from under him. He scrunched his nose, remembering their flowery speech, trying to force it to the socially inept little half-busted crankcase that was Jack. *It wasn't my intent to deliver such sorrows to you, blessed-of-my-heart. Please, vanquish this bitter portal and allow me to bear your troubles with you or I'll be forced to take out my rage on your current abode.*

"Open the door or I'll beat it the fuck down."

This time, when she ignored him, Jack's hands tightened into fists on a surge of rage. "All right, sugar. You were warned." He took a step backwards, leaned back, and put his fist through the door. Casually, he reached through and unlocked it. Then he yanked his arm back through the hole, twisted the knob and pushed the door open. "Okay, just shut up and listen while I—uuuhhh, Blaze?"

Blaze's shirt, piled in a corner by the door, was on fire. It was smoldering on the sleeves and down the front, working in slow, outward-spreading bubbles of flame. Blaze, for her part, appeared to be unconscious, tucked under a blanket, looking rather peaceful.

"Uh..." Jack said, glancing from Blaze to the burning shirt and back. "Why'd you set your shirt on—" Then he froze. He knew what this was. The feather. She'd *activated* it. And she'd been *crying*.

"Oh, oh shit, uh, okay, um, never mind, you just stay right there, honeybuns, and I'll take care of everything." He reached down to grab a fistful of the shirt, then howled when the tearstained cloth came into contact with his hands. "Ow, *fuck!*" He dropped it into a smoldering pile on the floor at his feet, shaking out his palm. When he examined his skin for boils, he found there were no burns, but it still hurt like a *bitch*. Like he'd reached into a blacksmith's forge and dragged out a handful of white-hot coals.

Then, realizing from the wisps of smoke coming from the hardwood floor under the smoldering wad of cotton that the shirt was about to set the *house* on fire, he squatted to pick it up again. Careful to touch the *back* of the shirt, Jack yanked it off of the floor, hurried over to the woodstove, and tossed the garment inside.

"Okay, sweetie, it's all better now," he said, locking the woodstove door behind it and coming back inside to peer at Blaze worriedly. She appeared to be sleeping peacefully, not even having stirred at his commotion. He frowned. "Blaze?"

When she didn't respond, he eased a little closer, then squatted slowly beside her bed. "Blaze?" he asked again. When she didn't stir, he reached up and touched her forehead. Immediately, he wrenched his hand away with a hiss. Her head was like *ice*.

"Okay, pumpkin," Jack said, trying not to hyperventilate, "you're scaring the shit outta me here, dear. What do I do?"

She just lay there, like a Yeti-sized ice cube, completely unresponsive.

"Fuck me," Jack managed, watching her. He tested her temperature again with his palm, just to make sure he wasn't overreacting, then decided when his fingers came back numb that, yes, there was definitely something very wrong with her. He ran upstairs, grabbed a thermometer from the owners' apartment, and came running back.

"Okay honey, open up," he said, sticking it into her mouth, not really caring what kind of cooties it had on it when she had the same general temperature as the inside of a commercial refrigerator.

Seeing that the little silver bar on the thermometer didn't even climb out of the bulb to pass to the first set of *notches*, Jack realized he had a serious problem on his hands. But what did you do with a *Fourth Lander* who was, to all appearances, dying in her bed?

The sun, Jack thought. He needed to get her into the sun. He dropped the thermometer back into its handy little plastic pouch and tossed it aside. "Okay, honey, you just hold on, I'm gonna take you outside, get you warmed up, okay?" He stood up and yanked back the blanket, intending to flip her over his shoulder, then froze.

"Oh," he said at her long ivory body, as perfect and unobstructed as the day she was born. He swallowed hard. "Oh." What *was* it with girls nowadays? Didn't they at least wear a *nightie* or something? Long-Johns? *Something?* No *wonder* she was cold. She didn't have anything *on* under there. She was stark *naked.* Nothing but pale, gorgeous skin, lily-white, delicate curves, perfect round breasts, with little spatterings of freckles down the stomach…

Jack realized he was staring. He quickly tucked the blanket back over her and tried to get hold on himself. "That was *your* fault for not wearing pajamas," he muttered, flushing hard enough to make his ears burn. "What kind of decent woman doesn't wear pajamas?"

If she heard him, his Yeti-sized ice-cube made no response. And, after *that* little blunder, Jack was pretty sure she wasn't faking. The Blaze *he* knew would've been hollering hidey-ho if she'd even *suspected* the hairy little curmudgeon wanted a look at what was under her 4-Extra-Long combat pants.

"Okay, gorgeous," he growled, wrapping her up in a blanket and heaving his Yeti-burrito over his shoulder. "I'm gonna go save your life. You get pissy with me, I'll just eat you." He carried her back out the ruined door, up through the lodge and out to the front porch, and laid her down gently on the creaky spruce planks. Squinting up at the sun, he unwrapped her and then quickly turned his back to make sure any nosy dumbshit neighbors kept their distance.

After a good hour in full sunlight, Jack reluctantly glanced back over his shoulder. The leggy Fourth Lander lay where he'd left her, soaking up the rays with that deliciously pale, curvaceous—

Jack quickly looked away again. Getting up, he *backed* up to her and carefully reached a hand behind him, aiming for an arm. His fingers hit what he was pretty sure was a warm, supple human breast. Crying out, he jerked his hand away. "Sorry!" he stammered. "Sorry, I was reaching for your arm and…"

The leggy Aphrodite continued to sleep peacefully.

"Okay, babe," Jack said, quickly grabbing the blanket and flipping it back over her. "You got your rays. Time to take you back inside 'fore you wake up and take all this the wrong way." Once he was sure she was good and *covered*, Jack turned, gathered up his Yeti burrito, and once more threw her over his shoulder. He trundled back down through the lodge and deposited her on her bed. Then, once she was tucked in, he went looking for a screwdriver.

As quietly as he could, he unscrewed the door from its hinges, pulled it aside, took it upstairs, replaced it for one in one of the far guest rooms where she wasn't likely to notice for awhile, and brought the fresh door down and screwed it into place. Then, when he was pretty sure he'd done all for her he could, he locked the inside latch and yanked the door shut behind him.

Then, sweating, he started pacing back and forth outside her door, cursing himself for locking it, wondering if he was going to have to make another trip upstairs with a screwdriver.

• • •

"Where are my clothes?" Blaze demanded, storming up the stairs to slap a Gigantor hand on the table beside Jack's plate of eggs. She was wearing a shirt that still had creases from the nice little department-store package she'd taken it from, because somewhere during the night, even through a *locked door*, her flannel shirt from yesterday had gone missing.

"Uh," the wereverine said, blinking up at her over the kitchen table. "What shirt?"

Blaze narrowed her eyes at him. "I said 'clothes,' not 'shirt,' Jack." Then, before Jack could spout some bullshit story about how, gee, this neck of the woods is inhabited by Marty the Shirt-Stealing-Marshmallow, she swiveled and started down the stairs.

"Where are you going?" he called after her, sounding a bit concerned.

"I'm gonna go run the dozer a bit." She went outside, yanked her boots on, and strode across the yard. She could feel Jack watching her through the second-floor window as she hopped up onto the wide metal track and climbed into the driver's seat.

Ignoring him completely, she turned the key in the ignition and cranked the engine over. For the first time in weeks, the engine roared to life, she lifted the blade, backed it up, and started attacking the edge of the forest once again.

A couple hours later, she was really settling into the groove, learning the machine, relieving all her tension in the upturned earth, when the engine sputtered and died.

Blaze frowned and turned the key again, but the engine cranked over uncooperatively.

"Sounds like it ran out of fuel," Jack called from behind her.

Blaze twisted to look over her shoulder.

The wereverine was sitting on the trailer, watching her, idly playing with a set of vice-grips. He dropped the tool back to the trailer and got to his feet, making the springs groan from the sudden release of weight. She expected a sneer or a quippy comment, but instead, he gestured for her to get down from the dozer. "Come on over to the fuel shed with me," he called. "Generator's running…I'll show you how to run the pump."

He seemed to hesitate, then, waiting to see if she would follow. Blaze turned again to look at the bulldozer's controls, then, reluctantly, she climbed out of the driver's seat and hopped off the track, into the soft earth. Seeing her get down, Jack started toward the smallest shed on the property.

Once Blaze arrived at the barrel-filled shack, Jack flipped a switch on the wall that made the ancient gas-station pump start to hum, then went and grabbed a yellow plastic gas carrier off a shelf and set it on the wooden planks between the barrels.

Blaze had to stoop to enter the tiny shack. Once she was inside, there wasn't much space to maneuver, and Jack's leaden arm brushed her stomach as he uncapped one of the barrels and stuck a metal-ended hose inside.

"This is diesel," he said, dipping his fingers into the liquid inside the barrel and holding it up to her. "Big rigs like the dozer and the backhoe are gonna use diesel. We keep the diesel in the green barrels." He wiped his hand off on his pants and went for the line of blue barrels opposite the green ones. After twisting off the cap with a 4-pronged metal lever, he dipped his finger into the second barrel and held it up to her. "Gas," he said. "Short for gasoline."

"I know what gas is," Blaze growled, scrunching her nose at the slight difference in smell.

Jack shrugged and recapped the barrel. "In the fuel business, we call gas 'gas' and diesel 'oil.' You don't say you need gas for your dozer. People will look at you funny, because you put gas in your dozer, you kill your dozer."

Blaze watched him suspiciously, trying to figure out why he was suddenly being so nice. Finally, she decided, "You're afraid I'm gonna take that cell phone out of your pay, aren't you?"

He blinked at her. "What?"

She made a gesture at the barrels. "Why you being so nice all of a sudden? What did you do? Aside from steal my shirt?"

Jack's brilliant green eyes widened for a moment, then he cleared his throat and turned back to his work, but not before she saw him redden. Instead of responding, he pulled the hose nozzle off of the ancient pump, then stuffed it into the yellow canister. "We use the yellow jugs for diesel, the red ones for gas."

"It says it on the side," Blaze commented.

Jack's entire body went stiff, and she saw his green eyes flicker at the lettering on the side of the canister.

Before he could get offended, however, Blaze squatted and pointed to the first letter on the canister. "That's a D. It's used for 'duh' sounds. Like drugs, dick, or dumbshit."

Jack's face reddened and he flipped on the pump. Liquid began to slosh into the yellow canister.

"Next two are I and E," Blaze said. "Usually, they have their own separate sounds, but English is a fucked up language, and in 'diesel,' they both sound like a hard 'E'. Like 'mean' or 'scream' or 'steam.'"

Jack cleared his throat uncomfortably, but she could tell he was paying attention. He finished filling the canister and switched off the pump.

"Next is an S," Blaze said, pointing. "Used for things like 'scumbag' or 'shithead' or 'stupid stubborn asshole.'"

He flushed crimson and looked away in agitation.

"That right there is another E," Blaze said, tapping it. "E can have a bunch of different sounds in the English language, but this time, it's kind of silent. The last one is an L." She smiled up at him. "Used for words like 'little,' 'laughable,' or 'lewd.'"

Jack glared up at her and yanked the canister off of the ground. "I'll keep that in mind." His big shoulders flexing under his blue flannel shirt, he stalked out of the shed and out toward the bulldozer.

Blaze grinned as she watched him go. *Maybe we can work together, after all.* Blaze again felt herself admiring the rock-hard features of his body, the clefts and bulges pushed tight against his well-used clothes. She was still watching him, appreciating his confident, sexy swagger, when she saw a light flicker out of the corner of her eye, near where her hand was resting on the door jamb.

Frowning, Blaze turned back to the shed.

The green speck winked out the moment she looked at it, and she was about to shake her head and write it off as the gas fumes getting to her, when it popped back into sight a few yards away, at the edge of the forest. When she turned to face it completely, however, the light slid deeper into the forest, then winked out. She saw it there, blinking off and on, keeping its distance.

Feeling a tightness work its way into her gut, Blaze backed up, then, when she was sure whatever it was wasn't going to lunge out at her, she turned and bolted for Jack.

Jack had just climbed atop the bulldozer and was uncapping the cap from the fuel tank on the side of the machine. He didn't even look up.

"I saw something!" Blaze cried, climbing up onto the dozer with him, putting him between her and the strange green light.

Jack grunted and pulled the collapsible tube from the canister, then leaned it up against the bulldozer and started to pour.

"A green light," Blaze babbled. "It was bobbing around near my hand, then took off for the woods when I saw it. Winking in and out. Size of a fist." She was panting, gasping for air.

"Fey," Jack said. "A young one. Don't worry about it."

"Fey?" Blaze said. "I thought you said fey would want the fea—"

Jack slammed the diesel canister back on the dozer and gave her a *look*. "Just 'cause you can't see 'em," he said softly, capping the gas tank again, "Don't mean they aren't out *there*, sweetie." With another scowl at her, he re-sealed the canister and hopped off the dozer.

"Where are you going?!" Blaze cried.

"I've got things to do," Jack said. "We're gonna need a *ton* of firewood come fall, and that green four-wheeler is knocking again. Think I'm gonna spend a couple hours tinkering with it before dinner."

"What do I do about the fey?" Blaze cried.

He raised a jet-black eyebrow at her. "What do you mean, 'do?' The fey want to hang around, you leave 'em alone." He grunted. "Besides. It's not the babies you need to be worried about. Anything with wings is gonna be more scared of you than you are of it. Moment you start seeing wingless teenagers running around, though, then you should start getting concerned. They're usually about a thousand years old at that point." He gestured at the fuel shed. "Little guys like that, though…" he snorted. "They won't eat much."

"You *saw* him," Blaze realized, horrified.

Jack wrinkled his nose. "*Smelled* him, more like. Always makes me nervous when they hang out near the gas shed. Smell a lot like ozone, and I always wonder if they're gonna set off a spark to make the whole place explode."

"But I thought you said the fey would—" Blaze began.

Jack stopped her with another *look*.

"Uh," Blaze said, reddening. "I thought you said you kept this place clean of intruders."

"I do," Jack said.

"Then why would you let them stay?" Blaze demanded.

Jack gave her a long look. "Like I said, sister," he said, "It's not the babies you need to watch out for. They don't know any better, and they're harmless little buggers. Annoying sometimes, but what youngsters aren't?" He scowled out at the forest. "Nah, it's the big ones that I'll rip rim from limb, if I catch them sneaking around on my land."

Blaze again felt herself tense at the way he said 'my' land, but before she could correct him, Jack had turned and started toward the 4-wheeler trailer, which was still piled with drywall from the last barge trip.

Blaze started after him to help.

She had taken two steps when Jack dropped the fuel canister on the ground beside the 4-wheeler and, as she watched, impressed, heaved an entire batch of drywall off the trailer at once and carried it inside the basement of the lodge, then came back and drove the 4-wheeler over to where Blaze had knocked down a dozen good-sized birch trees, threw on chaps, and started attacking the logs with a chainsaw.

Reluctantly, Blaze crawled back up into the bulldozer's operator chair, nervously scanning the woods for little green glowies. Fey. Like *fairies*. Of the *abracadabra* You Now Have Ears Like A Donkey kind. It was just too much. Maybe she could open a seasonal greenhouse outside Anchorage or start a farm in the Mat-Su Valley. Wasilla or Palmer. Something a little less…ambitious.

Blaze nonetheless started the dozer and lifted the blade, and found herself immediately comforted by the low rumble around her.

Then again, she thought, as she once more began to work the earth, watching Jack cut up the trees she'd downed for him, *I might be able to make do.*

Her land-clearing endeavors, she decided, would need to include sites for a major greenhouse and a couple of livestock buildings. Her first set of stock, according to the plan she had developed before beginning this mess, would be delivered a month after the lumber loads, in late-August. Goats, rabbits, pigs, two dogs, plus a good six dozen of various fowl.

Her plan included setting up fencing on a few acres of forested area, releasing the animals inside, and let the goats and pigs eat their way through the rest of the summer, supplemented with feed from Blaze's barge-runs. The rabbits and fowl would be penned separately, to protect from martins, foxes, and goshawks.

If it worked out, she would get a yak or two next spring, along with a few beef calves.

Excitement began to build with every new stroke of the bulldozer's blade. Finally—*finally*—she was doing something to see her dreams come true. Soon she would be neck-deep in endangered breeds of livestock, helping to carry on genetic diversity with critically rare breeds that had lost their commercial value due to hybridization or genetic 'improvements.'

Looking at the churned earth around her, however, Blaze realized she needed to stick with the plan, take it slow. She remembered one of her Algebra professor's favorite acronyms, K.I.S.S..

Keep It Simple, Stupid. Already, her fantasies were running away with her. She wanted her farm, and she wanted it *now*, and her brain was politely overlooking the fact that she had precisely diddly in the form of structures, pens, and paddocks, and that it wouldn't be very genetically responsible to have foxes or wolves drag off a few dozen animals from breeds that, for some, only had two hundred breeding individuals in North America.

"Just a little bit at a time," she told herself, as she rolled another ball of roots out of the way of her building-space. She would start small—goats, pigs, rabbits, and fowl. If that worked out, she could think about the rest in the spring.

That night, Jack met her by the woodstove with her smutty adventure book. He shoved it into her hands. "There ya go, Boss," he said. "Teach me to read."

Blaze, hearing the command in his voice, seeing that he fully expected to be obeyed, almost turned and set the book up high on a shelf, out of reach for him without use of a stool. She fought the urge, however, realizing he would probably just tear a few swipes through the wall until the shelf came to him. She forced a polite smile. "My name is Blaze."

He squinted up at her, green eyes narrowed. "Sounded to me like your name was Beatrice."

Blaze shuddered. "I'm getting it changed." Then she caught herself and frowned. "And that's none of your damn business. I want to be called Blaze, you call me Blaze."

"You can wanna be called the Tooth Fairy for all I care," Jack said. He crossed his arms over his burly chest and nodded at the book in her hands. "You gonna teach me to read that?"

Blaze narrowed her eyes at him. "You got one hell of a way of asking nicely."

"Who said I was asking?" Jack pulled a hand free and looked at the back of a fingernail. He stuck it in his mouth and started gnawing on it. "Way I see things, sugar," he said around his finger, "you need me a hell of a lot more than I need you." He spat whatever he'd collected from his nail onto the floor, scowled at his finger-tips, then re-crossed his arms. "I've gone my whole life without books. You, I'd wager, probably never changed a carburetor or pulled a spark plug in your life." He gave her a polite smile. "So, you gonna be reasonable?"

Blaze felt her lip curling in a snarl. "You are not the only one who can change a spark plug."

"Maybe," Jack said. He casually leaned back against a corner wall, "But I'm pretty sure that any other mechanic you hire won't stay long." He winked at her. "Considerin'."

I hate him, Blaze realized. And at the same time she wanted to rip out his guts and nail them to her wall, she was struck by how utterly sexy he was lounging against her wall, sleeves rolled up, big arms bunching against his chest.

Muttering, she set the book down and went into her room.

"Hey," Jack growled, unfolding from the wall to quickly follow her. "We had a bargain, there, missy."

Blaze ignored him and found her journal. She grabbed a couple sheets out of the back, ripped them free, and brushed past him to sit at one of the hand-hewn wooden chairs beside the fire.

"Sit down," she said, thrusting a heavy chair at him with her foot.

Jack grunted as it hit him in the legs. Scowling at her warily, he brought it up beside her and sat down with his upper body leaning over the chair's back. She heard the wood creak and wondered if he was about to snap off the backrest with his weight.

"How much do you weigh?" she asked.

As if knowing exactly why she was asking, Jack showed his teeth and leaned harder on the chair, and she heard wood pop under the pressure. *I break it, I'll fix it. You don't need to worry your pretty head about it.* That had been the excuse he'd used for everything from tearing holes in her drywall to shattering her sink because he'd cut himself shaving.

"It's *my* money we're using to fix *your* damages," Blaze growled, watching the chair strain underneath him.

He bared his teeth more. "Take it out of my pay."

She glared at him. "Maybe I will."

"Fine, honey. You do that." As if it didn't matter to him one way or the other.

After another moment of glaring at Jack, Blaze reluctantly looked back down at the notebook sheets, once again having to resist the urge to wad them up and put them somewhere out of reach. As legibly as she could, Blaze scrawled out the upper and lowercase alphabet on the top of the page. Her handwriting had never been particularly neat, described by most as deranged chicken-scratch, but she went slowly. She had to erase several times—penmanship had never been her strong suit—and bent over as she was, her hair kept getting in her face. She took a moment to pull off her hat, pull her thick carrot-orange hair out, comb the rats' nests with her fingers, and weave it back into a quick braid between the Q and the R.

"You got nice hair," Jack muttered. Like he was mentioning a pustule growing from her forehead. He hadn't looked up from the page.

Caught between frustration at Jack's complete, stubborn *maleness* and a little girly flutter of 'he thinks my hair is pretty,' Blaze quickly cleared her throat and ignored him completely. She tossed her boonie-hat on the chair beside her, leaving her braid pulled over one shoulder. Once she had all twenty-six letters aligned out in six neat rows, she slapped the pen down in irritation. "There," she muttered. "The alphabet. Twenty-six letters, both upper case—that's the big ones—and lowercase—the little ones."

When she looked up to make sure Jack was paying attention, he was staring at her, jaw open, appearing completely lost in thought. He didn't seem to notice she was talking to him.

"You paying attention?!" Blaze demanded, jabbing a finger at the letters.

Jack blinked suddenly. "Huh?" He shook himself, frowning, and glanced down at the page of notes. When he saw them, he reddened. "Yeah?" he growled, bristling. "So?"

"So that's the alphabet," Blaze said, handing him the pencil and paper. "All the letters in the English language. You try."

By the way he blushed, she might as well have asked him to strip down naked and pirouette for her. When he didn't reach for the proffered paper, she nudged him with it.

"That's just gibberish," Jack growled. "What am I supposed to do with that?"

"You *learn* them," Blaze sighed.

Jack snorted. "I don't need to do that to learn."

Blaze gave him a long look. When the wereverine just glared at her stubbornly, Blaze sighed and stood up. She went over to the nice, warm woodstove and opened the door on the front.

Jack flinched and lunged out of his seat, eyes on the papers. "What are you doing?" The panic in his voice was almost comical.

Blaze yawned. "I'm going to use this to heat my home, because it's obviously no use to you." She moved to drop it through the open door.

Jack jumped forward and caught her wrist, that feral growl deep in his chest. "Listen, missy," he snarled, "It's in your best interest not to piss off the wereverine."

She raised an eyebrow down at him. "Piss you off? Who said anything about pissing you off? I thought you didn't *care* about this 'gibberish.'" She moved to toss it into the fire anyway.

Growling, Jack yanked her hand away from the fire and took the papers from her. He snatched up the pencil with his other hand, then slapped it all down on the seat of his chair and squatted beside it, glaring at her. Then, huffing like an angry bear, he took the pencil up in a fist and started scratching at the words. When Blaze immediately stepped closer to correct him, his back hunched in a flood of fur and he sprouted teeth.

Blaze quickly found something else to do.

A few hours later, there was a knock at her door.

"So, uh…" He had his big fingers wrapped around the pencil in a fist. He hadn't made more than a half-dozen of the letters on the page, and they all looked like someone had been trying to write the alphabet with a wrench. "I can't…" His voice cracked.

For the first time, Blaze realized the big baby was about to cry.

She also realized that, if she made a big deal of it, things were about to get really, really ugly. "Okay," she said, quickly putting down her book, "Well, you're holding the pencil wrong. It's gonna be tough, but you gotta train yourself to hold it like this…"

She took his huge, calloused, somewhat-resistive hand and forcibly shaped it around the writing instrument. "Like that." She grabbed him by a meaty shoulder and pulled him back over to the chair and set the paper down on it. "There. Copy them." She tried to push him into a squat, but it was like trying to bend the knees of a granite statue.

"Oh, for Chrissakes!" Blaze cried. She grabbed his hand and pulled it down to the paper. "There. See that? Draw them like that."

Reluctantly, the wereverine did. As Blaze watched and helped with minor corrections here and there, he scratched out all twenty-six letters of the alphabet.

"See?" Blaze cried, happily slapping him on the shoulder. "You *did* it!"

Immediately, the wereverine's jaw went slack, and the pencil slid back into a fist. Seeing that, Blaze frowned, leaned in close, and re-adjusted his hand. "Gotta remember that position," Blaze said. "Can't write like a ham-fisted mechanic, okay? Gotta use finesse."

Instead of looking down at the way she had positioned his fingers, however, the wereverine was staring up at her, mouth open again. He looked like a fox that had just realized there was a new chicken in the coop…

…or a nerdy pervert imagining her in leather armor and broadsword.

Blaze slapped the papers onto the chair in irritation. Growling, she got to her feet. "I don't do the barbarian thing," she growled, glaring down at him.

Jack blinked up at her, the moment gone. "Huh?"

"I like sex just as much as the next girl," Blaze gritted, "But the moment you try to get me to put on a breastplate and chainmail, we're done."

Jack dropped the pencil and lunged to his feet. "Now hold on a second," he babbled, "I really don't know what you're—"

"I've seen that look," Blaze snorted. "I know what it means. It means you've got some creepy part of your brain tellin' you you wanna be dominated by a big Amazon with a battleaxe."

When he didn't deny it, merely stared up at her, Blaze made a disgusted sound and pushed past him, back to her room. She slammed the door behind her and locked it.

Then, quietly, she slid to her knees beside the bed and concentrated desperately on keeping her tears in check.

EIGHT

Yeti Wars

When Blaze crawled out of bed the next morning, her handyman was nowhere to be found. Stumbling, still groggy from lack of caffeine, Blaze was settling the coffee pot on the woodstove when she caught sight of the sheet of letters on the chair, right where she had left it.

Disgusted, she took out the filter, tapped the grinds into the compost, and refilled the percolator. She was yawning, trudging past the chair on her way back from the bathroom, when she realized the page looked different than before. She paused, frowning down at the letters.

Jack had filled the page with a crude alphabet, upper and lowercase.

When she picked up the page, she saw that the back, too, was covered with painstakingly-etched letters, as was the next two pages. Every square inch of surface area, he had filled with letters.

Blaze was still staring at it when she heard someone step onto the porch. She quickly put the papers back and arranged them roughly as she had found them, then hurriedly moved to the stove, pretending to warm herself as the coffee percolated.

A moment later, Jack yanked the door open and stepped inside with a bundle of firewood in one big arm. "Morning," he said as he shut the door behind him. "Boiler's been going since six, so there's hot water for a shower." His eyes flickered to the papers on the chair, then away again.

Now that he mentioned it, Jack looked...*cleaner*...today. When he grew close, Blaze thought she smelled cologne.

"A shower sounds great," Blaze said.

Jack paused in unloading the pile in his arms. "What, you think that was a suggestion?" He snorted and dumped the rest of the wood to the metal spark-guard surrounding the woodstove. "You stink like diesel fuel, and you *look* like you went rootin' around in the yard with those pigs you keep talking about. I got tired of smelling your grimy ass." He took something from his pocket and shoved something against her stomach.

When Blaze blinked down at it, her hands came away with a bar of soap.

Then Jack went back to stacking wood like he'd said absolutely nothing out of the ordinary.

Suddenly, something profound occurred to Blaze.

"You've never *had* to live with a woman before, have you?"

Jack hesitated in piling wood. "Don't know what you're talking about," he said, without looking up.

"This really long life you claim you've had," Blaze insisted, gesturing at him with the soap. "Throughout it all, you never had a woman, did you? You were too much of a crass, grumpy, egotistical prick. You ran them all off."

Jack deposited the last of the wood on top of the stack a bit harder than was necessary. Glaring up at her, he growled, "I've had women before."

"Oh yeah?" Blaze laughed, crossing her arms over her chest. "Like when?"

Bristling, Jack got to his feet and said, "Like 'bout six years ago, right before I found pieces of her scattered all over my yard."

Blaze froze, her blood running cold. "I thought you didn't know if she survived."

Jack shrugged. "Never found any particularly important pieces."

"You found *pieces* of her and you think she might have…?" Blaze thought she might be ill.

Jack gave her a flat look. "It's hard to kill a were."

Blaze glanced out at the verdant trees through the window. Suddenly, the alders and other low-laying bushes seemed to take on a new, more sinister, purpose. She wondered what kinds of things could be hiding behind the screen of leaves, just out of sight. Immediately, she shied a bit closer to Jack, swallowing hard.

"They're not coming onto my land again without a special invitation," Jack said, following her gaze. "I made sure of that."

"How?" Blaze asked, suddenly very much craving to hear how much of a badass her new business partner was.

"Sputched the pack leader and six of his lieutenants," Jack said, turning to look at her. "Sent the rest of them off to lick their wounds."

"How'd you survive?" Blaze whispered.

He grunted. "They're just puppies. As old as I am…it was like slapping around some toddlers.

Blaze squinted at him. He looked to be in his late-twenties, maybe as old as thirty. "Just how old *are* you?"

He gave her a wary look. "Might wanna use the upstairs bathroom. I'm gonna be re-grouting the floor on this one in the next few days and I don't want it wet." Then he turned his big back on her again, heading for the door.

"Hey!" Blaze snapped. "I already know you're a *wereverine*. What's it gonna hurt?"

Jack hesitated at the door. When he looked back at her, his green eyes were cautious. He sniffed, then rubbed a greasy wrist across his face, then fidgeted with some wood-chips clinging to his shirt. Finally, he said, "You know those barbarians you keep talking about?"

It took Blaze a minute to realize he meant Vikings, then she nodded, slowly.

"I was on the raid on Lindisfarne Abbey." The way he said the name sounded foreign, almost like he wasn't speaking English. Then he yanked the door open, leaving her frowning after him.

Blaze puzzled on that all through her shower, racking her brain as she tried to remember her freshman European History class. By the time she'd gotten out and toweled off, she had narrowed it down to one of two major attacks, both perpetuated by Vikings. Depending on which one, that meant he could be anywhere from a nine to twelve hundred years old.

She was laughing when she stepped out of the bathroom.

Head still wrapped in a towel, she stuck her feet into a pair of shoes and went marching out to the shop, where she found him bent over the innards of another chainsaw. He turned when he heard her coming.

"Do you actually mean to tell me," Blaze said, jabbing a finger into his thick chest, "That you were born a *millennium* ago?"

Jack didn't even flinch. "Never said I was born then," he said. "Just said I went on a raid." He went unconcernedly back to the chainsaw. "Not actually sure when I was born, but I'd guess five or six times that. Hard to tell. Never really kept track. Think I was made somewhere in Russia, though. Remember being a trapper's son, and he came home covered in blood one day. Bit me a couple months after, I think. Then the village killed him, chased me out into the woods, and I began my life on the fringe of society."

Blaze's mouth fell open. "You mean you can do stuff like..." she raked her brain for something completely absurd, "...make a sword?"

"What kind you want?" Jack said distractedly. "Bastard sword, longsword, rapier, Zweihänder, cutlass, saber, claymore?" He started fiddling with the greasy parts on the table in front of him. "Even spent some time in the Orient, so I can make a decent katana or talwar or jian, though I'm by no means a master at those." He plucked a little plastic piece from the mess and fit it back into the chainsaw. "Even tried my hand at Damascus steel, but that was a real pain in the ass. Had to get the mixture just right, and only about half of them turned out good in the end, anyway."

Blaze narrowed her eyes. "The process of making Damascus steel was lost in the seventeen-fifties." She knew, because she had done her European History term-paper on the subject. Several modern-day swordmakers claimed to make 'Damascus' steel, but none could compare to the real thing.

"Was it." He flicked a bit of grime off of a circular rubber ring and fitted it back into the chainsaw.

"You are *not* six thousand years old."

He gave her an irritated look as he replaced a screw into the main compartment. "Six thousand is nothing, dearie. You wanna be blown away, take a vacation up to the Brooks Range and go find yourself a dragon. They don't die of old age."

"And you *do*?" Blaze scoffed.

He grinned at her, and she saw fangs. "Not old age, per se. More like 'differences of opinion.'"

Blaze glared at him, still not sure he wasn't completely pulling her leg. "And dragons?"

He shrugged and wiped his greasy fingers on his pants. "Dragons are a bit harder to drag into a fistfight. Lots of posturing, very little fang. Well, the old ones, anyway. Would rather look down their noses at you and quote poetry and hold grudges than settle it like men." He slapped the cover on the chainsaw, used a screwdriver to cinch it down, then hefted it off the table. Grabbing the pull-cord in one hand, the front handle in the other, he said, "Stuck-up pussies." He yanked the chainsaw cord, and suddenly the machine came to life in his hand.

Blaze took a nervous step backwards, watching as he started the blade running along its track in a high-pitched whine. "So I take it you haven't had any differences of opinion?" she asked, when he made a satisfied nod and shut it off.

Jack dropped the chainsaw back to the table. "None I lost."

Blaze peered at him. "Six thousand years and you've never lost a fight."

Jack went to the wall and pulled down a set of what looked like cowboy chaps. These he cinched around his waist, then clipped around the backs of his legs. He found a set of yellow headphones hanging on a nearby peg and grabbed those, too. Then, picking up the chainsaw, he walked out of the shop.

"*Never*?!" Blaze demanded, following him.

He glanced over a big shoulder at her. "I'm still here, ain't I?"

She caught up to him. "You ever fight a *dragon*?"

He gave her an irritated look. "Do I look stupid to you?"

"Uh..." Blaze grinned.

Jack stopped, halfway across the yard toward the jumble of downed trees she had put there, and smirked up at her. Way too confidently, he said, "That's not the general idea I get every time I catch you starin' at my sexy ass, honey."

Blaze flushed crimson. She hadn't realized he'd noticed.

Jack got a smug look. "Thought so." He turned and walked away, and made a show of flexing his jeans as he went.

Before meeting the bastard, Blaze would have been so horrified that she probably would have hidden in her room and stayed there for a few days out of utter, humiliating shame, but after almost two months of dealing with his shit, she only narrowed her eyes and jogged to catch up.

"And what about you?" she asked, keeping stride.

Jack gave her an uncertain look. "What do you mean?"

"I've caught you staring," Blaze said. "Caught you staring last night, in fact. Twice."

Jack's face reddened to a faint purple.

"See?" Blaze cried, in triumph. *Two can play at this game, bastard.* "I totally turn you on, don't I?"

"Lady," Jack growled, setting the chainsaw down on a fallen tree while he adjusted his headset. He smiled at her, and it was vicious. "Seein' how you wanna play this game an' all, I should prolly clue you in a little bit. Only fair."

Frowning, Blaze said, "What do you mean?"

"I don't go for the tall chicks," Jack said, yanking the cord on the chainsaw. "Yeti isn't my style." He gunned the engine, then, as she stared at him, horror wreaking cold, twisting tendrils of shame through her stomach, he unconcernedly started driving the blade through the tree.

• • •

Jack winced as Blaze ran back to the house and disappeared in the basement. He cut the power to the chainsaw and lowered the blade to rest on the half-chopped log, his heart pounding. It had taken every ounce of willpower he had to look up into her eyes and tell her he didn't go for the tall chicks.

Fuck, *every* girl he'd ever fallen for had been taller than him. Hell, Mae Lae had almost matched Blaze for height. He *liked* 'em tall. More chimney to crawl up, damn it.

But she had *pushed* him and if she had *noticed*, that meant he was a hell of a lot more turned on than he had thought, and he *refused* to do that to a woman again. He couldn't let his damned hormones get another girl killed. He'd rather go dig his own grave.

An apology was necessary for sure this time, he knew. He'd stuck his foot so far in his mouth he was choking on calf. Desperate for some way to remedy the situation, he started trying to think of what he could say to patch up this particular cluster. He didn't want to hurt her, just keep her from sealing that claim by accident, because he *knew* she wouldn't trust him again after that, and with something as permanent as a mating link, he wasn't about to take chances. He racked his brain for something to say. *Hey, babe, you might be tall, but you're still sexy as hell, I'm just not interested.*

But he *was* interested. *Way* too interested. He was so interested it had gotten painful to listen to her sleeping through a *wall* because he wanted to be *in* there, watching over her as she dreamed.

Yeah, this was getting way, *way* too outta hand, and it was a damned good thing he'd warned her off. He needed to just step back and take a breather and cool his nuts on a goddamn block of ice and think about Life for awhile. A Fourth Lander like that was *not* interested in a hairy little Third Lander.

But, that startled little death-wishy part of his brain thought, *she is interested.* He'd smelled it on her, multiple times, and in a stupid, ballsy maneuver that still had his heart pounding, he'd just gotten confirmation.

...and then he'd utterly fucked it up and told her she was a Yeti.

"Fuck," Jack muttered, slumping to the half-cut birch log. The woman of his dreams and she was probably off bawling in her room, thinking he was about the worst asshole on the—

Then Jack flinched. *Bawling?* He dropped the chainsaw and hurriedly jogged over to the closest basement window, listening.

He couldn't *hear* her crying. But then again, would he be able to hear *tears*? He carefully eased himself inside of the house and snuck up to the edge of her brand-new door, listening.

"He's just an asshole," Blaze was patiently explaining to herself. "He doesn't think you're a Yeti." Then she paused and Jack heard a huge, wrenching breath. "Okay, so maybe he thinks you're a Yeti. Big deal. You've had what, like *two* guys in your life? Babe, you *know* you're a Yeti. So what? It's not *news*. The only *news* here, *tootz*, is that he's completely not interested."

But I am *interested*, Jack wanted to yell. So damn interested he was having trouble controlling himself around her. The *beast* in him wanted to dispense with the bullshit, claim her, and rut all over her like a dog in heat. The *man* in him was desperately trying not to be totally turned on by the way she seemed utterly unafraid of him, by the sexy way she kept pissing him off on purpose, by the delicate clockwork brain that was always in motion behind those pretty blue eyes. *I am interested*, he thought again, in misery. *I just don't want you to end up a goddamned bloody corpse, okay?*

Listening to her rant to herself, Jack glanced down at his big, rough, greasy mechanic's hands and bit his lip. By running her off, he was protecting her....wasn't he? Living with him was dangerous. He was doing her a favor. Keeping her out of the limelight. Keeping her safe from being swept away by the alluring whirlwind of death that was Jack.

And yet, *he* had insisted on moving in with *her*, a completely knee-jerk, Oh My Fuck I'm Not Letting This Thing Outta My Sight moment, the second he fully realized just what kind of beastie he had on his hands. So that argument kinda lost its merit, now that he thought about it.

Which meant he either needed to run her off for good, pack up and leave town, or dispense with the bullshit.

Jack glanced down at the little pile of papers that he had dutifully filled with letters for her and felt a wave of humiliation at his own failings. He might as well, he knew, take those papers and try to use them to get himself into Harvard. He didn't have a chance with her. He was a pauper that had found the Hope Diamond after it tumbled off somebody's crown, and he was doing his best to snatch it up and build a castle for it.

She's so totally out of your league, he thought, in misery, *and she doesn't even know it yet.* The moment she *did* figure it out, she was gone. She was gonna fly off into the sunset, baby, because there were *much* better prospects out there than a hairy little asshole. She seemed rather infatuated with dragons, for instance. Or maybe she'd go head off north to check out Thunderbird. She didn't *need* him.

And, in that moment, he felt a growl start to rattle in his chest. *Yes, she does*, that death-wishy part of him retorted. *And you sure as hell know that no dragon out there's gonna waste his precious time or hoard building her a* farm. And the idea of Thunderbird dirtying his hands changing out engines or getting sweaty hammering up a barn was completely laughable.

You've got a chance at this, he realized, stunned. *All you gotta do is stop screwing things up…*

Biting his lip, glancing back at the little sheaf of papers she'd left for him, Jack snuck back outside to begin unfucking his mistakes.

NINE

Meet the Neighbors

Blaze was still reading a book in an attempt to keep herself from crying an hour later, when she heard Jack thump up onto the porch and yank the door open.

She heard him stop outside her door.

"I drew up some plans for the barn and the first greenhouse," he grumbled through the wall. "Could use your help on a couple things."

Blaze, who was still in her towel and bath gear, put the book down, tore the towel off of her head, and started getting dressed.

"Hey Blaze?" he asked, his voice sounding tentative.

Blaze grabbed her huge man-pants, yanked them on her huge man-legs, jammed her huge man-toes into her huge man-socks, then rammed her Yeti feet into her man-boots. She laced them up in silence.

She heard him get out of the chair. "You okay in there?" he asked softly, outside her door.

With hard, rough brush strokes, she combed her hair, snapping off snarls rather than taking the time to comb them out.

"Bruce is gonna be here with the next load in an hour," Jack said.

Blaze found her jacket and tugged it on, then grabbed her booniecap off of the wall and cinched it down onto her head. She grabbed the bug-dope and sprayed it until her tongue was numb and her nose stinging.

"Blaze?" Jack asked again.

Blaze went to the door and jerked it open.

Jack looked up at her and took a surprised step back. Immediately, his nose scrunched in disgust. "What, you use half a can of DEET in there?"

Blaze gave him a smile filled with teeth. "In order to ensure that your *Yeti* doesn't board the flight back to town, your *Yeti* is going to go on a walk," Blaze said. "Take care of the supplies when they get here." She made a dismissive, uncaring gesture toward the lodge. "Or don't. Let Bruce pile them on the beach for all I care. Right now, I don't give a rat shit *what* you do. You wanna go get out the sandblaster and paint some buildings, that's fine. You wanna go sit up in the prow and smoke pot and recount all the wonderful things you've done with your really long life, that works. You don't wanna show up for work tomorrow, that would be good, too."

She brushed past him and slammed the door of her room, leaving a stunned-looking wereverine standing in the hallway as she yanked the outer door open. "Oh," Blaze said, looking back at him, "And *don't* follow me. You do, and I'm on the next flight out with Bruce. I don't care what I have to do, I'm gone." She gave him a bitter smile. "Not that you'd mind, seeing how you've gotta share living space with a *Yeti*." Then she pushed through the door.

At her back, she heard, "I don't think you're—" before she slammed the outer door shut behind her, busting loose the hasty repair job that Jack had given it.

Blaze knew that it would seem rather suspicious if she didn't show to help unload when Bruce arrived with her first load of supplies, but she also knew that if she got anywhere near the plane, she would find herself on it when it took off.

And she had put up with too much of the wereverine's horseshit to quit now.

I'm going to hire someone else, Blaze thought, striding down the path toward the lake. *I can't work with him.*

Though she had to admit he did a rather good job. Every worry she had, every unforeseen misfortune that had befallen the lodge in four years of abandonment, he had methodically been ironing out. He was competent, more competent in more things than anyone she had ever seen.

And he was a complete, heartless asshole.

Thinking about his last quip still made her guts roil in humiliation. Blaze looked down at herself as she walked. Freakishly tall, flat-chested, feet the size of Bigfoot...Tears once again tried to sting at her eyes. She had to look away, had to focus on the trees along the edges of her path to keep them down. She would *not* cry. The *last* thing she wanted was to end up unconscious and helpless in the middle of bear-territory.

Shuddering, however, her mind kept getting dragged back to the same horrible thought. Jack thought she was a Yeti. Maybe her father's money would have been better spent on a boob-job and a height-reduction. She heard they were making girls taller, in Russia. Breaking the legs, stretching them out, letting them regrow. Rinse and repeat. Why not shorter? Hell, that seemed easier, anyway. Just cut out a bit of bone here, another bit there...

One of the few men whom she had actually allowed herself to long for, a man who was so perfectly sculpted even a ninety-year-old *nun* would take notice, and he had looked her in the eye and called her an undesirable Yeti.

She sucked in a breath and fought down a sob. The bastard. The callous, heartless bastard.

Without any real goal in mind, Blaze reached the edge of the lake and started following the water's edge, just walking.

If she hadn't already sunk all of her inheritance into this place—and indebted herself for another two hundred and fifty thousand—she would have walked away already. She would have happily gone back to the city, plugged herself back into the Grid, and forgotten about her farm.

But the bastard had everything she owned sitting right there on 'his' land, and she'd already spent a good fifty thousand in lumber, barging, fuel, and supplies. The animals were gonna drive that to seventy-five, easy. That left a hundred and seventy-five to keep herself and her employee—whoever that ended up being—alive while they bought more lumber, built cabins, sank septic systems, drilled wells, secured advertising, and hired guides.

She should have waited.

Blaze bit her lip against another threat of tears. She would *not* cry, damn it. Jack could go fuck himself.

Still, she knew she should have gained a few years of experience working in someone else's business, managing someone else's staff, squirreling away someone else's salary, getting ready. Seeing her father's check, she'd gotten excited and jumped in too soon, and she was going to lose everything because of it.

No, her mind growled. *You haven't lost anything. Just tell the arrogant fucker to leave. It's* your *property. You paid for it. He doesn't like it, you can call the State Troopers and clue them in on this cranky little asshole that's squatting on state land.*

That made her feel minimally better, but not by much. At most, she could make the wereverine pack up and leave. She certainly doubted that the Alaska State Troopers had the means necessary to put him in a cell, if he didn't want to be there. And, further, she was pretty sure that if she ousted him, he would make his displeasure known by doing something horrible before he left.

Like, say, running the dozer through the basement, or leaving the chainsaw buried in the generator.

Or he could simply kill you, a disgusted portion of her brain thought. *Twist your head off and shove it in the woodstove. Bury the body with the dozer, go back to being an asshole in the woods.*

Blaze trudged along the lakebed, then continued out the same channel she had seen Bruce and Lance putter out to on floats. Here, the water lightened to a greenish hue and moved at a couple feet a minute. Blaze ducked under a fallen spruce and kept going.

The time had come, Blaze decided, to start taking control of the situation. She'd poured everything she had into this place, and the fact that her handyman had turned out to have special…attributes… shouldn't stop her from living her dream.

Thinking about it, she doubted she could make him leave. And, when she considered that option, she was pretty sure she didn't *want* him to leave, at least not until he'd taught her what he knew about the operation of a fishing lodge. She wasn't however, going to entertain any more stupid fantasies. They had a business arrangement, and that was all. She was going to take up residence in the top floor owner's apartment. He was going to stay in the basement. She wouldn't eat meals with him, wouldn't talk with him any more than necessary to get the lodge up and running, and would only continue her rudimentary reading lessons if it meant he would continue to make himself obsolete by teaching her how to take care of the place herself.

Something like an hour and a half later, she was standing on the banks of the Yentna River, watching as Bruce Rogers idled out through the mouth of Ebony Creek and into the swift gray waters of the Yentna.

As she watched, he gunned the big engine and got the large plane up to speed. It was a DeHavilland Beaver, he had informed her on one of his many previous trips, able to carry six times the load than the Cessna 206 his brother had used to drop her off—and almost twice as expensive at six hundred dollars an hour. As she watched, Bruce lifted the blocky nose and sailed into the air. Blaze felt a twinge of regret, seeing him go.

She glanced at the shore back the way she had come. She had scheduled two or three more such Beaver trips to the lake that day, depending on how much they could fit in each load. Either way, if she hurried, Blaze was pretty sure she could make it back to the lake before Bruce used up the four grand she had allotted him for the deliveries. She could still get out of here.

She turned her back on the urge, and instead started down the Yentna. The river was abnormally low, she had been told, which was why she wasn't having the barge run *now*, with an eighteen thousand pound cargo capacity at twenty-five cents a pound, and was instead hiring a six-hundred-dollar-an-hour airplane with a max load of a couple thousand pounds, about half of which would be used up on lighter things like towels and toilet paper, to deliver three loads of construction supplies, food, and other necessities.

Among the many disturbing revelations that Blaze had stumbled upon since May was the fact that Jack ate a *lot*. He'd worked his way through what *should* have lasted her all summer in the space of two weeks. And she was pretty sure that he was still hunting on the side.

Blaze had been walking for another hour and a half before she heard the second flight take off, far upriver and around the bend. She watched as Bruce Rogers glided overhead, gaining altitude, and again felt that pang of regret.

I'm not giving up, Blaze thought stubbornly. *That short, crass little jackass isn't going to make me give up my lodge. I just need to cool off.*

Now and again in the patches of silty gray sand interspersed throughout the gravelly riverbed beneath her feet, Blaze saw signs of life. Usually tiny, like bird or squirrel or even mouse, she nonetheless found a couple large moose tracks here and there, often with smaller prints accompanying them. That made Blaze smile. At one time, there had been only two hundred moose along the entire Yentna River. The moose population of the area had almost been driven to extinction by a black bear boom twenty years ago, and for ten years, Fish and Game had allowed subsistence moose hunts only and had instigated a heavy predator-control program to try and reverse the decline.

For the first time in twenty years, there were about two thousand moose feeding in the lakes and swamps along the river system between the Brooks Range and the Cook Inlet, and that number was climbing slowly. Fish and Game was still well below the six to eight thousand they required before they cancelled the predator control measures—measures that they had originally planned to only keep in effect for three or four years—and now Alaska was facing an upheaval in the political scene as to who was to blame, and why. Prey numbers all over the state had been dropping precipitously, especially the caribou herds north of the Brooks Range, and no one could seem to pinpoint the cause. The current head of the Department of Fish and Game had quietly resigned over the predator control controversy, and until today, Blaze had looked at the whole hoopla as a ploy by the media to sell more papers.

Now Blaze looked at the situation in a new light. Werewolves, werebears, dragons, and an ornery little wereverine...She wondered just how much food those creatures had to eat, and where they were getting it. She couldn't imagine that Jack was upkeeping his chiseled body on eggs and sandwiches alone, and the energy to transform into that slitty-eyed beast had to come from somewhere. And, judging by the way he'd decimated her food stores, requiring several more deliveries of groceries than she had been anticipating, he was more than a little desperate for sustenance. She actually wondered several times if he had been starving before she showed up. Of course, she couldn't mention it, not without getting that furry hackles-up scowl and, "*I don't need your money, sister...*" Right. He was only eating her out of house and home to make her *feel* better.

Then she remembered what Jack had said about killing new weres, and how there were too many of them already.

Suddenly, her farm began to take on a whole new potential. For years, she had been worried about the red tape involved with raising and selling livestock and dairy products in the United States. The equipment and processes involved for legal sale of a farm's goods were prohibitive, to say the least. Between the inspections, the fees, the codes, the structures, the facilities, and the fines for non-compliance, Blaze hadn't really considered large-scale production an option. But if she could quietly establish contact with her nearby neighbors and set up a system of trade for a cow here, a few pigs there, then she could bypass the need to clean and butcher entirely, thereby foregoing the need for a USDA-inspected slaughterhouse. She even wondered if she could make a contact to the north, and maybe shuttle cattle north of the Brooks Range...

...or have them come to her.

The thought of meeting a *dragon* left Blaze with a flutter in her stomach. She'd always enjoyed reading stories about dragons as a kid, would snatch them off of the bookstore shelves just because they had a dragon on the cover. The idea that they were *real*, and that she may someday meet one, left her feeling a mixture of excitement and anticipation. She could imagine the monstrous creatures landing in her yard at night to feed, and then trying to explain to the neighbors why five of her cows had gone missing sometime after dusk.

Blaze was still smiling about that thought when she heard the whine of a boat motor.

Pausing, she glanced up. A flat-bottomed river-boat was coming north up the Yentna River, toward her. Once it got close enough to make out the shapes against the glare of the gray glacier water, Blaze saw that it contained two women; one sitting in the back to run the jet, while the other huddled near the front against the wind.

Not really in any mood to talk, Blaze had hoped that they wouldn't see her and would motor on by. As it grew closer, however, the boat started to veer to the right, toward Blaze's beach, and her stomach grew tight with a lump of dread. The *last* thing she wanted to do was explain to her neighbors why she was out wandering the river without so much as a backpack.

"Hello there!" the lean woman in the back of the boat called over the roar of the prop. She was probably about five-ten, and even under her bundle of heavy jackets and floatation device, Blaze could tell that her body was the slender, hourglass-shaped figure that she had always wanted. Her eyes were blue, almost white, and she had long blonde hair that was even then loose in the wind.

"Hey," Blaze said, smiling and bracing herself for a conversation she didn't want.

"Why you out walking the river?" the blonde woman asked, as the aluminum hull of the boat scraped the shore near Blaze's feet and she shut off the engine. "Boat break down? Need a lift?" Taking up a seat in the bow, her companion was a tiny, brown-eyed, black-haired mouse of a woman who seemed to be hiding within her lifejacket, probably only five feet, max. She was cringing backwards in her seat, her dark eyes fixed on Blaze's face in horror. When Blaze stepped forward to offer the woman her hand, she just slid further away, looking like Blaze had approached her with a bloody hatchet.

The Walking She-Mountain strikes again, Blaze thought, disgusted at the fear she inspired in the timid woman. Fighting down another rush of self-loathing, she returned her attention to the blonde woman and her question. "Wanted to look around," Blaze lied. "We don't have the boats in the water yet."

The driver's delicately arched eyebrow—nothing like the thick orange masses on Blaze's forehead—went up. "You're new in the area, then?"

"Yeah," Blaze said. "I'm Blaze MacKenzie. Bought the Sleeping Lady Lodge from the Meyers."

"Oh!" the woman cried, sounding delighted. She tilted the engine and got up. "I'm Amber Stern, and this is Kimber Womac." She gestured to the child-sized bundle.

When both Blaze and Amber's attention turned on her, Kimber raised a tentative hand and gave a soft hello in a voice that almost sounded Arabic. Combined with the woman's dark skin, her jet-black hair, and her tiny size, Blaze guessed she was probably a military wife, brought over when one of the GIs from Elmendorf or Fort Richardson came back from a deployment. Like a lot of women when they hit American soil and started having to repeat their name to fat-tongued Americans, she had probably changed her name to something more pronounceable by her new Yankee neighbors.

"So where ya from?" Amber asked, as she climbed out of the boat.

Blaze moved to help the woman drag the vessel up the shore, but Amber had the prow resting on six feet of gravel before she could lend a hand. Blaze found herself impressed. For such a small woman, she was *strong*.

"Alaska," Blaze said. "First time in the Bush, though. Kinda jumped between Wasilla and Anchorage my whole life."

Amber smiled, her startling blue eyes flashing amusedly. Almost in the patronizing tone one would use on a child, she said, "The Yentna's a big leap from Anchorage. Why'd you move?"

Yet another Bushrat who thinks I'm a useless city-slicker. Bristling, Blaze shrugged. "Had some money come in. Thought I might try getting away from it all."

Amber's smile was still pleasant, but her ice-blue eyes narrowed almost imperceptibly. "What kind of money?"

"Inheritance," Blaze said, trying not to show just how rude she felt the woman's questions were.

She thought the woman's attention sharpened. "How much?"

How *much*? Blaze couldn't believe someone would have the audacity to ask. Then again, considering her experiences with Jack, she wouldn't be surprised if the people in the Bush were a little less up-to-date on their people skills.

"It was enough," Blaze said, shrugging against the odd sensation of the woman's complete attention. "Bought the Sleeping Lady outright. Now I've got Jack Thornton helping me fix it up."

The woman's face darkened to a thunderhead. "Jack Thornton." The way she said it, Blaze might as well have said that she had hired an undead intestinal parasite.

Blaze raised a brow, her curiosity getting the best of her. "You know him?"

"Who *doesn't*?" Amber snapped, and even the girl in the boat seemed to cringe. "He's the crankiest, most selfish asshole on the river. The world would be a better place if someone shoved a chainsaw up his ass and pulled the cord." The way Amber's lip twitched in a snarl, it was evident that she had *personal* experience with the bastard.

Blaze was grinning, despite herself. "I was beginning to think the same thing myself. What'd he do to *you*?"

Amber was scowling upriver, her shoulders hunched in obvious fury.

The petite woman on the boat reached out and touched a tiny hand to Amber's leg.

Amber's face seemed to clear immediately, and she looked back at Blaze with a smile. "Oh, nothing a rabid, lobotomized ape with anger issues wouldn't have done in his place." She glanced at the boat, then raised an eyebrow at Blaze. "You wanna go back to our place and talk about it?"

Blaze hesitated, glancing at the river behind her. She had told Jack she was just going on a walk…

Then she froze, thinking of something new. "You guys got a phone?"

Amber grinned. "Sure, why?"

"I need to make a call," Blaze said. "Get myself a new cell phone and a new Colt .45 shipped out here."

Amber raised a brow. "Oh?"

"Yeah," Blaze said. "Bastard broke 'em both."

Amber seemed to stiffen a bit. "He broke a *revolver*?" She gave Blaze a narrow look. "He must be really…strong."

"Or stupid and pigheaded," Blaze said smoothly, realizing her mistake. "Told me I didn't need 'em. He's got enough tools in the place that I'm pretty sure he could take apart a nuclear warhead, if he had the inclination."

Amber seemed to relax. "He took it apart." She seemed to shake herself and gestured towards the boat. "Come on in. There's a life-vest under the prow, and—"

Kimber's hand on Amber's leg again stopped the woman.

The petite woman was still staring up at Blaze, wide-eyed. Kimber gave a slight shake of her head and bit her lip.

Amber threw her hand off of her with a snarl that both startled Blaze in its viciousness and made the woman climb behind the seat, quaking. "She's coming." Glancing at Blaze, she smiled. "She's had to deal with Jack these last few weeks. I'm sure she could use the company."

Made uncomfortable by the display, Blaze uneasily tried to piece together the relationship between the two women. The smaller woman was quite obviously terrified, and Amber seemed to think absolutely nothing of it.

Amber's smile cracked when Blaze didn't get in the boat. "Don't mind Kimber," she said sweetly, looking back at her companion. "She's a little…" She cocked her head, almost thoughtful. "Off." Returning her attention to Blaze, Amber smiled and said, "She's sheltered. Raised in Skwentna, never left the Bush."

Raised in Skwentna? Blaze thought, thinking of the woman's Arabic features and voice. Then, shrugging, Amber added, "Probably never seen a woman over six foot in her life."

Blaze flushed and dropped her gaze.

Amber's interest seemed to sharpen. "Get in the boat," she said.

Blaze jerked her head up, frowning. That had almost seemed like a *command.*

Amber gestured at the vessel, waiting. Now that Blaze was looking closer, the pupils of her eyes seemed to be slightly misshapen…When Blaze didn't move forward, Amber's eyes narrowed. She lifted her head slightly, took in a deep breath through her nose that reminded her of Jack's flared nostrils whenever he caught a new scent on the breeze. Delicately, she unzipped her lifejacket and set it aside.

Every instinct in Blaze's body was suddenly humming, telling her to back away from the pretty blonde, and run as fast and as hard through the forest as she could go.

"Now," Amber said, as her pupils lengthened into slits. She smiled, and Blaze saw long ivory fangs emerge from beneath her lips. "We're gonna have a little fun with his newest toy."

Blaze's heart was hammering, now. She took a step backwards, though, after seeing Jack's speed, she knew that wouldn't save her. "I don't know what you're talking about."

"Oh?" Amber laughed. "I can smell his musk all over you. He's shifted in your presence, and you've put the little shit into a rutting mood." She took another deep breath, nostrils flared, sniffing the air between them. Her smile widened, and her face was elongating in the shape of a canine's skull, her ears stretching and growing silvery-white fur. "Tell me I'm wrong."

Blaze took another step backwards, arcs of adrenaline biting through her veins. "I hate the sonofabitch," she managed.

"That's not what your body is telling me." The woman hunched as her body grew, the hump of her shoulders rising above Blaze's head. Long white fur was sprouting from every square inch of the woman's body, and her lips and eyelids were darkening to an ebony black. She smiled, and as Blaze watched, the extra rows of teeth punched through the roof of her mouth leaving strands of bloody saliva dribbling from her jaw. "The body can't hide its own musk, girl. Now get in the boat."

Blaze eyed the boat, saw the ebony-black wolf standing beside Kimber's life-jacket like a very large, very muscular dog, and she bolted.

Blaze didn't even make the edge of the riverbank before pain ripped through her back and something heavy dragged her to the ground. She screamed and tried to kick away, but a leaden, clawed fist slammed into the side of her face, stunning her.

Dazed, unable to put up much resistance, Blaze groaned as she felt rough hands grab her wrists and drag them behind her back. "Get the anchor line," Amber snapped over her shoulder. Then, to Blaze, her hot breath licking the back of Blaze's neck, she said, "We're gonna enjoy ourselves taming Thornton's newest bitch."

Vaguely, Blaze felt the woman loop the rope around her wrists and pull it tight. Unlike Jack, however, Amber didn't make any attempt to be humane. She twisted the ropes until they were cutting off circulation to her hands, then yanked Blaze's ankles back and wrapped the line around them, as well.

She took a second piece of rope and, after stuffing a greasy, gas-smelling engine rag into Blaze's mouth, cinched it tight around her head.

Blaze was just starting to regain some of her senses when she felt herself hefted off the ground, then thrown into the boat, heedless of whatever got in her way. Blaze, unable to protect her face, felt her world explode in a burst of agony as her head hit the far side of the boat and something in her nose snapped. She gagged on the rag as blood started running down her face in rivulets, dripping on the boot-scuffed aluminum.

As she passed to return to her seat at the back of the boat, Amber shoved her aside with a foot, until her face was mashed against the back bench-seat, her knees crammed against the forward bench, wedged between the two with a painful angle to her neck. Then Amber threw a couple spare life-jackets over Blaze's prone body and started the back engine while Kimber pushed them off the beach.

The brutal treatment left a growing well of fear rising within Blaze's gut.

They don't care if I live, she realized, as she felt warm blood start dribbling down her ribs from the wound in her back. Which meant they didn't plan on leaving her alive.

She remembered Jack's last girlfriend, the wereverine that had disappeared, leaving only body parts behind. Suddenly, it made too much sense.

The boat trip seemed to take hours, but in reality was probably only about twenty minutes. Neither of her captors spoke, and for Blaze, with her busted nose grinding hard against the low metal seat, it was doing everything she could just to stay conscious.

When the motor finally slowed and the boat jolted as its hull slid up a sandy bank, Blaze was starting to feel dizzy. The blood dribbling down her ribs had slowed, but the bottom of the boat was crimson underneath her.

"Go get the pack," Blaze heard Amber growl. "Tell them to dig her a hole. I want this bitch underground before he realizes she's gone."

They're going to bury me. Her panic rising, Blaze made weak struggles against her bonds.

Behind the bench, Blaze heard Amber begin to bail out the bloody rainwater from the bottom of the boat. A moment later, Amber paused. Her voice was low and dangerous when she said, "I told you to go get the pack."

Kimber's voice was a timid whisper when she said, "Amber, I think we should let her go. When I look at her, she's wreathed in—"

The boat jolted as Amber leaped its length. A moment later, Blaze heard the sound of choking. "Did I *ask* you for your opinion?" Amber sneered.

"No," Kimber whimpered.

"Then *go*," Amber snarled. Blaze heard the sound of something heavy hit the sand. "Do as I told you. Next time, I won't waste my time leaving your head attached."

"Sorry, mistress," Kimber whined. "So sorry." Then there was the sound of running feet, and Blaze was alone with the werewolf.

"So," Amber said. Blaze felt the boat rock as she stepped back into it with her. "I'm sure you're wondering by now what you did to deserve to be buried alive." She stepped over the front seat, then squatted beside Blaze, her ice-blue eyes cold. "Well, nothing, really." She smiled. "Except maybe have really bad choice in men." Amber reached out, wiped a dribble of blood from Blaze's lip, brought it to her mouth, and tasted it. Smiling over her finger, Amber said, "See, the wereverine killed my mate, and six of my best friends. Every once in awhile, I gotta remind him why weasels don't play with wolves." She reached out and patted Blaze on the head, then got up and started bailing the boat once more.

She's going to bury me alive? Blaze thought, the idea taking a clammy hold in her gut.

A few minutes later, several heavy footsteps came running. Blaze, crammed as she was between the benches, couldn't raise her head to see who had approached.

"You get the cage dug up?" Amber demanded.

"Was right where we'd left it, mistress." A deep male voice. Low and submissive.

"Then throw the blanket over her and take her to the pit," Amber said. "I'll be along in a bit to see her off."

Then there were big bodies moving in the boat beside her, lifting Blaze off the ground, carrying her from the boat, shielded from the rest of the world by a tattered old quilt. Hanging from her shoulders and ankles, shrouded by a blanket, Blaze could only see the thin dirt track in the forest floor as it passed beneath her.

After a few hundred paces, the forest floor became littered with loose dirt and they dropped her suddenly amidst the soil-strewn bushes. Blaze, her sight completely cut off when the blanket fell around her, thrashed to get it off of her head.

A heavy boot slammed into her ribs, and suddenly it was all Blaze could do to breathe, each gasping lungful of air lancing jagged spikes of pain through her spine.

She felt movement around her, and heard voices. "That's a *girl*?" a man asked, sounding incredulous. "Why'd she pick *that* thing up?" A toe nudged Blaze through the blanket. "She's gotta weigh, what, a couple hundred pounds?"

"Boss said she's a rich brat," another replied. Blaze could *hear* the shrug in his voice when he said, "Got some sort of inheritance."

"And she's been fucking Jack Thornton," a third voice, female, piped in.

"Inheritance, huh?" the first voice mused.

A third male voice snorted. "What'd you *think*? A figure like that, Amber sure as hell ain't goin' for the sex appeal."

Blaze lowered her face to the ground and squeezed her eyes shut against the humiliation. Even before it killed her, Life was going to serve her one last dish of shame. For old times' sake.

A few yards away, she heard what sounded like something heavy and metal being dragged through the dirt, but with the blanket covering her head, she couldn't identify it.

The commotion seemed to build around her, with more and more people showing up and adding their opinions to the conversation. The general consensus was that Blaze was definitely an eyesore, but Jack needed a wakeup call and the pack could use the extra money.

I'm not rich! Blaze wanted to scream. She had the Sleeping Lady Lodge, and that was it. She had been able to secure a two hundred and fifty thousand dollar loan with her lodge as collateral, using every ounce of her knowledge as a Business major to convince the loan officer to sign on the dotted line. She was going to have to pay back three hundred and fifty thousand dollars, by the time she'd paid off interest.

But they weren't taking the gas-soaked rag out of her mouth, and every time Blaze grunted or moved, she got kicked for the effort.

I'm not rich, she thought, in misery. *I'm not.* Why they thought they could somehow access her accounts by making her disappear, she didn't understand. She hadn't brought out planeloads of cash, or buried a thousand pounds of gold bullion in the basement. She had *nothing* but a few hundred under her pillow, a couple debit cards, a credit card, and the deed to the Sleeping Lady. If they would only take the gag out and let her *talk* to them, she could explain the situation.

But they continued to talk around her as if she didn't even exist. By the number of voices, Blaze estimated twenty, maybe even thirty.

This is where all the moose have been going, Blaze thought, ridiculously. Human hunters were issued a permit for a single bull moose a year. Werewolves—especially werewolves who were willing to kidnap a woman and bury her alive—probably weren't going to bother applying for permits. They probably also weren't going to be selective on how old the moose was, or whether they brought down a bull or a cow.

They were like a cancer, Blaze thought, listening to more arrive. At least thirty, now. The dozens of voices around her were beginning to reach a roar. If what Jack had told her could be believed, six years ago, there had only been a few werewolves left. Now, she would have been surprised if there weren't forty of them gathered around her.

Maybe they're not all werewolves, Blaze thought hopefully. *Maybe the rest are just groupies.*

"She doesn't smell rich." It was a deep, husky voice, very near her head. She heard the sound of a match, then the acrid tang of cigar smoke swept under the blanket, powerful even through the smell of her own blood. She heard puffs, then choked as a cloud of smoke drifted under the opening between the quilt and the ground, directed there by whoever was squatting beside her. The same voice said, "She smells like that rat fuck who killed Raul." Whoever he was stood up and walked off.

As the talking grew louder and even more began to show up, even through the blanket, Blaze began to smell alcohol.

"Hey, get off me!" A woman's voice. Native. Slurred. Somewhere to Blaze's right.

"C'mon, baby," a man said, his voice also slurred. "It won't kill you to put out once in awhile."

Blaze heard what sounded like a sack of potatoes slamming into a tree, followed by a snarl. A drunken brawl followed, and she flinched as it neared her head.

"Come on, you idiots!" the deep, husky voice of the cigar-smoker growled. "Knock it off 'fore I rip off your damn heads."

That seemed to settle them a bit.

The crowd, however, had just gotten started. Conversation peaked, and it seemed like Blaze had been dropped in the middle of a cocktail party, not in the dirt and mosquitoes of the Alaskan Bush.

Finally, she heard the crowd go silent and instinctively knew that the approaching footsteps on the trail behind her belonged to Amber.

"So," Amber said, coming to a stop beside Blaze, "I see everybody's arrived."

"Everyone except Derek and Megan," someone piped. "Couldn't get the druggie bastards out of bed."

Amber sighed. "I thought I told you fools to stop feeding them. If they can't stop using, then we got no use for them."

"We did," another woman complained. "Derek went out last night. Dragged back half a moose calf and fed it to her."

Amber made a disgusted sound. "Tell those two if they don't get clean, they're going in the cage with the wereverine."

There was raucous laughter at that, and Blaze's attention sharpened. *The wereverine?* Then Jack's girlfriend was still alive…

Amber jerked the blanket from Blaze's body and smiled down at her, looking amused. "So, my very large heiress, perhaps you're still wondering why we're going to bury you alive."

But Blaze's eyes had already locked onto the squat metal cage sitting at the top of an incline leading down into a gaping dirt hole. The cage was about five feet square in any direction, and looked to be built of something resembling welded railroad track.

"It's because," Amber said, squatting down beside her, "We don't want you to do anything stupid after we've welcomed you into the family."

As she spoke, the werewolf's face lengthened, her teeth growing longer and more predatory. Her blue eyes became slitted, her body growing the silvery-white fur. All around them, men and women whooped and hollered, and then, as Blaze watched in horror, they, too, began to change. All of them. At least forty. While Amber only went half-way, staying in a semi-human form, the rest shifted completely into huge, four-legged wolves of every size and color. All of them staring at her, all of them waiting. The only one who didn't was a hulking black man who was leaning against a tree, at least seven feet tall, his violet eyes watching her with commiseration.

…violet eyes?

Then Blaze blinked, remembering what the woman had said. *Welcome me into the family?* her startled mind thought. Then she saw Amber's extra rows of teeth as they pushed through the roof and floor of her mouth, making blood well up against the woman's tongue and spill over her gumline.

"Oh my *God*!" Blaze tried to scream into the gag. She struggled, yanking at her bound hands as hard as she could.

"You have no right to do that, pup," the big black man interrupted, his voice coming from over Amber's shoulder. He had closed the distance, and had put his hand on Amber's shoulder.

"'Aqrab, shush!" the little black wolf snapped.

"But mon Dhi'b, she's a—"

"Control your slave, Kimber," Amber growled, without even looking up. Her slitted eyes were fixed on Blaze, bloody saliva dribbling from her open jaws.

Above Amber, the black man stiffened. "I am a *sheik's* son, you pustulent camel penis."

"Do you want to meet with the shadow again, 'Aqrab?" the tiny black wolf demanded.

"They break the *Pact*!" the huge black man snarled. "That doesn't *bother* you, Justicar?!"

"Open your mouth again, flamekin," the little black wolf retorted, "and you will be choking on darkness."

Towering above them, the black man looked like he would say more, then his violet eyes met Blaze's and she saw a twist of misery before he looked away. Without another word, he walked off to lean against a tree and cross his arms defiantly over his chest, watching the scene from afar. And, when Blaze desperately scanned the faces of the monstrous wolves gathering around her, no one else in the group seemed willing to help her.

Squatting beside her, Amber was grinning, enjoying Blaze's terror, her long ivory teeth glistening with mingled saliva and blood. "All right, then. Seeing how there are no other objections, here we go. Struggle all ya want, big girl. It'll only make the magic work faster." And then, like she was easing into a lover's embrace, she leaned forward and clamped her big jaws down on Blaze's shoulder.

Blaze screamed as a hundred needle-like teeth punctured the skin and muscle of her chest and back, then felt an odd rush as *something* raced outward from the wound, spreading in a icy, searing wave through her body. Suddenly, her heart was a thundering mass of fire, each vein a pounding coal, each capillary an individual inferno as hot and cold streaks started warring in her chest.

Blaze gasped, sucking in a chestful of gasoline-choked air, then emptied her lungs into the gag as the fires spread throughout her body, blazing through her blood and bones in angry surges. It felt like she'd been thrown into a vat of liquid nitrogen, dunked in diesel fuel, and lit on fire. Blaze screamed again, this time because her skin felt as if it were burning away, leaving bones and dust in its place.

Somewhere in the group of wolves, a small black one started backing away from the group.

When Amber yanked her jaws from Blaze's shoulder and pulled away, smiling, there was an odd silver luminescence to the werewolf's inner teeth, mingling with the blood, dripping down her jaw to glow in red-streaked silvery puddles on the forest floor below.

"There," Amber said, patting her wound. "Welcome to the family."

All around her, wolves began to howl.

Blaze shuddered and lowered her head to the ground, every beat of her heart a fiery blast of anguish. She felt her heart stutter, try to fail. Something kicked it back into gear, but then it stopped again, this time for good. For several long seconds, Blaze had the distinctly unreal feeling of stillness within her chest.

"Her heart stopped," the Italian-looking man with the cigar said, frowning.

Amber scowled and slammed a fist into Blaze's spine. "Why would her heart stop?"

The sudden jolt made the lump of fire within her chest shudder and thump again. The werewolf hit her again, harder, and Blaze began to feel dizzy as her heart staggered and thudded.

"You think he already claimed her?" the man asked, grinding his cigar out on the trunk of a birch tree. He came over to squat beside them.

"She's only been out here a couple months," Amber growled. "And he's got those fucking 'standards' of his."

"Maybe she's already a were?" the Italian man asked. He held his half-burned cigar in one hand, and was lowering a big palm to Blaze's forehead with the other. Blaze's vision was going hazy, her lump of coals dying in her chest.

"She didn't shift when we caught her."

From the group of wolves, the little black one whined, "Please put her in the cage, Amber. *Please*."

"I don't want the rich bitch to die on me," Amber snapped.

"That's the least of your concerns, now, demonkin," the black man laughed. He had stepped away from his tree, towering over all the wolves in the area. Even through Blaze's stupor, she knew his laugh was filled with bitterness. "Next time, listen to my mistress when she tries to tell you something, puppy."

"'Aqrab!" the tiny black wolf hissed, even as Amber stood up in a roar, teeth and talons bared. "This is *my* pack. *I* turned them, asshole. They answer to *me*. You try start giving orders round here, slave, you're gonna end up in the hole with the wereverine. Same for you, Kimber."

The huge black man narrowed his…*purple?*…eyes. "It may be your pack, but it will crumble to dust before I see my next decade." Turning his big back to her, he turned to stalk away. Over his back, he called, "Mon Dhi'b, when you fools are done with this stupidity, I'll be wandering the dunes." Then he vanished completely. Blaze didn't have time to think on that, though. Her heart had been utterly still for an entire minute.

"What's wrong with you?" Amber snapped, slamming her fist back into Blaze's spine again. Blaze felt more ribs snap under the abuse. "You already been claimed by the magic, girl?"

Blaze's heart stumbled back into gear, and she found her vision going fuzzy around the edges. Her chest was aching with the searing flow of molten metal with each combustive blast of her core. She vomited into the gag, then struggled to swallow it back down so she could breathe. She nonetheless saw silver dribble from around the rag, onto the ground beneath her head

"What's wrong with her?" one of the werewolves asked. She had shifted back to a human state, apparently unable to hold the half-state that Amber and Jack seemed to acquire so easily.

"Huh," Amber said, dragging a talon through the blood seeping through Blaze's punctured shirt. Peering at the silver-red mixture, she said, "Weird reaction."

"Looks like she's spitting out the magic," another suggested.

"Maybe she's part fey," another said.

Amber poked Blaze in the side. "You part fey, girl?"

Blaze groaned and tried not to feel the way the fire was arcing through her body with every beat of her heart.

"If you're fey, you better tell us. Moon magic'll kill an earth-bound."

Blaze's heart was still pounding, but she felt like she was panting out scorching gas with every breath.

"You turned Jen just last week." A man's voice. Nervous. "Maybe you ran outta venom."

Amber bristled at that, and Blaze felt her stand. "Put her in the damn cage and close the hole. She lives, fine. She doesn't, well, we can throw her in with the wereverine, for when we finally get Jack."

Blaze felt jolts of liquid fire race down her elbows and into her shoulders as two big men came up beside her and lifted her off of the ground. They lowered her to the heavy barred floor inside the cage. It took two of them to pull the massive steel door shut and affix the padlocks into place. Then a group of them was shoving her, cage and all, into the hole, the whole contraption moving on smooth metal sliders much like snow skis.

As Blaze neared the darkness of the hole, still struggling to breathe against the searing heat enveloping her body, she was assaulted with the overwhelming stench of rot.

The wereverine, Blaze thought, reeling at the brink of sanity as the second cage and its occupant came into view. This cage did not have metal sliders. This one was welded into place, with fused rebar jammed into the walls and a concrete pad to hold it in place. The corpse was resting in one corner, huddled against the bars. It was wrapped in rusty, putrid chains.

TEN

Jack and the Puppies

Jack set down the latest pages that he had torn out of the city-slicker's binder, glaring at the door in irritation. Still no sign of his boss. He checked the enormous timepiece that she had insisted on setting up prominently in the main room the moment she got to the Bush, then frowned.

Eight o'clock. He sniffed and went back to work scrawling out the letters she had made for him. His hand hurt from gripping the pencil, and his head hurt from concentrating. Even with all this practice, his still looked like poor imitations in comparison, and it was frustrating him. Aside from the ones he recognized from her galling rendition of 'diesel,' he still didn't even know what any of them meant.

Finally, at eight-oh-nine, he shoved the papers aside and scowled at the sun outside. Unless she'd somehow squirreled away some snacks inside her room, Blaze had missed breakfast, lunch, and dinner.

Jack thought of all the many dangerous things that could befall a city girl in the woods, then remembered her strict warning not to follow her. Feeling torn, he got up and started to pace.

What if she'd fallen in the river? Or broken an ankle? Or gotten lost?

There was a fun idea. Hunting her down at night, finding her wandering aimlessly in the middle of nowhere, utterly disoriented, yet utterly *determined* she knew where she was going, then having her bite, kick, and scream at him all the way home.

Jack felt the surge of liquid power as his hackles pushed through his skin and he quickly forced the prickly sensation back down. After a few millennia of practice, it was almost second-nature to him now.

She told me not to follow her, he thought, eyes on the clock. He'd screwed up everything *else* he had tried to do or say around the woman, and he was pretty sure if he screwed up again, she was going to make good on her word and go back to town, and he really didn't want to have to go sniff her out in the big city.

Still, he couldn't help but worry.

Muttering, he glanced again at the clock. Eight-twelve. He snatched up the book she had brought with her and started pawing through it, trying to recognize the letters she had outlined. Some of them seemed similar, but others seemed utterly foreign. Growling in frustration, he threw it aside and started pacing again.

She had told him not to follow. She'd made that clear enough, by cracking the door in half on her way out. Jack still needed to patch it. He glanced at the clock. Eight-fifteen.

He decided to go out to the shop and grab some carpentry supplies for another temporary patch-job. He went out, rummaged around for some scrap lumber and good nails, then strapped on his toolbelt and took the whole mess back to the door.

He paused on the porch, looking at the broken portal, calculating how many hours it would take him, then at the book he had discarded against the wall, the pages even then half folded-in on themselves from the fall. The clock said eight-thirty-two.

Jack dropped the carpentry supplies, went to the 4-wheeler, yanked the cart off the hitch, and fired it up. "You can kill me later," he muttered, kicking it into gear. He spun out of the yard and hurtled down the path to the lake, then along the lakebed, not even bothering to look for tracks, following her smell.

She had made for the channel, and he had to ditch his machine at the creekbed and walk in order to get over the fallen trees and down the very narrow beach.

He followed the channel all the way back to the Yentna River at a jog. The gray, slow-moving water was extremely low for this time of year, and had left five feet of beach to walk on, at the narrowest point. He found the marks in the sand where she had passed, disturbed that the scent really wasn't getting stronger.

Damn that woman can move, he thought, trotting down the beach. She must have been moving fast, not stopping to smell the roses as he had assumed.

Then another thing occurred to him. She had headed south, down the Yentna. Could she be trying to *walk* home? The more he thought about it—and the further he ran—the more obvious it became that that's exactly what she had done.

He felt the Third Lander's feral growl start again in his chest at the thought. He had offered his protection, damn it, taken her under his wing, and she was acting as if she hadn't even noticed—or cared. Like his protection was meaningless to her. What was worse, she was yet again ignoring him, aiming to put herself square into the wolves' territory.

"Zeus and Ares *damn* that woman," Jack growled. She was smart—hell, he could *smell* that much—but half the time she didn't seem to have any common sense.

You were young once, too, a voice chided him.

Jack scowled at the tracks in the sand. *Not this young.* He really needed to take her aside and have a long, sit-down chat with her, explain to her just what she needed to do if she wanted to stay alive out here.

He was halfway around a curve in the river when the smell of wolf suddenly hit him, carried on the breeze. The smell instinctively made the liquid power surge within him. Jack froze, heart hammering. *Oh no.* He felt his fangs instinctively settle, felt the painful pricks as his talons pierced his fingertips. *Oh gods no.*

His eyes followed the line of tracks up the river, disappearing around another bend. The stench of the she-wolf was unmistakable. Amber. The current pack alpha. And she had shifted.

Jack lunged into a sprint, his feet hitting the ground hard enough to shatter stones. Trees and water became blurs on either side, and he felt the moon's silvery current roaring within him. The wolf-bitch would hear him coming, but at this point, he didn't rightly care. He didn't like to hurt women—hence why he made the idiot mistake of leaving Amber and her packmates alive when he had annihilated the males he had assumed were leading them—but if Amber had harmed the city-girl, he would gut the wench and be done with her.

Jack came to a sprawling stop at the scuffed sand at the end of the footprint trail, all four limbs gripping the earth to slow himself down. His heart began to hammer as he smelled the unpleasant tang of Blaze's fear.

Oh no, he thought, his gaze catching the ribbed indentations of a river-boat's hull, where it had rested in the sand. Beside it, he saw droplets of blood. *Blaze's* blood. *No, no no…*

He got down and smelled it. Not heartsblood, he realized, with a pang of hope. Then his nostrils clogged with the scent of Amber's triumph. Unbidden, an image of the scene spread out in his mind; Blaze's terror, the poor girl trying to run, struggling, getting dragged to the boat by the she-wolf; Amber's cruel, tiny mind compelling her to detail out the horrible things she was going to do to Jack's latest plaything.

Jack dropped his head to the sand. He felt the old sorrow come rushing back, threatening to overpower even his millennia of control. He thought of the others, remembered how being close to him had brought them their deaths.

He would *not* let it happen again. Not again.

He lunged to his feet.

Amber would have taken Blaze back to the den. She would have tried to turn her.

And, more than likely, if he didn't find her in time, come morning, Blaze would be dead.

You just fucked with the wrong wereverine, Jack thought, anguish and rage building at the thought of Blaze, scared and alone, dying as the moon-magic worked its way through her system. He felt the sharp, sliding pain as his second teeth punctured the roof of his mouth. Seeing no one else on the river, he turned and bolted back for his home, lunging boulders and leaping fallen trees like they were pebbles and twigs.

As he ran, images of the past came to him, unbidden.

Six thousand years.

Six thousand years, and only four women. His companion for three millennia, a dragon with a taste for adventure. Sniffed out his little cabin in the woods and discovered his true nature. Dead for the other three, killed while he was off cutting firewood. A spritely fey girl, looking for a rough tumble. A thousand years of joy, companionship, and love. Killed by her own kind, for being impregnated by a human. One of his own kind, lithe and lovely, his first attempt to turn another, at her request. A whirlwind romance, ended only when the Inquisitors caught her, hunting for him. She'd died in a bewitched iron maiden, her magic bled out to power the Inquisition as they tried to get her to betray him. This latest wereverine—just a girl in comparison to him, but the start of something special. Killed by the wolves to try and lure him into doing something stupid.

Now Blaze. The tall, lovely Fourth Lander with the sunfire coursing through her veins. The first one in centuries who had offered to teach his cranky ass something he desperately wanted to learn—the one thing he had never managed to master, the development he'd had to watch from afar, as scholars and monks in their towers and abbeys created masterpieces while he loped at the fringes of society, shunned by humanity.

Damn the wolf. Jack had let them keep the territory, feeling bad about killing all the girls' mates. But now, as he fought every carnal instinct to go full Third-Lander, he realized it had been a mistake. He'd known that Amber had been the kind to hold a grudge—he had seen it in her icy blue eyes, when he was walking away, covered in her mate's blood.

Still, to inflict their feud on an innocent girl…

Such behavior was unacceptable, and had just been her death-warrant.

Jack knew that Amber was trying to bait him into doing something stupid. He also knew that the poor she-wolf didn't have enough experience to realize that a wereverine didn't last six thousand years by letting his anger control him. Fearless, he may be. Stupid, he was not.

Jack rushed up his front steps and threw open the door. Going to the living-room, he yanked the rug off of the floor and tore the hidden hatch from its hinges, revealing a dark room below. He dropped inside and started yanking weapons and armor from the shelves he had bolted to the masonry walls. Two rippling katanas, made by a master. Two patterned black longswords, made by himself. Riveted-link, fey-bewitched chainmail tunic, made to fit around his altered form. Breastplate of dragonhide, studded with a gargoyle's teeth. Chain and dragonhide pants to match. Dwarven-steel bracers, metal with a slightly greenish hue, marked and scarred from a thousand battles. Two axes, with the same greenish glint. A couple shimmering blue hatchets, tucked on either side of his belt.

Then, from the velvet-lined case in the back, he lifted out a Zweihänder. The weapon weighed in at fourteen pounds—six and a half feet of undulating Damascus steel. He slid it into a sheath over his back, then went for the smaller case inside the locked silver chest. Opening it with a cloth, careful not to touch the silver, Jack held his breath as the light in the room seemed to dim somewhat. Inside lay a dagger of void-titan bone, centered with the horn of a dread unicorn. Even then, the black spiral was leaking curls of misty darkness into the room, as if the owner were still trying to find and punish Jack for killing it.

Looking down at the dagger, Jack hesitated. He hadn't had to use it for centuries, and never on anything so common as a few wolf pups.

Still, he had smelled the growing stench of werewolf coming from downriver over the last six years. He had heard the tales of campers gone missing, of homeless and millionaires alike vanishing off the streets of Anchorage. He had seen the moose population stagger yet again. He knew she was building her army.

Yet he hesitated. Some gut instinct was saying to leave the weapon behind, that his problems would only get worse if Amber saw it.

Amber's not going to survive seeing it, Jack thought stubbornly. He was going to bury it in her skull and do the whole damn neighborhood a favor.

Jack carefully took the black dagger from its case and tucked it into the padded sheath on his belt, careful to avoid the razor-sharp tip. One scratch would create an instant necrotic reaction in a were, instant death in a mortal. A good plunge into the brain would cancel out the moon magic entirely, negating the very power that had made the were. It was as effective as silver, except its effects were instantaneous, on any creature.

You don't need it, part of him argued. *They're just puppies.*

But the puppies had pissed him off, and Jack intended to do some spring cleaning, starting with Amber's bad apple.

He turned and lunged out of the hole, then bolted through his living-room, leaving a good four-dozen weapons and armor still hanging upon the walls behind him. He ran down to his boat, shoved it into Ebony Creek, and hopped onboard. By the time he hit the gas and roared out onto the river—somewhere around ten-thirty—the sun was finally starting to edge towards the horizon.

Hold on, sweetheart, Jack thought, fighting a growing sense of unease at how long Blaze had been in the werewolves' paws. Holding tight to the upright drivers' console, he slammed the throttle all the way forward, putting the sleek boat up onto step and skipping across the river at about forty-five miles an hour. At this point, he didn't care if anyone saw him half-changed, motoring around in strange, scaly armor, bristling with swords and axes. He wanted—no, *needed*—to find the girl and bring her back safe. He'd offered his protection to too many women and failed.

He could *not* go through that again. It would end him, as thoroughly as the dread blade on his hip. Yet every time Jack got near Blaze, he felt that growing tug in his chest, felt himself aching for that shared link, that part of him that Oethynna had awakened when the ancient dragon took him to mate, so many ages ago…

…the part of him that she had left abandoned and so totally alone, the moment the royal hunters had severed her cord, dropping him to the forest floor at the agony within. It had been devastating. Like losing the other half of his soul. He hadn't been able to move for days, just wept into the mosses. When he finally found himself able to crawl back home, he had found her corpse stretched out upon the floor of his cabin, naked, the place stinking of a witch's-brew and sweat, and Jack had lost his mind.

The days that followed had grown so dark, so abysmal, that he became the monster the humans feared he was. He would have never done it again, had Mae Lae not simply hunted him down and *made* the link, not giving him a choice. After the fey princess's death, grief had once again driven Jack to solitude, and once again the Cosmos had wrenched him back from isolation with a pretty, innocent human peasant girl who got lost in the woods and needed his help. After two prior connections, that part of himself that the dragon had awakened had been starving, hungry for the companionship he'd lost. Like a fool, he'd formed the third link to Tavva almost instantaneously, and had spent years following her around like a puppy-dog until he finally got the balls to tell her he was a wereverine. Out of fear that she would grow old, he had given in to her demands that he turn her. And when he felt her body pierced by the iron maiden, slowly drained of its fluids for Inquisitional blood-magics, Jack had died inside.

When Henrietta had come sniffing, he had managed to keep his head on straight, had managed not to let that part of himself make the bond, and it was probably the only thing that had kept him from losing his mind all over again when the wolves killed her, becoming that beast of nightmare and legend.

…But Blaze was different. He didn't have the *control* around her, and something about her was tugging on him more strongly than anything he'd ever known, *demanding* that link, *commanding* it.

Jack let out an unsteady breath, the pull having become almost unbearable of late. It had reached the point where he was having trouble *thinking* around the long-legged vixen. He was playing a dangerous game, he knew. If he managed to get her out alive tonight, it would be all he could do not to simply surrender to the dragon-bond and claim her right there on the spot. Some deep and carnal part of Jack, after eight hundred years without that mating-connection, was desperate to make that link. He knew himself well enough to understand that the relief might overwhelm him, and he might seal the link just by accident.

Can't do that, buddy. She's outta your league. Top-tier to your vermin possession. The moment she figures it out, you're just the handyman again, bud. If she even hung around. If she stayed, Blaze was going to do for the area in a couple years what Fish and Game regulators had been struggling to do for twenty. He knew a dozen friends who would gladly pay cash money for a couple goats or a few chickens a week.

If she hung around. If he could *find* her. If she wasn't already *dead.*

Damn Amber, Jack thought again. She obviously didn't understand he'd left her alive out of *mercy*. 'Cause he couldn't hurt a damn woman. Damn it. Couldn't she see he was being *nice*? All he'd been able to bring himself to kill had been the males in charge of that clusterfuck, the ones that had led the girls astray. Seein' the girls all huddled together, scared to death of him after he'd ripped apart all their mates, had been too much. He'd felt something snap in his head and he'd just growled something about minding their manners and let them all live. Now she had some stupid *grudge*...

Once Jack reached the far edge of the Yentna, he shut off the throttle and drifted into shore. He set anchor, then slipped into the woods. The next three miles, he took slowly, weaving through the trees, every sense alert, looking for guards.

The stench of wolf was everywhere, and Jack was more than a little disturbed to find trash, empty whiskey bottles, and syringes scattered throughout the forest, becoming more prevalent the deeper he went into the wolves' territory.

He was even more unnerved at the lack of guard. The last mile into the wolves' territory, and *no one* stepped out to stop him. Surely, after doing something as brazen as kidnapping Blaze, Amber would have posted a watch.

She's utterly without fear, Jack thought, astounded.

Then, as he came within sight of the den, he realized why.

The old, ramshackle cabin that the wolves had used as cover for their burrow was crawling with weres. Most were slumped on the front porch drinking whiskey or vodka or some other form of hard alcohol straight from the bottle. A few were playing cards on a rickety little table off to one side, most smoking cigarettes or pipes or, in the case of one large black fellah leaning against a far tree, reading a book. Several looked to be smoking bongs, tainting the entire area with the bitter smell of cannabis.

Jack sniffed for Blaze. Her scent was here, but it was muted by the stench of a few dozen wolves. He grimaced, looking at the front door of the cabin. He had been in it once before, and he would rather not crawl down that tunnel again, if he could avoid it.

Carefully, Jack angled himself back toward the water, deciding he would pick up Blaze's scent where she had stepped onto shore and follow it that way.

There were no guards posted at the beach. Jack drew one of his black longswords and quietly began cutting the anchor-lines, sending the boats drifting downriver. He stopped at the boat that still stank with the smell of Blaze's blood. Someone had spent quite a bit of time trying to rinse the vessel clean, but Jack would recognize that scent anywhere. It smelled of desert sunshine and earth-fire, and it had been burned into his memory during his time in the East.

The puppies, Jack thought, his anger rising. *They have absolutely no idea what they've got on their hands.* Hell, the impulsive bitch had probably kidnapped Blaze for the simple fact that Blaze had hired Jack, and Amber didn't like Jack.

She needs to die, Jack thought again, remembering the cesspool that Amber had been building up around her. Even as he had the thought, however, his gut quailed. The last time he had killed a woman, she had already been dead, and the taste of her fear was still a filthy stain in his mind.

Jack cut the final anchor line and set the boat adrift. Then, carefully, he eased himself up over the riverbank and sheathed his longsword. He pulled a katana in either hand, then slowly moved down the path, every sense alert.

The first wolf saw him and shifted—his body growing to approximately double that of Jack's before he lost control and sank into full-wolf form.

Puppies, Jack thought, as the creature didn't even bother to raise an alarm, merely charged, in full throes of the moon-magic.

Jack, while smaller than a wolf in the half-form, was much faster than a wolf, and stronger. Wolves gained their strength in numbers—the more wolves belonged to a pack, the stronger they became. Wolverines gained their strength from age, pure and simple, and Jack was *old*.

Jack swung to the side just as the wolf left the ground, jaws wide to clamp shut around his throat. Twisting, he brought his katanas down almost distractedly, severing head from body and cutting the torso in half without even slowing down. He kicked the head aside, to seal the boy's fate. As he stepped over the corpse, Jack watched the silver moon-magic bleed out of the creature even as it tried in vain to piece himself back together.

The rest of the path was clear up to a split. One fork went towards the ramshackle cabin and the main den, while the other went to the left, deeper into the forest. From that direction, Jack smelled turned earth and…fire. He frowned, and took that path.

The trail took him deep into the woods, up to a large, half-dug tunnel buried into the side of a hill. A new den? Though Blaze's smell was everywhere, Jack didn't see her.

Instead, a tiny woman was sitting on the churned earth outside the hole in the hill, rocking back and forth, staring at the half-made tunnel. Jack recognized her as one of the survivors from six years before, one of the ones that had cringed away from him as he'd come out of the den, covered in her lover's blood.

Keeping low and quiet, Jack crept closer, katanas ready.

She sensed him just as he was getting ready to lay a katana against her neck, and, with a startled sound, she jumped backwards, away from him. She didn't, however, run or try to change.

Smart girl, Jack thought. It meant that, unlike the majority of the fools around here, her fear-response didn't automatically throw the moon-magic into control. Which meant she was probably old enough to know that, without her pack around her, she didn't stand a chance.

"Where is the woman your alpha took today?" Jack asked softly.

The tiny woman's brown eyes went wide and she pointed at the half-finished tunnel.

It took Jack a moment to comprehend. "You *buried* her?" He took an angry step forward, his hackles lengthening down his spine.

"I tried to tell Amber," the woman whispered, "I tried to get her to leave her on the river."

She's terrified, Jack thought, stunned. *And still she doesn't shift.* That took a lot of control, especially for a wolf. He frowned at the woman. "You aren't a were, are you?" He sniffed, and wasn't sure if the smell of wolf was coming from her or from one she had simply been spending a lot of time rubbing up against. For a brief instant, he thought he caught a whiff of feathers, but it passed. Her latest meal, perhaps? Older weres got better about hiding their scent, but by the way she was cringing, she probably hadn't had time to master that particular talent.

She licked her lips nervously and gave the forest behind her a calculating glance.

"Don't," Jack growled. "You're much too young to outrun me, girl."

She twisted back and Jack saw irritation in her brown eyes. She stood a little straighter and her voice was cold when she said, "She almost died from the initial bite, Shadowkiller. I've been monitoring her. She's rejected the Third Lander poison and is still alive, but barely. You want your pet back alive, you'll need to dig her out before it gets dark."

Then she shifted—as smooth and quick as polished glass—and Jack took a startled step back, again catching the scent of…*wings?* When he placed the *kind* of wings, he stumbled backwards. No. No way.

After giving him a long, weighing look with eyes that glowed yellow in the half-light, the small black wolf turned and bolted into the trees, flickering from tree to tree, so fast it might have been made of shadow itself.

That, Jack realized, his gut clamping, *was not a puppy.*

The last time he'd heard someone refer to him as 'Shadowkiller,' he had been working as the personal blacksmith for a sheikh during the construction of Baghdad.

He glanced up at the treeline. The sun was just at the edge of the horizon, and would probably dip beneath the trees within the next half hour.

Swallowing, he glanced back at the path back to the den. He wondered if the little black wolf was even then looping around, telling her kin of the wereverine on the property. If she did, and they caught him in the entrance to the tunnel, all the swords in the world weren't going to do him any good when they surrounded him.

Jack got the gut-wrenching feeling, however, that the little black wolf wanted Blaze alive just as much as he did, and, though she wasn't going to risk helping him free her, she wasn't going to betray him, either.

His gut was also telling him that the little black wolf was telling the truth, and that Blaze was going to die if he didn't get her back into the light before the sun went down.

Making his decision, he slid the katanas home through the cleaning-cloth and, with one last nervous look at the path, rushed to start flinging dirt out of the tunnel.

The scent of death hit him before he'd gone more than a foot. Jack's heart immediately clenched at the thought that he had been too late, but as he dug deeper, the smell grew so great that he knew it had to be coming from another source.

They put her down here with a corpse? he thought, disgusted. As he broke through the final few inches of soil, the blast of death and decay almost knocked him over. He smelled wolf—dozens of wolves had spent some time down here—and the overpowering scent of sunshine and fire. The rot, however, while definitely carrying the tinge of moon-magic, didn't smell like wolf.

It wasn't until he pulled away the last clods of dirt and looked into the vaulted chamber inside that he realized where the smell was coming from.

ELEVEN

Frontal Assault

Blaze heard thumps as something clawed at the dirt, and in her delirium, Blaze thought that the rotting wereverine was still alive. She screamed a long, miserable wail into her gasoline-soaked gag, and tried again not to vomit at the streaks of ember-hot fire that laced through her body with the motion.

They buried me alive with a ghoul, a terrified corner of Blaze's mind babbled, when the thumps in the utter darkness got closer. Blaze's heart, disrupted from the weak-but-steady groove that it had etched for itself over the long hours of drifting in and out of consciousness, started to hammer, lacing concussive blasts of coals throughout her body.

Each weak explosion in her chest seemed to bring the sounds closer, until they seemed to be right on top of her. Blaze babbled her terror into the vomit-crusted rag, and her fear only made the pain searing her body more intense. She felt every throbbing pulse like someone had injected a canister of jet-fuel into her veins and the electrical charge of her contracting heart was setting it on fire.

Blaze rolled back and forth in a struggle to get away from the sounds, but her motions were weak. What took a monumental effort on her part resulted in only an inch or two of movement, and it was utterly exhausting. Worse, Blaze knew that her panic was only making her bleed faster. She could see the glowing silver spreading outwards on the blackened dirt beneath her body, and as the flow increased, so did her delirium. It must have been her imagination, but it almost looked like there really *was* fire mixed in her blood. It seemed to swirl against the silver, orange-gold in the absolute darkness, except for little pops of flame here and there, where the blood came into contact with a root or twig.

No air, Blaze realized, in explanation for the strange visions. *They shut off my air.* She remembered the hallucinations of miners, trapped deep within the earth, and knew that she should probably try to slow her breathing, if she ever expected to survive this place.

The sounds near her elbow, however, were too close. The ghoul was wakening, and was slowly crawling towards her in the flickering darkness...

Blaze screamed again and felt her heart erupt against her chest, and panic made her vision dim. More blood dribbled forth, but this time, the flame lasted longer, eating at the very soil like someone had spilled diesel over the floor of the cavern.

Then light burst into her world, searing her eyes, leaving her blind. She saw a shadow, outlined against the sun. She peered at it, trying to make out the features...

A taloned fist wrapped around the heavy door of her cage and ripped it off its hinges. Blaze laughed in despair at this new vision, for her panicked, dying mind had given her that which she had most wanted—but not allowed herself to hope—to see.

The wereverine stood at the entrance to her prison, wearing pretty black scaly armor and a dozen different weapons, staring at the other cage beyond.

Weaving in and out of consciousness with the stuttering of her heart, Blaze turned her head. She saw the zombie, jumped back into the same position it had been before, pretending to huddle against the back of its cage, head tilted back, mouth hanging open, several rows of teeth showing in the roof of its open mouth.

Tricky zombie, Blaze thought, a part of her giggling hysterically. The other part of her was incredibly tired, and as each space between heartbeats grew longer, her humor faded and her sleepiness grew. *Don't trust the zombie*, Blaze thought, as the wereverine-hallucination grabbed her and tugged her from the cage. *She's faking it. She was alive a moment ago. She was eating me.*

Even then, she could remember the zombie crawling across the floor, lapping up the silver and gold juices flowing from her body as it watched her with its evil, rotted white eyes catch fire behind its bone-white skull.

...Couldn't she?

Blaze didn't think she'd ever been so tired in her life, and the warm heat of the sun against her face seemed to calm her heart just enough that the pain wasn't keeping her awake any longer. She closed her eyes.

She almost didn't hear the, "Gods have mercy," almost didn't feel the way her hands seemed to fall free, her huge Yeti toes slamming numbly into the dirt behind her.

Something strong rolled her over and tapped her face.

Blaze heard the flesh slapping from a distance. It was an irritation, but she was more concerned with her heart. She had thought she had felt it move, but couldn't remember the last time when her body had shuddered with a full convulsion.

A heavy weight slammed into her bruised chest, hard enough to crack more ribs. Blaze gasped and her eyes flashed open at the feeling of another detonation throughout her body. The wereverine was hunched over her, still wearing the ridiculous armor. Didn't he know he looked like something out of a nerd-convention? That black scaly stuff was so obviously fake, too. It wasn't even chipped, like *real* armor would have been, had it ever been through a *real* battle. And the weird, crescent-shaped blue-white hatchety-looking things on his belt...She couldn't even place an era in history where anything like that had actually ever been used in war.

He looks so damn pitiful, Blaze thought, giggling inwardly. *He really should study his history, rather than buying plastic crap off of Ebay.* She was getting sleepy again, and her eyes were sliding shut.

Something crashed into her chest again, and this time, the explosions rocking her ribcage continued in a panicked frenzy, arcing streaks of pain throughout her body. Blaze moaned, and was surprised to find she wasn't trying to breathe through vomit and gasoline. She opened her eyes again, and she saw Jack's deep green stare peering back at her, his face etched with concern.

"You gonna be okay there, sweetie?"

"You look ridiculous," Blaze managed. "What era is that?"

But Jack was shifting back into his hairy wereverine self, looking over his shoulder, and he was grabbing a big two-handed sword from where it was slung across his back.

When the blade slid free, the ringing sound got Blaze's attention. She frowned up at the randomly filigreed blue-black pattern on the metal. *Is that* Damascus steel? she thought, peering at it. Then her eyes caught on the katana he slid out in his second hand, and the rippled edge of the blade made her breath catch.

That's real, she thought, horrified. *That's a* master's *blade. And he's wearing it around like a toy.*

The toy proceeded to cut through a werewolf's skull, depositing half of it, jaws still twitching, on Blade's chest.

Blaze rasped a scream and weakly crawled backwards, trying to fling the snapping, biting thing off of her.

"Stay here, sugar," Jack said, distractedly bending down to grab her by the ankle with his katana-hand. He dragged her backwards, his eyes were on something behind her.

Blaze flipped the truncated cranium off of her chest and twisted to see what he was looking at.

Forty werewolves stood a few yards off, their slitted eyes glowing in the hazy light.

One of them, with silver-white fur and ice-blue eyes, stepped forward, body massive and monstrous in comparison to the wolverine hunched over her, swords dripping crimson-silver blood down their antique blades.

Very slowly, Jack slid the katana back into his sheathe. When he removed the twisted black spiral horn from his belt, its razor tip dribbling blackness that seemed to settle onto the ground in a void-like mist, Blaze knew she was dreaming.

Dreaming…or dead. Though, when Blaze swallowed, she was pretty sure that dead people didn't have to deal with the burning taste of bile.

"I'm taking her home with me, Amber," Jack said. "Don't try to stop me. You really don't want to deal with the consequences if you do."

"You actually think you're getting out of here, don't you, weasel?" Amber snarled, her blue-white eyes glowing like twin moons in the dimming light. She took another step forward, just out of range of the huge Zweihänder.

At the edge of the pack, the big black man boomed, "I'd let him go, if I were you, wolf pup." His violet eyes were focused on the strange black dagger, and his whole ebony body looked tense, ready to bolt at any second.

"Listen to the slave," Jack snapped. "I spared you once, you miserable bitch, but I'm not going to do it again."

Amber snarled a challenge and leapt.

Almost as if she were watching a slow-motion replay, Blaze watched as Jack stepped out of the way and slashed the tip of the darkness-dripping black dagger across the werewolf's face.

He didn't stab her, Blaze thought, frowning. If this were a *decent* dream, he would have *stabbed* her. And he also wouldn't be wearing such ridiculously stupid armor. Who did he think he was trying to imitate? The infamous Black Knight?

The howl of pain from the werewolf, however, made Blaze hesitate. As she watched, Amber changed form in mid-air and fell to the ground in a human ball, clutching her face.

"Anyone else?" Jack snarled, turning his attention to the forty wolves. Behind him, the woman was shrieking and clawing at her face.

"Take good care of that one," the big black man said, though if he were speaking to the wolves or the wereverine, Blaze wasn't sure.

The other wolves exchanged uneasy glances between the decapitated werewolf still twitching on the ground beside Blaze, the two halved wolves even then in their death-throes in the woods behind

Jack, and their leader, screaming like she was being eaten alive. Several took uneasy steps backwards.

Slowly, Jack slid the Zweihänder back into its sheath and reached down to grab Blaze. He pulled her into a sitting position, then, his eyes still on wolves, hefted her over his shoulder, the dripping black weapon between him and the others.

As Jack started backing into the woods, Blaze yet again face-down over his shoulder, she heard him say, "Anyone who follows me is gonna get the same." Then he turned, and Blaze felt her world blur and her body press into his as he lunged forward with more Gs than an F-15.

A couple minutes later, Jack leapt, and Blaze heard the soft sound of sand thumping under his feet. When she looked, the gray swirls of the Yentna River was moving along beside them. She heard a branch snap on the bank above them. Felt Jack tense and turn.

She heard the black man say, "You should kill her." A few yards off, at Jack's back, a little black wolf was standing beside the river under an overhang, watching them. Pretty wolfie. She was pretty sure that Jack didn't see the wolfie, because he was listening to the black man.

Then Blaze's heart started to hammer as she realized what the black man had said. *Kill me?* her fragmented brain cried. *But he just dressed up to rescue me.* Then she chittered inwardly, thoroughly amused by her joke. She dimly felt a line of silver and gold run down her neck and drip off of her chin, staining the driftwood...black? Was that *smoke*?

She felt Jack hesitate under her, meet the black man's gaze. "I don't kill women," Jack said.

"This time, it would be a mercy, Shadowkiller," the black man boomed. "She's lost her mind."

Shadowkiller? Blaze pushed off of Jack's back enough to turn her head and look. The effort required to see their visitor was monumental, and she was left panting at the big man leaning against the tree.

"Or maybe you're just craving a bit of freedom, eh?" Jack growled. He pulled a boat close and waded out to it. "She the one who bound you, slave?"

"I can only offer my advice," the black man replied softly. He uncrossed his arms and shrugged. "Whether you heed it is up to you."

Then Jack was lowering Blaze into the boat, still watching the man on the bank. "I don't deal with your kind," Jack growled. "Get the hell outta here, slave."

He's racist, too, Blaze suddenly realized, disgusted. *I really need to get myself a new handyman.* Someone suave and charismatic and helpful, not an ornery little shit with a bad attitude.

Then a disturbing thought occurred to her. What if *all* of this was a nightmare, not just the last few hours? What if she hadn't really received an inheritance from her estranged and eccentric father? What if she was still grinding away at an accounting job with the State of Alaska, aiming for that coveted full-time position? What if she really was going to burn to death in a fire, as that wide-eyed fortune-teller had told her?

Then again, a logical portion of her brain told her, she had actually *increased* her chances of burning to death in a fire by moving to the Bush, what with the open stoves and diesel fuel and cooking propane and barrels of gasoline.

The bottom of the boat was *cold,* she realized, as a wave of shivers overtook her. She heard her teeth chattering, felt her body start to tremble.

Then the boat jerked and began to drift on the current. A moment later, there was a wereverine standing over her, his bestial face somehow conveying concern despite his jagged, ivory teeth and his snake-like emerald eyes. "You gonna be okay there, honey?"

"Cold," Blaze whimpered. She felt like they were *in* the river, not floating down it.

Jack picked her up and propped her up against an upright steering console. She felt her head loll and her arms flop around as he shoved her into a lifejacket and zipped it tight around her.

Though the sleeves were much too short, Jack was able to close it with room to spare. Yet more proof that Blaze was a disproportionate beanpole. She made an unhappy sound into the wereverine's scaly chest.

"You've lost a lot of blood, sweetie," Jack said, stepping behind her to reach the console. He flipped the ignition switch and the boat's engine roared to life. "But I swear, just hang with me a little longer, and you'll be feeling better in the morning."

Jack was *warm*, Blaze realized, as she snuggled against him. He manned the steering wheel with one hand and kept his other arm wrapped around her, propping her up against him with the other. She barely felt the wind hitting her back, the bounces of the vessel's bow as it skidded across the water.

Warm, now, Blaze began to snooze.

"Hey," Jack growled, shaking her. "Stay awake, there, princess."

Blaze jerked awake in irritation. "Stop it, you illiterate bastard," she muttered. It came out as a slur. She frowned. That was funny. She didn't remember drinking…

She felt Jack crane his neck to look down at her. "You're lucky I just spent a bunch of time rescuing you, wench. Otherwise I'd just throw your big ass in the river."

"I don't have a big ass," Blaze slurred. She was proud of that fact, actually. Her ass was one of the *only* parts of her that had curves in all the right places. And oh my *God* she was warm. She felt herself sliding into the depths again, and felt her eyes sliding shut.

"Sure you do," Jack said, jogging her body against him. "Kind of like those pictures of Bigfoot I've seen in the papers.

Blaze's attention sharpened and she scrabbled back to the surface of the Void. "Bigfoot?" she growled.

"Yeah," Jack agreed. "Real big ass. Gorilla-like, almost."

"You asshole," she growled. "Let go of me."

"Sorry, princess. I drop you and you're liable to break that massive nose of yours all over again."

Blaze froze. She hadn't thought her nose was massive. *Was* her nose massive? Of all of her, she had thought it was rather petite.

"Rather equine, if I do say so myself," Jack said. "Hell, with the big feet and the massive nose, I'm still wondering where that Clydesdale hit your family tree."

She would kill him. She strained to push herself up, but couldn't manage more than a prolonged twitch of her left arm. Her right arm, heavy under the wound in her shoulder, wasn't responding properly.

It felt like a dead weight swinging from the joint, and Blaze wondered again when she'd been drinking. Then she remembered Jack saying he'd look for some hard alcohol that the previous owners had left behind, and she realized that *he* was to blame for her current state of sobriety.

Hell, he'd probably gotten her drunk so he could add that to his list of trophies: Tallest Woman Ever Fucked.

"You're a bastard," Blaze slurred.

"And you're one lucky little bird," Jack whispered.

God, she was tired. She closed her eyes and rested her head against his scaly black chest. Just a few minutes…

"Hey!" Jack called, shaking her rudely. "We're almost home, sister. Just keep your panties on."

"Why, so you can take them off?" she slurred.

"Maybe someday, tootz," Jack said. "Maybe once we're both on sensible, speaking terms, that might actually be nice." She heard him shut the engine off and felt a jolt as the boat scraped up the shore. "Until then…" Jack heaved her over his back again. "Just fantasize about my tight, rippling body as I take you home." He jumped out of the boat, into the water, and sloshed towards the bank.

Blaze got splashed, and she groaned and tried to push herself off his shoulder. She didn't even manage to get her left arm to move this time. Instead, she found herself staring at his tight, rippling buttock as it bounced against her face.

He's a monster, she thought, as his exquisite ass moved beneath her lips. She had to add 'molestation' to her list of abuse. This was definitely something they prosecuted for, back in the real world. Ranked right up there with bestiality and masturbating in public.

She felt him jog up the trail, her still face slapping against his tight posterior.

He is so dead, Blaze thought. *Gets me drunk, then hauls me around like a sack of potatoes instead of throwing me to the ground and ravishing me properly. He must have some sort of pony fetish.* It would explain the stubborn mule syndrome. She'd have to ask him, later. Pony fetishes she could handle, as long as there was good sex involved. Broadswords and leather armor, though…

Well, she thought, remembering his geeky getup, as long as *she* wasn't the one carrying the broadsword, she supposed she could handle it.

…Which brought a new train of thought skidding to a startled stop in her brain. Jack, naked, with a couple of these pretty reproductions he was carrying slung across his muscular body and strapped to his narrow hips. Now *there* was an image she could use next time she was bored. Hell, she'd be using it now, if she weren't so totally wasted. What did he *give* her? She hadn't felt this out of it since drinking a fifth of tequila as a sophomore back in the dorms.

"Still alive back there, missy?"

That, and her chest hurt. And her limbs hurt. And her ribs hurt. And her face hurt. It felt like someone was tracing coals through her bones and embers through her heart. She still tasted vomit, so she was pretty sure she had puked up most of it, whatever it was, but whatever was left was causing a god-awful reaction.

Then Jack was laying her down in the dirt, facing the yellow-green sky. The sun had dipped beyond the horizon, and it was at that fleeting time of day when the stars started overtaking the heavens.

Jack blocked her view, his annoyingly bulky body slipping between her and the spectacle above. He put his hand to her forehead, then hissed and yanked it away, shaking it out.

Wuss, Blaze thought, automatically.

"Stay there, sweetie," he said. "I'll be right back." She heard inhumanly fast thumping sounds as he ran away, once more leaving Blaze with a view of the emerging starscape.

From somewhere on the property, she heard a huge diesel engine start.

That asshole's using the dozer without me, Blaze thought, irritated. She liked bulldozing. It was fun, and it gave her something productive to do that didn't leave her looking like a bumbling city-bred idiot. She should've known that he couldn't handle her being competent in something, the insecure bastard. She decided she would teach him to spell his name as A-S-S-H-O-L-E. Oh yeah. Totally. *Of course I can help you with that, sweetie! You want to know how to spell your name? Right here. A-S-S…Oh, wow, you're doing great! H-O-L…See? 'J-aaaa—ck.' Now just finish that final 'E…'*

Then she heard the bulldozer approaching, and suddenly realized he aimed to run her over. Blaze whimpered and babbled that she wasn't going to teach him to spell it wrong, she was just joking, she swore. As the metallic rumble of the tracks grew louder, all she could think about were her legs. She couldn't feel her legs, but she knew—*knew*—he was going to crush them. As much as she tried, though, she couldn't lift her head far enough to look.

The earth began to rumble under her, and Blaze's breath came out in a low, terrified moan.

The engine suddenly fell into an idle, seemingly right on top of her, and she felt a thump in the earth as Jack jumped down.

Every breath was coming in a whimper, and Blaze rolled her eyes to look at his face in horror. "Please don't," she whispered.

"Oh sweetie," Jack muttered, looking torn. He glanced over his shoulder. "It's only gonna be a minute, all right? I've got to."

Blaze's terror ratcheted up a few more notches and she found a tiny bit of strength in her limbs, enough to flip herself over and start crawling away from the machine.

"Come on, now," Jack growled, snagging her lifejacket and holding her immobile. "Stop struggling. You're making yourself bleed."

For some reason, Blaze thought she smelled the acrid tinge of burning nylon.

Jack must've smelled it, too, because he frowned and unzipped the life-jacket. Then, even as Blaze was trying to bat his hands away, he roughly yanked it off of her, leaving her wrapped in cold once more. She whined and curled into a fetal ball.

"Stay there," Jack growled. He got up and she heard the engine rev once more.

It's the backhoe, Blaze thought, listening to the tell-tale metal creak and rattle as it dug out and redeposited soil in long, swinging arcs.

Then another spike of horror almost threw her over the edge. *He's digging my grave. He's gonna bury me, just like the werewolves.*

Then she frowned. What werewolves?

Then the backhoe shut off and Blaze heard another thump. She heard footsteps, then sprays of soil hitting the ground. Then Jack was back in front of her, his hand once again on her forehead. "You gonna be okay for another minute, girlie? I need to go start the generator and get some water."

I don't want water, Blaze said, *I want to sleep.*

Jack gave her a concerned look and bit his lip, glancing over his shoulder. He was still wearing the ridiculous, blood-stained reproductions.

Blood-stained?

"Okay," Jack said. "Stay here, tootz. I'll be back in two minutes, okay?"

Blaze stared at the trampled earth under her nose, too cold to respond. She heard him get up and run off, and a moment later, the generator rumbled on.

She tried to shiver, but couldn't seem to find the strength. The bastard had taken her coat. Of all the stupid, asshole things to do. Even now, she could see it smoldering over in a pile, just out of reach.

...*Smoldering*?

Blaze strained to focus her eyes on the little wisps of smoke. So she *had* smelled burning nylon, she thought, in triumph. Not only had the bastard drugged her, but he'd also tried to set her on fire.

And now he was going to bury her. He had her grave all dug out, ready to plant a six-foot-four Yeti.

The hairy, malicious little monkey, Blaze thought. She would have to get pictures of him and send them to her mother. She thought *her* stomach hair was bad...

But her mother was dead. Car accident. Slid through intersection, T-boned by semi, *squish-squish*. Blaze giggled, or tried to. Her breath seemed to be caught in her chest. For that matter, her heart felt funny. She felt her eyes sliding closed again, felt the warm darkness enveloping her.

TWELVE

Thunderbird

Blaze woke to the smell of fried eggs and bacon, artfully presented alongside a couple slices of buttered toast, on a platter a couple inches under her chin. Blaze moaned and dumped it on the floor.

Jack, who had been wolfing down his own breakfast in a chair beside her bed, paused, his mouth half-open, fork poised to stuff another piece of egg into his mouth, eyes fixed on the pile on the rug.

Slowly, the wereverine lowered his fork. "Not hungry, I take it?" It sounded like every syllable was being pushed through concrete.

"You think I'm ever eating anything of yours again?" Blaze groaned, putting a palm to her forehead at the throbbing in her temples. "You sick bastard."

Still scowling at the pile of food, Jack jammed the piece of egg into his mouth and chewed. "You know," he said, "I'm not cleaning that up."

Blaze glared at him from underneath her fingers. "*I'm* not cleaning it up."

Jack shrugged. "Your room." He went back to eating.

Blaze slumped back to the pillow to stare at the ceiling. "So what's the peace offering for, anyway? You sodomize me? You get me pregnant?" She paused, turning her head to look at him, an eyebrow raised. "You give me some sort of venereal disease?"

Jack choked, spraying egg particles across the room. Glowering, he shoved a fork in her direction. "You," he growled, jabbing with the fork, "Have an awfully funny way of saying 'thank you.'"

"*Thank* you?" Blaze scoffed. "Thank you for what? Getting me drunk? Making a deposit at the bank? Taking your beaver cleaver and going skinny-dippin'?"

Jack narrowed his eyes at her. "How about, 'Thank you, Jack, for rescuing me from another bout of my own stupidity.'" Then he cocked his head at the wall, thoughtful. "Or better yet, 'Thank you, Jack, for dragging my dying ass out of a hole and pounding some life back into me?'" Then he waved his fork and shook his head. "Nonono. Here we go. 'Thank you, Jack, for proving to me yet again how utterly awesome you are, while bathing in the blood of my enemies?'" Then his green eyes refocused on her flatly. "Or how about just, 'Thank you, Jack, I'm sorry I just dumped your food on the floor?'"

Blaze snorted. "You broke my nose." She remembered that much.

Jack scowled at her. "The *wolves* broke your nose. I straightened it for you."

...*Wolves?* It triggered some memory just under the surface, tantalizingly close. Blaze frowned, trying to remember. Last time she had heard about wolves, the Department of Fish and Game commissioner was resigning due to claims of mismanagement.

Jack must have seen her confusion, because his jaw fell open. "You honestly don't remember, do you?"

"I remember you breaking my nose," Blaze growled. And, now that she thought about it, somehow molesting her with his ass.

"Oh for the gods' sakes, *nothing* is easy with you, is it?" Shaking his head in obvious disgust, Jack went back to his food.

A bit taken aback by his obvious irritation, Blaze hesitated. "You mean we really didn't have sex?"

"Nope," Jack growled, around another egg. He had, Blaze noticed, an entire plate of them. Probably a couple dozen or so.

"I *knew* it," Blaze said, watching him.

"Knew what?" Jack asked, sounding not the least bit interested.

"You've been sneaking off to hunt all this time, haven't you?"

Jack shrugged. "You didn't bring enough food."

And now that she had, he was working his way through a month's supply in a single morning.

"So what *did* happen yesterday?" Blaze asked cautiously. She peeked under the covers, found herself topless, but still wearing pants.

"Well, for one, it wasn't yesterday," Jack said, without enlightening her further. "How much you remember?"

Blaze scowled. "You called me a Yeti."

"Yeah, and?" The way he said it, he might as well have said the sky was blue.

Narrowing her eyes, Blaze said, "And I decided to fire you."

"Uh-huh," Jack said, around his food. "That before or after you walked off in a tiff and got yourself captured by werewolves?"

Blaze snorted at that ridiculous accusation. "I didn't get captured by—"

Suddenly she remembered a woman's icy blue eyes, boring into her, as several rows of hypodermic teeth sank into her shoulder. "*Welcome to the family.*"

Blaze shrieked and crawled up the wall. "They *bit* me!" she cried, patting her shoulder, trying to find the wound. Did that mean she was a werewolf? A *beast* like the one sitting beside her bed?

Jack raised an eyebrow, but didn't stop his meal. "You know, I've been meaning to tell you…Nice tits."

Blaze's world came to a crashing halt. She slapped her hands over her breasts in horror and snapped, "Get me a shirt."

Jack paused in chewing, his mouth half ajar. With a little frown, he raised an eyebrow at her, jabbed a thumb at her scattered pile of clothes behind him, said, "Plenty of 'em right there," then went back to masticating his food.

"Get out of my room so I can dress!" Blaze cried.

"Ain't nothin' I haven't seen before, honey," he said, still eating. Around eggs, he said, "*Multiple* times."

Seeing the wereverine continue to stuff food into his face, realizing that arguing with him would have the same general effect as arguing with a retarded chimpanzee, Blaze slid back under her covers, glaring at him.

"So," Jack said, finishing his last bit of eggs. "While you were snoozing, I called in a favor upriver. Thunderbird's gonna be here at three, to tour your garden and have dinner."

Blaze froze, her heart suddenly pounding at the idea of once again being face-to-face with the electric-eyed rain-god. "He's going to *help* me?" she squeaked.

Jack winced, rubbing the back of his neck with a callused hand. "Uh, well, no promises on that one. You can't really buy the sonofabitch. Only way you can get him to cooperate is to convince him it will make him prettier." He shrugged. "But he says he'll come out for dinner." Putting his plate aside, he said, "Oh, and I built you a coop. When you gonna send those chickens out here?"

Blaze blinked at him, her brain having trouble going from having *dinner* with *Thunderbird* to populating a chicken coop. "Uh…" she stammered. "Soon?"

"Good," Jack said. "It's high time you got this farm running. I'm getting tired of cold sandwiches."

Blaze peered at him, disconcerted by his new…willingness to please. "Why are you being so helpful all of a sudden?"

She thought she saw his eyes widen before he slid a talon from his finger and started pulling splinters from the arm of his chair. *Scratch-snap. Scratch-snap.* Blaze had long ago given up on trying to curb him of that nasty habit, with the understanding that he would repair it later. To the arm of the chair, Jack said, "Just figure you ain't paid me yet, and it's high time I started importing some real food around here."

Blaze's mouth fell open. "You will *not* be eating my chickens."

"Then what the hell's the point?" Jack cried.

"They're a rare heritage breed," Blaze replied. "I'm going to be ensuring their survival by raising breeding stock. You can't *eat* them."

"The goats, then," Jack said.

"You will *not* be eating my goats until I've established a breeding population," Blaze growled. "And once I do, you *ask* me which ones you can eat. You don't, and I'm going to shove a snub-nose revolver up your nostril and pull the damned trigger."

"Pigs?" Jack demanded.

"Same thing for the pigs," Blaze growled. "They're an extremely rare variety. Only about two hundred breeding individuals in existence."

Jack glared at her. "I just saved your life, so you owe me. I'm also not letting you out of my sight, which means I'm not gonna be hunting anymore. Get me something to eat."

It took Blaze a couple minutes to realize he was utterly serious.

"We don't have the lumber for the barn," Blaze growled. "And *won't*, until the river comes up and we can start barging it in."

"Oh yeah?" Jack asked, crossing his arms. "How much you need?"

Remembering her calculations, Blaze made a disgusted sound. "Only like fifty grand worth."

Jack got up, went digging through her clothes, and tossed a shirt at her. "Get dressed. I'm taking you for a ride."

Taking it, Blaze slid further under the covers and pulled it over her head. "What about the werewolves?" she demanded.

Jack snorted. "Those puppies? They're gonna hide away awhile, licking their wounds."

"And when they come over here and massacre my stock?" Blaze demanded.

"They set foot on my territory and they're dead."

"The animals I'm going to be getting are *critically endangered*."

Jack gave her an irritated look. "I said I took care of the problem." He turned and started out her room. Over his shoulder, he said, "C'mon. I got something you'll probably like to see."

Blaze, muttering, crawled out of bed and stared down at her huge, Yeti feet. He hadn't even bothered to take her boots off. Even then, she could see spatters of gore on the leather. And, when she thought about, a good portion of her pants were a huge bloody stain, with crumbles of dirt still clinging to her—

Blaze flipped back the covers in horror.

A Yeti-sized brown smear was covering her only set of nice flannel sheets.

"There's *dirt* in my bed!" she shrieked.

"Next time, I'll remember to wash you off, first," Jack retorted.

Blaze froze at the idea of having Jack languidly run a wet, soapy rag over her body, his muscular arm bunching as he…Clearing her throat quickly, Blaze threw on her gear and went to meet him. Jack was already on the four-wheeler, cart attached, wearing his toolbelt.

…and a sword.

Blaze hadn't seen it in the room from the way he'd been sitting, facing her, but now that she had a good view of his broad back, she was pretty sure it was some sort of Hollywood-style black longsword.

"Nice sword," she muttered, coming outside. "Where'd you get it? Ebay?"

"Made it," Jack said. "Forged void-titan bone."

That definitely sounded like something one of her nerdy dorm-mates would have spouted during one of their all-day Dungeons and Dragons sessions on the middle of the common room floor. "So is that a plus-one or a plus-two sword?" she asked, squinting at it. "Actually, no, it kinda looks like a plus-three. It's *black*."

Jack blinked over his shoulder at the hilt of his sword, then back at her. "It's void-titan bone."

"Yeah, whatever," Blaze said. "Next you'll be slaying adolescent black dragons and using their scales for armor." She sat down on the cart, peering up at the Sleeping Lady. When she considered, she was actually rather pleased with how fast Jack had been putting it back together.

On the front of the machine, Jack leaned around to look at her. "You sure you don't wanna sit up here with me?"

And run her hands down his nice, tight thighs while the machine bounced her against his muscular back? Yes, thank you very much, I'll take two.

"No," Blaze lied.

"It's gonna be a rough ride."

"I can handle it," Blaze said.

Jack grunted. "Suit yourself." He gunned the engine, and Blaze found her teeth being rattled out of their sockets as the four-wheeler turned off down a path she hadn't noticed before, hidden behind the big diesel machine-lot. Then Jack gunned the engine and suddenly it was all she could do just to hold on as Jack found every branch, root, and rock and drove them over it at about Mach 15.

By the time he finally shut down the engine and swung his muscled leg over the back of the machine to dismount, Blaze's spine hurt and she was pretty sure she'd cracked a tooth.

"So," Jack said, gesturing at a big blue tarp with moss and algae growing on top of it. It was covering something approximately the size of an elephant. "What do you think?" Now that Blaze looked, there were clusters of moldy tarps all around them, with baby birch and cottonwood trees growing up in all the spaces between.

"What is it?" Blaze muttered, pushing off of the cart.

"Sawmill," Jack said. "Owners bought it a couple years before they left. Got a couple logging permits for the state land upriver and spent a couple summers milling. Were planning on building cabins." He walked over to one of the man-height piles, and sure enough, when he peeled back several layers of tarps, spilling algae-stained water onto the ground below, there was a pile of boards several feet high and several feet deep, neatly stacked with spacers in between. Beside that one, there were at least a dozen more, like blue, algae-covered lumps in the woods.

"Uh," Blaze said, as her brain underwent an overload and politely shut down upon seeing at least a hundred thousand dollars of lumber staring her in the face, "That's…a lot."

"And we can make more," Jack said. "Just tell me what you want, and where you want it, and I'll get it built. They already had the concrete for the cabin foundations shipped out here. They're under tarps out at the site. Insulation and roofing will have to wait for the barge, but we got plenty of tarps. I can jury-rig something to keep the structure dry until we get the rest of the materials."

Blaze was still staring at the lumber, slack-jawed. Jack glanced over at her and frowned. "You listening?"

"Just give me a second," she said as she struggled to think. The owners hadn't listed a sawmill on the equipment list, and her logical mind was frantically coming up with reasons why the fortune in lumber wasn't rightly hers. She glanced around, looking for property landmarks. "You sure this belonged to the Olsons?"

"Helped Bill move it out here," Jack said. He pointed down the trail. "That heads out to state land along the Yentna, where they'd gotten their logging permits. Earned some pretty good cash helping Bill haul spruce logs back here, for Susan to cut up." He pointed. "See that little tractor over there?"

Blaze glanced at the little red machine, barely visible against the brush that was overtaking it. "Yeah?"

"She used that to load logs onto the mill. Pretty slick." He grunted and started pulling the tarp completely off of the stack. "So yeah, it's yours. Help me load it onto the trailer and we'll go start building you a barn." As he spoke, he grabbed a big armload of boards—six to eight times what Blaze could lift—and hefted them over his shoulder like they weighed nothing at all.

Blaze glared as she watched him show off. "Looks like you got things covered," she muttered, when he laid them out on the trailer and came back for more.

"Yeah," Jack winked, "But I love to see your face when I put all this lean meat to good use." He flexed an arm for her and kissed his bicep, grinning.

Blaze's mouth fell open. "You're an arrogant prick, you know that?"

"Maybe," he said, picking up another load, bigger than before, then split it into two halves so he could flex each of his massive shoulders, "But with a body like this, who's to blame me?" Still grinning up at her, he delivered the bundles to the 4-wheeler. That time, the trailer's tires actually squatted under the weight.

He made two more trips, strapped the lumber down with a handful of bungee cords, then mounted the four-wheeler, giving her a wonderful presentation on the form and function of the gluteus maximus, then started the machine and spun the cart around.

"You coming?" Jack asked, slowing beside her.

Blaze eyed the cart anxiously. "It already looks like it's gonna pop a tire."

"That's why you'll ride up here with me." He patted the seat behind him.

Peering at the overgrown trail, remembering what happened last time she had gone off in the woods alone, Blaze decided she really didn't want to walk. Reluctantly, she climbed aboard the four-wheeler with him.

"*Whoa*," Jack whistled, as the four-wheeler squatted precipitously. "Just how much do you weigh, woman?" He gave the tires a concerned look.

Blaze reddened and started to get off.

"I'm joking," Jack laughed, grabbing her knee, "I built this thing solid, to hold my heavy ass. A few hundred extra pounds isn't gonna make much difference."

A few hundred…? she thought, shocked. She stared at the back of his head as they started moving down the trail, imagining it imploding, sucked inward by the inescapable vacuum that was his brain. "You want to learn how to spell your name?" Blaze asked, through gritted teeth.

Jack frowned over his shoulder at her, his green eyes suspicious. "Why?"

"No reason," Blaze said. "Just bored."

His eyes flickered nervously across her face. "Maybe later," he said slowly.

"Begins with 'A,'" Blaze offered.

Jack glanced back at her again, uncertainly. "'A,' Huh?"

She smiled and nodded.

"I'll have to keep that in mind." Then he was paying close attention to the trail, and Blaze couldn't help but notice where his nice, hard body was tucked up against her—and where his ridiculous reproduction sword was thoroughly getting in the way.

Blaze grabbed it by the handle and yanked it free.

Jack let off the throttle with a cry of, "Hey, now!" He stood in the stirrups and turned, frowning at her. "Just give it back, honey."

The way he said it, she was holding some sort of holy relic from the days of King Arthur. Blaze rolled her eyes and tried to figure out what kind of enamel they'd used on the blade. Whatever it was, she wouldn't mind trying to replicate the process, once she had her renaissance resort up and running. When she looked closely, though, the void-black coating was probably too deep to be cost-effective. Even scratched, she couldn't see any silver shining through from underneath. Blaze tested the sword's edge. And cut herself. She jerked her hand away. And cut herself again, when the blade slid through her denim jeans and bit into her thigh.

"Holy *shit* that's sharp!" she cried, jamming her thumb into her mouth, holding the blade at arm's length as she stared at it, wide-eyed.

Jack snatched it from her and rammed it back into its sheath, scowling. "I could've told you that."

"Where'd you *get* that thing?!" Blaze cried, hastily examining her leg to see how deep the blade had sunk into her thigh. Not far, thank God, though it was starting to bleed like a stuck pig.

"Told you," Jack said, sitting back down, "Made it." Then they were moving again, the 4-wheeler bouncing them down the overgrown trail as if Blaze were not sitting on the seat behind him, bleeding.

"I need a Band-Aid," Blaze muttered, looking at the split in her thumb.

"Could try the first-aid kit upstairs," Jack offered.

Blaze stared at the ebony hilt, bouncing under her chin. Now that she was looking, the scrollwork on the guard and pommel were much too elaborate to belong to something that was stamped out in a factory at thirty cents a blade. "Did you really make that?" she asked softly. "It looks like a masterwork."

"Someday," Jack said, "I'll show you my collection."

"So you *collected* it?" Blaze demanded.

"Yes," Jack said. "From a void-titan's thighbone." He grinned over his shoulder at her. "The dragon I was with at the time got everything else—greedy sonofabitch—otherwise I'd probably have made a suit of armor out of the stuff." He shrugged and went back to driving. "As it is, I got a couple longswords and a dagger hilt, so I'm happy. Trellyn did most of the work, anyway. I just kinda stood around and hacked at his feet when he was distracted."

"You know a dragon?" Blaze whispered, her heart making an extra excited thump.

"Several of them," Jack said. "And if any of them set foot on my territory again, I'm going to drive a crow-bar through their skulls and twist."

"That's…brutal," Blaze said.

"They're snooty, higher-than-thou, two-faced thieving bastards," Jack said. "About as interesting as a cardboard cutout, and as selfish as a troll." He waved a disgusted hand at the north. "Thunderbird pretty much keeps them at bay, I'd say. I haven't heard of any of them heading south out of the Brooks Range, and good riddance."

"I'd like to meet a dragon," Blaze said, biting her lip at how ridiculous that sounded.

Jack twisted in his seat to give her a long look. "Missy," he said, "If you survive the next couple of years, I'm pretty sure you're going to." He pulled the four-wheeler around the big-diesel lot, then rolled to a stop in the churned earth beside her bulldozer.

Blaze frowned. "Why's that?"

Jack glanced at her and dismounted. This close, he clinked as he moved, and Blaze realized that he was wearing some sort of chainmail underneath his shirt. Jack started freeing the bungees from the lumber pile.

"You didn't answer my question."

"What question, sweetheart?" He tucked the bungees away on the back of the 4-wheeler and started kicking out an even patch of ground.

"Why do you think I'm going to meet a dragon?" Blaze demanded.

"You're out in the woods," Jack said vaguely. He threw down a few blocks to keep the lumber off of the ground, then started taking the rest from the cart and laying it out in rows.

Irritated at his evasiveness, Blaze climbed off the 4-wheeler. She was about to start helping him when her eyes caught on a green shape a few yards off. An abandoned life-jacket. Frowning, she walked over and picked it up. Something hard and lumpy against her hand caught her attention. She turned it over.

The jacket was melted inside, almost like someone had dribbled burning kerosene on it.

Blaze had just the faintest tantalizing memory before it was gone, buried back under the surface of the Void. Frowning, Blaze held it up so Jack could see the burn marks. "You know what did this?" she asked.

Jack looked up, then stumbled. Righting himself quickly, he made a nonchalant shrug. "Caught on fire, probably."

"Well, that's obvious," Blaze growled, tossing it aside.

"Then why'd you ask?" He finished unloading the lumber, then climbed back aboard the 4-wheeler. He started the engine, obviously waiting for her.

Muttering, Blaze stalked over and, after a brief deliberation over whether to ride on the vertebrae-shattering cart or the soft, padded, shock-absorbing seat of the 4-wheeler, she climbed up behind Jack.

It took several trips to relocate the pile of lumber from the abandoned clearing in the middle of the forest to the fresh new dirt pad out behind the lodge. Then, as Jack dragged her around gathering up concrete sacks from yet another abandoned clearing to the west, various tools and supplies from the shop, and began to set it up beside the pile of lumber, Blaze had that funny, world-shifting realization that he was serious.

He's gonna build me a barn, Blaze thought, stunned to tears. Realizing she was about to put herself into another coma, she quickly took several deep breaths and held a palm over her eyes to calm herself, thinking about her last Business Statistics exam in order to keep from falling into another 'grief-triggered psycho-emotional collapse.' Fucking overpaid hack doctors and their 'self-induced psychosomatic' bullshit.

When she lowered her hand, she realized Jack had been watching her. He cleared his throat, his face reddening, and he glanced up at the sky, "So, uh, we should probably start dinner."

Blaze looked out at her parched garden and winced. "You really called *Thunderbird* for my *garden*?" She peered at Jack. "You really think he's coming over?"

"He better," Jack said, "as many times as he's called me over as his home-fucking-repairman, he better be here right on time, a smile on his face, or he's gonna be swimming in his own crap for a few centuries." At her stare, he said, "What, you think the North American rain-god uses an *outhouse*? As full of shit as he is, he's lucky he only overloads his septic tank twice a decade." He made a disgusted sound. "Come on, I'll never hear the end of it if we don't feed him. Hospitality and all that."

North American rain-god. Blaze suddenly had a flutter of worry that she and Jack had the audacity to bother such an entity with something as silly as her *garden.* Then a bigger, more pressing matter occurred to her. What *did* you feed a North American rain-god?

"I hear he likes spaghetti," Jack said, when she asked. "And nachos, on game nights."

Blaze peered at him. "He watches football?"

Jack shrugged. "Flies in to his place in Chugiak once a week to watch the game."

"So you *have* been to town before," Blaze cried. Chugiak was smack-dab between Anchorage and Wasilla, and as far as she knew, there weren't any Bush-plane charter services operating out of Chugiak.

Jack gave her a funny look. "No, I don't give a rat shit about his place in town. He hires someone for that. The place in town is just so he can watch the game. His main place is a cabin upriver. Drags my ass out of bed at the crack of dawn—he's an early riser—a few times a year to take a miserably cold boat-ride up the Yentna to fix whatever he busted." At Blaze's stare, Jack shrugged. "When he works on engines and batteries, he tends to make stuff explode."

They decided to make spaghetti with the last of Blaze's precious fresh vegetables, and Jack insisted on dumping a whole palmful of oregano into the sauce as it simmered, despite the recipe's listed 'one tablespoon.' They spent two hours preparing, cooking the noodles, simmering the sauce, filling the entire lodge with the delectable scent of fresh-cooked Italian food.

"Okay, now," Jack said, as he stirred the sauce, "a couple things you should probably keep in mind 'fore you do something stupid."

Blaze knew he wasn't talking about putting too much olive oil in the spaghetti noodles. "Like what?" she asked, nervous, now.

"It's like this, sister," Jack said. "This guy's like a walking powerhouse. He gets pissed at you, you're dead, *capiche*? Not even the dragons will fuck with him. Well, not the smart ones. Younger ones still have pissing contests and shit, but he could sputch 'em dead if he really wanted to, you understand?"

This was reminding Blaze of his previous lectures about How To Not Sputch Yourself Running A Fishing Lodge. "Um," Blaze said, looking down at the strainer of noodles, "are we sure we want him over?"

"He's mostly harmless," Jack said. "But, uh, yeah. Watch your step around him. He's already a bit touchy. I think I might've pissed him off the last time I chased him through the woods. Said some pretty unkind things about his sexual orientation, and I think maybe he took offense."

His *sexual orientation*? Suddenly, the lack of rain made a lot more sense to Blaze. She narrowed her eyes. "Are you saying this place has been a desert because you—"

"What I'm *saying*," Jack said, flushing, "is don't insult him, don't raise your voice around him, and for Chrissakes, don't tell him he's an effeminate prick."

Blaze thought she could handle that. Hell, if she had her way, she would keep her distance and let Jack do the talking, maybe smile and nod if it was necessary. She was still trying to get over the idea that she was about to entertain a *god*. With *spaghetti*.

A couple hours later, Blaze was starting to wonder if their guest was actually going to show up when Thunderbird just *arrived*, a crack of lightning out of a perfectly clear sky, scorching a good swath of her desiccated front lawn. He was fashionably late, dressed in black and red Spandex, a fluffy white towel draped over his wiry shoulders. He was also *gorgeous*. He oozed a startling, almost sexless beauty, much like the Japanese bish⊠nen. Tall and slender, but with a presence of *power*, his long Athabascan face had a handsome agelessness to it, and his long ebony hair was braided into a thick rope that trailed up the steps behind him.

"You know, weasel," Thunderbird said, making every hair on her body raise in a wash of static electricity as he climbed up the stairs of the front porch, glaring at the wereverine. He pulled a fuzzy black exercise headband from his brow and tossed the headband onto an Adirondack chair. "I was in the middle of my salsa class. I have *triplets* in that class, weasel. *Triplets*. But no, I am *here*, on your front porch, after flying from *Anchorage* to talk to you about *gardening*." He made a disgusted sound. "*Tell* me you are serving something other than spaghetti."

Blaze blushed, thinking of the pot of red sauce even then bubbling on the stove.

"Oh for fuck's sake!" Thunderbird cried, throwing the towel onto the chair with his headband. He jabbed a manicured finger at Jack. "*Every* time I've come to your beck and call like a trained pet monkey, it's undercooked spaghetti. Have you not a single creative cell in your entire testosterone-saturated body?" The rain-god gave Blaze an irritated look, and she saw, in shock, that his eyes were no longer glowing, but a very pretty shade of blue.

A moment later, Thunderbird remedied that by yanking two contacts from his eyes and stuffing them into a little white case he carried in a convenient little fanny-pack on his hip. "All right," he said, waving a disgusted arm at the backyard. "By all means. *Show* me this garden of yours, weasel."

"It's *her* garden," Jack growled, crossing his arms over his chest. "And stop being an asshole."

Pot. Kettle. *Black*? Blaze stared at Jack, wondering if he'd popped something important in the forest, hefting all those big boards.

"You should find it refreshing that I'm dropping to your level," Thunderbird said, peeling off thin cloth gloves and dropping them onto the pile upon the towel. "Half the time, I'm not sure you even understand civilized conversation."

Then Jack said, "Generally, I don't give a shit, but there's a lady present."

Blaze's mouth fell open. Just what *were* the symptoms of an aneurysm, anyway?

But instead of laughing and dissolving into a little raincloud and floating away—or jolting Jack into oblivion—Thunderbird twisted to look up at Blaze. "You're taller than me," he said. Like he found it annoying.

Blaze, who had fully intended to stay *far* back and let Jack plead their case for them, suddenly found herself stammering. "Uh, yes, well, I—"

"Just show me the garden, feed me your slop, and let me go back to my triplets," Thunderbird said. "You have…" He yawned and checked his fancy gold watch. "One hour." Then he crossed his wiry arms and peered up at her, one brow raised impatiently.

"Well, go *on*, tootz," Jack said, when Blaze could only stare down at Thunderbird, completely at a loss as to what to do or say.

"Uhhhh," Blaze said, "can you please make it rain?"

She thought she saw the rain-god's face darken. Thunderbird sniffed, glanced at the sky, then out at the parched brown lawn, then at his watch. "Fifty-nine minutes."

Blaze, realizing she'd probably just committed a horrible faux pas, just *asking* the god of rain to wet her crops, babbled her apologies. "Sorry, Mr., uh, Thunderbird," she managed. "I didn't mean to offend, sir. I thought Jack was gonna do the talking. I really don't know how to do this properly, and I…" She hesitated, mouth open, realizing she was about to ask someone what kind of sacrifices he preferred to be made in his name. Yeah, following Yeti Isn't My Style and Werewolf Abduction, the Return To Anchorage column was definitely gaining the lead.

Thunderbird just peered up at her impassively, that weird tingle-before-a-lightning-strike lifting the hairs off of her skin. "You're just wasting your own time, Fourthlander."

Fourth…Lander? Was that like 'Highlander?' Lots of people thought Blaze looked Scottish, what with the freckles and fiery red hair. Her parents' surname only heightened the effect. Blaze swallowed, glanced at Jack, who was scowling at Thunderbird, then said, "My garden's out back."

"By all means." Thunderbird made a dismissive gesture towards the back yard, boredom showing in his electric eyes.

Seeing the rain-god's disdain, Blaze swallowed hard. "Okay, uh, this way." She led the demigod off of her porch, rubbing her arms at the weird way every hair in its follicle was standing on end. Thunderbird yanked his dance shoes off, tossed them on the chair, picked up his ten-foot-long braid, wrapped it carefully around a shoulder, and followed, barefoot, across the lawn. Behind them, Jack followed at a distance.

Rounding the west side of the Sleeping Lady, the sad state of Blaze's test-garden was readily apparent. Dust lay in thick swaths, painstakingly pulled into neat mounds by Blaze's constant effort. Well-marked signs indicated each type of heritage crop. *None* of it was growing. The little specks of green that had stubbornly worked their way out of the ground as a result of her tediously-applied buckets of lake-water looked dried and shriveled, like salad-sprouts left out overnight. Seeing that, Blaze wondered how long she had been asleep.

"So this is my garden," she said, walking Thunderbird over to it, as Jack continued across the yard to turn his attention to the lumber pile, leaving her alone with the rain god. "Not very impressive right now, for obvious reasons."

Thunderbird grunted and picked grass bits from the end of his braid.

"I'm trying to grow heritage crops," Blaze offered. "Really rare stuff. The kinds that still taste good, that haven't been bred to produce wads and wads of cardboard with little or no nutrient value. Stuff our *grandfathers* used to grow." She hoped that Thunderbird, being what he was, might sympathize with goals to resurrect dying agricultural legacies.

"I don't have a grandfather," Thunderbird said. He surveyed the dusty rows with something between boredom and apathy. "It looks horrible."

"It hasn't rained at *all*," Blaze blurted. She gestured at the painstakingly-tended quarter-acre of dusty rows. "Alaska's the perfect climate for a lot of this stuff, but it's rained everywhere *but* here. The neighbors talk about getting flooded, down on the river, 'cause of all the rain they're getting north of us, and the farms in the Mat-Su valley are having the best year they've ever seen, but we haven't seen a drop."

"Of course not," Thunderbird said. "The weasel insulted me."

Blaze's mouth fell open.

"But," Thunderbird said, "I'm interested to see what kind of platitudes he has in store for me. The petulant little shit actually thinks I'm going to let him con me into letting it rain around him. Ever again. I've heard drought does interesting things to one's pantry, and moon-kissed are notorious for their appetites."

Blaze stared at him, her heart pounding at the thought of watching her entire thirty acres dry up to dust. "Please let it rain again."

Thunderbird sighed and glanced again at his watch. "Fifty-four minutes." His eyes fell to Jack, who was a dozen yards away, arranging the lumber they'd hauled out of the woods. "I find it particularly underhanded that he tried to get a *woman* to do his dirty work for him. I think I'll maybe add a few tornadoes, for that."

Blaze swallowed hard, realizing he was utterly serious. "So, uh, I guess you're already aware. The weather's not been cooperating with me."

"Weather doesn't *cooperate*," Thunderbird said, swiveling on her with a sudden flash of irritation in his glowing white-blue eyes. Waving a disgusted hand at the quarter-acre of dusty rows, he said, "Too many people on my continent think that weather is just another thing to be controlled. Cloud-seeding, hurricane tracking, preventing tornadoes, weather *predictions*. The *arrogance*. Weather is a force of Nature. You work *around* it."

"I tried," Blaze growled, face heating at the rain-god's irritated stare. "I carried up buckets of water from the lake. Like a hundred gallons a day. It just dries up. Evaporates."

"You obviously weren't trying hard enough," Thunderbird said. And that, Blaze realized, was what he thought on the matter. As if to heighten the effect, Thunderbird pulled out a pink nail file from his convenient little fanny-pouch and started running it across his nails, then held them up and blew the dust off of them. Returning his file to his fanny-pack, he said, "Are we done here? I'm hungry."

She felt something twitch in her brain as she looked down at the Spandex-clad rain-god. "How hard would it be for you to make it rain here?" she demanded.

Thunderbird sighed, deeply, and started to turn towards Jack. Raising his voice to the wereverine, he called, "Feed me that slop so that I may be on my—"

Blaze grabbed the man by the shoulder, twisting him back around to face her, angry, now. "How *hard*? We talking a few hours? A few minutes? A *thought*? What?"

Thunderbird pulled himself out of her grip with a look that made it obvious he thought she might give him some sort of grow-tits-and-drop-nuts disease. "I am a *god*."

Which meant with a *thought*. Blaze's eyes narrowed. "But you're making me beg. For nothing. Because you don't intend to let it rain. Because he called you a fag."

Thunderbird sighed again. "Jack!" he called, turning. "I will eat your disgusting food and then fly back to—"

"No," Blaze snapped, grabbing him and dragging him back around again, "you *won't*."

For a long moment, the very air around them seemed to gain the scent of ozone, and Blaze's hair started to stand on end, floating around her face in a little halo as Thunderbird once more removed her hand and they scowled at each other. Very slowly, Thunderbird said, "Excuse me?" His voice sounded like the crackle of electricity, and she thought she saw the blue flash of current sizzling in the back of his throat.

"It's my land, my lodge, and *my* food." Blaze jabbed a finger into his breastbone. "You showed up, let me make an ass out of myself begging for something you never intended to give me, and then called my food 'disgusting slop.'" She raised her arm and pointed towards Anchorage. "You can get the fuck off my property. Right now."

Judging by the way Thunderbird's eyes lit up and the tingling she started feeling in her feet, Blaze honestly thought she was about to be electrocuted out of her shoes. Jack, too, seemed to think this, because he dropped the boards he was carrying and started running towards them, yelling, "Hey now! No need for that, Brad, goddamn it."

But Thunderbird never took his eyes off of Blaze. "What kind of food?"

"Spaghetti, you dick," Blaze snapped. "We thought you *liked* it."

"I do," Thunderbird growled. "What kind are you *growing*?"

Blaze frowned at him, caught a little off-guard. "Anything I can."

Thunderbird sniffed. For a long moment, he simply continued to scowl up at her. Eventually, he reached up, scratched his nose with a slender finger, then took a deep breath, sighed, and put his hands on his hips. Turning back to face the garden, he said, "I like peas. Green Arrow, two rows of fifteen feet each, with the vines held up by five-foot fencing, full sun, a good walkway, and a bucket nearby."

Blaze stared at him, absolutely shocked by his arrogance. "I don't give a fuck *what* you—"

"Sounds great, Braddy-ol'-Boy," Jack cried, jogging up and shoving Blaze aside. "We'll get that up and running for you ASAP."

Blaze's mouth fell open and she stared at Jack. "You have *got* to be shittin—"

Her words ended with a jab of Jack's elbow. "Remember Zeus," she thought she heard Jack mutter to her.

Thunderbird sniffed and rubbed his nose with his manicured hand again. He cocked his head up at Blaze with a sideways look, then walked out into the garden, stepping *on* her desiccated rows, and stopped in the nicest, most central part of the garden. He glanced up at the sun, then at the rows around him. "And I want it to be right here." He then proceeded to mark off a row with one bare toe, then paced off fifteen feet and marked another spot, dislodging what few zucchini plants Blaze had gotten to grow.

Blaze stared at him, a little ball of rage unfurling in her stomach. "Get out of my—" Her words cut off when Jack stepped on her foot, hard.

Padding out of her garden, tromping over *more* of her carefully-laid beds, Thunderbird nonchalantly said, "What kind of rain?"

The college student in Blaze was stunned to recognize the sound of a business negotiation, and she had to suddenly backtrack to figure out what she had missed. Then, stunned, she said, "*Peas*? You'll do it for *peas?*"

"The ones in the supermarket are tasteless," Thunderbird said. "And I fly past here often enough. I like peas. Might stop in a time or two this summer and grab a couple handfuls. You will keep both of my rows pristine, unpicked, free of weeds, however. I do not like to waste my time searching for them."

Blaze felt her heart start hammering, realizing she was amidst weather negotiations with a *god*. "Um. Okay, but it's much too late in the season to—"

Jack stepped on her foot again, even as Thunderbird's eyes narrowed.

"Sounds good," Blaze said, clearing her throat.

"So what do you want?" Thunderbird said, yawning and checking his watch again. "What kind of rain?"

Blaze scrambled to come up with something specific that wouldn't get her plants waterlogged and drowned, while at the same time making best use of daylight. After a few mental calculations, she said, "I want heavy rain, four times a week, for five hours at night. Full sun during the days. No hail."

"Sure, sure." Thunderbird said, dismissively. "And I suppose you'd like me to avoid the tornadoes and hurricanes, as well?" Like he was discussing his Daily Planner.

Blaze froze, realizing he was dead serious. "Alaska doesn't have—" Then she realized who she was talking to, swallowed hard, and said, "Yes, please."

"All right," Thunderbird said. He turned to Jack. "You put oregano in it?"

"Butt-tons," Jack said.

"Good. Let's eat."

THIRTEEN

Christening the Barn

That night, it rained. Hard. Blaze lay in bed, listening to the patter on the tin roofs, biting her lip in happiness. It stopped five hours later. To the minute.

The next morning, Jack *insisted* on replanting her freshly-moistened rows, despite the fact it was already late June, and the first frost in Alaska usually came in mid-September. They reworked the center of the garden to accommodate Thunderbird's peas, then spent the day replanting everything that had withered and died. Blaze was actually starting to pick up a bit of Jack's enthusiasm by dinner time, for which they shared a ham-and-turkey sandwich on the back porch.

Well, Blaze had a sandwich. The wereverine fried for himself an entire tray of eggs and a commandeered an entire loaf of bread, slathering mayonnaise on each slice just long enough to wrap it around a couple eggs, then stuffing the whole mess down his throat in a grotesque display that reminded Blaze of something out of a sci-fi horror show.

Despite the massive amount of food he ate, Jack finished first. He sat on the porch and gave the back yard a thoughtful look as he licked mayo off of his hands. Blaze took her time to finish her sandwich, feeling somewhat obligated by Jack's appalling lack of etiquette to eat *extra* slowly, as an example of proper eating habits. If Jack noticed, he never mentioned it.

When she was done, Jack jumped off the porch and motioned her to the pile of barn lumber they'd left there the day before. "Come on over here, a minute," he called to her. He spread out a sheet of notepaper already covered with building designs over the top layer of boards, then pulled a pencil from behind his ear. "Okay, so you want something with two levels, right? Pigs and goats down below, feed and rabbits upstairs. Nesting boxes, stalls, cages, feed storage, water pipes, staircase, gangplank. Something to catch the rabbits' pee so it don't fall through the floor…" He started drawing up plans for a two-story barn that, off the cuff, was more functional and well-thought-out than anything Blaze could have come up with given a week of planning and research. Watching him methodically hash out the little details, Blaze once again felt more than a bit insecure.

Then she realized that, throughout it all, he hadn't marked down a single measurement.

"How are you gonna build that without any math?" Blaze asked, eying the elaborate structure dubiously.

He gave her an irritated look. "I eyeball it."

"Come on!" Blaze cried. "You aren't even gonna use a tape measure?"

He scowled at her and folded up the paper. "I was building houses without a tape measure since before the Bronze Age." Then, discussion apparently over, he picked up a board and started expertly counting off handswidths.

Blaze narrowed her eyes. "You're using a tape measure."

"This is faster," Jack said. He stopped near the end of the board and marked it off with a pencil.

"You wanna learn your numbers or not?" Blaze demanded.

Jack, who had already started on another board, hesitated, then frowned up at her.

"Stay there," Blaze said. She turned on heel and went into the shop, pulling down the one tool that Jack hadn't used since he got there. She took it out to the pile of lumber, set it down and held out her hand. "Gimme that paper a second."

Jack gave the tape-measure the same look he would have given a coiled snake, but he handed her the pen and paper anyway.

"Okay," Blaze said. "How big are you making this thing?"

"Uh," Jack said, "Forty feet by eighty."

"How'd you plan on doing that?" Blaze demanded. "How much do you know about math?"

"I can count to a thousand," Jack said. He was flushing, now, looking hard at the wood grain of the lumber beneath his face. He lifted a hand to one of the boards and Blaze saw a talon slide from his fingertip, sinking into the wood.

Blaze rapped his knuckles with the pencil. "Stop it."

Jack raised a lip and snarled, but he pulled his hand away.

"Okay," Blaze said. "So you know your numbers? What's this one?" She wrote '482' down on the sheet."

Jack looked at it for several moments before he muttered, "Two hundred eighty-four."

"Four hundred eighty-*two*," Blaze said.

"Well, shit!" Jack snapped. "The Romans switched stuff around on me, too, and the Japanese and the Chinese and the Germans and the Egyptians...Everybody had a different system, and just when I thought I'd started to pick it up, I had to pack up and run and start over someplace new, so give me a damn break, okay?" He was panting, his face crimson, and he looked for all the world like he wanted to bolt.

"Okay," Blaze said softly, "Easy." She laid a palm on his forearm. As he frowned down at the touch, she prodded, "So you ever had anyone try to actually *teach* you before?"

He snorted bitterly. "Only about a hundred times."

Blaze's breath caught as she realized what was going on. "I think I just figured out what your problem is."

Jack bristled, and she saw fur sprout against his back. "My problem, huh?" He yanked his arm out from under her grip and went back to counting out his handwidths on the board.

But Blaze was sure of it, now. "You had too many different teachers and not enough time in one place to learn any one system, so they're all jumbled up in your head and making it even harder for you."

He hesitated, his broad back still turned toward her.

Blaze then began to tell him everything she knew about basic math. Starting from the very building blocks, and working her way up.

Slowly, Jack turned back to face her, biting his lip. She thought she saw tears in his eyes, but she pretended not to notice. "Okay," she said, finally returning to the drawing he had made, "Forty feet—" she marked it, "—by eighty." Another mark. "You can read those?"

"Yeah," he said, reluctantly. It was the first word he had spoken in a couple hours.

Thus began Blaze's career as an architect. She gave him numbers to add or subtract to get a total, and he would scowl over every inch, poring over the numbers on the tape with the same concentration of someone who only half understood, but who was determined to figure it out. Sometimes, due to the fact that Blaze *wasn't* an architect, it was hard to translate what he *wanted* to do onto paper. The roof, for instance...She had no idea what he meant by 'eight-twelve pitch' until he put two boards together, perpendicular, then, looking at her as if she were an utter imbecile, made eight measurements with his palm straight up and twelve measurements outward from the T, creating a triangle with a steep outward side. The 'pitch,' as he explained to her.

For his part, Jack taught her how to mix and form concrete, how to smooth it out with a trowel, how to use a table saw, how to work a level, and how to properly pound nails. Blaze had never realized that there was an actual *method* to pounding nails, and was amazed to watch him set and drive nails with two rapid blows, then flabbergasted when he showed her to do it herself.

It took almost two weeks, during which, Blaze had to order another Beaver load of groceries—mostly meat and eggs—but by the time the barn was finished, and the two of them were standing outside, admiring their handiwork, Blaze was feeling much more confident about her usefulness in the woods, and Jack wasn't acting like an asshole anymore.

In fact, more than once throughout the construction process, Blaze had caught him staring at her, mouth agape, and the 'Yeti' and 'Clydesdale' comments had all but faded from his vocabulary.

"Well, how's it look?" Jack asked, leaning back against the four-wheeler, shirt off, covered in a day's sweat, a root beer in his hand as he surveyed the two-story barn. "Think your goats'll like it?"

Seeing it there, completed, Blaze felt a welling of joy that she had to share. She leaned over, put both huge hands on either side of his head, and kissed him, right on the lips. "It's perfect," she said, beaming. "Thank you."

Jack went crimson and immediately found his feet very fascinating. He scuffed them in the dirt. "Yeah, well, thank you, too." *Scuff, scuff.* "Was nice to, uh, learn something new." Even then, the neon-green tape-measure stood out proudly against his hip, taking a spot beside his hammer on his tool belt. When he looked up at her, his green eyes were filled with gratitude.

Looking at him, Blaze's breath caught. The sun, coming in at a slant just above the horizon, was painting his body in the golden light of late evening. Shirt off, still sweating from climbing around on the roof, he was beautiful. Blaze had to clear her throat and look away, lest he catch her staring. "So, uh, I guess fencing is next?"

"Might be a good idea," Jack agreed, pushing off of the 4-wheeler. "Tomorrow, though." He stretched and yawned, and Blaze watched in awestruck appreciation as his big shoulders worked. "Too tired to keep my eyes ope—"

This time, he *did* catch her staring. He grinned and flexed with one arm downward and one arm bent upward, giving her an excellent view of the musculature of his back.

Blaze's heart began to pound and, face flushing, quickly found something else to do. She stood up and started gathering up her root beer and work gloves, then reached for the bug dope to take it inside.

"Hey Blaze."

Jack was close, almost right behind her.

Blaze turned in confusion.

He was grinning, his green eyes twinkling with that mischievousness she had come to associate with backhoes and Manual Labor 101.

"What?" Blaze asked, suspiciously.

Jack opened his mouth, and then his grin faded. He got this funny frown on his face, like he was trying to concentrate. Then he wrinkled his nose, closed his mouth, scowled, then opened it again. "Your smile… is…" He grimaced, then shook his head. Biting his lip, his green eyes filled with consternation, he said, "Your face…"

"My face?" Blaze winced. "What, do I have something in my teeth?" She *had* forgotten to floss that morning. At his look of horror, she cupped her hand to her mouth, blew into it, and sniffed. No, it didn't *smell* like something was rotting in there.

Jack flushed red and scratched at the back of his neck, then licked his lips and got that funky constipated look again. "Your hair. *Tall.*"

"My *hair*?" Blaze glanced down at it. Yeah, she supposed some of it had fallen out of the braid while throwing up the rafters and she probably looked like a sweaty orangutan. She sighed. "Okay, so what is it? I'm a gangly-ass Yeti who needs a shower and a haircut? My buckteeth are blocking your sun? What?"

He just stared at her. "I'm *not* that much of a dick."

Blaze just laughed. Shaking her head, she chuckled and said, "I'm gonna go get that shower before I try really hard to figure out which part of me you were insulting this time." She started to turn.

Jack stepped closer suddenly, until their bodies were *touching*, and grabbed her wrist, tugging her back abruptly. "Truth is…" he said hesitantly, his eyes searching hers.

"Truth is?" Blaze whispered, her heart already starting to pound where he was holding her in place, his hard body against hers. Lord, he was *strong*…It was all she could do not to go all mushy inside at the way he held her there with all the power of a grizzly, yet those iron-crushing fingers having all the gentleness of a teddy bear.

He's insulting you, a part of her reminded. *Just save that thought, sister.*

Jack's green eyes must have found whatever they had been searching for, because a slow grin spread over his face as he looked up at her. "Truth is, I kinda got a thing for Yetis." And he reached up with a powerful arm and pulled her head down into a kiss.

Heart hammering like a machine gun, Blaze dropped the items from her hands and returned his embrace, leaning into him, melting under the strength of his kiss. He wrapped a big arm around her waist as the other reached up and his fingers dug into her hair, holding her firmly in place. Blaze shuddered at the feel of something so completely *male*, so utterly close. This was *not* a geeky roleplaying college nerd. This was something *entirely* different, and he was making that clear to her with every heart-pounding second.

"Oh my God," Blaze gasped, when he released her to breathe. Her head was swimming, and she had to slump to the 4-wheeler seat to keep from falling on her ass.

Jack was grinning at her as he reached down for something hidden behind the 4-wheeler's front tire. "So, uh, wanna christen the barn?"

Blaze was on her feet and dragging him stumbling across the yard before he'd finished his sentence. Inside the barn, she shoved him against a wall and started ripping his clothes off—and Jack grunted and grabbed her hand, stopping her.

Blaze stared down at him blankly.

Jack held up a bottle of wine between them like a holy symbol. "*Christen* it," he said, shaking the bottle. It was a brand she didn't recognize, which, considering her wine-snob of a father, probably meant it was very expensive indeed. When she just stared at him, Jack offered, "You know, drink a *toast*, say a few words, splash a little over the sides for good luck?" He was shying away from her uncomfortably, and was looking at her like she'd just tried to shove her hand down his pants.

...Which she had.

Blaze couldn't have been more horrified if she had somehow had all of her clothes disintegrate in the middle of the Wal-Mart electronics department. She quickly stumbled backwards, her face on fire, unable to understand how she had just made such an utterly, incomprehensibly stupid blunder.

There was a long, awkward silence between the two of them before Jack glanced down at his bottle of wine, then at her, bit his lip, then said, "We should probably save it for when we get the greenhouse built, huh?"

Blaze was struggling against tears. *I am* not *going to let him see me cry over this*, she told herself. But, unfortunately, he was standing between her and the door. "Probably best," she managed. It came out as a whisper. "I think I need to go finish out those rabbit hutches upstairs."

"I'll come help you," Jack quickly said, setting the bottle aside.

She didn't want his help, didn't want to be anywhere *near* him, but when he strapped on his toolbelt and offered her hers, she was still so horrified that all she could do was take the belt and clip it around her waist.

Jack gave her a long look, his green eyes searching, his breath catching like he wanted to say something, then bit his lip and looked away. He snatched up his hammer and the bucket of nails beside the wall. "Come on," he said. "We can probably get them finished tonight." He started thundering up the stairs, his huge weight making the barn rattle, giving Blaze little way to save face except to follow.

How could I have read him so wrong? Blaze thought, in despair.

Blaze was still thinking about that, several hours later, when she and Jack put the finishing touches on the rack of hutches. He had avoided her all night, even going so far as to work on the cages opposite her, to stay out of her way, and had Blaze not already committed herself to helping him—and spent the last two weeks falling into a routine of working with him—she would have gone back to her room to try and piece together what had just happened.

Jack had his head shoved inside a rabbit hutch, pounding the final trim pieces on the inside corners to help keep out martins, and Blaze, finding herself with nothing to do, went to the window—sans glass—to look out at her new home.

A man was creeping across the yard, towards the back door.

"Jack," she whispered, her heart suddenly a wildfire in her chest. "There's someone out there."

Jack was pounding away inside the box, unable to hear her through his hammering on the plywood.

Out in the yard, the man hesitated, sniffing at the still night breeze. He glanced around him warily, every step very carefully placed, paying special attention to the entrance to the barn. He was extremely short, only about four feet tall, and his long black hair was elaborately crafted into a hanging network of braids, all pulled back from his eyes with a single hoop of metal, all tumbling almost to the ground at his heels. He wore a long, silvery cloak that seemed to alternately shine and fade in the moonlight.

The man hesitated at the discarded life-jacket that Jack had slung over the burn-barrel for the next garbage burn, picked it up, turned it inside out, examined it, then slowly lowered it back to the ground. He glanced again at the barn, warily. Then he was slinking forward again, low and quiet, moving towards the steps of the back porch. On his hip, he carried what looked like an extremely sharp, translucent, flat-bladed rapier, but it glowed silver in the dusky light.

"*Jack*," Blaze hissed.

The man in her yard twisted suddenly and looked straight at her. His eyes widened and he vanished.

"*Jack!*" Blaze screamed, backing away from the window. "*There's someone in the yard!*"

Jack was out of the nestbox and in wereverine form in an instant, snapping the plastic clip of his toolbelt as his body expanded, dropping it to the floor. He glanced at her, then at the window, then leapt over the edge of the loft, not even bothering with the stairs.

Leaving her alone again. Blaze huddled against the wall, staring at Jack's discarded toolbelt, trying not to think about just how utterly terrified she was.

Minutes seemed to tick by like hours, and Blaze was beginning to worry that something might have happened to the wereverine by the time Jack came trudging back up the stairs, a frown on his face.

"Fey warrior," Jack said. He gave her a meaningful look. "Likely come sniffing out that item of which we do not mention or otherwise give any hint of its presence."

"He's still around?" Blaze whispered.

"Probably somewhere in the room," Jack growled, glancing at the rafters, sniffing. "Little bastard's got the mage-gift. He's been casting glamours ever since you spooked him."

"What does he want?" Blaze managed.

"I know what he wants," Jack snarled, peering at the room around them. "I also know what he's going to *get*, if the little prick doesn't get lost." He seemed to be talking to the walls.

Thoroughly unnerved, Blaze glanced out the window. "What do we do?"

"For one," Jack said, "We go get it. I'll take the damn thing and put it somewhere *no one* can touch it."

Blaze frowned. "But I thought we already…"

Jack's attention sharpened, but only for an instant. "Already what?"

"Already buried it," Blaze blurted.

She seemed to see a flash of recognition before the Jack snorted. "True, but I, for one, don't want the little thief to dig it up while I'm snoozing."

"Oh," Blaze said, frowning.

"So," Jack said, "Let's go get it." He gestured at the stairs down.

Blaze hesitated. "But I thought you said…"

Jack sighed. "The jig's up. We might as well go grab it and hang onto it until he gets bored and wanders off. Now *hurry up*."

Blaze moved to the stairs, but frowned at Jack as she passed. "But you said it would help my garden grow."

Jack's attention snapped to her. "He did, did he?"

Confused, Blaze said, "Didn't you?"

Jack shrugged. "Maybe. Maybe not. All depends on the weather."

Something wasn't right about the man, and in that moment, Blaze realized it.

He's wearing his toolbelt, she thought. Icefire ran in cold waves through her veins as her eyes caught on the object on the floor, identical to the one now on Jack's hip.

"So," Jack said, urging her forward. "We need to hurry up and get a shovel before the little shit realizes what we're up to."

Blaze's heart was thundering. Now that she was thinking about it, she had spent the last two weeks feeling the barn shake with Jack's every footstep, but whatever *this* was had barely even disturbed the planks.

"Okay," Blaze said, heading toward the ground floor, her back on fire as she could barely even feel the creature's steps behind her. Then, at the base of the stairs, she spun, slammed a fist into the creature's groin, and bolted for the yard. "Jack!" she screamed. "*Jaaaaaack*!" She heard something light tumble the rest of the way down the stairs and saw Jack's image flicker in and out on the concrete pad, replaced with the picture of the man that had been sneaking towards the back porch.

Oh my God, she thought, as the creature groaned and sat up, glaring at her. "Jack!"

She went to the 4-wheeler, grabbed the sword that Jack had leaned there, yanked it free.

The man—she *thought* it was a man—stood up, snarling. He shoved a stocky finger at her, his brown eyes glinting with Athabascan fury. He looked, for all the world, like an Alaskan native man who had somehow failed to have a growth spurt…and had somehow developed slight points to his ears, chin, and teeth. "Put it down and get a shovel. Now."

"*Jaaack*!" Blaze screamed, keeping the sword between them.

"He's halfway to the Cook Inlet by now," The creature sneered. "I led him on a merry chase to nowhere, and while the fool is still figuring that out, *you* are going to get me his artifact and hand it over."

"*His* artifact?" Blaze said, frowning.

"If you *don't*," the tiny man growled, pulling the slender, glowing sword, "I've got no qualms running a mortal through, if she's bearing a blade."

Blaze looked down at the weapon in her hands, then back at the tiny native man. She had absolutely no idea how to wield a blade, and she guessed by the way he swished his back and forth in an effortless motion, he did.

She turned the blade upside-down and rammed its tip into the earth. Lifting her hands, she stepped away from the sword.

The man strode forward and yanked Jack's weapon out of the soil, peering at it. "That's void-titan," he said, sounding surprised. He hefted it. "This'll fetch a pretty penny, at the market."

"That's not yours," Blaze said, sick to her stomach that she had handed over Jack's blade.

"You put it down," the man said, looking up at her. "You obviously didn't want it anymore." He hefted it again appreciatively, then carefully wrapped it in the cloak he had been wearing and tucked it under his belt. Then he nodded at her. "Go get a shovel and dig me up this artifact he's so proud of. I can feel it nearby."

Blaze didn't move. She bit her lip, wondering where Jack was.

The man narrowed his eyes and stepped forward, his glowing, translucent, razor-thin blade lifting to meet her stomach. "I will *gut* you, human."

Blaze felt the way the blade seemed to melt her shirt away from its glass-fine edge, and a rush of terror felt like coals being pushed through her veins.

"Now!" the man shouted. His blade flickered, and suddenly, Blaze was bleeding down her front.

She stumbled backwards and fell to her ass in the yard, blood oozing from a gash in her abdomen. Seeing the blood, remembering his threat, Blaze whimpered and slapped a hand over her stomach. Her heart was hammering blasts of liquid wildfire through her veins, and suddenly it was all she could do to breathe.

The man rolled his eyes. "I didn't gut you, mortal," he growled, stepping forward. He grabbed her hand and yanked it away from the wound. "It's just a scratch, see?. Now get up, and go get a shovel, or—" Suddenly, he stopped, looking down at his hand where it held her wrist.

Slowly, his hazel eyes came up and met her face. In their liquid depths, Blaze saw shock. The man released her suddenly and took a quick step back, wiping his hand on his shimmery pants. Blaze frowned when it seemed to make a golden stain before the garment returned to its normal silvery hue.

Then, in the distance, the forest started to crack and rustle, getting closer at inhuman speed.

The man swallowed, looking at her, then looking at the forest, licking his lips, looking like he wanted to say something.

Then Jack was *there*, a raging, snarling ball of fury, and the creature flickered aside just as a big taloned paw swept through the air where he had been. Blaze, still on the ground, watched in horrified fascination as the creature easily flitted around the wereverine, slashing him with the glass-like weapon here and there as Jack roared and spun, trying to get a hold on him.

Then the tiny man paused, gave Blaze a look that left a chill in her gut, then flashed out of existence again. This time, for good.

For a long moment, Jack stood over her, snarling, panting, that creepy animal rattle loud in his chest as his big body hovered over her on all fours, head swinging left and right as if he expected the little man to appear one last time and drag Blaze off with him. Then, after a moment, he straightened and glanced at the 4-wheeler. He seemed to slouch upon seeing the empty sheath. "The bastard took my sword." The words came out in defeat; exhausted, spent.

"I gave it to him," Blaze whimpered. Then, when Jack's attention sharpened on her, she quickly said, "I was trying to use it but I chickened out when he told me to put it down."

Jack gave her a long, irritated glance, but eventually muttered, "You probably saved your fool life. If you'd kept it, the Faefolk Code says he could sputch you." But she could see the longing in his eyes, the heart-pangs in him as his eyes once again fell on the empty sheath.

"I'm sorry," Blaze whispered.

Jack shrugged. "It was just a blade." His face, however, was dark as he turned away. Transforming back to human shape as he walked, gave her a very good inspection of his naked backside as he went into the barn to retrieve the wine bottle. A few minutes later—much longer than necessary—Jack returned, his lips tight, as he went to the 4-wheeler.

"I'm sorry," Blaze said again, biting her lip.

Jack stopped beside the machine to pick up his gloves, hat, and empty soda can. "He came here looking for something else," he muttered. She thought he was trying to make her feel better until he said,

"Probably wouldn't even have noticed it was there if you hadn't picked it up."

Blaze glanced away, ashamed.

"I need to teach you the rules," Jack sighed, leaning forward on the machine, hanging his head. "A fey can't take something from someone that they made themselves." He turned to look at her tiredly. "The moment that item is given away as a gift, though, they consider it fair game. You picking up the sword probably translated, in his small and twisted brain, to that I had given you leave to use it. Which made it a gift. Which made it his."

"You could ask for it back," Blaze said softly. "Tell him what happened."

"And have a fey admit a mistake?" Jack gave a disgusted snort. "They'd rather pluck off their own damn wings." He yanked his gloves off of the seat and, scowling at her, said, "Let's get back inside. The bugs are pissing me off."

Then, without another word, he strode back towards the lodge, yanked the door open, then slammed it behind him, leaving Blaze to get up on her own.

Asshole, Blaze thought, getting to her feet. Then she saw the sword's empty sheath, still lying against the 4-wheeler front tire, and felt another wash of guilt. It had been a treasure of his, something he'd bled for, something he'd created with his own hands, and she'd lost it for him.

Swallowing, she followed him back to the lodge.

When she stepped inside, Jack was already in his room, the door shut.

"Jack?" she said, tapping lightly on his door.

"Not right now, sugar," Jack growled. "Just go to sleep. I'll see you in the morning."

"I'm sorry about your sword," Blaze said softly.

She got no response.

Feeling like shit, Blaze went to her room and closed the door. She picked up her journal, tried to describe what had happened that day, then tossed it aside in disgust. What had possessed her to try to tear off Jack's clothes? Or pick up the sword? She'd never been trained in swordsmanship, and she should have known that this wasn't a ren-faire, and anybody swinging a sword out here *would* be trained.

Suddenly, all the confidence that two weeks of learning construction had instilled in her seemed to vanish with that simple thought. As much as she learned how to start a generator, run a bulldozer, or pound a nail, she still wasn't going to fit in. She'd thought that living out in the Alaskan Bush would mean a couple years of learning the equipment and easing into the rhythm of the seasons. She had never considered that she would have to forever depend upon a short, cranky wereverine to keep her alive.

The more she thought about it, the more a greenhouse outside Wasilla was sounding like the better alternative.

Then she thought about the fun she had had building a barn with Jack, and remembered the glorious feel of his rock-hard body in that long, passionate kiss, and she felt a welling of despair at the thought that she had ruined it all.

First time a real man takes an interest and Bigfoot assaults him and gives away his most valued possession, Blaze thought, disgusted. In ten years, she'd never had anyone so incredibly sexy so much as look at her. She had been forced to settle for roleplaying nerds who wanted to see what it was like to bed an Amazon. They had wanted to be pinned to the bed and taken. They had expected her to take charge, leaving their smaller, weaker bodies to be used as some strange scenario played through their twisted heads. She had seen it in their eyes—a kind of dreamy, distant look—as she had held them down and ravished them. Yet Jack had so overwhelmingly *taken* her with his kiss that she was just glad she wasn't fertile—if she had been, it probably would have made her freakin' ovulate.

Back in Anchorage, thinking about the number of single men in the Bush, Blaze had optimistically opted to renew her Implanon—three years of hormone-stimulated birth control. It had been a nerve-wracking procedure, utilizing a needle approximately the size of a roofing nail, but she had endured it, powered by the hope that maybe some hunk in the Bush might see the Yeti and not run away screaming.

And now that she had found one who didn't, she'd ruined it. Utter and completely ruined it. She doubted he would even want to talk to her again, so thoroughly had she screwed the pooch today.

Blaze got in bed dreading the repercussions in the morning, wondering if she would ever feel him wrap his arms around her again, have his rippling body holding her tight, to be ravished by his kiss.

It doesn't matter, she told herself, miserable. *There's more to life than good sex.*

She knew that, but it didn't help. After so many years of feeling awkward and different, the girl that none of the guys in the bar wanted to approach, the one who was stuck on the sidelines at every dance, something deep and carnal just wanted a man to treat her like a normal woman. After a lifetime of fantasizing about her perfect kiss, only to have Jack blow it completely out of the water, taking her so thoroughly it left her panting and breathless, Blaze knew she had been forever spoiled to the geeky computer nerds—the only ones who had ever even looked in her direction before this.

And you fucked it up royally. You fucking assaulted *him.*

Remembering the uncomfortable way he tried to slide away from her, the way he'd avoided her afterwards, Blaze was struggling not to cry as she finally fell asleep.

FOURTEEN

The Condom Age

Blaze woke to the smell of fried eggs and bacon, and to the sound of someone in the room with her. Squinting, she started to sit up.

"Oh no you don't," Jack laughed, quickly tugging the platter off of her chest. He held it while she sat up, blinking at him.

He doesn't look *angry*, she thought, peering up at his face.

Jack set the platter down on her lap, then sat back down in the chair he'd once again dragged in from outside.

Blaze peered at the doorknob. She was pretty sure she had locked it.

"Honey," Jack said, when she asked, "You're dealing with a blacksmith." He winked and went back to his food.

Blaze looked down at the platter of eggs and bacon, with two buttered pieces of toast on the side, then tentatively picked up a fork, feeling a bit like she'd woken up in the Twilight Zone. She stared at her food, almost afraid to eat.

Jack's eyes flickered to her plate and he cursed. "Shit. Forgot salt and pepper." He got up and ducked from the room. Strapped to his back was an ebony longsword.

When he returned with the two shakers, Blaze took them with a frown, her eyes on the leather straps across his shoulders. "Did the fey give it back, then?"

Jack snorted. "No, this is my other one. Half a thighbone for one, half a thighbone for the other. Just enough left over for a dagger hilt." He sighed, poking at his eggs with a fork. "No, I'm pretty sure the little bastard's already through the tween zone to go sell it to some fey warlord for a few centuries of breeding privileges." He scraped up the eggs and stuck them in his mouth, chewing violently.

"I'm sorry," Blaze said again, heartfelt.

"You didn't know," Jack said, shrugging. "And I hadn't told you, so it's just as much my fault as yours." He jerked his thumb over his shoulder. "Besides, I got a spare." Then he made a dismissive wave. "Was just a bit upset last night because I'd had the blasted thing almost five millennia. Put a few thousand hours of my sweat and blood into it, after cutting it out of that damn titan. Saved my life more than once, in the years after." He shrugged and went back to piling eggs into his mouth. "No biggie." Around a mouthful, he said, "It was bound to happen, sooner or later. 'Specially with me doing something as stupid as planting myself right next to a fey superhighway."

Blaze stared at him, confused by this new and understanding Jack. "You mean you're not pissed?"

Jack gave her an annoyed look. "I said it was fine. I'll just twist the little bastard's head off later, next time he comes snooping." He gestured at her platter with his fork. "You gonna eat your eggs?"

Reluctantly, Blaze turned to her meal. Though she began to get uncomfortable when he just sat there, watching her every bite.

Eventually, after enduring his scrutiny for almost ten minutes, she looked up in irritation. "What?"

Jack made a nervous laugh and rubbed the back of his neck. "I, uh, well…" He swallowed, looking at her. "I like you."

Blaze flushed with the sudden, overjoyed beating of her heart. "I like you, too," she admitted. "It's nice to find someone who doesn't mind…" she gestured at her huge form.

"Yeah, well, I like crossbreeds."

Blaze's attention sharpened. "Crossbreeds?" She thought that maybe, finally, he was going to tell her what he knew about her that he had been withholding all this time.

"Yeah," Jack said, grinning. "Always been fond of Clydesdales, and Yetis add a bit of hardiness to the mix. They live in the Himalayas, you know."

Blaze stared at him, caught between wanting to kiss him and throw her platter at him in disgust.

"So, uh, yeah," Jack continued, "I like you." He swallowed, looking pained, obviously having more to say.

Blaze narrowed her eyes. "And?"

"And, uh, I mean I *really* like you. And, uh..." He was blushing, his face beginning to dot with sweat. He wiped his brow, then sniffed his underarm, then groaned. "Thor's balls, I'm no good at this."

"No good at *what*?" Blaze demanded.

It all came out in a tumble, so fast that Blaze had trouble understanding the words. "I know that I'm a dick, but it seems like you like me, too, so we should probably get married before something goes wrong," he blurted.

Blaze felt both of her eyebrows shoot skyward. Her mouth fell open. "*What*?"

"Uh," Jack said, flushing crimson at her reaction, "Well, you obviously aren't a virgin, so you must know a little bit about the way things work."

She cocked her head at him. "The way *what* things work?"

He made a nervous chuckle and rubbed his arms. He glanced at the door like he wanted to bolt. "I, uhhh, can't, uhhh." Another nervous chuckle. "I mean, I, uh..." He swallowed, hard, peering at her. "Well, maybe you just don't know. A guy and a gal have...relations...and the girl is gonna get pregnant."

A wave of understanding washed over her in a blessed burst of relief. "Ohhhhhh," Blaze laughed. "Okay, I get it." She reached out and patted him on the hard shoulder. "Don't worry about it, bud."

His face darkened and his spine stiffened. "I won't be producing a bastard." The vehemence in his words was highlighted by the way his talons were suddenly gripping into the chair arms. "I seen enough kids in my life that ain't had a daddy. I won't let it happen to one of my own."

Blaze slapped her hand over her face and dragged it down. "Okay," she said. "What do—" She hesitated at the strange look that Jack was suddenly giving her. Like a combination of someone who had just won the lottery, someone who was having chronic constipation, and someone who had just been diagnosed with some weird brain tumor that gave them visual and auditory hallucinations. Suspiciously, she said, "Why are you staring at me like that?"

Jack jerked and blinked at her. Scratching behind his ear, he muttered, "Well, uh, to be honest, I thought you were gonna be more stubborn than that. Woman these days are so…gun-shy…about marriage. Just flit from guy to guy, have kids with whoever, never settle down. Like they don't trust their man to hang around and protect 'em anymore." He stood up abruptly. "I'll fly a pastor out here." He started towards the door, looking as if he were going to go do just that.

"Sit down!" Blaze snapped, louder than she had meant to.

Jack froze, mid turn. He slowly sank back into his chair, eying her as if she had suddenly grown nine-inch fangs.

"Now listen to me a sec," Blaze said. "You saw Bronze Age, the Iron Age, and you may or may not have seen the Stone Age. This is the Condom Age. Today, we have ways to keep girls from getting pregnant from a night of hot, mind-blowing sex."

Jack flushed so hard she thought his face might explode. He started to get up. "I think maybe the fire needs a few more—"

"*So*," Blaze continued, cutting him off, "Seeing how this glorious Condom Age allows us to manipulate our hormones in the name of fucking like bunnies, I went in and got *this* stuck in my arm." She pointed to the scar where the ten-gauge needle had pierced the skin of her bicep and held it out for him to see.

Jack leaned over and sniffed it. Frowning, he looked up at her. "What's it do?"

"Magical things," Blaze said, dropping her arm back to her side. "Three years of unprotected sex, kids-free."

Jack's eyes widened at the scar. "They can *do* that?"

She grinned at him. "Wanna find out?"

But he looked thoroughly unnerved. Jack flushed again, appearing acutely uncomfortable. "I don't know…I'm pretty potent. My moon-magic might overwhelm it, and then the seed would take hold…"

"Can't overwhelm it if it can't stick to the sides of the uterus," Blaze said, getting out of bed. "Can you pass me a shirt?"

Jack, who was staring at her, twitched, then hurriedly snatched up a shirt and tossed it to her. Then he blurted, "Gotta go check the fire," and bolted.

Blaze stared after him, stunned and more than a little irritated by this new development.

They had the fencing up by evening four days later, which was a good thing, because Jack had just about polished off the rest of the eggs, meat, dairy, and anything else remotely resembling protein that Blaze had had shipped out on the last grocery run. Since Jack had frustratingly kept Blaze phoneless—still not trusting her not to 'hit the rag and do something stupid'—they went to his house and Jack powered up the generator so she could make a few calls out to a few farmers she knew in the Mat-Su Valley. Yes, she knew it was last minute, yes, she was going to need feed, yes, she was actually going to fly them out to the Bush in an airplane.

"Okay," Blaze said, putting down the phone, "Hope you like goat milk."

"Was raised on the stuff," Jack said.

Blaze peered at him, trying to determine if he was joking. He was leaning back, picking his teeth with a distracted air. Slowly, she said, "We're lookin' at sixteen meat kids, five adult milk does, and a meat buck, plus twelve breeding piglets."

Jack nodded. "And a butt-ton of fowl and rabbits. I heard."

Blaze gave him a narrow look. "You aren't to eat any of this stuff unless you've got my go-ahead first. All right?"

He raised an eyebrow at her. "They're livestock. They're meant to be eaten." The way he said it, he was going to walk into the barn whenever he got hungry and eat the first thing that got underfoot.

"They're *rare* livestock," Blaze said. "Those pigs are Mulefoot Hogs and Gloucester Old Spot Pigs. There's fewer than two hundred of either breed in North America."

"And the chickens?" Jack growled.

"Jersey Giants," Blaze said. "I'll let you eat some of the roosters, when they hatch." She gestured. "Mostly, we're gonna keep you fed on eggs and rabbit. Standard rex. I've got American Blue and Silver Fox rabbits coming, too, but you can't eat those."

"Why not?" Jack demanded, bristling.

"Because they're *endangered*," Blaze growled.

"Eggs and rabbit and a chicken now and then?" Jack growled back.

"And some ducks and turkeys and geese. And the meat goats and some of the pigs, when they grow up."

"Some," Jack muttered.

Blaze looked him up and down, then tried to calculate how much he ate. "That's not gonna be enough, is it?"

"I've been starving myself this last month," Jack growled. "I need *real* meat, and lots of it. I've been losing muscle with how little I've been eating lately."

Blaze looked him in the eyes, thought about the massive plates of eggs he'd wolfed down, saw he was serious, and went back to the phone to call a few more friends. Her feed bill was going to be astronomical, but then there were discounts for buying in bulk.

Thus, the next morning, when Bruce Rogers' DeHavilland Beaver brought in the first load of yaks and unloaded them, mewling, on the shore, the whole neighborhood turned out to stare.

"Whatcha gon' do with yaks?" Joanne Klein, the neighbor from the little shack on the mouth of Ebony Creek, asked. Somehow, news of their plan had spread, and seven neighbors had met them on the beach that morning, asking about their new farm.

"Eat them," Jack said, gathering up the yak calves' leads and hauling the entire eight-calf herd through the crowd, up the path toward the lodge. Blaze, unable to handle the stares she was getting from the other residents of the area, followed him up the hill.

By the third Beaver trip, this time dropping off the piglets, rabbits, and bags of food, Blaze was getting not-so-polite chuckles and smirks behind hands.

By the sixth, this time filled to the brim with kid goats, some of the neighbors were laughing outright. Jack ever-so-politely told them to fuck off.

It took seven trips total, and about thirty thousand dollars in plane, food, and animal costs, but when the day was over and Blaze was sitting in her yard, watching her ten dozen chicks peck at the ground while the goats, pigs, and yaks explored the boundaries of the fence, she had her farm. The thought gave her a warm glow, and sitting beside Jack, feeling his strength beside her, she wondered how life could have gotten that good.

Jack roasted goat for dinner. Despite her protestations, Jack said that, seeing how her Boer meat goats were the one 'decently edible' thing she'd brought onto the property that wasn't an endangered breed, should he end up eating them all, she could just buy more. And then he promptly took a young buck out back, cut its throat, and skinned it, all with the practiced ease of someone who had done it many, many times in the past.

Blaze then watched in shock as he ate half of the entire goat by himself in one sitting, probably close to twenty pounds of meat, the spectacle so gruesome she finally gave up eating just to stare. "You full?" she asked, when he was finished.

Jack grunted. "One or two of those a day should work."

Her brain did a quick mental calculation. Thirty pounds of meat a day, multiplied by three-sixty-five…

"No *wonder* the moose population around here's taking a hit again," Blaze cried. "You guys have been eating them all."

"Hey," Jack growled. "That's why I've got ten square miles and run a salmon fishwheel."

"But the wolves," Blaze said. "They've gotta be hitting this place hard."

"Fifty percent drop in moose population in one year," Jack said.

Blaze flinched. "I hadn't heard that." From what she'd heard, when she was doing research into good areas to establish a hunting lodge, the general consensus had been that the Yentna area was recovering.

Jack shrugged. "Yeah, well, the Fish and Game guys don't want it made public, considering the stink going around right now about predator control. They're trying to blame it on the heavy snows last winter."

"Wow," Blaze whispered. "That can't be good…" She tried to calculate the amount of food that forty werewolves were eating, and found her brain sputtering to a stop. "*Moose*? Is that where the wolves are getting their food?"

Jack took another swig of his root beer. "Moose, bear, fox, rabbit… Anything they can get their hands on, I'm sure."

"Oh my God," Blaze whispered. "There won't be anything left."

"Hey," Jack said, shrugging. "There's a reason why we try to keep our numbers down, honey. The wolves are the ones with the annoying habit of starting populations the ecosystems can't support. The rest of us try to keep it to one or two every twenty square miles, which usually does us pretty good. Times are getting tougher, though, so lately we've had to squish closer and closer together, and frankly, yeah, I've been thinning down the population some. I've been hoping you'll help with that."

"How?" Blaze asked, turning to him.

He reddened. "Your feather. Leave it in the ground long enough, the ley-lines will carry its magic outward and stuff will start to regenerate."

"Yeah," Blaze said, "But *forty* werewolves? What can recover from that? I don't care how much magic is in the soil…they're probably going through a moose or two a week."

"Try more like one or two a day," Jack said. At her stunned look, he shrugged. "Wolves eat more than wereverines. They got more mass."

When she just stared at him, he shrugged. "Way I see it, eventually the wolves are gonna eat themselves out of a home, and then they'll have to move to greener pastures and won't be my damned problem anymore." He finished his soda and crushed the can. "Just gotta hang in there 'til they do."

Blaze bit her lip. She was looking at her ability to attract and retain hunting clients this fall and next spring dwindling to nothing.

Seemingly reading her mind, Jack patted her on the back and said, "Just worry about getting your farm up and running and those fishing clients in here next summer. I'm thinking the wolves will probably move north this winter, probably go up the Yentna and challenge a dragon for its territory up in the Brooks Range. Amber's the kind to do something that stupid, and when she does, good riddance."

Disturbed, Blaze looked out the window at the goats that were even then munching their way through the cranberry bushes. "What will keep them from coming out here and eating everything we just flew out?"

Jack gave her an irritated look. "I told you. I took care of it."

Blaze squinted at him. "Took care of it…*how*?"

He gave her a long look. "I have a dagger," he said finally.

"Oh yeah?" Blaze said. "That one of titan bone?"

"Titan bone and dread unicorn. The evil kind. A unicorn that went bad. Necromancers. The horn will destroy any living flesh it comes into contact with. Kind of like a really bad spider-bite, but faster."

Blaze frowned, remembering the snippets of conversation she had overheard from her friends Dungeons and Dragons parties in her living-room. "I thought necromancers raised the dead."

Jack grimaced. "It does that, too."

Blaze stared at him so long her mouth got dry. Finally, clearing her throat, swallowing several times, she squeaked, "You have something that will raise the *dead*?"

"I don't *use* it for that," Jack cried. "Even a *fool* knows not to do something that stupid. I only use it when I have to. It will take down just about anything, and as much as I love a good, old-fashioned fistfight, if you're gonna go toe-to-toe with the big boys, sometimes you gotta play rough."

Blaze suddenly didn't feel good. "Where is it?"

Jack stiffened. "I'm not telling you that."

She raised her brows. "Why? You think I'd use it on you?"

"No," Jack growled. But he didn't say anything else.

"What if I need to use it?" Blaze demanded.

"You won't," Jack snapped.

"What if you're not here and I have to defend myself?"

"I'll be here."

Now he was just making her mad. "You said you wanted to show me your weapons collection."

"Not *that* part of my collection," Jack growled. His hackles were pushing through his skin, raising the shirt on his back.

But Blaze wasn't satisfied. "So why do you think that this dagger is so scary that Amber's gonna keep her distance?"

"She got a taste of what it can do," Jack said.

Blaze gestured at his hip. "I don't see you carrying it."

"I don't *need* to," Jack snarled, slamming his fist into the hewn-log table, making the massive thing jiggle precariously. "Now drop it, before you piss me off."

Irritated, Blaze got up. "I've gotta go check the barn."

"You do that," Jack growled. "I'll clean up my mess." He grabbed the uneaten half of the goat by the spine and turned toward the fridge.

Blaze's mouth fell open when he opened the refrigerator door. "You can't mean to put that—"

He stuffed the carcass into the center rack, still dripping juices, then slammed the door.

Staring at the refrigerator, Blaze managed, "I'm going outside."

"You already said as much," Jack said, dumping both plates of left-overs onto the table and tossing them into the sink. Then, grabbing a bowl from the central island beside the stove, he slid the load of bones and salad remains in a greasy smear across the table and dropped them into its basin. He shoved it at her. "Put this out there. The chickens and the pigs will go apeshit."

Eyes on the grease-smear that was even then soaking into the wood, Blaze managed, "Are you going to clean that up?"

"I did clean it up," Jack retorted. He gestured at the bowl. "See?"

Someday, she would have to bring him up-to-date with twenty-first-century food sanitation codes. If she started that argument right now, though, Blaze was pretty sure that the grease dribbling out of the fridge and down onto the floor would still be there in the morning and she'd only have a new window for her troubles, where Jack had hurled a half-eaten goat carcass through her wall. She could see it now. *"You don't want it in your fridge? Then* fine*! Let's put it back outside!"*

Blaze took the bowl down the stairs and deposited its contents in the pig trough that Jack had made. The piglets, it turned out, didn't really have the chewing capacity to work their way through the bones, but they nibbled the meat and gristle off of them and spread them around the yard.

Sighing, Blaze started picking up the scattered bones, dropping them back into the bowl to be put into the compost heap later, when she saw motion in the trees over the fence. She stood up to look.

The four-foot man with the hundreds of tiny braids was standing beside a birch tree, watching her, his black hair gleaming iridescent purple-green in the sun. As soon as their eyes met, he disappeared.

"Jack!" Blaze screamed, dropping the bowl. She turned and bolted for the lodge.

The wereverine was through the back door and into the yard before she even made it over the fence. "What?" he demanded, coming to a running halt in front of her.

"I saw him," Blaze babbled, pointing to the birch tree where she had seen the fey. "He was standing over there, watching me."

Jack lifted his nose and sniffed the air. "Yeah," he growled, bristling. He shoved her behind him, facing the woods. "It's him."

"Please don't leave!" Blaze cried, grabbing him by a shoulder that was even then growing in fur and bulk. "Just stay here, okay?"

"Little bastard needs his *ass* kicked," Jack snarled at the forest. He looked half-tempted to take off after the fey, anyway.

"Please?" Blaze asked. She hated the way it almost sounded as if she were pleading.

Jack turned to look at her, a single eyebrow going up. "Well, I guess if you're gonna beg…" He looked genuinely surprised.

Blaze blushed against the shame of feeling so helpless without him. She looked away.

"Hey, honey," Jack muttered, his face melting, "Come here." He grabbed her by the waist and pulled her into his arms, giving her the choice of falling against his perfectly muscled chest or having him snap her spine. She stumbled forward, her mother's nagging voice in the back of her mind lecturing her about independent women and how she should be kicking him in the gonads right now, but her relief of being *held* overwhelming the impulse. She just swallowed and let herself feel the wereverine's body around her, taking carnal comfort in the fact he seemed perfectly willing to shred someone alive for getting too close.

Her mother, she decided, had never been stranded in the Alaskan Bush, with only a crabby little wereverine between her and a multitude of horrifying creatures who grew fangs and swiped at her with glowing silver swords.

Jack seemed to sense her inner struggle. Looking up into her eyes, Jack said, "You're not a warrior, all right? There's no shame in that. World needs all types. Hell, I wouldn't *want* you to fight, not when you've got me to take care of this sort of thing. I'm a warrior, through and through. I'll fill that role for you. I've done it before, and I'll do it again."

His sudden gentleness, so soon after her panic, tried to bring on a wave of tears. Fighting them viciously down, because she would *not* swoon into a coma in his perfectly masculine arms, Blaze bit her lip and lifted her chin with that surge of Independent Woman she'd learned from her mother. "I want to learn to use the sword. If I could use a sword, I wouldn't have to have you save me all the time."

Jack stroked her hair, holding her. "Okay, honey. I'll teach you. Hell, you can play around with a sword all you want, but when it comes to stuff like this, let me fight your battles for you, okay? I don't want to see you get hurt, and you aren't built to take the sort of punishment I am. I was born and bred for this stuff. I can hold my own against a fey. Even the lords, if I've got the right equipment. You...You've got another purpose in life."

Remembering his demand for marriage, Blaze pulled away and narrowed her eyes down at him. "What, like cooking food and raising babies?"

"Yeah," Jack said. "Like cooking food and raising—" Then he frowned at her scowl. "What?"

"So let me get this straight," Blaze said, her indignance rising. "You want me to play the part of the housewife, all barefoot and pregnant, while you do the macho thing and defend me from the big bad world, is that it?"

"Oh Zeus and Apollo," Jack moaned, rolling his eyes. "I just want to keep you safe."

"So that I can pump out kids for you," Blaze accused. She jabbed a finger at her bicep. "So should I get this taken out, then? Maybe start early? Since I won't even be able to defend myself? Better reproduce as much as possible *now*, because who knows when my genetics are gonna be completely wiped off the map because I'm a helpless woman whose only purpose in life is to make your babies."

Jack made a disgusted sound and let go of her. "I said I'd teach you to use a sword, not have sex with you."

Blaze's mouth fell open at how easily he said that. Fury bubbling up from within, she snarled, "And then you went on to say, 'I'm gonna teach you to use the sword, Blaze, but don't ever try to use it when it really counts. Just go have fun with make-believe while I go fight your real battles for you.'"

He glared at her. "I didn't say that."

"Yes," Blaze said, "You *did*."

Bristling, Jack turned and started walking back to the house. Over his shoulder, he said, "I'll be inside, when you come to your senses."

"I think I'll sleep in the barn!" Blaze shouted back.

"You *do* that," Jack returned. "Maybe your friend will come back, give you a chance to show him how macho you are!" Jack stomped up the steps and slammed the door behind him, making the window-panes rattle.

Blaze glared at the back door until the sounds of animals in the yard once more brought her attention to the gate she had left open in her blind panic. She shooed the animals back inside, then shut it behind her and went to collect the bowl of bones.

When she stood up, the tiny man was there again, watching her. Closer this time, squatting under a spruce.

"Fuck *off*!" Blaze screamed, waving her arm in the general direction of the forest, scattering chickens and goats.

Then, without waiting to see what he did, she turned her back on him and went to the gate.

Jack was already on the porch, giving the woods a concerned look. "He come back?" he asked, as she walked up to him. Blaze brushed past him, set the bowl of bones inside the house, then started walking towards one of her 4-wheelers.

"Where are you going?" Jack demanded.

"Going to make a phone call," Blaze said. She got on a 4-wheeler and started it.

"Now hold on a second," Jack cried, coming to stand in front of the machine. "What's going on? I said I'd teach you the sword. What form you want? I'm a master in dozens. I've studied in Japan, China, Egypt, Turkey, Germany, Spain, Italy…You looking for fencing or just wanna hack at stuff with something big? Katana or rapier? Shield and long-sword or a couple of cutlasses? Kenjutsu or San Cai Jian? You wanna use a dao or a gladius? A claymore or a falchion? What?" He looked desperate, and a bit scared.

Blaze looked him in the eye and said, "I want a gun."

Jack flinched. "Why's that?"

"A gun is faster," she said sweetly. She formed an L with thumb and forefinger, pointed it at his forehead, and said, "Bang."

Jack narrowed his eyes. "A gun doesn't do much against a were," he said. "Works well enough against a fey, but good luck getting them to hold still for it."

"I think I'll go for silver bullets," Blaze said, gunning the engine. "And a machine gun."

Jack jumped out of the way, but grabbed onto the back tie-down bar as she passed and dug his feet into the dirt.

Blaze found herself sitting immobile, the machine spinning all four tires and flinging soil everywhere.

"We," Jack grunted, over the roar of the engine, "Need to have a sit-down chat, you and I."

Blaze grabbed a hammer off the front cargo bin, swiveled, and slammed the head into Jack's fingers. Jack swore and released the 4-wheeler, which suddenly lunged forward, and Blaze, with only one hand on the handlebars, accidentally pulled it sideways, and the machine hit the side, rolled, threw her off the seat, and ended up on its side, pinning her body under a tire.

A few seconds later, Jack walked up, sucking on his knuckles, glaring at her.

Blaze, who had been unable to push the thing off of her, and was finding it hard to breathe, just glowered up at him.

Jack took the machine in one hand, lifted it, still sucking on his knuckles, and set it right-side up beside her. Scowling, he bent and offered a palm, lips still wrapped around his other hand.

Blaze accepted his grip, reluctantly, and struggled to her feet. Her lower half felt like she'd just taken a beating with two-by-fours, and she was pretty sure her ankle was sprained.

Jack peered up at her with a long look, which Blaze returned, glaring down at him, and the silence was only marred by the still-running engine.

"You know," Jack finally said, "For something that is half draft horse, you've got the stubborn streak of a mule. What kind of gun you want?"

"A .45 Long Colt, a .308 NATO AR-10 Armalite, a Desert Eagle fitted for .50 caliber Action Express, and an AK-47."

If he was surprised that she was able to rattle off makes and calibers, he didn't show it. "You know your guns," he said simply.

Still holding his gaze steady, she said, "I also want a bullet press, bullets, steel jackets, a dozen cases of brass, extra lead, a crucible, powder, silver ingots, and silver nitrate."

He stiffened at the last two. "You really know your guns," he said softly.

"My father was a wealthy gun snob, among other things," Blaze said. "Some of it rubbed off." He'd gone shooting at least three times a week, and Blaze had often tagged along.

Jack gestured at the lodge. "What about what you brought? I saw some rifle cases on that last grocery run. Those won't work?"

"Not for what I'm gonna need them for," Blaze said. "I brought a couple shotguns, a few bolt-action hunting rifles, and an antique muzzleloader my dad gave me before he died. I can use the shotguns, but I'm going to have to re-pack the ammo. I'm thinking silver and steel buckshot." She cocked her head at him. "The fey *are* allergic to steel, aren't they?"

Jack was looking pale. "It's as poisonous to them as silver is to a were. Steel and iron."

"So yeah," Blaze said. "A ton of steel bearings. And a metal mold, to make some silver beads." She smiled. "Oh, and a ballistics table and a scale, so I can get the weight measurements right."

"Uh," Jack said, "I don't mind the steel, honey, but no offense, but I'm not letting you anywhere near me with silver nitrate."

Blaze snorted. "I'm not gonna shoot *you* with it."

"No?" Jack said. "And what about your little friend out there, when he slices your hamstrings and takes the gun from you?" Then he gestured in a southerly direction. "Or Amber, when she catches you alone and rips it out of your hands?"

"I thought you said you took care of Amber," Blaze growled. "So if she's taken care of, and we're *not* going to be attacked by werewolves, what's the problem with me carrying something to defend myself?"

"It could *kill* me, that's what," Jack snapped.

"So?" Blaze asked. "You can 'sputch' me where you're standing. Just twist off my head and throw it across the yard."

Jack glared at her. "I'm not going to do that."

"Then you should trust I'm not going to pepper you with silver buckshot." Blaze started back towards the 4-wheeler.

Jack grabbed her hand. "No."

Blaze stopped and turned, scowling down at his grip, which held her like a vice, then up at him. "*No?*"

"You've already got guns," he insisted. "Pull them out and use those. Load your shotguns with buckshot and blast the little bastard next time he shows up. Leave the silver out of it."

"Let go of me," Blaze growled.

"No," he said. "No goddamn silver. That stuff is…" He hesitated, gave a slight shudder. "If you had any idea how much it *hurts*, even a stray flake getting caught on the skin, you wouldn't even be considering it."

"I said I wouldn't pelt you with the stuff," Blaze bit out. "What's the problem?"

"Look," Jack said softly, holding her gaze with his green eyes, "I like you, but I don't trust you." When Blaze frowned at him, he added, "I'm old. Hell, *ancient*. And I didn't get that way by trusting someone with something like that. You wanna bring a bullet press and all the goodies out here and make your own steel-core bullets, that's fine. No silver."

"We have forty werewolves for neighbors," Blaze growled, "And you said yourself they were gonna run out of food and go looking for greener pastures, probably to the north. We're north."

"I said no," Jack said stubbornly. "I see that shit anywhere near this place, it's all going in the river. Guns, press, bullets, everything. I'm dead serious about this. No silver."

Blaze glared at him, then reluctantly hobbled over to the 4-wheeler and switched the engine off. "Fine." She started towards the porch. "I hurt like hell and I'm going to bed. Lock the chickens up when you come in, okay?" She had limped twenty feet before Jack threw his shoulder under her arm and gave her some support. "Thanks," she said, honestly grateful for the reprieve.

"You break anything?" Jack asked, giving her legs a worried look as they walked. "It landed right on top of you."

"Bent my knee backwards a little bit," Blaze said. "Think it sprained an ankle. My hips are aching from where the tire landed on them. Other than that, though, I think I'll be fine."

"I can get you some help if you need it," Jack suggested.

Blaze snorted. "And pay the hospital fees when they MedEvac my ass to Anchorage?" She shook her head. "I quit my job with the state. No insurance. Something like that, it'd use up the funds we need to get ready for next summer."

"Oh," Jack said, as they reached the steps and climbed across the porch. "Well, I was kind of thinking of a more locally-produced home remedy."

Blaze laughed. "Like what? Cranberry wine? Spruce needle vodka?"

He licked his lips as they stepped inside the threshold. "Well, there's some whiskey in it. And some root beer."

Blaze hurt. A lot. It was only then starting to sink in, as he helped her to her bed. "Well," she said, "Frankly, I feel run over. A little alcohol might help."

Jack helped her to her bed and eased her under the covers. "Okay, hold tight a minute. I'll be right back."

Blaze lay back against the wall, staring at the ceiling, wondering what the hell she had been thinking. She probably *should* take the flight to Anchorage. She'd heard of internal bleeding from things like this, and her hips were throbbing like someone was raking coals across the bones.

What Jack brought back smelled like watered down root-beer, with a faint splash of whiskey, and it had odd berries and spruce-needles and what looked like tree bark floating in it. She sniffed at it, giving it a dubious look.

"Drink it," Jack muttered.

She gave it a tentative sip. Blaze grunted when the first taste made her arms go tingly. "Holy crap," she said, looking at it. "What *is* this?"

"Somethin' I learned a long time ago," Jack said. "Drink up."

And Blaze did. The effect was almost instantaneous. "Wow," she cried, staring at the pieces of bark and berries in the bottom of the cup. "We need to figure out how to package that up and sell it."

Jack bristled. "I'd rather not."

"Screw the hunting lodge," Blaze said, amazed at how suddenly revived she felt. "We could get rich bottling that stuff. What's in it?"

"It's a secret recipe. I'm not sharing it with anyone."

She raised an eyebrow at him, then shook the contents of the bottom of the cup at him. "It's not so hard to figure out." She picked out an unripe cranberry, held it up. "See?" She squished it, tasted the bitter green juice, and winced. She dug through the bottom. "Birch bark, spruce needles, some tree fungus, moss...Yep, I could make this." She looked up at him, grinning. "You really need to work on your clandestine potion-making skills."

"I suppose I will," he growled. "You feel better or not?"

"Feel great," Blaze said.

"Good," Jack growled, taking the cup from her. "Stop over-analyzing everything all the time." He turned and stalked out, leaving Blaze feeling blissfully warm and tingly.

Wow, she thought, as she closed her eyes and started to fade, *That's some really potent whiskey.*

FIFTEEN

Jack's Adoring Fans

The adult Jersey Giant chickens didn't lay eggs the first day. Which, Blaze knew, wasn't surprising, considering their sudden new change of habitat. This left Jack to drag the goat carcass out of the fridge and finish it off in front of her, while she picked at a bowl of cereal she had put together from what remained of the jug of milk that Jack had chugged that night.

Even having seen it several times before, Blaze had to stop and gawk at how much Jack ate. Looking at him, and looking at the goat he had picked clean, Blaze didn't think that she could fit that much meat on a *plate*, let alone in her stomach. She once again thought about the werewolves and how they were devastating the landscape.

"How did you survive all that time?" Blaze asked, watching him. "There must've been times when you ran outta food."

Jack flinched. Too slowly, he said, "I went hunting."

"You mean you *never* went hungry?" Considering how much he ate, she found that hard to believe.

He cracked a rib bone in half, started sucking out the marrow. "Let's just say that the people hated weres for a reason. We get hungry, we get...cranky." He threw the bone aside, picked up another. "A starving were is about the closest thing to an honest-to-god hell-hound that I can think of, and it eats everything in sight."

"Even people."

Jack stiffened, then immediately tried to hide his reaction by nonchalantly picking meat from his teeth with a talon.

"You ate people, didn't you?" Blaze asked.

Jack grimaced and glanced out the window at the yard. "We should probably go open up the barn, let the animals out."

"*Did* you?" Blaze demanded.

He gave her a flat, irritated look. "That's none of your damn business."

"I'm living with you," Blaze growled. "I think it's my business."

"It won't happen again."

"So you *did*!" Blaze cried. She took a step backwards, appalled.

Scowling, now, he growled, "You get that hungry, you don't really think straight."

"And the wolves?" Blaze asked. "Is that what we're gonna be dealing with this winter, when they start heading to greener pastures?"

Jack grimaced. "I'm hoping that Amber was smart enough to set up contacts in town, get meat shipped out to her." Then he sighed and shrugged. "But maybe."

A cold feeling started worming its way through Blaze's veins. She found herself really, really wanting some silver nitrate. Jack's threat, however, had left no room for misunderstanding—he saw it, it was going to disappear, along with all her guns, gun packing materials, and ammunition.

"So when did you eat people?" Blaze asked.

Jack's body tensed, every muscle going taut. "I really don't want to talk about it." He stood up, grabbing the goat carcass. "I'm gonna be outside, working on the greenhouse. You wanna come help, that'd be nice." He hesitated and looked back at her. "Could always use some help with the designs, right?"

Blaze smiled, despite herself. "Sure."

To her surprise, Jack didn't seem at all fazed by all the exotic ideas she had had and wanted to try. She detailed them out, from a small single-story greenhouse that incorporated rabbit hutches to an extensive two-story generator-powered setup with pigs, cows, and chickens on the upper story, their excrement washed down through gunnels by a sprinkler system where it hit a vat, fermented, created methane to run the generator, and then was fed through a hydroponics system directly to the roots of the plants she was trying to grow.

They decided on a big two-story setup, generator-lit through the winter, irrigated, insulated, and heated, with space for trees to grow up through catwalks above, the catwalks themselves filled with places to plant tomatoes, peppers, and vining plants, with rabbit cages and nest boxes hanging underneath. They staked out the thirty-by-eighty base for the greenhouse directly over the spot where they'd planted the feather, and Blaze might have imagined it, but she almost thought she felt a tingle when she walked directly over its hiding place. That gave her a little thrill of anticipation, as she considered what Jack had told her it would do to her plants.

And then they built it. Blaze was amazed at how easily Jack seemed to put her different ideas together into a cohesive whole. "We're gonna need insulated glass," Jack said, once they had the frame up. "That's gonna be the expensive part."

Blaze, who hadn't considered that part, winced. "How expensive?"

"That much glass?" He considered. "Probably sixty thousand. If you got a bulk discount."

Blaze cringed.

Looking at her, Jack shrugged. "But we can cover it with Visqueen until we've got the money for glass, grow stuff through the summer months until we can make it permanent."

"Let's do that," Blaze managed.

They got the rolls of Visqueen and a dozen tomato plants shipped out the next day, and between the two of them, they managed to get the massive rolls of plastic stretched over the frame in a day of tugging, pulling, cursing, and struggling with the breeze.

"I'm rapidly becoming Bruce's best client," Blaze muttered when they were finished, eying the greenhouse. Her plans were to use it to keep the lodge supplied in fruits and veggies, instead of having to hire a plane to fly groceries out twice a month. She needed something permanent—the area routinely had six or more feet of snow accumulate during the winter, which would shred the flimsy plastic—but Visqueen would have to do for now.

Jack gave an unconcerned shrug and took another slug of his root beer. He'd taken his shirt off again, though he still wore the chainmail tunic and his sword. "I saw some boxes of seeds in the first supply runs," he offered.

Thinking about planting the greenhouse, Blaze got a thrill. She quickly curbed the instinct, though. "It's the first week of August. We'd never get anything to develop by the first frost in September." She had been planning to start the seeds that winter, in the big sunny windows of the front prow of the lodge.

Jack winked at her. "Trust me. You'll want to plant them now."

"Right in the *ground*?" Blaze demanded.

"Hell, you should call those friends of yours, get some trees and stuff sent out. Whatcha like? Grapes? Apples? Mangoes?"

The thought of growing mangoes in Alaska left Blaze utterly flabbergasted. All she could say was, "We didn't insulate it."

"Winter might give 'em a bit of a jolt," Jack agreed. "But I'll bet you anything they survive."

She turned to face him, suddenly wondering just how much a *blacksmith* knew about *gardening*. She squinted at him. "You didn't grow your own food much, did you?"

He slugged his root beer, then crushed the can and cracked the top on another. "All the damn time." He grinned at her. "Told you, honey, you've got a secret weapon." At first, Blaze thought he was talking about himself, but then he gestured at the greenhouse and the feather buried underneath.

A magic feather…

Curious to see just how *wars* could be fought over something like that, Blaze humored him. They planted about a dozen different varieties each of tomatoes, peppers, melons, and cucumbers, planted a twelve-by-twelve area of nothing but herbs, and hired yet another charter to bring out a load of exotic fruit trees that Blaze had ordered through one of her friends in town.

By now, news had once again spread—Blaze was pretty sure that someone at Bruce Rogers' charter service knew someone out on the Yentna—and the neighbors had stopped by to watch the process, the most polite pretending to need to borrow this wrench or that before they stopped to stare, while the rest just stopped to stare.

Jennie Mae Hunderson, the owner of the Ebony Creek Lodge, was the loudest amongst the starers. "You think you're gonna get *mango* trees to grow in *Alaska*?"

"Got the soil tested," Blaze said. "It's supposed to be pretty good."

Jennie Mae scoffed. "But *mango* trees?"

"And avocados," Blaze agreed.

"You're wasting your time," Jennie Mae laughed. "I have trouble getting my *cucumbers* to grow. I get a single, fist-sized watermelon a year, if I'm lucky."

"She's got a green thumb," Jack growled. It was the first time he'd spoken since the neighbors started to show up, and Blaze could tell he was not enjoying the company.

Jennie Mae peered at him. "And what you doin' dressin' up like that for, Jack Thornton?" The way she said it, she was a disapproving aunt. She gestured to the sheath he carried slung over his back. "You gonna protect those pigs from bears with a sword?"

More chuckles from the spectators.

"This whole thing is ridiculous," Jennie Mae said, seemingly powered by the crowd around her. She gestured to the greenhouse, the barn, the livestock. "Who keeps pigs in the woods? Everyone knows the bears'll get 'em. You're just flushing your money down the toilet, girl."

The low rumble in Jack's chest was hopefully only audible to Blaze, who was standing right beside him. Bearing his teeth, he said, "People used to raise pigs in the woods all the time, before they started depending on some huge factory to raise them in crates, who then sends 'em to a slaughterhouse that kills a thousand of 'em in an hour for their bland, barely-edible 'meat.'"

Jennie Mae didn't take the hint. "And *yaks*?" she sneered. "This is America, not Mongolia."

Blaze thought she saw the first bit of hackles sprouting on Jack's back, and Blaze quickly stepped in front of him and said, "I did some research on hardy livestock for out here. Stuff that doesn't eat much, can withstand the cold, and has lots of uses other than just meat. Yaks and goats topped the list. Can't hurt to try, right? I'll invite you all over when we butcher our first one in the fall. Should taste a lot like bison."

"You're gonna *eat* them?" The way the woman said it, Blaze had just suggested they all eat maggots. Blaze flushed, suddenly feeling every eye on her, suddenly acutely aware of her awkward body and the amused scorn in their faces.

I must look like a retarded giant, Blaze realized, miserable.

"All right," Jack snapped, slamming the shovel into the dirt, "I'm sure you all have something better to do than stand around on someone else's land, gawking at them like a bunch of fucking idiots. Get the hell lost."

Jennie Mae gave them an almost smug look before she turned and stalked off, taking the neighborhood with her.

"That wasn't very nice," Blaze muttered, watching the last of their backs disappear around the shop. "I want to be friends with those people." To be truthful, however, she was relieved they were gone.

Jack snorted and picked up the shovel again. "They were being rude."

They finished planting the trees that evening and went up on the catwalks to sit and watch the plants grow. Once they got to a reasonable height, Blaze thought she would introduce chickens, to see if they would help control pests like aphids and chickweed. The rabbits were already in the hutches, their manure falling at the bases of the new trees.

"You think this is gonna work?" Blaze asked, listening to the rustle of rabbits and the mulling of animals outside, feeling her first real pangs of anxiety about her whole plan.

"You need this stuff for the lodge, right?" Jack asked. The needy look in his eyes added, *And your pet wereverine?* He had, she'd noticed to her dismay, taken quite a liking to goat.

"Yeah…" Blaze said tentatively. "Barging food out here is so expensive…" Guy Meyers, the man who ran the barging service, didn't even *make* enough barge trips to cover that kind of food bill. Not to mention what it would cost to *buy* it.

"So we make it work," Jack said. And that was the end of the discussion.

That night, while feeding the chickens, Blaze saw the tiny fey man again. He was standing at one end of the greenhouse, examining the door curiously. He pried it open just enough to look inside.

"Hey!" Blaze snapped.

The tiny man jumped, his braids gleaming iridescent green-purple as they swung in the sunlight. He backed up, drawing his sword. In the sunlight, it almost appeared to be a very long, very thin shard of milk-glass, cloudy, but not too cloudy to be opaque. Then, glancing nervously behind him, he suddenly flashed out of existence.

"This is *my property*!" Blaze shouted. "I see you again, I'm going to pepper you with steel buckshot, you thieving little bastard, you got that?!"

If the fey man heard or cared, he made no sound.

Cursing, Blaze strode back to the lodge, went into the room, and started unpacking her shotgun from the case.

"You see him again?" Jack asked, coming to lean against her doorjamb, watching her.

"Was sniffing around the greenhouse," Blaze muttered. "I see him again, I'm gonna give him something to think about." She started jamming buckshot cartridges into the chamber, then slammed the pump, loading a round.

"Just so you know," Jack said, "You shoot a fey with buckshot, you're looking to start a war."

"What, it doesn't matter that the thieving bastard's snooping on my property and already stole your sword?" Blaze demanded.

Jack gave a dismissive shrug. "They take pride in that sort of thing. It's like a rite of passage for most of the tribes."

"So what you're telling me," Blaze growled, "Is that I'm supposed to just stand around while some adolescent critter snoops out my treasures and takes what he wants?"

Jack scratched at his scalp, then examined the results. "Fey have a really good case of A.D.D.. I've been hoping he would get bored." Then he frowned. "It's actually strange he's still sticking around. That was like, what, three weeks ago?" He peered at her quizzically. "You didn't tell him what we've got, did you?"

Blaze winced. "I told him you said it would make stuff grow."

Sighing, Jack said, "Probably not the smartest thing you ever did. The fey thrive on that sort of stuff."

"I thought he was *you*," Blaze growled.

"So you just randomly told *me* something that I told *you* because apparently I have these gaping holes in my memory that needed refreshing?" Jack raised his eyebrows, waiting.

Muttering, shotgun in hand, Blaze pushed past him.

"Where are you going?" Jack demanded.

"To start a war." Blaze yanked the door open, stepped out onto the porch, and slammed the portal shut behind her. She crossed the yard, let herself into the barn, climbed the stairs, and sat in the open window, watching the yard, shotgun resting in the crook of her elbow.

Around midnight, Jack came out on the porch and called up to her, "You plannin' on sleepin' tonight?"

Blaze waved him off.

Heaving a huge sigh audible even to her perch in the barn, Jack went back inside the house. Sometime after that, Blaze dozed off.

She woke to the sound of a scream and wood splintering.

Blaze jerked awake, frowning at the lodge. Had she imagined it? Seconds ticked by, and all she heard were strange, low thumps, seemingly coming from the basement. In the yard below her, the animals were huddled together against the barn, almost climbing over each other in their attempt to get closer to the middle of the pile.

Then something huge and furry came hurtling through the back door of the lodge, Jack fully transformed, sword in hand, only an instant behind it.

Oh my God, Blaze thought, her body suddenly electrified with adrenaline, *That was a werewolf.*

Five more followed the wereverine, rushing through the door in a flood from behind. Jack, almost half their mass when fully transformed, nonetheless kept them at bay, his ebony blade flashing like the Void in the hazy Alaskan half-light of early morning. He gutted the one on the ground, gruesomely slicing the main body in half and kicking it, still twitching, apart before whirling on the next. His movements were almost too fast to see, and Blaze found herself quailing unconsciously into the barn at the feral, beastly screams that were ripping across the yard from both wolf and wereverine alike.

He cut down three others, his blade sliding through heads, torsos, and hips as easy as if he'd been cutting through water. Where the three died, however, their bodies still fighting well past the point where a human should have bled out, there were six more to take their place.

The lodge was *crawling* with them, Blaze realized, horrified. She saw them on the roof, circling around from the front, coming out of the shop…

I've got to help him, Blaze thought, watching Jack slip and take a werewolf's claws across his chest, before cutting off the offending limb. He was completely encircled, the only thing keeping the much bigger creatures off of him being the light-eating flash of his sword.

Heart thundering, Blaze took aim with the shotgun and pulled the trigger.

A couple of the werewolves nearest her roared and swung around to face her.

Jack's sword took them in the backs, cutting cleanly through the first, but getting stuck halfway through the second.

That was his mistake. As Blaze watched, a dozen werewolves rushed him, throwing him away from his weapon, pinning him to the ground. As Jack struggled to reach something on his belt, a big silvery-white wolf stepped on his hand and drew it herself.

Oh no, Blaze thought, seeing the liquid blackness swirling from the blade's tip. It was bringing back a strange memory, something about a hole in the ground…

"So, Jack," Amber's voice sneered. The woman stood up, and Blaze saw that one half of her face was showing nothing but bone and sinew. "I thought maybe you'd appreciate dying by your own weapon." As she examined the twisted black blade, Jack struggled and snarled amidst the werewolves holding him.

That's his dagger, Blaze realized, her heart lodging in her throat. *The one that raises the dead.*

Hands trembling, she cocked the shotgun again, aimed for the pile of werewolves, and pulled the trigger.

The werewolves broke in confusion as the buckshot peppered them, and it gave Jack just enough freedom to slip free. His eyes glowing like green embers, now, he ripped the head off of the nearest wolf and threw it across the yard. Blaze re-cocked the gun and aimed it at another cluster of werewolves, then fired. In the chaos that followed, werewolves attacked werewolves and Jack was able to down another two of the brutes with his bare hands, ripping one's jaws completely open and exposing the skull inside, and stepping on the neck of another while yanking the legs upward, tearing the head free before throwing the body into the woodpile. Blaze picked another likely cluster, cocked the gun, and pulled the trigger.

Amber's head came up, pinpointing her in the barn window. "Go kill the bitch!" she snarled, wiping specks of blood from her chest and forearms where the buckshot had penetrated.

Two gray wolves immediately turned and headed for the barn, inhumanly-fast.

Jack saw the two headed for Blaze's hiding-place and was turning to intercept when Amber stabbed him in the gut.

"Enjoy *that*, you bastard," the werewolf said, looking into Jack's startled eyes before she pulled the black dagger free. "Spent a long time thinking about where I'd stick you before I decided on the gut." Amber smiled, baring her long white fangs as Jack started to thrash and scream, holding his abdomen. "Should take you a *good* long time to die." Where the blade had punctured, an eerie blackness was spreading outward, exposing his organs within.

Seeing that, Blaze's heart gave a painful shudder. Fear and adrenaline and made a fiery mixture in her veins, and suddenly it was all she could do to breathe, her very lungs feeling as if they were filled with searing gas, not air.

Amber kicked Jack off of his feet, then turned and started walking back towards the lodge. "We'll make this the new den," she heard Amber say to the cluster of wolves following her. "Enough food here for a couple weeks."

She's going to take my farm, Blaze thought, rage beginning to add its own caustic fire to her limbs. *She just killed Jack and she's taking my farm.*

Her heart began a concussive explosive rhythm in her chest, and Blaze thought she smelled the acrid scent of wood smoke.

What were they burning? Her lodge? Her shop? Her barn? A dozen different possibilities raged through her mind, and it was the last straw. It left a rising, indignant fury boiling up from within, and Blaze fired another couple shots at the werewolves in the yard, pumping and pulling the trigger until she ran out of rounds.

Then two werewolves were throwing open the doors of the barn and seeking a way into the loft. Powered by adrenaline and fury, Blaze jumped down through the window and started running, fire burning through her veins in searing, painful arcs.

She heard the werewolves thunder into the loft, heard their snarls of rage when they saw her running across the yard, toward the gas shed, felt the *thumps* as their great bodies hit the ground behind her—much too close—and started after her.

Blaze was running as fast as she could, but feeling them gain distance at inhuman speed, instinctive, terrified panic flipped some sort of switch in her brain. Her fear dissolved, suddenly, and she slowed to a stop. She felt the adrenaline within her body sizzle her blood and bones, and smelled the scent of smoke, all around her. A moment later, the werewolves were on her, and Blaze's world exploded into a wash of pain and searing, throbbing agony.

SIXTEEN

Tears for Jack

Blaze woke up cold, trembling from head to toe, her body wracked with shivers. She groaned and tried to pull a blanket over her, but then felt the oddly warm, fluffy texture under her skin shift, her hand sliding against stones and pebbles. Frowning, she opened her eyes.

She was naked, lying in a circular bed of ash in the middle of the back yard.

Blaze started up quickly, heart hammering over the low whine of mosquitoes. The light was starting to lighten the sky again, probably around three or four in the morning. She racked her brain, trying to remember what had happened the night before. The werewolves had set something on fire, and the fire had spread…

Even as she thought of it, her eyes caught on two charred humanoid shapes, a few yards away. She saw bones through the blackened gristle. Immediately, she looked to the gas shed, expecting to see the roof blown off, the forest on fire.

The shed was intact.

It was then that Blaze noticed the small, childlike shape crouched on one knee a few feet away, his arm to his chest, his head pointing at the ground, his body facing her. Laid out on the ground in front of him was Jack's sword. Blaze blinked, wondering if she was imagining things.

A low moan from across the yard caught her attention and she turned.

Jack was laying in the driveway, clutching his gut, whimpering. *He's still alive*, she thought, horrified. Blaze got up and ran to him. The fey man stayed where he was, motionless, as she hurried past him and knelt beside the wereverine.

"Jack?" Blaze asked, shaking him.

Jack whimpered, his face deathly pale. His eyes were shut, his face sweating.

"Jack!" Blaze snapped.

"He's unconscious, Lady," the fey man said softly. "The dread horn is killing him."

"Get the *fuck* off my land!" Blaze snarled, twisting on him.

The fey man's eyes widened and, biting his lip, he got up and flickered out of existence, leaving the sword where it was.

"Jack," Blaze growled, lifting his head off of the ground, peering into his face. After a moment of watching the wereverine's eyes twitch behind the lids, she realized that the fey man was right. He was whining in his sleep. She lowered his head gently and reached for the wereverine's hand. With some effort, she managed to pry it from his stomach.

Underneath, she could see the white gleam of ribcage and spine.

"Oh my God," Blaze gasped, scooting backwards, staring at the grotesque wound. By every medical fact she knew, he *should* have been dead. "Jack?" she whispered.

The wereverine didn't answer her. His upper body was trembling, but his legs were absolutely still.

It's severed the spine, Blaze thought, horrified. At the same time, the stench of the wound hit her, the smell of rancid meat. Seeing the slow pulsing of his discolored organs inside his chest, Blaze's stomach clamped. She rolled to the side and retched into the gravelly yard, though her stomach could bring up nothing but bile.

Once she'd regained control of her guts, Blaze backed out of reach of the smell and frantically tried to remember the concoction that Jack had made for her.

Grow up, a part of her sneered. *Root beer and whiskey and some woodland herbs aren't going to heal something like that. He's dead, tootz.*

But then, she thought stubbornly, it had healed a sprained ankle and possibly a cracked hip.

But twigs and berries? a part of her demanded. *Come on.*

She bit her lip as tears of shame and anguish threatened to boil up from within. *He can't be dead*, a selfish part of her whimpered, desperate. *I just found him.* She had spent her whole life searching for someone who could look up into her eyes and not feel insecure, and now that she had, he was dying in front of her, obviously in horrible pain, all due to her own stupidity. Granted, while not insecure, he was crass, abrasive, and rude, and it took a hell of a lot of patience to put up with him, but she was still more than willing to see where they could go from here. She felt more tears stinging her eyes, biting like acid, as well as the first tug of exhaustion that always followed. *No*, she gritted, *this is* not *the time to start crying*. She blinked and wiped her face on her forearm, trying desperately to collect herself before she could wind up helpless again.

She knew Jack was dead. No one could survive a wound like that. Yet, even as she watched him moan in agony, miserable, unable to ease his suffering, something was telling her she had to help him. Some subconscious voice was telling her she needed to act fast…

…but to do what?

Thinking back on Jack's draught, she tried to imagine what could have been so powerful about the random woodland herbs he had deposited in the drink. The more she thought about it, the more she realized the wereverine *had* to have put something else in it. It had tasted so watered down…

Blaze's breath caught. *He used the feather.* The way he had been so vehement about not putting it in her animals' water…A new hope searing up from deep within her, Blaze scooted forward to touch the wereverine's face. His forehead was ice cold, yet doused with sweat.

She got up quickly and rushed to find a shovel, pausing just long enough to take in the fluffy bowl of ash she had woken in before continuing to the shop. *Ash*, she thought, something twingeing in her brain. Her father had said he'd found her in a bed of ash. She had a brief moment where she felt two synapses trying to connect, then, *No way. No fucking way.* The werewolves had been playing with fire, that was all.

Inside the shop, leaning against the wall, she grabbed two shovels. When she came out, she slammed one into the dirt outside the shop and shouted, "I've got a deal for you, you thieving little shit!" Nothing happened. Jack continued to groan on the ground. Desperation raising the pitch of her voice, Blaze shouted, "I know you're out there! I have a deal for you! Can't resist a good deal, can you?"

For a moment, it seemed as if the fey man would not answer. Then, almost reluctantly, he seemed to walk out of her woodpile, only a few feet away.

Seeing him, Blaze held out a shovel. "What's your name?"

The fey flinched, eyes on the spade. For a long moment, it looked like he wouldn't speak. Then, softly, he said, "Runt, Milady."

"Help me dig something up, Runt, and it's yours after I'm done with it."

The man's liquid brown eyes widened and he licked his lips, looking in both directions. "You would *give* it to me?" He said it in an awed whisper.

That damn thing is just as valuable as Jack said it was, Blaze thought bitterly. She saw her dreams of having a farm in the Bush go up in smoke, but she knew she didn't have a choice. "My friend is dying. His life for the feather."

The little fey man glanced at the dying wereverine, then licked his lips again. "I already took one thing that didn't belong to me. The elders made me return it. If I show up with an artifact like *that*..."

Frustrated that they weren't *digging*, Blaze threw a shovel at the ground in front of him. "I don't have *time* for this shit. You help me, or don't, but I need to go get that feather." Without waiting to see what he would do, she stalked off towards the greenhouse.

Behind her, she heard a shovel gingerly slide off the ground, and soft footsteps, following.

Blaze yanked the greenhouse door open and found the spot where she and Jack had 'planted' the feather. It was in the new addition, a second, connected structure that Jack had insisted on adding after her lesson on Manual Labor 101. Tomato seedlings—only a couple days old—had already sprouted and were working on their third set of leaves. Blaze tilled them aside, her bare foot aching on the shovel as she rammed it home.

I'm naked, she thought, ridiculously. *I'm naked and I'm digging in the dirt for a feather while somebody's* dying *on my doorstep and I'm not even going to go get pants on and call the cops. I'm gonna dig in the damn dirt until my feet bleed.*

Oh, man, the lawyers were gonna have a field day with this one.

If she lived that long.

The fey came up beside her and tentatively stuck the shovel into the dirt beside hers. He set his soft-booted foot on the spade, and, though he grimaced at the steel head, started to dig.

It took about an hour of fast digging. Blaze eventually broke down had to go inside and get boots and clothes after the first ten minutes of wearing her soles bloody. When the first tinges of the feather showed in the bottom of the pit, however, the little fey didn't dart it and grab it, as Blaze had half-expected. Instead, his eyes went slightly wide, but he quickly looked away.

Blaze jumped in, pulled the feather free, and ran inside to get a glass of water. When she came back outside, the fey was nowhere to be seen.

"How do I make this work?!" Blaze shouted at the empty yard, holding the glowing, flaming length in one hand, the glass of water in the other. She held it up, waiting for some sort of guidance. The last thing she wanted to do was to put the feather out.

The woods remained silent, and it was obvious she was not going to get further help from the fey. Furious, Blaze dipped the feather into the glass.

The fiery glow continued to writhe and swirl around the feathery tendrils even underwater. Like it was made of pure sunlight.

Not knowing what else to do, Blaze held the feather there for over a minute, determined to get a stronger brew. Then she pulled it out and tossed it to the ground. "There you go, you little prick. Take it and get the hell out of here." She didn't wait to see the fey man blink in and snatch the feather, just knelt beside the wereverine and lifted his head.

"Okay, asshole," Blaze said, prying his mouth open, "Drink this." She poured a dribble into Jack's open mouth. The wereverine coughed, sputtered, and swallowed.

Blaze thought she saw the color of his organs flash orange, followed by a more healthy wave of natural flesh-toned shades before the wound faded to black once more.

"Try dribbling some on the wound," the fey suggested. He was standing behind her, holding the feather in both hands like a sacred treasure.

"Aren't you gone yet?" Blaze growled, but she did as he suggested. She got the same result. A golden flash—like liquid sunshine—that overpowered the black before the magic of the dagger once more overcame it.

Blaze used up her first cup of water and went back for a milk jug. Yanking the feather back out of the fey's hand, she dunked it inside and for several minutes watched its fiery tendrils twist and curl in the liquid, completely unaffected by the water in the jug. The fey made no objections, and Blaze thought that if he had argued at that point, she would have gone for his throat with her bare hands.

At the sound of a long, agonized moan from Jack, Blaze pulled the feather out and began sloshing water from the jug into his wound.

It bubbled and hissed and steamed, but the blackness refused to fade.

Blaze tried two more jugs, force-feeding Jack one of them, pouring the rest into the cavity of his abdomen, before she realized it wasn't going to do any good. Whatever the horn was, it was stronger than the feather's magic, and the size of his wound was growing.

"Lady," the fey man said softly.

"Go away," Blaze whimpered, bringing her knees to her chin, watching Jack in silence.

She wasn't going to be able to help him. There was no miracle cure, no way to bring him back from the depths. She was going to watch him die, and there was nothing she could do about it.

The more she sat there, brooding over it, the more Jack began to moan with the agony, and the more Blaze realized that there was really only one thing left that she *could* do—she needed to put him out of his misery.

Another low groan, this time part whimper, escaped his pasty-white lips.

Steeling herself, Blaze got up and back at the yard, looking for the shotgun. She found it, melted into a rock-studded puddle, in the ash.

Blaze stared at the ruined weapon for some time before slowly setting it down in the gray powder and peering at it from a distance. Then, feeling as if she were in a dream, she went into the lodge for a rifle.

When she came back, Jack's breath was coming in tiny pants. Blaze tucked a cartridge into the chamber, then slammed the bolt home, her eyes burning.

"Sorry," she whimpered, aiming the gun at him. She was crying, now, tears dripping down her cheeks, hitting the ground by his body. She tried to squeeze the trigger, but found that all she could think about, looking into his too-pale face, was the way he had thought she was sexy, when no other man would.

This is all my fault.

He had tried to protect her—he had saved her *life*—and it had gotten him killed.

Gasping, Blaze dropped to her knees beside Jack, her finger leaving the trigger.

Her whole world was crumbling around her. As the guilt started to twist at her innards, wrenching more tears from within, she realized she should have listened to all the people that snickered behind their hands when she dove into excited conversations about sustainable farming in the Alaskan Bush. What did she know about running a business in the woods? She was a rich city brat, not a Bushrat.

The few times she'd set foot in the Bush before stepping off of Bruce's plane, she had been on a chartered fishing trip with her father, led around by the hand by two well-paid guides, sleeping in well-appointed cabins rented for the purpose, ushered around in luxury river boats, and deposited back in Anchorage before the week was up. And the renaissance fair? She only had some vague contact in Washington, insisting that if she could create the right place, he could dredge up the right people. She'd trusted him on his word alone, and had poured hundreds of thousands of dollars into finding a suitable place to meet all her goals. She had been stupid, and stubborn, holding onto her dream even after she realized that the people in the wilds around the Yentna River weren't what they appeared.

Her grandmother, in her innocence, had said it best…

A woman? Running a fishing lodge? Why, who would pay for that?

Blaze's chest was a tangle of hurt, self-pity, and loss. She felt like she had had her dream in her palm, had actually *grasped* it and held it close, only to have it break into a thousand pieces and scatter to the winds. She felt tears stinging her eyes like hot, caustic acid, and flung them from her face in bitter violence. As she did, the fey man jerked away from her with a look of horror.

"I told you to take the feather," Blaze told him. "It's yours. Just get the hell off my land and don't come back."

He cringed, but didn't move. He almost looked like he expected her to raise the gun, aim it at his nearest pointy ear, and pull the trigger.

She glanced at Jack, whose breathing had seemed to go strangely calm.

He's close, she thought, tears welling up again. She bit her lip and looked away as her eyes stung like hot coals. She blinked, and they fell into the ground near the fey man's feet. He jerked, eyes fixed on the place where they had fallen, then looked up at her, wide-eyed. Seeing her face, he stumbled away from her like she suddenly had sprouted horns.

Blaze rubbed her forearm across eyes and wiped it on her pant leg, but the burning in her eyes continued. Already, the exhaustion was unfurling in her chest, pushing outward like a void swallowing the flames of the sun, leaving her numb. "Look," she said, trying to keep her words from cracking apart, "I'm new here, and the guy who was helping me figure all this out is over there dying in my yard, and there's not a medic in the world who could help him. I'm about a fraction of an inch from taking this damn gun and blowing my own brain tissue all over the place. If you could please just get off my land and leave me in peace, I'd really appreciate it." She sniffled again, and again, she caught the tiny Athabascan man staring up at her face in horror.

Like I'm a ten-foot-tall monster, Blaze thought. She felt tears threatening again, and reached up to brush them away.

"You can't!" the fey man cried, arm flung out like he meant to stop her.

Blaze hesitated.

Seeing that she had paused, the fey man swallowed, hard, and looked in all directions. Then he began babbling nervously and started fumbling with the pouches on his belt. He found a tiny blue vial, uncorked it, and dumped out the contents on the ground. Then Runt was kneeling beside her, holding the tiny blue jug under her face. "If you would allow…" he whispered, his words tinged with awe. Then, his hands moving like lightning, he began catching her tears.

It was so ridiculous, so utterly beyond her comprehension, that Blaze just watched him do it, grateful for the company. She closed her eyes and cried for Jack, for herself, for her father and mother, for the critically endangered breeds she had failed to give a home, for the pretty greenhouse she was going to leave to rot in the woods…

When she was done and opened her eyes, the fey man was still there, looking at her with anxious concern. He reached up, slowly, and when she didn't stop him, he carefully wiped the rim of the jug against each of her bottom eyelids, then capped the contents and handed it to her. "Your tears, Lady," he whispered, his voice soft with what almost sounded like respect.

Looking down at the thing, Blaze had to squash the sudden urge to hurl it across the lawn. "Thanks," she managed, though she didn't know what she was thankful for. She felt utterly spent, every ounce of energy wept from her body, her limbs barely even functioning enough to hold her upright.

As thoroughly as she always did when she cried, she felt *exhausted.*

It was all she could do to keep from slumping over right there in the yard and close her eyes. A few yards off, she heard Jack moaning, his body jerking against the gravel. *I'm sorry,* Blaze thought, as her awareness even then started to fade. *I can't help you.*

Runt glanced nervously at the Sleeping Lady. "Do you need to sleep?"

How could he know? Blaze thought. She had always gotten so extremely tired after crying—so much so that her over-protective parents had often taken her to the Emergency Room whenever she'd experienced a particularly painful heartbreak—and until now, her adrenaline had been thrumming through her veins, its fire keeping her conscious. Now her exhaustion was all hitting at once, and suddenly she wasn't sure she could even make it to the house.

Fist wrapped around the tiny blue jar, Blaze started crawling to the back door. Somehow, she made it onto the mattress, and was grateful when the fey man flipped the blankets over her and tucked them around her gently. Like a sleep-deprived narcoleptic, Blaze slid into oblivion immediately.

She never felt the little fey man take the vial from her open hand.

SEVENTEEN

Stocking Up

Blaze woke up the next morning feeling about as bone-tired as she had felt falling asleep that night, except maybe more so. She groaned and flipped the blankets off of her. She peered at the open door, frowning at the yellow cast to the trees through the far window. The golden color was such that she had either slept very little—which was what she felt like—or much too late—which was what the sinking feeling in her gut was telling her.

After one of her particularly bad crying spells, she'd fallen into a near-coma for five days afterwards, and nothing the panicked doctors had done had dragged her out of her stupor. Judging by the loud mewling of the farm animals outside her window, she guessed that they were missing a meal…

…or three.

Reluctantly, she crawled out of bed. Jack's sword was propped into a corner of her room, in its intricately-tooled sheath. After taking a moment to try and remember how it had gotten there—and how she had fallen asleep—Blaze slipped on her shoes and went outside.

She'd always had trouble with sleep. A random native medicine woman had stopped her in the streets of Anchorage, on one of Blaze's quick shoes-shopping trips in the Northway Mall in between classes, and had told her that the doctors weren't going to find a cure, and oh yeah, while you're at the mall, you should invest in an extra-large swimsuit and spend more time sunbathing, getting that all-important Vitamin D. This had been back in her late teens, when she'd been struggling with heartbreak and class deadlines, and the random three-day comas were wreaking general havoc on her grades. The native lady's prediction had come true the next morning, when the CAT-scan results had come in the mail: Negative. Absolutely nothing wrong with her. Oh, and by the way, here's a twenty-thousand-dollar bill for your dad. Thank you, do come again.

Outside the lodge, the ground was soaked, the grass covered with glistening moisture, probably from the dark thunderclouds that were even then sweeping to the northeast. The air smelled of rain, and there were puddles in the yard.

Blaze went to the barn and started feeding her animals, carefully ignoring the corpse lying in her driveway beside the shop. She was walking back, past the greenhouse, when she noticed color inside that hadn't been there before. Frowning, she opened the door and peeked inside.

The tomato and pepper seeds that she and Jack had planted were already three inches high, and sprouting their fourth and fifth leaves. The hole she and Runt had dug in the center of the greenhouse had been filled in, the shovels removed, the seedlings re-planted.

And the trees were flowering.

Blaze stared at them, sure she would have remembered flower buds, when Bruce had dragged them out of his plane. Further, it looked like the branches had spread out, the trunks a good half inch thicker than when she had collapsed in her bed.

How many days was I asleep? Blaze thought, horrified. She remembered the five-day comas of her youth and swallowed hard.

Blaze shut the door, too early in the morning with too little coffee to think about that. Finally, deciding she had to face the inevitable, she turned towards Jack. Upon seeing his hair and clothes soaked by the storm, lying in a puddle of runoff from the roof, she grimaced.

She hadn't even bothered to pull his corpse out of the rain. She'd just crawled to *bed*.

She lowered her head in misery, taking a moment to collect herself. She had two options. She could call the police and try to explain to them why there was a man with a half-rotted hole in his gut in the middle of her yard, wearing ripped-up chainmail, and then spend the rest of her life in jail. Or she could try to get rid of the evidence and *maybe* save her farm from werewolves. Half of her wanted to call the police. But, reluctantly, she picked up the shovel from where it leaned against the greenhouse. It was her fucking farm, damn it, and she wasn't going to let one sexy little corpse get in the way of that.

She wondered if the authorities would even come looking for Jack, considering he probably hadn't registered in any of their systems. Hell, in all likelihood, he hadn't even acquired a drivers' license. *Could* he, if he was illiterate? Still, the neighbors would know who he was, and where he had last been seen, and it could probably get ugly pretty fast, especially if they brought out cadaver-sniffing dogs...

Which made her glance around the yard, looking for the other bodies. She had been sure she had seen at least seven or eight before she'd checked out. Had the werewolves come back to claim their losses? Or did their bodies disintegrate over time, and she was just panicking for nothing?

Yet she couldn't leave a body lying out in the middle of her backyard, waiting to test that theory. What she decided to tell the authorities afterwards, she could decide later. Right now, she needed to get it out of sight before Jennie Mae Hunderson came over to borrow a dozen eggs and gawk at her yaks.

Blaze went and got the 4-wheeler, hitched it to the trailer, then backed it up to the wereverine's corpse.

When she reached down to pick him up, however, Blaze was stunned to find the wereverine's wrist was still warm. When she put a hand on his chest, she realized he was still breathing, his torn chainmail shirt rising and falling in even breaths, a certain rosiness to his waterlogged face. She fell to a crouch beside his rain-matted head, frowning. "You're *alive*?"

Blaze pulled Jack's hand away from his stomach—she actually had to fight him, this time, so strong was his resistance—and was stunned to find the hole in his abdomen closing, the blackness gone, leaving just healthy muscle and organs throbbing in its place. She stared down at the wound, utterly sure that she *should* have been examining a dead body.

Staring at Jack's face, she managed, "You stubborn, lucky shit."

She didn't know much more about magic than what she had overheard in those brief snippets of snickering Dungeons and Dragons nerd-fests in passing between the fridge and her room in between writing business papers, but she could have *sworn* that the feather hadn't worked.

Yet she was looking at pretty convincing evidence that it had.

Change in plans, Blaze thought, looking at the 4-wheeler. She had to get him *inside*....All four hundred and fifty pounds of his heavy ass.

She went into the shop and pulled out the little wheely-thingie that Jack had used to crawl underneath the big machinery to do his repairs. Lining the path between the wereverine and the door with boards, she settled the wheely-cart on the boards and began the frustrating task of rolling the wereverine onto the roller.

She had to grunt and strain for every inch. He was unnaturally heavy, like he carried lead in his bones. Four hundred and fifty pounds was a low estimate. For his part, instead of doing anything to aid the process, the wereverine had once again slapped his hand over his wound and held it there, eyes shut, groaning.

Well, at least he's not mauling me for the effort, Blaze thought, tugging him over the cart as best as she could. It was a struggle. She had to rope him down, just to keep the weight of his legs from pulling him back off the cart.

Once Blaze had finally gotten him up the ramp she'd made over the porch steps, she paused to catch her breath. Panting down at Jack, she cried, "Why do you *weigh* so much?"

"Depends on who you ask."

Blaze cried out and turned.

The fey man was standing behind her, giving Jack a disgusted look. "You ask him, he will tell you it is because he is carrying the magic of the moon in his blood. And it is true, moon magic is heavy. Just look at the tides." The tiny man gestured to the west.

Blaze struggled to remember what had happened the night before. The man was named Runt, she remembered. But why was he still hanging around?

"But," Runt said, "if you ask the Folk, it's because they carry their demons within them."

Blaze's eyebrows went up. "Demons?"

"Surely you've seen the beast," Runt offered.

Blaze remembered the slitted eyes and the hypodermic teeth. "That thing's a *demon*?"

"Not in the Christian sense," Runt said quickly. "Consider it more of a possession from the Third Lands. A supernatural entry-way created by the creatures' bite, that gives the Unmentionables access to the victim's body. The younger ones are usually controlled by it. They get small-minded and violent and dangerous and generally take on the personality that possessed them from the Third Lands. The older ones..." He looked down at the wereverine. "Well, sometimes the possessed becomes the possessor."

"You think he's *possessed*?" Blaze cried.

Runt gave her a wry look. "You can see why it is not a popular theory amongst the moon-blooded."

"He said it was just a magical plague, of sorts." The thought that Jack was possessed was making her uncomfortable.

"Well, there is magic to it," Runt said. "The Third Lands are ruled by moon magic—bathed in it, even. It is a place that is locked in perpetual darkness, the light of the moon taking center stage in the sky, never moving. Everything there is similar to the plants and animals we have here, but more...vicious...and most are desperate to leave."

"So they possess people?"

Runt shrugged. "It is the only way for a Third Lands creature to withstand the light of the sun. They need the body of a First Lands creature to protect them, otherwise they will simply turn to dust."

"Like a vampire."

Runt winced. "Yes, actually. A vampire is a very good example of a Third Lands creature that has found passage into the world. Probably a great magus who opened a portal." He looked back down at Jack and shrugged. "The rest, though…They're not willing to take that chance. They opened a gate, but they sent an animal through, instead, one that was linked to their own blood, trained to bite only humans. When the animal bit and deposited the moon-magic in a victim's system, they and all of their kin suddenly have access to the body, so it's usually snatched up immediately."

Blaze thought of Amber's ice-blue eyes as she sank her teeth into her shoulder, remembered the oozing silver liquid as it hit the ground beneath her. "So how long does it take to show symptoms?" she asked softly.

"Of possession?" Runt shrugged. "A few minutes to a couple hours. With so few of the demonkin still passing on the plague, every opening is fought for." He glanced again at the wereverine. "Like I said. The Third Landers are desperate."

Blaze was about to ask 'why,' then she remembered the otherworldly thing that Jack transformed into when he was angry. She looked at the wereverine, sleeping peacefully on the willow mat. She tried to imagine a world filled with those creatures, where the light of the sun was only a myth, and her gut clenched.

"I would have let him die," Runt continued, following her gaze, "But you looked as if you wanted very much to see him live."

"I did," Blaze admitted.

"I admit that I broke a rule of my people," Runt said, his words coming out hesitant. "The Second Landers have no love of the Third Landers, and would like to see the Unmentionables' plague stopped for good, because it upsets the balance."

She glanced at him warily, once again beginning to get the sense of a malignant voice recording. "What does that mean?"

"It means, Lady," Runt said, "That if you value my life, you will not tell the feylords I helped him survive."

"Feylords." Blaze snorted and waved a dismissive hand. "Yeah, I think we're safe from that."

Runt bowed again. "Then you have my gratitude." And just like that, he was gone again. Probably once more spying on her from afar.

Blaze was beginning to understand why Jack had claimed to hate the meddling little bastards. The irritating shit had stood around watching for hours as she struggled with Jack's body, then popped in just long enough to spout irrelevant nonsense that only served to creep her out, then disappeared again, making no offer to help her get the wereverine the rest of the way inside.

Though, Blaze decided reluctantly, *If he healed Jack like he said he did, I guess I can't begrudge him a few hours dragging the ornery old prick around.* In fact, she probably owed him a pretty big favor, and if anything she knew about the fey was actually true, that was a Very Bad thing. She got a sick taste in her mouth when she wondered when he was going to try and collect.

Blaze spent the next hour trying to hoist the wereverine's roller-cart up and over the doorway and into the lodge. She got him as far as the foyer before Blaze realized that it would be about ten times easier to move the *bed* to *him*, and she went and got a mattress and slapped it down inside the basement door. Then it was a struggle to roll the wereverine onto it, and when he fell, belly-down, all but crushing the mattress to the floor, Blaze decided not to attempt the frustrating task of trying to flip him back over. She waited just long enough to make sure he was still breathing, then stalked back to her room, grabbed her best rifle and a box of shells, and went to the 4-wheeler.

In light of recent events—and the fact that Jack couldn't stop her—she needed to make a phone call.

Blaze took the long, winding trail to Jack's home at a breakneck pace, trying to fight down that little fear-instinct that something inhuman could be on the trail behind her, catching up. She came to a stop in the grassy driveway outside Jack's house and her breath caught.

While the wereverine's home was fashioned solely of logs, it was much bigger than a cabin, with many extra rooms and additions that made it both fanciful and unique. Its entire makeup screamed of craftsmanship, from the river-stone chimney to the little cobbles leading up to the front porch. It was a beautiful work of art.

...It was also completely destroyed.

Blaze switched off the engine, her heart pounding. Through the smashed-in door, she could see that the cabin had been utterly wrecked, with pillow stuffing and food packaging littering the porch and surrounding yard. Slowly, warily, she got off the machine and started toward the front porch.

Claw-marks raked the logs and furniture, and just about every usable material in the building had been dismantled, spread across the living room and yard in tiny pieces. The hides and wall-hangings were shredded. There was a huge, gaping hole in the floor, almost like something had fallen through. The entire place smelled strongly of urine.

Grimacing, Blaze briefly took another look at the hole in the floor. A bit startled, she realized that the edges of the hole were precisely cut, and that there were still the remnants of hinges on what had used to be a door. Some sort of root-cellar, then?

She went to the generator house, first. The fuel canisters were missing, the batteries cracked and leaking acid onto the wooden planks. The generator had been ripped asunder, its pieces spread in metal fragments across the shed. She avoided them gingerly as she stepped into the shed.

Though she wasn't a mechanic, she was pretty sure that what was left of Jack's generator and battery system wasn't useable.

Cursing, Blaze stepped back outside, aiming for the house. Inside, the phone was in several pieces against the far wall, shards of white plastic from its impact still embedded in the logs. When she stepped up to the gaping hole in the floor, however, Blaze began to get a tingle of dread.

She found a pack of matches amidst a pile of piss-smelling glass and ruined cookware that had been thrown into a pile in the corner. Matchbook in hand, she started down the steps into to the hole in the living-room and struck a flame.

The tiny light was just enough for her to see that the interior of the hole was rather spacious; maybe sixteen feet in any direction. Racks and hooks and display cases covered every spare inch of surface space—all empty, smashed or overturned. The whole room was utterly cleaned out.

Remembering the black void-titan sword, his scaly black armor, and the darkness-dribbling black dagger, comparing them to the dozens upon dozens of vacant weapons' racks scattered around the room, Blaze suddenly felt like throwing up. She stepped back up out of the darkness feeling as if she'd been hit by a freight train.

We are in so much trouble. Blaze once again considered chartering a flight back to Anchorage, and then after that, somewhere in the Bahamas. Maybe she could wait on tables for tourists and completely forget that there were werewolves and Thunderbirds and other nasty critters that liked to tear each other apart up in the Land of the Midnight Sun.

But if she left, then Jack really *was* going to die. And she was at least partially to blame for this. Hell, *mostly* to blame.

Who are you kidding, Blaze? He was talking about enchanted weapons and armor. *You don't need to be a D&D nerd to know that's gonna screw with your world. Hell, he had a dagger that could create* necrosis. *Oh, and did we mention* raise the dead*?*

Then, remembering the wolves' conversations about her animals, Blaze realized, *They're probably going to sell them for food.*

And if they sold Jack's swords, Blaze didn't have enough money to get them back.

But that is exactly what she knew was going to happen. She was a Business major. It was basic numbers. Amber had to keep her little 'den' stocked with food somehow or her precious 'family' was going to revolt, which means she needed to find the cash to buy herself the equivalent of a cow every day or two. Blaze's lips twisted as she remembered the squatter atmosphere of the werewolf den, the drunken brawls and drugs. If what she had seen was any indication, the werewolves weren't really working for a living.

That's why she needed to get those weapons back *now*, before the wolves had the chance to pawn them off to tourists on the streets of Anchorage. Throwing her rifle over her shoulder, she went back to the 4-wheeler and started it up.

It was time she visited the neighbors.

• • •

"So whatcha need silver ingots for out in the woods?" Jennie Mae asked, once Blaze put down the phone. If she felt at all awkward that she had been shamelessly listening to Blaze's phone call, she didn't mention it.

"Haven't you been listening to the news?" Blaze asked, swinging her rifle back over her shoulder. "The economy's on the verge of collapse. Silver and gold are about the only things that are still stable."

Jennie Mae grimaced. "Ain't that the truth." The woman peered up at her. "You really gonna eat yaks?"

"When the government comes crashing down around us?" Blaze said. "Yeah, I'm pretty sure I'll eat yak."

Which launched Jennie Mae into a dissertation on the current dismal state of the U.S. government, and how nobody in Washington seemed willing to make any changes, and how the economy was being run by a bunch of crooks. "They're just lining their pockets with *our* money," Jennie Mae growled, and nobody's got the balls to stop 'em. "All those earmarks and pork...You listen to Limbaugh? He's got the whole nation in an uproar about that predator control stuff. Federal government's trying to step in, when what we *really* need to do is kick all them wildlife cops out and start managing it ourselves. Leave it to the men and women who *live* here, not some office worker in Anchorage. Mother Nature's got cycles, and those dumb bureaucrats back in Washington don't have the first clue about how to 'manage' our resources. Can you believe it? The *federal government* trying to take over Fish and Game? Like we don't even own our own damn state anymore..."

Blaze listened as long as she could, making polite nods here and there, but eventually she began to itch to get back home to check on the wereverine. The Ebony Creek Lodge was a beautiful place with plenty of exposed wood and a nice homey feel, but Blaze kept seeing the wrecked insides of Jack's cabin, knowing that if she didn't do something soon, sooner or later, the wolves would do the same here.

"I hate to do this to you," Blaze interrupted after a pause in Jennie Mae's tirade, "But I've really gotta go get back to the lodge. I left Jack to watch the lodge, and he's got about as much interest in it as a caterpillar's got earholes."

At mention of Jack, Jennie Mae's face darkened. "Don't know why you had to go hire that man. He's a rude, ornery jerk. No offense, but most of the neighbors are hoping some hydraulics fail and he guts himself on a tractor blade."

Blaze grimaced at that idea. "I'm the one running the bulldozer."

"Well, you get the idea," Jennie Mae said, stepping to the door, but not opening it. "He's a bastard. Nobody likes him."

"He gets the job done," Blaze said, trying to fight the bristling impulse to tell the woman to get out of her way. "Anyhow, I gotta get going." She gestured meaningfully at the door.

Jennie Mae didn't take the hint. "You know, Blaze, he may be good at swinging a hammer, but my boy Ralphie could do the same thing. You need a mechanic, well, Ralphie's been learning everything his dad knows. Works for cheap, too."

Because it was obvious the woman wasn't going to let her out of the lodge without either continuing the conversation or Blaze shoving her over, Blaze said, "How old is he?"

"Thirteen," Jennie Mae beamed. "And he already rebuilt his own four-wheeler. It's that one, out there," she said, pointing through one of the many enormous windows of the lodge.

The 4-wheeler in question had a lift-kit that put it approximately four feet off of the ground, with a set of steps to climb into the driver's seat. The front was completely covered in a truck-sized cow-catcher—just in case it slammed into a moose, of course—and the whole vehicle was painted a nice, shiny black. It also looked ready to tip over the moment it went around a sharp corner.

"Wooow," Blaze said, biting down her wince. "That's really...big!"

"Did it himself," Jennie Mae beamed. "My boy can do anything he puts his mind to."

"I can see that," Blaze said. "Well, I'll have to keep that in mind."

That seemed to satisfy Jennie Mae, because, smiling and nodding, she yanked the door open, saying, "You do that, you do that. We'll see you again soon, Miss Blaze."

She said her goodbyes quickly and made a hasty departure, stepping out onto the porch where Jennie Mae's two big Great Danes were curled on either side of the door. They lunged to their feet and growled, hackles bristling, as she tried to pass. Blaze came up short, eying the feral look in their faces nervously.

"Must be the smell of Jack on you," Jennie Mae offered, pulling the dogs inside. "He's gay, you know."

Blaze almost tripped over herself, choking. "*Gay?*" She had a brief stab of fear, remembering the way the wereverine had brandished the wine between them like a shield, and wondered if *that* was why Jack had tripped all over himself the next morning, offering marriage vows.

"Sure is," the portly woman insisted. "I arranged for twelve different girls to go have dinner with him over the years—*nice* girls, too, ones who were working at the lodge for the summer—and he just sat there and insulted them until they left in tears." The big dogs, still growling, only reluctantly allowed the loud, round woman to drag them inside the lodge. "Said the last one had buckteeth and a Ben Franklin forehead, and asked her where the *donkey* was in her family tree. Can you believe that?"

"Oh," Blaze said, letting her breath out between her teeth in relief, "That explains it."

"Uh huh," Jennie Mae said, nodding. Shutting the door behind her, Jennie Mae said, "Besides, that Jack Thornton gives Duke and Daisy fits, and dogs *know*. That man ain't no good, I'm telling you." She gestured at the mutant 4-wheeler. "You just give my Ralphie a call. He'll help you out."

"I'll do that," Blaze said, finally realizing why Jack, out of all the people on the river, didn't have a dog—and why he had stalwartly refused to let her have one to guard her stock.

She took the 4-wheeler back on the dirt path down the riverbank from the Ebony Creek Lodge and back through the woods to the Sleeping Lady at speeds she normally wouldn't have felt comfortable with, except now, with the idea of a werewolf running along behind her, wasn't fast enough. *Could* werewolves flit in and out of view, or was that just the fey? Blaze kept checking over her shoulder, keeping the machine at a breakneck speed, paranoid they could do just that.

She slid to a stop in the gravel driveway behind the Sleeping Lady and jumped off the 4-wheeler, her back prickling with that anxious feeling of being watched, though Blaze couldn't tell if that was just her nerves or an *actual* feeling of being watched. She had about as much ESP sensitivity as a kiln-fired brick.

Rifle in her hands, Blaze began walking around her property, assessing the damage to her lodge. Overall, she was relieved. The werewolves hadn't ripped the place up as badly as Jack's cabin, and she had an irritated feeling that it was because they had planned to use it as their home base. A few walls in the basement floor were busted, and the woodstove was slightly crooked on the spark-catcher where something big had slammed into it, leaving burnt fur on the iron. Her animals, for the most part, were alive, though she would have to buy more yaks.

Later. Once she got the wolf problem under control.

Oh yeah? a part of her demanded. *And just what are you gonna* do *there, girlie? You're dealing with* werewolves, *or had you forgotten?*

Blaze's fingers tightened on the rifle. So what if they had a dagger that could make a person's flesh rot? They were *not* taking her dream from her.

And yet, all the woodsy experience Blaze had ever had had come from hunting trips with her father. What was she going to do...go to their camp and start picking them off until they figured out where she was hiding and gutted her? Hell, in all her father's hunting trips, Blaze didn't even have the stomach for gutting her own kill. A fault in the extreme, to most serious hunters, who considered it a lack of respect for the animal. So, to avoid having to see the requisite blood and gore—and withstand the disapproval afterwards—Blaze had simply started to make excuses whenever her father scheduled his yearly hunting trips, explaining how *busy* her Econ class had gotten, or gee, that's sad…her Government Club had already planned a trip to Juneau that week to meet with the state reps on important student issues, and she just *couldn't* afford to miss the talks about technology funding and teen pregnancy. Sorry, Dad.

It was one of the many things she had begun to regret in her life. Not only had she given up perfectly good life experience, but she'd seen that much less of her old man before he finally kicked the bucket.

Sounds like you blew that one, tootz, Jack's irritating drawl said in the back of her mind. *So whatcha gonna do 'bout it?*

Shoot them, for one. While Blaze didn't really have the stomach for gore, she had spent enough time with her dad packing ammunition and sighting-in rifles that she had a pretty damn good idea how to put a good-sized dent in the werewolf numbers. If, of course, the legends—and Jack's irrational fear of silver—were to be believed.

The question was, of course, whether or not they would catch her before she thinned out the herd.

…and whether the Alaska State Troopers would come investigate all the shooting.

Have to make myself a silencer, she noted. It was easy enough. A milk jug packed with insulation would do the trick.

What Blaze *really* wondered, though, is whether or not she could go through with it. She could melt silver and load ammunition from now until the End of Days, but the first time she pulled the trigger and saw someone fall, was she going to lose her nerve?

The full consequences of her plan hit her, then, and she just about dropped her rifle in the dirt, right then. And what the hell was she *thinking*? She had trouble killing *moose*, and here she thought she could just traipse around killing *people?*

She just didn't have the stomach for gore. Hell, the one time her dad had forced her to clean her own fish, she had puked all over herself and gone into something akin to shock. It had been one of the times her parents had shipped her to the Emergency Room, too, earning her a place on the not-so-hallowed list of patients whose symptoms were 'self-induced.'

As in, she was a rich brat who did it for attention.

Yet she had to do something. The wereverine was down for the count, and she had absolutely no idea when Amber's pack would be back, looking to finish the job.

She realized the elf was watching her from behind her barn. Upon seeing her, he reluctantly stepped into view. "You should go back to where you came from," he said in his stiff, stilted English. "The moon-kin will be back. Maybe not tonight, but soon. This is their territory, now. They laid claim when they defeated the wolverine."

For the first time, Blaze felt a rush of viciousness surge up in a rising fury. "This is *my* land," she growled. "They step on *my* land, I'm gonna show 'em a few things about modern warfare."

Runt gave her a dubious look up and down. "How?" he finally asked. What he left unsaid was, "You may be twelve feet tall and have boots big enough to crush a hippopotamus, but you don't even know how to use a compass."

Blaze smiled, gaining some nerve in the fact that the little fey man obviously thought she was insane. After all, she had twenty-five years of practice in having people look at her like she was some sort of alien. "Silver bullets, silver buckshot, silver nitrate hollow point, a colloidal silver sprinkler system…Stuff like that. They step on my land again, they're gonna be wishing they hadn't."

"Oh," Runt said. He glanced at the Sleeping Lady Lodge, then back at her and shrugged. "Well, it's your grave you be digging." Then he turned and did his annoying little fey thing, vanishing into thin air, leaving Blaze with a whole new wave of goosebumps trickling down her back.

EIGHTEEN

The Third-Lander Within

On August 28th, Blaze was pulling her very first ripe tomato off of its vine, staring down at it in flabbergasted awe, when Runt came running inside the greenhouse, wide-eyed, hand clutched protectively around a growing bruise around his throat. "The demonkin is awake. He's asking for you."

As if on cue, from the open lodge door, she heard a load roar of, "*Blaaaaaaaaaaaaaaaze*!"

He probably smelled the silver. Blaze unconcernedly began walking down the greenhouse aisles, checking on her rabbits. They had bred like, well, rabbits. Even now, the cages were overflowing with all of them, and it had only been three weeks since the greenhouse had been constructed.

"Blaaaaaaaaaaaaaaaaaaaaaaaaaaaaze!" the wereverine roared again. The Visqueen vibrated with the anger in his voice. Blaze opened a cage to change the water-dish.

Runt glanced over his shoulder nervously. "I shouldn't be here." And then *poof*, the little bastard was gone, leaving her to deal with the wereverine on her lonesome.

Blaze had been rehearsing for this. She knew the wereverine wasn't going to take kindly to her use of silver, so she'd taken great pains to place little pockets of silver ammunition, silver nitrate, colloidal silver, and silver ingots wherever she could think to stash them. This time, she had no intention of going anywhere unarmed.

The heavy weight of the Desert Eagles bouncing against her hip giving her comfort—even then chambered with alternating silver slugs and silver nitrate hollow-points—she continued unhurriedly meandering through her greenhouse, listening to the wereverine rant.

When something heavy went hurling into a wall, however, Blaze paused at a poblano plant with a frown. Sure enough, she heard another roar, and something else went flying into another room with a crash.

"Oh God damn it," Blaze growled, throwing aside the pepper and rushing to exit the greenhouse.

Inside, Jack was still lying in bed, but both the heavy rough-hewn chair that Blaze had been using while monitoring his condition and the rough wooden bench beside his head were both scattered pieces down the hall. He was in the process of lifting the coat-rack, hefting it over his shoulder, aiming at the pile of broken furniture down the hall. "Blaaaaaaaaa—"

Blaze grabbed the coat-rack and yanked it from his hands, surprised she could do so.

Jack turned, startled. When he moved, it was only with his upper body. His legs and abdomen remained more or less motionless.

"What the *hell* do you want?" Blaze snapped, slamming the coat-rack down, well out of reach.

Jack sniffed, his eyes going to the holster on her belt, but he surprised her by whining, "Food. Please." There was a feralness to his eyes that was disturbing, like he was on the very edge of losing control.

And, if what Runt had told her was true, that was not something that Blaze wanted to see.

"I can make you some eggs," she said. "The hens started laying."

Jack whimpered. He collapsed back to the bed, shaking.

"Not enough?" Blaze asked, more than a little unnerved by the way his body seemed to be shrinking before her eyes.

"The Unmentionable is waking up," Runt commented beside her. "It's been asleep for three weeks. It's hungry."

Seeing Jack's musculature shriveling like a concentration camp victim starving on time-lapse video, Blaze dropped her tomato and ran for the barn. She hauled a goat to the back door, put a Desert Eagle to its head, and was about to put a silver bullet in its brain when Runt's translucent blade flickered from its sheath and cut the animal across the neck.

Blaze winced, realizing she had been about to feed Jack silver nitrate.

She tucked her gun back into its holster. Then, picking up the limp, bleeding form, she carried it into the room.

Jack's body was fully changed, his slitted eyes glowing an otherworldly emerald green. As soon as he saw her, he let out an animal snarl and his big claws started ripping chunks out of the wall and floor as he tried to pull himself out of bed, towards her.

Keeping her distance, not knowing what else to do, Blaze threw the dead goat at him.

The wereverine dismembered it, ate it all, and resumed snarling, reaching for her legs. The way he was panting, teeth bared, green eyes feral, Blaze knew that if he got hold of her, she would not survive the experience. She scooted backwards out of the lodge, listening to the wereverine's animal snarls from the porch outside.

Biting her lip, she went to get more goats.

It took six more of the beasts, several turkeys, and a couple dozen rabbits—all consumed head, hair, feet, and all—before the wereverine's chest-rattling growl began to quiet and his head went limp against the mattress, claws still dug into the floor in his attempts to get closer to her. She heard snores.

Relieved, Blaze started to take a step towards him, to check his vitals.

Runt's hand suddenly appeared on her stomach, stopping her. "The Unmentionables are a crafty breed," the fey man said, watching the wereverine closely. "The creatures of the Third Lands are almost all predators, and very smart."

Blaze scowled down at the tiny dark-skinned man. "Why are you hanging around?" she demanded, impatient. "He's asleep."

The fey removed his hand and shrugged. "Very well. Like I said before. It's your grave you be digging." He stepped back, gesturing impudently for her to continue.

This time, though, Blaze hesitated. She watched the wereverine sleep for several minutes, trying to judge the authenticity of his snores. They seemed a bit too...calculated. Or was that her imagination? Surely the damn thing wasn't *baiting* her. That was just paranoid.

...Wasn't it?

Uncertain, Blaze watched Jack sleep for much longer than she thought necessary, a bit unsettled by the way the fey was hanging around a few feet behind her like some kid eager to watch a fox rip apart a rabbit.

After a bit, Jack's snores cut off abruptly with a chuckle. The wereverine's head came up, his hypodermic teeth exposed in a malicious smile. He started snarling again, digging at the floorboards once more. Only his legs, like dead logs attached to his hips, kept his now-skinny arms from pulling his way towards her.

Blaze stumbled backwards, stunned. The fucker had been trying to *eat* her.

"It's like I said," Runt said, lips twisted in disgust as they watched the insane motions of the wereverine on the mattress. "There is no telling how long he might stay like this. He was unconscious for three weeks. A demonkin starved that long..." He hesitated, liquid-brown eyes fixed on the wereverine's mindless animal movements. "It might be a mercy to kill him."

Blaze narrowed her eyes. "More goats."

She fed him fourteen meat goats before the Third Lander's appetite finally began to wane. Watching his inhuman jaws expand to take down huge portions of meat and bones he by all rights should not have been able to swallow, it was all Blaze could do not to be sick.

"Where is he keeping all of that food?" she whispered, watching the wereverine as he forced the last of a goat's haunches into his mouth.

Runt shrugged. "He feeds the beast." The fey seemed to be finding the helpless wereverine amusing enough not to flicker in and out of sight, and was instead staying rather close by, though never attempting to help her with anything. The little dweeb.

Then, when the wereverine snarled another inhuman scream at them and again began trying to drag himself across the floor, towards them, Runt's eyes narrowed. "Or the beast feeds itself."

"What's wrong with his legs?" Blaze asked, nervously. She knew that the wereverine's paralyzed lower half was probably the only reason she wasn't already in his gut.

"The dread horn's necromancy ate away his spine," Runt said. He didn't sound too upset about the fact. Blaze wondered just what kind of relationship the wereverine had maintained with the fey in his area. So far, Runt had seemed willing to help…but not *too* much.

"I thought you said you healed him," Blaze said.

The fey's eyes flickered towards her too quickly, then he just nodded. "I did. However, my magic is warring against the dread horn's, and we have yet to see which will be the victor."

Seeing them standing there, talking about him, the wereverine screamed in impotent rage and hurled a boot at them from where they were stacked against the wall.

Runt dodged it easily.

"Is he paralyzed, then?" Blaze asked.

"Time will tell," Runt said. "The Unmentionables give their victims untold regenerative capability, and phoe—" he hesitated and looked up at her, clearing his throat and blushing. "The magics I used are the most powerful healing energy known in the Five Realms, but there is no greater breed of necromancy than the dread unicorn. That he survived at all is a miracle."

The wereverine hurled another boot, screaming his rage.

"Well," Runt amended, his face souring. "That he survived is definitely interesting."

"What is wrong with him?" Blaze demanded. "We fed him. There's enough gore covering the walls of this place to paint a slaughterhouse. What happened to Jack?"

Again, the fey shrugged. "Jack could be dead." With the amount of feeling he gave his words, he might as well have been talking about the last mosquito that landed on Blaze's arm.

Blaze turned on him, heart giving an extra thump. "What?"

For a moment, the little fey man got the look he always did when he was considering whether or not to blow her off and just disappear. Then, with a sigh, he said, "When the beast within him woke, it began to consume everything in its hunger." Runt shrugged. "It is possible that you didn't feed him in time and he died." Again, he sounded as if he cared as much about Jack's demise as he did about a bothersome insect.

Blaze remembered the terrified look Jack had given her, the pleading in his voice, the way he had curled into a ball and started to shake as his body began to shrivel.

"He's alive," Blaze said, with more conviction than she actually had.

"Mayhap," Runt said, noncommittally. "But if you leave him down here in the basement like this, he might cause problems if Jack is indeed deceased. Especially if you have visitors." Then he turned, and Blaze knew that, now he had dropped *that* particular bomb, he was about to disappear, the responsibility on *her* shoulders.

"Wait!" Blaze cried. "Do you have a better idea?"

Runt paused and glanced back at her, then at the wereverine. He pursed his lips. "The demonkin Jack and my elders will already be upset that I helped you..." The way he trailed off at the end and looked up at her expectantly, however, left Blaze realizing he wanted to make some sort of trade.

"What do you want?" Blaze demanded, taking a lesson from Jack and being too tired to deal with fey bullshit to beat around the bush.

The little man licked his lips and glanced out the door, as if he was worried someone else might overhear. Then, like an excited child trying very hard to hide his anticipation, he leaned closer and Blaze had to lower her head to hear him say, "More of your tears."

Blaze straightened, squinting at him. "That's *it*?" she demanded.

His eyes widened and he cleared his throat and feigned boredom. "Uh, yes. That's all. Just a few more tears. Nothing really important."

She scowled at him, remembering the little blue jar that had disappeared. "What are you doing with them?"

The sudden red-faced shame on his face was all Blaze needed. The little bastard was probably using them in love potions or some bullshit like that. He licked his lips again, then looked like he was going to do his Houdini routine anyway.

"Never mind," Blaze barked. "I don't care what you use them for." Then she hesitated, remembering Jack's 'rules' and how the fey could take that to mean something completely different than she had intended. "I mean, I *do* care, but you're not using them to hurt anyone?"

The tiny fey blinked up at her. "How could I?" He seemed thoroughly perplexed.

And Blaze certainly wasn't about to start giving the little bastard ideas. "Fine," she said. "Help me take care of *that*," she gestured at the insane wereverine, "and we'll figure out a way to get you more tears."

"Faewire," Runt said immediately, "And that big yellow metal beast."

"The bulldozer?" Blaze asked.

Runt nodded. "The dozer of bulls. Yes. I wrap him in enough faewire to keep him occupied, then we pull him out of the basement using the dozer of bulls."

"Bulldozer," Blaze said.

Runt frowned. "That's what I said. The dozer of bulls."

Blaze felt a muscle in her neck twitch, but she kept her mouth shut. "So we drag him a ways out into the woods where no one's likely to stumble upon him, and then what? We leave him there for a week or two to see if he improves?"

Runt nodded enthusiastically.

"Out in the elements," Blaze repeated.

"He's a demonkin," Runt said. "It won't hurt him."

Still, Blaze hesitated, trying to think of a way of keeping Jack somewhere warm and comfortable for his recovery.

Then the wereverine grabbed a handful of discarded viscera from the piles on the floor and flung it at her in an animal scream of rage, spattering her from head to toe in blood and entrails.

"On second thought," Blaze said, pausing to wipe the crimson bits of excrement and organs out of her eyes. "I think that sounds like a *fine* idea." She gave the wereverine a sweet smile and turned to get the bulldozer.

Once she'd backed up to the porch, Blaze shut off the dozer and frowned, listening to the ruckus inside.

"You stay here," Runt said, popping into existence at the base of her machine. He was panting. "I think the demonkin Jack has made it off of the mattress."

Indeed, even as she stood there, she could see long talons clawing at the wood, powered by too-skinny arms and a malevolent, leering snarl as the wereverine peeked around the corner of the basement, dribbling saliva.

"That," Blaze said, watching the thing slide slowly closer, "Is not natural."

"Not for the First Lands," Runt agreed. He opened one of the pouches on his belt and tugged out a bundle of what looked like glowing blue-white fishing line. He carefully plucked one end of the filament out and slid it from the bundle, and it came without a tangle. He handled it very delicately, his thick fingers moving with an inhuman precision and speed. Then, deftly holding up one end of the filament, he held the tangled bundle out to Blaze.

"If you would hold that?"

Blaze gingerly took the glowing bundle in both hands. "What do I do with this?"

"Just hold onto it whilst I gather up our heavy friend." He started pulling the line out, the luminescent filament slid easily out of the ball in her hand without snarling. At about ten feet away from the wereverine, Runt paused, seemed to brace himself. Then, like a flash, he suddenly darted forward, the only thing visible of him being the luminescent thread where it floated in the air.

In an instant, he was over the porch and into the foyer beyond, and in a motion almost too fast to see, he wrapped the filament around each of the wereverine's wrists and knotted it. Then he lunged away, and would have made a clean escape, but his foot caught on the doormat at the last moment. Reeling, Runt popped back into existence stumbling out of the wereverine's reach just as the creature's massive talons rent a hole in his shirt. Runt lurched backwards through the door, falling onto his rump on the deck as he stared at the wereverine with wide eyes, then glanced down at his chest like he expected to see his own beating heart.

The wereverine, for his part, was yanking at his hands, screaming his rage as the slim little line refused to break.

Gingerly, touching the lightly-bleeding scratch in his flesh, Runt got back to his feet, his dark skin looking more pale than usual. He walked back to Blaze backwards, eyes still on the wereverine.

"If you would allow me?" Runt asked, once he reached her. He held out his hand for the twine.

When he went to tie it to the bulldozer, Blaze frowned. "Is that really enough to hold him?"

"It's unbreakable, Lady," Runt said, as he started draping shimmery blue-white line over the hitch. "Only an earth-touched may untie it."

Then a new thought occurred to her. "Won't that bite through the skin of his hand?"

"He's demonkin," Runt said with a shrug. "He'll heal." Then he was gingerly knotting the glowing glacier-blue line around the large metal ball-hitch on the back of the bulldozer, careful not to actually touch the metal.

When he made the second knot, the rest of the twine fell to the ground in a bundle, leaving only the knot that held it in place. Picking up the tangle, Runt stuffed it back into his pouch, looking satisfied with himself despite the gaping hole in his iridescent green shirt. "You may wake the dozer of bulls," Runt said, waving at the machine. "We should take the demonkin Jack somewhere distant, where there's no chance that someone will wander across him on the trails.

Blaze knew just the place.

She got on the dozer and, as the wereverine struggled in vain to free his hands, she started the machine moving forward.

As Runt had promised, the line held, and as the wereverine's cries turned from rage to pain, Blaze bit her lip and hit the gas, dragging him out of the basement. As he screamed and snarled behind her, Blaze took him down the overgrown path to the abandoned mill, then beyond. She picked a spot that looked like it hadn't seen a single soul in about ten years, then pulled off of the trail into the forest, checking periodically to make sure the wereverine was still attached.

He was, and if anything, he looked even more demonic than before. Seeing that, Blaze gained more confidence in the fey's knots, since she was pretty sure that, had the wereverine been able to break free, he would have done it as soon as she started dragging him across the yard.

By the time Blaze had shut down the engine, yanked the key from the ignition, and hopped off of the track, the wereverine was a snarling ball of slitty-eyed hatred. He watched her as she made a wide circle around him, then met Runt on the path. Stopping to look back at him, Blaze hesitated, looking for some sign of Jack.

Only malicious animal fury stared back at her.

Clearing her throat, Blaze said, "We're gonna give you a few days to think about stuff. We'll be back tomorrow to check on you."

"He can't understand you," Runt said. "The Unmentionable is in full command, and they're much too simple to—"

"I'm going to enjoy gutting you both in your sleep," the wereverine said, as perfectly precise as a Yale attorney. "Your friend is dead. I devoured his soul and took what was left." His words sounded like the eerie baying of hounds, and it took Blaze a moment to realize that the creature's mouth remained closed throughout.

Runt had his glassy blade out and was putting an arm out in front of her, pushing her backwards. "Lady," he whispered, "That thing needs to die."

Blaze's heart, still in her throat from the alien words, flinched and glanced down at Runt in startlement. "Needs to die?"

"That's a full magus of the Third Lands," Runt whispered. "They deal in *blood*. He needs to die."

"Not if you want your tears, you don't," Blaze growled, grabbing the fey man by the back of his shredded shirt. "Come on, I want him alive."

At the wereverine's insane cackle that followed, every hair on Blaze's body stood on end. She took an instinctive step backwards, trying to resist the primal urge to bolt. Runt followed her, holding the opalescent sword between him and the creature as if he were afraid it would suddenly get up and charge.

"*How* old was the demonkin Jack?" Runt whispered.

"He didn't know for sure," Blaze lied, having that sudden gut feeling that if she said the wrong thing, Runt was going to slit Jack's throat, regardless of her polite requests.

"Long enough for the Third-Lander to reach full magus," Runt said. "Not good, not good."

Blaze eyed the immobilized creature, biting her lip. "What are the chances he'll get loose?"

"I know you were fond of this demonkin Jack," Runt said softly, "but I would very strongly suggest we kill the Third Lander magus. He knows what you are, and if he doesn't, he will soon figure it out."

Blaze frowned. "What do you mean, 'what I am?'"

Runt bit his lip, then glanced at the wereverine, who looked like he was listening intently, rounded furry ears pricked forward with interest. "Back at the lodge, Lady. Not here. Please."

Meeting the glowing green eyes staring back at her through the underbrush, Blaze just nodded.

Sword still out, Runt led her all the way back to the porch, facing their back-trail, before he slumped down on the back steps, staring at the path to the sawmill. He still looked pasty-white, and he wasn't putting his sword away. Softly, he said, "If you would allow me, Lady, I would like to go back tonight and destroy the Third Lands magi."

"What were you saying earlier?" Blaze demanded.

The tiny man shook his head, still staring at the forest. "That looked like the kind capable of making a host-leap. He might have been a magus before he took demonkin Jack. How the mortal *ever* overpowered him, I will never understand."

"You were going to tell me what I am."

"Miss Blaze, truly," Runt whispered, pale-faced and sweating. He turned to gesture at the forest. "That is a creature that should never walk the First Lands. If a mortal found it in the woods, a simple scratch and it could switch bodies—"

Blaze grabbed him by the iridescent green-purple braids and spun his head around to face her. "Listen, you little 1-800-number twit," Blaze said. "I woke up in a puddle of ash three weeks ago. My best shotgun was a melted mess. I saw fingerprints in the slag. Why is that?"

The man's native face paled and he vanished.

Blaze felt herself snarl, looking at the empty back yard. "You better not hurt him!" she yelled impotently at the barn.

If the fey man heard or cared, he never responded.

NINETEEN

Bears

Amber's face throbbed as she smiled. She felt her pack slip through the trees on either side of her, willing to die at her command. *She* was a true leader, not the little bitch and her oathbound coward who were even then sharing the same cage in the newcomer's pit, for daring to argue with her plans. She should have killed them, but with the wer-everine as such a compelling example, she felt like a slow death would be more meaningful to them.

Amber came to a halt, nose up, as they approached the little cabin beside the creek. The entire area stank of grizzly bear. The man, a broad, somewhat husky oaf of about five and a half feet, was hoeing potatoes in the little garden behind the house. The woman, a petite, narrow-waisted remnant of an obsolete tradition, was sitting out in a parasol-shaded chair beside him, wearing a sunhat and a corseted dress, stitching a quilt.

A quilt, of all things.

"Subdue them," Amber said.

Her pack melted away from her, spreading into the couple's yard.

The woman looked up first, her nose to the wind. "Osgood," she said softly, as Amber's betas slipped out of the forest, surrounding them.

The man stiffened, his grip tightening on his hoe. The woman slowly got to her feet, setting her quilting gently aside.

"What do you want?" the man demanded, backing until he was side-by-side with the frilly bumpkin woman, a stupid expression on his face. His piggish eyes seemed to catch nervously on the swords and axes her pack now carried, donated by the ever-so-talented wereverine, and he gripped the hoe as if to use it. "We're just minding our own business, folks, keeping to our own selves out here in the woods." His words carried a dimwitted slur.

Amber stepped forward smiling as her pack parted for her. "Good morning," she said, stopping a few yards off from the wary couple. Addressing the man, she asked, "Do you have any food or valuables stashed away on the property?" Peering at the dirt under her talons, Amber said, "If you do, tell us, and perhaps we will spare the life of your cute little damsel, over there."

The man stiffened with a growl. It was the petite woman, however, who spoke. Her frightened doe expression had faded, leaving nothing but rigid ice behind. She was glancing at the swords that Amber's pack carried. "Those weapons do not belong to you, sugar," she said. Her voice had the soft tilt of a Southern Belle.

"They do now," Amber said. "Considering that their last owner is sadly departed." She smiled at the woman. "Which brought me to an epiphany, of sorts. Old fools seem to hoard valuables they can't use. I don't suppose we'll find a similar collection, in your basement?"

The tiny woman's smile was glacial. "You assume much, puppy."

Amber drew the black dagger almost thoughtfully. She heard the woman hiss as its twisting ebony blade swallowed the light. "Something like this, maybe?"

"Where did you get that?" the woman demanded.

"The wereverine gave it to me." Amber smiled. "After he died."

"Wynflaeth," the man whispered to his wife, "Isn't that the blade that raises the—"

"Shhh," the petite woman hissed, too quickly. She cast Amber a quick glance.

Amber frowned at the nervousness she saw in the woman's face. *Raises the what?* She thought of the way the blackness had eaten away her face, leaving throbbing bones behind. Suddenly, it struck her. This was a *necromancer's* blade. Necromancers killed the living...

...and commanded the dead.

Slowly, a smile spread across Amber's face, knowing just the use for such a tool.

The petite woman's eyes narrowed. "You're never leaving here alive, pup." And she began to change, her tiny body morphing into a brown, eight-foot, grotesque melding of woman and bear. Beside her, her husband did the same, his head reaching ten feet as they towered over the yard; fat, rippling masses of tooth and talon.

The woman fell to all four hairy legs and charged, heading directly for Amber.

Amber darted backwards into the woods, allowing her pack to take the brunt of the bear's attack. The woman hit them and threw them aside like bowling pins, such power in her massive arms that she ripped a startled packmate's ribs in half and scattered his entrails in a swath across the woods with one swipe.

Amber slid further into the trees as her packmates distracted the female. She came around behind the male, who was howling in rage as the faster wolves were darting around him, slicing his body apart with their new blades. When he turned to swipe ineffectually at another attacker, Amber lunged in and sank the blade to the hilt in his back.

Then she darted backwards, grinning as the huge beast screamed and started clawing at his own chest.

"*Osgood*!" The female had been faring better than the male, but upon seeing him slump to his knees, startled mouth gaping wide, she went into a frenzy. She was faster and smarter than her mate. She caught one of Amber's submissives in the ear with a powerful swing, knocking the man's head through the woods until it exploded against the trunk of a birch tree. Seemingly oblivious to the sword cuts from Amber's packmates, she charged Amber again, this time ignoring all else, her insane brown eyes aglow with hatred.

Seeing the charging bear, knowing what she intended to do, Amber actually felt a spasm of fear, knowing that, should the creature get hold of her, she would fare no better than the man whose brains were even then sliding down the birch tree.

Amber tried to run, but even with her pack around her, this woman was faster. Bleeding from a dozen different wounds, half of her furry face torn away by an axe blade, the bear chased Amber down through the woods, as single-minded as a rabid terrier. Amber tripped, fell. She rolled in terror, watching the feral beast approach her, scrambling backwards, babbling apologies that flowed from her in panic.

The bear caught the hand that held the dagger and drove it into the ground. The other paw pinned Amber by the skull, talons digging into the sides of her head. Suddenly realizing what she meant to do, Amber grabbed the woman's thick wrist in a panic, to keep her from twisting off her head.

Her muzzle glistening with tears, the bear managed, "Why did you kill him? You stupid little bitch…*why*?"

As the massive fist tightened around her head, Amber realized the bear didn't *need* to pull her head from her shoulders to kill her. Staring up into the woman furious face, Amber babbled in terror, unable to come up with an answer she thought would save her life.

"We would have given you our land," the bear whispered. "We just wanted to be left alone."

Amber whimpered, so afraid she couldn't even find words.

The bear's brown eyes hardened. "Osgood was a good man." The claws buried in her scalp started to squeeze.

One of Amber's favorite submissives leapt atop the bear's back, skewering the woman between the shoulder-blades with the rippling two-handed sword. Amber had given the sword to him as a gift, due to his loyalty. The bear flinched, but tightened her grip. Amber felt her world shudder as her skull started to crack.

Her submissive yanked the sword free and swung again, hacking at the bear's neck.

The sword lodged halfway and stuck in the bear's spine.

Twisting, the bear caught the man's head between her paws. She slammed her palms together, then threw aside pieces of skull. Then, choking, she fell back to all fours, looking down at the blade in her neck. Silvery blood bubbled up over her brown lips, spattering the ground beneath her. She wobbled slightly on her feet, the blade itself obviously blocking circulation to the woman's brain.

Sensing her opportunity, Amber lunged forward and made a nice, long slice down the woman's ribcage.

As the bear screamed and made a crude swipe at her, off-balance, Amber ducked around and did it again, to the other side.

Then, stepping back, Amber watched smugly as the woman let out a low, gurgling scream and fell to her knees, the blackness beginning to expose her ribs, heart, and lungs. She shifted back to human form, her petite body twisted in agony.

"I killed him," Amber said, returning the blade to its metal sheathe on her hip, "Because he was a stupid pig."

The bear moaned as her organs began to turn black, pulsing under her ribcage like sacks of black gelatin.

"What was his IQ, anyway?" Amber laughed, walking around the dying woman. "Seventy? Sixty-five?" Amber snorted. "I bet you had to teach him not to drink out of the toilet."

The bear began to cry as her organs disintegrated, and the overwhelming stench of living rot filled the forest. Amber held her hand to her nose in distaste. She reached out and jerked the huge blade from the woman's neck.

"So what was it like, being married to a dog?" Amber asked, grinning at the pain and hatred she saw in the woman's brown eyes. "Was the doggie good in bed?" She made a disgusted sound and gestured at the carcass in the yard. "The fat fuck certainly wasn't much of a looker, so you must have kept him around for something."

The woman went suddenly still, looking directly into Amber's eyes. For a disappointed moment, Amber thought the woman had died already. Then, in a deep voice that sounded eerily hollow, deep and ringing, almost as if it had an echo, the dying woman said, "You are but a speck of dust compared to what is coming, fool. When the Guardian of Morning offers your corrupted flesh to her pyre, your death will be a grain of sand in the desert of her life."

Amber's heart began to pound at the alien tone of the woman's voice, but then she realized that the odd sound must have had something to do with the way the woman's lungs were turning black.

With the last of her breath used up in poetry, the woman collapsed. Amber sighed, wishing she had made it take longer. The bear had been almost as arrogantly infuriating as the wereverine.

...Whose death was yet another that she hadn't been able to appreciate thoroughly, thanks to the—*thing*—that had exploded to life in the yard, hurling balls of liquid fire that had flawlessly hit their targets, even careening around sheds and behind fences to engulf their victims, and nothing, absolutely *nothing*, had been able to land on it.

Between it and the wereverine, Amber had lost thirteen of her number that day. When she and her pack had come back to the den, badly burned and a quarter of their number missing, with nothing but the wereverine's arsenal to show for it, the tiny black coward had been waiting on the doorstep with her slave, their faces smug.

"*Told you,*" she had said.

Amber had endured that tiny act of insolence in stride, but the next day, when Amber had begun making plans to spread northward, taking the old ones' hoards as they passed, the black bitch's balking had been the last straw. Amber had thrown her into the cavern with her useless slave, then sealed her inside.

But now, thinking of the bear's stupid slip about the dagger, Amber had something she wanted to try.

Inside the werebears' cabin, Amber and her submissives found a handful of massive swords and axes wrapped in a quilt and tucked under the bed, their grips too big to be effectively used by Amber or any of her pack.

The real treasure was the jewelry. Gold necklaces, gems, bracelets, rings, antique coin, tiaras, and brooches, all stuffed into a gold-and-ironwood chest and hidden under a few false boards in the floor. Most of the jewelry was plain, but Amber knew its real value was in its age. Any one of the pieces, she guessed, would keep her pack fed for a year.

This was such a good idea, Amber thought, staring at the loot that her submissives spilled onto the floor at her feet. Her mind briefly drifted north, to the great dragons that occupied the Brooks Range, and she felt a welling of glee in her chest. *They'll never know what hit them.*

Amber claimed the nicest tiara—a golden Celtic knot-pattern dripping with sapphires—to compliment her eyes. Then she and her pack feasted, cleaning out the werebears' impressive freezer and pantry.

Once they were finished eating, she led them home, the werebears' stash distributed amongst her submissives.

We'll need more, Amber thought, looking at the moving bodies around her. So many had already fallen, leaving only the strongest, the healthiest to survive. She would have to replace those lost with fresh blood. Fishermen, most like. She was beyond caring what the authorities thought. She glanced again at her dagger, touching it for reassurance. With equipment like this, nothing could stop her. She would create her army, then march north, taking the Thunderbird and then the dragons.

But first, she had an experiment she wanted to try…

They returned to the den, then Amber sat and drank a glass of wine as her submissives dug out the little black bitch and her minion.

Except, when they pulled out the cage, it was empty.

Seeing the door still locked from the outside, ice slid down Amber's back in a wave.

TWENTY

Crippled

Jack opened his eyes and groaned at the mosquitoes in his ears. He moved to swat them away, but something caught his wrists. When he looked at them and saw the glowing blue-white faewire, encrusted with his blood, a growl started in his chest.

Then he saw the bulldozer, and he knew the fey wouldn't have bothered using it to drag him anywhere.

Blaze, Jack thought, irritated. But where had she gotten the faewire? And *why the fuck was he tied up?*

He gave the wire a tentative tug, found it secure, and didn't bother wasting his time. He sat up, intending to trot over to the bulldozer, fire it up, and drive it back home.

Except he couldn't sit up.

Frowning, Jack glanced down at his legs.

They were still attached, but he couldn't feel them. And nothing from his stomach downward would cooperate with him. And, now that he was paying attention, he could see a crusted stain of filth on his groin, and the air stank of crap.

Jack tried again to move his legs.

Again, they failed to twitch.

And, as he watched, he saw the dry, crusted stain on his groin grow in a pool of wetness, and smelled urine.

Panic began to take an icy grip on his heart as he watched the stain spread. "Blaze!" he cried, wanting to crawl away, wanting to do *anything* but stare down at the limbs that he couldn't feel, the growing wetness on his pants.

He watched a mosquito land on his knee. Watched it suck his blood, its abdomen fill with silvery crimson, watched it retract its proboscis and fly away. Through it all, he felt nothing.

"*Blaze*!" Jack screamed, horror driving wretched pangs through his being. *Oh no*, he thought, his fear ratcheting up a notch. He must have survived the blade. Despite all odds, his moon magic had somehow reversed the dread horn's necromancy. Then his eyes narrowed.

Unless…

Sprawled on the ground, unable to sit up or twist, he looked again at the faewire. He leaned close and sniffed it.

Over the scent of his own blood, he caught the little wretch's stink.

He told her, Jack thought, fury rising like an ice-storm within him. He felt the moon-magic surge, trying to take control, but he instinctively fought it down. No, he wouldn't need the beast to wring the little bastard's neck.

"Blaze!" Jack screamed, scooting in the churned earth as best he could on his elbows. His arms felt weak, and when he looked, they were a third the size they should have been.

Jack froze. He remembered the last time that had happened, and what had caused it.

Oh no, he thought. *He got loose again.*

"*Blaaaaze*!" he shrieked, losing his self-control. "*Blaaaaaaa—*"

He heard a 4-wheeler motor come rumbling down the trail at high-speed, then heard a thump as someone got off in a hurry. "What the fuck is it now?!" Blaze demanded, with much less compassion than Jack would have expected. Somewhat cowed, Jack had to twist to see her as she came off the trail, stepping into view well out of reach of the tether. "I already told you, you piece of shit—you keep screaming and we're just gonna have to move you further away from the lodge, you get it?"

Jack was taken aback by the rage and frustration in Blaze's face. "Uh," he said, "I'm swimming in my own shit over here."

"Oh *really*?" Blaze said, her tone dripping with sarcasm. "Hmm... Well, maybe I should just come closer and change you into something more comfortable."

Jack stared at her. "Have you lost your fucking mind?"

Blaze narrowed her eyes at him, then turned to leave him in the woods.

"Wait!" Jack cried, desperate, now. "Why am I tied up? Please, I can't feel my legs!"

Blaze snorted and got back on the 4-wheeler. Over the roar as she started the engine, she said, "Keep it quiet. You'll get fed again before bed. I hear you screaming again and I'm coming back and firing up the dozer."

Then he heard the sound of dirt flying as the 4-wheeler did a quick circle and disappeared into the distance.

Jack stared after her, in utter disbelief. When he realized she wasn't coming back, he turned his attention to the overcast sky through the tops of the birch trees, feeling dazed. As if to add insult to injury, it began to drizzle on his unprotected body, leaving him shivering in his own shit.

Hours later, he was calculating just how to best broach the subject of what an utter bitch she was being when he heard the sound of a 4-wheeler again. Jack instinctively tried to sit up, but his body refused. He gritted his jaw, fighting back the burn of tears.

When Blaze stopped the 4-wheeler on the trail, Jack tentatively cleared his throat. "Why am I tied up?"

"Gee," Blaze said. She was wrestling with something on the bed of the trailer.

"What are you doing?" Jack asked.

"Feeding your ungrateful face."

When she dragged the goat out to him and threw it on the ground beside his face, uncooked and bleeding, Jack just stared at it.

Well out of tether-reach, Blaze hesitated. "You aren't going to eat?"

"Uh," Jack said softly, "Why isn't it cooked?"

Blaze gave him a look of utter fury. "You're lucky I feed you at all." She turned her back to him and started back to the trail.

"Wait!" Jack called, sickened by the way he was unable to slide out of the path of the blood oozing from the goat's neck. "What's going on?!"

"That innocent *bullshit* isn't going to work again," Blaze growled. "You almost got me the *first* two times." He heard the shocks creak, heard her switch on the ignition key.

"*Tell me what I did*!" Jack screamed, desperate, now. He remembered losing control to the moon magic. He didn't, however, remember what had happened afterward. A bad sign, and one he hadn't experienced in over a thousand years.

Blaze ignored him and hit the ignition switch. She drove away to the rattle of a cart and the hum of a 4-wheeler engine.

Jack spent the night staring into the dead face of a Boer goat.

When she returned in the morning, a cartload of dead rabbits behind her, Blaze hesitated upon seeing the goat. She frowned at him, towering just out of reach. "Why didn't you eat it?"

"Because I'm not a fucking animal," Jack said, feeling wretched and humiliated under her pitiless stare. He had wet himself again, and the slurry of shit in his pants had just gotten thicker overnight.

To his surprise, Blaze laughed. "Fine. I'll come back tonight."

"Wait, goddamn it!" Jack snapped, as she turned. "Can you at least tell me what's going on?"

Blaze's shoulders hesitated and she turned, slowly. Her eyes, however, were exhausted and wary. "I'm not falling for it again," she finally said. She turned again.

It was at that point, between the dead goat, the uncontrollable bowel movements, the lack of feeling in his legs, the faewire around his wrists, that Jack simply lost it. His fear and humiliation came tumbling out in a sob. "Please tell me what's happening. Please."

Blaze didn't stop. He heard her climb back upon the machine, heard the engine start, heard it drive away.

Jack spent the rest of the day watching flies land in the dead goat's open mouth. A black bear wandered just out of reach of the tether, sniffed at the air anxiously, eying the goat, then wandered off. Jack began to count the types of birds chirping, trying desperately to ignore the smell of his own shit.

• • •

It had frosted that morning, and Jack had still shown no improvement. He was still playing head-games, still trying to lure her close enough to rip her limb-from-limb. Blaze looked down at the three nasty scars up her right arm, where his claws had raked through her skin like Jell-O. He'd almost killed her. And that had been crippled from the waist down, with both hands tied to a bulldozer.

She sweated now, just thinking about it.

Now, facing the final days of September, Blaze was warily counting the days until it snowed, wondering how she was going to protect the wereverine from the elements, wondering when the wolves would next attack. Her whole life had become a waiting game. Several times, she'd thought she'd seen something in the forest, dark, furry shadows sliding past, then slipping back into the woods before she could get a clean shot.

It was a waiting game, and Blaze was rapidly running out of time. Whatever it was that had kept the wolves at bay so far was going to wear off, eventually. Between waking up and reaching for a gun at every tiny sound in the darkness and listening to the wereverine scream and rant at her at all hours of the day, Blaze hadn't gotten much sleep.

Still irritated at the stubborn way the demonkin had refused to eat the goat, Blaze was trying to figure out what to do with a five-gallon bucket of mangoes when the two Alaska State Troopers walked around the corner of the shop. One was tall and angular, looking as if he spent too much time running and not enough time eating, and the other was short and barrel-chested, the kind who could rip his opponents' arms off in a fistfight. They hailed her, then came to a halt a few feet away, scanning the yard, lodge, and outbuildings with alert, even nervous, eyes.

"How you doing today, Ma'am?" the shorter of the two troopers said, holding out his thick hand to shake. "I'm Pat Amsden and this is Matthew Wellsboro."

"Blaze MacKenzie," Blaze said, returning the gesture as she fought down a growing sense of dread. She thought of Jack, stuck out in the woods within shouting distance, and prayed he didn't open his mouth.

"Ma'am," the shorter of the two said, "We're with the Alaska State Troopers. It seems that there's been a rash of disappearances in the area, and we're curious if you've noticed anything strange lately."

*As a matter of fact...*Blaze thought ridiculously, thinking of the wereverine tied to the backhoe. But she frowned. "What kind of disappearances?"

"Fishermen, mostly," the man said. "An entire lodge down at Lake Creek has been abandoned, owners and all, and nobody knows where they went. They usually hold about fifty to sixty people at a time, and this is prime trout fishing season. Not as popular as salmon season in July, but the place should still be at least half full."

His angular partner nodded. "But we got no calls, nothing. The only way we even found out about it was that the last group of fisherman dropped off by a charter service never made their pre-arranged pickup on the island. The pilot went looking, and sure enough, everyone was just...gone."

"Seems really odd nobody would say where they're going," the taller trooper added. "No calls to family, no signs of struggle, and a good portion of them already missed their flights out of Anchorage. Everyone just vanished, Roanoke-style."

"Weird," Blaze whispered, thinking of Amber.

The man nodded. "It's looking like over eighty people so far, with the lodge and the nearby cabins. It's more or less centered downriver around Lake Creek, but we're advising everyone in the area to stay in their homes until we figure out what's going on."

"Okay," Blaze said.

"*Have* you seen anything strange?" the smaller trooper asked, watching her anxiously. "Right now, anything would help."

Blaze hesitated, trying to decide just how much to tell the officers. Finally, she said, "You should talk to Amber. She was acting…strange… the last time I saw her."

"Amber Stern?" the smaller trooper asked, a little sharply. He gave his partner an 'I Told You So' look. "She's one of the only ones *not* affected by the disappearances."

Blaze shrugged. "I dunno. Last time I was walking the river, she pulled up in a boat with Kimber Womac and told me to get inside. Jack, my handyman, came to my rescue, but I'm pretty sure she had something unpleasant planned for me back at her place."

The troopers' gazes sharpened. "She use any weapons or any other forms of coercion?"

"Just herself," Blaze said. Then, when the troopers hesitated, obviously calculating how petite little Amber could have coerced a Yeti to do anything, Blaze shrugged and added, "She was fast and strong. I think she knew martial arts or something."

The shorter of the two pulled out a pad and started taking notes. "You said she tried to force you on her boat?"

Blaze nodded.

"Did she have any motivation that you could see?" the man asked. "Any reason for wanting you to come with her?"

"I wasn't sure at the time," Blaze said. "I think she might've been on drugs. You go anywhere near her place and there's syringes and alcohol bottles everywhere."

"All right," the man said, giving his partner a pointed look, "How long ago was this?"

"Around June 22nd," Blaze said, trying to remember. "It was almost two months after Bruce dropped me off on Lake Ebony in early May."

They seemed disappointed with that news. "These disappearances were all within the last couple weeks."

"Oh," Blaze said.

"Other neighbors have mentioned seeing wolves at night," the barrel-chested trooper suggested. "We got a couple folks complaining of wolves before they disappeared. You seen anything like that?"

"You think *wolves* are getting people?" Blaze demanded.

"We aren't ruling anything out right now," the skinny Trooper said. "You seen any predators around here?" He glanced at her barn and its fences of livestock with obvious interest.

"I saw a wolverine," Blaze said. "Crawled in my basement. Ripped stuff up."

The shorter man gave his partner a meaningful look. "Wolverines are pretty rare around these parts," he said, obviously to make her feel helpful. "Nasty little critters."

"You got that part right," Blaze said, narrowing her eyes.

"But probably not overly dangerous to humans," the skinny Trooper added slowly.

"Oh, I don't know about *that*," Blaze said, showing them the claw-marks on her arm. "Ornery shit sliced me up good before I put a shot-gun blast between his eyes."

"That looks rather nasty, ma'am," the barrel-chested man agreed, looking uncomfortable. Too late, Blaze realized that Troopers were probably technically supposed to turn her over to Fish and Game for violating the season on wolverines. She tried not to let her relief show when the skinnier man cleared his throat and added, "But we're really out here checking out stories about wolves."

"No wolves," Blaze said.

There was an awkward silence, and she definitely got the feeling that it was probably the troopers' jobs to ask her what happened to the wolverine, considering they were out of season.

The taller trooper cleared his throat. "I see you're packing some nice handguns," he said, looking at her Desert Eagles. "Bears?"

"Wolves," Blaze said. "Heard stories they were bad around here."

The tall trooper grimaced. "We're really hoping that's not what's going on. Last time a wolf pack did anything like this..." He shook his head. "Was in the Middle Ages."

"Kinda makes you wonder about those old stories of werewolves, huh?" Blaze ventured.

The two troopers chuckled and gave each other nervous looks. The taller one glanced at the dirt and scuffed the ground, while the other one cleared his throat uncomfortably. "Well, miss MacKenzie, we've got to get moving," the barrel-chested man said finally. "Got six more places to interview before tonight, but just keep your eye out, okay?"

"And lock your doors," the taller trooper said. "Are you here alone?"

"Pretty much," Blaze said.

"Definitely lock your doors," the angular trooper repeated firmly, giving the Sleeping Lady another nervous look. "These wolves...if that *is* what's causing it, and I'm not saying it is for sure...are nasty. They're getting into places they shouldn't have access to."

"Okay," Blaze said, shaking their hands again. "Stay safe. And let me know if you find those guys."

"Will do," the taller, angular man told her. He fished into his pocket, pulled out a card, and handed it to her. "And if you hear of anything, give us a—"

"*Blaaaaaaaaaaaaaaaaaaaaaze*!" The wereverine's scream shattered the man's sentence like a sledgehammer. Blaze froze. The last thing she wanted to try and do was explain why she was keeping a paralyzed man tied to a bulldozer in the middle of the forest.

The troopers turned toward the sound, the anxiety in the air increasing exponentially. "That someone you know?" the stockier of the two asked. Jack yelled again, louder, drawing out her name in a long, indignant scream.

"The handyman," Blaze growled, her hand clenching on the bucket handle. "Hired him to take care of the place. He's taken to ordering me around like a serving-wench ever since. Something I *really* wish I'd known before I headed out to the Bush—the men out here all seem to be chauvinist pricks."

The stocky trooper snickered behind his hand, but the taller one was frowning at the woods. "He always sound like that? Almost sounds hurt."

Jack called again, droning out her name so that it rang in the treetops, the final note dwindling on the wind.

Shut the hell up, Blaze thought at Jack. "All the damn time," she muttered. "He's out working on the sawmill, waiting for lunch. Too lazy to come back to the lodge to get it, so he whines." She turned toward the trees. Raising her voice, she shouted, "All *right* already! Give me half an hour!" She turned to the troopers. "I've gotta make sandwiches. You two interested in staying for lunch?"

"No thank you, Ma'am," the taller one said quickly. "Like we said, we've got six more cabins to visit today."

"Okay," Blaze said, even as Jack yelled her name again. She grimaced. "Well, if you have any mechanic buddies who would be willing to live out here in the Bush for about twenty grand a year, let them know where to find me."

"Will do, Ma'am." The two troopers glanced again at the source of the screams, then, shaking their heads, went back down the trail out to the lake.

Blaze waited until they were well out of sight, dropped the bucket of mangoes, and went to get the 4-wheeler.

• • •

When the girl returned the fifteenth or sixteenth time and hesitated, staring down at the rotting dead goat, then at him, before starting to turn away, Jack lost all control he had on his temper.

"Listen, you gangly Yeti *bitch*," he snarled. "You leave me here another night and I'm going to pack up and let you run your own goddamn fishing lodge."

"I'd like to see you do that, tied to a bulldozer," Blaze said, but she paused, a frown on her face. "Why didn't you eat the goat?"

"Because it's *not cooked*!" Jack screamed back. "And it's covered in *flies* and *maggots* and it *stinks*!"

Blaze peered at him. "That hasn't stopped you before."

Jack's breath caught in his throat. "How long was I asleep?"

"As far as I know, you haven't been. Not for a month." Blaze grabbed the rabbits she had brought along and flopped them back on the trailer.

"Listen to me," Jack said, "Whatever I did, that was the moon magic, not me."

Blaze snorted, and her face darkened. "Sure. You said that last time, and the time before, and the time before that…" She hesitated, seemingly to consider, "Oh yeah, and the time before *that*…Right before you tried to *gut* me." She pointed out a series of scars up her right arm, then dropped it again, glaring at him. "I'm beginning to think Runt has it right. You're not letting him wake back up. We should just cut off your head and get it over with." She stepped out of sight and he heard her climb back onto the 4-wheeler.

Jack knew that he needed tact to pry himself out of his current situation, but all he could come up with was a feral, animal roar. The moon-magic surged within him again, and he felt his hackles sprout as he started flailing at the wire for the first time since waking.

He heard the 4-wheeler start and drive off.

He spent the night staring at the moon, wondering which god he had insulted to gain this kind of wrath. Loki, probably. The malicious shit. The goat, beside him, had really started to stink, and it made his gut roil as he fought the urge to eat it anyway. He was *hungry*…so hungry he was beginning to get close to losing control again. He watched the white orb travel across the sky, racking his brain for something he could tell her.

When Blaze appeared the next morning, frost had crystallized on Jack's eyelashes and he was close to weeping with hunger.

When she saw the goat had remained untouched, Blaze seemed to be taken aback. As she stared at it, frowning, Jack said, "I'm attracted to you, you goddamn Yeti."

Blaze's head jerked up, and he thought he saw a flash of gold behind her blue eyes.

"From the first time I touched you, when I made you shake my hand," Jack said. "It was all I could do not to just tell you right then. I felt that surge and I just…Gawd. I just like to play with fire, okay? Some death-wish or something, I don't fucking know. Mated a dragon and a fey and a wereverine. Rest o' the girls didn't really set off my alarms enough to interest me. I gotta get that little gut-twitch of apprehension, you know? And, honey, you gave me a gut-twitch that almost made me run for the hills. You've had this poor little wereverine panting the moment you pulled yourself out of that lake. I looked up as you went by and *boom*, done, gone, no saving me, light my ass on fire and send it up a tree, 'cause I was a goner the moment you stepped off that plane."

Blaze gave him a long, hard stare. She obviously didn't believe a word, but at least she was *listening* this time.

"I'm rude and pigheaded and stubborn 'cause I don't want you to get too close, *okay*?" Jack cried, so hungry and desperate he was trembling. "I get those tingles when I get close to you and I just wanna drop everything and bolt in the other direction, 'cause outta four women, I got *all* of them killed. All four. Imagine that, for a minute! Everyone that meant anything to you, dying *because* of you, and in *unspeakable* ways? Girl, I'd be willing to wager you scare the crap outta me a hell of a lot more than I scare the crap outta *you*."

"You tried to kill me," Blaze said.

He swallowed, hard. "That wasn't me. That was the beast."

"Obviously."

"Look," Jack babbled, "I understand why you're keeping me out here. It probably scared the holy living bejesus outta you. But for the love of Thor, if you're going to leave me here like this, at least get rid of the goat and treat me like a human being. I need something hot to eat. I'm close to losing control again."

A flash of understanding crossed Blaze's face before her guard went up again. "How do I know this isn't another trick?"

Jack had considered that, all night long, and the best he could come up with was, "I kind of like crossbreeds." He gave her a weak smile. "They've got that hybrid vigor thing going on."

Blaze's eyes widened. "Jack?" she whispered.

"I'm really, really hungry," Jack whispered back.

Blaze bolted for the 4-wheeler, and in the half an hour that followed, Jack stared at the dead goat, fighting the impulse to wrap his jaws around the frozen, maggot-infested head and swallow it down.

When Blaze got back, she had a couple gallons of milk, a bowl, two boxes of cereal, and a pot of scrambled eggs.

It was the fey, however, who untied him. Jack narrowed his eyes, but didn't resist as the tiny man put the faeglass sword to his throat and held him there, pinned to the ground, as he fidgeted with the faewire knot.

"I *really* don't think this is a good idea," the little prick kept saying as he fiddled with the string.

"I'm not going to hurt—" Jack began to protest.

The fey simply pushed the blade neatly into his throat, forcing Jack's head back to the ground. "Move again and I'll gut you, demonkin Jack," the youngster said unconcernedly, obviously trying to mimic the total detachment of the fey elders.

"What are you afraid of, twerp?" Jack growled, his spine pressed flat to the ground as the fey worked. "I'm paralyzed from the waist down."

"Tell that to my basement," Blaze muttered. "We only just finished scrubbing the gore off the walls."

Gore? Jack glanced at her, swallowing over the faeglass sword. He wanted to ask what kind of gore, but he couldn't find the courage.

After another few minutes of fiddling with it one-handed, Jack's tether fell free, and the fey darted out of the way so fast that his blade punctured the skin of Jack's throat. Jack grunted and put his hand to his neck, but was so happy to have his hands free that he didn't complain.

"Still hungry?" Blaze asked, watching him with obvious suspicion.

Using both hands, Jack was able to force himself into a seated position. Holding himself there with one hand, he gestured at the cart. "Whatever you got. Hurry."

It was the fey who delivered the pot of eggs, dropping it just out of reach and then sliding it forward on the tip of his sword. They didn't give him a fork, so Jack ate it with his fist, swallowing eggs as fast as he could, barely pausing to chew.

After he had finished his third bowl of cereal, the food had begun to quell the hunger, giving him a better hold on the magic. Jack slowed down, trying to go more carefully, enjoying the first real food in over a week.

The experience was ruined when he yet again smelled fresh shit.

Jack set the bowl aside, trembling. "Blaze," he whispered, "I need you to do something for me."

Blaze raised an eyebrow at him. "If it includes coming over there and giving you a great big hug, you're dreaming."

"I need your Desert Eagle," Jack said, motioning to the gun on her hip.

Blaze's mouth fell open. She glanced at the fey. "I think the wer-everine lost his mind."

"I can *smell* the silver in it!" Jack snapped. "Somehow I healed… partway. I am a warrior. I am *not* going to spend the rest of my life smelling my own bowels."

"You want me to give you my gun…so you can 'sputch' yourself." Blaze sounded like she didn't believe him.

"*Look* at me!" Jack growled, gesturing to his withered limbs and his useless legs. "It will be a mercy."

Blaze seemed to consider, then sighed and pulled the Desert Eagle off of her hip. Instead of handing it over to him, however, she pointed it at his skull and put her finger on the trigger. "The silver buckshot only seemed to make you scream," she warned, sounding unconcerned. "This one's got silver nitrate. Won't be able to work it out this time, once it hits."

She shot me with silver? Jack was horrified, wondering how much of the past days he had lost. He closed his eyes and waited, knowing that nothing could possibly be worse than the pain of a necromancer's blade. He waited for several minutes as she worked up the courage to do it.

"Jesus," Blaze said. He heard her arm drop. "I think he's serious."

Jack opened his eyes to the fey man saying, "Demonkin *do* have a penchant for stupidity."

• • •

Blaze shut the 4-wheeler off and glanced back at the wereverine, who was releasing the rope dragging behind the trailer and collapsing forward with a low sob. Neither she nor Runt were willing to get close enough to him to heft him onto the back of the trailer—not after the beast had tried repeatedly to coax them into believing he was Jack. Aside from the scars up her arm, Blaze still had a ragged scab on her neck, where he'd raked her with his claws in an attempt for her throat, after sweet-talking her for over an hour.

Blaze watched the exhausted wereverine pant into the gravel, his chest heaving with low, miserable whimpers. For the first time since he'd almost killed her, she felt a pang of guilt. Either the creature had devised a whole new category of deception, or the wretched, sobbing wreck on the ground really was Jack.

There was one way to find out.

Blaze removed her gun holsters and set them on the front 4-wheeler basket. Then, tentatively picking her away around the trailer, she squatted beside him.

Jack looked up, saw her coming, and quickly turned his head away, tears wetting his cheeks. "Just kill me," he said, for the thousandth time.

When he stayed in human form and didn't lash out at her, Blaze found the courage to touch his arm. "You'll get better," she offered.

Jack refused to look at her. His emaciated arms, she saw, were trembling with the strain of holding his upper body off of the ground.

"All right," Blaze said, sidling closer, "I'm gonna pick you up. You bite me or anything like that, it's back to the bulldozer, all right?"

Jack let out a hopeless sound that wracked his whole body, and dropped his forehead to the ground as he cried.

I just threatened a cripple, Blaze thought, ashamed. Feeling guilty, she eased herself closer until she was squatting over him, half-expecting the wereverine to sprout fangs and attack her.

When he just continued to weep, however, Blaze gingerly slid her arms under him. Jack didn't struggle. Blaze braced herself, expecting a couple hundred pounds, at least. What she lifted off of the ground, however, matched the withered limbs she was seeing. The wereverine weighed sixty, maybe seventy pounds, most of which was bone. And, now that she was close, he *smelled.*

"Okay," Blaze said, standing with him in her arms, "We're gonna take you inside for a bath."

Jack avoided her gaze, twisting to look at the ground.

Blaze carried him inside, feeling ever-more guilt-ridden as he clung to her, trembling in her arms. She sat him down on the clean white tile in the bathroom, then went to start a fire in the boiler. Thirty minutes later, she had hot water, and went back to the bathroom and closed the door. The wereverine didn't look up when she entered.

"I'm gonna strip you down," Blaze said. "Then shower you off. Then draw a bath."

Jack said nothing, only stared down at his hands. She could see the defeat rolling off of him with every breath.

Carefully, Blaze unbuttoned his jeans and pulled them down off of his hips.

The smell of excrement was suddenly so overwhelming that Blaze choked, pausing midway, horrified.

Jack let out a shuddering breath and turned away.

Swallowing, Blaze finished with his jeans, then peeled his crusted, shit-covered underwear away from his hips. She threw the result into the trash, then, bit her lip. "I'm gonna need to roll you over."

Jack just nodded. She saw tears in his eyes. Crouching beside him, Blaze gingerly turned the wereverine so she could see the damage.

The tile beneath him was a puddled brown mess, and his entire backside from the base of his spine to the base of his thighs were covered in it, the edges crusted and dry, as if it had been there several weeks.

...Which it probably had.

Feeling another wave of guilt, Blaze grabbed a roll of toilet paper and started cleaning him as best she could. Jack, in his humiliation, just stared at the floor in silence.

"Okay," Blaze said, rolling him away from the mess. "I'm gonna start the shower."

The wereverine said nothing, just stared at the floor.

She got the water going, made sure it was hot, then gently lifted him from the tiles and into the tub. She took the pitcher from beside the tub, filled it, and rinsed as much of the stuff off of his withered frame as she could. As soon as the water rushing down the drain began to run clear, she ended the shower, flipped the plug into place and started filling the tub. Then she grabbed a washcloth from the rack, lathered it, and handed it to him.

For the first time, Jack looked up at her as he took the cloth, and there was a pitiful mixture of gratitude, despair, and confusion in his eyes.

"You clean up while I get rid of this," Blaze said, gesturing at the pile of wadded toilet paper. "Take as long as you need." She hesitated, seeing the running water, half afraid he would try to drown himself, but then quickly hurried off to find garbage bags and a dustpan.

When she came back, the tub was overflowing, and Jack was collapsed against the back wall of the tub, watching the water spill over the tub's edge in silence.

"Shit!" Blaze cried, realizing her mistake. With the wereverine's useless legs between him and the other side of the tub, he had no way to reach the faucet. Blaze rushed to shut it off. She let out some water, then replaced the plug. "Doesn't matter," she said quickly. "Just take your bath. I'll take care of the rest." Already, the pile of excrement and toilet paper was growing soggy, the smell of the place amplified by hot water. Blaze slid what she could into garbage bags using the dustpan, then used one of the towels to start mopping the floor.

She carried four bags out to the furnace, the towel and his clothes in the final bag, before the place had stopped smelling like a latrine.

When she returned, Jack was still scrubbing. His water was thick and cloudy with soap.

"Here," Blaze said, changing the water for him.

Jack continued scrubbing. It was getting violent, now, and Blaze saw fiery red skin under his ministrations. When he finished, he tossed the washcloth in the garbage, had Blaze get him a new one, lathered it, and started over again. Blaze watched, uncomfortable, wishing she could say or do something to ease his mind.

"Would you like me to leave?" she finally asked, as he dropped the second washcloth into the trash and started rinsing.

Jack nodded.

Blaze set a stack of washcloths beside the tub, then backed from the room and shut the door.

Two hours later, when he still hadn't called her, Blaze gingerly tapped on the door.

She heard water swish, but she got no response.

Tentative, she opened the door.

Jack was leaning back in the tub, staring at something between his legs. He had tears in his eyes.

"Hey, now," Blaze said, "It's not so ba—"

She froze when she saw the brown lump of barely-congealed feces half-floating between his legs, rubbing against his genitals. Biting her lip, Blaze grabbed the pitcher and scooped it out as best as she could, then flushed it down the toilet and replaced his water.

Instead of washing, Jack said softly, "Take me out back, put the Desert Eagle to my head, and pull the trigger."

"Why?" Blaze demanded.

"Why?!" Jack glanced up at her, gesturing to his legs.

"So you can't move your legs," Blaze said. "So you can't stop from wetting yourself. So you're a cranky little curmudgeon that enjoys calling me a Yeti. So what? I like you anyway."

Jack seemed to hesitate, scanning her eyes before dropping his attention back to his useless legs. "No woman is gonna understand. It's different for a man."

Blaze crossed her arms and raised a brow. "Different how?"

"A man can't do his job if he can't walk."

"And what job is that?" Blaze demanded. She had put the Desert Eagles back on her hips on the last trip out to the furnace.

Jack tensed. "Don't make me say it, woman."

"No, go ahead," Blaze said, "Because I'm honestly curious. What is it that's so important for a man that he can't be a cripple, but a woman can?"

Jack snarled at the word 'cripple.' His green eyes fierce, he growled, "A man's gotta protect his mate. He's gotta provide for his family and keep them safe. He's gotta do the important jobs—"

Blaze laughed. "The 'important' jobs? Wow. Someone really needs to introduce you to the twenty-first century."

Jack narrowed his eyes. "So the woman can raise the children with love and respect, unhindered by the stresses of outside life."

"Impressive," Blaze said. "So what the hell were you doing, teaching me to use the bulldozer?"

Jack actually flinched. He looked her up and down, and Blaze actually expected him to say, 'You look close enough to a man, you might as well act like one.' Instead, he just glared at her.

"Well?" Blaze demanded.

"You're a maid," he finally growled. "You haven't had a child yet."

Blaze refrained from cracking her skull against the ceramic sink basin, but only barely. "So let me get this straight. You, being the man, can't do your 'job,' and therefore need to be put out of your miserable existence. Me, being the woman, should follow suit, because I couldn't possibly survive without a man to do the important stuff for me and I would certainly starve to death when I ran out of food in the fridge, or possibly even freeze to death because I wouldn't even *think* of collecting firewood on my own." She raised a hand, palm-up, and shook her head. "Huh-uh. Too dangerous. Something could fall on me and I could *die*. Yes, a bullet to the head is definitely quicker. More humane than shivering in a corner, wondering why some man somewhere isn't throwing wood on the fire."

Jack narrowed his eyes at her. "You're mocking me."

"Yeah," Blaze said. "How's it feel?" She smiled at him.

"Like I want to crawl out of here and throttle your leg," he muttered. His face, however, cleared. His eyes again caught on Blaze's Desert Eagles. He sniffed, and his nose scrunched with distaste. "Has Amber come back?"

"Not yet," Blaze said.

"How long's it been?"

"About six or seven weeks," Blaze said.

Jack frowned. "Did you kill her?"

"Runt assures me she's still alive," Blaze said. "Though from what I saw, she probably lost about a dozen of her wolves."

Giving her an odd look, Jack said, "I only killed half that."

Blaze shrugged, uncomfortable.

"You used silver?" Jack demanded.

"Uh, not quite," Blaze managed. "Uh…" She swallowed, remembering the bed of ashes. "There was some sort of a fire."

Jack peered at her.

Shrugging, Blaze said, "There were some corpses when I woke up." She laughed uncomfortably. "Burned all to hell." There. Let him make of that what he would.

But Jack's eyes went wide as if he knew exactly what she was talking about. "You woke."

Blaze's heart gave a sudden, unhappy thud and she made an awkward shrug. "Not really sure what happened. I woke up in a pit of ash." Talking about it made Blaze uncomfortable in much the same way, she imagined, that someone with Multiple Personality Disorder didn't want to hear about what their alter-ego did that night in the bar.

"So you didn't wake." Jack cursed. "Do you think you could you do it again?" His attention had intensified on her. "Maybe feel your way back through it, if you had to?" The way he talked about it, he was already taking it for granted that Blaze might have had something to do with the crispy werewolves.

Blaze scoffed. "I'd have a better chance of swimming to the moon."

It was actually cute the way the wereverine roared and slapped the water with his scrawny arms until about half the bathroom was wet and dripping. Wiping her face, Blaze raised a brow. "Tantrum over?"

"I swore to protect you," Jack muttered, staring down at the water between his legs.

"Yeah," Blaze said. She grabbed a towel off of the rack and threw it over her shoulder. "So?"

"*Look* at me!" Jack cried. He almost sounded like he was on the verge of weeping again. He flung a disgusted hand at his feet. "I can't even move my own damn legs."

"Runt tells me it's temporary," Blaze lied. She went to the bath and lifted him out, then set him on the floor, wrapped in a towel. "So I had a wheelchair delivered on the last barge trip."

Jack gave her a narrow look, but his voice was soft when he said, "The thieving prick said it was temporary?" The hope in his voice was so strong it was painful.

"Yeah," Blaze said, trying not to let him see the way the lie was making her face flush. "He said that. I'm gonna go get you some clothes and the chair."

She had ordered adult diapers from Wal-Mart after a quick discussion with a Palmer Public Health nurse over the phone. The best thing, the woman insisted, would be to put him on a backboard and send him in to the Mat-Su Regional Hospital to prevent further damage to the spine. Blaze, wincing as she remembered dragging the wereverine around through the woods with a bulldozer, said that she would take that under advisement.

When Jack saw the diapers, though, he shook his head and tried to scoot away. "Huh-uh," he growled. "I'm a grown man. No way."

Blaze looked down at the 'Adult Incontinence Product' and then shrugged. "Fine. But sooner or later, you're gonna run outta pants, because I am *not* putting that in my washing machine." She gestured at the place on the floor where she had carefully scraped several weeks of excrement from his body, then turned and threw the package of diapers into the trash. Then she shook out his pants and bent to start pulling them onto his legs.

Jack eyed the trash nervously. He licked his lips. "Wait…"

Blaze hesitated. "Oh? You want the diaper, then?"

Jack's face flushed crimson and he muttered something about Yetis and Clydesdales.

"Fine," Blaze said, going back to working his limp legs through the pants.

He kept casting nervous looks at the jeans, then at the box of adult incontinence products. Finally, he grabbed the waistband of the jeans, stopping her from working it further up his thighs. He muttered something softly under his breath.

"Oh *what now?*" Blaze cried, standing up to glare at him.

"Diaper," Jack grated.

"Sorry?" Blaze asked, grinning. "I don't think I heard you correctly. Did you say you wanted me to swaddle your ass?"

"Give me the damn diaper, wench!" Jack snarled, hair prickling through his emaciated back.

Chuckling, Blaze went to the trash, retrieved the incontinence wraps, and proceeded to pull one free of the packaging. Then, holding it up to the light, she gave it a long, curious inspection. "Awww," she said, "It's almost like a pair of Huggies. For big people." Then she grinned, noting the pink color. "Guess I should've stated 'boy' adult incontinence products, eh?"

"Fine!" Jack growled, his face purpling. "Throw it away. I don't need it."

Ignoring him, Blaze bent over him, diaper in hand. "Push up," she ordered, sliding one half of the diaper under his rear.

Reluctantly, Jack obeyed, pushing down with his fists, lifting his butt awkwardly off of the ground. Blaze tucked it in place and cinched it down with the adhesive straps. Then she stood up, admiring her handiwork. "You know," she said, "I should get a camera. You look absolutely adorable in pink."

Jack hunched over like an angry weasel, glaring up at her. "I'll remember this, when I'm back on my feet, Yeti wench."

"Uh-huh," Blaze said. "Until then…" She reached down, finished tugging on his pants, and then lifted him into the wheelchair. "Here's your shirt." She tossed it to him.

Glaring, Jack put his skinny arms through the sleeves, then flinched and looked down at the way it hung from his bony body. "This can't be happening," he whined.

"What?" Blaze asked, "I pick the wrong color plaid?"

"I'm a blacksmith," Jack growled, holding up a scrawny arm. "*Look* at me."

"So you got some filling out to do," Blaze said. She shrugged. "It'll come back."

He peered up at her, long and hard. "Did you cry for me, Blaze?"

She flinched from the suddenness and oddness of his question. "Uh…" She remembered the coma, remembered waking up alone, not knowing how many days had passed until she switched her phone on. "Kind of…" she admitted.

Jack lowered his head to look at his legs. "Hard?" he asked softly.

"Pretty hard," Blaze managed.

Jack twisted to look up at her. Tentatively, he whispered, "Think you might cry for me again anytime soon?"

Blaze snorted. "Not if I can help it."

Jack jerked like she'd hit him. "Why the fuck not?"

"Why *should* I?" Blaze demanded. "You're fine now. Don't need me going and putting myself in a coma again for no damn good reason, do we?"

Jack's hackles went up. "What, I'm not worth a good cry?"

The self-loving, egotistical prick. Blaze laughed at him. Jabbing a finger into his chest she said, "Not on your *life*, you asshole. You've been such a pain in my ass…hell, after you *asking* me to, I doubt I *could* cry for you, even if I wanted to. Go take your crippled ass somewhere else to wallow in your self-pity. I won't have any more part of it."

Jack stared at her, mouth slightly ajar, looking deeply wounded. Before Blaze could figure out what she had done wrong, the wereverine closed his mouth and, glaring at her, turned suddenly and started wheeling himself out of the room in a huff. His wheel got caught on the door-jamb and he cursed. Before Blaze could move to help him, he had violently shoved himself off of the door and scooted away, snarling at her to keep her distance.

"What's wrong?" Blaze called after him, confused.

The wereverine turned a corner and a door slammed.

TWENTY-ONE

The Curmudgeon

Almost a week went by with Jack scooting around the basement in his wheelchair, muttering and cranky, and Blaze having absolutely nothing she could do to cheer him up. She toted all of her guns and silver upstairs the first day, which was a good thing, because one of the first things he did, once she left the house to tend the livestock, was go looking for them. When she came back, her room was a mess and Jack was glowering at her from a pile of clothes, where he had fallen out of his chair. Sighing, Blaze scooped him back into his chair and once again sent him on his way, grateful for the few added pounds of weight he had gained in the interim.

Yet neither his legs—nor his incontinence—seemed to get any better.

The longer he was in the wheelchair, the more grumpy the wer-everine became, until it was a dreaded chore just to take dinner down-stairs and eat with him each night. More than half the time, it ended with Blaze getting frustrated and storming off—or Jack throwing his plate across the room.

Jack began to complain about everything, from the way she cooked to the way she wiped his ass. He insulted the weather, he insulted her, he insulted the clothes she'd picked out for him. His entire life, trapped within the basement of the lodge, seemed to become a mission to see how miserable he could make Blaze's life. He griped and puttered around the bottom story of the Sleeping Lady like a bitter old nursing-home fart who'd lost the will to live, but couldn't get his pesky heart to cooperate.

"That's *it*," Blaze finally growled, after the second week of Jack's deteriorating mood. She grabbed the wereverine by the back of the wheelchair in the middle of yet another griping-puttering mission, twisted him around, and started for the back porch.

"Now hold on there, Yeti wench," the wereverine growled, trying to slow the chair. In the last fourteen days, 'Yeti wench' had been a more common term than her name, used with loving care in such sentences as, 'My bath is cold, Yeti wench,' or 'We're out of firewood, Yeti wench,' or 'So where does a Yeti wench like you learn how to cook? 'Cause that last meal tasted more like charcoal than duck.'

Blaze ignored him and kept pushing the wheelchair towards the back door. "You," she said sweetly, "Are going to start making this place cripple-accessible." She gave him a little shove through the door, stopping him just before he flew off the back porch. "I'm tired of your griping about not being able to do anything."

Jack swiveled to glare up at her, his animal growl once again rattling in his chest.

"Here," Blaze said, reaching beside the door to grab the supplies she had collected. She dropped a hammer, a box of nails, and some boards into his lap. "First order of business is gonna be for you to make me a ramp."

Jack squinted at her, and for the longest time it looked like he was going to tell her to get lost. Then, tentatively, he said, "A ramp?"

"You want to leave the lodge? Then make yourself a way to do it." She gestured at his chair.

Jack peered down at the tools in his lap, then gave the back porch a dubious look.

Then Blaze raised a brow. "Unless you don't think you can…?"

Jack bristled again. "I'm going to need some ten-foot two-by-sixes, a level, a planer, a sander, tape measure, pencil, paper, skillsaw, and lunch, Yeti wench."

"Okay," Blaze said, fighting down a surge of excitement that he seemed to be interested in something again. Then she hesitated. "What's a planer?"

Nose in the air, with all the delicacy of a carpenter detailing his trade to a very retarded dog, he explained it to her. And she went and got it for him, along with everything else on his list. Then Blaze allowed him to direct her as she got everything situated where he wanted it, then helped the wereverine down out of his chair, to sit on the ground, propped up by the porch.

After settling in, Jack picked up boards and started measuring and sorting them. Blaze watched for a few minutes, feeling like a nervous hen, but the wereverine had seemed to forget she existed.

Runt came up to stand beside her, the soft black fluff of a baby Silver Fox rabbit in his hands. He petted the bunny with a distracted air, frowning as they watched the wereverine grumble and mutter over his project. "Are you sure he's capable of building anything in his condition, Lady?" the fey finally said.

"I'm sure," Blaze said, though once Jack started casually busting out the beautiful hardwood railing and flinging the debris haphazardly across the yard, she found she had to go do something else before she thought about yet another part of her lodge that the wereverine was breaking.

Getting the wereverine to build himself a ramp, it turned out, was a mistake.

Now, instead of being restricted to the basement, he was free to gripe and complain all over the property, and did so with great enthusiasm.

At least, she thought, watching him weld a piece of steel to his 4-wheeler that enabled it to be shifted by hand, as opposed to by foot, *He's being a* productive *asshole, now.* She went back to gathering eggs from the chicken coop.

• • •

Jack was propped up beside the 4-wheeler, welder in hand, when he saw the pale, naked form limp around the back of the shop. It was just for an instant before the main body was hidden by the little Jeep he had pulled out of the woods and gotten running the day before, leaving only the ghostly white calves and feet visible under the car. He frowned and pushed his welding mask out of the way, trying to get a better look around the 4-wheeler and other equipment blocking his view.

Finally lowering himself almost level with the dirt to look beyond the 4-wheeler's undercarriage, Jack managed to catch another glimpse of the naked ankles. And, now that he thought about it, they had an odd color to them, almost grayish. The odd, stilted shuffle set the little hairs along the back of his neck on end.

And, like a blow, the wind carried with it the sudden stench of rot. *Horus be merciful*, Jack thought, scooting away hastily. Even though Jack had made no efforts to be quiet, he watched the bare feet continue their shuffle towards the far side of the yard, their goal elsewhere.

Jack, frowning, wedged himself up to see what the creature was aiming at.

Across the yard, Blaze stood with her back to him, picking eggs from the additional coop that they'd had to build to support her growing flock.

Examining the creature's trajectory, Jack heart began to hammer.

Then, as the corpse of the last woman he had ever loved lurched into sight around the 4-wheeler, his heart stopped altogether.

• • •

Blaze placed the last egg into her basket, leaving the two broody Australorp hens to hatch their clutch, then turned to head back to the lodge. Jack was probably getting hungry again—ever since he'd started carpentry and mechanicking again, he had been needing a constant supply of food—and she wouldn't have minded a quick lunch herself. As for the Second Lander, Jack's first analysis that all fey had an extreme case of A.D.D. seemed to be pretty accurate. Runt was gone again—doubtless with a rabbit, gosling or some other form of small, cuddly animal—and probably wouldn't have wanted eggs, anyway. As far as Blaze had seen, the little imp ate only fruit, berries, and herbs.

...and her hot peppers. *All* of them. Once the fey had gotten over the fact that they had enough heat to blow the top off of a nuclear power plant, he had taken to eating them. All. Of. Them. Blaze had yet to catch the little bastard at it, but she hadn't managed to make a single spicy meal in three weeks, despite having an overabundance of sweet peppers.

Muttering, she was closing the fence to the yard when she caught movement out of the corner of her eye. She turned, expecting Jack and his wheelchair.

A naked, too-pale woman was slowing down a few feet away, her washed-out eyes fixed on Blaze's face, her head cocked curiously. There was something familiar about her, something about her face that Blaze was sure she had seen before. Yet, whoever she was, she was *sick*. Blaze winced at the grayish color of her skin.

"Are you okay?" Blaze asked softly.

The woman swallowed, rasped something, then swallowed again. Blaze had to resist the urge to gag at the smell of her breath. It was definitely the worst case of halitosis she'd ever experienced.

"What happened to you?" Blaze asked, panicking, now. "You get robbed? You need some clothes?" She racked her brain trying to remember where she had seen the woman before, but it kept slipping under the surface of her mind. She frowned. *Why* was the woman giving her such goosebumps? In the distance, she heard Jack start the 4-wheeler, and found herself irritated that the self-absorbed prick hadn't tried to help the woman.

The gray-skinned woman worked her throat again, and the rasp that came out resembled something akin to, "I need...blaze."

"A fire?" Blaze asked, glancing at the house. "We've got a wood stove. Come on." She turned to head into the lodge.

The woman's hand was like ice when it grabbed her wrist. "I need… blaze. Are you…her?"

Blaze was surprised at the strength in the woman's hand. The woman couldn't have been more than five-five, but with a single hand, she had stopped her, dead in her tracks. "I'm Blaze," she said, frowning.

In that moment, the woman's face began to morph, stretching and elongating into a roughly ursine form.

A *dead* ursine.

The woman's fur sprang forth in scabby patches, the flesh began to fall off in clumps, and the woman's slitted pupil was distorted beyond glowing white cataracts. The smell of rot was so strong that Blaze's stomach heaved.

"Told…kill…Blaze," the creature said, as the hypodermic teeth slid from the top of her jaw, ripping flesh loose from the roof of her mouth, producing no blood when they punctured the skin.

Blaze dropped the basket of eggs and tried to step back, but the woman's grip was like iron. It was like a cold, clammy vice, and no amount of twisting would allow Blaze to so much as wiggle her arm.

"Told…kill…Blaze," the creature said again, as its toothy jaws stretched wide, snake-like, and tilted to the side, reaching for Blaze's throat.

A 4-wheeler slammed into the creature from the side, knocking it to the ground under a tire, violently tearing it away from Blaze's arm.

Blaze looked down at the gashes left in her wrist by the woman's talons, then quickly wrapped her hand around it, seeing the blood spurt to the ground. Heart hammering, she backed away.

Jack had slid off of the 4-wheeler and crawled over to the dead woman, who threw the machine off of her with a roar. It went tumbling across the yard like a toy. Even then, she was getting back to her feet, her gaze once more fixing on Blaze. The creature took a step forward…

Then screamed as Jack's axe took off her right foot at the ankle. The wereverine was transformed, his hackles puffing out his shirt, his face stretched in a wolverine's fanged grimace. He swung again, but this time his axe only embedded itself in the bone of her leg, and as he was trying to wrench it free, the woman turned on him.

"Jack?" The low, fleshy rasp was just barely audible through her death-blackened teeth. Instantly, the woman's animal features slid away, leaving ripped and puckered skin. Her face, twisted out of proportion by the wereverine's snout, was only half in place, the rest sliding downward, revealing white bone around her cheek and eye-socket. "Is that you, Jack?"

Jack hesitated, his shoulders tensing as he stared at the axe bit, buried in the woman's unbleeding leg. A low rattle building in his chest, he yanked the axe free.

"They told me you were dead, Jack," the dead woman rasped, as she fell to one knee in front of him. She stretched out a grisly hand.

Jack swung again, catching the woman in the arm as she reached for him, taking it off.

If the woman noticed or cared, she made no indication. She seemed enraptured with the paralyzed wereverine. "I waited for you to come, Jack. I spent a month down there in that hole, waiting. I thought I would never see you again."

Jack slammed the axe into her knee, breaking it sideways, cutting through the rotten joint.

She fell to her hands and knees. "I was scared, Jack. I thought I was going to die down there."

Jack cut off a wrist. Then another. The woman tried to get up, clumsy, then noticed the axe in his hands, her stumps of wrists. Her delicate face tightened in a frown. "Jack?" she asked, looking up at him, confused.

Jack started screaming as he worked the blade, slamming it into the creature's flesh, ripping it apart, piece by piece.

When at last the body was in a hundred unmoving pieces, Jack let out a wretched bellow, threw the axe aside, rolled away, and cried. Blaze watched his shoulders shake, looked down at the reeking corpse, and remembered where she had seen that face before. She stumbled backwards, horrified.

Amber had…*resurrected* her?

Looking at the pile of bones and putrefied flesh, the air clogged with the stench of decay, Blaze's stomach heaved again, and this time, she wasn't able to hold it down. She vomited into the grass, still holding her hand tight over her injured wrist.

As she sat there, staring at the wereverine and his former mate, suddenly, Jack's proclamation that she wasn't a warrior felt a thousand times more accurate. Blaze bit her lip out of shame. Throughout it all, she hadn't even thought to use her Desert Eagles.

• • •

Jack used the backhoe to bury the woman's remains, then wheeled himself inside the Sleeping Lady and didn't leave the house for days. He just sat on his bed, his sword in his lap, staring at the wall, eating if Blaze happened to put something in front of him, sleeping if she left him alone.

And, for the most part, Blaze left him alone. She had no idea what to say to him that would make up for the troubles she had caused.

She was out collecting firewood from under the eaves of the shop, wincing up at the October snow-flurries that were coming down in huge, heavy flakes, when she saw the two State Troopers from three weeks before once more trudging up the path.

Shit, Blaze thought. A paranoid corner of her brain wondered if that the hole that Jack had dug hadn't been deep enough to hide the wretched smell of the dead woman, and one of her neighbors had turned her in for the disappearances. She forced herself to put on a smile.

"Hello, officers," Blaze said, dropping the firewood back on the stack.

"Hello Miss MacKenzie," the gangly officer said. He came to a halt a few feet from her and glanced at his partner. "Well, we found out more information on those disturbances."

"Sure did," his partner muttered, nodding.

The slender man took a deep breath, then let it out reluctantly. "I'm really sorry to do this, Miss MacKenzie, but do you mind coming down to the station with us?" The way he said it, it wasn't a question.

Blaze's heart began to hammer. "Why?" she asked.

"Well," the barrel-chested man looked up at her and said, "We talked to Mrs. Jennie Mae Hunderson over at Ebony Creek Lodge and she says she saw you hack a woman apart with an axe on the fourteenth of October. We're gonna have to search the property."

Blaze's heartbeat was rushing through her ears in powerful, fiery thunder, now. So *that* was why she hadn't heard from Jennie Mae in days. "Uh, I didn't hack anyone to pieces."

The taller man gestured at her bandaged wrist. "Where'd you get the wounds, Miss MacKenzie?"

"One of my pigs bit me," Blaze lied.

"That's not what Mrs. Hunderson said," the smaller, barrel-chested Trooper said.

"Jennie Mae is *lying*," Blaze blurted, so scared she was panting. "Amber's doing it. She's a *werewolf*."

The two Troopers looked at each other, hiding smirks. "Oookaaay," the barrel-shaped Trooper said, "Look, Miss MacKenzie, we know we came out here talking about wolves, but we figured out what was really going on. Took us awhile, but we figured it out."

Blaze swallowed down her rising dread. "What's really going on?"

The thinner man smiled at her, but there was no mirth in his look. "*You're* what's been going on, Miss MacKenzie. You're the new blood out here. Only thing that's changed in like twenty years."

"First the lodge at Lake Creek, then the cabins down there, but then you got lazy. Started sticking closer to home. Took out the couple to the west of you, then the fishermen, then your *handyman*..." He nodded at her livestock pens. "You been feedin 'em to your pigs, Miss MacKenzie?"

Blaze's mouth fell open. "No...I mean, it wasn't *me*." Then she frowned. *Who told them that Jack was dead?*

"Sure it wasn't, Miss MacKenzie," the rounder one said. "Would you mind putting your hands above your head and facing the woodpile while my partner removes your weapons?"

Shit, Blaze thought, as she obliged. *Shit, shit.*

"Just stand still," the Trooper said as he moved closer. "Now put your hands behind your back."

Behind him, his partner began to say, "Blaze MacKenzie, you have the right to remain silent..."

Shit!! Blaze's panicked mind began to scream as she felt the cold shackles of metal touch her wrists and snap into place. Amber was pinning the whole thing on her, and now there was a hacked-apart dead body buried in her backyard, right under a fresh new hole Jack had put there with a backhoe. She was gonna go to jail, *forever*, and there wasn't a damn thing she could do about it.

The shorter trooper continued, "Anything you say can and will be used against you in a court of law. You have the right to an attorney. If you cannot afford an attorney, one will be provided for you. Do you understand the rights I have just read to you?"

Oh God, Blaze thought, each beat of her heart a thundering wave of fire. Then she realized she had to help Jack. If they took her away, he wouldn't be able to feed himself.

She cleared her throat. "Officers, I have someone..." Before she could finish telling them about the cripple she was caring for in her basement, however, the thinner cop shoved her against the woodpile and his hand reached for her pistol.

"Fuck," the thinner cop said, pulling the gun from her belt. "She's using fucking *silver*." Blaze heard her gun thump out in the yard behind them, followed by her other.

"I knew the gigantic bitch smelled funny," the other cop said. "No wonder Amber wanted nothing to do with her."

With those words, Blaze felt every hair along her back stand on end.

The smaller cop kicked her in the back of the knees, forcing her to the ground. "Still. I wonder what the boss was so afraid of," the thinner Trooper growled. "She's not even a were."

"Not very smart, either," the barrel-chested trooper replied. "Gave up her guns without a fight." He snorted. "Hell, this was *easy*." He sounded disgusted with that fact. In that moment, something heavy shoved Blaze bodily to the ground, so that her face was pressed into the eighth-inch of fresh snow.

"How should we kill her?" the thinner Trooper demanded. "Dig a hole and bury her?"

"Boss said to have some fun first," the barrel-chested trooper said. "Then we can kill the big bitch." She felt him kneel behind her and suddenly a rough hands was gripping the back of her hair, hauling her face off of the ground. Into her face, the man said, "This *is* a bitch, ain't it?" He sniffed her neck, then, dropping her head unceremoniously back to the ground, stuck his face between her thighs and drew in a breath. "Oh yeah," he chuckled. "It's got a cunny, all right." Rough hands started gripping Blaze between the thighs, rubbing hard against her womanhood.

Panting in terror, now, Blaze twisted her wrists in the cuffs, trying everything to yank them loose. Her big hands might as well have been barbells for how much give they had inside the metal bands, and the barrel-chested man had a hand in the middle of her back, pinning her to the ground as he ran his hand up and down the inside of her leg.

"I don't know, man," the thinner Trooper said, sounding uncertain. "It's our job to stop that sort of shit."

"*Fuck* the job, man," the thicker man chuckled. "Do *you* really wanna go back to that boring crap?" He snorted and leaned down to lick Blaze's neck. "Oh yeah. Damn she tastes good. Come on. Help me undo her pants."

"Dude," the thinner cop said, as Blaze began to hyperventilate. "Leave her alone, okay?"

"We're gonna kill her anyway," the barrel-shaped man muttered. "Besides, Boss told us to have some fun." He drove his hands under her waist and started unbuckling her pants.

"Hey, goddamn it!" the thinner cop growled. "She may have bit us, but that doesn't make us goddamn animals, all right? Get up, let's kill her and get this over with."

"Matt, just go fuck off for a half hour or something, okay?" the barrel-chested one snapped. He grabbed the back of Blaze's shirt and, with a brief flash of pain as it tightened around her neck, she felt it rip away like paper. Then he flipped Blaze over, face up at the falling snow, back to the icy ground, and gave her a dangerous snarl that showed slitted blue eyes. Before Blaze could pull her legs back for a kick, he leaned forward and said, "You kick me, bitch, and I'll eviscerate you slowly, ya got me?"

Terror drove through Blaze's core like a stake. She lowered her legs, shaking. As if he had just warned her about the weather, the barrel-chested trooper started tugging her pants and panties down her legs, exposing her lower body to the falling snow. Blaze bit her lip and shivered, but was unable to close her eyes to the beast as he crawled over her.

To her horror, he started to *change*. His slitted blue eyes started to glow, and his body grew larger, heavier, and heavy gray fur sprouted from his arms and face. Suddenly, there was a wolf kneeling over her, leering down at her with his unnatural, hypodermic smile. Blood from where his teeth had punctured the top of his mouth was dripping on Blaze's exposed chest. "Figured you wanna know what it is to be a real bitch," her assailant said. "Got just what ya need here, sweet cheeks." He leaned down and licked his blood off of her belly in long, wet strokes. Blaze trembled, whimpering.

"Pat," the thinner Trooper warned, "That isn't how we do things." He leaned down and took the wolf by the shoulder.

Her assailant whirled on Matt and swiped a taloned hand at his arm. "I said *fuck off*!"

In a move too fast to see, Matt yanked Pat off of her. With a roar of fury, Pat pulled himself off the ground and leapt at Matt's chest. Snarling, they went tumbling towards the woodpile in a frenzy, causing half of the pile to fall down atop them.

Ten-pound chunks of birch flying like matchsticks, the werewolves started tearing at each other amidst the firewood, blood and fur staining the air. Blaze screamed when the first piece of firewood hit her in the stomach, and started kicking backwards, trying to get away from them. With the pants locked around her ankles and the cuffs around her wrists, however, she could barely move more than a few inches at a time. She scraped her naked arms and back against the icy gravel, sliding towards the house, as far away from them as she could get.

Matt screamed suddenly, and Blaze saw Pat rip the other wolf's chest open, collecting a handful of heart and lungs before shoving his opponent aside into the ruined pile. Matt's mouth was open, blood draining from his open ribcage onto the birch quarters. Pat threw his heart and lungs aside in disdain, still twitching.

Letting out a little whine of terror, Blaze flopped herself over onto her stomach and tried to get her feet under her.

There was a fresh drag-mark in the snow off of the back porch. Blaze hesitated, following it with her eyes.

Then the wolf was flipping her over, pink drool dripping from his bloodstained lips. "Where do you think you're going?" he growled, pinning her shoulder to the ground as he started to reposition himself over her. "I ain't done fucking you yet."

"Hey puppy," Jack said.

Above Blaze, the wolf hesitated and looked up.

The blast of a gunshot made Blaze flinch.

The wolf stiffened above her, then rolled to the side and began to scream.

Another gunshot shattered the yard, followed by another.

The wolf started to thrash, howling.

Blaze felt Jack's warm body slide past her as he crawled up to the flailing wolf. He took two more shots, then the wolf went quiet.

"Hold on there, sweetheart. I'll get the keys." She sat up to watch Jack crawl across the yard to where the Trooper's pants had been shredded and shed. He dug around in the pockets until he found what he was looking for, then crawled back to her, head down, a determined look on his face. By the time he got close enough to touch her leg, he was red-faced and sweating. He dragged his body the last few feet behind her, then grunted as he flopped onto his side. "Just hold still a minute." She felt him fiddle with the cuffs at her wrists, heard a metallic click.

Blaze was shaking all over when her hands fell free. Partly out of terror, partly from the cold, every muscle in her body was suddenly trembling, and all she could do was stare down at herself in shock.

Behind her, Blaze heard another metallic click. Numbly, she turned.

Jack was holding the pistol to the side of his head, looking at her torn and shredded shirt. The hammer was back, his finger on the trigger.

Blaze tensed. "Don't," she whispered.

Tentatively, Jack met her eyes. "I can't go through this again," he whimpered. His words came out as a plea. "Fly out of here. Go somewhere the hell else. I can't do this. Not again." He closed his eyes and took a deep breath. For a horrible moment, she knew he was going to pull the trigger.

"I'm going to kill them," Blaze said, and she knew this time she meant it. "You shoot yourself, I'm going to go find them and kill them all."

Jack hesitated. Slowly, he opened his brilliant green eyes and looked at her. Gun still to his brainpan, he growled, "You know that's the most retarded thing I've ever heard, right?" The way he said it, Jack no more thought she could kill werewolves than she could waltz onto a dance floor and have every guy in the place vying for her arm.

Blaze gestured at the gun. "Can't be worse than threatening to sputch yourself across the yard because you just saved my life, leaving me shivering here, naked, with your gore all over me."

Jack narrowed his eyes. For a long moment, he just kept the gun to his temple, glaring at her. Then, reluctantly, he let it drop into his lap. "I moved my toes this morning," he muttered at his knees.

Blaze felt a surge of hope. "That's *great*!" she cried.

He looked up to glare at her. For a long time, he said nothing. Then, "Go inside and get me my chair, Yeti wench. My ass is getting cold."

Naked, shivering, Blaze narrowed her eyes at him. *Well, at least his attitude is back.*

TWENTY-TWO

Back to Anchorage

They buried the wolves with the backhoe, then Blaze bulldozed it level and they put up more fencing. Despite Jack's taste in goat, the hairy little beasts were multiplying. Hell, everything that was within a hundred *yards* of the greenhouse was still vibrant green, despite the three inches of snow on the ground. What was even more amazing, the goats, which had a gestation period of a hundred and fifty days, were kidding at around thirty, and goats that normally had one to two kids on average were having four or five. Even more stunning, the woods where they had penned them—that Blaze had thought might last two, maybe even three weeks before the little brush-machines completely devoured all signs of life—wasn't even showing indication that they'd been munching on it.

"You know, *someone's* gonna notice this," Blaze said, as she re-stacked blood-spattered firewood under the shop eaves. She gestured at the green trees in the snowstorm. "They're not dropping their leaves."

Jack twisted in his chair, his thigh squishing the Desert Eagle on his hip. He peered at the greenery an unconcerned moment, then shrugged. "Anybody asks, you can call it a weird virus or something." He went back to concentrating on his feet. He was getting them to twitch slightly, one after the other.

Considering that, Blaze said, "I haven't seen Runt in awhile."

"They hibernate," Jack said. "Little twit's probably sleeping. Good riddance."

Blaze frowned. "Do wolves hibernate?"

Jack just watched his feet, a frown of concentration on his forehead. "You know, Yeti wench, I could use a drink of water."

Blaze dropped a piece of firewood on the pile a bit too abruptly. Jack looked up.

"You are perfectly capable of getting your own water."

Instead of appearing chagrined, however, the bastard returned his attention to his toes and said, "I know, but I want you to do it. It's easier for you."

Blaze felt a muscle in her neck twitch. Ignoring him, she picked up another birch quarter, this one covered in blood and long gray wolf hair. *Wolf* hair…She paused, staring down at it, her forehead tightening in a frown, as the ticklings of a new thought began tugging at the back of her mind.

"You know, Yeti wench," Jack said conversationally, "My thirst will not quench its—"

"Shut *up* a second!" Blaze snapped, looking down at the wolf fur. She frowned at him. "You only killed *one* of those Troopers, right?"

Jack was giving her a startled, somewhat irritated look. She saw the bits of fur poking from under his shirt and realized he probably didn't like being told to shut up. "You know, Yeti wench, I don't appreciate—"

"Answer me!" Blaze growled. She held up the gore-stained hunk of wood. "*You* didn't kill the first one, right? His partner did that?"

Jack sighed like a professor tasked with teaching an incompetent student. "The moon-magic grabs the young ones and don't let go until it wants to. Once they hit wolf form, they do all sorts of stupid shit."

Blaze frowned. "So when they're possessed, the Third Lander is completely in control? That why you blacked out?"

"Now *hold on* a minute there, missy," Jack growled. "I don't know what that little shit was tellin you, but I ain't possessed."

Blaze met his eyes and held it. "But you *did* black out."

Jack narrowed his eyes. "I'll be in the basement." He spun his chair around and started for the back steps, his big back having already regained most of its prior definition.

Blaze grabbed his chair and spun him around.

Immediately, Jack's shirt puffed out with fur and he sprouted fangs. "I ain't possessed," he snarled, his slitty eyes glowing.

Blaze decided to leave that sore subject for later. Instead, she squatted in front of him, still holding the birch quarter. "Those two, when they died, were *wolves*. Ugly, misshapen, nightmare wolves with way too many teeth and fucked-up eyes, but *wolves*."

Jack peered up at her as if she had just grown peach fuzz and testicles. "Huh?"

"We don't have human bodies buried in my backyard," Blaze said. She shook the quarter of birch and its glob of hair at him. "We have *these* things, and *these* things were happy to kill each other, given the right provocation."

Jack squinted at her, but the fur was starting to sink back under his skin. He eyed the block of firewood like she intended to beat the idea into his skull with it. "So?"

"So how do we get the whole pack to change into *these* things?" Blaze demanded. "They'd take care of the problem for us."

Jack snorted. "If it were that easy, they'd have all sputched themselves the moment Amber took them on their first hunt."

Blaze shook her head and tapped his chest with the gory block of wood. "No. I mean, once they're *there*, they can't change back unless the Third-Lander wants them to. They'd be kind of *stuck* there if we can give them a reason for the Third-Lander to stay in charge."

Jack's hackles went up again. "I don't like the way this conversation is going, missy."

"What would a Third-Lander want more than anything?" Blaze demanded.

Jack frowned at her, and it almost looked like he wouldn't respond. Then, reluctantly, he growled, "You mean aside from not being in the Third Lands?"

Blaze nodded.

"Power," Jack said. "As much power as they can get their hands on."

"What about a magic feather?" Blaze asked.

Jack's eyes went wide. "Oh *hell* no. The *last* thing I'm gonna do is give Amber a dread unicorn's horn *and* a magic feather. That's just about the dumbest thing I've ever heard. Don't you even *think* about it."

"Would the Third-Landers recognize it?" Blaze demanded. "If they all got a good look?"

A rattling growl started deep in Jack's chest. "I said no."

"But..." Blaze started.

Jack spun on her, and when he did, his face was a nightmarish mass of fangs and fur. "*No*." So vehement was the fury in his eyes that Blaze decided to abandon that particular idea.

"Okay," she said. "We'll leave the feather where it is." Blaze glanced up at the Sleeping Lady with a twinge of regret. "I have another idea."

"Stuff it," Jack said. "I don't want anything to do with it." He tried to turn and scoot away again.

Blaze yanked him back and shoved the block of birch under his nose. "Listen here, you ornery little *weasel*. You are going to help me *fix* this, or I'm going to leave you out here to wiggle your toes while I go take a high-powered rifle and stake out a spot across the damn river from the werewolf camp and shoot them until they figure out where I am and eat me. You *get* me?"

Jack laughed. "You'd never be able to pull the trigger."

"I pulled the trigger on *you*," Blaze growled, shaking the firewood, "when you tried to eat me, and again on those werewolves Amber brought with her the night they gutted you. Now are you going to *listen* to my idea or am I going to have to take a *skillsaw* to that ramp you made, install a *deadbolt* on the bathroom about *six feet high*, and run over your chair with my *bulldozer*?"

Jack eyed the block of wood as it hovered near his face with a chagrined wince. "Uh. Sure, Boss. What's your idea?"

Blaze lowered the block of wood. "I want that fire extinguishing system I brought out installed in the lodge."

Jack snorted. "And I want my legs to work again."

She raised a brow, then went to get her high-powered rifle.

"Now hold on a minute, missy." Jack grabbed her by the pant leg as she passed his chair, dragging her up short. Once his chair stopped rolling, he released her jeans to glare up at her. "You spent six hundred thousand of your 'hard-earned' dollars on this place. You sure you wanna go burn it down?"

Blaze grinned down at him. "Wouldn't need a fire extinguisher if I was planning on doing that, now would I?"

Jack got all squinty-eyed and wrinkled his nose as if he smelled something nasty. "I'm not sure I like where this is going."

Blaze glanced back at the yard where she had buried her silver bullion. "You know how to make colloidal silver, Jack?"

"*Bullshit!*" Jack cried, backing his chair away from her. He pointed a taloned finger at her, snarling. "I *knew* I wasn't gonna like this. You bossy damned Yeti, *fine*, go get a gun and plunk away at wolves until they come eviscerate you. I'm gonna stay right damned here."

Leaning over the wereverine's chair, Blaze said, "Listen. My mother was a health nut. Thought colloidal silver was like the Elixir of Life or something like that, but even with as much money as she had, she didn't want to go buy the stuff for twenty bucks a bottle. So she had Dad make it in the shop, by the gallon."

"I said I don't wanna talk about silver," Jack growled.

"I'm telling you we can *make* it," Blaze insisted. "I have the silver wire. Drop it in a glass jar of water, hook a car battery to it, and voila! An hour later you've got colloidal silver."

"A fat lot of good that does us," Jack muttered. Reluctantly, he added, "If we're gonna talk silver, we should be talking silver nitrate or silver bullets. Colloidal's like, what, a drop of silver to a gallon of water?"

Blaze grinned. "There's about ten parts per million, on the low end. Can get it higher, if you do it right."

Jack blinked at her. "Ten parts per *million*? Are you *crazy*?" He snorted. "That's like dunking 'em in itching cream. All it'll do is piss 'em off."

Blaze nodded, smiling. "Exactly."

The wereverine stared at her for a long moment before saying, "Anything you want to *add* to that, sister, or are we planning on letting them *itch* themselves to death?"

When he saw that she planned on letting them do just that, the wereverine threw back his head and cackled. "Just go," he said between spasms, gesturing at the lodge. "You big bumbling city-slicker brat. You're gonna get yourself sputched anyway. At least the wolves'll get a couple day's meal out of your huge carcass."

Blaze shrugged, went inside, found her rifles and ammo still safely where she had stashed them on the second floor, and came back with them strapped over her shoulder. Jack was where she had left him, bristling with fur and teeth. She paused thoughtfully. "You think I should bring food? Think I'll survive that long?"

Jack narrowed his eyes, but said nothing.

Blaze sighed and resettled the rifle over her shoulder. "Probably not. I'll see you later, Jack." She started walking down the path towards the lake.

Jack hunched in his chair and watched in silence until she vanished around the shop. Blaze kept going, though she was beginning to get worried he was simply going to let her wander off to die when she heard a distant shout of, "Get your Clydesdale ass back here and find me a damn wrench!"

Blaze grinned and went back.

Over the course of the next two days, she was Jack's arms and legs as together they installed her state-of-the-art sprinkler system, which had been part of the bank's requirement for the loan.

"There," Jack growled, when it was finished, "Now you can set your house on fire—or burn the toast—and it'll set this baby off." He tapped the sprinkler system and frowned up at her. "We might as well kiss our asses goodbye, you know."

"Whatever," Blaze said. "Help me board up the windows."

Jack scowled. "Why? We going somewhere?"

"Yeah," Blaze said, "Back to Anchorage."

Immediately, the wereverine stiffened. "No. I ain't goin' anywhere near that cesspool. Huh-uh. I'll stay right here and hold down the fort."

He jammed a finger towards the floorboards under his chair, twitching a leg with the vehemence behind his words.

"Leg moved," Blaze noted.

Narrowing his eyes but without taking his gaze off of her, Jack muttered, "I saw."

Blaze shrugged. "The point is moot. I already chartered the plane," Blaze said. "During your last bath. We leave tomorrow at noon."

"You already chartered the *plane*?" Jack demanded. "I'm not going anywhere!"

The way he sounded like he was panicking made Blaze squint at him. "You've never been on board a plane before, have you?"

Jack flushed red. "I prefer good ol' Gaia. Screw flying."

"You've never *flown* before, have you?" Blaze cried, gleeful. "And you call *me* 'out of touch with reality.'"

"Last thing I flew," Jack growled, "Was a dragon as it pinwheeled into the ground after a void-titan knocked it out cold. I would like to avoid a repeat experience."

Blaze opened her mouth to again ask him about dragons, then realized he was diverting her attention from the subject at hand. "Don't change the subject. We're going flying. The point is moot."

The wereverine sprouted fangs and slitty green eyes. "The point isn't moot if I start taking pot-shots at the plane when it comes to take me away," Jack snarled, a big hand gripping the Desert Eagle on his hip.

...Or when he starts clawing up the insides of the cockpit because we hit a little turbulence, Blaze thought, with a wince.

Shaking off that thought, she said, "You're going. Now help me with the damn windows."

Jack narrowed his slitted green eyes at her in that stubborn, I'm Deciding Whether Or Not To Tell The Yeti To Go Screw Herself look, then finally muttered, "Hammer. Nails. I piled the plywood out behind the shop."

Grinning inwardly, Blaze went to go fetch the supplies. She was halfway around the yard when she saw the jet black werewolf watching her like a statue in between the tractor and the bulldozer, only a few feet away. "Jack!" she screamed, backing up, fumbling for her gun.

The wolf spun and disappeared.

"Jack!" she screamed again. Her hand was shaking where she held the gun, and her finger felt weak on the trigger. Her heart was in her throat, and her arms felt like they were on fire.

"What the hell is it now?!" Jack demanded, pushing his chair around the corner at speed. He saw her standing with the gun out, shakily pointing it at the woods. She heard him draw his own weapon, cursing. For a moment, they just stood there, waiting for the attack.

"Wolf?" Jack finally asked, sniffing the air.

Blaze nodded.

Jack lowered his weapon, scowling. "I wonder why she's hanging around."

"Huh?" Blaze asked, turning.

"Kimber." Jack shook his head. "Probably smells the meat." He gestured dismissively at her barn. "Come on. Let's get those windows boarded up and get you out of here."

• • •

Amber was reclining upon a futon her submissives had dragged from the Ebony Creek Lodge when one of her number came back at a run. There were so many of them now and such a huge turnover rate that she hadn't bothered to learn all their names. Maybe someday, she could afford that leisure, but camaraderie was one of the many things that Amber had sacrificed in the name of expanding her family's empire.

"Yes?" she asked, as the scout slid to a stop, still in full moon-form.

"Mith Blathe ang Thornthon fwoo aw—"

"Oh for Chrissakes," Amber snapped. "Don't sit there slurring like a goddamn beast. Shift!"

Her submissive—a pretty gray with a bit of black on his rump, whined in shame and he lowered his belly to the dirt, probably in hopes that she wouldn't force the issue. The young ones had such poor control of themselves, most of them, it seemed, actually *preferred* the moon form.

"Misthreth, pleathe..." her submissive whimpered.

Amber sighed and looked at her fingertips. "I'm not asking again." Then, frowning at the dried blood under a few of her nails, she used one of the pretty translucent faeglass daggers she and her pack had acquired in their latest raid—a group of fauns, most of which had run through their precious portal back to the Second Lands in a panic—to pry the flaky brown crust from the nail bed.

While Amber waited impatiently, it took him a full five minutes of struggling against the moon-magic to shift back into his human form. Of course, as young as he was, she supposed she was lucky he could get out of moon-form at all...

The young man who ended up naked at her feet looked a bit dazed. A pretty enough specimen, though, Amber decided. A fly-fisherman she had caught pike fishing up in the chain of lakes beyond Lake Ebony. He might make a decent enough mate, if he could learn a bit more control. She *hated* the way the new ones tended to transform mid-act. She found it rather vulgar, and while she didn't mind a good screw in the middle of a hunt, she would much prefer the species at least remain the same throughout.

"Mistress?" the man asked, from his knees.

"You were telling me about our gasoline-loving heiress and her dead wolverine slut."

"Oh, uh..." He blushed, then frowned. The fool actually had to think about it. Amber realized she probably should start teaching them all the importance of maintaining control of the moon magic, but she just didn't have the time of late. Too many miserly old fools to kill, too many wonderful stashes to discover.

She flicked the milky tip of the faeglass blade at him. "Let me guess. You don't remember much of what happened after you changed."

The man looked up at her and flinched, his face reddening in shame. "Uh...No Mistress."

Well, at least he was smart enough to get the 'Mistress' part down. Amber probably would have gutted him before this, had he not. And why not? She had two dozen who would happily take his place, and could make two dozen more with a simple kiss.

"Perhaps I can jog your memory," Amber said. "I told you to go figure out what happened to our boys in blue."

The man frowned, hard. "Uh…I remember the change. And running through the forest…" He peered at the ground in front of him as if he were looking into a very deep well. "And I remember reaching the lake…"

Amber sighed, looking him over for blood. "Did you kill anyone?"

The man—a liberal-minded bleeding-heart doctor by trade—cringed. She had already broken him of *those* particular pretentions to squeamishness, when she'd made him shift and set him loose on a group of female captives she'd bloodied up for him. The new ones simply couldn't control themselves around the scent of blood, and Amber's pack already had too many females for her tastes.

"I don't think I killed anyone, Mistress," the man whispered. His brow was knotted in concentration. As a former doctor, Amber supposed that being incapable of remembering certain things was rather new to him. As was having to crawl on his belly around her, she was sure. That's why she made them do it. If too many submissives got the idea that their pack leader wasn't in complete control, the moon-magic might spurn them into doing something unpleasant.

"But there was some reason you came rushing in to talk to me," Amber suggested, rather enjoying his embarrassment. She'd never liked doctors. Always stuck-up, too full of their own modern medicine that they wouldn't know magic if it bit them.

Which Amber routinely made sure it did, she thought, grinning.

"I remember!" the young man cried with sudden excitement, like he'd unearthed some great archeological find. "The lodge is completely boarded up and abandoned. All the food's still there. Left lots of food out, though. I think they're planning on coming back."

Amber dropped the faeglass blade and looked up from her nails. "What lodge? And who is 'they'?"

But her submissive was babbling excitedly, now. "The Sleeping Lady. Blaze MacKenzie and Jack Thornton. They left it. I was rounding the edge of the lake and I saw Blaze and the wolverine get onboard. They taxied out to the river and flew off.

Amber frowned. "You mean she carried the weasel's body out of the Bush? On a plane?"

"No, no." The man frowned, obviously concentrating. "The wolverine was alive. His legs weren't working, though. Paralyzed, I think. Waist down, it looked like. She had to help him into the plane."

"He's *alive*?!" Amber was out of her futon and on her feet, half-transformed, in an instant, snarling down at her submissive. "And you let him *leave*?!"

The man cringed against the ground, whining up at her. "The girl was with him. And the pilot—"

Amber reached down for the man's neck and dragged him off the ground until they were eye-to-eye. "You think I give a *crap* about the pilot? He killed my *mate*!" Her fist was squeezing of its own accord, and the submissive peed himself as his moon-magic once more took hold. In full wolf-form, however, he was even more helpless to avoid the claws around his neck. He whined and struggled, his pretty blue eyes pleading with her.

"He was paralyzed and you let him *get away*," she screamed, utter rage flowing through her system, now. Her fingers squeezed until the whining stopped, the man's windpipe blocked off. Other submissives were coming out of the trees to see what the fuss was about, yet keeping a good twenty-foot distance when they saw her half-transformed.

The man dangling from her hand looked like he desperately wanted to say something. Amber reached up and ripped the top half of his skull off, then threw it aside. She'd never liked doctors, anyway.

To the rest of her submissives, who were staring at the twitching body with trepidation, she snarled, "Pack our stuff. We're moving the den. I want everything inside the Sleeping Lady by the end of the day. That rich brat decides to come back, she's gonna have a big surprise."

She stalked off towards the river to clean the gore from her fingertips.

Unfortunately, it seemed that the wereverine was smarter than he looked. He'd probably convinced the mountainous heiress that she was safer in the city, with her money protecting them. Damn him. Amber would have to schedule a family vacation to Anchorage someday, once she figured out where the rich bitch was hiding.

Until then, there was a good week's supply of food milling around the Sleeping Lady. They could rest there, then gather their strength and move north to find the caribou herds beyond the Brooks Range.

In the meantime, Amber needed to make a phone call. She had no intention of letting the cranky little curmudgeon hit up his friends in Anchorage—if the rabid little weasel even *had* friends—and then escape off to some remote village in Nevada. No, she was going to head him off and finish the job she started.

This time, she'd jam the dagger right through the weasel's *skull.*

Amber marched into the cabin, bypassed the massive hole in the floor that led to the main den, and yanked the satellite phone off of the far wall. "Someone start the generator!" she yelled out the open door, then settled down with her address book. She found the number she was seeking at the same time she heard the stuttering rumble of the generator kicking into gear.

Grunting, Amber dialed the number to Bruce Rogers' Flying Service.

TWENTY-THREE

Packhorsie

"You sure you two got everything?" Phil Russels of Wasilla Air Taxi asked, eying Jack's progress dubiously. The muttering little wereverine was crawling into a harness strapped to Blaze's back, as Blaze stood patiently on the spongy muskeg of the lakeshore, steadied by the airplane's wing support.

"*Damn* you're heavy," Blaze grunted, as the wereverine's full weight hit the harness. "I *really* hope I don't end up carrying your useless ass the rest of my life."

She saw Phil Russels give her a startled look.

"Oh don't worry," Blaze said, waving a dismissive hand at the pilot, "The crass little jackass dishes out a hell of a lot more than that every time he blows his nose."

"Stop moving, you goddamn draft-horse," Jack snarled, yanking sharply on the harness as he secured it. "I can't believe you talked me into this. First you dump me in the lake trying to get me on the plane, then you take me in the air and I puke my guts out all over Bruce's cockpit, then that asshole in the taxi tells me I smell like wet dog—wet *dog*—and now you plan to cart me around like a freakin haunch of moose…Hell, I should just end us both right here and let the gods sort things out."

"Uh..." Phil said, chuckling nervously, "If you guys want to go back to town, I'm headed that way anyway..." His eyes were on the Desert Eagle strapped to the wereverine's hip. "I mean, it's snowing out, and it's not every day someone wants to go hiking through the woods who's paralyzed from the waist down."

Blaze almost toppled over when the wereverine swiveled on the man and snarled, "I am *not* paralyzed, you potbellied fuck."

Phil reddened. "Was just saying..." He gestured to the wereverine's legs.

Strapped to her back, the wereverine growled, "Sayin' what, exactly?"

The pilot from Wasilla Air Taxi cleared his throat uncomfortably. "Well, I hope you guys got a good plan."

"Oh, we got a *great* plan," Jack snapped. "The Yeti thought of it herself."

"I mean..." The man cleared his throat again. "I don't see you packin' much in the way of food. And two guys alone in the woods..." He caught himself and flushed suddenly, looking up at Blaze. "I mean... A guy and a girl...I mean..."

"I know what you mean," Blaze said, years of practice putting a smile over her embarrassment.

Jack made a clucking sound that reminded Blaze of Old West movies. "Let's go, Bessie," the wereverine said. "Don't want this poor mortal's head to explode."

Deciding that was definitely *enough*, Blaze spun around, careful to knock Jack's head solidly against the wing support as she turned to face the pilot. Holding out a hand for Phil to shake, Blaze said, "I'm really sorry about my poor, retarded brother. He kind of came out like this, and, well, he's never been very...cultured."

"Now *listen here*, Yeti wench!" Jack snarled. She felt him wave his arms around, throwing her balance off a bit.

"You should probably go," Blaze said, gesturing for the pilot to get back in his plane. "My brother and I will be fine. I own a cabin just through the woods."

"All right," the pilot said reluctantly. "Just tryin' ta make sure you two stay safe, seein' how you're carrying around a cripple, 'n all."

"A *cripple*?!" Flinging this way and that on her back, the wereverine snarled, "The only thing that isn't safe is your *face* when I sink my claws into your—"

Blaze connected his skull with the wing-strut again, hard. Phil winced at the resounding rattle of his aircraft's frame. "Oh!" she cried, peering over her shoulder at the wereverine. "I am *so* sorry…" She glanced back at Phil. "Is there anything else you need?"

"Uh, no," the pilot from Wasilla Air Taxi said. "Uh, you two have a safe trip, all right?"

"Thank you kindly," Blaze said, even as Jack snarled, "Just screw off already."

She helped the pilot get launched, then held her hand up against the blast of wind as the prop wound up and the float plane started out across the lake.

"Someday," Jack said, "I'm going to break your legs and tote *you* around in a haversack."

"It's technically not a haversack," Blaze said, smiling and waving at the plane as it departed. "It's a glorified baby-carrier."

She could *feel* Jack's hackles push up against her back, through his shirt. "Miss Blaze," he said, and it came out in a bit-out snarl, "Since when did 'pissing off the wereverine' start to sound like a good idea to you?"

"Do you have the compass?" Blaze asked, picking up her small backpack of water and snacks and handing it to him.

"I don't *need* a compass," Jack growled. "I can smell our way there."

Blaze narrowed her eyes at the vanishing plane. "You left it in the cab, didn't you?"

"Don't need it," Jack insisted stubbornly.

"Don't need it…or don't know how to *use* it?!" Blaze demanded.

"I got the sun and the stars," Jack snapped back. "That's all I need."

Blaze jabbed a finger at the overcast sky. "And when *that* happens?!"

"…I can smell our way there," Jack growled. "Start trotting, horsie. 'Fore I make good on my threats and put us both out of our damn misery."

He just called me a 'horsie', Blaze realized with that dreamy half-aware state of a scholar making a note on a rather interesting form of insect, *And I wanted to get this bastard into my bed.*

"Giddy-*up*!" Jack said, slapping her on the thigh. "Better get *going* if you wanna get there by sunset."

Blaze took a deep breath to quell the urge to cut the straps from her back and dump the wereverine into the water. Getting that impulse under control, she looked at the forest behind the swampy edge of the lake. "Think this is gonna work?"

Strapped to her back, Jack laughed. "No."

"Why not?" Blaze demanded.

She felt his hand wave around as he gestured at the forest. "Just get going. You'll see."

Blaze very soon *did* see. Trudging through the woods, she quickly discovered, was *not* the same as meandering along a nice, pre-cut path, clearly marked with pink surveyor's tape for your convenience. It was a spongy, marshy, jumbled mess, where every step was either getting her soaked to the knees or making her trip over herself as the cranberry bushes and hidden logs caught at her ankles and dragged her down.

"I'm not paying you to *fall*," Jack laughed, after the fourth time she went sprawling, "I'm paying you to *walk*, pony."

Fury was the only thing that got her back to her feet, that time. Legs trembling under the strain, Blaze dragged herself up the trunk of a spruce tree. "You," she panted, clinging to the tree's rough branches, "Are really close to getting left in the woods you petulant little *shit*."

Jack went quiet after that.

Knowing she wasn't going to make it back to her feet if she fell a fifth time, Blaze picked her way carefully, keeping her shaking legs straight, trying desperately not to think about how much dead weight was clinging to her spine.

When they finally made it to the old mill trail, Blaze let out a whimper of happiness. She lurched onto the relative solidity of the trail and caught herself on a spindly birch just before she went sprawling.

Her legs, by this point, felt like trembling knots of liquid muscle, and she didn't trust her knees to hold her up.

"You're doing good," Jack said softly. "Just another mile."

It was the first thing he had said for a couple hours, aside from telling her to turn right or left, and that he was speaking now irritated Blaze.

"What, no Clydesdale comments?!" she snapped. "No telling me I'm a city-slicker who can't even carry her own damn weight in the woods?"

When the wereverine didn't respond, immediately, Blaze laughed bitterly and looked out at the trail ahead, trying to divine how she was going to get them both another *mile*. She barely had enough strength to cling to the tree, much less stand there.

"Blaze," Jack said, "I told you this was impossible when you first told me your stupid plan. I told you you'd be too worn out from the trek through the woods to carry my ass."

"So you were right," Blaze snapped. "Good for you. Does the wereverine want a cookie?"

"…and you already went three times as far as I thought you'd get us," Jack said. "I honestly started off the day thinking you were gonna leave me stranded in the woods."

"Haven't *not* left you stranded, yet," Blaze reminded him.

"I was pissing you off on purpose earlier," Jack said. "Trying to keep you going." She felt him move a little in the pack. "Now, if you don't mind, I'd *really* like it if you got us the rest of the way there, so we really have a chance of making your plan work."

"My legs aren't working right," Blaze confessed. She looked down at her trembling knees. "Hell, I don't know if I can move."

"You can do it, Blaze."

The confidence with which he said it gave her a little flurry of hope…

…Which was squashed just as soon as Blaze took another look at how *much* of the trail she had to go. She groaned and looked back down at her huge feet.

"The lodge is just a mile up the road," Jack insisted. "You get us there, we'll be like Vikings raiding an abbey."

"Bet that was pretty easy," Blaze muttered.

"They had boiling oil and crossbows," Jack said. "It sucked."

Blaze took a deep breath and glanced again at the snowy trail. "All right. But you owe me a massage after this."

"Hell, woman," Jack said, "You get us through this, alive, and I'll give you a massage every night for an entire *year*."

"I'm holding you to that," Blaze said, taking a reluctant step forward and releasing her grasp on the tree. "Every night for a year. Naked."

"Every night for a year," Jack agreed. "Na—*wait*, what?"

Chuckling at the panic in his voice, Blaze said, "Sounds like a good deal to me. I mean, here I am carting your sorry ass through the woods as you gripe at me and alternate between calling me an abominable snowman and a strange new form of draft horse." She took another wobbly step.

"Who's gonna be naked?" he asked, suspiciously.

"Why, you, of course," Blaze responded, planting another foot and gingerly taking the weight with a tremulous knee. "I'm just the one getting the massage."

"You know," Jack said, "I did spend some time in Japan as a Geisha…"

Blaze tripped suddenly, and almost sent the both of them sprawling in the snow.

On her back, Jack was laughing. "Only in your dreams, tootz. Let's get this day over with. Then we'll talk."

"Naked," Blaze muttered, taking another step. "Or I drop your ass in the snow."

"You drop my ass in the snow and you'll have to worry about those wolves all by your lonesome," Jack reminded her, "Oh, and your knee-caps, when I blow them away." She heard the sound of metal as he patted his Desert Eagle.

"That's my gun," Blaze growled.

"Maybe," Jack said, "When you pry it from my cold, dead fingers."

The wereverine, to her irritation, had taken a liking to her gun. Which gave her an idea…

"Naked," Blaze said, taking another step. "And you keep the gun."

"Fine," Jack said, "But I get breakfast in the morning."

"*Breakfast?*" Blaze scoffed. "If you get breakfast, I get to be pounced on, pinned to the ground, and thoroughly taken with some hot wereverine sex."

Jack went quiet.

Too late, Blaze remembered the little brown turd in the bathtub, and Jack staring down at his genitals in complete despair. "Uh…" she stammered, "I mean…"

"Where and when?" Jack barked.

Flinching, Blaze said, "But your legs aren't—"

"*Where*," the wereverine growled, "And *when*?"

"Okay, uh," Blaze said quickly, racking her brain for a time far enough out that the wereverine would forget, but not so far out he thought she was insulting him. "The kitchen. Two weeks from now. Once we've both recovered." She laughed nervously. "As it is, I don't think I'll be able to walk for a week."

Instead of complaining of CDC regulations that *specifically* forbade the exchange of bodily fluids on counter-tops, Jack said, "You got it, babe." He reached down and patted her ass around the backpack. "Though I'll take it nice and slow. Don't want you to get hurt or nothin."

She blushed furiously when she realized he wasn't talking about claws or fangs. It was one of the things she couldn't *help* but notice, in the multiple times she'd helped him in and out of the bath. Clearing her throat, Blaze quickly changed the subject. "I, uh, think I need a drink of water."

Jack obligingly handed her the water-bottle from where it was strapped beside his elbow. Blaze took it over her shoulder and flipped the cap off, drinking deep.

"I think you're big enough to handle it," Jack said thoughtfully. "Though I have had problems in the past."

Blaze sprayed a mouthful of water across the snow and sputtered, "Size has *nothing* to do with it." Meaning, of course, how proportionate her body was to her insides.

She could hear Jack's grin when he said, "Oh, believe me hon... Size has *everything* to do with it." Pride oozed from his words like an over-filled balloon.

Blaze narrowed her eyes. "We're getting close. I think we should continue the rest of the way in silence."

Jack just laughed.

• • •

The last mile took Blaze an hour and a half. Her feet had never hurt this bad in her life. Every step left her feeling like she was tearing her arches from the bone. Her thighs and calves had long ago ceased their intended function and had just become throbbing masses of pain strapped to her legs. Her shoulders and back hurt so bad it felt like the wereverine was driving a stake through her spine. Every few minutes, she had to stop, entire body shaking, to cling to the closest tree and catch her breath. Jack, probably in the interest of his own safety, kept his quips to a minimum.

When Blaze finally reached their modest weapons-cache at the base of one of the large cottonwoods overlooking the lodge's spacious backyard, she slumped to the ground, legs finally collapsing under her. She stared at the snow underneath her in an exhausted fugue as she felt the wereverine unbuckle himself from the harness on her back.

"Perk up, sister," Jack whispered. "We still need your legs."

Blaze groaned inwardly and fought tears. She didn't think she could get back to her *feet*, much *less* cross the entire backyard.

Can't cry, she thought, in panic. *Don't you dare cry. That would put you out for a week, and Jack needs you right now.* At Jack's raised eyebrow, she just nodded numbly, the entirety of legs from the thighs down a hot-tingly buzz of liquid gelatin.

She heard the muffled snaps as the wereverine buckled himself to the harness at the base of the tree, then the shuffle of undergrowth as he shouldered the guns and ammunition at the base of the cottonwood.

"You gonna be able to do this?" Jack demanded softly.

Blaze, who had been feeling the need to vomit for the last hour, tightened her lips against the impulse and just nodded again.

Beside her, the wereverine grunted and she heard the faint squeak of a pulley as he started hauling himself up the tree. In their practice-runs, Blaze had enjoyed watching the wereverine's muscular back work as he pulled himself hand-over-hand up the tree. Now, she didn't even have the strength to turn her head. She had *never* been this exhausted before. She didn't think she would have been able to keep *breathing*, if it weren't an automatic response.

And the worst part of it was that she wasn't *tired*. If she was just tired, she could simply close her eyes and sleep it off, and it wouldn't have been so bad. But Blaze was so *beyond* tired that all she could do was stare at the blueberry and lowbush cranberry bushes peeking from under the white between her knees, her mind replaying the hike through the woods in a monotonous, never-ending reel. Time, she realized, no longer seemed to exist except to be measured by her intermittent breaths.

Plunk. A tiny cottonwood branch landed in the thin layer of snow beside her right hand. Blaze's eyes twitched towards it dazedly. *Plunk.* Another one, this one hitting the brim of her hat. With enormous effort, Blaze lifted her head and looked up the grooved bark of the cottonwood tree until she found the wereverine, who was sitting in the massive crotch of three gigantic branches about fifty feet off of the ground, strapped to the trunk. He was frowning at her in question.

When she didn't reply, he made a walking gesture and pointed at the lodge.

Deliver the payload, lock 'em up, set off World War III. Easy-peasey. Just like they'd planned. Except, when they'd been planning it, Blaze had been leaned back in a soft, cushy chair, a clean towel wrapped around her freshly-washed hair, her bare feet up beside a hot woodstove, a beer in her hand.

He wants me to walk across the yard, Blaze thought, in horror. Back when she'd been making the plans, she'd assumed that her biggest fear, at this point in the game, would be getting eaten by werewolves, but now that she was actually *here*, experiencing it, her biggest concern was that the backyard was four or five hundred feet from the treeline to the lodge, and that she had as much control over her knees as if someone had sliced her hamstrings.

She lowered her head back to stare at her legs. The muscles were twitching in funny places, little jolts here and there, and everything from the waist down felt like it'd gone through a chemical reaction that somehow melted the cell walls of her muscles into electrostatic pudding.

Oh, wait. That's what strenuous exercise *did*. Hell, she'd heard of guys in prison squat-competitions who experienced necrosis of tissue in their legs because they'd overdone it. Like pouring the contents of a car battery over their thighs. Mmmm, yeah. Feel that burn.

Except Blaze couldn't really feel *anything* except how wonderful it was that she was sitting down, instead of walking across the yard.

Another stick plopped in the snow-covered cranberries beside her, making Blaze twitch. Above her, Jack was giving her the What The Hell gesture, and pointing at the sky. It was, Blaze noticed, definitely starting to get darker out.

Seeing her lack of response, the wereverine's face became a thunderhead and he reached for a much larger stick.

Damn the cranky little old monster. Before he could snap off the branch and lob it at her, Blaze crawled to the cottonwood, used the fissures in the bark to drag herself back to her feet, and stood there, dizzy, as her head stopped swimming. Her knees felt like ionized gelatin, completely unresponsive to her commands, and the sweat that had soaked through her jacket was now like ice against her back and belly.

She shrugged off what was left of the backpack and let it drop in the snow. Ahead of her, through the last ten feet of brush, she could see the general open area of the back lawn. Beyond that, the barn loomed like a nervous giant, guarding its flock. Outside its walls, she could see dozens of goats and fowl in the muddy, trodden area beyond the fences.

Seeing that her stock was still alive, Blaze frowned. Had the werewolves not even shown *up* yet? She had made sure to call all the neighbors and let them know she was heading back to town until the disappearances could all be sorted out. And, with the speed with which word traveled along the river, *something* should have gotten to Amber.

Unless she had already eaten all the neighbors…

Blaze was just about to curse and go stomping across the yard for a hot bath when she saw the dark shape exit the basement door of the lodge, go over to the goats huddled inside the fence, and grab one of the cowering animals by the neck. She heard a sickening popping sound as the shadow twisted the goat's head by the horns, then watched as it slung the limp carcass over its shoulder and carried it back inside the lodge to shut the door.

Blaze quickly shrank back against the side of the cottonwood, her own survival once more taking precedence over the numbness in her legs.

This is suicide, she thought. *Total suicide.*

Something small hit her in the skull, dropped from a height. Blaze narrowed her eyes and looked up at the weasel, who made an insistent jab at the lodge.

Already, night was falling. It had to be like seven-thirty. She didn't have much time, and they both knew it.

Oh God, Blaze prayed, watching the back of the lodge, *please let me get out of this alive.* Then, reconsidering, she amended, *Then again, if I* have *to die today, at least deliver me to a place with a hot bath and a masseuse.*

Another stick hit her in the top of the head, this time bigger than the others.

Bristling, telling herself that she could get the weasel back later, Blaze stumbled forward through the brush.

What if they have guards? she thought, in panic. *What if they rip me apart the moment I step into sight?*

Somehow, she made it out into the open. She took three tentative steps across the lawn…

And then her legs collapsed and she went down on her hands and knees, staring at the snow under her head, wondering how it had gotten there.

I can't do this, Blaze realized, looking up at the distance to the back of the lodge. Then she glanced over her shoulder at the wereverine, who was securely settled in his cottonwood tree, rifle in hand, homemade silencer fitted over the barrel and affixed there with a wad of black electrical tape.

Looking up, seeing the anxiousness in the wereverine's face, Blaze realized she *had* to do it, because no one else could. She pushed one knee under her, lodging an aching foot on the ground, then used both hands on her thigh to prop herself up to a one-legged kneeling position. Gritting her teeth, using her own knee as leverage, Blaze forced herself to stand.

Just four hundred feet, Blaze thought, stumbling forward. *You can make four hundred feet.* With each transfer of weight, her knees kept trying to dump her on her face. Up ahead, she could hear the rowdy roar of merrymaking reverberating against the inside of the lodge. Listening to it, she staggered across the open area of the backyard like a corpse, knowing that, at any moment, the wolves inside were going to throw open the back door and see her there, yet she had reached the point where she was just too exhausted to care.

Blaze stared at the ground beneath her as she trudged onward, trying not to think about how glacially slow the inches of churned snow and gravel were passing under her feet. Her world became a monotony of step after struggling step.

Somehow, she made it to the back porch. She only became aware of this fact, however, because suddenly she ran out of snow-packed gravel and her foot thumped against the elegant 2x6 ramp that Jack had made for himself.

Looking up blindly, she found herself staring at the partially-open door of the back of her lodge.

Clinging to the post holding up the porch roof, Blaze climbed the last two steps and stumbled to the back door. Her breath coming in little pants, now, she reached out, took the latch in a gloved hand, and yanked it shut.

"We said *leave it open* you fucktard!" someone called from the inside. "It's too hot in here!"

Blaze stared at the door, her heart beginning to hammer fiery blasts of liquid metal through her veins. She glanced up at the huge iron brackets that Jack had welded together and bolted to the door and the wall, then her eyes fell on the huge 4x4 that they had left leaning against the wall, amidst a pile of scrap lumber. In that heart-pounding moment, she recognized the second huge miscalculation that she and the wereverine had made, in their final plans three days before.

While Blaze had been able to heft the 4x4 into the brackets and dance off of the porch with practiced ease back in their trial-runs, to her current eyes, the board looked approximately the same size as a Sitka Spruce, and the porch was approximately the same height as Denali.

Inside, she heard a curse and heavy footsteps headed her way. It was sheer terror that spurned her to yank the heavy 4x4 from the pile and struggle to lift it up to the door.

Arms trembling, she couldn't make it. Her body just didn't have the *energy*...She felt her arms drooping, heard the nearing footsteps, and Blaze knew that her life was over.

An ebony shape flitted past her from behind and suddenly a petite woman was wrenching the 4x4 from her grasp and shoving Blaze away from the door. The warning in the woman's deep brown eyes was clear.

Oh God, Blaze thought, recognizing the tiny, Arabic-looking woman as Amber's second hand. She knew she had failed, then, and Jack would spend the rest of his short life plinking away at wolves until he ran out of ammo and they cut him out of his tree with a chainsaw.

"I guess we're about to find out if you're as lucky as the gods are making it appear," Kimber finally said to her, hefting the 4x4.

Blaze cringed, instinctively protecting her head with her arms.

Then, as Kimber's clansman tried to pull the door open, the black wolf turned and yanked the door back shut and dropped the heavy length of board into the brackets Jack had made for it.

Blaze stared at the woman, stunned.

"*Finish the job*!" the tiny woman roared, bearing slender white fangs. Though she couldn't have been more than five feet tall, her voice sounded like the thunderous bellow of a big predator, and Blaze instinctively took a step backwards.

Seeing her stumble, Kimber reached up and grabbed Blaze by the front of the jacket and jerked her back. Like she was made of solid titanium, the woman yanked Blaze down until their faces were only inches apart. Hair sprouted from the skin of the woman's nose. Saliva dribbled from the woman's fangs. Her brown eyes, close enough that her lashes almost touched Blaze, were so dark that Blaze had trouble seeing the slits.

"You," the woman snarled up at her, "are going to help me finally right my wrong. *I'm* cursed, but *you* aren't. You must finish what the weasel started and kill them all. Do you understand?"

Something slammed into the other side of the door, making it rattle against the bar. Kimber released her suddenly, shoving her towards the shop.

Towards the...shop? Immediately, Blaze's mind remembered the little lever that Jack had installed inside the shop, near where the pipes out of the boiler connected to the pressure-tanks and the lodge beyond. She remembered the little black wolf, darting away as she and Jack discussed strategy. *She'd been* watching, Blaze realized, in shock.

"Finish it," Kimber growled. Then she turned back to face the door and half-shifted, becoming a hunched mass of muscle and fur and talons.

She's...helping...*me?*

Trying to process that, Blaze stared at the ebony werewolf, who was braced against the porch like a Floridian expecting a hurricane, then glanced at the shop, and the tiny lever Jack had installed.

"*Now*," Kimber shouted, jerking as something smashed into the door yet again, splintering the 4x4. An instant later, something shattered the portal and leapt through. Kimber caught it by the throat and, though it seemed to be three times her size, flung it back inside the lodge as if it had been a toy.

Spurred by the horrible sounds behind her, Blaze stumbled off of the porch and into the shop. She fell to her knees beside the tiny lever, which led to the huge new hot-water tank that Jack had requisitioned for the purpose. *Here goes nothing*, she thought, reaching out and yanking the lever down.

Inside the lodge, she heard the tinny sound of the alarm going off, and the subsequent screams of the werewolves.

Colloidal silver, it seemed, when applied in the form of a high-intensity shower, did not a happy wolfie make.

Blaze collapsed back against the red metal sheeting of the boiler and closed her eyes. The rest was up to Jack.

TWENTY-FOUR

Up in a Tree

Agony wracked Jack's soul as he watched Blaze stumble across the back yard, weaving like a drunkard, staggering in her exhaustion, yet doggedly aimed for the back porch.

She carried your sorry ass seven miles through the woods, Jack thought, anguished. *Because you weren't man enough to put a damn bullet in your head when you had the chance.* He kept the muzzle of the rifle aimed at the door, but his breath was coming in quick pants, now. *Great Roots of Yggdrasil, you should be down there with her, but you're hiding in a tree like a goddamn coward. You're a* warrior *and she's a* healer *and you're forcing her to her death. She's going to* die *because you—*

Out of the corner of his eye, he saw a black shape slip out of the brush near the edge of the clearing and start loping across the yard, following Blaze's progress.

Jack jerked his rifle to level it on the wolf that followed her, his heart rate spiking so suddenly that it drove the moon-magic out through his flesh. He felt his eyesight sharpen, felt the punctures in his fingers as his talons pushed through his fingertips, felt his body grow and strain against the straps holding him in place.

Come on, Jack thought, *Just hold still…*

On the ground, Blaze stopped and just stared at the ground in between her feet for a minute, panting. Behind her, her stalker hesitated, giving him a clear shot.

Jack caught a whiff of gold and sun and sand just before a big, black, African hand appeared out of nowhere and grabbed the barrel of his gun, yanking it up to point at the sky. Violet eyes met Jack's in warning, and the rest of the djinni appeared, seated casually in the tree right beside him.

"There will be none of that," the djinni said softly. "Tonight, Northman, our goals are the same."

Jack, whose every hackle always went up around the crafty, word-twisting djinn, yanked his gun free of the massive man's muscled arm to once more peer through the scope.

Indeed, the tiny black wolf continued to creep behind Blaze almost tentatively, as if she knew she had a gun sighted on her flank. "She's turning on her own kind?" he demanded.

"She is helping to correct a mistake," the djinni said. "One she does not intend to make again."

Suddenly, Jack understood. "She *made* them, didn't she? Amber. And Travis. And Michael. All of them."

"She only made one," the djinni said. "One who turned on her the moment she made her."

Thinking of the petty white bitch that had stabbed him in the *gut*, Jack's fingers tightened on the gun. "Amber." It came with a wave of fury, realizing that he'd *assumed* it had been Michael and the others leading the pack. And he'd left her *alive*. *Damn* it.

The djinni simply nodded, watching the wolf's progression.

"You're hers, then?" Jack said, following the small wolf through his scope. "Others aren't old enough."

The djinni's black face twisted in disgust. "The others are possessed infants."

Jack bristled at the word 'possessed,' his knuckles whitening on the gun. Following Blaze's movement across the yard, he growled, "What'd she do to claim you, slave? Found a treasure hoard from the Old Country? Paid a witch-doctor? Sputched a few Romani? What?"

"We dueled," the djinni said. "Soul-for-soul."

Jack froze, every hair on his body pulling up from his skin. "She's a *magus?*"

"One of the only First-Lands magi who still exists," the djinni said, his violet eyes watching the wolf as it slunk across the yard behind Blaze. "Hence why you really don't want to pull that trigger."

She's a magus, Jack thought, raking his brain. *Not a wolf, then...* Then he tensed when the small black wolf suddenly darted up after Blaze and ripped the 4x4 from her hands. His hands tightened on the gun as he watched the wolf through the scope.

"Careful, moon-child," the djinni warned. "She means your little bird no harm."

"Why the fuck do you care if I kill her?" Jack demanded. "It'll set you free, right?"

Jack saw pain in the djinni's eyes before the man looked away. "All you have to understand," the djinni said softly. "Is if you kill my mistress, you will die tonight. You have my word."

Jack frowned as the wolf yanked the door shut and slammed the 4x4 into the brackets. Then the wolf grabbed Blaze by the front of her shirt and dragged her down as she sprouted fur and fang, and with the wolf half-transformed and snarling at Blaze, it was everything that Jack could do to stay his hand. "When this is over," Jack gritted, watching the altercation through his scope, "I'm going to have a sit-down chat with your owner."

It was the djinni's turn to stiffen. "She is not my 'owner'."

"Are you soul-bound?" Jack demanded.

The djinni looked away, violet eyes dark.

Sensing a weakness, Jack pressed, "Can you weave the Wyrd, do *anything* without her permission?"

"Harm the wolf, you will regret it." With that warning, the djinni vanished.

Jack laughed. He'd never liked djinn. The tongue-twisting assholes always said one thing, then did another, then blamed *you* for not understanding their words. *His* general thoughts on the common magus pastime of trapping djinn in the First Realm was that if someone managed to beat the word-weavers at their own game, more power to them.

A moment later, Blaze stumbled off of the porch and into the shop. At the same time, the front door exploded, and a flash of blue fire made the wolves inside the lodge stagger backwards.

A magus, Jack thought, stunned. *Mighty Thor, she doesn't need our help.*

Yet for all the little wolf's flashy lights and pretty pyrotechnics, Jack didn't see the bodies falling that he would have expected. He began to frown. *Why isn't she just killing them?*

And then he heard the sprinkler system engage inside the Sleeping Lady, and boarded-up windows began to shatter as the wolves leapt through, screaming. The little black wolf, for her part, vanished like a fey.

One after another, wolves came pouring from the lodge in full throes of the moon-magics, the pain of the silver having drawn it out. Snarling, angry, locked into moon-form by the sprinkler system, they formed a tense, uneasy knot in the back yard as they regrouped. Saying a prayer to Zeus, Jack brought his rifle up to bear and fired at a wolf in the center of the mass. Aiming for the haunches, he hit the wolf in the hip, then chambered another round as the injured creature turned on its already pissed-off packmates and delivered a painful blow to the chest.

Sorry I can't get down there and join in the fun, boys, Jack thought, firing again. *Guess I'll just have to watch.* He chambered another round, again aiming to create more pain than to kill, and fired. As Blaze had so thoughtfully pointed out, while a cripple Jack may be, those in the grips of the moon-magics were fully capable of doing Jack's job for him, given enough provocation.

And, true to form, after six or seven shots intended solely to wound, the knot of werewolves had devolved into a wild, roaring blood-fest. It was then that Jack re-loaded and started aiming for the head.

TWENTY-FIVE

Gold

Her pack was dying.

Amber felt her power lessen as their lives slipped away, one after another.

Someone's killing them, Amber thought, frantically. She threw open the door of her family's Wasilla ranch, looking to the north.

More fell, one after another. She felt their cords snap tight, then dissolve. One by one. Only seconds in between.

Someone is killing my famil—Amber froze, suddenly realizing why she had been able to find no trace of the wereverine's stench in Wasilla, Palmer, or even Anchorage.

The weasel had gone back. He and his six-foot ape were killing them all.

Amber knew, then, that she should run. She had stabbed the weasel right in the gut with the necromantic dagger, and somehow he had survived. On that fact alone, Amber knew that she should take the three weapons she carried with her and the fifty grand in her bank account and flee to Siberia, where she could start a new pack, a new family, a new life. Yet not only was there the fact that Jack survived a *dread horn*, but he was being protected by some sort of flame-slinging monster, something that Amber had never seen before.

Add that to the fact that Jack had survived the un-survivable and it meant he had powers beyond what she herself possessed, even with her pack at her feet. Powers of healing…

Amber frowned, remembering the column of fire that had killed so many of her family in her last encounter with the weasel. She had thought it had been a trick of her imagination, but she had almost thought it looked like a *bird*.

Something tingled at the edges of her memory, and Amber scrabbled to categorize the creature she was dealing with, suddenly certain discovering its identity was more important than saving what remained of her incompetent family. Not a djinni, like the pathetic creature Kimber carted around with her wherever she went, but certainly a similar denizen of the Fourth Realm. Something made of sunfire…

Amber's eyes narrowed when she remembered the greenery around the Sleeping Lady, when she and her pack had gone to claim it. There had been animals everywhere. Rabbits overflowing their cages. A *mango* tree in the greenhouse…She'd been too excited by the prospect of a few decent meals to really *think* about it, but that just wasn't possible. Not even a feylord's green thumb could grow *mango* trees in *Alaska*.

As Amber felt the last family strands snap, leaving only the ones between herself and the annoying runt Kimber in place, it dawned upon her what she was dealing with and she smiled.

She didn't need to flee to Russia. She had everything she needed right here.

She remembered back to her times as a younger were, when she would gather everyone around the fire each night while the family told stories. The djinni, especially, had told interesting stories. Stories of a legendary bird that tantalized emperors with its ability to heal, whose feathers had astonishing powers to nourish, to grow…

A bird who flew on wings of sunfire, who could bring the wrath of the heavens upon its enemies with a single thought. A bird that died only once every five hundred years, to be reborn again with a single feather as a keepsake. A single feather that was its key to awakening…

…or its capture.

A bird of the Fourth Lands who, just as mortals in the First Lands were to mercury, as the fey in the Second Lands were to iron, and as the moon-kissed of the Third Lands were to silver, was deathly allergic to gold.

TWENTY-SIX

You'd Like To Report a *What*?

Blaze listened to the werewolves' chaos outside and shakily pulled out her Desert Eagle from the holster on her hip. Careful to avoid the pipes leading out of the boiler, Blaze pushed herself deeper into the crevice against the wall of the shop. Almost immediately, she felt the uncomfortable heat near her lower ribcage. Instead of starting a wood fire in the furnace—which, when the pumps were switched on inside the lodge, would supply hot water to the flooring of the lodge—or simply lighting a fire in the woodstove in the basement, the wolves had lit the diesel boiler—usually used only in the coldest part of winter, Jack had told her—and had left it running as high as it would go, pumping a continuous stream of extremely hot water through every floor of the Sleeping Lady.

Beside it, the generator matched pace, left on despite the inverters on the wall both having switched to float, indicating, as Jack had so politely informed her, that the generator was no longer charging the batteries.

Yet for once, Blaze was grateful for the loud roar of the generator drowning out all other sound. As Jack had demonstrated, those touched by the Third-Lands seemed to have an uncanny set of predatory senses, and at the moment, Blaze's heart was doing approximately a thousand beats a minute, her breaths were coming in ragged, choppy pants, and she was pretty sure she stank of fear and sweat. At least, with the generator roaring beside her, the smell of grease and diesel thick inside the shop, she figured she had a better chance of going unseen until Jack had finished cleaning up.

Oh God, Blaze thought, listening to the inhuman sounds outside, *Please let this work.* The screams were getting fewer and further between, the commotion quieter in general, but Blaze knew it would only take one survivor to rip her into tiny Yeti pieces. She had seen the kind of power these creatures had in a single swing, and knew she didn't stand a chance against that kind of devastating strength.

Gun clutched in trembling hands, Blaze waited. She'd gambled everything on this night. Her farm, her lodge, her *life*. Hell, she'd even gambled Jack's life on it, and not given him a choice in the matter. Now, listening to the horrible sounds outside, feeling the reverberations through the walls as five-hundred-pound bodies slammed into the woodpile or the thumps in the concrete pad under her ass when they were driven into the gravel driveway, she began to wonder what the hell she had been thinking.

Just *one* of them needed to survive, and both she and Jack were dead. Just *one*.

She heard something heavy land on the roof, then long metal screeches as something scrabbled up the eaves, doubtlessly rending huge holes in her tin sheeting as it climbed towards the peak.

Another something hit the roof, and then the very walls of the shop shook as the creatures above her screamed and thrashed, making the ceiling above her bow, their weight and struggles threatening to collapse the structure.

Then the scream ended in a sudden gurgle and one of the combatants above thumped to the sheeting and started rolling down the roof. Roaring, the survivor launched himself from the shop, making several of the rafters crack from the sudden weight. Little bits of sheet-rock fell from the ceiling and landed on the 4-wheeler Jack had pushed inside to repair back in August, speckling the handlebars with white plaster. On the yard outside, something landed with a *thud* that Blaze felt through the concrete floor. Blaze flinched, clinging to the gun, adrenaline searing through her veins as her heart radiated fire in her chest.

Outside, she heard the sounds of heavy canine feet loping between the firewood stacks, towards the door of the shop.

I didn't close it, Blaze realized, with sudden horror. *I never latched the door!*

She drew her knees up tight against her chest, gun clenched in trembling hands as the loping stride paused outside the entrance. A moment later, a crimson-stained muzzle pushed through the crack, sniffing at the dimly-lit air inside the shop from the darkness beyond.

Go away, Blaze pleaded, her hands tremulously lifting the gun. *Please just go away.*

But the nose pushed inside further, revealing a huge lupine head, gray but with strips of black. It sniffed again, its blue eyes focused a bit of sheet-rock that slipped off of the 4-wheeler to crunch against the floor. Blaze saw it glance up at the break in the ceiling, then step fully into the room, a massive beast the size of a tiger, trailing a line of intestines through the sawdust on the floor behind it.

Oh God, Blaze thought, seeing the streak of blood it left on the grease-stained concrete as it limped through the shop. Even then, the creature's innards were pulling back into its body, ropes of pinkish intestine flipping back and forth unnaturally as it returned to the stomach cavity.

The wolf slunk to the far corner of the shop—only ten feet from Blaze's hiding place—and settled against the wall, whining. She could see several rows of teeth glistening red behind its fangs, and its slitted yellow eyes glowed like twin flames against the dimness of the shop's single overhead light. As Blaze watched, the last of its woodchip-covered innards slipped back into its abdomen and the huge gash in the flesh there began to seal. Still whining, the nightmare-wolf began to lick the blood from its stomach in long, slow swipes with its tongue.

Blaze's eyes flickered toward the darkness beyond the door. Could she make it back outside before the wolf was fully healed? The sounds of fighting were dulling, now, and she was pretty sure there were only a handful left still standing, and they were probably too distracted to make much note of a helpless mortal bolting across the yard…

Who was she kidding? Every kid in Alaska got taught in grade-school that you don't run from predators. Running triggered something in their minds, completely wiped out the uncertainty that came with the smell of human, leaving raging instinct in its place. It was like offering yourself up on a silver platter marked PREY: PLEASE EAT.

Not daring to move more than her eyes, Blaze glanced down at the gun in her hands. Sweat was making the grip slick in her palms, and her own paranoia kept feeling the Desert Eagle sliding, like it was going to drop onto the concrete at any moment.

Outside, the last howls went silent. The werewolf curled against the inside wall pricked its ears forward, listening, but kept panting and whining, shaking its head and intermittently and scratching at its face, neck, sides…

The silver, Blaze thought, stunned that the colloidal sprinkler system had worked. She thought about the gun in her fingers, and how Jack had emphatically told her not to shoot a were if she could avoid it, because most shots would just 'piss it off,' even with silver. And she had shot Jack in the *head* with a *shotgun* and he had still tried to rip off her face afterwards. What was one little bullet going to do if a *shotgun* blast to the *head* didn't kill them? She swallowed, her heart hammering as she tried to decide what to do. She heard no sounds outside, so she assumed that the fight had ended.

Unfortunately, that also meant that Jack, up in his tree, thought the situation was under control. She could already imagine him lowering himself from the cottonwood, rifles slung over his shoulder, so that he could crawl across the yard and come figure out why she hadn't at least taken a few pot-shots at wolves from inside the shop.

The werewolf whined again, rubbing its nose against the shelves behind it, making the loose chainsaw chains jingle where they dangled from a peg. Then it lifted its big head toward the door and growled, an unearthly rumble in its chest that left the hairs on Blaze's arms and legs prickling.

Still growling, it began licking itself again.

"Blaze?" Jack's voice called from outside. "Where'd you go, sweetie?"

Blaze flinched as the werewolf froze, its ears pricking forward, its unnatural eyes narrowing as its lips pulled away from ivory fangs. Though Blaze was close enough to hear the low growl that issued from its tensing chest, she knew that the noise from the generator would keep the wereverine from hearing it.

Still moving only her eyes, trying desperately to keep her breathing under control, Blaze glanced again at the door. *Could* she get outside before the wolf caught her? At least if she was outside, Jack would have a chance to shoot the thing, if it came after her.

"*Blaze!*" Jack shouted, sounding worried, now.

I can't answer you, Blaze thought, agonized, *There's a monster curled up beside me.*

Even as she had the thought, she watched the drool drip from the werewolf's fangs to puddle in the metal-shavings and woodchips covering the shop floor. It got up slowly, unfolding with an easy grace of a quarter-ton predator, head low, facing the door.

You have a gun, you coward, part of her snapped. *Use it.*

Blaze felt her heart rate skyrocket with that thought, and suddenly the blood sizzling in her ears was drowning out even the sound of the generator.

"Blaze!" Jack called, getting closer, "Where are you, you damn Yeti?" She heard the scuffling of the wereverine dragging himself between the woodpiles to the door. Inside the shop, the werewolf was moving closer to Blaze, putting its back to her, getting into the shadows furthest from the door.

Point the gun and pull the trigger! a part of her screamed. *It's right there*...kill *it.*

Watching the creature's haunches bunch as Jack pushed the door open, Blaze slowly raised her gun to the back of its head, now only inches from her. Her sweat-slickened finger tightened on the trigger. Her hands started to shake.

The werewolf backed further into the shadows with her, until its bristly gray fur was brushing Blaze's face and chest.

Jack crawled into the shop on his elbows. He paused, lifting his nose tentatively to the air and sniffed. "Blaze?"

Blaze wanted to scream, wanted to shoot, wanted to *warn* him, yet all she could do was sit there in complete terror, the creature's fur brushing her face, as it waited in the shadows to ambush Jack.

"You fall asleep in here, girl?" the wereverine demanded, frowning. Blaze saw his eyes catch on the bloody smear leading into the shop before he started crawling further into the room…

The werewolf leapt.

Jack rolled to meet it, transforming in the span of a single heartbeat, talons out, fangs bared, his blonde and brown fur puffing up his shirt and ripping apart his pants. The werewolf landed with the wereverine's hand around its throat, and they tumbled in a ball of snarling teeth and claw, slamming into the 4-wheeler and scattering bits of drywall across the floor.

It didn't last long. Throughout it all, the wereverine kept a firm hold on the wolf's throat, talons digging bloody red holes into the sides of the wolf's red neck. After a few moments, the wolf's movements grew weaker, its struggles less violent. Eventually, Jack took a second grip on the wolf's skull and Blaze heard the snapping of bones as he twisted.

Knowing what would come next, she winced and looked away.

She heard a wet popping *crunch*, then a wet thud as something the size of a watermelon hit the back end of the shop.

"So," the wereverine said, not even sounding winded, "You all right over there, sister?"

When Blaze looked, Jack was leaning against the front tire of the 4-wheeler, wiping blood from his mouth and depositing it on what remained of his pants.

Blaze looked down at her gun, still clutched between trembling fingers, and felt a huge wave of guilt settle deep in her gut. *You're such a damn cowar—*

"Don't worry about it," Jack said. "Your kind…hell…they don't kill 'less it's important."

"My *kind*?" Blaze managed, self-loathing embittering her words. "You mean *women*?"

"Women?" Turning to level his green eyes on her, Jack snorted. "Girl, you obviously ain't never heard those proverbs about a woman scorned." He shook his head, seeming to find what she had said highly amusing. Turning his head to the side, he spat a gob of red onto the dusty floor of the shop, then turned back to peer at her, something akin to concern in his emerald eyes. "He rough you up some, then?"

"No," Blaze bit out, "I was perfectly functional and unharmed the entire time. I just couldn't find the balls to pull the trigger."

Jack grunted. "Don't take balls to pull a trigger." Casually flicking a shred of flesh off of his arm, he said, "Besides. You'da pulled that trigger and he'd've sliced you up like a birthday cake 'fore I could get to him."

"Instead, I just cowered in my corner and let him ambush you," Blaze bit out. "This was *my idea*, just like the lodge, just like the farm and everything else, and once again, *you* did all the work."

Jack shrugged. "I knew he was in here. There was a damn blood trail leading in from outside." He gestured at the dark smears on the concrete floor, giving her an irritated look. "Why the hell you think I made so much noise coming in here to get you?"

Suddenly, it dawned on Blaze…"You *knew* he was in here waiting for you?"

"Watched him walk inside," Jack said. "Was just hoping you'd manage to keep your head down 'til I could come rescue your pretty behind."

Blaze narrowed her eyes at the wereverine. "I do *not* need rescuing."

He raised a single, manly eyebrow at her.

Disgusted, Blaze stood up and stormed towards the door. Before she yanked it open, however, she hesitated. Over her shoulder at the wereverine, she asked, tentatively, "They're, uh, all dead?"

"Place is all yours again, princess," the wereverine said, gesturing grandly at the door.

"Good," Blaze said. "You stay here. I'm gonna go call the cops."

Propped against the 4-wheeler, the wereverine's pretty green eyes went wide and he said, "*What?*" just in time for the shop door to cut off the rest of what he was going to say.

Blaze took out the new cell-phone she had purchased while the wereverine had stayed stubbornly cooped up in the hotel room, and dialed 9-1-1. Behind her, she heard the tell-tale scraping as the wereverine crawled to the door, and she yanked it shut, then set the latch.

On the other side, she heard the wereverine grunt, then strain, then slam his fist against the door. "They can't know about us!" he shouted. "You'll start an all-out extermination!"

"Don't worry about it," Blaze said, waiting for the line to connect.

"*911, what is your emergency?*" a polite female voice on the other end asked.

Looking out at the multi-colored carcasses strewn about the yard, Blaze said, "Uh, yes, I'd like to report a wolf attack."

• • •

Blaze and Jack watched from the basement window of the Sleeping Lady as Fish and Game and the Alaska State Troopers loaded the last of the werewolf carcasses into the ADF&G helicopter that had landed in the enormous crimson bloodstain that was her backyard.

"Lucky to be alive. Pfft." Jack snorted and popped the cap off of his beer with a thumbnail. "I should've stuffed my fist down that little prick's throat."

The 'little prick,' in this instance, had been a six-foot, rather muscular wildlife officer who had taken their statements while his comrades collected bodies, made a few on-the-spot autopsies, and then quickly started packing whole wolves—viscera and all—into body-bags the moment that they found a human hand in the first animal's stomach.

Outside, the racket was intense. Multiple news crews had been flying in helicopters overhead ever since Jack had ever-so-politely told the first camera crew to get off of his property at the wrong end of a twelve-gauge.

Never mind that it isn't even his property, Blaze sighed.

The troopers, of course, seeing the sad state of the interior of the lodge, the gashes raked into the metal on top of the shop roof, and the gore spattered for six hundred feet in any direction, had given the cranky little curmudgeon a bit of a break. The shotgun was even then somewhere in the back of the troopers' chopper, on loan, the 'little prick' had assured them both, until they could finish cleaning up and be on their way.

The 'cleanup,' unfortunately, took the entire day. It was dark again by the time the officers finished taking pictures and collecting bodies, and it wasn't until seven-thirty before an officer knocked courteously on the back door and carefully leaned the shotgun inside against the steps before jogging back to the chopper.

By the time the troopers had all climbed aboard and the helicopter began to lift off, Blaze had gone a day and a half in clothes that still had the faint white lines of salt-crystals where her sweat had dried on them. Thus, the first thing Blaze did once the police and news crews finally departed was go out to the shop, light a fire in the furnace, and start the water circulating to the hot water tank.

When she came back inside, Jack was still staring out at the blood-darkened snow of the backyard, his empty beer sitting on the window-sill beside him. "What bothers me," he growled, without looking at her, "Is you just went and told the whole world there's werewolves in Alaska. I mean flat out *told* them they were all werewolves."

Blaze snorted. "And I was an exhausted and frightened female that was hyperventilating and talking about how they'd tried to eat me. Telling them I thought they were *werewolves, oh my god, werewolves!!* was going to make that as the least likely solution in their minds, because they're all big, strong, rational men who are going to immediately pat the terrified woman on the head and go find the *real* answer to what happened here."

Jack peered at her. "That was pretty convincing, you know."

"What was?" Blaze asked, confused.

"The whole babbling and hyperventilating thing," he said, with the start of an evil grin. "Makes a man wonder if you've had practice."

Blaze narrowed her eyes. Sniffing, she said, "You don't really think anyone's gonna see this and scream 'werewolf!' do you? Hell, I overheard one of the biologists talking. They think it's a missing link.

Something ancient that survived the Ice Age, precursors to both wolves and foxes."

Jack turned to give her a flat green stare. "You're kidding."

"It's what they were saying," Blaze said, shrugging. "Slitted eyes and all. Freaked 'em all out a little at first, until someone mentioned it could've been a forgotten branch of the lupine family tree, and then they all got real excited, kind of like a bunch of nerdy kids with a science project."

Jack stared at her a minute, then turned back to the window, grunting.

"Modern man just isn't ready to see magic," Blaze said. "Even when it's biting them in the ass."

"Still," Jack growled. "It's gonna be all over the news."

Blaze shrugged again. "It was gonna be all over the news one way or another. At least this way, we're not going to be implicated as mass murderers, considering that we were the only survivors."

Jack's face twisted. "I can think of someone else who survived who'd I'd sorta wished she hadn't."

Blaze's heart began hammering, realizing there was really only one person who had survived that she could think of. *Me?* a girly, insecure part of her thought, horrified and anguished. *Does he really think I'm that much of a dead weight that he—*

"That Jennie Mae Hunderson from Ebony Creek Lodge was on that first news helicopter. They dropped her off at her place and did an interview. Said she and Russ and Ralphie all took a family vacation around the end of August for a vacation in San Diego. Went to the zoo and everything."

Blaze was caught between joy that the Hundersons had survived and irritation at the wereverine's lack of charity. "That's not very nice," she muttered.

"She's a loudmouth gossip," Jack growled, bristling. "Has been riding my ass since she got here thirty years ago to go find a girl, and when I finally told her to bugger off a couple years back, she started telling the neighbors I was gay."

Blaze winced, remembering her conversation with Jennie Mae.

Jack scowled at her. "She told you, didn't she?"

"What," Blaze asked innocently, "That you were gay? That's nothing to be ashamed of."

"Th-That I'm…" Jack sputtered. "…*not gay*!"

"You know," Blaze said, "It's becoming a perfectly acceptable thing nowadays, to be gay. Guys like you are coming out of the closet all the time."

A rabid growl started rumbling in the base of Jack's chest and she saw hair sprout against the shirt on his back.

Feigning disinterest, Blaze yawned and crossed the basement to the downstairs bathroom, utterly grateful that the commotion had finally settled and the police had departed. "I need a shower. Then I'll want my massage." She grabbed a towel from the closet—one of the only things that the werewolves *hadn't* ransacked—and ducked inside the bathroom, trying not to think about Jack's big hands playing up and down her spine, kneading out the tension in her thighs and calves, rubbing the knots out of her shoulders…

After all, she doubted he'd really do it. She was pretty sure it had just been something he'd said to keep her from dumping his ass in the woods and leaving him there to insult the passing magpies. And maybe, if he got lucky, a moose.

Thus, when Blaze stepped out of the bathroom wrapped in a towel, she was rather shocked to find the wereverine seated in his wheelchair in all the glory that God had given him upon his birth.

And then some.

Through some tantalizing moon-magic phenomenon, he had rebuilt most of the muscle he'd lost, even in his legs. All that upper body workout, though, had left his torso, shoulders, and arms a rippling mass of sexy Adonis manmeat that completely took her breath away.

"You said naked," he muttered, at her shocked look. "That was just you foolin' around, then?" He plucked at a frayed peeling edge of vinyl on his chair, refusing to look at her.

"Naked works," Blaze managed, and it came out as a strangled sound in her throat.

Hearing it, Jack yanked his head up to peer at her suspiciously. "It does, does it?"

"Sure," Blaze said, swallowing. To think that those big hands were about to work their way over her body while the rest of him moved and glistened nearby…"Uh, where do you want me?"

Jack seemed to contemplate that a bit longer than necessary, studying her face for long moments before saying, "It'd honestly be easier for me to do this on the floor."

Blaze winced, glancing at the shards of splintered wood, broken glass, and chunks of wet drywall that made up the floor of the basement. Tomorrow, the place was going to get a top-to-bottom inspection and an overhaul. Today, she had just planned to curl up on one of the unshredded mattresses with her Desert Eagle and try to sleep.

"Okay, uh, lemme go find a broom," Blaze said.

She found half a broom—the important half, thankfully—embedded in the wall of the upstairs kitchen, and once she had finished sweeping aside a blanket-sized spot on the floor beside one of the unharmed downstairs beds, threw down several layers of blankets as padding. Then Blaze helped Jack out of his chair and laid herself face-down on the floor in front of him.

The first thing the wereverine did was yank her towel from around her waist and toss it up on the bed. Blaze gasped, skin prickling at the sudden cold, but fought the impulse to sit up and reach for it. She completely forgot her protests, however, when the wereverine started kneading his fingers into her back. Within minutes, she was so limp she was drooling, head tilted at an angle on the blankets, staring at the ruins of her lodge in a dreamy half-haze.

"You know," she slurred, "I'm finished."

"How's that?" the wereverine asked, running his hands along her shoulders, turning them to mush. "Someone take your Himalayan ancestors to a Chinese wildlife preserve? They need you to hire a lawyer to get them out?"

Blaze felt something twitch in her neck, but it was quickly massaged back into place by expert hands. She sucked up the drool that had been about to hit the blankets.

"You were saying something about being finished," Jack said, shifting over her, using his big hands on the small of her back, now. She felt his warm, naked torso moving against her ribs with the rhythm of his massage.

"Blaze?"

"Uhhhnng," she managed.

Laughing, he pushed himself away from her and dropped lengthwise beside her, so that he was leaning on an elbow, looking down at her. "You were saying?"

Blaze's eyes caught on the jumbled mess on the floor around them and sighed. "Yeah. I took out a two hundred and fifty thousand dollar loan to get this place on its feet." She gave a despairing laugh. "Now it's soggy, the inside's tore to shit, glass everywhere, and I was counting on being able to use some of that cash for advertising for the fishing season next year. I'm finished. Kaput. Done. Sell it all off and send me home, sir, 'cause that's all she wrote." She snorted. "Hell, maybe I can go find an apartment in Anchorage with a greenhouse and sell mangoes to the local farmer's market." She sighed, twisting her head to look up into the wereverine's green eyes. "Of course, no one would believe I grew 'em myself."

The wereverine seemed to consider that, then glanced around them and grunted. "I can help you fix it up this winter."

Blaze laughed. "Have you *seen* how expensive drywall is, nowadays?" When Jack just gave her a blank look, she said, "It's like nine dollars a *sheet*." She flopped a limp arm to include the lodge in general. "And *look* at this place. There isn't a piece of wall *anywhere* that isn't punched to shit. Ten thousand square foot lodge, that's like," she paused to do the math, then decided she was too relaxed to do the math, "...at *least* a million dollars."

Jack winced. "That's a lot."

"Uh huh," Blaze said, nodding up at him. "Then we start looking at the cost to replace the windows, the floors, the doors that got ripped out of the walls..." Blaze snorted. "I'd be lucky if I could sell this place for a couple hundred grand, after this. 'Bout the only thing worth anything is the stuff in the shop, the heavy machinery, the barn, and the land we're sitting on. And I already burned all my loan money on sprinkler systems, barge trips, and farm animals. I'm screwed."

"Hmmm," Jack said. "So you need a million dollars?"

"Oh, at least," Blaze said. "Ten million would make things easier, though." She yawned into her blanket. "Shit, I could sleep right here." She lifted her head just enough to peer at him pointedly. "You may *continue*, by the way."

"Oh," Jack said, jerking as if he'd been lost in thought. "Sure thing, tootz." He propped himself back upright and put his big hands back on her spine, and Blaze lost her train of thought. In fact, she was pretty sure she started drooling again immediately, considering the way her cheek kind of squished up toward her eye socket in bliss when he started kneading the backs of her thighs.

She must have fallen asleep sometime after that, because Jack woke her with a low, throaty rumble of, "I do have one concern about what happened the other night, princess."

Blaze, delirious, raked her brain for what could have happened between them, and came up empty. "You mean inside the barn?" she mumbled, peering up at him bleary-eyed. Sometime during the night, he had pulled a cover over them both, and he was seated beside her, propped up against the bed with the Desert Eagle in his lap.

He frowned at her a moment, then shook his head. "The wolves. I don't think we got Amber."

That made Blaze sit up in a hurry. "You *don't*? Why the hell didn't you say something?!"

"Didn't want to spook you."

Blaze's mouth fell open. "Didn't want to *spook* me? What *did* you want? Me to die completely oblivious, like the blonde ditzes in a horror show?" She grabbed a fistful of bad-bleach-job-orange hair and held it out to him, shaking it. "You know, people like me don't last long, when there's serial killers on the loose. We tend to run screaming from the building and get stabbed by the guy with the machete standing outside the back door." She cursed. "And you let me take a *shower*. You *ass*!" She started frantically reaching for her clothes.

Jack gave her a look like she had just hacked up a loogie and spat it on the blanket before painstakingly rubbing it into a little green smiley-face with her thumb, giving Blaze the distinct idea that he'd probably never watched a horror movie in his life. Or, for that matter, *any* movie. She certainly didn't remember seeing a TV in the wreckage of his house.

"For one," Jack said, as if she hadn't spoken, "Amber's a bone-white little beastie, and the only white one we got was a male."

Staring at him, Blaze managed, "You know, we really need to work on catching you up to the twenty-first century." Drawing a rectangle in the air with a finger, Blaze said, "Nowadays, there's this wondrous thing called tel-e-vi-sion." She pronounced every syllable slowly, so that he could understand. "It is a '*magic box*'"—airquotes—"…that allows you to watch mo-tion pic-tures and D-V-Ds. *Also* magic."

"For two," Jack said, "I couldn't find my dagger anywhere. Found the swords, found the armor, found *other* people's swords and armor, found *everything* but the dagger, and Amber would've kept that on her at all times." Indeed, there was a stack of weapons, armor, and other valuables near her head.

Blaze peered at the tidy pile of valuables, then reached for something that looked like a crown.

"Wouldn't do that if I were you," Jack said. "Pretty sure that one's cursed."

Blaze laughed, despite herself. "Sure, and it'll decrease my intelligence to three and give me halitosis of twelve until I go to a high-enough-level cleric who can remove it." She was about to grab it anyway, then she remembered that she had just fought a battle with silver bullets, was growing mangoes in her backyard, and that the stale odor of wet-dog seeping into the walls was the lingering smell of werewolves. She pulled her hand back and frowned at the jeweled circlet. "You're serious, aren't you?"

"About Amber or about the curse?"

Somehow, Blaze found the idea of a cursed object more disturbing than a megalomaniac werewolf. She said as much.

"Oh," Jack said, looking down at it, "Yeah, you live long enough, you start to gain a smell for those sorts of things." He wrinkled his nose. "I'm pretty sure that little trinket spent some time in an old Norse king's grave. Has the smell of Odin on it." He chuckled. "Hell, it'll probably make you go blind in one eye."

"That is so not funny," Blaze said, vigorously wiping her palm on her pants. "What are we gonna do about Amber?"

"*Do*?" Jack snorted. "In case you hadn't noticed, girlie, I'm a bit home-bound, at the moment." He slapped his thigh and gestured disgustedly at his legs. "I won't be *doing* much of anything."

"So what can *I* do?" Blaze demanded. "She's going to come back."

Jack snorted. "We just took out her entire pack. She's smarter than that."

"Wait," Blaze said, yanking her shirt over her head. "Doesn't that give her all the more *reason* to want to stab us?"

"No," Jack growled, "That gives her all the more reason to tuck her tail between her legs and run."

"...or sneak up in the dark and stab us both," Blaze said.

"She's not coming back," Jack growled. "Discussion over."

Blaze peered at him, then at the gun in his lap. "If she's not coming back, why are you sitting up, awake, in the middle of the night, holding onto that Desert Eagle like you're afraid it's gonna run away?"

"I'll protect you," Jack snarled. "Go back to sleep."

"So you *do* think she's coming back!" Blaze cried. She looked at the devastation around her, panic beginning to set in. "Tonight?" she demanded.

"I don't know when," Jack muttered. "Just go back to sleep. I'm sorry I woke you."

"Oh, we are *definitely* going to work on your communication skills!" Blaze cried, scrabbling for the rest of her clothes. "Is she out there right now?"

"I said I don't *know*," Jack snarled. "If she's smart, she won't be back."

Blaze stared at him. "Somehow, that is not encouraging."

"I'm gonna be up awhile, anyway," Jack growled. "The moon-touched need less sleep, so you might as well catch some Z's." He gestured impatiently at the bed he was leaning against. "Go sleep. I'll keep an eye on things tonight."

"You tell me something like *that* and then expect me to *sleep*?" Blaze cried. "You might as well tell me the earth was about to get hit by a gigantic asteroid!"

"Could you do anything about it, if it was?" Jack demanded.

Blaze blinked at him.

...And then the mountain of shame hit her when she realized Jack was absolutely right. Even when she had a werewolf at point-blank, with its *back* to her, she hadn't been able to bring herself to pull the trigger. What was she gonna do when Amber showed up, all fur and fang and talons?

Pee herself, most like.

Muttering, Blaze dragged a blanket up onto the bed behind Jack and sat there, contemplating the dark, boarded-up window in silence. With most of the windows in the place busted and the outdoor temperatures already reaching into the low twenties at night, the Sleeping Lady was having trouble retaining heat. She pulled the blanket tighter against the cold and dragged her own Desert Eagle closer.

"You know," she said wistfully, into the long silence that followed, "We're gonna have to abandon this place."

"Like hell," Jack snorted. "Pipes'll freeze, and you let the pipes in an infloor heating system bust, and you might as well throw gasoline over the whole deal and light a match. Replacing the floor like that... Place won't be worth *anything* if we let it freeze."

Blaze snorted. "It gets *forty below* out here in winter, Jack. It's still *fall* and it's *freezing* in here."

"So we throw blankets and Visqueen over the holes until we can get some new windows freighted in," Jack said. "We got all winter."

Blaze squinted at him. "Okay, I know numbers might be a problem for you, so let me put this in terms you can understand. As your boss, I feel it is my obligation to inform you that I am *out of money*. That's it. No more. Zip. I have like seven hundred and sixty-two bucks left in my bank account and a couple grand in cash that I withdrew when I was in town. Hell, I don't even have the money to pay you your wages for the last three months—though I guess you did spend about two months of that asleep, bedridden, or making me do your work for you." She sighed, glancing out at the wreckage of the inside of the lodge. "I figured I could pawn off some of the machinery to the neighbors to pay you, then go back to town and see if I can sell the lodge to some handy-type as a 'fixer-upper', 'cause I'm pretty sure the werewolves wrecking my place didn't fall under 'Acts of God' in the insurance policy."

"Don't need to pay me," Jack muttered, still looking out at the door like he expected a pretty white werewolf to tear it off its hinges at any moment.

Blaze sighed. "Jack, I know you got that whole manly pride thing goin' on and all, but I feel I owe you just a teensy bit for saving my life, even if you were a jackass every step of the way."

"Don't want your money, Yeti," Jack growled. "Don't need it."

"Oh-ho!" Blaze laughed. "So let me see here. You, jobless, and certainly without the social skills to be a guide or run a lodge, basically *begged* me to let you work for me out of the goodness of your own heart?"

"Pretty much," Jack muttered. "I caught a whiff of something on that first check you wrote. Wanted to get a better look at what I was dealing with."

"Come *on*," Blaze laughed. "Stow the poor man's pride, already. I'm gonna give you your salary."

"Woman," Jack growled, "I was a *Viking*. Before that, I worked as a personal blacksmith to a *sheik*. You know that wolf that raised Romulus and Remus? Lemme tell ya, tootz, it wasn't a damn she-wolf. Hell, I trapped and traded my way across America in the days of Lewis and Clark because I got bored making swords for the Japanese shogunate. I came to Alaska during the *gold rush*." He gestured dismissively at the cursed circlet. "That little trinket's *nothing* compared to the treasures I've got buried out in the woods. Not just old stuff, either. Bought stock in Microsoft, GM, and Ford, just to name a few. Oh, and Sony.

You know? Those 'tel-e-vi-sions' you were talking about? Got those certificates buried out there somewhere, too."

For a long moment, Blaze could only stare at him in stunned shock. *He's been patronizing me since the beginning*, she realized, horrified. She felt tears beginning to burn her eyes, along with the first wave of exhaustion.

Jack twisted back up at her to give her a superior grin. "I said I was illiterate, sweetheart. Not stupid."

Blaze lowered her eyes to the claw-marks in the bed beneath her. Compared to the other rooms, this one had been the least devastated, yet it, too, had been badly ransacked. She had the sudden urge to ask Jack for a loan, fresh hope giving her the illusion that maybe she could still hold onto her dream. But, with as many times as he had told her this was 'his territory' and how he had treated *her* as the interloper, Blaze knew he'd been waiting for the helpless woman to fail since all the way back in May, when he had first told her she looked like a Clydesdale.

"What?" Jack asked, snorting. "Not going to ask me for a loan?"

Blaze blinked away tears, and turned away from him. "I'm getting very tired," she whispered.

"It's 'cause you're crying, you dumb ox," Jack growled softly, his eyes on the stains on the blankets. "Stop it."

Dumb ox. Add *that* to his repertoire of name-calling, and suddenly his choice in words all this time seemed to make sense. Draft animals, Yetis, hippopotami…None of them were known for their rocket-science. Blaze sniffled, but the burning inside kept surging forth, stinging like fire in her eyes until she swiped them away.

"Horus's balls!" Jack cried, jerking away from her. "Watch where you throw those things!"

Startled by the vehemence in his words, it took Blaze a moment to realize he was talking about her tears. She sniffled again, then dragged her hand across her face and stared down at the liquid in her hand.

"Uh," Jack said beside her, "We're probably gonna need to burn those blankets."

For a moment, the tears on her fingertips *seemed* to glow with an inner fire, but she knew that had to be a trick of the flashlight. She wiped her hand on the mattress.

"Oh, uh," Jack said, wincing as his eyes caught on the bed. "Uh." He glanced back up at her, looking almost timid. "You mind sparing a couple of those for a cranky old wereverine?" He was biting his lip. "Please?"

He's asking nicely, Blaze thought, absurdly. She lowered her head and shook it in despair. "Whatever, Jack."

"Okay, honey." He inched closer, like he was a rabbit approaching a sleeping fox. Then he frowned at her. "Why *are* you crying, anyway?"

Suddenly, Blaze couldn't hold back the superheated pressure overflowing from within. "*Because you're an asshole!*" she screamed, so angry she was trembling. She closed her eyes, whimpering as the exhaustion increased its tug at her soul. "If you didn't want me on your land, you should've just let me go home that first day," Blaze said. "Like I'd *wanted* to."

"Hey now," Jack said his massive shoulders bunching as he awkwardly dragged himself onto the bed beside her, "I don't know where you got the idea that I didn't want you here, tootz."

"Oh, gee," Blaze snapped. "You tell me I've got Clydesdale in my ancestry, you belittle me by telling me I'm a big, stupid Yeti, you let me feed you endangered livestock on my dime, making it out like you've been starving out here, you call me an *ox*..."

"Never said I was starving, sweetie." Jack reached up and wiped the tears from her face. Blaze actually thought he was making the gesture in tenderness until he swiped his thumb across his thighs. She thought she saw a brief glint of gold where his thumb touched his leg before it was gone.

Almost instantly, the wereverine balled his fists and gritted his teeth. "Gods, that hurts worse than getting poked by a dread horn." He proceeded to pound the bed a few times with a fist, his breath coming out in a low groan between his teeth.

Suddenly, in her growing exhaustion, Blaze understood. "Tears," she said. "You're using them to *heal*."

"Fuck. It *burns*," Jack growled. He was sweating, and Blaze could feel a sudden heat radiating off of him, like something that had been left out in the sun too long. He gave Blaze a wary look. "This *is* what you did to fix me the first time, isn't it? Tell me I didn't just mix moon and sun magics in a way that's gonna get my ass burned off."

Runt used the tears, Blaze thought, remembering the absurd way the little fey had caught each individual tear as it fell from her eyes. Interested, now, she sniffled, then rubbed her eyes again, taking what was in them and dropping them on Jack's legs when he was preoccupied with pounding on the bed.

"Oh *shit*," Jack howled, jerking away from her suddenly. "I didn't ask you to—Ow, ow, ow, *fuck*!" Hissing, he fell onto his side, grabbing his thighs in both hands. The heat pouring off of him again made Blaze think of a stone that had been left in the desert heat. He started panting and whining, which developed into low, anguished moans. Throughout it all, however, he didn't even grow the slightest bit of fur.

"You want more?" Blaze asked, wiping her eyes again.

"No more!" Jack screamed, rolling away from her, falling with a crash onto the debris-scattered floor. "Fuck, it burns! My legs are on *fire*!"

"Well, at least you're *feeling* them, right?!" Blaze snapped, more vindictively than she would have thought herself capable.

The wereverine didn't hear her. He had devolved into a long string of curses, imprecations, and invectives that left her ears burning…

…And her exhaustion finally hit her like a sledgehammer. As the wereverine rolled around on the floor, moaning and screaming like he was dying, Blaze slumped to the bed in a near-stupor, knowing she probably wasn't going to wake up for a few days.

I hate crying, she thought, as the blackness enfolded her.

TWENTY-SEVEN

The Truth Comes Out

"So, uh, you feelin' ready to wake up yet? You been sleepin' three days, tootz. I already gave you a good sunbath. You keep sleeping, it's just you bein' lazy."

Already gave you a good sunbath? But before she had a chance to think about *that*, Blaze felt something poking her in the ribs and she moaned and rolled away, pulling the covers over her head.

She heard Jack sigh and walk around the bed.

Walk around the bed? Blaze peeked out from under the blankets. Jack was looking down at her with a platter of what smelled like steaming eggs balanced in one hand, and a book balanced in the other. He tossed the book so that it landed by her nose, then lowered the plate of eggs to the mattress beside her stomach.

"Teach me that," Jack said, gesturing at the smutty romantic adventure novel, "and I'll consider it a fair trade."

Frowning, Blaze sat up and said, "Consider *what* a fair…" She didn't finish when she realized that the drywall of the room had been stripped to the two-by-four studs, and that through the now-transparent walls, she saw that the rest of the lodge seemed to have suffered similar treatment, though she could see no evidence on the floors.

Blaze was so flabbergasted that all she could say was, "You *swept*?"

"I only just started on it," Jack said, almost sounding apologetic. "But we've got all winter. Place was needing an upgrade anyway. Already took the liberty of scheduling a few freight-trips in with David Foruke. He's got a nice snow-machine rig he runs up the river after freeze-up." He gestured at the plate of food. "But you eat something. You been asleep for three days."

Most people, Blaze knew, would have been freaking out and calling the EMTs in Anchorage if someone they knew just suddenly decided to fall asleep for three days. Jack just treated it like it was a matter-of-fact. He was also walking again. Easily. Like he hadn't just spent a month in a wheelchair, wearing a diaper.

"Why did my tears heal your legs?" Blaze demanded.

Jack winced. "Uh, well…"

"Just spit it out," Blaze growled. "I'm about ready to use my last bit of cash to charter a plane back to Anchorage."

Jack narrowed his eyes at her. "It's freeze-up, missy. You ain't chartering a plane nowhere 'til the lake freezes up enough for something to land on it."

"The world has this marvelous new invention called a 'helicopter,'" Blaze said. "I'll charter one of those." And it would probably cost her *all* of her cash, too, but it would be worth every penny to finally wash her hands of this mess and return to a place where people weren't trying to kill her and she had enough control over her emotions not to put herself into a coma every time her neighbor looked at her funny.

Jack's lip lifted in a bit of a snarl. "So that's it, then? You're just going to take off and leave your dream here to freeze as soon as the weather turns?"

"You've been *hiding* something from me since I *got* here!" Blaze snapped. "So *yes*, I *am* about to pack up and leave."

Jack glared at her for a long moment before he crossed his arms and leaned against the wall. "You're a phoenix," he muttered. "You got little tricks you can do, no big deal."

A phoenix. Blaze's mouth fell open as things suddenly fell into place for her. "And you didn't think this was important to tell me *why*?" she blurted.

He gave her an irritated look. "Didn't think you needed to know. Seemed to have been doing fine on your own. Why bother you with something like that?"

Then Blaze remembered the way the dread unicorn's horn had instantly knocked him out of his Third-Lander shape and back into human form, then similarly how he had been rolling and howling three nights ago, yet for all his screaming, had remained perfectly human.

"The tears yank the moon-magic out of you, don't they?" she demanded.

Jack's eyes widened slightly and she saw a tinge of sweat as he unfolded from the wall. "Who told you that?"

"Despite what you keep claiming," Blaze growled, "I don't have the IQ of a farm animal. Every time you get so much as *irritated*, you start growing fangs. Yet you were rolling around screaming last night and you looked more human than you do now."

Indeed, the nervousness in his green eyes was beginning to lengthen the pupil, elongating his teeth…

Licking his lips, the wereverine looked out the now-drywall-less walls, avoiding her gaze.

Suddenly, Blaze understood. "You're afraid of losing your power."

Jack jerked his head back to face her suddenly, eyes too wide. He quickly replaced his bored mask, but not before Blaze saw the fear, there. "It's only temporary," he muttered.

"Okay," Blaze said. "So keep my tears to myself. Gotcha." She snorted. "Shouldn't be hard. Hell, it's not like I ever learned how to cry on command. I spent the last twenty-five years of my life training myself *not* to cry." She gave him a weak smile. "You get told your comas are 'self-induced' enough and you stop really believing in the whole medical establishment. I got really *good* at not crying, until I met you."

Jack watched her tentatively, something akin to understanding in his eyes, but seemingly had nothing more to add.

"So," Blaze sighed. "That the only reason you don't want me on your land?"

The wereverine jerked. "Don't *want* you here? What gave you that idea?"

Blaze gave him a long, level look.

"Oh." Jack chuckled nervously and scratched at the back of his neck. "Uh. Truth is, tootz, I'd kinda like you to stay."

Blaze could not believe it. "So let me get this straight," she said, "In some strange, weasely part of your brain, you've somehow decided that calling a woman a draft animal was akin to telling her she had a pretty smile."

"Uh..." Jack swallowed again. "Bad habit, I guess."

Then Blaze remembered his little monologue whilst tied to the bulldozer, in which he had babbled about playing with fire. Suddenly, something clicked in her head. All the insults, all the rude innuendo, all the posturing, all the *bullshit*...He was acting like a kindergartener who tugged a girl's pigtails because he couldn't figure out a better way to say he liked her.

Blaze's mouth fell open.

Jack gave her a nervous look and scratched at the back of his neck. He was *sweating*, Blaze noted, and his eyes flickered sideways like he wanted to put a new hole in the wall and bolt.

Why did I not see this before? Blaze wondered, caught somewhere between awe and irritation. To test her theory, she said, "That day tied to the bulldozer...You weren't just saying that to get me to let you loose, were you?"

Immediately, the wereverine bristled like a puffer-fish. "Of *course* I was making that shit up," he growled. "You had me swimmin' in my own goddamn shit, you inconsiderate orangutan." But the anxiety in his eyes betrayed him.

Blaze's mouth fell open again.

Looking up at her, Jack swallowed. He licked his lips and turned his attention to picking a splinter from a nearby two-by-four. "Why are you looking at me like that?"

"You like to play with fire," Blaze said, only able to stare. "You've known *all this time*, haven't you? From the day I stepped onto 'your' land."

"Had about a six-foot-five suspicion," Jack admitted.

Blaze narrowed her eyes. "I'm six-foot-four."

Jack laughed. "When you're that big, tootz, nobody's really counting."

"You like to play with fire," Blaze repeated. Jack flinched, and the way he looked up at her uneasily cinched it for her. "Oh my *God*," Blaze cried. "You've wanted to get me naked *all this time*, and you just let me *stew*?"

He puffed up again, looked like he wanted to say something loud and obnoxious, then swallowed and gruffly muttered, "I don't bed a girl 'cause I'm bored."

Maybe he *was* gay. Blaze eyed him carefully. "*How* many women did you have in all that time? Four?"

He peered at her suspiciously. "You get as old as I do, anything less than a decade or two don't really count."

Oh, great, Blaze thought. *So the sly little bastard isn't as chaste as he's been leading me to believe.*

"But yeah," Jack said, picking at the splinters again, "Four."

Blaze peered at him. "That 'Wereverine' four or 'American English' four?"

"Four," Jack growled. "Not that it's any of your damn business. You gonna teach me to read or should I just pack up and head home and let you deal with this beat-to-shit mansion in the woods by yourself?"

Blaze grunted. For the longest time, she looked down at the book, trying to add up things in her head. "So," she said tentatively, "Just so I can get this straight. You're telling me you'll help with…uh…costs…if I teach you to read this?" She hefted the book and held it up between them.

"That's the deal," Jack said.

Blaze peeked up at him. "And you'll keep giving me massages."

Jack raised an eyebrow. "You haven't been making breakfast."

Blaze's jaw fell open. "I've been *asleep*!"

"I noticed," he quipped. "While I was hard at work fixing walls and repairing water-damage."

"I healed your legs," Blaze growled.

"Your *tears* did that, tootz," he said, infuriatingly. "All you did was have a little pity-fest on your own behalf."

Blaze narrowed her eyes. "Compliment me."

The wereverine blinked down at her, looking startled. "Huh?"

"Compliment me," Blaze repeated. "Do something other than pull my damn pigtails."

Jack stared at her. "You ain't got pigtails."

"Do it," Blaze growled. "You know, like, 'wow, your hair is pretty this morning, Blaze.'"

"It's a rat's nest."

Blaze caught her reflection in one of the broken chunks of mirror propped up against the studs. It did, indeed, look like something a particularly nasty rodent would have called home. Frustrated, she said, "Fine, tell me I smell nice."

"Sorry to break this to you, tootz, but you haven't showered in three days." The wereverine sniffed at the air. "And I'm pretty sure you pissed yourself somewhere along the way."

Blaze flushed furiously, remembering all the awkward, messy mornings she'd experienced waking up after a sob-fest, particularly in her teenage crush years. "You," she muttered, feeling like her face was on fire, "are missing the point."

"What's the point?" the wereverine asked her, looking thoroughly confused.

Blaze's mouth fell open. "I'm trying to get you to comp—" She frowned. "Waaaiit. Do you even know what a compliment *is*?"

"I thought we determined I was illiterate," Jack growled, looking ruffled, "not stupid."

"Okay," Blaze said, crossing her arms, "Then compliment me."

"Why?" Jack demanded, looking suspicious.

She narrowed her eyes at him. "Because I asked you nicely."

"No you didn't. You *told* me to."

"Yeah," Blaze growled, "Well now I'm asking."

"Don't feel like it," Jack muttered.

Blaze stared at him long enough that Jack coughed nervously and looked away. "So let me get this straight," she growled, throwing the blanket off of her and standing up to stare down at him. She poked him in the chest. "You were offering to *marry* me and there's *nothing* you like about me?"

Jack stared down at her finger, poking him in the chest, then lifted his head to peer up at her. "Men have had their arms ripped off for less than that," he said.

Blaze narrowed her eyes and poked him again. "There's *nothing*"—poke—"that your little pea brain"—poke—"can come up with"—poke—"that you like about me." She thumped his breastbone one last time and left her finger there, waiting. "And if you say I excrete a bodily fluid that cures what ails ya, I'm gone, *tootz*. Packing my bags and *outta* here."

He squinted up at her in the same way he had squinted at the hotel manager, when he had handed them plastic cards as 'keys' to their room. Sounding leery and confused, he said, "Why do you want a compliment so bad?"

"At this point?" Blaze cried. "Just idle, random curiosity to see if you can even *do* it."

He peered up at her so long that Blaze began to wonder if a wire had crossed in his brain and the thoughtful look to his green eyes was actually an irreparable short-circuit. She was about to snap her fingers in front of his face when, finally, each word like pulling teeth, he muttered, "I like your hair."

"You just told me it was a rat's nest," Blaze growled.

"It is," Jack muttered. "Still like it." He reached up and lifted a red-gold lock from her chest and rubbed it between his fingers. "Pretty. Like fire."

He likes playing with fire. Heart suddenly slamming like hot thunder in her ears at his sudden closeness, Blaze managed, "Kids in school thought I dyed it."

Jack gently released the lock of her hair, then traced it up to her face. "Pretty ears, too," he noted. "Got the cheekbones of a princess." Blaze tried not to tremble as he traced the ridges under her eyes, then across the bridge of her nose. "Soft skin," he noted, still tracing. "Gentle eyebrows." He drew his finger down the center of her face.

"Cute nose." He gently brushed her lips and then ran his finger down her chin. "Full lips, nice pert chin."

Blaze closed her eyes, each heartbeat a nuclear explosion in her chest. Her whole body was on fire, again, and every one of her senses was zeroed in on the rough, male finger that was tracing its way under her chin and down her throat. He was so *strong*, so perfectly *close*...

As if to answer her, he stepped closer, until his big chest was touching hers, and one of his powerful arms wrapped itself around the small of her back, pulling her hard against him.

Even as Blaze's mind did a startled double-take at that, he reached up, slid his fingers through the back of her hair, and took a firm grip against the back of her head. "Pretty eyes, too," he whispered, against her throat.

Blaze's eyes flashed open and she looked down to see him looking up at her, grinning mischievously. "That's more like it," he purred, and pulled her down for a kiss.

Once again, the wereverine took her breath away. The touch of his body to hers, the feel of his chest against her breasts, the inescapable pull of his arms as they held her in place, the total *maleness* of the man holding her...Again, she was made perfectly aware of the fact that this was *not* a nerdy college kid with a hardon for Amazons. This was a virile, infinitely strong, perfectly potent *man* who put everyone else she'd ever had to shame, and then some. All of it combined into a hot sizzle ripping through her loins where they touched his, until she was *thrumming* with the need to rip his clothes off and drag him to the bed. Returning his kiss, she started angling that way, until her knees were touching the back of the mattress.

Breaking the kiss, Jack glanced down at the bed behind her and wrinkled his nose. "Yep, you peed it. I'll go get the hot water started. Might wanna get your pants in the wash, too. Pretty sure that's gonna leave a stain." Then, as if she wasn't standing there, red-faced and panting, he turned his back and walked off, leaving her with a cold plate of eggs and a pee-stained sheet, staring after him in horror.

• • •

"You smell nice," Jack said pausing in the hallway when Blaze stepped out of the bathroom—or the blanketed-off area that was *supposed* to be the bathroom—fully dressed and still steaming. A bundle of lumber over one shoulder, he popped what looked like a cherry into his mouth and chewed on it thoughtfully as he looked up at her hair, which she had combed out and braided. "Hair's pretty." Then he strode past her down the hall, his pile of two-by-fours swaying easily on his shoulder.

Blaze brandished her brush at his back. "Now you're just being petty."

"Stop threatening me with your hairbrush and get some shoes on," Jack said, without looking, "Today I'm gonna show you how to repair trusses." He popped another of the red balls into his mouth and dumped his load of lumber beside a ruined wall.

"Are those *cherries*?" Blaze demanded.

"Hope so," Jack called, as he picked up a pre-cut board and fitted it into position along the ruined wall. "That little tree you planted in the corner of the greenhouse is covered with 'em." Sticking another in his mouth, he chewed on it as he arranged the 2x4, then easily nailed it into place. The pit, Blaze noticed, got ejected onto the floor when he was done with it, joining a couple dozen others that she could see in the immediate area.

I have a cherry tree in my backyard, Blaze thought, a little stunned. *In the middle of winter.* She'd always thought she'd have to live in Washington to get cherries to grow. "So, uh, what's a truss?" she asked, as she went to examine his handiwork. She nudged the cherry pits with her foot. "Got any of those for me?"

He dug into his pocket and handed her a palmful of cherries and lint. Keeping one for himself, he said around a cherry, "A truss is what holds up a roof. Barn didn't have 'em, it had a ridgepole with rafters. The shop has trusses. They're the little triangular things that hold up a roof."

The hole in the roof, Blaze realized, remembering the werewolves fighting atop the shop. "That sounds like fun," she said.

"It's gonna be a bitch. Hand me that short two-by-four." He pointed with the handle of his hammer.

Grabbing it and handing it to him, Blaze said, "So what do you know about…what you said I am…anyway?"

Jack missed a beat in hammering the board into place. Pausing, he looked up at her, still bent over to reach the floor. "What, a phoenix?" Then he gave her that little suspicious look and said, "Or you talkin' a Yeti?"

Her neck twitching again, Blaze said, "A phoenix."

"Oh," he chuckled. "Well, ain't much to tell." He grabbed another board and hammered it into place, then spat another cherry pit onto the floor.

"Why not?" Blaze demanded, once he was finished pounding. "Seems like you've been withholding some pretty important information."

Jack grunted. "Not my job to tell you what you are. Can you hand me that one right there?"

Blaze handed him the board and reluctantly tasted one of the fruits Jack had given her. It was *exquisite*. Nothing like the dull, tasteless cherries that spent two weeks on a barge, getting up to Alaska. "Oohhh," she moaned. "This is so *good*." Then she jabbed a finger at him. "And yes, it *is* your job, because I'm clueless."

Jack gave her a sideways look. "That happens."

"Happens how?" Blaze demanded.

"When you die," Jack said. He shrugged. "You go nuclear, rattle a few tectonics, maybe leave a crater. Then you show up all fresh and new and cute."

"The baby in the firepit?" Blaze asked.

"That's the one," Jack said, around a cherry. He made a general gesture to her and the back yard with his hammer and said, "The rest is pretty obvious."

Bristling, Blaze said, "Enlighten me. Use small words, if you have to."

"Hmm." Jack slapped another two-by-four into place, then paused, leaning against it. Frowning at her, he said, "You really don't remember nothin' at all?" His green eyes sparkled with curiosity.

"What you see is what you get," Blaze said. "I've been bigger than my classmates all my life, my hair's got that weird red-orange color that looks like a bad dye-job, and my eyes are somewhere between yellow, orange, and albino red."

Jack flinched, looking up at her. "Your eyes are blue."

"Those are contacts," Blaze growled. "You have *no idea* what it's like to walk into Wal-Mart and have every kid in the store pointing and saying 'Mommy Mommy, her eyes are *orange*!' while their parents are trying their damndest not to stare, but doing it anyway."

Jack grunted, apparently seeing her in a new light. "Orange, huh? Well, that makes a lot more sense. Hell, here I was thinking you were a halfblood or something. Orange." He nodded his approval and went back to his construction.

"So tell me about a phoenix," Blaze said. "What the hell is a phoenix?"

Eying her in between setting boards into place, Jack said, "Very rare, for one. Back in the day, kings and emperors had groups of huntsmen out looking for your kind all the time. Would pay a pretty penny to have one caught alive. Made really nice gardens."

Hearing that, Blaze bristled. "And here you've got one making its nest right next door, eh?"

Jack eyed her warily. "Yeah. So?"

Blaze deflated, realizing again how alone she was in the world, and how little it mattered that she was sharing her living-space with a cranky wereverine. At least he wasn't trying to sell her to the highest bidder or something. Hell, he even seemed bound and determined to *protect* her. "So they caught them? To, what, put in their zoos?"

"Uh, well..." Jack flushed and rubbed the back of his neck with a callused hand before peeking up at her under a flop of black curls. "Uh. Yeah, they did stuff like that."

"Stuff like *what*, exactly?" Blaze growled, not liking the way he seemed to be avoiding the subject.

"Uh." Jack wiped sweat from his forehead and gave her a long look. "Not good stuff. Really awful stuff, actually. It's why you guys never spent much time around people. Got dangerous if you didn't have someone you could trust, what with the crying and all that."

"What kind of stuff?" Blaze prodded.

He winced. "Uh. Technically, I probably should've sent you packing for dragon territory the minute I figured out what you were. At least until you were awakened. But Hell, even a dragon would..." He hesitated. "Uh. At least unicorns can disappear whenever they feel like it. The fey blood and all that."

Blaze peered at him. "I'm a unicorn?"

"No," Jack growled, "You're a phoenix."

"Okay," Blaze said, "So why would you send me packing?"

Jack took a deep breath and gave her a long, measuring look. She could see the debate behind his eyes before he finally said, "Because I could go out back right now, dig up that feather, and force you to do my every whim for the rest of your life." He popped a lint-covered cherry into his mouth and chewed it thoughtfully. "You could see where that might get unpleasant, right?" He hesitated. "Specially me bein' a guy, you bein' a girl, and back then, all the rulers were guys, and they were all sorts of interested in crossbreeds and that sort of shit."

Blaze swallowed uncomfortably. She *did* see, and it was making her nervous as hell. She had to try several times before she could get her throat to work enough to say, "You're telling me that *feather* is a danger to me?"

"Not a danger, as much as something to watch out for," Jack said. "Kind of like Spiderman's Kryptonite."

"That's Superman," Blaze said.

Jack blushed. "Uh. Yeah. I only had pictures."

"I'll teach you," Blaze assured him. "An hour a night until you can read that book." She hesitated. "Until then, uh, I'd really like to know what you know about being a phoenix."

Jack took a deep breath. "Well, you're *supposed* to have a temple in Egypt, another in Mexico, and a third in China where you all can congregate and learn from each other and do your phoenix thing, but I'm guessing that you guys stopped doing that around the same time they put out the Bounties."

"Bounties?"

Jack grunted and waved a dismissive hand. "Catholic Church. Inquisition. You read about it in the history books."

"They wanted to kill…us?" Blaze asked, frowning.

Jack snorted. "Hell, no. Sure, with most, like the moon-kissed, they just wanted to use the magic in enchantments and artifacts, stuff that would help them expand against the pagans, so they bled that out of us. Critters like phoenix and unicorns, hell, they'd keep them alive indefinitely. Probably *still* have some tucked away, in odd places. Stuff like that…" He shook his head, then looked at her sideways. "You ever wonder why the Catholic Church is one of the biggest land-owners in the world?"

Blaze thought she was gonna be sick. "They *bled* you?"

Jack's face darkened. "Some of us."

Remembering his former wives, Blaze went quiet.

Jack popped a cherry into his mouth and chewed on it, glaring at the pile of lumber he'd dragged inside. "Good cherries," he noted.

"Thanks," Blaze whispered. All the different facts were slamming together into her head, making the world a hell of a lot bigger—and scarier—than she had ever thought possible.

As if sensing her growing dread, Jack spoke softly, "I've got your back, sister."

Blaze swallowed against impending tears. "Why?" she managed. "I've been nothing but trouble for you since I got here."

He much-too-carefully picked lint from a cherry, then, once it was completely clean, handed it to her. Meeting her eyes, he said, "'Cause I do."

Numbly, Blaze took the cherry, though she couldn't bring herself to eat it.

"The ones that are left, we kind of stick together." He was looking up at her tentatively. "The old ones, anyway. Not like Amber…The ones who know better." Then he made a disgusted sound and his words took on an embittered tinge and he gestured at the woods around him. "But every year, a couple more of us die, usually to stupid crap like this. Cities are spreading outward, crowding us all into tighter quarters, and the Bounties are still out there." He sighed and scuffed his foot against the floor. "Hate to say it, Boss, but things ain't been lookin' too good for the Home Team for a few centuries, now."

"What's the bounty for a phoenix?" Blaze whispered.

He cocked his head, intelligence in his green eyes. "Same as that for a unicorn, last I heard."

Blaze got a sinking feeling in her gut. "What's that?"

Jack almost looked like he didn't want to answer. Reluctantly, he said, "A hundred bars of gold. Probably more now. There were a lot more of you guys flying around back then. Hell, I ain't even *heard* of one for a couple centuries."

A hundred bars *of gold*...Blaze suddenly didn't feel so good. She knew from her Econ classes that a single Good Delivery gold bar in the world's gold reserves cost over seven hundred thousand dollars. "You're saying those bounties...they're *still* out there?"

For a moment, it looked like Jack would lie to her. Then, his face darkened and he snorted, "'Course it is. What rich fuck wouldn't wanna have mangoes in December?" Jack gave her a wary look. "Or everlasting health?"

Suddenly, it was like the world had just collapsed around her, leaving her drifting in the rubble of What She Once Knew. People wanted to kill her. Or capture her—Jack hadn't really been clear on that. People she had never even *met*.

"Are you *sure* about that?" Blaze whispered. "That I am...uh...that thing?"

"What, a phoenix?"

Blaze grimaced, not liking to hear it out loud.

Jack grunted. "Pretty sure. Smells right. And there's the feather out back. And you just about set me on fire when you splashed those tears on me."

Blaze thought of all the ways she couldn't defend herself against werewolves, dragons, and the rest of the nasties of the world, and she suddenly felt very small and insecure, for a woman about the size of Goliath. "You said you could go out back and dig up that feather and control me? How?"

Jack grimaced at her. "I ain't gonna do it."

"*How*?" Blaze demanded. "I think I deserve to know, don't you?"

Grunting, Jack said, "You ain't gonna like it."

"Oh, would you fucking *tell* me already?!" Blaze snapped. She jabbed a thumb at her chest. "I can handle it, okay?"

Jack grunted. "Sure, okay. Fine. You noticed how delicate I was when I carried the damn thing around, right? Like it was made of freakin' crystal?"

She peered at him. "Don't you *dare* tell me that thing breaks in half and my spine cracks in two."

Jack winced. "Said you wouldn't like it."

Staring at him, she growled, "You're kidding. A *feather*? My whole...*existence*...is bound to a *feather*?" She didn't believe that. Not a whit.

"Well, not all like that," Jack said. "Uh, I don't think it could actually kill you to snap it in half, but it'll hurt like hell. Guess a good way to look at it is the spine of the feather is like the bundle of nerves running down your spine. Each of the floaty little branches on the feather is like a branch of nerves running through your body. Except instead of nerves, think life-fire."

Blaze peered at him. She *wanted* to tell him that he was wrong and he could go take a flying leap off a cliff while she packed her bags and left this insanity in the Bush, but there was that little nagging voice in the back of her head that reminded her of the fire that flowed through her veins when something disturbed her calm.

"So," she said tentatively, "You're saying it's connected to me."

"You pluck a feather, it's gonna hurt," Jack said. He shrugged. "Ain't that big a deal, long as you keep it out of sight."

Suddenly, buried in the back yard didn't seem *half* as safe as something like that needed to be. "Where can we put it that nobody's ever gonna find it?" Blaze demanded.

Jack bristled immediately. "It's good where it is. Told ya, tootz, I'll protect you."

"What about putting it in a metal box and dropping it to the bottom of the Mariana Trench?" Blaze demanded.

Jack balked, paling considerably. "Uh…no…sweetie, that would be very bad."

Once again, she was getting the distinct feeling that he knew more than he was telling her. "Spit it out," Blaze growled.

"Uh…" Jack rubbed the back of his neck and she was pretty sure she heard 'Yeti wench' in the muttering that followed, but finally, after peering down the hall, then at the Visqueened windows, then at the ceiling, then at the cherry stones on the floor, he just looked straight at her and said, "You can't wake up if you don't have that feather."

"Wake…up…" Blaze said. She frowned. "Enlighten me?"

"Wake up," Jack said, gesturing at her. "You know. Grow wings and hurtle across the sky in a blaze of fire? All that wonderful phoenix stuff?" He frowned. "Well, I mean, I guess it's not *impossible* to do it without the life-link, but it's damn hard."

"In English, please."

He narrowed his eyes at her and spouted something that sounded French. Then repeated himself in Chinese. Then German. Then… Gaelic??…then Russian then Japanese then another dialect that sounded Chinese—

"Enough!" Blaze cried, "Jesus!"

Still scowling at her, back all puffed up and hairy, Jack growled, "I said I'm illiterate, not stupid."

"I didn't *say* you were stupid," Blaze growled, jabbing her thumb at her chest again, "I said *I* didn't understand. This is important to me. You and your goddamn touchy pride can take a flying fuck at a rolling goddamn doughnut. *Tell me what you meant in terms I can understand.*"

The wereverine sniffed and glanced beyond her at the door out the basement of the lodge, and for a moment, it looked like he would simply wander off. Then, muttering, he said, "You take the feather, pierce your heart with it, and boom, you take its power back, which triggers a reaction inside. Kind of like setting off magnesium shavings. You get all burny and glowy and it hurts to goddamn look at you, okay?"

"Uh," Blaze said. "Why would I ever want to do that?"

Jack's mouth fell open and he stared at her like she'd just offered to shove leeches up her nose. "Why…?" he stammered, obviously confused.

"Yeah. Why?"

He peered at her. "Well, you could fly, for one."

"I could buy an airplane."

Giving her a somewhat startled look, he said, "Because it's your *power*. You have someone show up on your property you don't like, well, you tell them to leave. They don't wanna leave, you scatter their ashes across half the valley."

"You said stab me in the heart with a feather. I'm still trying to get past that part."

"Uh, yeah," Jack said, frowning. "So?"

Then Blaze remembered who she was dealing with, and just how many times he'd had his body ripped asunder, and realized getting stabbed in the heart probably wasn't such a big deal to him. "And this big, glorious ball of fire that you can't even look at…that's gonna be my M.O. the rest of my life, post-feather-stabbing? I just walk around having people shield their eyes?"

"No," Jack said, frowning. "That just lasts a couple hours. It kinda fades with nightfall."

"So I'm a great big, really pretty fiery birdy that flaps around setting things on fire, is that what you're telling me?"

Jack was obviously confused by her line of questioning, because he said, "Uh, yeah, I guess. If that's what floats your boat."

Blaze snorted. "No, I think I'll stay just like I am, thank you. Yeti beats 'unapproachable avian bonfire' any day. Hell, you said it yourself…with how few of…those things…are out there, I'd probably never have sex again."

Jack stared at her. "They don't *just* have the bird-form. They can change. Human and back."

Blaze froze. "It's like a possession from the Fourth Lands, isn't it? Instead of the Third Lands, like werewolves?"

Jack stiffened immediately and growled, "There's no possession involved. You imbeciles left the Fourth Lands through the portal in the sun. Fled the wars in your home lands and thought it would somehow be better here. Little did you know they would seal the portal and leave you here with a bunch of monkeys who think they got a right to run around killin' stuff that they don't understand."

Blaze peered at him for a long moment before saying, "All right. Say I believe you about...what I am...and say I just leave that feather right where it is instead of punching it through my ribcage. What'll happen to me?"

Jack gave her an irritated look. "Nothing. That's why I wasn't gonna tell you about it."

"And if I *do* decide to stab myself with it, then what happens? Big, glowy birdy for a few hours, then back to regular old Blaze, but with a few upgrades?"

"Your eyes will glow," Jack said. "Uh, so will your hair. And it'll float, too. Kind of like the way the filaments on the feather do."

Ooooohh, yeah. Blaze could so totally live *without* that. "Anything else I should be aware of?" she asked, trying not to look as thoroughly spooked as she felt.

Jack grunted a moment, then sighed and gestured out at the greenhouse. "You know the trees you planted?"

"Yeah," Blaze said.

"Okay," Jack said, "You take the feather away, they'll start to die. You put an awakened *phoenix* in its place, and everything within twenty square miles is going to look like the Garden of Eden within a decade or two. You know that nice lush area of Mesopotamia, where the Tigris and Euphrates made it so easy for people to start their nice new civilization? It wasn't just the rivers, baby. Had a phoenix living there, at least in the beginning. Ran him off eventually, of course, but that's where everything started."

"Uh," Blaze said, looking down at the cherries in her hand. "Twenty *miles?*"

Jack shrugged. "I dunno. Twenty miles in a decade's probably a bit of an embellishment, but I do know the longer you're in one place, the further it goes. Guy on the Tigris, hell, he had been living there close to his full lifetime before they drove him out. Had a good hundred miles growin' like weeds. Prettiest thing you ever saw."

Blaze peered at the wereverine for a long moment, finally starting to understand why he wanted her to hang around. "You want that to happen here."

He flinched and gave her a nervous look. "I, uh, ain't gonna force you into nothin' girlie. Already told you that. You just take as long as you need. Hell, wasn't even gonna *tell* you until I was sure you could handle it. You forced my hand and made me. Wasn't like I was gonna drag you outside and stab you, you know, so no need to take it the wrong way. Sure, I want you to stay, and yeah, some extra greenery around would be really nice, but you ain't gotta rush it."

The way he was suddenly babbling made Blaze wonder, "How many phoenixes have you known?"

Jack went quiet.

"One? Two?"

Reluctantly, looking up into her eyes almost timidly, he said, "They're kinda rare."

Hence why, when the curmudgeony old fart had one dropped in his lap, he broke her cell phone and otherwise removed her ability to leave.

Blaze took a deep breath, then let it out slowly. "Okay. So, what, you're offering your protection so I'll hang around and make your plants grow?"

"Already said that," Jack growled. "First time you asked it."

"You didn't say *twenty square miles*!" Blaze cried. "Jesus! That's like..." She tried to think of a way to describe what people would start saying if twenty square miles of the Alaskan Bush suddenly started growing pomegranates, with the Sleeping Lady at its epicenter, but discovered she couldn't find the words. Instead, she dropped her face to her hands. "I'm so screwed."

"Look, you ain't alone in this, honey," Jack said hurriedly. "I'm here. And Brad...He's a vain and arrogant shit who struts around in robes and Spandex and panics if he gets dirt under his nails, but he'll probably come to your aid, if we ask nicely. Same with the dragons." He winced. "Well, *half* the dragons. The other half would spirit you off and tuck you away in their cave so you make their mountain thrive."

Glaring at him, Blaze said, "Kind of like you?"

"Now hold on there a minute, missy," Jack growled. "I never kidnapped you."

"You ran me down in the woods and dragged me back over your shoulder," Blaze growled. "Twice."

"Three times, if you count saving your ass from the werewolves," Jack growled. "I was just doing my job and keeping you safe."

"Your…job…" Blaze gritted, deciding that was something they needed to examine under a more careful light, "is *what*, exactly? Telling me I'm a draft animal and giving me just enough of a taste of your chiseled body to leave me in a state of constant sexual frustration?"

Jack gave her a long, irritated look, then picked up his hammer and said, "I'm gonna go fix some trusses." He started to walk past her.

Seeing him about to leave, Blaze suddenly had every bit of her pretenses stripped away, realizing that at any moment, he could decide to leave her to deal with these things alone, unequipped and ignorant. "Wait," she whimpered, catching him by the muscular arm. "Please. I'm sorry. I'm scared, all right? It's like a kid who never watched the Care Bears because their parents decided it was too violent suddenly discovering there's rapists and murderers out there, and, gee, some of them are living right down the street." She held his arm until he stopped. "Please," she whimpered. "I don't think I've ever been this scared in my life, and we just fought *werewolves*."

Jack looked down at her hand, then slowly up at her. There was compassion in his green eyes. "I'll help any way I can, sugar."

The revelations, the fear, the wereverine's sudden kindness…It was too much. Blaze bit her lip and felt the first wave of fatigue as tears stung at her eyes.

"Hey now," Jack said, giving her a worried look. "No need for that. Here." He yanked off his shirt and carefully brushed the tears from her eyes with it. Softly, looking up at her, he said, "You're gonna be fine, girl. It ain't as bad as it seems." Then he grinned. "Besides, you got a grumpy old wereverine on your team." A big, callused hand holding her arm to steady her, he lowered the shirt and peered into her face. "Feel better?"

"Could use a hug," Blaze managed.

"Oh, darlin," he said, pulling her close. "Okay, here." She felt him wrap his arms around her, heavy and strong, felt his thick chest hard and firm against her breasts, and she lowered her chin to his shoulder, suddenly feeling a lot better. She felt tears burn her eyes again, followed by the requisite wave of exhaustion. She blinked, and one dropped.

Under her, Jack hissed and immediately stuffed the shirt under her chin. "Don't mind hugging your Yeti ass," he growled, through a clenched jaw, "but that fucking hurts."

Blaze laughed, despite herself. She pulled back and wiped the tears away with her arm. Before she could fling them aside, however, Jack snagged her wrist and, with his shirt, less-than-gently ran the rag up and down her arm. "Listen, tootz," he said, as he worked, "Eventually, you're gonna get things figured out, but until you do, *please* don't go throwing liquid sunshine on a nice tongue-and-groove wooden floor." He caught her eyes with an impatient scowl. "Really messes up the epoxy."

Blaze frowned at him. "Huh?"

Finishing with her hand, Jack gave her an irritated look, strode over to the fireplace, and threw his shirt into it. Then, casting her *another* irritated look, marched across the hall to the room where she had slept and came back with a scorched blanket in his hands. Gesturing at the black, melted holes in the dark blue material, he said, "Kept a good eye on it, as you slept, and put out the ones that actually took, but yeah. Not a good idea."

Blaze frowned at the blanket. "*I* did that?"

"No, it was probably the Easter Bunny."

She glared at him. "I had total sob-fests as a teenager and my house never caught fire."

"Probably hadn't touched the feather yet, either." Conversation over, Jack threw the blanket back into the bedroom and went to retrieve his hammer. As he passed her on the way to the back door, he said over his shoulder, "If you wanna keep from passing out, you should probably come hang out in the sun with me for a few. It should help."

Indeed, Blaze felt absolutely exhausted, and all she wanted to do was crawl into bed. When she saw Jack hesitate at the back door, giving her a pointed look, she realized that she could either follow him, or he would probably come back to demonstrate his Yeti-shouldering technique. Reluctantly, though every part of her body was begging to go to the *bed*, Blaze followed him.

The wereverine led her to the south-facing front porch and had her stretch out in one of the Adirondack chairs arrayed there. And, sure enough, the sun helped. Blaze felt herself pep back up in only fifteen minutes, when she was pretty sure she would have slept the rest of the day away, left to her own devices. "How did you *know* that?" Blaze asked, stunned, having rolled up her pant legs and shirtsleeves at the wereverine's suggestion.

Oddly, the wereverine, who had been casually leaning against the porch railing, watching her, blushed purple and began to fidget. "I, uh…" He cleared his throat loudly and grimaced. "Lucky guess." He gestured at the shop. "So you done screwing around over there? I still got work to do."

They spent the rest of the day working on the shop roof, trying to repair the damage that the werewolves had left behind. Blaze was standing up on a ladder poked through a hole they'd cut in the drywall, holding a board in place for Jack, when a thought occurred to her. She could *fly*? She remembered the excitement of being like plastered to the window of that Cessna 206, watching the ground pass underneath her, and she got another thrill, like that was what she was *meant* to do. To *fly*…

"You know," she said, "If I ever work up the balls to stab myself in the heart, there's really nothing keeping me tied to one spot, right?"

She saw Jack flinch before he quickly hid his reaction by pounding in a nail.

"I mean, seems like that would be a better way of not getting found…" Blaze continued. "Fly all over the place, don't spend too much time in one spot. I mean, hell, you can see the green from that *feather* from the air. If a whole *river* started to grow like that...Kind of paints a flashing neon target on my back, wouldn't you say?"

Jack held the hammer over the nail head for a long moment, staring at it, before he turned to her slowly. "I think," he said softly, "Part of what's wrong with the world nowadays is that critters like you feel compelled to do what you just described to me. They take off and stay on the run, never staying too long in one spot, taking their magic with them. Where's that leave us? In a damn, desolate, hungry time. That's where." He met her eyes evenly. "I swear to you. If you stay here, I will do everything I can to protect you. I'll put my life down, in a heartbeat, to protect you."

"Why?" Blaze whispered, trying not to let her heart flutter at the fierce way he was giving her that look. "You don't even know me."

His eyes flickered across her face. After a moment's hesitation, he said, "I think it's time we started reversing the process, you know what I mean?"

"Reversing it...how?"

Jack turned back to the nail. "Lay our claim. Make a stand." He shook his head and lowered his voice until it was almost a whisper. "Somethin." He pounded the nail the rest of the way in and moved to the end she was holding.

Blaze watched him work for several minutes in silence, contemplating that. "I'll stay," she said finally. Then she gave a nervous laugh. "I mean, hell, aside from you, I don't really *know* anybody. I don't have any family. People avoided me in college, so I just kept to myself. And boyfriends..." She made a pathetic sound. "Right. Boyfriends." Nervously biting her lip as she watched him, she said, "So yeah. Uh. Seeing how we're both single and all...What do you think about that?"

Jack hesitated. When he looked up, she saw a spark of dumbstruck awe in his eyes, but it was quickly hidden when the wereverine returned his attention to the truss he was working on. A gruff, "Sounds good," rumbled from where he was peering much too closely at the nail he wasn't hammering. "I mean, you ain't got a problem with it, I ain't got a problem with it." He hesitated a moment and she saw him swallow, hard, then looked up at her, nervousness in his eyes. Then, almost timidly, he said, "Just to be clear...Are you talking about what I think you're talking about?"

Blaze felt a flush under his stare and started picking old paint spatters off of her ladder. "Well, yeah, I think so."

Jack went pale and got that constipated look again. "I, uh..." He cleared his throat, opened his mouth like he wanted to say something, but when he tried, only a rough airy sound came out. Swallowing, his brow knotting, Jack glanced down at the hammer in his hand. "I gotta find a file and sharpen the claws on my hammer." He started to climb down his ladder.

Blaze leaned over to peer at his hammer. "Those need *sharpening?*"

The wereverine's face went crimson and he swallowed again, without looking at his hammer. "Uh, yeah. Standard procedure, tootz. Can't talk now. Might forget." He jumped the rest of the way off the ladder and *ran* from the shop, pulling the door shut behind him so haphazardly that it cracked open again, revealing a band of brightness outside. Still clinging to her ladder, Blaze could see several files sitting out on a workbench, where he had recently used them on an axe.

TWENTY-EIGHT

Jack the A-S-S-H-O-L-E

"*I've gotta sharpen the claws on my* hammer?" Of all the retarded things he could've said…Groaning, Jack paced back and forth out behind the back woodpile, once again cursing his own thick tongue. He'd *wanted* to warn her, to tell her that he'd been taught how to life-bond with a dragon and how, once he'd tasted *that* ambrosia, he could never go back, and how he'd done it with every serious girl since. He wanted to tell her how, either by an act of the gods or some crazy phoenix thing, she was as receptive to it as anyone he'd ever met, hell, *more* than receptive to it, like *pulling* him to do it, *demanding* it, like a lightning rod jutting up into the swirling mass of a thunderstorm, and how he'd almost already *accidently* done it, with Blaze, while she *slept*, because he had gotten too *close* to her.

He'd almost claimed her for his mate. While she was unconscious.

And she wanted him as a 'boyfriend.' Which meant, in city-slicker terms, she wanted him in her *bed*. As a fun little disposable werever-ine sex-toy. She didn't *understand*. He couldn't *do* that. It just wasn't *in* him to do that. Hell, just *kissing* her had almost settled the bond, both times. He'd been fighting every impulse to drag her into another kiss ever since he almost lost control the last time.

Somehow, he didn't see it going over too well if she woke up one morning, feeling his body beside her—and feeling with a deep and inner knowing exactly how uncomfortable his boner had gotten over the night of listening to her breathe beside him. Or the fact that Jack was really having trouble with the whole asshole thing, and some of those tactless, dumbass things he'd managed to keep himself from saying were going to roll down that connection and pop into her head anyway and she was gonna realize just how incredibly crass and cluster-fucked he really was. Or, gee, the fact that all Jack could think about lately was *her*, and she probably didn't want to catch little snippets of him fantasizing about her in the shower.

By Puck's Tongue, he was so *screwed.* Hell, just the *smell* of her had slowly begun to drive him insane. Like sunfire and desert stones, making him unable to think about anything except *exactly* where her body was placed, in relation to his own. Just up there in the trusses with her, pounding nails, smelling that hot, heat-baked sunlight, it had been everything he could do not to turn around, grab her, put his forehead to her own, and cement the mating bond right then, covered in sweat and insulation.

*Odin's Eye, boy, you've got it bad…*Swallowing hard, Jack continued pacing behind the woodpile, the hammer clenched in a fist.

He couldn't just *take* her, regardless of how startlingly *easy* it would be. So easy, in fact, that Jack was starting to worry that even *working* with her was going to set it off, much less her nightly massage. Somehow, he had to *explain* to her that she needed to pull her fucking lightning-rod out of the clouds before she got zapped. But *how*? He didn't understand magic, not really. Oethynna had tried to teach him, but only the stuff about the bond had really stuck. And *Blaze* didn't have a freakin' clue. A phoenix wasn't a magus. They were like a magnifying glass pointed at the sun. They didn't work *magic*. He started talking about bonds and lightning rods and she was gonna look at him like a hairy little ape babbling fairytale bullshit.

"Damn," Jack muttered, pacing again.

This was not going to go well. It was gonna be a stain. No matter which way he went, whether he told her she needed to back off for her own safety, or whether he just went the fuck ahead and sealed that permanent bond—either way, she was about to become a very pissed little bird.

Thus, when Blaze came around back and leaned against the woodpile to watch him, Jack froze. Even at that distance, he could feel the tugging at his core, her little lightning-rod aimed at his thunderstorm. *Fuck, fuck!* he thought, shying away. As soon as he did, her face took on a dark look.

"Looking for this?" Blaze growled, holding up a file.

Jack blinked at the file, still thinking of heat-baked sunlight and thunderstorms. "Why the fuck would I want a file?"

Blaze stared at him for a long moment, then tossed the thing down at his feet and turned on heel. Over her shoulder, she snapped, "I'm taking a shower. The insulation is making me itch."

Jack stared at the file, confused. Why the Hell had she given him a—

Then he realized he was still gripping the hammer in his other fist, and he flinched.

Yep, Wonderboy Jack Thornton had done it again. Groaning, he reached down and plucked the file from the grass. He looked down at it, then at his hammer, and considered slinking off to spend a half an hour sharpening the claws to razor-points, just so she didn't think he was out back here pacing because of *her*.

Then he heard her enter the basement of the Sleeping Lady and his mind went into sudden neutral, thinking about the fact that she was about to expose that pale, smooth skin, and that *he* had just missed his chance to *be* there for it.

Pissed-off bird be damned. He could deal with pissed off. He couldn't deal with not being able to touch her anymore. Not when she gave him such delicious goosebumps every time he started her nightly massage…

Hearing her start the shower, Jack broke into a jog. He dropped the hammer and file off on the edge of the woodpile and hit the basement at a run. Praying she took a good *long* shower, he started moving his stuff into her room. There. Let her argue with *that*. He was dropping off the last duffel bag of clothes when she came out of the bathroom, towel wrapped around her slender body, steaming like a volcanic goddess, and saw him leaving her room.

Instantly, her face darkened, and she lowered her brush from her fiery hair in irritation. "What are you doing?"

Immediately, Jack tried to think of something eloquent to say, some twist of words that a djinni would spin to make everything better.

In combining our living-space, we engage on an exciting new journey—

"I'm putting my stuff in your room." Even as he said it, Jack winced at how defensive it had sounded. He tried to smooth that over with, "The whole you need a boyfriend thing."

Blaze stared at him so long that Jack swallowed and started to fidget. She started to swipe at her hair again, eyes still leveled on him, absolutely no indication of her thoughts on her face. Then again, judging by the way she'd narrowed her eyes, Jack was pretty sure that there was *some* indication of her thoughts, but it wasn't an indication that he wanted.

He cleared his throat uncomfortably. "So, uh, that *is* what you were talking about, right? Needing a boyfriend?"

Blaze continued to yank the brush through her hair, and Jack was pretty sure he heard snarls snapping.

"Uh," Jack said, at her silence, "you want me to work that rat's-nest out for you? Before, you know, you make yourself go bald?"

"You're in my way."

Seeing that his wide shoulders were taking up most of the entryway, Jack stepped back, letting her enter the room with him.

As soon as she stepped past him, she turned, facing towards him and the open door as she kept ripping her brush through her hair. "You're in my room."

Jack scowled, at that. "Hey, babe. I just told you. It's *our* room, now, tootz. You said you need the company."

She continued to brush her hair as she glared down at him. "You need a shower."

Jack jerked. He did? He sniffed under his underarms, then winced. "Oh. All right. Well, uh, maybe next time we can shower together. Being how you need a man and—"

"*Get out while I dress*!" Blaze snapped.

Thinking he saw gold flash behind her eyes, Jack did.

• • •

That night, Blaze went and got more pages from her journal and waited outside the blanketed-off 'bathroom' as Jack took a shower. She accosted him as soon as he flipped the blanket back, making him give the papers in her hand a wary look.

"Come on," Blaze said. "Your room or mine?"

"It's the same room," Jack said, hackles lifting. He had, quite stubbornly, insisted that he move in with her, 'because she needed a man.' Blaze, on the other hand, *refused* to let him lead her on any more than he already had, and, while she could deal with a lack of sex, she certainly couldn't deal with a lack of sex *and* having his hunky body stretched out on the floor a few feet away from her, where he'd piled a neat little sleeping-roll and a few layers of blankets, 'in case she peed the bed again'. No, she was pretty sure she would try to molest him in his sleep, and she wasn't interested in finding out what a startled wereverine did when he was shocked out of a dead sleep by a full-blown sexual assault.

"Your room, then," Blaze said. She had spent the time he'd been showering re-locating all of his carefully re-located belongings, moving them from the piles he'd placed around her chosen room and into a fairly un-damaged room across the hall.

Still wrapped in a towel, Jack stepped past her, towards *her* room, steam rolling off of his bronze, muscular torso. Seeing the current placement of his stuff, Jack paused in the doorway and growled, "You an' I need to have a chat about who's in charge, here, tootz."

His words came as such a surprise that Blaze actually laughed. "Who's in *charge* here?" she demanded. "Maybe I'm missing something, but this is *my* lodge."

"Yeah, well, your lodge on *my* land."

"Oh?" Blaze demanded. "Well, I have a deed to *your* land in *my* safe-deposit box."

"Couldn't prove it by me," Jack said, showing teeth.

Blaze narrowed her eyes. "We have a business arrangement. You made that *perfectly* clear earlier today, when you told me the reason you are keeping me around. In the spirit of keeping things professional, *these* are now your quarters, while *I* will be sleeping across the hall."

Jack frowned at her. "What do you mean, 'the reason I'm keeping you around'?"

"The Garden of Eden thing," Blaze said, waving a dismissive hand in the general direction of the greenhouse. "I get it now. It's all business. Phoenix magic means more game means happier wereverine. I finally cued in on that."

Jack's green eyes looked slightly confused. "Girl, as far as I remember, you were thoroughly enjoying your kiss this morning."

Blaze flushed. "And then you ended it with, 'Yep, Blaze, you peed the bed. Toodles!'" She waved a frustrated hand in the direction of the bed they had vacated. "Like I wasn't *panting*…hell, I woulda gotten naked right there on the *floor* if you'd—"

Throughout her tirade, Jack's grin widened, until he simply reached up and cut off the rest of her monologue with another heart-pounding, toe-curling, loin-searing kiss that she couldn't have pulled away from if she'd tried. When he released her to stumble away from his shower-warmed body, Blaze was dizzy. "But…" she stammered, patting her hair down, "Why…?"

Jack shrugged. "You gave me a date. I intend to stick to it."

It took Blaze several moments to make the connection in her mind, and when she did, her mouth fell open. "Two weeks," she said. "You're waiting two weeks."

"Uh-huh." He gestured at the papers in her hand. "Kitchen, right? What are you doing with those?"

"Bullshit!" Blaze threw the papers aside and grabbed him, and dragged him over to the bed. She was actually rather lucky he decided to cooperate, because she was pretty sure she could have had better luck tugging her bulldozer across the front yard as moving the wereverine if he hadn't wanted to be moved.

"What's all this, now?" the wereverine asked, as she flopped him to the bed, the towel sliding up one shower-flushed, muscular leg.

"You," Blaze said, breathlessly jabbing a finger at him as she stood over him, "are *not* waiting two weeks."

"It's only ten days, now," Jack said, giving her a mischievous grin. He leaned casually back on the bed, looking up at her with a thoughtful expression. "Besides. Thought you wanted me to do the taking, not the other way around, missy."

Blaze's mouth fell open to retort, then she realized she was standing there, *telling* him to seduce her, acting every part the Amazon that she absolutely was not.

Jack's grin only widened. "Way I see things, I got you all alone out here with me in the woods during Breakup, when nobody can get out here without use of a helicopter, and I'm gonna have my way with you for a day, when you're least expecting it. Might be in ten days, might be longer. Who knows?" He took his spare towel and started rubbing the water out of his black curls. From under the cloth, he said, "But *I'm* gonna be the one doing the taking. You made that pretty clear that's what you wanted."

"I was *delirious*!" Blaze cried. "I'd been packing your crippled ass through the *woods* and I *wasn't thinking straight.*"

Jack shrugged. "Deal's a deal." He gestured at the papers she had deposited on the floor. "Speaking of deals. I already made some calls, got the ball rolling to get this place fixed up. You wanna tell me what the paper's all about?"

Blaze felt herself caught between wanting to scream and wanting to molest him anyway. She could see the latter ending unpleasantly, however, especially when he did something like, oh, embed her in the ceiling.

Numbly, Blaze went and collected the paper, willing the tiny fiery explosions in her chest to subside enough to concentrate. "I, uh, am gonna teach you to write your name."

Jack's smile was so bright and genuine that it caught her off-guard. Nodding, he said, "You said it starts with A."

Blaze's mouth fell open again as she tried to think of something to say to that. Now *what do you tell him, tootz?* "Uh. No I didn't."

Jack's smile faded. "Yes you did."

"I said J-aaaay," Blaze said. "Totally different."

Jack continued to scowl at her. "You said A. That one that looks like a triangle. I memorized it."

"Jay," Blaze said. "*Then* 'A'."

Jack sniffed the air between them, then gave her a suspicious look. "You're hiding something."

"No I'm not."

"Woman," Jack growled, "I got a memory like a steel trap. You said A."

"Well, maybe I did, back *then*," Blaze said. "But today I'm feeling generous."

His suspicion increased severalfold. "How generous do you have to be to teach me my name?"

Blaze shrugged. "I dunno. Generous. Hell, someone without any morals, well, shit, they could teach you to spell your name as 'asshole' and you'd never know the difference. So just bear with me, okay?"

He gave her a somewhat crestfallen look. "So it doesn't start with A?" Then he frowned, raising an eyebrow. "Or are you trying to get back at me for not sexing you thoroughly just now?"

"Fine!" Blaze said, "Fine. You know what? Never mind. Learn your own goddamn self. I'll just go take my feather and start up a home-remedies business in the Everglades."

Jack reached out and snagged her arm as she was turning, and the grip that held her might as well have been wrought iron. In a low growl, he said, "What I want to know, missy, is why you tell me 'A' one day, then 'J' the next. That's what I don't quite understand." He got slowly to his feet, the towel falling from his waist as he held her in place, that deadly glow to his green eyes.

Blaze looked down at her wrist, which was now thoroughly locked in the wereverine's grasp, and had the sudden, vivid image of her arm sailing across the room, sans body.

"Uh..." Blaze said, her face heating.

Jack was looking up at her much too acutely. "What *does* 'asshole' start with, anyway, Blaze?"

"Uh..." Blaze squeaked.

"Best not to lie to a moon-kissed, honey," Jack said, as he grew fangs and slitty eyes. "Things can go...wrong."

"'A'," Blaze whimpered, squeezing her eyes shut. "Please don't sputch me."

Absolute silence reigned for the next minute and a half, until Blaze finally worked up the courage to once more look down at the monster holding her arm.

Jack was looking up at her, the look in his eyes utterly dangerous. "You know what?" he growled, as his perfect, muscular body remained exposed fearlessly before her, "I think I might make that earlier, rather than later."

"My...sputching?" Blaze babbled, trying to back away, but failing due to wereverine attachment. "Uh, I'm really, really sorry. I was just being a twit. I apologize. Really. I wasn't gonna let you think you were an asshole forever." Then she winced. "Well, I mean, you are an asshole, but I wasn't gonna let you—" At the fur that sprouted suddenly from Jack's naked body and the demonic growl that began to rattle in his chest, she cried, "I wasn't gonna do it, I swear!"

"Oh really," the wereverine snarled, saliva dripping from three-inch ivory fangs as he leaned up towards her throat. "You were just gonna, what, let me sign it on my checks a few times?"

"No," Blaze babbled, her heart sending blasts of molten fire through her veins. She tried to back away from him, but he easily tugged her back. "No, I was just—"

"Just what?" Jack growled. He was moving around her, cornering her in the room. "Just going to let me *humiliate* myself a few times? After I *trusted* you to help me?"

"Oh God," Blaze panted. "Uh. I am *so* sorry. I'll never do it again, I swear."

"You got *that* right," Jack snarled. It sounded way too…final.

Thus, when he reached up for her throat, Blaze screamed and tried ineffectually to jerk her hand free. "I'm *sorry*! Really *sorry*! Oh God, *don't eat me*!"

There was a sudden ripping sound and Blaze jerked her head down to her suddenly-exposed chest. The wereverine tossed her shirt and bra aside, which he'd torn away by a downward swipe from the collar.

Ridiculously, she thought, *He's plucking me like a turkey, exposing all that pretty breast meat…*

When the wereverine threw her onto the bed, however, she screamed. *Really* screamed, this time, because he crawled on top of her, all tooth and fur, and pinned her there so thoroughly with his heavy body that she was utterly immobilized. After a few futile struggles—because really, how did a girl, even a gigantic ape of a girl, fight a four hundred and fifty pound beast besides clawing at his slitty eyes and getting a hand gnawed off—Blaze closed her eyes, her heart hammering a thousand crazy beats a minute in her chest, and waited for him to rip out her throat.

A low, throaty chuckle near her jugular made her flinch. "Do you surrender, little bird?" the wereverine rumbled, his warm breath grazing her ear.

Surrender? Her panicked brain did a double-take and Blaze's eyes snapped open.

The wereverine was sprawled out lazily on top of her, not a sign of fur or fang anywhere, grinning demonically, his green eyes twinkling. Naked.

Her mouth fell open in indignation. "You *scared* me, you prick!" she cried, throwing him off and standing up.

…or not.

What actually happened was that she grunted and strained as she pushed on his meaty shoulder, which remained thoroughly in place, pinning her quite effectively to the bed.

"So," Jack said, propping himself up on his elbows on either side of her head, leaving his naked abdomen holding her immobile, "Should I take you now or later?" The considering way he said it, and the thoughtful expression he had on his face as he did so, made it very clear to Blaze that he thought he had full right to do just that. Then, his demonic grin widening, he said, "Or maybe both?"

Mouth falling open, Blaze stammered, "Get off of me!" She tried to wiggle out from underneath him, but she might as well have been pinned by the hull of an aircraft carrier.

"Hmm," Jack said, lowering a hand to trace it across her face. "You've been a real pain in the ass, Miss Blaze. Mixed signals and all that." He stroked a callused finger down her throat, then between her breasts, leaving tingly traces of ecstasy in its path.

Blaze grabbed his wrist before his finger could find something important. "Mixed *signals*?" she growled. "You are the *king* of mixed—"

Jack grabbed one of the wrists she was using to keep him at bay, pulled it effortlessly over her head, and held it there while he retrieved the other.

Blaze felt her heart give a startled thump as she twisted her head to look up at her pinned wrists. "Uh, what are you..."

The wereverine casually left her arms tightly imprisoned with one hand and resumed tracing his other hand down her naked body.

Shuddering, arms pinned above her, Blaze sank into the bed underneath him, melting under the touch, unable to escape it, her breath coming in tiny pants. "Uh," she managed, suddenly realizing how utterly helpless she was, "what are you doing?"

"Workin' on makin' some better signals," Jack said distractedly. He shifted slightly over her, and she felt his attention move to an areola.

Oh shit, Blaze thought. He was *serious.* That made her all sorts of...well...horny. And a little anxious. She'd never *been* on the bottom before. *Well, tootz, you so totally asked for this,* she thought, between panic and elation. *You got a hunk pinning you to the bed, about to molest the hell outta you.* Now *what are you gonna do?*

Then Jack lowered his mouth to her nipple and her spine arced of its own accord. She saw his eyes flicker to her face and felt him grin around her tender flesh as he suckled. *Oh my God...*Blaze thought, her mind going into neutral as she felt his hard, unyielding body shift above her. Unable to control herself, Blaze strained against the hand that held her arms to the bed, but Jack kept her firmly in place, his greater strength easily pinning her down as he played with her.

"Like that, do you?" Jack chuckled, releasing her breast just enough to breathe on it, sending a whole new wave of pleasure through her body. Blaze moaned and squirmed, suddenly all-too-aware of how many parts of her body were on fire, and where, and how she couldn't move to relieve it.

"God," Blaze groaned, as he turned his attention to her other breast, obviously taking pleasure in her contortions. "Let go of my hands," she blurted. "I can't..." Couldn't *what*? Couldn't roll on top? Couldn't mash his face into her breast? What?

Jack's grin widened from where his mouth hovered over a breast. "I think you're stayin' put, tootz." His hot breath touched her skin again and Blaze gasped, unable to pull away.

Then his words brought Blaze's mind to a wrenching halt. Staying... *put*? She'd never actually considered how a guy would take charge in bed. And, as her eyes widened with understanding, Jack's emerald eyes started to dance as he simply continued to hold her in an unrelenting iron grip. "That's right, sugar," he growled, obviously reading her thoughts. "You're getting taken."

Blaze felt a jolt of heat rise through her being, realizing he wasn't going to let her go, and she couldn't pull her arms away if she tried. *Oh my God,* she whimpered inwardly as he moved over her, kissing down her chest, her nipples perking up in aching little nubs, unattended, *He can't be serious.*

But it became quite evident that he *was*. She started to pant as Jack just grinned at her, then *blew* on her nipples, obviously enjoying her frustration, she lifted her head from the bed and slammed it back in despair, crying, "My *hands*, Jack."

Instead of obediently releasing her, the wereverine made an irritated grumble and shifted over her, still pinning her arms above her, his groin holding hers firmly in place on the mattress, giving her no movement in any direction. "You havin' fun?" he demanded.

Blaze's face reddened, feeling her sensitive areas stretched, exposed for him. To be honest, it was *thrilling* her to feel him hold her in place and have his way with her, but that little mental babble in the back of her head was sifting through all her previous sexual experience and telling her she needed to take control of the situation. "Ummm..."

"'Um,' huh?" Jack sighed and lowered his lips to her earlobe. "Okay, tootz. I guess we could do something else." Taking her ear gently in his mouth, he nibbled it. Then, releasing her arms, he pushed himself up on his elbows and grinned down at her. "Something...*completely*... different."

Blaze's mouth fell open in horror, realizing he was talking about, oh, say, overhauling an engine. Still pinned underneath his leaden body, Blaze grabbed him by the hair and tugged down, yanking his head to her face with a startled wereverine grunt. "Listen, you demented *turd*," she panted, nose-to-nose. "This is the *last straw*. Do *not* start something you don't intend to finish, or I will *end* you."

Jack peered down his nose at her a long minute in silence, a little grin twitching on his face. Then, softly, his breath against her lips, he said, "I wanna see your eyes."

Blaze's stomach gave an instinctive pang of fear. "You've seen my eyes."

"You know I haven't."

Blaze's heart began to hammer, looking up at him. Without her contacts, she felt naked. Exposed. *Ugly*. Like a freak. She bit her lip as Jack watched her. She never went anywhere without her contacts. Not even her parents had seen the real color of her eyes in fifteen years. Hell, *she* didn't even see them, after she'd learned how to put them in without a mirror. She *hated* her eyes.

And this wereverine wanted to *see* them. Was *insisting*. "Please," she whispered, "You don't want that." She was shrinking into the bed, wishing she could slip under the covers and hide her face from his scrutiny. She *knew* Jack was going to cringe away from her the moment she showed him what she *really* looked like, once he saw the red-orange streaks, once he began wondering if she were bleeding in the iris, or in the *brain*.

"Show me," Jack whispered. He kissed her gently on the tip of her nose, then waited, looking down at her.

Blaze bit her lip and looked askance.

Jack gave her a long look, waiting, then, when it was clear she wasn't going to show him, he sighed and pulled back. He started to roll off of her. "Guess you might as well show me to write my name, then."

"Wait," Blaze whimpered. When he hesitated, still half-suspended above her, Blaze took a deep breath and lifted a trembling finger to her eye. She touched the film of plastic, pulled it aside.

Above her, Jack's breath caught.

"I need to get the case from my pocket," she said, bitterly, reaching under him to get at her thigh. Refusing to look at Jack, she twisted the caps off and dropped the lens inside. Above her, she felt Jack's entire muscular body remain tense, his breathing shallow. Committed, now, she took the other from her eye, then dropped them disgustedly onto the tiny cups of liquid, two little round blue rings taunting her from inside the contact case.

Above her, Jack just stared.

"You happy now?" Blaze demanded, blinking hard against the sensitive surface of her long-protected lens.

Jack said nothing, just gingerly reached out and tried to take the contact case from her fist—Blaze's hand spasmed, at first, not wanting to let go—and then, once he gently pried it from her fingers, lowered it to the floor beside the bed, eyes still on her face. "Miss Blaze," he whispered softly, "I don't know what's the matter with you—"

Oh, that was *it*. She started to sit up in disgust.

Jack gently pushed her shoulder back down. "—but that's the most beautiful thing I ever saw."

Even as her mouth fell open, he grabbed her wrists again and firmly replaced them over her head, giving himself an unobstructed view of her face. He stayed there for long, heart-pounding minutes, her soul bared for his perusal.

He actually likes them, Blaze thought, stunned beyond all words as he held her arms back, giving her no way to avoid him.

Slowly, still meeting her gaze, Jack lowered his lips and kissed her between the eyes. Then he started making a satisfied, predatory growl as he sank lower, returning his mouth to her ear and neck, sucking, nipping…*Nipping?*

She heard the wereverine inhale against her sensitive throat, heard him groan. Was he…trembling? Pressed into the flesh of her abdomen, she could feel his manhood harden through her pants. Then he was nibbling the sensitive skin along her jaw, kissing her chin, then moving down the other side.

Oh no. Blaze could *not* handle this. She moaned and tried to twist her hands free, even as heat was rushing up her core from the wereverine's breath against her throat. He lowered himself slowly, until his warm chest was once more pressing against her breasts, pinning her completely beneath him. He started kissing her collarbones, then moved up the sensitive hollow in her throat.

"Why won't you let me touch you?" Blaze whimpered.

"Pretty sure you said you wanted 'to be thoroughly taken with some hot wereverine sex,'" Jack rumbled, his naked chest vibrating against her breasts. "Like I said. I'm fulfilling your request. Now shaddup while I do this right." He moved up to her ear, nibbling on her other lobe. Blaze moaned and tried to return in kind, but he held her perfectly pinned, one hand on her wrists while the other explored downward, giving her no leverage to squirm. Above her, his sunkissed body rippled as he moved, kissing, nipping, his big hand seeking the most sensitive ridges and clefts of her body while she lay helpless beneath him.

"Not…" she gasped, straining against his grip, "…fair."

"Sweetie," Jack chuckled against her throat, "who said anything about being fair?" It was then that she felt soft fur against her jaw, felt the gentle nip of sharp teeth against her skin. *Oh shit*, she thought, as that little prey instinct kicked into full gear feeling his warm teeth against her neck. *Oh shit, oh shit.* She renewed her struggles again, panic surging through her chest. Jack, for his part, did not relent. His voice had that deep, rumbling growl against her throat when he said, "'Fair' is for wolves and other pussies." He nipped her again, right under the jaw, making it perfectly clear in her mind just how totally she was at his mercy.

Oh my God, Blaze shivered, that hot feeling of surrender melting at her core as she realized that Jack was going to have his way with her. He was giving her no way to pull her neck out of his reach…and she *loved* it. It made a little thrill rush back down through her center, and she felt that hot fire racing through her chest as she panted breathlessly beneath him. He continued to nip her down her throat, a low rumble in his chest, those deep intakes of breath against her collarbone, followed by his shudder.

"Zeus and Apollo, woman, you smell good." When she looked, Jack was grinning at her, wearing a soft covering of fur and sprouting a bit of fang, but his eyes were still human…and filled with mischief.

Still holding her arms in place, he kissed his way back down between her breasts, then caught a now-rock-hard nipple in his mouth and started sucking on it. Then she felt the tiny nip of teeth, electrifying the flesh, drawing heat from her loins in an arc. Breathless, Blaze tried to reach down, tried to make him speed up, tried to do *anything*, but he simply held her and continued at a slow, leisurely pace, grinning at her contortions beneath him, obviously enjoying her torment. He was so *strong*, so utterly masculine above her…

"Oh *God*," Blaze cried, straining, unable to take any more. "I can't *move*!"

"That's the point of being taken," Jack said. "Unless I missed something?" He lifted his head and gave her another raised eyebrow.

"*Please*, Jack!" Blaze moaned, so frustrated and in *need* that she had goosebumps. She tried to thrash, to touch her nipples to his chest to ease the tension, there, but he easily stayed out of reach. "Oh please, God."

To her horror, Jack slid sideways off of her, still holding her, using his heavy leg to neatly pin hers to the bed. She felt a prickle against her breast, then realized he had a talon out and was gently tracing patterns on her body with his finger. The same talon that could rip sheet-metal to pieces was now sliding easily along the top of her skin, kissing it just lightly enough to make a gentle scratch.

"Ohhh," Blaze managed, quivering, unable to flinch away. "Ohhh, um..."

"Tell me something, Miss Blaze." Jack lazily traced his free hand down her naked belly, doing slow circles with his talon to the top of her pants. Her skin went pink underneath his touch, then white, leaving ultra-sensitized flesh behind. He casually leaned down, caught her closest nipple between his teeth, and slid his tongue along its surface, sucking the heat up from her loins, until it was a fiery wash through her chest and back. His other hand found the button of her jeans and started removing them.

"Tell you what?" Blaze whimpered, her hips giving tiny thrusts of their own accord.

Jack's mouth released her breast. Still dusted with a light covering of fur, his voice still carrying the deep rumble of the wolverine, he said, "Just how much experience *do* you have, here?"

"I'm not a virgin," Blaze babbled, and even to her lips, it sounded like a plea. She was covered in goosebumps, and was quite literally shaking with the need to relieve the pressure in her loins. "*Please*, Jack."

The thick muscles in Jack's big shoulders seemed to lose a lot of their tension. "Good. Just, uh..." He lazily started tracing more designs against the ultra-sensitive flesh of her abdomen, making her whimper. He seemed to be fascinated with the lines of her belly as she strained. "I've been...holding out...awhile now. Things might get a little rough, and I don't want anybody to get hurt."

"The only one who's gonna get hurt is the *wereverine* who's about to get his *head ripped off* if he doesn't *finish the job*!" Blaze cried, trembling, panting under his touch. She'd never been so horribly out of control of her body in her life.

Jack chuckled, his green eyes playful. "Girlie, I think you got some misconceptions about who's in control, here." He started tracing again, reaching upwards towards a breast, *away* from the pounding heat in her groin. "'Sides. There's some things I wanna discuss with you."

"Oh *God*," she whimpered, straining under him, unable to avoid the delicious sensations as he lazily traced her curves.

"I've got a problem, Blaze." He took his time to reach her nipple, tracing slow patterns across her belly and chest, leaving liquid fire in its wake.

"What kind of problem?" she whimpered.

"The mating kind." When his touch reached the hard, aching, rigid peak, he flicked it gently with a talon, and Blaze shuddered from head to toe.

"Condom...Age..." she panted.

He chuckled again and started tracing the soft fur of the back of his hand across her abdomen, stroking exquisite softness across the ultra-sensitive skin. "Okay. Say that's true. I'm not really worried about that part of it. What worries me is what you're gonna do *afterwards*, if I stake that claim."

Whereas in most cases, Blaze would have been irritated at the wereverine's old-time views on women and sex, now all she really wanted was for him to do just that. "Take me," she managed. "Please, Jack. However you need to. I'll be fine with it after. I *swear*."

Jack jerked and she saw a tiny frown before his face cleared. "You don't really know what I'm asking." He said it with a sigh.

She was shuddering with Jack's every languid motion, now, the heat in her groin building to a painful *need* that left her body a single massive ache for completion.

"Please, dear God, Jack, please." Twisting her arms desperately underneath his grip, she turned her head to face him, biting her lip. "If you're not gonna do it for me, at least have the *mercy* to let me do it myself."

Grinning at her, his green eyes dancing, Jack started working her jeans down her hips, then the big pad of his finger—*not* his talon, thank

God—started tracing pathways through the orange curls between her thighs.

Moaning outright, now, Blaze arced her back, trying again to speed his descent, to make his touch harder, faster, *anything*. He took *centuries* to reach her sensitive center. Then he found the little nub at the base of her mound and she cried as he began to rub, ever-so-gently. Not hard enough, and not fast enough, however, to do anything but make that heat racing through her body build and build…

"I can't do this," Blaze whimpered, once it became unbearable. "I can't." Her mind was being thrown into neutral, and her body was becoming one arcing, straining mass of pleasure. "Please, Jack."

"Please what?" Jack rumbled in a chuckle. Toying with her. As if he didn't *know*.

Oh God. He was so strong, so *male*…His body hot beside hers, pinning her down, *playing* with her. Panting, Blaze managed, "Take me. Please."

Jack seemed to consider that a moment, then slowly pushed himself from the bed and shifted back over her. This time, she felt the hardness at her groin, felt the heat rolling off of him, and she whimpered, rolling under him to bring her body against his rigid chest and abdomen. He lowered himself over her, bringing his lips back to brush against her ear.

"Just stay there a second," Jack whispered, against her neck.

Her mind did a startled double-take when he suddenly released her arms and backed away…

…And then he yanked her jeans free of her legs and spread her thighs wide, a deep groan of appreciation in his chest as he lowered his face to her—*crotch?*

Blaze had just enough time to do a startled double-take before waves upon waves of spine-arcing pleasure began pounding through her, doubling her over, curling her toes until her feet cramped with each flutter of his tongue.

"Jaaaack!" Blaze cried, grabbing him by the scalp and reflexively pulling him tight against her. "Oh Jesus, Jack! What are you *doing*?!"

Jack lifted his head to look up at her curiously. "Never had anyone play with you before, little bird?" He sounded a bit startled. And amused. "What kind of two-bit pussies—"

Blaze was getting dizzy with need. She pushed him back to her womanhood, not really caring what he was about to say.

His green eyes met hers from betwixt her legs and he chuckled against her folds, which built into a massive, shattering explosion within her, sending her body into an arc of clenching, spasming heat. She felt herself bucking against his face, which only seemed to make him chuckle and try harder, alternating his tongue's rhythm, sometimes suckling, sometimes plundering, sometimes lapping. And, while the first orgasm was the best Blaze had ever had, the next one completely knocked it out of the ballpark. She devolved into mindlessness, riding each wave of pleasure as it came, so far gone she didn't even see Jack's smile when she bucked against his face.

And he *didn't stop*. Blaze, who in the recent past had never had more than one tiny orgasm before she had to wait for her body to reset, suddenly couldn't control the pounding waves of pleasure driving through her, again and again, jerking her body like a puppet on strings. Her mind switched off and she felt herself go completely over the edge, losing herself fully in the experience, so far gone that, somewhere along the way, she simply lost consciousness.

• • •

Jack watched Blaze's pale body finally stop quivering against the bed and, after several moments of suckling her clit with no response, he gently pulled his face from her warm center, now covered in the sweet scent of her musk. He'd brought her to orgasm so many times he'd lost count, and watching her lithe, beautiful body buck and roll underneath his attentions had almost brought him to release on his own. *Oh gods*, he thought, kissing the tip of her womanhood in parting as his eyes swept up her stomach, adoring the smooth lines of her passion-slickened body. Her glistening, flat stomach was still rising and falling with the fervor of her orgasms, her pert breasts still peaked with the swollen pink knots of her rock-hard nipples, tantalizing him, begging to be kissed, nibbled, licked…

Throughout her contortions, it had been everything he could do to keep from staking that claim. The whole time she'd been moaning and thrashing against him, he had been struggling with her lightning-rod to his storm, stoppering up that energy, forcing it back before he formed a link they would both regret. He was *still* struggling with it, seeing her stretched out delicate and inviting beneath him.

Even then, her long, exquisitely pale legs were spread wide to him in her sleep, exposing her hungry pink clit, swollen from under its protective hood. Beneath it, the lips of her womanhood were engorged, waiting…

Jack traced a finger down a perfectly pale thigh to the blazing orange fur of her center, biting his lip. She was so beautiful. Beyond beautiful. Like a Norse goddess come to steal his heart away. He tentatively looked up at her face, then, anxiousness once more tearing at his soul. She seemed so strong, and yet so innocent, as well. He was pretty sure she had no idea just how terrified she made him, each time she'd tried to bring them to this point. He wanted her, wanted her so badly it hurt, and yet he was afraid of what would happen to her if he did. He struggled with another overpowering urge to claim her, to make her his mate, to wrap his protective arms around her and hold her close as he took her for his own. He knew, beyond a doubt, that all the control he had managed to maintain throughout the night would disintegrate the moment he sank himself into her core. The link would form. She'd be *his*, and no amount of apologies would change that.

He was so afraid…What if he formed the link and she *rejected* him? He was a *demonkin* and she was a *phoenix*…Part of him knew she just didn't realize how big that difference was, and it terrified him that he was letting her in, opening his heart, making her his own, entrusting *everything* to her, and someday she was simply going to fly away. She could have any man she wanted. Why *him*? Why would she want a short, insecure, uneducated little wereverine? And, as she had made so perfectly clear as they'd fixed the trusses, she knew it. She could go *anywhere*.

Yet she obviously wanted him, so badly she'd spent over an hour moaning, thrashing, *begging* for him to take her. To *claim* her...The heat of that still rushed through him like blasts from a furnace, warming his heart, opening him further to her, and he almost lost control again right then. *Damn* it...

Her lightning rod to his storm. He bit his lip, eying her warily. He was already riding the very edge. He couldn't take her and continue to keep the mating link at bay. He just didn't have the control. Half of him wanted to run away screaming, and the other half wanted to cement the bond right then.

Blaze moaned and moved slightly in her sleep, making his breath catch at her exquisite, smooth lines. Her breasts stood up high on her chest, as dually assertive and as delicate as the rest of her.

He lowered a trembling hand to her tantalizing stomach, felt the pounding of her heart in the flat of her belly. She was so graceful, so elegant, so *fragile*...She obviously wanted to be pinned and taken, obviously wanted him to be strong and forceful, yet he was terrified he'd gone too far. He'd been walking a fine line, trying to give her the thrill she wanted, to let her feel his power at its best, to let her soak up that strength and know it was there to protect her, and yet terrified he was going to cross the line and have her eyes darken, see her shields go up, hear her tell him he needed to leave.

And through it all, he'd seen the *need* in her eyes and it had been all he could do not to give her everything she wanted right then—*all* of it.

Even now, his manhood was a throbbing ache against his stomach, so hard that it pressed tight against his abdomen of its own accord. Seeing her, spread beneath him, her exquisite body waiting, Jack felt the heat in his groin increase and he had to look away. It had taken every ounce of self-control he had not to give in to her demands, not to thrust himself home within her, savoring her enveloping heat, loving the arc of her back and her little pants of need as he took her slowly, savoring the ambrosia of the link.

Jack pulled away from her before that thought could trigger that lightning-strike. He couldn't do that. Not yet. Not until he was *sure.*

Slowly, he got up and levered himself to the side, careful not to wake her, lowering himself to the bed until he was leaning on an elbow, looking down at her smooth form from eye-level. Her light, flowing hair reminded him of flames, and those strands that had fallen from her braid in her feverish orgasms were now plastered to her sweat-soaked face.

Her eyes were closed—*such beautiful eyes,* he remembered, his heart skipping a beat. Like tongues of sunfire leaping outward from the pupil, twisting against a ruby backdrop. They'd stopped his heart, the first time he'd seen them. And, as she'd clung to him and thrashed, moaning in ecstasy, he was pretty sure he'd seen a flash of an inner inferno before it had been gone, hidden by the way they rolled into the back of her head and her legs tightened against his ears. He'd *almost* been afraid she was going to awaken right there, thighs clamped to his face, his tongue burrowing into her musky feminine center, his mouth blissfully suckling at her engorged lips.

Now, though, her head was tilted softly to the side, away from him, exposing the smooth lines of her graceful neck. Her breathing had slowed to a gentle rise and fall of her breasts. He could see her pulse still pounding her throat, however, her heartbeat still singing in his ears.

Jack leaned back, admiring the beauty sharing his bed. Of its own accord, his hand found her braid and tenderly pulled the band free, then, biting his lip and watching her gorgeous face for any sign of arousal, he tugged the fiery locks free with his fingers and laid them out along her glorious body.

Her hair spilled forth from his fingers like liquid fire, flowing over her breasts and stomach, tantalizing against the U-shaped ridge of her perfect, swim-model belly-button. Seeing that, Jack felt his breath catch again. He rearranged the glorious locks around a nipple, leaving the pink nub saluting through the waves of fire, then idly began stroking his fingers along her curves, tracing her lines, learning her.

Underneath his caress, Blaze gave a soft moan and one of her legs slid down, relaxing against the bed.

With a gentle touch so as not to wake her, Jack ran his fingers across her impossibly smooth skin, reveling in the softness of her shoulders, the utter femininity of her long, sexy body, the milky smoothness of her pale thighs. His hands found her fire-orange mound and hesitated there, circling, reveling in the texture and color of her mons. Against his better judgment, he let his hand dip downward, felt the thrill as he traced the tip of her slick womanhood, circling her hot clit. He started to slip his fingers into the waiting warmth beneath, to prepare her for his claim, then hesitated, eyes once more catching on her sleep-slackened face.

She's not yours yet, you old fool, Jack reminded himself, reluctantly pulling away.

"Why'd you stop?"

The soft whisper, coming from the other side of the bed, preceded Blaze's head turning, her flame-and-ruby eyes catching on his. Once again, Jack felt his heart stop, riveted by the beautiful streaks of fire in her eyes. "Uh..." He found himself unable to speak, caught between a horrible desire to climb over her and stake his claim, and the horrible, soul-piercing fear that she was just passing time, that she didn't *really* want him. Not like that...

But her eyes flickered down to his groin, and her face cleared, a little smile playing upon her full, arousal-moistened lips. "Oh." Her husky voice sounded...naughty.

Blindly, Jack tilted his head down to see what she was looking at.

His manhood, rock-solid and almost purple in its throbbing need, was greeting her like an old friend.

"Oh," Jack said, flushing, "Uh, yeah, sorry, I'll go find some pant—"

But she rolled onto her side, facing him, and her delicate fingers found his sensitive flesh, ending his words in a strangled sound as his breath left him from the electric tingles of her touch. He gave a tiny moan as her fist closed around the head of his member and tightened, pulling back the foreskin to show the glistening head underneath.

"You never finished?" she whispered, her breathtaking eyes once more finding his face, curiosity there.

"Miss Blaze," Jack said, trembling under the building heat in his loins, "I don't want you to take this the wrong way, but I mate for life."

But she wasn't listening. "Oh my God," she whispered, barely able to fit her feminine hand around the shaft itself, "does this even *fit*?"

Again, Jack found himself wondering what kind of ball-less pussies had mounted this beauty in the past, and felt another kindling of rage that he should have had to share her. Then his mind did a startled double take. *Share* her? She wasn't even *his* yet.

"I can't even close my hand around it," she giggled, trying.

"Well," he admitted, watching anxiously as her smooth fingers slid across his skin, "I *have* had problems in the past."

Then her slender hands were sliding down, cupping his balls, moving against his most tender parts. Jack, already oversensitive from watching her body thrash under his ministrations earlier, had to grab her wrists to stop the sensations before they drove him over the edge. "Listen, Miss Blaze," he panted, his whole being tingling with heat and passion. "I don't think you really understand. I—"

The rest of his words choked off when she leaned down and caught his nipple in her teeth and gave it a playful tug, sending shockwaves of pleasure through his system.

Growling, Jack rolled back over her, once more pinning her wrists above her head. "Listen here, missy," he rumbled down at her, "I was in the middle of telling you something important."

She looked up at him, her ruby-flame eyes dancing with mischief. She gave him a devilish grin as she began to wiggle underneath him, and it took him a moment to realize that she was positioning the throbbing head of his member to the wet heat of her womanhood.

With a groan, Jack quickly retreated and pinned its length between the two of them, confining her firmly to the bed. "*Listen* a moment," he said, breathless.

"You're no fun," she pouted, still smiling. She strained up against his grip, leaned up with her head, her pert chin reaching for his chest again.

Just for that, Jack lowered his lips to the taut pink nipple sticking up from between her locks of hair, and her chest arced under him with a gasp, her firm belly pressing into his abdomen as she moaned his name.

...his name?

Releasing her nipple, Jack lifted his head to stare down at her, caught between panic and elation. Panic, that she didn't understand what she was asking. Elation, that she seemed to crave his touch as much as he wanted to give it.

"Miss Blaze," Jack said softly, lowering his head to nip up her jaw-line. She moaned as he reached her earlobe and nibbled. Into her ear, he whispered, "Will you let me mate you?"

"Of course," she cried, tugging in vain at her wrists. "Hurry the hell up before something *explodes*."

Jack pulled back so he could see her eyes, his heart hammering like an anvil against his chest. "You're sure? It's...permanent. Can't take it back."

Wriggling ineffectually under him, she finally lifted her head and slammed it back to the bed in frustration, surrounding her face in a halo of fire. "*Yes*!"

"I don't want your decision to be one of passion," Jack growled. "Think on it. Whatever you decide tonight, goes."

It was then, trapped beneath him, still slick with passion, he saw the sharpening in her eyes, saw the understanding. "Mate...Like *wife*?"

He winced at the harsh way she said it. "Yes, like 'wife,'" he managed. But it was so much more, such a deeper connection than that... In a rush, he decided to lay it out for her logically, so that she could make an educated decision instead of a slap-dash one they would both later regret. "It's like this, Miss Blaze: You're a prize. I ain't arguin' that point. Any man in Alaska'd be happy to crawl up your chimney. And anyone who knew what you *were*? Hell, you'd have dragons knockin' down your doorstep to get you. But I got experience, I got blades, I can *protect* you, okay? You just say the word, and you will have a wereverine watching your back the rest of your damn life. You understand? I been lonely a long time. I ain't the best conversation, and I'm a bit of an asshole, but I get around you and my heart starts thumping out of my chest and I can't hear myself think. If you had ears like mine, you'd already *know* what you do to me. Those kind of feelings, I only had those four times in my life, and each one lasted a *long* time. You get me? A *really long* time. I just want to make sure you know what you're dealing with, before it goes too far and you can't take it back, you know?" He winced as he finished, knowing he'd babbled, but unable to form the words properly in his head.

"Somehow," she said softly, "I don't think you're talking about marriage."

Jack winced. "Uh, yeah, uh…" It was hard to ignore the hum of potential between them, the waiting for that thunderclap, that surge of energy that would change everything. Tentatively meeting her orange-on-ruby eyes, he managed, "It's…a connection…between lovers. A dragon forged the first path, when I was young, and I've been unable to lock that part of me down ever since. It's…uh…been wanting to connect with you ever since you stepped on my land. You're really…uh…ripe for it. Basically, I let that bond form and *boom*. You're mine. For good. I've had to avoid you to keep it from happening." Catching the sharpening in her gaze, he winced and dropped his head. "Sorry."

She gave him a long, considering look. "Is it safe?" she finally asked.

Jack, thinking she was going to demand what the hell he was thinking, a hairy little wereverine thinking he could claim a phoenix, was caught off guard. "*Safe*?" he sputtered. "It's *wonderful*…"

"Wonderful how?" She was still naked beneath him, still pinned to the bed, but she had all the poise and rapt attention as a realtor negotiating a land sale, and it made him nervous as all Hell.

Jack cleared his throat uncomfortably. "It, uh, opens us to each other. Stuff is shared that can't be shared otherwise. Feelings. Uh. Pleasure…"

She raised a single fiery eyebrow at him. "*Pleasure*?"

He bristled at the sarcasm in her voice. "The alternative, missy, is I pack up my stuff and leave. I hang around, I'm gonna end up doing it on accident, and it's *not* reversible. Get me? I make you mine, you're *mine*. There's no going back. I make that connection, you can tell me to fuck off 'til you're blue in the face, and I won't budge a goddamn inch 'cause it won't *let* me. I made my *claim*."

She gave him a long, hard look, and he saw the debate in her eyes. Finally, she said, "You like tall chicks?"

Jack blushed. "Might."

"You like *this* tall chick?"

Ducking his head, Jack muttered, "Already told ya I did. Long time ago."

"Okay," Blaze said.

Jack waited for her to finish her sentence.

Then, as Blaze just peered up at him, a slow smile working over her face, Jack squinted at her. Remembering the last time they'd had this conversation, he said, "Okay what?"

"Okay, take me," Blaze said. Her gaze was smoky, full of sexual heat. "Yes. Mate me, claim me, whatever you want to do with me. Do it."

Jack felt his heart start to hammer violently in his chest, the undeniable desire in her eyes making his raging hardon so painful that he had to ease the pressure between them. He couldn't believe it. He'd been ready to pack his things and head to some other part of Alaska, unable to withstand watching some other man take his place, and here she was *accepting* him…

All he could manage was, "Why?"

Blaze kissed his thick forearm where it passed near her face, holding her willowy wrists down, and her voice was silk as she said, "Not only are you the single sexiest *stud* I have ever met, but you saved my life and helped me build a farm. Not only that, but you even seem to dig tall chicks. Hell yes, I'd be honored."

Jack's heart was pounding at her words. He tried to think of something poetic to say in reply, something that could be remembered through the ages, but all he could come up with was, "Stud, huh? Guess this is your first run-in with a real man, there, sister?"

She narrowed her eyes and looked like she was going to retort, but he caught her full lips in a kiss and began working his way across her smooth, sinuous body with his free hand, roaming, teasing, tantalizing. Then, shifting his weight slightly to accommodate, his fingers found that luscious, velvety center, and she let out a long moan underneath his lips and ground her breasts against his chest, gasping, begging for him to release her, to let her finish before she exploded.

He didn't, of course. Jack, enthralled, kept her at the very edge, soaking in her porcelain body as it contorted under him, his own passion rising in a crescendo.

• • •

Just when Blaze thought she was completely spent, her body devolved into a moaning, twitching, sweaty mass of pleasure underneath the wereverine, he removed his hand from between her legs. As Blaze moaned and tried to reset her world, he shifted over her and his hardness was *there*, hot against her engorged lips. When she moaned and gave a weak thrust, trying to meet him, Jack quickly pulled back. "Careful, Miss Blaze," he whispered. His face was covered in sweat, and he was trembling. "I'm gonna claim you, but I gotta do it my way, or I might just lose it."

Blaze felt a spasm of fear at his words, but she quickly brought it into check. "How?" she whispered, imagining some horrible, violent wereverine ritual to mark his mate.

Jack swallowed hard, sweat standing out on his brow as he met her eyes. "You're sure? I can't take this back, darling."

"Tell me how," Blaze repeated, swallowing back dread, now. "Are you gonna bite me or something?"

"Not a bite," Jack replied. His body trembled, and she realized he was panting. "Blaze, I can't hold it back much longer. Yes or no, babe. Hurry."

Blaze bit her lip, looked up into his emerald eyes, and said, "Yes."

Jack groaned, and with no further ado, dropped his body to hers and touched their brows together abruptly. Suddenly, his whole body shuddered, and Blaze felt something hit her like a warm, electric sledge-hammer to her chest, gut, groin, and head, spreading outward from her heart, superheating and tying those parts of her body to... what?

Then she felt him, hovering over her. She felt the strain in his arms as he held himself above her, felt the throbbing heat at his groin, felt the startling softness of her skin, felt the nagging worry that he was hurting her with his weight.

"Oh," Blaze managed, feeling herself breathe *under* him, *through* him. "Oh God."

Very slowly, Jack lifted his head until they were eye-to-eye, and she saw his open-faced surrender, so plain on his face it was as if he'd written it in a book. Shyly, he smiled. "Hey."

Blaze stared at him, so totally lost in the *understanding* of him that she forgot to breathe. She knew who he was, why he did things the way he did, how he struggled with his words, how much he *hurt* from losing his previous mates, how worried he was that he would accidentally hurt her...

"You're not hurting me," Blaze managed, just so totally overwhelmed by that which was *Jack*, so much depth, so much more profound than she ever could have imagined. A living, breathing, *thinking* being...and she was *part* of it.

Jack glanced down at where he still held her arms above her head. "You *like* it rough." He sounded stunned.

Blaze flushed, realizing that, apparently, the link wasn't just one-way. "Um," she babbled, looking away, trying to find a good lie. "I don't really know what you're—"

But then he was lowering himself atop her, he began suckling her nipple again, and Blaze felt both her own racing arc of electricity shoot up from her loins, as well as his thrill of pleasure at *her* pleasure. The duality was so intense, so completely foreign to her that it instantly drove her to the edge.

"Oh gaaaaaawd," Blaze moaned, tossing her head back and forth in panic, straining to pull her arms free before he unmade her. "Too much. Can't..."

"Oh, honey," Jack said, grinning around her nipple, "it's pretty clear you *can*."

His words, paired with her inability to stop the sensations ripping through her body, left her body straining against him in another long, violent orgasm. Her speech, already impaired, now became unintelligible. Every one of Jack's movements above her wrenched a moan, a whimper, or a plea from her lips...and all of it was amplified with the *thrill* that it gave Jack to see her writhe beneath him.

Finally, when she could stand it no longer, Blaze felt Jack shift his weight, felt the hard heat press slightly against the entrance to her womanhood, felt his *need* as if it were her own. She moaned and gave another weak pump of her hips, trying to draw him in, trying to ease that burning heat in him. To her desperation, he backed away, refusing her. Then he waited. Blaze opened her eyes in confusion.

Jack hovered over her, sweating. Immediately upon meeting her eyes, Jack's face lit up in a grin. Holding her gaze, he eased himself home, slowly, methodically, the dual satisfaction compounding, multiplying, making it impossible to think, to breathe, until Blaze cried out and wrapped her legs around his waist in an attempt to pull him inside her.

"Slowly, Miss Blaze," Jack whispered, trembling. "Not too fast. Can't...control it..."

Blaze moaned and writhed, aching for him to continue.

Jack did, but too slowly. And he *kept holding her down*. She got so frustrated she wanted to scream, but all she could do was pant and moan and try desperately to free herself from the maddening, slow easing of his manhood into her folds. "Jaaack," she whined. "Mercy." Blaze felt how much he needed it, felt it like a pain in her own groin, and couldn't understand why he was refusing her.

Jack hesitated above her, concern on his face. "It's too much, then?" He reached up with his free hand to tenderly caress the hard pink tip of her nipple.

That was it. Blaze's brain hit orbit, her body left cartwheeling back to earth. "Noooo," she moaned. "No more."

Jack bit his lip. "Sorry, honey. I know I'm big..." The hot, throbbing shaft within her began to recede.

Blaze's eyes flashed open, pinning the wereverine with her gaze. "You," she bit out, lifting her head as far as she could with him holding her arms down above her, "Had better keep going, or I am going to *skin you alive* when I get free."

Jack's mouth rounded in a little O. "You mean," he said softly, "that didn't hurt?"

A wave of frustration made Blaze slam her head back to the mattress in despair, every nerve in her body completely on fire, the wereverine's manhood half-buried within her, teasing, and there was nothing she could do about it.

The link must have done *something* right, because Jack pushed his hips the rest of the way down to meet hers.

Blaze gasped as she felt his curly black fuzz meet the sensitive flesh between her thighs. When Jack gave an experimental thrust, however, and she felt his groin grind against her clit, her eyes again rolled into the back of her head as she felt her body spasm around him, the sudden pressure of him moving within her triggering waves of pleasure spreading outward around him, through her groin, coursing through every fiber of her being, then magnifying when she felt *herself*, hot and twitching around him, wrapping him in sweet bliss...

"Oh *Jaaack*!" Blaze cried, as he pulled back experimentally and buried himself again, this time to the hilt. She began desperately rising to meet him, but again, he slowed her down, pressing a big, callused hand against her stomach.

"Honey," Jack whispered, looking pale, "I can't."

Blaze's eyes flashed open and narrowed. "Oh yes you *can*." She locked her legs behind him and *took* him, even with her hands pinned, even with his hand against her abdomen, trying to stay her thrusts. She wrapped her legs and dragged him close, forcing him to fill her completely.

Jack shuddered, then, hunching over her with a low groan. "Oh, birdie," he whispered, "Please don't move." She could feel the surge of pleasure starting within him, felt him fight it down.

"Oh *bullshit on that*," she blurted, wriggling, thrashing, panting, *dying* for the need to climax.

She saw his beautiful green eyes widen, saw him reach the tipping point, saw his back arch. "Oh gods," he moaned, as he started moving, harder now, faster, *taking* her as thoroughly as she'd ever been taken before...

...And Blaze completely lost control of her senses. She felt the pressure within give one final, perfect explosion, saw him driving himself almost violently into her own body, then her back was arcing into the bed, her chest bowing to brush her nipples against his hard chest as he continued ramming himself home, his breath coming out in a heated moan, filling her with each pounding thrust of his hips. Then, groaning, Jack threw his free hand under her arced back and drew her close, so solid it was like iron, and the hard, steady thrusts became more desperate, more wild, until he was shuddering and convulsing against her, his hips slamming home with such power Blaze's breath was taken away with each desperate plunge.

...and Blaze felt that pleasure all over again, from him, the exquisite rush as he buried himself within her softness, his body reaching a tipping point and tumbling into the abyss, the surge of pleasure within him as he took her.

"Oh...fuck...oh...*Blaze*!" Jack roared, as he met her eyes in his final, violent throes. He held her suspended above the bed for a long moment, almost painfully tight and immobile against his chest, straining against her body with enough force that Blaze once again had that tiny nagging reminder of just how easy it would be for him to snap her spine.

Then, groaning, Jack relaxed into the bed, allowing Blaze's back to return to the mattress, and settled atop her with a long, low, contented growl.

"Wow," was all Blaze could manage, once she had caught her breath. She could feel the dreamy happiness rolling off of him, as palpable as if it were her own.

Still hovering above her, Jack's green eyes flickered up at her with a nervous look. "Uh. So, yeah. That's the link." Even then, she was experiencing the thrilling dual sensation of his blood rushing through his veins while she felt his heartbeat thumping against her chest.

"It's nice," Blaze managed, because words simply could not describe how *fully* she felt him, understood him. "How close do I have to be to feel it?"

Jack grinned down at her slowly. "Closer you get, stronger it is," he said. Very tenderly, he kissed her neck, and she felt the tingling warmth both in her throat and in his own lips. "But the real question, missy, is how far I'm gonna let you get away from me. 'Cause, after this, I ain't letting you outta my sight."

And, Blaze realized, looking up into his open surrender, feeling the fierce, protective wall of wereverine that was perfectly willing to lay down his life to defend her, knowing, at the very core of her being, that her every word had just become his Gospel, and knowing that, disconcertingly, she had offered him the same, Blaze thought she could handle that.

TWENTY-NINE

Concessions

With Jack slowly-yet-methodically teaching her everything he knew, and with Blaze making her best attempt to pound her own knowledge through his mulishly hard head, and with all the amusing playtime in the interim—after all, Alaska, in winter, could be a very boring place—time for Blaze seemed to speed by at Mach 3. By mid-January, it came to the point where Blaze and Jack were shipping food and livestock *out* on every freight-trip *in*, just to keep the numbers of heritage breed fowl, goats, and pigs under control. Neighbors up and down the river received turkeys, geese, and full-blown hams for Christmas, and Jack took her on a snow-machine trip up the river to Skwentna, where they dropped off a sled-full of fruit, half of which got frozen on the ride.

After which, Blaze had to spend an hour over hot chocolate explaining why she had just decided, out of the goodness of her heart, to deliver mangoes, cherries, apples, and pecans in the dead of winter. Nervously skirting questions of, 'Does Costco even *sell* them at this time of year?' and 'Wow, these cherries are so *good*, where did you buy them?!', Blaze was more than happy to return home to the Sleeping Lady to wait out the rest of the winter.

With Jack's assistance, Blaze managed to secure her first guests for two nights on the weekend of March 3rd, the start of the Iditarod. Fifteen people, each paying a hundred and seventy a night, wanting to use the Sleeping Lady as a home-base to watch the Iditarod as it made its way up the Yentna to Nome. It was a bustle of nerves, early mornings, late nights, frantic cooking, dishwashing, bedmaking, and finally cleanup, but once the final roar of the last guest's snow-machine pulled out of the back yard and Blaze was holding six thousand, five hundred and thirty-two dollars in cash, checks, and tips in her hand, she felt the biggest swell of pride she'd ever experienced in her life.

The guests, she discovered in notes tucked under pillows or folded around the tips, really liked the food.

And, while technically she wasn't supposed to serve them food that hadn't been inspected in a USDA-Approved slaughtering and packaging facility, Blaze didn't think she was in much danger of them turning her in. Jack, of course, had offered to gut any 'panty-waist government shit' that tried to file a complaint, but in between the guests raving about the citrus—she had expanded her greenhouse and ordered a variety of lemon, lime, grapefruit, and orange trees—and moaning over the pulled pork and roast duck, several of them had asked to take food home with them, and had offered to pay accordingly.

Blaze, already overwhelmed with the produce coming out of her own backyard, had been happy to send sleds-ful of food home with them, as a complimentary gift. Hence, she assumed, the rather hefty tips.

"You can't just keep sending food out for free like that," Jack said, his sleeves rolled up and a beer in his hand as he relaxed in the sudden peace and quiet. He took a swig, and she felt the coldness along his esophagus as he swallowed. As Blaze closed her eyes and enjoyed that, he pointed the mouth of the bottle at her. "People are gonna get suspicious."

"We just made six thousand dollars in two nights," Blaze said, feeling a little giddy as she returned her attention to the money. "It's gonna work. I'll be able to pay off my loan!"

Jack grinned. "Honey, you get this place running full-throttle and you'll be making ten grand a *day*, and that's *after* you pay your help." He gave her a conspiratory look. "Fishing's where the big bucks are. That's chump change."

Blaze sighed, still quite happy with her six grand. Tucking it carefully—bill by bill—into a little leather money-satchel, she said, "Well, I guess I suppose I should thank you for not eating any of my guests."

Jack sprouted a little fur and grinned fang, and she felt the painful prick of the fur piercing the skin, the fangs growing through the roof of his mouth. "Who, me?" He finished off his beer and went to the fridge for another. Popping the cap across the kitchen with a talon, he said, "That was actually kind of fun. Didn't know you could cook like that." He leaned back against the fridge, watching her.

Blaze flushed, then zipped up the money-envelope and tucked it into a drawer. Her mother, as a diehard Independent Woman, had refused to cook, and had insisted that cooking was the first step to being barefoot and pregnant to some potbellied couch potato. Blaze swallowed down a rush of embarrassment at the wereverine's raised eyebrow.

"Independent Woman, huh?" he said, sipping his beer again, grinning at her. "You mom can get fucked. You cook great."

Even through her embarrassment that, yes, she had someone standing six feet away that was hearing her *thoughts*, Blaze felt his rush of pride like a warm, happy blanket around her, and she released herself to its embrace. Glancing shyly at the floor, Blaze managed, "Uh… cooking was a…hobby…of mine. Kinda took well to the culinary arts as an elective."

Jack grinned at her. "And here I've been teaching you construction." He tisked, shaking his head, and took another long swig of beer. "How long were you planning on holding out on me?"

Still blushing furiously, Blaze said, "Uh, well, there hasn't really been the occasion."

He raised a brow. "Thanksgiving? Christmas? New Year's?"

She narrowed her eyes. "I fed you turkey. And ham."

Jack grinned at her and said, "You should cook more."

"Thanks," Blaze said, ducking her head, overwhelmed by the pride he felt for her. The link was...different...than anything she'd ever experienced, and it had *readily* become apparent that they could not maintain any sort of anger towards one another. It *hurt.*

Their first argument, in fact, had been over the Desert Eagle she continued to wear on her hip. "I *can* protect myself, and I *can* do anything that a man can do," she had argued, when he first commented on it. Her mother, a true believer in sexual equality, had drummed that into her from the day Blaze was old enough to listen to bedtime stories.

It had been, Blaze quickly discovered, a personal affront to Jack's pride that she wore it, and Jack had stalwartly opposed her carrying the firearm from Day One, insisting he was fully capable of protecting her. Blaze, in her ignorance, had told him to fuck off. In the six days of emotional agony and mental turmoil that had followed, they had finally come to an accord. Blaze would wear the gun, and Jack would pretend it didn't exist. Though Blaze could still feel the unhappiness rolling off of him, every time his eyes caught on the pistol's holster.

For his part, Jack was hell-bent on staying armed, at all times. Even then, he wore her other Desert Eagle on his hip and two swords crossed on his back. The guests had given him funny looks, but he'd shrugged them off completely. And, somehow, the utter confidence he had in carrying those weapons, the complete indifference with which he returned their confused looks, had left Blaze warm and fuzzy inside, and, to her own surprise, grateful for the protection, despite all of her mother's careful feminist teachings and her status as an Independent Woman.

At that point, Blaze knew, looking into Jack's eyes, that she was no more independent from him than if she had two bodies, two souls. She found herself staring, overwhelmed yet again. Jack lowered the beer and returned it, a bashful smile on his face, contentment rolling off of him in waves. Then his eyes once more found the gun on her hip and that contentment quickly morphed into anxiety and unhappiness before he cleared his throat and looked away. He coughed, and for a moment, Blaze felt his urge to go downstairs and stew.

Then he turned back to her, met her eyes, and he smiled again. "So, uh, think we can skip the writing lesson tonight?" He gave her a sly grin and drew her close, pulling her up until she could feel their mingled heartbeats, playing against one another through the flimsy fabric of their shirts. His arms locking around the small of her back, careful to avoid the gun on her hip, he confessed up to her, "I mean, we *can*, but I kinda made plans..."

Blaze grinned down at him. "We could probably skip a night." She'd been teaching him to write, nightly. Even during this last weekend, with guests in the house, Jack hadn't missed his one-hour of study-time, their naked bodies entwined as they searched for fun new ways to add to his vocabulary. And, in return, he had spent every spare minute teaching her hairy-chested skills such as power-sanding, slab-pouring, drywall finish-work, nail-pounding, and engine-repair—stuff that she could now do with him, chatting with him about grout or metric bolts or carburetors while they got dirty working together, enjoying the other's enjoyment, sharing the camaraderie of the work itself.

In fact, once Blaze had figured out that, while arguing with your boyfriend was annoying, arguing with your mate was *excruciating*—and once Jack had figured out that insulting her actually *hurt* her—time had seemed to become a blissful blur. In fact, only last week, her first bill from the financial institution managing her loan had come in the mail. Just under four thousand dollars, due April 26th. Delayed a year, for her convenience. And she would be able to *pay* it, she thought, ecstatic. With her *own money*.

"Yeah," Jack said, grinning. "You're on your way, tootz." He reached around her to drop his empty bottle into the bin in the kitchen marked Glass Only. His grin grew sly and she felt a little thrill in her stomach when he grew a little fang and said, "Now whaddaya say we go celebrate?"

• • •

"This," Jack's voice said, close to her face, "has got to stop."

Blaze swam out of her dark, foggy delirium to open her eyes and peer up at him. "Huh?" She'd stayed up late the night before reading a fantasy novel, and hadn't gone to bed until 4:00 that morning.

Jack held up a five gallon bucket of eggs. "You got any ideas what to do with these? I already fed the pigs a couple buckets, ate my fill, and I think those poor birds out there have eaten so many scrambled eggs they're getting the wrong idea. That's what's leftover." He made a disgusted gesture at the bucket. "Do you *know* how long it took for me to sniff out all their nests? I'm thinking about doing a roundup here tomorrow and sending a lot of them off to birdy heaven. I'm sure as *fuck* not letting them hatch any more. Oh, and…" He bent down, grinning, and planted a kiss on her forehead. "Good morning, sugar."

Grinning back up at him, feeling the warm happy glow of his contentment, Blaze sat up. "And you want twenty square miles of this?"

"'Course I do," he said, breaking out into a predatory smile. "Never ate this good in my life." He lowered the bucket to the bed beside her. Its contents were a jumble of brown, peach, white, greenish, and almost black eggs of all different sizes. And, indeed, this close, Blaze could feel the contentment of a full stomach rolling off of him like a satisfying fog.

Still groggy, Blaze glanced at the bucket. "You offered any to the neighbors?" she suggested.

"Only like six dozen apiece," Jack said. "Oh, speaking of that…" He pulled something from his pocket and tossed it at her. "Miss Kendall, upriver, insisted on paying."

Blaze glanced down at the ten dollar bill that fell in her lap and mentally added another ten bucks to the money she could send off to a nice, friendly, out-of-state banking conglomerate. "The money bag is upstairs," she said, still feeling as if she'd been run over by a Mack truck. She ran a palm over her face. "You couldn't let me sleep in?" She glanced at the window. "And why was Hannah here that early?"

"'Cause Breakup's on its way, baby," Jack said. "Gotta use the snow-machine trails in the morning, before the sun has a chance to turn 'em into slush-puddles." He gestured at the sunlight that was even then glaring through the window at 10:00am. "Hell, give it another week or two, and nobody's gonna be able to use the river 'til the ice goes out." He raised a brow at her pointedly. "On that note, you got any mail you need sent out, now's the time."

Blaze thought again to her bill on her loan, but said nothing. She'd take care of it in April, once she took the money to the bank to get it deposited. After all, she couldn't send them four thousand in *cash*. She also needed to start work on taxes and take a look at the budget for the summer fishing season. Oh, and figure out the advertising situation. *Alaska Magazine* and *Fish Alaska* were both a good place to start, and she should've done it months ago, but just didn't have the cash. So many things to do, so little *time*...

"Also, some more good news," Jack went on. "That agent we hired in Florida. Sounds like he just did a tour through the South and then spent a couple weeks over in Europe, took our brochure to every sportsman's show in the civilized world. Anyway, got a really good call this morning. He's already got you booked for a group of six people for a week in June for king season, then eight more for silvers in July, mostly couples, about four to five days apiece."

Blaze tempered her thrill that followed with a businesswoman's logic. "We don't have a guide."

Jack grinned and she felt the rush of pride down the link as he opened his mouth to say, "We've got *me*. *I'll* guide them."

It took Blaze a moment to realize that was not what he said.

"Excuse me?" she asked, blinking in confusion. "What?"

"You'd make a great guide," Jack repeated, still flooding her with pride. "You're nice enough, you don't have the unfortunate habit of growing teeth and breaking arms when they give you a funny look, you can tell a good story, and you're smart. That's all it really takes." He frowned at her. "Why are you looking at me like that?"

Blaze realized that she was staring, her mouth hanging open. Very slowly, so as to make *sure* she wasn't misunderstanding him, Blaze said, "Did you just say you thought *I* should be a guide?"

"Sure," Jack said. "It'll be a damn shame to lose that kind of cooking, but hell, sounds like you'd be happier out there on the water, anyway. We'll just have to get your guiding license this spring. I think you got enough hours on the river last summer to qualify, and if you didn't..." He shrugged. "We can fudge it."

Still unable to comprehend the words that were coming out of his mouth, contrasting with the *pride* she was feeling from him, Blaze said, "I'm sorry, I must be hearing things. Did you just tell me I can guide for us this year *and* compliment my cooking?"

"What," Jack snorted, "You think *I* could guide those fat, lazy, money-bloated, upper-crust snots?" He chuckled. "In your *dreams*, sister. Last time I tried to do that, I ripped the engine off the boat, threw it into the river, and made them swim home. Pretty sure some of them told stories to their grandkids about this creepy guy on the river who sprouted fur and fangs back in the seventies, too, but never really stayed in touch." Jack gave her a wary look and she felt his alarm. "Are you all right? Need more sleep or something?"

Blaze realized she was staring, again. She consciously closed her mouth and cleared her throat. "Uh, no."

But Jack was grinning at her. "You look gorgeous this morning, babe." And Blaze felt the *truth* in his words, bed-head and all, and had to clear her throat and look away, because two more seconds and she knew she would have launched herself at him and they wouldn't get anything done for another couple hours.

"Thanks," she said to the bucket of eggs. She was pretty sure he'd figured out—the sly little weasel—that complimenting her made her feel good, which in turn made *him* feel good, and had been doing a *lot* of it lately.

"Just say it 'cause it's true," Jack said, reaching up, running a rough, callused finger upon her jaw.

Blaze shivered with their sudden combined need and quickly struggled to return the conversation to something productive, before they spent another day lounging in each other's embrace. Such diversions were blissful, yes, but were not conducive to a fully-operational, functioning fishing lodge come June. And Jack, as productive as he was when he was on a job, was also *very* easily distracted. "So, uh," she said desperately, as Jack's heart started to pound and his masculine fingers started tracing towards her collarbone, "I can't start a boat. Not reliably, anyway. Not those big engines."

Jack hesitated a moment and she saw the desire in his eyes, felt it as her own, and she knew that he was about to take her anyway. For a breathtaking moment, he continued to trace her. Then, heaving a big sigh, he dropped his hand. "Always business."

"I'm a Business major," she said weakly, still shuddering, trying desperately to recover from the desire he had invoked in her.

Jack grinned, and she got a thrill at the predatory surge within him. "Ya know, one of these days, I'm not gonna let you distract me, and I'll just pin you down and take ya anyway."

Blaze's heart hammered at the very real potential of that, rolling off of him, and sure enough, he reached for her again. "Boats," she managed.

Jack rumbled a predatory growl, but dropped his hand. This time, he heaved a *huge* sigh and said, "I've already been working on a quick-start system for your boat. It's a little battery-operated deal with a key and an ignition switch like mine. Means you won't have to fumble around and throw out your shoulder yankin the cord."

"You know there isn't a female guide on the whole river," Blaze said.

Jack's brow creased, and she felt his irritation like a blast of cold air. "So?"

"You never wondered *why* that was?" Blaze asked.

The wereverine gave her a long, hard look. "You tryin to tell me you can't do it?"

Blaze frowned at him. "Of course I can do it."

"Then do it, and stop whining and pussyfootin around," Jack said. "You wanna do somethin other than cook and make babies? Fine. Not that I'm against cookin' and makin' babies, but if you feel you gotta get out and prove you can do manual labor and swim with the sharks, by all means, *do* it, and stop whingeing about it." He gestured at the lodge. "We could really use a guide, and you'd be perfect for it. Hell, I'll roll up my sleeves and cook for a couple weeks, if I gotta. Ain't too bad at it, neither. Had enough damn practice." The rest he said with a grumpy huff, and he crossed his arms disgustedly and nudged the bucket of eggs with a toe.

Blaze was so completely flabbergasted that she could only say, "You'd cook?"

"Sure," he said, "But I'd want serving wenches."

Immediately, Blaze felt her face darken. "What?"

"Wenches," he repeated. "Barmaids. Waitresses. You know. A *wench*?" He gestured upstairs, towards the kitchen. "I ain't washin all those dishes by myself. If you're gonna be off entertainin, then we'll need to hire some kitchen help."

And kitchen help, Blaze knew, was a hell of a lot cheaper than hiring a guide. Guides got paid between a hundred and three hundred dollars a day, depending on how much experience they had, and how well-known they were for producing fish. Hell, there was a whole culture of young men living in the Bush who made all the money they needed to survive the brutal Alaskan winter on just a few weeks of fishing season in the summer. Between wages, tips, and the Permanent Fund Dividend, those that were money-savvy could afford to spend the winter crafting, tinkering on mechanics, or working on their cabins.

"You've already been working on a starting system?" Blaze asked, suspicious.

"Been thinkin 'bout it for months, now," Jack said with a shrug. "Figured I didn't really wanna bring it up early, seein how you're so sensitive about the subject."

Immediately, Blaze's eyes narrowed. "What subject?"

"The manly subject," Jack said. His eyes dropped to the Desert Eagle holster on her dresser and she felt another wave of unhappy irritation.

Flushing, she said, "I'm not sensitive. You're just an *in*sensitive boor."

"All right, tootz," Jack said, sighing, "Fine. We'll find someone else to guide those guests. There's a guy upriver, Kyle Chelson—"

"I'll do it," Blaze growled. "Never said I wouldn't."

"Never said you *would*, either," Jack retorted, "and gave me the general impression that it would be unseemly for you to be out there rubbing elbows with the big boys. This Kyle guy's had his license five years, now. Works freelance. Real good with guests."

"Jack," Blaze said carefully, "if you try to hire this Kyle guy to spare me the manly behavior of driving guests around on the Yentna, I will drag your stuff outside into a nice, big pile in the backyard and set it on fire." She gave him a sweet smile. "Thanks to you, I know where the gasoline is."

Jack paused, frowning at her so long that she began to wonder if she'd caught a nosebleed or something. Finally, the wereverine said, "Six thousand years, and I will never understand women."

Blaze sniffed and glanced down at the eggs in the bucket. "You got breakfast ready?"

Looking a little ruffled, a wave of guilt and irritation riding down their link, Jack muttered, "It's ten in the morning."

Which meant, no, he'd just come to wake her up because he was tired of her sleeping. But, now that Blaze *understood* just how much Jack enjoyed the company, and how hard it was for him—who only had to sleep two or three hours a night—to leave her alone for *eight*, she found she couldn't really get mad at him. Crawling out of bed, Blaze went to start her day.

Breakfast, for Blaze, was a fruit medley consisting of mango, citrus, grapes, cherries, and apples, all fresh, all picked and eaten as she toured her two-thousand-square-foot greenhouse. As part of the 'repairs' he'd been financing, Jack had shipped in a few hundred enormous, glass windows, and he still was refusing to tell her how much they cost.

Probably more than the damn lodge, Blaze thought, looking up at the crystal blue sky through the triple-paned glass. She sat down on a bench under her twenty-foot mango tree, watching the Jersey Giant chickens—some of the larger roosters of which had to be twenty-plus pounds—as they strutted around inside the greenhouse, dust-bathing and seeking out bugs. Out in the yard behind the barn, she could hear the snuffles and grunts of pigs, and heard goats playing on the huge boulder she had uncovered while bulldozing the barn's footprint.

As she sat there, one of the rare white Jersey Giants wandered up to her and, with the friendly, big-dog syndrome the breed was known for, jumped up onto the bench and eyed her mango, then Blaze, then her mango. Giggling, Blaze held it out for him. The rooster proceeded to peck gooey orange chunks from the pit until it had downed a good quarter of the fruit, then settled down on the bench beside her and puffed out his feathers in contented sleep.

Sitting there, life bustling all around her, Blaze had to hand it to Jack. The wereverine knew how to make a woman feel at home.

Then she sucked in a startled breath as a sudden, horrible pain streaked up her arm, like every tendon, bone, and ligament was being ripped apart, pulverizing her flesh. Out in the yard, Jack howled, "You *goddamn piece of shit*!" She heard something heavy and metal clang against something solid.

Blaze sighed. Her mango tree was *overflowing*, and she needed to grab a pail and start picking some for the pigs before they started falling from the tree and cluttering up the walkway. She got up to find a bucket.

Jack yanked the greenhouse door open and leaned inside, one side of him covered in blood. "I just ran my arm over with the dozer and I was wondering if you remember where I put my spare jack." Then he frowned at the chicken beside her. "Hey now. Don't you dare get sweet on the damn birds. They're taking over. We're eating him. His name is Thanksgiving. That's final."

Oh shit. Blaze had promised him she wouldn't fall in love with the chickens, because chickens were *food*. Desperate to divert the conversation, lest Jack take it upon himself to walk inside, grab the adorable little rooster by the neck and politely decapitate it for her, she said, "That *hurt*, you know." She rubbed her arm, which was still throbbing in tune with Jack's wounds. "Could you *please* be a bit more careful?" She thought perhaps making Jack feel guilty for hurting her would aid in helping her keep the chicken. She *liked* the Jersey Giants. They were such sweeties.

Jack gave her a flat look. "Thanksgiving."

Blaze bristled, dropping her hand. "They're mine. I decide if they stay or go."

Jack rolled his eyes. "Careful, tootz. I might just go ahead and change it to Easter."

"I don't know where your damn jack is," Blaze growled. "Have you checked the septic tank?"

Blaze felt a wash of amusement before Jack grunted and left. Thanks to the total honesty of the link, Blaze had been shocked to discover, among other things, that the kinky little wereverine actually *enjoyed* her sass.

Blaze spent a few more minutes sitting in the sun inside the greenhouse, considering. Jack had completely blown her away by suggesting she guide for the lodge. It had come completely out of left field, and it kind of disarmed her whole theory that he was only out to get her barefoot and pregnant, spending the rest of her days cooking casseroles in the kitchen and making his bed.

Blaze glanced at the chicken. "I think I'll call you Snowball."

"I heard that!" Jack roared, from across the yard. She winced and peered through the triple-layered glass at the fuzzy shape puttering around the shop. Just how good *was* his hearing, anyway?!

Then a somewhat comforting thought occurred to her. If Jack could hear her clearly from inside the sealed, climate-controlled greenhouse, from all the way across the backyard, with poultry, goats, and pigs creating a cacophony in the background, maybe he really had a chance of catching an intruder in time to stop another full-scale invasion.

That, and by Jack's own words, he could 'smell a rat fart at a hundred miles.' She noticed him stopping often throughout each day, nose to the wind, a little frown of concentration on his face as he tested the breeze.

Maybe he really can protect this place, Blaze thought, reluctantly. She certainly had to admit that he seemed much more 'on guard' than he had been before Amber's attack. Maybe he'd just needed a wakeup call.

With that thought, Blaze realized she had gone outside the lodge without her gun for the first time in months, and she had a little moment of panic when she noticed the now-empty spot on her hip. She was halfway out of her seat to go retrieve it when she hesitated.

Out back, a yak that had wandered close to the barn grunted as it fed on the fresh grass sprouting up in the melted spots around the greenhouse. A little further away, a goat kid bleated and bounded playfully to its mother. A duck quacked in the distance, followed by the ringing trumpet of a goose. In the main yard, a Black Spanish turkey gobbled and spread his marvelous, iridescent tail to the sun, strutting on the melting snow.

Slowly, Blaze sat back down. The mid-March sun was filtering through the glass, warming the mango leaves over her head. Everything around her practically *buzzed* with life. If she watched the pink flowerbuds on the cherry tree too long, she could almost believe that she saw them opening before her eyes.

I could live with this, she realized, feeling the flourishing energy around her. It felt…right. Fulfilling, somehow.

Now, if only she didn't have the sinking dread that somebody, somewhere, was going to try to take it from her.

Or take *her* from *it*. Jack hadn't been incredibly clear on that part. He seemed to suggest that a phoenix would make a better prize than the feather alone, but how did one control a winged ball of sunfire if it decided it wanted to go on a walk? Blaze decided she really needed to have another chat with Jack about that, and soon.

With the gentle ebb and flow of life around her, however, and Breakup hitting full-swing within the next week or two, thoroughly blocking off the stresses of the outside world for a couple weeks as the rivers thawed and the ice flowed out to the ocean, Blaze found it easier to relax.

In one fell swoop, Jack had alleviated her fears. Instead of offering to buy her a washing machine that didn't chew up the laundry or a commercial-grade dishwasher so she didn't have to wash every dish by hand, Jack had offered to set her up with a boat that started with the turn of a key, cook, do dishes, *and* clean the guest bedrooms, all while she was off making money.

Blaze thought of the details involved with running men—men who were, according to Jennie Mae, raucous, crude, and utterly chauvinistic—up and down the river for long days of salmon fishing and her heart fluttered, both with nerves and excitement. Though she'd never really made many friends, Blaze had the gift of gab. She could keep an entire room of people enthralled for hours as she told stories of things she had seen or heard. It was a talent she'd learned from her dad, who was constantly schmoozing the Alaskan elite, and a talent that had served her well on several occasions, like scholarship interviews and conferences with the dean.

And, she would imagine, such a talent would come in handy when stuck in a sixteen-foot aluminum boat with four to six men for fourteen hours on end.

She just hoped that the total enthrallment she'd gotten from her audience was, in fact, due to her storytelling skills, and not the fact she was six-foot-four and had hair that looked like she'd been accosted by a mad friseur.

"You gonna sit around all day or you gonna come help me change the track on *your* bulldozer?!" Jack called from just outside the shop. "I need another set of hands, and this fucker already bit me once."

Sighing, Blaze got up off the bench. Snowball the Thanksgiving rooster looked up at her curiously, then went back to sleep. Idly, Blaze wondered if she could sell some of the nicer roosters as breeding stock, instead of eating them all. Seemed such a shame to waste good heritage genetics.

Unfortunately, selling roosters wasn't very feasible a hundred miles from the nearest road. For the rarer breeds, she might be able to get seventy-five dollars for a particularly nice specimen. With transportation being restricted to Bush plane, riverboat, or snow-machine, it would cost that much just to ship it anywhere.

"You wait much longer and I might just put a fifty-cal through the crankcase and call it good!" Jack hollered.

"I'm coming!" Blaze snapped. Then, under her breath, "Impatient old curmudgeon."

"Heard that!"

She yanked the greenhouse door open, got a quick jolt as the forty-two degree outside air hit her skin, then went to see what the wereverine wanted.

• • •

The next morning, Blaze woke to the sound of the wereverine puttering nearby. She got up, dragged a shirt over her head, then went hunting for a pair of pants. As she dressed, her eyes caught on the Desert Eagle she had left beside her bed, still in its holster. Jack hadn't touched it, despite getting up before she did—of all the stubborn, asshole things he'd done, he still hadn't crossed that line, and for that, Blaze hesitated. She picked it up, felt its heavy weight in her hands. Not really reassuring. Just...heavy.

She was still standing there, staring down at the gun in her hands, when Jack opened the door and looked inside. His eyes immediately fell to the Desert Eagle. "Felt you wake up," he said. "You want hot water for a shower?"

"I can wait," Blaze said. As the days got warmer, they'd been letting the fire die overnight and shutting off the pump from the furnace, and it probably would have taken him a full forty-five minutes just to heat up enough water for a shower. Hot water, in the Bush, was worth its weight in gold.

And yet he still asked. Every morning.

Slowly, Blaze set the gun back on the bed. Leaving it on the pillow, she turned her back to it and looked at him. "You want breakfast?"

Eyes on the gun on the bed, Jack said, "Wouldn't mind."

"All right," Blaze said. "Any preference?"

"Whatever you're making."

Which, with as many poultry as they had on the farm, meant eggs. Maybe bacon, once the slabs that Jack had showed her how to hang and smoke were done curing. Leaving the Desert Eagle on the bed behind her, Blaze ducked past Jack, who gave her an odd look as she passed.

Blaze filled a non-stick soup-pot with eggs, leftover turkey, onions—Jack routinely insisted he was not a vegetarian, but he didn't mind copious amounts of onion, peppers, or other spicy additives—cheese, salt, and black pepper, then mixed it up and left it to simmer. She supposed it was a *good* thing that they were getting as many eggs as they were, because they used up about six dozen every morning for breakfast: Three for her, sixty-nine for the wereverine.

"Smells good," Jack said, sitting at the bar with his daily writing 'homework.' Pencil and paper in hand, he was watching her like a martin trying to piece together a hunter's trap.

"Thanks," Blaze said, stirring the pot. The eggs never had the standard clumpiness she was used to with scrambled eggs cooked in smaller portions, but Jack didn't seem to mind. It was always satisfying to see how quickly the wereverine wolfed them down.

She went to the fridge, grabbed a mango, some cherries, an apple, and some oranges for fruit salad. As she set them down on a cutting board to start slicing them into a bowl, Jack continued to watch her like he expected her at any minute to suddenly twist the knife around in her grip and launch it at him, blade-first.

"Bad dreams?" Jack finally asked.

Blaze smiled, remembering the long, tantalizing dream of being in the wereverine's arms. "No. Pretty good, actually."

He squinted at her, but said nothing else. Reluctantly, he went to work scrawling down the words she had given him the night before.

By the time the eggs were done, Blaze had finished the fruit salad, made coffee and set out dishes. She served Jack's eggs in a huge ceramic mixing bowl—the only dish in the house big enough to hold it—and then sat down beside him at the bar with her own meager pile of eggs and fruit. She ate thoughtfully for several minutes watching the sunrise on the back lawn while listening to the not-so-pretty sounds of the wereverine initiating the digestion process. As usual, he didn't bother to use the spoon she always pointedly laid out for him, diving in with his hands and face, instead.

When she was done with her meal, Blaze got up to put her dishes in the sink and retrieved a wet rag for the wereverine.

"Thanks," Jack said, taking it to wipe grisly bits of egg from his hands and mouth. In the same span it had taken Blaze to eat three, Jack had wiped out an entire *henhouse* worth of eggs, *and* had time to lick the inside of the bowl, afterwards. Still not so sure she wanted to know the mechanics of that, Blaze said, "I've gotta go feed chickens." She hesitated, feeling the emptiness at her hip and the nagging fear of werewolves. Tentatively, she met his eyes. "You, uh…" She bit her lip, feeling as if her heart was sliding out, within striking-range. "…gonna be out there?" she finished softly.

Jack seemed to understand, because his face melted until he hid it by picking egg off of the table. "Of course," he said gruffly. "Always am, aren't I?"

And, Blaze realized as she went about all of her daily chores, Jack *did* stay close. Always within sight. He even went so far as to drag a tarp out onto the backyard and drop a snow-machine on top of it so he could fiddle with the engine nearby while she tended her greenhouse, all the while nonchalantly pretending as if he had planned to do his work there on the cold, slushy ground anyway, instead of in the warmth of the shop.

She bit her lip. "Thanks," she whispered.

The rush of joy and pride singing down the connection was completely belied by the masculine grunt that followed.

That afternoon, Blaze selected four geese—she'd been around the wereverine long enough to judge his appetites such that, if he had had a rather easy day, like today, he needed to eat just under four large birds, or a ham off a pig, or a half a goat, or a quarter-haunch of a yak just to maintain his body weight. All in all, about a thirty to forty pounds. If he'd been stressed or working hard, that doubled or tripled, depending on the activity. Birds picked, she got the wereverine to help her butcher them.

Plucking a bird, Blaze had very quickly realized upon her first chicken-butchering venture, was something that almost *required* two people, just to keep from going insane with boredom. And Jack, with his big hands and firm grip, was good at plucking. He settled down beside her on a fold-out chair and together they spent the next two hours dumping feathers and down from her extra American Buff ganders into a five-gallon-bucket for use in pillows or blankets later. Every few minutes, he would lift his nose to the wind, often pausing in telling her some enthralling story about his past to sniff the air with a look of concentration before picking up where he'd left off.

If there was one thing that Blaze marveled at about the wereverine, it was that he had no qualms with helping to cultivate his own food. From the random times he'd filled in for her at feeding time, to slaughtering, to final preparation, he was always there, if she needed the help, always ready to lend a hand.

"You wanna eat it, you better damn well be ready to kill it," Jack said, when she commented. He pointed a bloody, feather-covered finger toward his mouth and grinned. "And honey, much as I like mangoes, these babies ain't made for chewin' veggies."

"Yeah," Blaze said, shaking her head as she dropped another handful of white and khaki-colored fluff into the bucket. "I think too many people have kind of lost touch with that part of it. I mean, I hear plenty of people tell me they love to eat beef, chicken, pork...but the moment I mention butchering my own, they're like, 'Oh no, I could *never* do that.'"

"Hypocrites," Jack said, as his eyes darkened. "Part of where this country went wrong."

Blaze almost opened her mouth to tell him that's what *everyone* said whenever they didn't agree with the general populace, then flinched. Jack had *been* there. He'd been *part* of it, from the beginning. He would *know*.

"Can burn the rest off with my torch," Jack said, dropping the final gander on the picnic table beside her. Then, without preamble, he went into the shop, grabbed the little portable propane torch they used for starting fires in the furnace, and brought it back to the table. Blaze watched his body move like a lithe cat, for the first time truly appreciating the simplicity to his way of life. The wereverine truly was a relic of the past, and as such, gave her a window into an existence before machines, before factories and agricultural conglomerates and massive slaughterhouses. An existence that, until now, she could only dream about.

As Blaze finished up her last goose, Jack burned away what was left of the feather fluff from the other three, then went inside to get a tray.

Piling the four birds on top of it, he carried the heavy lot upstairs while she held the door open for him.

There was an awkward moment when Jack hesitated in the kitchen, like he wasn't quite sure who was going to be making that night's meal, but then he seemed to relax as Blaze started cooking one of her grandmother's favorite Christmas recipes—roast goose with apple stuffing. The wereverine hovered nearby almost nervously for a few minutes, then he wandered off into the living-room, and she heard a vacuum-cleaner pick up nearby.

Blaze had to give it to the wereverine—he was *clean*. Each time Blaze cooked, she realized, thinking back, he had done the dishes. And, to his credit, he'd even picked up that bottlecap he'd popped across the room. It had been gone when she'd woken up, no doubt swept up in yet another of his random cleaning sprees.

As had been routine since the wereverine had taken up residence, Blaze fired up both ovens to cook the geese, then went downstairs and started on finances while they roasted. A few minutes after she had settled in with the books, Jack unobtrusively dragged an engine chunk from the snowmachine he'd disassembled inside and set it down on the far end of her table, making the table jump under her paperwork with its weight. Then, as if it were nothing at all out of the ordinary to disassemble an engine inside the basement, he quietly started taking it apart as she worked.

Overall, finances were not great, but she was pretty sure that, with the guests already scheduled for the summer, between bed tax, federal taxes, food, gas, diesel, and replacement parts, she could struggle through the monthly bank payments until the next year. The most difficult part of the year, for the Sleeping Lady, was going to be early spring and late fall, in those months between summer and winter where there would be no snow-machiners and no fishermen to help keep the business afloat. Those payments, she knew, she would have to save up from the fatter times in the summer, and it certainly wasn't going to help that taxes would be due smack in the middle of the leanest time of the year.

"How's it lookin, Boss?" Jack asked as he picked at his project.

Blaze squinted at the grease he was smearing on the table. "Better than expected, I guess. Are you going to wipe that up?"

He looked up with a single raised eyebrow, then went back to work.

She peered at him. "Wouldn't that be easier in the shop?"

"Probably," he said. He was wearing, she realized, both of her Desert Eagles and two of his long, light-eating black swords. A third sword leaned against the wall beside his chair, a curved blue scimitar with ripples in the metal that looked like water-splashes. *Damascus steel,* she thought, still stunned by that fact. *And he made it himself...*

"Someday," Jack said, squinting at a tiny piece that popped off into his hand, "you'll have to help me take a look at my books. I could really use the extra set of eyes. See where I stand, ya know?" He looked up at her and she felt his *terrifying* vulnerability before he quickly hid it by grabbing the rag and wiping down the tiny piece in his hand.

Watching him, Blaze was stunned. She'd never realized how deeply humiliating the illiteracy had been for him, and how much of his pride had been built around it, and how desperate he was to appear intelligent to her, regardless. It had just taken everything he *had* to ask for her help.

In that moment, Blaze felt a glowing swell of gratitude towards the wereverine. "I'd be happy to," she said softly. "And thanks."

"Thanks?" Jack frowned up at her and she felt a wave of confusion, almost dizzying in its intensity.

Blaze gestured at the swords he carried.

To her amazement, the wereverine blushed. "Uh, yeah," he said, ducking his head, happiness once more rolling off of him like a warm blanket. "No problem." He went back to tinkering with his part, discussion over. She was pretty sure that, had she brought up the second Desert Eagle at this point, he would have simply told her to get bent, so Blaze politely forgot to mention it.

After a couple more hours, when the tantalizing smell of roast goose began wafting down the stairs, Blaze packed up the accounting books and headed to the kitchen to finish the rest of dinner. Jack relocated with her, picking an out-of-the way spot along the bar to continue working on his project. Blaze winced at the heavy *clunk* it made on the Formica of the bar, but distracted herself with chopping potatoes and carrots to drop into the bubbling gravy accumulating around the base of the geese.

"You should cook more," Jack said, as the savory scent of goose and herb-roasted vegetables began wafting through the lodge. "Smells heavenly."

Blaze felt a little swell of pride, grateful beyond words. Cooking was one of those things that she loved to do, but had always felt this nagging fear of enjoying too fully. Her mother had trained her that cooking was not worth the time of a modern, independent woman, so she was still adjusting to the idea that she could do something she *enjoyed* and have Jack appreciate it for what it was, not take it to mean she wanted to get pregnant and hand him all of her bank accounts and credit cards while she got to work making babies. "During the slow months, if we don't have guests, I might just do that."

Jack grunted and returned his attention to his grease-stained metal.

Just as Blaze was getting ready to pull the roasts out and serve dinner, she was interrupted in grabbing a hot-pad by a knock on the basement door.

Jack rolled his eyes. "If Jennie Mae wants more eggs, just tell her to go *collect* them. She doesn't have to come over and *chat* about it, if you know what I mean."

Blaze sighed and gave him a pointed look. "It's good to have neighbors."

"Oh yeah?" Jack demanded. "Why? So they can eat your food and you can go haul their incompetent asses out of the river when their boats flip over?"

The knock came again, tentative, and, when it was clear that Jack wasn't going to get up to get the door, Blaze went downstairs to answer it.

THIRTY

Here, Kitty...

As soon as Blaze opened the door, she froze. A dark-haired, Asian-looking man stood on her back porch, probably around six feet, thickly-built, but packing more fat than the wereverine. As soon as she tugged the door open, his eyes widened and he tugged his ballcap off of his head and held it in his big hands. "Uh," he said, by way of introduction, "Name is Nicolai Sikhote. I just bought a cabin downriver. Moved my family in just before Breakup. Uh..." His nose twitched and he lifted it to the air, then his eyes came to a rest timidly on her face. "Thought I'd go meet the neighbors."

"Oh, well, that's nice," Blaze said, smiling. "I just cooked a goose. Come on insi—"

Then she was being thrown out of the way as a four hundred and fifty pound wereverine came hurtling down the stairs and shoved the man backwards off the porch, all fur and fang.

"*Jack*!" Blaze cried, "What are you *doing*—?"

But the man in the yard merely picked himself up off of the slushy ground and gave Jack a nervous look. "Uh, so, yeah. Just introducing myself."

Blaze started to get goosebumps at the way Jack stood there, snarling, saliva dripping from inch-long teeth, and the man only looked slightly perturbed. Like Jack had spat on his shoe. She swallowed and took several steps back into the Sleeping Lady.

"Heard there were some vacant land 'round these parts," the man said, eying Jack. "Not meaning to offend anyone."

"Well, ya done introduced yourself, now *git*," Jack snarled. "An' don't come back without a fucking invitation."

The man's shoulders tightened, and Blaze thought she saw a flash of yellow-green in the man's hazel eyes before it was gone. He slapped his ballcap back over his head and turned, shaking his head.

"Wait!" Blaze called.

The man in the back yard hesitated, looking over his shoulder.

"Come on in for dinner," Blaze said, stepping past the wereverine. "We got plenty."

"No we don't," Jack growled, stepping past her again, irritation and—*fear?*—strong down the link. Fear…for *her*?

"Jack," Blaze said gently, "this is my place. I want to invite the neighbor over for dinner, you say 'yes Boss' and go set the table."

"Oh, for chrissakes!" Jack snapped, his wariness and unhappiness and anxiety and fear all mingling in a tight knot in her chest. "The kitty's just *here* 'cause he can smell the *food*." Cocking his nightmarish head at the man in the yard, he said, "Ain't that right, sweetcheeks?"

Blaze saw the man tense. "I'm not a thief," the man growled.

"He's not saying you are," Blaze said quickly, trying to step past the wereverine again. "Come on in. Jack, *go*."

"Not gonna happen, honey." Jack solidly blocked her passage with an arm that may as well have been iron, keeping himself between her and the stranger. The wereverine just stood on the porch, glaring at their visitor. He wrinkled his nose and sniffed the air, and Blaze watched him level his glare back on the stranger. "You got kids an' a wife. You like 'em *alive*, you're gonna fucking keep your hands to yourself. Get me?"

Horrified, Blaze cried, "Oh for fuck's—"

"Shush, honey, the kitty and I are coming to an understanding," Jack said, never taking his eyes off the stranger. "He touches you, ever, I'll destroy his whole fucking family. *Capiche*?

The Asian man narrowed his eyes and again, Blaze thought she saw a flash of yellow-green. "I think we're clear on that."

For a long moment, Jack just stood there, glaring. Then, with a growl, he muttered, "Fine, you can come in, but I got silver and I got blades, and you so much as *fart*, buddy, and your ass is getting buried in the hill. Blaze, back up, sweetie."

Still keeping his body between them, Jack started backing into the Sleeping Lady.

"For *fuck's sake*, Jack!" Blaze cried, shoving around him. "Don't worry," she said to their guest, "it's nothing you did. He's always an asshole. Come on in."

The stranger tore his eyes from the wereverine and lifted them back up to Blaze. He tentatively sniffed the air again. "Uh. Thanks, miss…?"

"Blaze," she said, extending her hand.

The stranger came back up onto the porch and, giving Jack a wary glance as the wereverine stiffened like wrought-iron beside her, took it gently, and in that moment, she watched goosebumps crawl up his arm just before he released her quickly. "Uh…" he said, taking a noticeable step backwards and peering up at her. Gingerly, he took off his hat for the second time. "You sure, Miss?"

"He's just a harmless ball of fluff," Blaze said. "Pay him no mind."

"Fifty-three dead wolves would beg to differ," Jack growled, hovering beside her.

Blaze slapped her face to her palm. Doing her best to ignore the nervous-henning wereverine, she said, "Come on in. You drink coffee? Tea?"

"Whatever's hot," the man said in that soft-spoken tone that she'd noticed of many Asians. Still watching the wereverine—who was scowling at him like he was some sort of unwanted pustule—nervously, the man stepped inside after her and took his shoes off in the entry before padding up the stairs behind her, the wereverine in tow.

Jack carefully leaned against the bar, none-too-subtly putting his body between the newcomer and Blaze once they had entered the kitchen. Still glaring at Nicolai with slitty green eyes, he yanked a fistful of eating utensils from the drawer behind him, not even bothering to make sure they were the *right* utensils, and shoved them at him. They went sliding across the counter in a metallic tinkle, scattering against Nicolai's arm.

"Jack, dammit," Blaze muttered, but her heart was going out to him. She *understood* why he was so upset, and she wanted to make it better…But she also wanted to establish whatever social connections she could in this barren place. She *refused* to live in a cultural desert. Very politely, she said to the newcomer, "So, you said you've got a wife?"

"*I* said he's got a wife," Jack growled. "One who's gonna get her head ripped off if—"

Blaze slammed the coffee mug onto the counter, startling them both. Forcing a smile at Nicolai, she said, "You should bring her over sometime. I'd love to meet her. Not a lot of girls around here. She like gardening?"

Nicolai, who still hadn't fully sat down, reluctantly settled into a stool at the kitchen island, watching Jack nervously. "Loves it."

"Great," Blaze said, pouring him coffee as he settled onto a stool at the kitchen island, "So where you from, Nicolai?"

"Siberia," the man said, at the same time Jack said, "Russia."

Blaze frowned. "You two know each other?"

Jack shrugged and plucked a heavy-looking engine part from the counter behind him to start fiddling with it. "Wild-ass guess."

"So," Blaze said, flipping off the oven and retrieving hot-pads, "just so there's no confusion, you're moon-kissed, right?"

"Yes, Ma'am," Nicolai said, blushing. "'Bout a half a millennia, now."

Jack snorted. "Kitten."

That made the man bristle, and for the first time, Blaze saw a slice of ivory fang before it was hidden by his lips.

"Allll *right*," Blaze said, slamming the first goose down on the counter with a resounding *thump*, "Jack, this is *my* house and I *just* got finished replacing the drywall. There will *not* be fighting inside. There is, and I see so much as a *scratch* in the *paint*, and I swear to *God* I will *spit* you and roast you *both* alive just as tenderly as these damn birds. You *read* me?"

The man seated at her island went pale, and even Jack looked a little chagrined. Bending his head back to his grease-stained hands, he muttered, "Sure, Boss."

"Okay," Blaze muttered. "Let's eat." She ended up serving each of the weres two of the geese, and took a small part from Jack's meal to finish out her own.

"Why don't you take some off of *his*," Jack whined, watching the thin portion of goose settle onto her plate. "*He's* the freeloader, here."

Blaze's eye twitched and she was about to explain to Jack the meaning of hospitality when the newcomer reached into his back pocket, retrieved a billfold, and dropped a hundred-dollar bill on the table between them. "There," he said, nudging it across to her. "For your generosity, Ma'am."

"*Her* generosity," Jack snorted. "It's *my* dinner you're eating."

Blaze groaned. "Jack, for once, could you just stop being an asshole? For once? Please? Just once?"

"It's okay, Miss," Nicolai said, "I've dealt with his kind before."

And, by the way he said it, Blaze was pretty sure he didn't mean 'have a friendly chat and work things out diplomatically for the betterment of our two peoples.'

Apparently, Jack heard it, too, because that low rattle started in his chest again.

"For *chrissakes*!" Blaze snapped, standing and jabbing her finger at the wereverine. "*Eat*, or I swear to *God* you are sleeping in the shop tonight." She swiveled on the newcomer. "And *you*. Stop saying things that will piss him off. He's delicate. Talk about something benign, like the weather. *Now*."

The man quickly bent his head to the meal. "It's good food," he managed. While he wasn't wolfing it down with the enthusiasm of a starving piglet—*unlike* Jack—he was certainly putting a dent in it rather quickly.

"Thank you," Blaze said, relaxing back into her chair. "So you said you've got family out here?"

Nicolai's eyes darkened and flickered to Jack before he nodded and said, "Aside from my wife, two little girls."

"Weres?" Blaze asked.

The man twisted and gave her a horrified look. "No, Ma'am. They're six and twelve."

...which answered her question as to whether or not a were would breed more weres. Blaze glanced at Jack, rather pleased with that revelation. The wereverine had buried his face in his goose and was ignoring the both of them pointedly. "So," she offered to Nicolai, "I suppose you heard about the wolves?"

The man's face reddened. "Uh, yes Ma'am. Heard about it on the news. How I figured we could come on out here. Figured there'd be some territory up for grabs."

"Who said I didn't grab it?" Jack muttered into his meat.

The man winced, giving the wereverine a nervous look. "It's taken, then?" He seemed perfectly willing to go home, pack up his wife and kids, and head out of the Bush on the first flight out, after the rivers cleared enough for a plane to land.

But the wereverine muttered, "You're fine, kitten. Just don't come callin too often and you an' me we won't have a problem."

"Oh," the extreme relief that washed over the man's face was almost painful. "Thank you, sir."

Jack made an irritated gesture at Blaze with greasy fingers. "Thank *her*. *She's* the one who made it so I don't need any more huntin' grounds.

At mention of Blaze, Nicolai looked back at her and licked his lips nervously. "Uh, so she is, uh...?"

"*None of your damn business*!" Jack roared, even as Blaze calmly said, "A phoenix."

Jack's mouth fell open and he stared at her. "Now I gotta sputch him."

Indeed, Nicolai was paling again. He started fidgeting with his hat, and Blaze saw the white tips of claws pricking from the end of his fingers. Sweat was beading on his forehead. "Uh, Miss, I'm *really* sorry to have bothered you."

He thinks he's gonna have to fight his way out, Blaze realized, horrified.

And Jack, she realized, was thinking the same thing. Nicolai looked nervously at the wereverine, who was growing fur, and then glanced at the stairs to the basement.

"Now *wait just a minute*," Blaze said, slapping her hand to the tabletop, making both Nicolai and the wereverine jerk. "I'm a businesswoman," she growled. "I see an opportunity here for a mutually beneficial arrangement. You got a family you need to feed. I got food. *Lots* of food. And as long as I stay here, safe and sound, there's gonna be an abundance of it, or so I'm told."

Nicolai, sweating, tore his eyes off of Jack to look at her timidly.

"*So*," Blaze continued, "You bring us some firewood, money, gas, something to trade, maybe send your little girls over once a week to help with chores, and I'll send you home with more food than you know what to do with."

Nicolai swallowed, hard, and it was pretty clear he still thought he was about to be in a fight for his life. But he tentatively said, "Food?"

"Just take a walk out back with me," Blaze said, gesturing at the backyard. "It's everywhere. We can't get rid of it fast enough."

She saw a little flash of hope in his eyes. "My wife would appreciate that, Miss. She's been trying to make do on what the wolves left behind, and it really ain't much..." He hesitated. "We been feeding the kids first, of course, but mostly just rabbits, some voles..."

That settled it. Blaze stood up, grabbed Nicolai by the hand, and tugged him out of his seat. "Come on," she said.

"What...?" the man asked, still eying the suddenly-bristling wereverine nervously, carefully tugging his hand out of her grip. Jack seemed to relax when he wasn't touching her anymore. *God* she was going to have to work on his people skills.

"You are taking a yak home with you," she said, ignoring Jack, giving Nicolai an appraising look. "You *can* carry a yak, right?"

"Those are *my* yaks!" Jack snapped, irritation surging across the link. Then, when Blaze whipped around to glare at him, he lowered his face to the pile of bones under his chin and muttered, "Don't see why you're giving stuff away, anyway."

"Because," Blaze gritted, "as you keep pointing out, we're getting *overrun*. He can take some of it off our hands to feed his kids and everybody's happy."

Nicolai watched the exchange, nervously wringing his hat in his hands as his gaze flickered between them. "Look, I don't want to cause problems," he began tentatively.

But Jack was already getting out of his chair, a thoughtful look on his face. "You like chicken, Nick?"

Blaze frowned. "I said a yak."

"Oh, he can have that, too," Jack said, going into the kitchen. He came back with a burlap potato-bag from the pantry. "He's also taking some of them damn fowl with him. We got too many eggs, and those damn crowers are keeping me up at night."

Blaze winced, not really looking forward to the wereverine thinning out her flock, but realized it was as good a compromise as she was going to get from Jack.

In the end, she watched the wereverine shove a good twenty headless, still-thrashing birds into the sack and shove it at their neighbor. "Come back for more *any*time," Jack said, grinning and showing teeth. "With my *blessings*, pal."

Then she and Jack stood together on the back lawn, watching the man drag the yak off through the woods by a single fist on its horns, the sack of chickens hung over his wide shoulder.

"So what was he?" Blaze asked, once he'd disappeared amongst the birch.

Jack shrugged, turning back to the lodge. "Smelled like big cat."

Blaze felt goosebumps crawl down her spine. "What, like *Siberian tiger* big cat?"

He gave her an irritated look. "Now don't go all gooey-eyed on me. All those fools and their cat-fetishes." He snorted. "They're just haughty, arrogant, stuck-up, self-centered assholes."

"Ah. And you are so much better."

"Uh-huh," he agreed, "*So* much—" Then he caught her sarcasm and he narrowed his eyes. "I'll be upstairs doing dishes."

Chuckling, Blaze followed, and, careful to avoid the huge grease-smear and the snow-machine engine, sat down at the bar with her notebook to scrawl out his next set of practice-words while Jack cleaned up after dinner.

"Probably a good thing," Jack muttered, wiping down the last of the plates.

"Huh?" Blaze said, glancing up, having been thoroughly concentrating on his latest series of 'eat' words.

"That you didn't let me kill him," Jack said, matter-of-factly. "I guess we might as well share. No harm in it." The way he said it was grudging, like every word was wrenched from his chest quite unwillingly on his part.

"You're right," Blaze said, returning her attention to the worksheet she was creating. "And if you really want to make that stand you were talking about, I think the first step is to make some *friends*, instead of running everybody off who sets your hackles up."

Jack wrinkled his nose, but didn't argue. He tossed the drying-rag aside—he still wore his swords while doing dishes, Blaze noted—and said, "Massage?"

Blaze grinned and handed him his next writing assignment over the counter. "Sounds superb."

THIRTY-ONE

Heartache

Five mornings later, as Spring was hitting with a vengeance, rotting the ice on the river and making huge patches of mud on the snow-machine trails, Blaze awoke to the sound of goats bleating.

A little note beside her head, written in painstaking, childlike script, said, "IM AWF TO CHEK MAI PLAS. BAK IN A CUPPL OURS."

Feeling a little thrill at the note, overjoyed with Jack's progress, Blaze was nonetheless stunned that he would leave her alone. He hadn't left her out of his sight for *months*. And, without his presence nearby, without that flood of feeling that was *Jack* hovering at the edge of her awareness, she also felt *alone* for the first time in months. It was a bit startling, and more than a little unnerving. She wondered why he hadn't just waited for her to wake up.

Her mind chewing on this, she didn't catch the odd silence of the house around her until she got out of bed. The furnace, she realized, wasn't pumping hot water, which in turn wasn't making the comforting low ebb of flowing water under her feet and over her head. Neither was there a fire crackling in the woodstove outside her room. Further, the lodge was cooler than normal, almost chilly.

"Jack?" Blaze called, frowning out at the empty hall. It was early morning and no lights were on, but the sun was already illuminating the place like mid-day in December. She guessed it was probably around 7:00am.

She felt a rush of irritation at the wereverine, running off to do errands in the middle of the night, leaving her *alone*. She still hadn't gotten over that. After his constant presence all winter, it was almost… creepy.

Well, at least he didn't howl at the moon. Sighing, Blaze pulled some pants on and found her boots. She guessed he'd probably walked, considering that the four-wheelers were still stowed in the shed for winter, and the snow was just the right slushy-wet consistency to get a snow-machine stuck for *good*. Judging the distance between here and Jack's—at least a mile, maybe two—and the rough, soggy terrain in the interim, she realized he was probably doing some manly Spare The Woman The Wet Walk Through The Woods routine.

It actually made her disappointed. She really could have used the walk, and she *loved* sharing the outdoors with Jack. Walking with him, feeling his protective presence, trusting him to keep her safe, was almost like some deep, instinctual communion, something that went all the way back to humanity's humble beginnings.

Besides, she was sadly out of shape. Already, winter flab made a sort of pooch at her stomach, and for a woman known as 'Flagpole' for most of her school years, it was definitely time to start getting active again. The Alaskan Bush, she had quickly discovered upon arrival, did not have a conveniently-located, keycard-operated, 24-hour gym. Instead, its weight set was seemingly-never-ending loads of firewood—cut, split, and stacked—and its treadmills were navigating the woods, rivers, and trails on the thousand little errands necessary each day just to survive.

Unfortunately for Blaze, most of *that* took place in the summer. Winter, in Alaska, was generally not very active. Aside from the lunatics who liked to get helo-dropped atop mountain peaks to snowboard to the valley below—and hopefully not trigger an avalanche along the way—most people stayed inside their homes and thought of spring.

Blaze went upstairs and got the coffee-pot brewing, then tugged her coat on and went to feed the fire, that nagging sense of being *alone* making the little hairs on the back of her neck prickle. Yes, she was definitely going to have to have a talk with him about this. Next time, he would *wait* for her, dammit.

As soon as she opened the furnace in the shop, Blaze paused. The coals had gone out. Which meant Jack hadn't added wood all night. She frowned, knowing that the wereverine maybe slept two, possibly as many as three hours throughout the time she was asleep. Puzzled, she glanced out the shop door to the yard beyond. The goats were milling in a tight cluster up against the barn, and the yaks were nowhere to be seen.

It was the brown footprints heading out of the greenhouse, however, that made her heart pound.

Dirt. Lots of it. Piled up against the windows from the inside.

Oh no, Blaze thought, dropping the firewood, swallowing down a bolt of terror. She spun and ran for the back door—

—But a blonde woman in designer shorts and a tank top stepped from behind the firewood stacks, blocking her exit from the shop.

Amber sneered, half of her beautiful face showing bone through stinking, black flesh. "Hello, little bird."

Blaze's first thought was, *Oh God, Jack...*

Terror making it hard to breathe, Blaze took a step backwards, her blood becoming molten iron flowing through her veins. "What did you do with Jack?" she whispered, her eyes dropping to the dagger on Amber's hip. She recognized the smooth ebony pommel.

Amber cocked her head, looking patronizing. "The cripple? Oh, you needn't worry yourself with him, little girl." From her shirt, she drew a long, wispy fluff of molten sunfire. "Step out into the yard with me," the werewolf commanded, stroking the feather. "Now."

Eyes on the feather, her heart a concussive blast of coals in her chest, Blaze took a step backwards, angling for the door on the opposite end of the shop.

Amber chuckled. "Oh? Pretty birdy thinks she's gonna fly away?" She stopped stroking the feather and pinched a single golden strand between her fingers. "Step out here. Now. I have some friends that would like to meet you."

Blaze's eyes caught on the hiding-place of one of the many silver-filled guns that Jack had stowed around the place. She lunged for it, throwing the rags aside, reaching for the weapon. She was in the process of pulling the shotgun from the rack when a sudden, fiery blast of agony hit her like a freight-train.

Screaming, both Blaze and the gun hit the floor in a clatter of muscle and steel.

"Yep, that's the bird," a dispassionate male voice said, from outside. He seemed to almost have a Spanish or an Italian accent. "Definitely still linked."

Trembling, Blaze pushed herself up from the floor, her entire being a pounding wave of throbbing hurt. "Please," Blaze gasped, just trying to regain her bearings against the wracking pain. "I never hurt anybody. I just want to be left alone."

"Frankly," the man with the Latin-ish accent said, "We don't care what you want, demon." Two black shapes moved into the shop with her as men—*in combat gear*, Blaze realized, horrified—came to either side of her and each grabbed her roughly under an arm with a black-gloved hand.

"Bring her out here in the light," Amber commanded. "I'll get her to tell us where the wereverine is fast enough."

"Careful about giving orders, *demon*," the man beside Blaze said. "We came here today to fight the *moon-cursed*, regardless of Zenaida's *pardon* for you." He said the words with a disgusted twist of disdain. "Wolf, wolverine…I don't see much difference if you just disappear along with him. So watch yourself." But he nonetheless yanked Blaze to her feet and dragged her outside. More men bent to help, hauling Blaze painfully across the gravel and wood-chips and out into the still-frozen slush of the backyard. Nearby, she heard a strangely-muted, whuffling *thump, thump, thump* of a helicopter, and as she numbly tried to push herself to a kneeling position, she saw a sleek black shape slide into view over the treeline, as more men in black rappelled to the ground on wriggling, snakelike ropes.

Suddenly, a hand on Blaze's chin yanked her head back around, until she was looking directly into Amber's blue-white eyes. "So where's the weasel?" Amber asked, her honeyed voice filled with poison. "They want him, too."

"The bird's our primary target," the first man in black said, sounding annoyed. He pulled out a radio and said into it, "Put down on the front lawn. Bird is in custody."

"We're *not* letting him get away. That was the deal." Amber sprouted fur and fang in a snarl and twisted back to Blaze. Her slitted eyes drawing close to Blaze's, she said, "I want Jack. You tell me where he is, my delicate little birdy, and I won't hurt you anymore."

"The weasel can wait," another man in paramilitary black growled. "This has already taken longer than it should have. We should be in the *air* already." He was reaching down, fitting something spiky around Blaze's neck…

Jack's alive, Blaze thought, with a surge of hope. Then she felt the metal click as something snapped into place, and her neck started to burn where the little prickles touched her skin. Eyes widening, she automatically reached up to pull it off, but only succeeded in driving the pinpricks deeper into her neck.

Gasping, she released the metal band, her blood roaring through her ears in a furnace, now, as the pinpricks burned like liquid nitrogen where they touched her skin.

"In case you get any ideas about flame-throwing," Amber said sweetly, gesturing to the thing around her neck.

"What is it?" Blaze whimpered, as the cold seemed to seep outward, throbbing like a ice-cream headache.

"Gold," Amber said, still smiling. "Can't do your little birdy-thing if you are wearing gold." She started petting the feather again. "Where's Jack?"

"I don't know," Blaze lied, reaching up to touch the throbbing metal band around her neck. "Please, this hurts." The helicopter had moved to land in the front yard, and she heard the *thump*, *thump*, *thump* of the rotor blades rattling the windows of the lodge.

"Oh?" Amber said. "I was sure this would hurt a lot more." She plucked another filament from the feather.

Blaze doubled over, emptying her lungs in a scream as an arc of fire seemed to lance down her spine, from her scalp to her toes. Nothing in her life could rival the kind of pain that was coursing through her body, ripping hot coals through her being, tearing the very energy from her limbs, leaving her sobbing and trembling and spent on the ground.

"Damn it, demon," the man in black snapped. "Give me that fucking feather."

Amber ignored him completely, her gaze riveted to Blaze. "Tell me where to find the weasel!" Amber snapped, impatience burning in her blue eyes.

"I don't know where he is!" Blaze screamed, from a fetal position on her side. With the remnants of the agony still throbbing through every vein, the icy pinpricks of the collar didn't even register on her awareness. Blaze squeezed her eyes shut against tears, bawling onto the frozen ground beneath her face.

Amber's slitted eyes narrowed and Blaze saw insanity, there, as the werewolf reached for another filament.

Beside her, the man snarled and drew his pistol, aiming it for Amber's head. "Fucking demons. I'll just get rid of you now and deal with Zenaida lat—"

A sudden distant gunshot ricocheted off of the surrounding birch trees, followed by another. Immediately, the man lowered the gun and put the radio to his lips and shouted, "Was that us? Who fired, who *fired*?" as he and several other soldiers bolted for the front of the lodge. Seeing them go, Amber chuckled and shifted into a half-form, saliva dripping from her fangs. "Well. Looks like they decided to give us some time alone, there, birdy," she chuckled, squatting beside Blaze. The malicious way the woman said it left no question—Amber planned to pluck the feather clean.

Using every ounce of strength that she still possessed, Blaze swiped tears from her face with a hand and slapped her palm to the naked skin of Amber's shorts-clad leg.

The werewolf jerked back, suddenly, frowning down at her leg in total incomprehension, then gasping, dropped the feather, her fur and fang sucking back into her small human form as if the demon had been yanked from her body and cast back to the Third Realm. Suddenly fully human, Amber fell into a crouch and reached for the feather again, teeth gritted in a low, agonized moan.

Taking a moment to collect them *all*, Blaze slapped more tears to the woman's arm, and Amber's eyes went wide in an open-mouthed scream. She hit the ground sideways, all of her muscles seemingly locking into place. As her legs started to thrash on the frozen ground, Amber's hand went to her side and she caught the pommel of the ebony dagger and pulled it from its sheathe.

Blaze saw the black tip oozing voidlike fog against the ground and knew she was looking at her own death in the twisted curl of horn. Amber was again reaching for the feather, hands fisted, panting, her face flushed and sweaty.

While every ounce of her wanted to crawl away from the dread blade and lock herself in the shop, Blaze found herself reaching for the feather, instead. Her trembling fingers found it just before Amber's and she dragged it out of the way, holding it out of the werewolf's reach.

Her body too weak from Amber's torments to get up and run, Blaze held the feather for a terrified moment, knowing that she had to get it away from the werewolf if she wanted to survive. She scooted backwards with pain-sapped legs, until her back was touching what was left of the year's firewood.

"Thank you, bitch," Amber chuckled, getting awkwardly to her feet. Her body was still spasming, and she looked like she was in great pain, but the hatred and insanity in her eyes was like a demonic light animating a doll. The horrible wound on her face, Blaze noticed, was closing, the blackness fading, a golden light drawing skin over the gleaming white bone. "I needed that."

Not having the energy to stand, knowing she couldn't run away with it, couldn't do *anything* to keep it out of Amber's reach, Blaze fought a sudden wave of despair. She felt the feather's magic pulsing through the filaments, whispering, calling to her very soul as the tendrils sank into her fingertips.

Seeing the werewolf take a rigid step towards her, Blaze took a deep breath. She knew if she gave it up, she would never see Alaska again. Jack had made that much clear: Whoever these people were, they looked upon her as an artifact, a *prize*, not a person. They planned to *use* her, and her imagination could come up with a dozen horrible scenarios, none of which involved Jack. Blaze tightened her fist around the filaments, then, with a prayer to God, slammed its sharpened tip home into her chest.

As soon as the feather's shaft made contact with the fiery coal of her heart, it exploded in a hungry, jubilant greeting. Flames rolled outwards along her spine, pulling the feather inward, sucking it inside of her, until Blaze was watching it sink into her chest, creating a growing pit of molten yellow between her breasts.

Then, like a spark igniting a drum of jet fuel, the feather detonated. The trembling coal that was her heart suddenly erupted in a violent explosion of heat and flame, and the concussive wave of heat that followed shattered the closest windows of the lodge. White fire lashed outwards, melting her bones, liquefying her muscles, sculpting her body into a column of living, breathing inferno that billowed and grew, moving and dancing as the snow underneath her bubbled and steamed away.

Fly, part of her said. She felt part of her shift, felt the flames spread outward, aching for the skies.

But the thing around her neck was like ice, the tiny prickles like needles, drawing away the fire, leaving numbness in its place. She couldn't fly. She couldn't *change*. The gold was seeing to that. It was keeping the fire contained, refusing to let it press outward…

Suddenly, like another dimension unfolding around her, Blaze realized she could see and feel every trace of life around her, every touch of sunlight in every glittering ice-crystal, every glistening water droplet. She felt the joyous tickles of energy shining in Amber's hair, warming her sweating face, dancing against the surface of her widened eyes. She felt the black fabric of the paramilitary men on the other side of the lodge as their clothes soaked in the energy, heating in blessed wave after wave of perfect, undulating sunli—

Amber lunged forward and plunged the dagger into Blaze's gut.

Leaving it there, the werewolf slumped backwards onto her elbows, laughing up at Blaze's startled expression. "Aren't so clever now, are ya, birdy?"

Blaze felt the sun dim around her, felt the world lose its energized tinge as even the dancing water-crystals went bleak and dark.

On the ground, Amber frowned, a tiny twitch of her perfect lips.

Trembling, Blaze looked down at the ebony hilt, buried to the guard in her stomach. Swallowing down the revulsion of the vileness even now seeping through her body, Blaze wrapped her hands around the dagger and awkwardly pulled it out.

"Gonna enjoy watching you curl up and die," Amber was saying, "Right before I force Jack to moon-form and skin him alive. Could always use a good fur for my new mansion. They gave me eighty million, you know. Technically, was only supposed to be seventy, but the last ten was a bonus. Said they thought you were all extinct."

Looking blindly at the werewolf, the dagger in her hand, Blaze fell to her knees in front of Amber.

"Poor birdy," Amber sneered, as Blaze numbly reached out for her. "Guess you just can't win, if you're stupi—"

Blaze rammed the dagger to the hilt in Amber's perfectly human eye.

Amber screamed and yanked her head away, her body going into a twitching, jerking, writhing mass of shaking muscle and bone, but she didn't die. The tears were warring with the dread blade, so Blaze retrieved it and did it again. And again. She stabbed the woman until her skull was a rotting, red-pink slurry and her body had stopped twitching. Then she dropped the blade beside the dead woman and stood, feeling the energy of the area pull to her, sealing the wound in her gut.

I'm sorry, she thought to the darkened world that now suffered for her survival. She felt the land her feather had touched wither, the leaves droop as she retrieved the energy she had left there, her very existence battling the burning black cancer in her abdomen. She formed it into a cocoon of liquid fire, then pushed it from her body, allowing it to spatter on the corpse beneath her feet.

Amber's body exploded in a blast of heat, charred muscles quickly giving way to bone, which simply disintegrated into ash. Watching it almost distantly, Blaze released her hold on the sun's light, allowing it to once more spread back outwards, touching the plants that now stood brown and desiccated, tenderly re-kindling the tiny sparks buried within.

A shadow moved in the yard before her, and Blaze felt it as a shifting in the balance of the sun, the placement of the rays as they bounced to Earth and then away again. She looked up.

A man was stalking towards her, low against the grass, rifle up, barrel aimed at her chest. She saw a flash, watched the sun play off of a lumpy metal pellet as it arced towards her, then watched as it became one with her body in a joyous exchange of molten energy. She closed her eyes. Felt the man's face as the sun's rays danced upon his cheekbones. Felt his dry lips twist in a smile. She bent the energy around her again, warping it inward, concentrating it into a single spot in the yard.

An instant later, she felt the sunlight dance joyfully across tiny bits of fluff that drifted on the wind. *So pretty*, Blaze thought. She followed it with her consciousness, admiring every rainbow facet of every particle of dust.

Another flash.

Eyes still closed, Blaze watched the metal arc, watched it hit and meld into the area between her ears. She followed it back to its source, found the sunlight playing upon the unnatural twists and bends of cloth in the woods, and focused the light again.

A tree caught fire beside the dancing wisps of dust. Blaze watched the flames course up the side of the birch, feeding on the resin-soaked bark. They grew as they climbed, increasing in strength and number until they had enveloped the upper branches, a massive bonfire in the withered leaves above.

Another shift in sunlight caught her attention, drawing it from the flames.

Cloth soaked up the sun in the yard. A man-beast watched her, in a half-crouch. He was covered in dancing, glistening blood. The light played off the crimson surface of it in rainbow patterns as it dribbled from his fingers and face, slicked across his clothes in shiny streaks. Odd bits of flesh here and there also played with the light, glinting, flashing in the sun. As did the creature's pretty green eyes.

Blaze closed her eyes, taking in the water glinting along the edges of his eyelids, feeling the light bounce across his lashes and sparkle on his blood-wetted cheeks. Eyes still closed, Blaze examined him, top to bottom, reveling in the light as it played across the gleaming fur along his shoulders and down his back. She caught the sun, caressed him with it, focused it…

After long minutes of that, the creature said, "Hey, sweetie, uh…" He cleared his throat with a nervous tremble. "Not to be a party-pooper or anything, but after watching Mumbo and Jumbo over there go War of the Worlds on me, that sorta makes me uncomfortable."

Blaze opened her eyes.

Jack was standing very still in the center of the yard, watching her like a mouse that wanted to run from a cat, but didn't want to provoke its attention, in case the cat had somehow missed his presence. "You, uh, all right over there, honey?" He licked his lips, slowly lowering the glittering steel handgun he carried to the ground at his feet and leaving it there, backing away, hands up. "Did Amber get away, then?"

"Amber's dead." Blaze startled herself at the raspy sound of her voice, almost windy, but with the hint of fire and coal. She swallowed at the cold that was even then tugging icy fingers through her head and chest. "My throat hurts."

"Okay, honey," Jack said, "I'm gonna come help you, okay?" Even at this distance, Blaze felt his fear down the link. Fear and an image of *fire?* A woman of molten *fire?*

"It's hard to breathe," Blaze managed, swallowing again. Ice lanced through her neck and down her spine. Then she frowned. She *wasn't* breathing. Not with her lungs. Her *body* was breathing, as it moved and twisted around her.

"I know, honey," Jack said, "It's gold. It's gonna do that. But right now, what I'd like to do is get your assurance you're not about to go nuclear on me or in any other way make this little wereverine's life unpleasant."

She dropped to her knees in the ash, whimpering.

After what looked like a moment of indecision, Jack took a hesitant step towards her. "Hey honey, you just sit tight, okay? I'm gonna help you."

"Then *help already*!" Blaze cried, falling to her hands and gripping at the warm gravel underneath the ash, fisting her hands around the stones. Her throat *hurt*, and it was spreading outward, like tendrils of blood-poisoning lacing up an infected limb. She lowered her forehead to the ash and moaned, breathing little swirls into the dust against her lips.

The sunlight moved gently as the wereverine lowered himself beside her, though he made no move to touch her. She could *feel* his awe. And his fear. Of *her*. The dismay of that was enough to wrack her soul.

"Please get it off," Blaze whimpered, unable to think of anything but the horrible, throbbing ice. Long heartbeats followed, each one dragging an agonizing streak of cold through her body. "Please, Jack."

She felt a burst of inner agony from Jack, shame and fear. "Okay," Jack said. Sunlight glinted off of his tongue as he licked his lips. "*Blaze*. Honey. You're just about cooking me alive as it is…you think you could tone it down a bit so I can lean in there and get a hold of that thing?" Indeed, through her new dance-of-light-sight, she saw his fur going up in little wisps of smoke, where it was exposed to her.

Blaze whimpered and shook her head. Streaks of liquid nitrogen were running down her spine, through her buttocks, throbbing into her legs, stabbing stakes through her toes.

"Fuck." Jack glanced at her, then at the shop. More indecision, more fear. "All right, tootz. Just stay here a second, okay?" He got to his feet again slowly, then backed up like she was some sort of wild bear that was gonna attack the moment he moved too suddenly or turned his back.

"*Get it off*!" Blaze sobbed at him. The thing around her neck was *eating* her, devouring her from the inside, swallowing her heat and leaving icy agony in its wake.

Jack jerked and ran.

He came back with a five gallon bucket of water and a wet rag. "You are not gonna like this," he muttered, "But I gotta do it." The water danced and glistened in the light, and the beauty of the glimmering surface inside the bucket was enough to distract Blaze from the ice in her veins for a few short—

Jack dumped the bucket on her.

As Blaze gasped at the glacial cold and felt herself bubble and steam with a horrible, *disgusting* wetness. As she let out her breath in a scream, Jack reached into the column of steam with his soggy rag, placed it around the metal ring in her neck, and, with a hand on either side, flexed his massive shoulders as he pulled.

She heard a metallic snap just as metal prongs pierced her skin, raking across her throat, and a simultaneous blast of ice shattered her system. Blaze shrieked and fell into a ball, coldness throbbing through her numbed skin, her hold on the world of sunlight slipped irrevocably from her grasp.

"That was it, sweetie," Jack said, throwing the metal band aside. "Worst is over, I swear." He was backing away from her, hands up, blood-crusted calluses facing out, panic racing down the link at her. "All done. Big bad wereverine is leaving, now. Okay? I'm just backing off, so no need to get disagreeable. Got it?"

The ice was receding slowly, giving her a peek back into the realm of sunlight as it went.

Jack, true to his word, left her alone. She could feel his body bending the sunlight a couple miles distant, drifting through the woods in a wide, agitated circle.

Blaze lay on her side for the next hour or two, drifting in and out of body-consciousness, reveling in her senses as she felt the sunlight tumble to the earth nearby. It played upon the world around her in showers of rainbow color, skipping across the rotor blades, bounding over the tin roofs of the lodge and the shop, waltzing through the brown and withered leaves of her mango and cherry trees, sliding through the jittery rainbow crystals littering the ground around her.

Blaze soaked it all up in amazement. Eventually, her awareness sharpened enough to notice two holes in the sunlight, two rips where the energy simply disappeared, leaving no trace.

Lifting her head to look, Blaze saw the two golden pieces that Jack had torn from her neck. About the thickness of an orange peel, Blaze winced at the tiny, pin-sized metal barbs ringing the inner band. They only extended an eighth of an inch from the band itself, barely enough to make her bleed, yet the *cold* she remembered…It had been overwhelming.

Then she had a new thought. The coldness at her throat was *gone*. She was *free*.

Buoyed by that realization, she felt her body shifting, fire rippling outward, stretching into long, rolling filaments down her arms, down her tail.

Her…*tail*?

The woodpile beside her lit up in shimmer of light as Blaze twisted her head over her shoulder to look, spreading the long, diamond-shaped hackle-feathers on her neck.

…*hackle-feathers*? Blaze blinked at that. Under the rolling waves of fire, she had *feathers*. Tentatively, she spread her wings, almost twelve feet in either direction, and marveled at the red-orange-yellow flicker, the flames dancing upon every curve. She made a tentative flap of her wings, saw the fire course outward and engulf the woodpile. She giggled, watching it lick up the eave-supports, dancing against the roof.

Turning, she looked out over the yard. Her animals were hiding in clumps against the barn, as far away from her and the helicopter as they could get. Immediately upon seeing the open space of the lawn and the pasture beyond, Blaze's heart leapt. *Fly*, a part of her sang. *Spread your wings*. And, instinctively, she started hopping, wings out, pummeling the air, aiming for the treetops.

Almost immediately, she was airborne, gliding over the first pasture fence, setting it ablaze beneath her. Gravity, she found, didn't seem to tug at her as it had before, and all she really needed was the thought of *up* and she was soaring. She slammed her wings in glee anyway, rising above the open ground, climbing, veering in a half-circle, spiraling above the Sleeping Lady, joy rising in her like an ocean, flooding all of her senses as long tendrils of sunfire twisted and undulated in the air current behind her, caressed by her flight. She felt the sun racing through her feathers, felt her energy spread outward, infusing the land, and laughed. It came out as an eagle's scream.

Startled by that, Blaze let out a nervous little giggle, which translated as a smoky chirp. All around her, the sunlight rippled and played on melting snow, on trees, on ice, and she could feel it *all.* The further up she went, the more she could feel. Happiness lifting her in a tide, the Sleeping Lady's green cluster of roofs growing smaller and more distant, Blaze soared away from Lake Ebony, gaining loft, aiming for the sun.

She surged upwards, until the sky became darker and darker blue, and then black and filled with stars, a wispy blue haze in any direction—through the *atmosphere*, Blaze thought, startled. Her fires had dimmed, now, but she continued to soak in the light of Sol, every feather glowing like it was made of liquid sunfire. Turning, she looked down at the Earth, spinning beneath her.

Like a cerulean gemmed globe, it twisted against a backdrop of stars, taking her breath away.

Oh wow, Blaze thought. On a whim, she decided to start following the curve of the Earth, seeking out that hemispherical shadow that cast half the world in darkness. Awestruck at the way the Earth itself seemed to disappear against the backdrop of the Universe, Blaze ducked down to flit with the enormous shadow. Taking great joy in the breathtaking beauty below, dancing across the land that was even then meeting that stunning half-light of dusk, Blaze was completely unprepared for the way her wings suddenly abandoned her the moment she submerged herself in the darkness of night.

Like a meteor plummeting back to Earth, Blaze screamed and flailed in the horrifying fall that followed. Blaze had a brief, sickening moment of realizing she was *not* going to be able to stop, then her rational side kicked into gear. She tucked her arms and tilted her body and tried desperately to aim herself for a large, moonlit lake that was growing bigger by the second, frantically thinking that water would be an easier impact.

She didn't make the water. The last thing she thought before she impacted the sandy *bank* of a continental lake was the disgusted realization that she had missed the water by four feet.

Blaze woke sometime later as the foreign land—she thought China??—waited in strange, total darkness around her. Unlike springtime in Alaska, the darkness of midnight here was all-consuming, utterly complete. She felt it closing in around her like a void, and it left her feeling numb. Groaning, Blaze lifted her head. She had hit hard enough to put a three-foot-deep human-shaped impression in the ground, into which ran a trickle of water from the nearby lake.

The first thing Blaze realized, once she regained consciousness, was that she was remarkably still alive, and, from the looks of things, relatively unscathed. The second thing that came to her attention was just how much space-to-ground impacts *hurt*. Like flinging oneself in front of a Mack truck, taking every one of the massive sets of double-wheels down the spine, then pausing so the driver could hit reverse.

"Oowwww," Blaze managed, as water started sizzling over her body, surging upwards in pillars of steam all around her, draining her energy into a golden puddle around her.

Draining her…energy?

Blaze sat up with a groan, surprised she was able to sit up. Sure enough, the water around her knees was shimmering like sunlight itself, and she suddenly wasn't feeling so good. Her whole body was a bone-deep ache, she realized, that had nothing to do with the fact she'd just plummeted from the stratosphere like a six-foot-four meteor, and had *everything* to do with the way the water was glowing brighter and brighter gold around her feet.

Weakly, Blaze crawled out of the hole she'd made and slumped to the ground beside it, peering in a daze over the edge as more water rushed in from the lake, diluting the golden glow, which was even then lighting up the dark lakeshore around her brighter than the moon overhead.

Even more disorienting, bolstering the light cast off by the glowing puddle was her *hair*. Even now, Blaze was actually having trouble seeing *past* her hair, because it was floating around her head like little orange neon tendrils, making it hard for her eyes to focus to the darkness beyond. Brushing her hair out of her eyes, Blaze tried again to regrow her wings.

Nothing. Just frustrating emptiness, and a world that no longer sang to her with light.

It was then that Blaze realized how alone she really was. And, she knew, this time it had been of her *own* making.

"Jack," she whispered, shivering as the heat of her re-entry started to bleed off of her, leaving her exposed to the chilly air.

Thousands of miles away, the wereverine was well out of range to tell her everything was going to be okay.

Naked, cold, stranded on some unknown lake on an unknown continent, Blaze forced herself up into a seated position and dragged her knees up to her chest, biting her lip back against tears as she glanced at the alien foliage around her, trying not to think of what could be lurking in the forest, watching the glowy Scottish chick that had just plummeted out of the ozone layer. She would *not* cry. She would *not* leave herself helpless in the wilderness.

But it was hard when she was feeling a wall of grief from the link.

Jack, Blaze thought, anguished. He thought she had abandoned him.

And…she had. Just like he had feared, just like he had told her when he laid his heart bare. He had *told* her that the first thing he thought she would do when she took back her feather was grow wings and fly away and leave the cranky little wereverine to putter around in the woods alone. She had assured him, repeatedly, that she wouldn't. That she would stay with him. That she would never leave him.

But she *had*. Without even *thinking*.

She just, she realized in agony, hadn't *thought*. There was no *thought*. It had just been joy. Fiery, passionate *joy*. Feeling the sunlight around her, bounding upon the land, it had taken every care and swept it completely from her mind, leaving her bathing in *joy*, in *creation*. Her every movement had been one of awe and respect for the life around her, for the dance of light playing across the world. She just hadn't *thought.* And now Jack was suffering for it.

Ashamed, Blaze looked up at the moon and listened to the strange sounds of insects around her, feeling Jack's grief over the link.

Jack, I'm so sorry, she thought. *I'll be back. Please understand...*

The torment on the other side never ebbed.

• • •

Jack watched the phoenix rise and depart, and his stomach twisted on itself as he felt the link sail away with her. Groaning, he sank to his ass in the slush, despair clawing gashes through his chest as he stared at the vanishing orange blot on the sapphire sky.

Stupid. He had been so *stupid.* He'd sealed the link, knowing *full well* she wasn't going to hang around. That Blaze didn't understand how permanent it was. That she was going to someday grow wings and fly away.

Above him, he heard her shriek, felt the blast of overwhelming joy down the connection before it was once more muted by distance.

Stupid. Just a lonely, foolish, cracked little crankcase, trying to hoard the Hope Diamond.

Out in the yard, his eyes located the stripe of lawn and fencing she had set afire in passing. Beyond that, he saw flames crawling up the side of the shop, weaving through the woodpile.

She set the shop on fire and she doesn't even care, he thought, as a greater wave of despair sank in his gut. He had *felt* that joy, that freedom. She wasn't coming back. She didn't *need* to. She could go *anywhere.*

He watched the flames lick at the tin roof, climbing slowly over the pile of wood under the eaves, towards the rest of the structure. All that remained of his mate, Jack realized in misery, was a cluster of frightened animals, an abandoned lodge, and a smoldering woodpile. Jack couldn't find the strength to stand, so he let it burn.

All the years of hardening himself, all the decades of trying to prevent his heart from opening up to another girl, all of his attempts to keep Blaze at bay, and here he was watching her soar away, leaving the stupid, hairy little wereverine to guard his lonely little patch of woods on his own.

Jack watched the flames lick up the eaves of the shop, up the rafters, towards the main structure. His chest was in anguish, each breath unbearable. He watched the fire spread from afar, not really able to bring himself to care, yet some distant, practical part of him knowing he had to *do* something.

Somehow, Jack dragged himself slowly to his feet, not bothering to brush the slushy snow from his shredded pant legs as he stood. It was more out of a reluctance to see something useful burn than any real hope that the phoenix would ever return that Jack went to the pile of wood crackling under the eaves and swatted the whole thing out into the half-melted lawn, then spread it around until the fire went out. Then he grabbed the bucket, went to the spigot, filled the bucket, and doused the tentative flames under the eaves that were even then sputtering, without the heat of the woodpile to keep them growing.

Then, tossing the bucket aside, he went to the lumber-pile under a tarp behind the gas shed, yanked the plastic back, drew out a couple nice four-by-fours, and carried them into his shop. Getting out his tape, Jack marked the boards to the proper length, cut them, drilled the bolt-holes, and carried them out to the fence with a wrench. Dropping them at his feet, he un-bolted the charred remains of the fence, tossed the blackened chunks aside, and began installing the new pieces.

Once the fence was repaired, Jack stood there. He watched the animals milling. Smelled the charred wood and the blood. He looked down at the wrench in his hand, then over at the dark and quiet lodge, then up at the empty sky. From his location, he could see the slim edge of a rotor-blade, sticking past the front wall of the lodge. A single black body lay in the yard, a few hundred feet away, the snow smeared with red.

Dropping the wrench onto the ground, he went to fire up the bulldozer.

He bulldozed a brand new pasture out in the woods, then got the backhoe and dug a huge trench. A distant, detached part of himself then dragged all the bodies to the massive trough in the earth and threw them inside. After that, he began carefully dismantling the helicopter, taking it apart, piece-by-piece. He found the two trapped fey-lords that had been powering the rotors, forced into a kind of stasis in an enchanted box in the ceiling, drained for their magics. When the tall, slender, too-pale fey tentatively sat up from the box, holding their arms up to shield the light, babbling their gratitude in their silver tongues, Jack told them to get the fuck off of his property. He drained all the fluids from the helicopter's engine and put them in buckets in the shop, to be disposed of later. He then dumped every particle of the Inquisition, from the guns to the headsets to the rotor blades, into the pit, and covered it all up with the bulldozer.

It was well past dark by the time he was finished. Still in that thoughtless fugue, Jack shut off the bulldozer, right on top of the pit, and went back inside the Sleeping Lady, ignoring the scattered firewood and the smell of char as he passed. He went and lay down and spent several hours staring at the ceiling, smelling her in the pillows, the blankets, the sheets, the *walls*…

Jack got up and went out into the dark and fed the animals. Most never even stirred from their slumber as he dumped buckets of fruit and grain into their troughs, instead of the scoops that they were accustomed to. He let one drowsy-looking goat eat out of his hand for a few minutes, then went to the shop and started the generator. He sat there, watching the little lights on the inverters, until one switched to FLOAT, then shut the generator off. When he stepped back outside, dawn was rising on the horizon. Seeing the first rays of sunlight dancing on the treetops, Jack swiped his arm across his eyes, then started out towards the greenhouse.

A glint of light-eating black lay in the fluff of ash outside the shop door. He hesitated, then bent and retrieved the dread horn. He watched the shadows drip from its curves, falling to the ground like black dye through water. His hand fisted around it and he carried it to the greenhouse with him. He still had to pick fruit. Blaze always picked fruit in the morning, because if she didn't, they would fall off and start to rot on the ground by midday, with more growing to take their place.

Jack stepped inside the greenhouse, dropped the dread horn on the nearest bench, yanked the door shut, grabbed a bucket, and went to start picking. He hadn't gone more than three steps before he stopped and stared at the wilted, ruined fruit trees. Dead. Leaves brown and twisted. Because she'd *gone*. Because she'd yanked her energy from the land and *left*. Unable to avoid it any longer, Jack sank to the bench and let the tears come.

• • •

As dawn rolled over the pretty blue waters of the foreign lake, Blaze breathed a horrible sob of relief when the first rays touched her body and she found she could spread her wings again. Excitement once more bubbling up from within, she leapt into the air to again seek out the sun, setting more trees on fire in her passing. She pounded upwards, gleeful, spiraling into the deepest blue of the sky, feeling the brilliant rays of sunlight dancing all around her, flitting upon the ground in perfect harmony—

Misery.

It was like a cold punch to her gut, making her fires flicker, her wingbeats stumble. Blaze gasped at the horrible feeling in her chest, unable to place where it could be coming from when she was so *happy*, so *free*...

And then, in one horrible rush of understanding over the ecstasy of power, Blaze remembered. *Jack*. She had *left* him. Even then, when she concentrated, she could feel the despair on his end, the hopelessness leaking down the link, curdling in her gut, hollowing out her heart.

Oh God, Jack...Blaze thought, guilt sinking like a stone in her stomach. She spun, then, and with more speed than a *jet*, she arced back across the sky, flame billowing behind her like the tail of a comet, plummeting across the sapphire planet, towards the cluster of green roofs and the source of that link, growing stronger with every moment, the despair growing into anguish, desolation, despondency so powerful she felt it hard to fly those last few feet towards him.

Her shift back to human occurred naturally, not really a conscious push, but more of an idea that took form, borne of desire. Then she was running, surging towards the greenhouse, where she could *feel* him, a welling of such grief that she was choking back tears.

"Jack!" she cried, flinging the door open.

The wereverine was seated on the bench, the tip of the dread horn resting against the muscle of his chest. He jerked and blinked up at her, a wash of startlement flooding the link.

"Oh my God, Jack!" Panic powering her, now, Blaze rushed up, grabbed the tip of the dread horn and wrenched it from his hands. Then, as he stared at her in open shock, she took an end of the dagger in either hand and snapped it over her knee. Even as the blackness of the horn was fading, leaving a pearly white luminescence in its wake, she focused everything she had on the broken blade, dissolving it into dust. "You fucking *asshole*!" she blurted, in rage borne of terror. Gasping in relief and shame and *horror*, Blaze threw the fistful of ashes aside and dropped into Jack's embrace, wrapping her arms around the wereverine's thick neck, her breasts tight against his chest.

"I'm here," she whimpered. "I'm so sorry, Jack."

She knelt in front of him for several minutes before she felt his hands tentatively reach up and touch her hair. Over the mating connection, she felt *awe*. "Pretty," Jack whispered. She heard his voice catch in a sob.

Blinking back tears, Blaze pulled back far enough to see what he was talking about. He held a wisp of her hair, floating like liquid sunlight in the air around her, staring at it dumbstruck. Then, slowly, he turned to face her, and Blaze saw the tears in his eyes, felt the disbelief as if it were her own. "Why?" he asked, softly.

"Because it was *evil*," she growled, preparing for a fight. She knew as she was doing it that Jack would take offense to losing such a valuable treasure, but at this point, she didn't care. "It caused too many problems. I wasn't going to have that disgusting thing on my land, ever again." *And because you almost rammed it into your chest, you stupid bastard,* she thought.

"I wasn't talking about…" the wereverine swallowed, then wiped his face with a sleeve, peering back at her with a confused emerald gaze. "*Your* land?"

"*My* land," Blaze repeated. "I've got a safety-deposit box that says so."

For a long time, the wereverine simply stared back at her, something between disbelief, shock, and deep, unending love and gratitude washing over her from him. Then, almost tentatively, he said, "I don't really see how a slip of paper does you much good out here, tootz."

Blaze smiled at him, reveling in his love, his heartbeat. "I'm sure we can work something out."

That slow, predatory smile spread over Jack's face, and he eased slowly out of the bench, pulling her up with him. "I think we got something else to work out, first." And then he *flung* her over his shoulder and stalked off to the Sleeping Lady, and Blaze found out what it was *really* like to get taken by a wereverine.

That night, they retreated to the front porch to watch the sky, wrapped in a blanket. Blaze was soaking up Jack's presence, idly watching her glowing wisps of hair burn against the springtime half-light as they floated around her face, when the wereverine spoke.

"So," Jack said, shifting where he held her, "What the hell were they thinking?"

Blaze glanced up at his face, confused. "Who?"

"Amber," Jack growled. "Why'd they *stab* you with it? They could've used it to hold you, make you sing like a freakin' canary for the rest of your damned life."

"I took it from Amber and stabbed myself," Blaze said, cuddling into his arms.

Jack took a moment to digest that. "Hope ya got a spare set of contacts," he said gruffly. "'Cause you burned the last set."

She grinned up at him. "Yeah, well, you look funny bald."

"Then next time," Jack muttered against her ear, "maybe you'd like to avoid setting me on fire."

Next time. Blaze considered that. "So where are we gonna go now?"

"Excuse me?" Jack asked.

She gestured to the lodge, and the place where the helicopter had landed in the front yard. "They found me."

"Good for them," Jack said. "Remind me to send condolences to their kinfolk."

Blaze pulled away a bit, frowning up at him. "You don't think they'll be back? Isn't that a bit…" She sought out a way to put it delicately, so as not to offend the wereverine's prickly pride, "…overly optimistic?" She frowned, trying to remember. "Aside from Amber, I only killed two of them." She couldn't *remember* the helicopter taking off, but it was no longer in the *yard*, so she knew they were in trouble.

"Oh, they might," Jack agreed. "But I sputched them all and buried their chopper. Might make the others think twice."

"You *buried* the *chopper*?" Blaze cried, stunned. She glanced back at the forest, and suddenly, the bulldozer on that flat new piece of pasture had a more sinister purpose. She tried not to think of how many dead people were now buried on her land, feeding her trees.

He gave her a vicious smile. "'Sides. They get too many ideas, I might start mounting heads on the roof, so they get a good look at their predecessors before they decide to land. This is *my* land, and I'm gonna fight for it."

Blaze grimaced. "I don't think so." Then something troubling occurred to her. "Why were you gone so long? On your trip to your place?"

Jack shrugged. "Kept catching a whiff of something, here and there, so I decided I needed to get out of sight. Turns out, they were sneaking up for an ambush."

Blaze placed the flat of her hand against his chest and pushed him back until she could look directly into his face. "You used me as *bait*?"

"I had things under control, honey." And the pride that flowed off of him at that point made her realize that he did, in fact, think that he'd had the entire situation under control, from Ground Zero.

"Men in *combat gear* dropped from the *sky* and *assaulted me*," Blaze cried, feeling the fire in her veins glowing a little hotter.

"All part of the plan," Jack said. "I had to wait for the helicopter. Knew they were gonna try to pack you out of here somehow, but didn't wanna play all my cards until they put theirs on the table." He shrugged. "Once they landed, I just gutted them. Ripped up the inside of the chopper getting at the pilot. Bent a couple rotor blades. Took out the rest on my way around to find you."

He used her as bait. The *bastard.* Narrowing her eyes, she said, "And what would you have done when Amber decided to stab you?"

Jack snorted. "This ol' moon-kissed blacksmith didn't get old by being stupid. I was gonna shoot her. From a distance. Had a rifle all set up in the woods, just waitin. Decided maybe you ain't had such a bad idea in that respect, after all—one poke of a dread horn was enough, thank you." Then he kissed her forehead and rumbled, "But then I saw Mumbo and Jumbo kinda explode like the bags on a vacuum-cleaner and decided maybe toting a gun through the woods at that point wasn't such a hot idea."

Blaze frowned, trying to remember. "Vacuum cleaner bags?"

Jack peered at her. "The two blokes who shot you?"

She vaguely remembered the light glinting off of metal as it sped through the air before melting into her body. "Uh…" She swallowed, looking down at her naked body. "I was *shot*?" Then something more pressing occurred to her, remembering the brown leaves of the greenhouse. "The feather…" she managed. "It killed everything when they dug it out?"

"No," Jack said, "Now that I think about it, I'd imagine *you* did that, when you were making people explode like little puff-balls." He pushed a glowing strand of hair that had floated into his face back and tucked it down around her ear. "It's something you birds can do, if you get desperate. Whatever magic you put into the land, you can take it back out and use it, if you need to."

Blaze remembered how the world had dimmed as she'd fought the necromancy of the dagger, remembered the brown, wilted plants in the greenhouse, then swallowed. "Are my trees dead?"

"Uh," Jack said, wincing. "Well, let me put it to you this way, tootz. I think it's gonna be a couple months until you're eating mangoes again."

But when she concentrated, Blaze could feel the tremulous threads of life, tentatively working their way back up the roots snuggled within the earth. "It'll be sooner than that," she said.

Jack cleared his throat awkwardly. "So…uh…talking about *eating*, I was kinda thinkin' 'bout pork, though I wouldn't be too opposed to taking a yak to the front firepit and spit-roasting it. Expended a lot of energy ripping heads off yesterday. Figured your pet wereverine should get a treat, right?" He sounded almost…hopeful.

He's asking permission to eat one of my yaks, Blaze thought, a little stunned. Since when did the crabby little asshole ask permission to do *anything*? She peered at him until he started to fidget under her stare. Finally, Blaze said, "You're afraid I'm gonna set you on fire."

"You already did it once," Jack growled, on a wave of embarrassment. Then, quickly, "And I'm not afraid of anything. Just bein' polite." He sniffed and glanced over at the bulldozer as if he found the machine infinitely more interesting than her face. "Guess I could go eat a Thanksgiving or two. Maybe a Christmas. Got enough of the bloody things running around."

"Yak sounds great," Blaze said, not really wanting to see what 'or two' meant, in Wereverine. She was pretty sure, in his current state, he could decimate what was left of her flock in a matter of hours. "You sputch all my chickens and you're gonna find out what it's like to be dominated by an Amazon."

Jack grinned down at her, and she felt another rush of wereverine happiness swallow her in a warm embrace. He bent down and kissed her, long and hard, and then, just when Blaze's lungs were screaming for air, he released her and pecked her forehead. "Thanks for coming back, tootz."

THIRTY-TWO

Kimber

Breakup came and went, and by the time Blaze and Jack had to go to town to make her first loan payment scheduled for April 26th, the neighbors were already commenting about how the snow seemed to be melting faster this year, and how the grass was already starting to pop up under the trees and along the south face of buildings. For her part, Blaze would have *preferred* to go to town herself, simply due to the fact that she didn't think the wereverine had enough experience with bureaucracy not to go slitty-eyed and furry on a bank teller, but Jack was absolutely adamant in going with her. Wearing chainmail. And swords. And an *axe*. And *two* Desert Eagles. He *would* be staying in the car.

At least he looks the part, Blaze thought, considering her far-future plans of a renaissance resort, once they had the Sleeping Lady making money in other areas.

It was the morning of April 22nd, and Blaze was at the edge of Lake Ebony, leaning against the four-wheeler at with Jack, waiting for Bruce Rogers to arrive to fly them to Willow, trying not to bite down the urge to *once again* ask Jack to at least leave the swords behind. Finally, though, the pressure became inescapable. After scuffing her boot and twiddling her thumbs and fidgeting with her shirt, she blurted, "What's an Alaska State Trooper gonna think, flying down the road, look over, and see this guy bristling with antique weaponry?"

"Should I add another katana?" Jack said, over crossed arms. She felt his amusement and knew he'd been watching her…and had absolutely no sympathy for her point of view. At current count, she saw six swords, a massive greenish axe, a dozen daggers, a couple *hatchets*… He'd added the axe after she had complained the first time, the hatchets when she complained the second.

"I can't *begin* to describe to you how unnecessary that all is," Blaze gritted. "You're gonna be a walking neon sign that says, 'I'm a freak, stare at me.'"

"I've got another scimitar, too." He patted the curved scabbard at his hip.

Blaze twitched and tore her eyes away from the hairy medieval weapons-rack and peered out at the lake. "Swans are back," she growled, finding the clusters of white dots out against the far shore.

"Might have to cook us up one of those, when we get back," Jack said.

"Swans are *protected*," Blaze repeated, for the thousandth time. Jack, who seemed to have a penchant for swan, simply did not seem to understand the concept behind the Migratory Bird Conservation Act. Conservation, to Jack, seemed to involve stuffing half a goat inside her refrigerator, to save it for later.

"You'll have to grow me some swans. I like swan."

Considering that an adult swan cost somewhere between five hundred to a thousand dollars, *before* the four hundred dollars'-worth of shipping across the continent to Alaska, and considering that Jack could probably eat four of them in a sitting, Blaze told him he could wait.

Jack was doing an excellent job of pouting about her 'lack of culinary compassion' when an ebony shape the size of a very large dog slid out of the woods nearby and began approaching the two of them at a wary stride. Nearby, a much bigger, very *black* man appeared, leaning against a tree near the boat dock, muscular arms crossed over his chest, violet eyes watching the whole situation from afar.

"Oh shit," Blaze whispered, touching his arm. "Jack." Seeing the wolf smoothly shift upwards into a tiny, wretchedly-thin Arabic woman, she suddenly didn't begrudge Jack his swords at all.

"I'll take care of this, sweetie," Jack growled, putting his hand on the hilt of a katana with that gut-deep surge of fierce protective fire that Blaze had come to learn was *not* going away, despite the fact that she had spent a morning growing wings and exploding armed men like vacuum-cleaner bags. And, in this case, Blaze was grateful for that. Bank tellers, Blaze could handle. Angry werewolves and giant men who vanished in a blink of an eye, she could not.

Jack stepped smoothly forward, putting his body between Blaze and the approaching wolf. They waited for the tiny Arabic woman to get within speaking distance, then the little woman stopped, a good twenty feet off, looking at Jack cautiously.

"You're on land that don't belong to you," Jack said, in a low rumble.

Almost tentatively, the wolf said, "'Aqrab tells me the Fourth Lander awakened."

"Don't see how that's any of your business," Jack offered.

Kimber glanced back at the huge, mostly-naked man looming in the woods behind her. "My servant and I...We've discussed it at length. We would like to stay and help you protect the Fourth-Lander."

Jack laughed. "You mean you're starving and you noticed a bit of extra meat runnin' around and you thought we'd be stupid enough to throw you a bone." Jerking a thumb over his shoulder, he said, "Take your slave, pack your shit, and hit the road," Jack growled, "'Fore I decide to find out what you taste like, bitch."

Courteous, lovable old Jack. Blaze wanted to strangle him. Even as Kimber's face was darkening in a mixture of humiliation and fury, both her and her 'slave' turning to leave, Blaze stepped in front of the wereverine and said, "Hold on."

The werewolf hesitated, her back to them. Then, slowly, she turned back to face Blaze.

"You…want to stay?" Blaze said.

Kimber gave her an analyzing look, then the Arabic woman shook her head and said, "It's not to be. If the weasel is opposed to the idea, we don't want to make the youngling uncomfortable." She turned to go again. In the trees, the black man vanished.

"*Fuck* the weasel for a moment," Blaze cried, stopping Kimber in her tracks, knowing that she was about to disappear forever. "You want to stay? *Here*?"

"Of course they do," Jack snarled. "*Look* at her. Without her pack to help her hunt, the runt is starving. They've got a phoenix in the neighborhood, game is scarce, and she thinks I'm gonna let her go hunting on my land."

"It's *my* land," Blaze said, without looking at him. Tentatively, she said, "Your name is Kimber, right?"

The wolf, who had been watching the exchange with intelligent brown eyes, inclined her head slightly.

"You know how to make beds, Kimber?"

"Oh *fuck* no!" Jack roared, jumping between them again. "You have three perfectly good candidates waiting in town for their interviews. I will *not* have a wolf in my house."

"Good thing the Sleeping Lady isn't *your* house, then, isn't it?" Blaze said, without taking her eyes off the wolf. To Kimber, she said, "The Sleeping Lady is mine. I was just about to fly to town to hire a helper or two for the summer. Would you like me to cancel the interviews? I'd be happy to keep it local."

The little woman licked her lips and glanced at Jack, who was even then beginning to emanate a low, chest-rattling snarl. She saw the debate in the woman's liquid brown eyes, the desperation, the nervousness there.

"Jack," Blaze said calmly, "Remember the vacuum-cleaner bags."

The wereverine's growl cut off in a strangled sound. For a long moment, Jack glared at Blaze, then at Kimber, then back at Blaze, and she felt fear, mixing with anxiety, mixing with that hot, protective *need* in his gut. Finally, he threw up his hands in disgust. "Okay, tootz." He was talking to Kimber. "But if either you or your slave so much as *touches* her, you and I are gonna go toe-to-toe, and I fought plenty of magi in my life. You'd die like the rest of 'em."

Kimber's face twisted and her eyes began to glow yellow. "The moment I blithely take threats from a *man* is the moment I cut off my—"

"Just hold on!" Blaze cried, getting between them again. "Okay, Kimber. I wanted to thank you for helping me. You saved my life back there, when I was too tired to move because I'd just carried *Jack* through the *woods*." She said the last with a pointed look at Jack before turning back to the wolf. Blaze had an innate people-sense, and she suddenly found herself *desperate* to help this woman. Something told her that there was something much deeper going on, some inner working that had the little Arabic woman on the very brink. She racked her brain looking for something to offer her to smooth over Jack's insult. Knowing the way the Third Lander in Jack seemed to be appeased with food, she blurted, "We all know I've got lots of food. You're hungry? I can make you something to eat."

She saw the twitch in the woman's face. The pride. The indecision. The *need*. Then the woman's eyes once more found Jack and her face twisted. "I don't need—"

"She's starving," a deep voice boomed from the air beside her. Blaze froze, seeing no one nearby, then gasped and stumbled backwards when Jack snarled and shoved her out of the way just in time for a huge, shimmery black shape to appear before them like a heat-wave, glaring down at Jack. "The weasel wasn't far off," the huge African man said, his arms crossed over his chest as he peered unconcernedly down at Jack, who had sprouted fangs and fur and had a rippling blade in his taloned hands, its razor point aimed at the black man's massive chest. "My mistress is unable to kill."

Jack suddenly stopped snarling. His head twisted to look at the woman, whose face reddened and she looked away, hands fisted at her sides. His brown and gold fur slipped back under his skin and he straightened, blinking. "Oh," Jack said. And, for the first time, he looked speechless, glancing from the wolf to the big black Houdini and back. "*Oh.*" He swallowed, hard, and Blaze saw sympathy in his face.

"I was cursed," the woman muttered, lowering her head to look at her feet. "Long ago." Her eyes flickered towards her huge companion before drifting away again. "I would eat whatever you deemed worthy to give me."

Pausing to give the black man a long look, Jack reluctantly slid the sword back into its sheath. She felt a wash of wariness from him, anxious and tingling, along with a distinct band of dislike for the black man. Dislike and…fear?

Buoyed by Jack's anxiety, Blaze found herself peering up at the huge African man nervously. While Blaze knew she was big, this man stood at seven feet, if he were an inch. There was something *familiar* about him, too, something tingling at the back of her memory that prickled the hairs on her neck and left her ill-at-ease…"Uh…" She licked her lips. "Do I know you?"

The man smiled slowly, showing brilliant white teeth that contrasted sharply with the ebony of his face. "You know of my kind," the man said, still grinning. He almost sounded…shy? "Or you doubtless did, at one time. My kinfolk rule the Fourth Lands, much as the dragons rule the First."

Fourth Lands. Runt had said something about that. "Fey?" Blaze asked tentatively.

"Fey are Second Landers," Kimber said softly. "He's what's called a 'djinni.' A flame-demon." She cocked her head slightly, searching Blaze's face, and added, "He hails from your homeland."

A *flame demon.* And good ol' Jack had tried to pick a fight. No *wonder* the wereverine was giving him a wide berth. Blaze swallowed, looking up at the man. "Uh, okay. Are you hungry, too?"

The African man beamed at the question. "Actually, I am famished for a taste of home." For a paranoid moment, Blaze thought he was going to do something horrible, like grow fangs and chew on her head, but he and Kimber just stood there, casting nervous glances at the wereverine, waiting.

Realizing that the three of them were waiting for *her* to say something, Blaze cleared her throat. "Uh," Blaze said, glancing up the four-wheeler trail, trying to decide if she had time to stay another day or two before heading to the bank. "I gotta make a quick trip to town to buy groceries and do some banking. Wanna come along? I'll treat you to Subway or something."

Immediately, Kimber flinched, suspicion suddenly clear and tight on her face.

"My mistress will not fly in a beast of *steel*," the djinni snorted. As if there were some better way to fly.

"Technically, it's aluminum," Jack said. But he was watching Kimber all-too-closely, now, and Blaze felt the strange tingle of curiosity rolling down the link.

Kimber shot the black man a glare. "I'm sorry," she gritted, returning her attention to Blaze, "I think I made a mistake, coming to you. We will leave now. Our welfare is none of your concern."

"No, wait!" Blaze cried, digging for her new phone. "I'll call Bruce. Postpone my departure a couple days. Get you guys situated." She knew that, even if she by some miracle convinced Jack to stay behind and 'settle them in,' she couldn't leave the two of them alone here with the wereverine while she went off to run errands in Anchorage. She might as well turn on all the burners on the propane stove, empty a few drums of gas on the living-room floor, and stick a sock in the toaster to smolder a little bit while she was gone.

Jack, for his part, only grunted. Some part of the conversation seemed to have made him relax a bit, though he was still giving the djinni wary glances, and still kept his body physically between Blaze and their visitors.

Kimber also seemed to settle just a bit, and both the werewolf and the djinni watched her as she dialed the number to Rogers' Flying Service and rescheduled her flight for two days later.

"Okay everybody," Blaze said, ending the call and lowering the phone. "Come on. Let's go back up to the lodge." She started up the 4-wheeler trail that wound up the hill, but stopped when she realized no one was following her. Seeing the two newcomers facing off the wereverine, Blaze had a sudden surge of panic. *Oh God, Jack, please don't turn this into a fight...*She was nonetheless frozen in place, knowing that, at this point, she needed to let the three of them come to their own understanding, and that trying to heavy-handedly defuse the situation would only make it explode.

Kimber remained where she stood, giving Jack a long, analyzing look—the look of a wary cat. Finally, softly, she said, "May 'Aqrab and I pass, Shadowkiller?"

Jack sniffed, rubbed a hairy arm across his nose, then squinted at her. Snorting, he tilted his head and looked up at the nearest tree-top as if it had something incredibly interesting in it, then wrinkled his nose again and glanced at the muddy stones at his feet. "You the Blade o' Morning?" he finally asked.

Kimber froze, paling. She swallowed, hard, and started to back up.

"Just checkin'," Jack said. "Not a big deal." He gestured at the djinni. "You got the gorilla under control?"

Kimber had stopped backing away, though she was still pale. "Thoroughly." It came out as a hoarse whisper. Even as she said as much, a look of pain crossed the black man's face before he simply vanished.

Jack grunted. He sniffed again and glanced out over the lake. Then he glanced down at his foot and dug his boot into the muck of the lakebed. Very reluctantly, he muttered, "You like goat?"

"You have my oath that I will do everything in my power to protect the phoenix." It sounded...desperate. And the woman, Blaze realized, was trembling, her arms much too thin, her legs almost emaciated.

"I don't know about staying, but we'll get you something to eat," Jack said gruffly.

Blaze saw the disappointment in the werewolf's eyes, the hopeless depression at Jack's words. *She's looking for a home*, Blaze realized. *She needs help.*

Oblivious, Jack gestured at the 4-wheeler. "Take a seat. I'll drive you up."

The werewolf stiffened, eyes locked on the red padded seat of the four-wheeler.

Immediately, the air above Jack's head growled, "My mistress does not touch beasts of metal and coal, Third Lander." Like Jack had asked her to smear excrement upon herself and dance naked under a full moon, chanting Voodoo curses.

Jack snorted and opened his mouth, and before he could say something rude, Blaze blurted, "That's all right. We need to leave it down here to collect groceries when we get back from town, anyway. We can walk up. Get you guys settled in."

Very slowly, Jack and Kimber both turned to her. She saw the indecision in Jack's face, felt his frustration, then he just shrugged and started walking towards her. Blaze let him take the lead, falling back to walk beside Kimber, the huge African man drifting in and out of the woods off to the side.

"So, uh," Blaze said gingerly as they walked, "how long has it been since you had something to eat, Kimber?"

The werewolf glanced at her, brown eyes nervous. "I found a dead rodent on Monday," Kimber managed. Indeed, it looked like she was having trouble keeping her balance. Ahead of them, Jack glanced back with a look of...*concern*?

"Jesus," Blaze cursed. "Are you all *right*? You look so thin...like you can barely stand. Why are you not shifting and trying to eat me?"

The black behemoth was instantly back in sight, looming between them dangerously. "The demon has no control over—" he began.

Kimber made an irritated gesture and the djinni narrowed his violet eyes, but then made a...sarcastic?...bow and slipped back into the ether.

"I have more control than the child you're bedding," Kimber said.

And, oddly, the wereverine did not retort, though Blaze saw his shoulders stiffen.

"The Third-Lander slime has not had control for a thousand years," the djinni said, pride thick in his deep, rich voice. "My mistress conquered the beast centuries ago."

A flash of anger crossed the little woman's face, and she turned on the djinni in irritation. "You are not *wanted* here, 'Aqrab."

The big black man bristled. "I am within my rights to hold a *conversation*, mon Dhi'b."

The darkness in the woman's eyes made Blaze cringe, realizing there was something *very* wrong, here. "I will be the judge of that, djinni." It sounded like a warning.

It looked like the huge man would argue, then the djinni simply gave a disgusted sound and vanished. Turning back to Blaze, Kimber said, "So you intend to stay? For truth?"

Blaze felt uncomfortable at the blatant hope in the woman's eyes, so soon after...what? Anger? Rage? "Uh, yeah. That's my plan, anyway."

The wolf sounded relieved. She bit her lip as she watched the wereverine's back, a few paces ahead. "That is *very* good news." She gestured at the woods with an emaciated arm. "These lands...they have needed it for some time."

Blaze gave an awkward chuckle. "Well. Like I told Jack. I'm here to stay until someone in combat gear drags me off in a helicopter."

Kimber's eyes narrowed, and there was a deathly chill in her words when she said, "That will not happen again." The vehemence and confidence in the woman's words was unnerving.

"Damn right, it won't," Jack agreed, up ahead.

"Uh," she said, suddenly feeling self-conscious beside the tiny, assertive, *beautiful* woman. Kimber's commanding attitude, combined with her delicate body and graceful steps—even half-starved—reminded Blaze of Hollywood portrayals of Arab princesses, or wives of sheiks, acutely making her feel like an elephant trundling beside a gazelle. "Well. I'm glad you think so."

"My mistress has done war with the magi of the sons of Christ and won," the air somewhere near Blaze's head said, in a voice meant to soothe. "She does not think. She knows."

"Ibin himaar, 'Aqrab!" Kimber snapped. "*Go*! I will summon you again when you are necessary."

The voice said nothing more, though Blaze could feel the sunlight shifting on something unseen nearby, just out of reach. She decided to keep that information to herself, however, as the effort that the tiny woman had expended in barking at the djinni had left her shaking.

"Come on," Blaze said, hurrying her pace to catch up with Jack. "Let's get you something to eat."

Blaze butchered two goats—judiciously deciding that the two moon-kissed probably would be adverse to sharing—while Jack took the wolf inside and fed Kimber scrambled eggs, yak milk, and cherries. Then the wereverine hung off to one side as Blaze roasted the meat in her ovens, still watching the wolf with wariness.

For her part, the wolf graciously ate everything they put in front of her, and even while starving, she dined on Blaze's offerings with a thousand times more delicacy and finesse than the wereverine had on his best days.

"There," Jack muttered, once the seasoned goat haunches came out of the oven and Kimber had spent two hours carefully carving off strips of meat and neatly devouring the carcass to the bone, "you fed her. Now she can leave." He gestured out the window. "Give her a yak for the trip."

For his own part, there was a smear of grease and gristle across the kitchen counter, which had dribbled onto the floor in his haste to stuff meat into his mouth, and Blaze was pretty sure she saw spatters on the ceiling that she hoped weren't going to stain the paint.

"Kimber's going to be staying," Blaze said. "As is 'Aqrab." Her tongue stumbled over the Arabic word, but Jack got the point.

"Bullshit!" he roared. "I will not tolerate a slave in my house."

"*Eyreh be afass seder emmak*, rodent," the air said nearby.

Though Blaze did not understand the words, Jack did, and the rush of fury that followed made her wince. Sure enough, Jack bristled and startled to growl.

Delicately, from the counter, Kimber said, "Please stop provoking the child, 'Aqrab."

"I'm merely holding a polite conversation," the air said. "He is the one spewing insults."

"Please tell me how 'my dick in your mother's ribcage' is somehow furthering our endeavors here, djinni," Kimber said, her brown eyes narrowing at the air.

"It was just a thoughtful suggestion," the djinni said.

"Stop hiding like a yellow-bellied coward!" Jack snarled, talons snapping from his fingertips.

The djinni chuckled, a deep melodic sound. "I believe I'm making the rodent nervous."

"Show yourself, 'Aqrab," the werewolf sighed.

Immediately, the enormous black man appeared directly in front of Jack, leaning casually against the wall, arms crossed, peering down at him with amusement.

Seeing how close the djinni had been, Jack growled and took a step backwards, sprouting fur, snarling up at the djinni like a martin facing off a brown bear, and Blaze could *feel* how close he was to once again destroying her drywall.

"Jack," Blaze said, firmly. "They're staying. We could use the help."

Jack sucked in a breath to argue, then glanced at her, saw the pleading in her eyes, and deflated. "I don't *need* their help," he muttered, sulking. But he put the Third Lander away and started picking at a splinter in the hardwood trim they had installed that winter. Digging it out and snapping it off, he started using it to pick his teeth. Blaze shuddered against the urge to yell about splintering her trim, and instead forced a smile, deeply grateful that he wasn't going to continue making a scene. "Maybe you don't *need* them," she offered gently, "but they could use our food, and Kimber *did* help us take care of Amber's pack. Besides, it would make me feel better about the whole assassins-dropping-from-the-sky thing."

She met Jack's green eyes, felt the anxiousness there, the desire to keep her safe warring with the desire to keep her happy—which, in this case, was letting the werewolf and her...friend?...stay—and gently reached out to touch his hand, letting him know she understood.

Kimber must have seen it, too, because she said, "We're all on the same side, here, Shadowkiller. We want to see the phoenix safe as much as you do." Then she bit her lip and glanced out the window at Blaze's pastures. "But we will not stay where we are not welcome. Tell us to go and we will go." She looked back to Jack. "However, if you *allow* us to stay, neither my servant nor I will in any way interfere with your daily life, nor try to claim your territory. We will defer to your rule, here, in all things."

"I would rather *drown* than defer to this *child*," the djinni rumbled.

"You may leave, 'Aqrab," Kimber said.

"Look what happened *last* time you made such concessions," the djinni snapped.

"Now."

The huge black man bristled, but flashed out of existence in a wavering flicker. Blaze felt him lingering nearby, stalking back and forth across the kitchen floor.

Still standing at the head of the stairs, Jack had narrowed his eyes at the werewolf. He glanced quickly at Blaze, then, almost tentatively, he cleared his throat and said to Kimber, "*My* rule, huh?"

"When it comes to the defense of this land and our use of its resources," Kimber said, bowing her graceful neck in agreement, "you shall command us."

At that, Blaze felt the fourth presence in the room disappear entirely.

"Will you allow us to stay, Shadowkiller?" Kimber insisted, bowing low.

Jack wrinkled his nose, eyes on the top of the werewolf's head. "Guess so," he muttered, under his breath. Then, quickly, "But we're building you a cabin out back. Like hell you're living with us."

"You wish your privacy," Kimber said softly. "This is understandable."

"No more making baby wolfies, either," Jack growled.

"Never again," Kimber agreed. "It was a mistake I only made once."

Jack grunted. "And you're going to tell your slave to stop with his damned vanishing act." He gestured where 'Aqrab had disappeared. "We're going to have guests this summer, and the last thing we need is a three hundred pound African gorilla vanishing while serving dinner."

Kimber gave a slight nod. "I will inform 'Aqrab of his new restrictions."

Jack grunted. He wrinkled his nose again, then licked his lips. Blaze thought she saw a bit of uncertainty in his green eyes when he said, "You're…uh…a magus?"

Again, Kimber gracefully lowered her head in acknowledgement.

"You…uh…" He swallowed, glanced at Blaze, then reached up and scratched the back of his neck. "Think you could place some wards around this place?"

"Of course," Kimber said. "What do you have in mind?"

"Well, for one," Jack said, "Make it less obvious what's happening here from the air. Give anyone flying overhead the impression they're just seeing more woods, all normal-like. We'll let the world know when we're damn good and ready."

Kimber nodded again. "As you say, Shadowkiller. I will do that tonight."

For once, Jack's eyes scanned the werewolf and he actually looked a bit guilty. "I, uh, you look kind of…hungry…still. Whenever you get around to it would be fine."

"I thank you for your generosity," Kimber said softly. "You are kind beyond words."

Jack grunted, looking decidedly embarrassed. "Uh, yeah. No problem. Uh." He cleared his throat, flushing, and Blaze felt the discomfort from Kimber's gratitude rolling off of him in a wave. Scratching his neck, he said, "I, uh, gotta go change the oil in the generator." Then, turning, he bolted down the stairs, leaving Kimber and Blaze standing in the kitchen alone.

Once he was gone, Kimber sounded amused when she said, "Aqrab could have defended himself." The way she said it, the thought that Jack could have hurt her friend was akin to the idea that a teddy bear could rip off a grizzly's legs.

"I was really worried about the drywall," Blaze confessed. "It's been a rough year, and I'm getting *really* sick of drywall."

Kimber peered up at her face for long minutes before tentatively saying, "You truthfully intend to let us stay?" The withheld hope in her voice was almost painful.

"I'd be very *grateful* if you stayed," Blaze corrected. "For as long as you and your…friend…decide you want to make this place your home," Blaze said, hesitating over the djinni's exact wording. She hated calling someone a slave, and somehow couldn't see this tiny woman perpetuating such a thing. Jack must have simply misunderstood.

"My slave will do as he is told," Kimber said, her voice suddenly harsh. "I suspect that too much time has passed since he was reminded of that fact, and he has forgotten his place."

Well, I guess that answers that *question.* Blaze winced, suddenly not even wanting to be in the same room as the tiny woman, with the dangerous glint in her brown eyes. "Oh." Licking her lips nervously, she said, "Uh, well, you're both welcome, regardless."

Kimber glanced around the lodge, examining everything she could see from where they stood in the kitchen. Then, turning back to Blaze, she lowered her voice. "Is he gone, then?" she whispered.

Instinctively, Blaze knew the woman was talking about the djinni. "Uh, I felt him…leave…when you were talking with Jack."

"Good," Kimber whimpered.

…*whimpered*?

Blaze watched the sheet of calm masking the woman's face suddenly break, revealing a roiling wash of agony underneath. "Thank you, flamekin. Your generosity…" Her voice cracked. "I was about to give up, and let 'Aqrab go home."

By 'go home,' Blaze got the gut feeling that Kimber wasn't talking about chartering a plane back to Africa. She was pretty sure it was something else, something deeper that bound the man to this Realm.

The despair in the woman's soft brown eyes held the answer Blaze sought.

She was going to kill herself, she thought, horrified.

Then, as Blaze was still trying to comprehend that, the tiny woman stepped forward and wrapped her delicate arms around Blaze's man-sized midsection. Before Blaze had really figured out how to deal with *that*, the woman started to sob as she clung to her, weeping in long, heart-wrenching wails against Blaze's shirt.

There's more here than meets the eye, Blaze thought, returning the tiny woman's embrace tentatively. She'd never had someone cry in her arms before, much less someone who could rip her arms off if she patted her wrong.

"Thank you so much," Kimber sobbed, as Blaze held her awkwardly. "I had nowhere else to go."

Blaze returned the woman's hug tighter, then, deciding right there that she and Kimber had much more in common than she first assumed. "You have a home here," she assured her. "Make yourselves comfortable. We have extra food, as you noticed. All the fruit, dairy, and meat you can eat, whatever strikes your fancy. And if there's something else you'd like that we don't have here, you say the word, I'll have it shipped in."

The werewolf gave a timid laugh. Backing out of Blaze's embrace, she wiped her eyes and sniffled. Her voice soft and shy, she said, "I'm rather fond of dates and pomegranates. It's been too long since I've tasted home."

Blaze winced inwardly, but didn't let the little werewolf see it. Mangoes were bad enough, but *pomegranates*? She might as well post a huge neon sign on the lodge that screamed, SOMETHING WEIRD IS GOING ON HERE, but she kept the thought to herself. "I'll buy the seeds off eBay when I'm in town," she assured the woman. Cocking her head at Kimber pointedly, she said, "Are you going to be all right?"

Kimber gave her a sideways look and bit her lip. She took a deep breath, and for a moment, it looked as if she would explain. Then, softly, she said, "It is nothing you can change, flamekin. By giving us a home, you have helped enough." Then the mask of calm was back in place, the only indication that the werewolf had just been sobbing in Blaze's arms being the redness to her eyes and the wetness against her lashes.

Distressed, wishing she could help the woman, yet knowing she couldn't pry, Blaze decided to change the subject. "Would you like a tour? I can show you around."

"I'm still hungry," Kimber admitted almost fearfully. Almost as if she expected to be slapped for the audacity of not being full.

Blaze stared at the woman. *Amber was starving her,* she realized. "Okay," she quickly said, gesturing out the second-story window at the farmstead beyond. "We've got a little bit of everything out there. Take your pick. Yak, turkey, rabbit, more goat, a pig, chicken, waterfowl..."

Kimber flinched at 'a pig' and tentatively cleared her throat. "Perhaps you will show me where you grew these cherries?" She paused, looking up at Blaze, for all the world like a nervous teenager in a friend's mother's house. "If you did grow them, that is..."

"I grew them," Blaze said quickly. "Come on. They're in the greenhouse." She twisted towards the stairs, a bit too fast, and Kimber suddenly flinched away from her, like a whipped animal.

*That was...weird...*Blaze thought, making a mental note to move more slowly around the woman as she led her out to the greenhouse.

It took Blaze the next hour of observation, watching the woman's timid reactions as she guided her through her farm, before she understood. *This woman is* terrified *of me*, she thought, a bit startled. Despite the façade of total calm, and perfect collectedness, the woman was absolutely *terrified.* And it wasn't just Blaze that scared her, she realized, looking out at the yard. The way the woman nervously eyed the yaks, the way she jerked when a chicken flapped its wings, and the way she had let out a breath when the djinni had gone...She was afraid of *everything*.

And when Jack came out of the shop wiping his greasy hands on a rag and started assisting Blaze with the tour of the property, the wereverine must have also recognized it, too, despite the immediate icy calm that doused the woman's features upon his arrival. As Blaze watched, he actually started curbing his crass behavior and kept his gestures slow and muted as he explained how the Sleeping Lady worked.

And, for once, through it all, the wereverine had the good sense to keep his mouth shut.

After watching the wereverine keep a tight rein on himself for the following two days, in fact, Blaze was reasonably sure she could trust him alone with the werewolf and her companion. With two days of preparation and some sort of illusory spell that Kimber cast on her at Jack's request, Jack had reluctantly agreed to let Blaze go alone while he kept the 'backward idiot shits in line,' and Blaze re-scheduled her flight out with Bruce Rogers.

In between buying groceries—mostly things like toilet paper, flour, sugar, salt, and other necessities—taking her guiding class with the Alaska Department of Fish and Game, buying feed for those animals that needed the extra boost, depositing money and making her first loan payment, three nights of hotel rooms, and paying Bruce for the flight back, Blaze had exactly seventeen dollars left to her name by the time she got back to the Sleeping Lady, and no idea how she was going to buy the fuel, groceries, and other supplies necessary to begin the fishing season.

Some Business major I am, she thought unhappily. *Less than a year and I've already bankrupted myself.*

Then, a logical side of her brain noted, *Well, you did have help with that.*

Had it not been for the brawls in her living-room, she was pretty sure she could have scraped by with enough cash from her savings, her last two paychecks from her part-time apprentice accountant internship with the State of Alaska, her loan, and her PFD to get her well into next winter, even without a single guest for the lodge.

Wincing at the 'brawls in the living-room' thought, Blaze began to have a very bad feeling that she was going to be making a few more trips to Home Depot as Bruce Rogers dropped them on the deep black surface of Lake Ebony and began taxiing to shore. She wouldn't have left Kimber and the wereverine alone if she could have helped it, but her loan *had* to be paid, or she might as well have just grabbed the deed to the Sleeping Lady and kissed it goodbye. She just hoped that hiring Kimber and 'Aqrab instead of some bright-eyed young kid in Anchorage hadn't been a horrible, drywall-crushing mistake.

Jack was waiting for her on the beach, hip-waders pulled up to his thighs, as Bruce cut the engine and the plane drifted to shore. The wereverine grabbed the plane by the float, then held it steady as Bruce and Blaze climbed from the cockpit of the Cessna 206.

As soon as Blaze was out of the plane, Jack grabbed her, swept her off of the float, and carried her up the bank in his arms, his hard body holding her tight as he grinned down at her. "Missed ya, sweetie," he said, kissing her long and hard, in full view of God and everyone, and Blaze clung to him, enjoying the feel of his warmth, his love, his heartbeat. Then, setting Blaze breathlessly on dry land, Jack turned and waded back out to Bruce, who was giving the wereverine a look like he'd grown antlers.

Reddening, Jack said, "You need another dunkin', asshole? Your mama never teach you not to stare?"

Bruce Rogers quickly started unpacking the plane. Between the three of them, they got the Cessna 206 unloaded and packed onto the trailer cart in under ten minutes.

"So, uh," Bruce Rogers called, half-inside his airplane, giving Blaze a nervous chuckle as they carried their last loads up the beach to the 4-wheeler. "Watch out for werewolves, eh?"

Both Blaze and Jack swiveled on him. "Why's that?" they both demanded, at once.

Bruce gave an uneasy laugh and gestured at the woods. "You haven't heard? That's what all the kids on the internet are calling those wolves you guys killed. Got a whole kind of pop-cult goin on, tryin' ta raise money to stay at your place. Say they're gonna go hunt werewolves. It's kinda funny, but not really. After all the damage those things did…" He just shook his head. "You just be careful, okay?"

Blaze and Jack glanced at each other, then Jack grunted and started securing the trailer load with bungees.

"Thanks, Bruce," Blaze said, meaning it. She dropped her armful of paper towels on the trailer, then waited as Bruce Rogers got situated in the cockpit and Jack got the Cessna turned around and pointed in the right direction. Then she and Jack stood on the beach, watching Bruce taxi the plane across the lake and out Ebony Creek.

"I know what you're thinking," Blaze said, as the plane disappeared around the bend, "And I think it's a horrible idea."

"Aw, come *on*," Jack chuckled. "I would have *so* much fun making those panty-waisted city-slicker asswipes run screaming through the woods."

"They might bring silver bullets," Blaze noted.

Jack considered. "I'll scope 'em out once they get here. They look like something other than a geeky college kid with his father's pea-shooter, I'll take it easy."

Blaze frowned at him. "You almost make it sound like you *want* to be hunted through the woods."

"Sugar," Jack said, looking up at her with an infernal grin, "Obviously you got some misconceptions about who'd be hunting who." The way he said it, he'd already been planning it in his mind.

Blaze dropped her face into her hands and dragged her fingers down her cheekbones. "You got some calls already, didn't you?"

"They're coming out this Thursday," Jack said, teeth glinting in mischievousness. "Twelve of the little fucks. Six days. Already put down a deposit." He grinned out at the woods. "I'm gonna give 'em a week they'll never forget." Then he shrugged. "If they stay that long." His grin was demonic when he said, "Prolly won't last the night."

"You will *not* be eating my guests!" Blaze cried.

"Oh no," Jack said, laughing. "That'd spoil the fun."

Groaning, fighting the urge to tell him to cancel their arrangements, her business mind began tabulating numbers. Curious, despite herself, she said, "How much of a deposit?"

"Hmm," Jack said. "Lessee...They didn't want guides, so I cut 'em a break. Knocked a couple hundred off the daily price. Think it ended up being close to ten grand. They wanted to write a check, but I told 'em to wire it to your bank, considerin it was such short notice." He gave her a suspicious look. "Why? You ain't gonna go all wet-blanket on me and try to refund 'em, are you?"

*There's ten thousand dollars in my bank account...*Thinking about that, Blaze grunted. "Well, as long as they're not shooting silver bullets and you're not hurting anyone, I guess I can't complain about another ten grand."

"Good," Jack said, a slow smile spreading across his lips, showing long, ivory fang. "'Cause Kimber and I'm gonna have a blast. We already talked about it. Won't let the silly bastards go home 'til they all peed themselves."

Well, they must be getting along okay, if Kimber has agreed to it, Blaze thought. Then, wincing, she realized that, while they might be getting along *now*, it was quite possible they hadn't gotten along for a couple *minutes*, yesterday afternoon. She said a mental prayer for the preservation of her décor, then said, "You know, scaring the crap outta a bunch of teenagers isn't gonna do much for keeping your cover, once they get photographs."

"Let 'em." Jack grinned wider. "I'll be sure to break their cameras."

And she was pretty sure he didn't mean that in the metaphoric sense.

Groaning, Blaze also realized it would probably be the highlight of some kid's life, to be chased around the woods by a wereverine.

That, and Jack was just *way* too excited to rain on his parade.

"Fine," she said, jabbing a finger at his chest, feeling her finger hit home on his breastbone as if it were her own. "But no blood, and no letting them get pictures."

"Darlin'," Jack said, looking up at her lazily, "Just who do you think you're dealin' with, here?" Face still smeared with that wolfish grin, Jack reached up, tangled his big fingers in her hair, and dragged her head down for another heart-pounding kiss. Then, releasing her, he climbed aboard the four-wheeler and started the engine. "Now let's go. King Kong's got steaks cookin."

Blaze winced, deciding she was *definitely* going to have to work on his people skills.

THIRTY-THREE

Thrillseekers

It took Bruce Rogers three trips with his 206 to bring all twelve kids out that Thursday. Against her better judgment, instead of calling to cancel at the last minute, Blaze found herself standing on the beach of Lake Ebony with Jack, Kimber, and 'Aqrab, waiting to greet the first load of guests as Bruce's plane taxied toward them from the middle of the lake.

"No blood, no pictures," Blaze said, through her smile. She waved at the plane, as it approached.

"Honey," Jack said, also through his teeth, "Me an' the wolf got this shit *covered*. It'll be like icing a cake."

"Icing a cake is hard."

"Hell," Jack said, as if he hadn't heard her, "We even hired that Nicolai guy downriver to help us out."

"The *tiger*?" Blaze cried, turning to face him, her jaw open, now.

Jack continued to smile and wave at the plane. "Figured it's 'bout time he started earning all those yaks."

"They *might* have mistaken a wereverine for a were*wolf*," Blaze said, "but I'm pretty sure a *tiger's* gonna stand out."

"'Course he is," Jack said, still waving. "You want the little turds to come back, don'tcha?"

"I suppose," Blaze said, reluctantly. What she *really* wanted, at this point, was not to have a huge liability lawsuit on her hands. She glanced down at the waivers in her hands, trying to avoid the sick building of dread in her gut.

"It'll be fine, sweetie," Jack insisted, as the plane loomed closer. "You remember everything?"

They'd rehearsed every moment of the kids' stay for several days, and Blaze had the nagging suspicion that all four of them were going to jail by the end of it. Jack's plan was horrifyingly simple—turn the Sleeping Lady into the centerpiece of a week-long scare-fest that left the kids with nightmares. Starting with kidnapping one of the students—hopefully a pretty blonde—and dragging her off to the 'lair' that Jack and Kimber had dug out off the mill trail. Oh, and the phones going down, the power going out, and all the keys pulled from the 4-wheeler ignitions.

This could go so bad so quickly, Blaze thought, trying to decide how, exactly, she was going to tell the judge she had conspired to just *temporarily* kidnap a pretty young girl and haul her off into the woods.

And then Bruce cut the engine and Jack was wading out to catch the airplane's float, keeping the big Cessna from running aground

Please *let them not be professional serial killers*, Blaze thought, seeing the heads watching her from behind the dim windows of the airplane's cab. Bruce piled out, followed immediately by a striking young blonde woman in hunter's camouflage.

Yep, Blaze thought, wincing inside, *she's the one.*

Then Jack was walking forward, smiling, holding out his hand and welcoming the girl to the Sleeping Lady Lodge, and oh how he *really* hoped she enjoyed her stay...

"Dude, that is some *freakin' awesome* chainmail!" one of the kids cried. "Are those *real swords*?" Blaze actually watched the kid give Jack a plus three against werewolves in his little mental stat-sheet.

We're going to Hell for this, she thought, fighting down a pang of guilt as all the geeks crowded around Jack, taking pictures, cooing about his 'cool gear.'

What was worse, the girl in camouflage looked to be one of the more serious of the contestants of Jack's 'festivities.' Whereas all the others carried pepper-spray and cameras, she carried a *gun*.

Yep, Blaze thought again, watching her sling the .375 H&H rifle over her shoulder with professional ease, *she's gonna spend a week in a hole*.

"I'm Sarah Evans," the blonde said, stepping up to give Blaze a firm handshake. "I hear you got wolf problems."

The woman couldn't have been more than five-foot-three, but Blaze got the general idea that she was *just* the right sort of Type-A personality to sue their asses completely into the ground when Jack finally allowed Blaze and the assorted heroes clamoring off of the plane in various colors of green to 'rescue' her from his 'den.'

We are sooooo dead, Blaze thought, forcing a smile down at the woman. "We haven't had many wolves around here since the attack," Blaze said. "It's mostly been real quiet."

Sarah's eyes sharpened in that I've Been To Law School look that a lot of Blaze's father's friends had gotten, whenever they heard something that disagreed with them. "*Mostly*?"

Oh yeah. They were screwed. Clearing her throat, Blaze slipped the stack of papers out from under her arm and said, "Look, before y'all go any further, we're gonna have to get you guys to sign a release of liability. This really isn't our thing here at the Sleeping Lady, and I would've cancelled had my *mechanic* not already allowed you to put down deposits." She started passing out the bleached white sheets to the knot of kids forming on the beach. "We're not a hunting lodge, and these woods are *dangerous*, as you well know, and we really don't want this to come back and bite us in the ass."

"It won't," Sarah said, but she signed anyway. She even went so far as to collect the papers from her friends and hand them back to Blaze. "So," she said, in an all-business, no-nonsense attitude, "Where would you say is the likeliest spot to catch them, if you were gonna go do it?"

Blaze's eyes flickered to Jack, where he was carting luggage off of the plane and dumping it on the 4-wheeler trailer. "Uh, well, I got some ideas, but I wanna stress, they're *really* dangerous." Then, inwardly biting her lip and praying for forgiveness, she lowered her voice and said, "Don't tell anyone, but I don't really think they're *wolves*."

While that seemed to make the knot of youngsters' eyes light up, Sarah just gave a curt nod. "Don't worry, Miss MacKenzie," she said. "We'll take care of the problem for you." She patted her rifle. "My marksmanship team took nationals, a few years back."

Blaze narrowed her eyes. Yes, this one was *definitely* going in the hole.

• • •

The kidnapping, unexpected *escape*, then re-kidnapping of the pretty blonde took Jack the first couple days. Then, when it was 'clear' that they had to rescue the girl 'without the authorities' help,' 'Aqrab, Blaze, and all twelve of the kids spent the next five days scouring the woods, getting their tents ripped apart, firing lead-filled Desert Eagles blindly into the night, and generally getting the crap scared out of them when Jack, Kimber, or Nicolai materialized out of nowhere and ripped apart a few tree-trunks 'trying to eat them.'

In the end, the kids rescued the maiden, who, with great surprise lighting her face, described the beast that kidnapped her as 'a total gentleman with a lonely streak' and her time with him as 'a Beauty and the Beast moment,' where she spent time 'calming his tormented soul.' The blonde, in fact, seemed so enamored with the 'forlorn monster' that it didn't even sound like she was going to try and press charges.

Thus, Blaze was all-too-happy to give them the additional day at the lodge 'for free' and shoo them off with Bruce just as quickly as she could get what was left of their stuff packed and on the plane. Under the guise, of course, that 'the beast might be back'. After all, according to reports, he'd spent untold hours down in the hole with the girl, recounting his lonely, unhappy life.

"You laid it on pretty thick, I hear," Blaze said, as they watched the last plane take off.

"Yeah," Jack said, grinning like an imbecile, "but I'll betcha they'll be back next year."

Blaze groaned. "You want *more* kids running around in the woods?"

"It was ten grand," Jack said. Then he cocked his head. "That, and Sarah's got a crush on me," Jack said, showing teeth like the Cheshire cat. "I can *smell* it."

Blaze whirled on the wereverine and grabbed him by the scruff of the neck. "You," she growled down at him, "had better ease up on the 'tormented soul' routine before you start giving people the wrong idea."

Jack shrugged, but happiness rolled off of him as he grinned up at her. "I'll bet you a hundred bucks we've got ten more reservations by the end of the day."

Ten, it turned out, was a bit off. As soon as tales of their 'encounter' hit the web, the phone started ringing off the hook. Blaze actually had to start switching it off at night, due to the fact that so many people in opposite time-zones didn't bother to look at the time-charts before deciding when to call. Or they simply mis-calculated, adding when they should have subtracted, or read 'am' when they should have read 'pm.'

"You know," Blaze said, as the lodge booked its seventh straight weekend, "This could eat into fishing time."

"Already told 'em June through September was off-limits," Jack said. "They posted it on their website."

"Yeah, but—" Blaze started. The phone cut her off, ringing for the sixth time that day alone. Another potential guest, this time wanting to bring his wife and kids.

"I'm sorry," Blaze ended up telling the man, "but that's just too dangerous. Call back when they're all eighteen." She hung up and gave Jack a tired look. "We're gonna have to limit it to groups of six or more." Then, wrinkling her nose at him, she added, "And *you* are going to have to come up with a different shtick."

Jack chuckled. "Aw, I think the 'lonely werewolf' motif worked rather well."

Blaze opened her mouth to argue, then her words kind of died in her throat. It *had* worked, and it had allowed all the young, geeky boys to rescue the damsel in distress, who in turn got all gushy over the big, beefy werewolf who'd captured her. Typical Stockholm Syndrome at its best. Hell, they'd all been so high on their own awesomeness afterwards that they'd completely forgotten the fact that Jack had been nowhere to be seen for much of the screaming-and-running-through-the-woods bits.

This is going to work, Blaze realized, looking around her at her new home in awe. She had enough money to make her loan payments, had her farm up and running in a *year*, instead of a *decade*, as she had first planned, and she had so much food growing on her property that she was having to *beg* her neighbors to take it off of her hands. Runt, once he returned that spring, had taken up gardening and cuddly-animal-tending duties in return for the lion's share of her hot peppers, packing out huge, shimmering sacks of them and returning with a fancy new hairpin here, a rainbow-glinting cloak there. Judging by the substantial increase in quality of his attire—and the added bounce in his step—Blaze suspected he was selling them for obscene profits in the Second Realm, but from the way he was keeping the garden and greenhouses immaculate, she found she couldn't begrudge him a few peppers.

Through the window out back, Blaze could see Kimber planting flowers beside the new cabin that Jack and Blaze had built for them, while 'Aqrab sat in a lawnchair in the sun reading the Shakespeare tome Blaze had bought for him on her last trip to town. The djinni, she had found, not only set tables and delivered meals with a smile on his face, but made an excellent conversationalist when everyone gathered for dinner, winding stories of love and adventure and keeping their guests so enthralled that half the time, they forgot to eat. And Kimber, while quiet and reserved around their clients, had made herself utterly indispensible cleaning rooms, vacuuming, tending the grounds, making beds, and doing dishes.

Leaving Jack to manage repairs, tidy, and tend the mechanics, and Blaze to schmooze, run finances, and share cooking duties with the wereverine.

"Wow," Blaze managed, suddenly overwhelmed. "Jack, I think we did it."

"Ain't no question, sugar," Jack said. He wrapped a heavy arm around her waist and grinned up at her, and his pride was overwhelming through the link. "So...Yak tonight?" He sounded hopeful.

She grinned down at him. "Yak tonight."

And Here's a Sneak Peek of...

GUARDIANS OF THE FIRST REALM:

ALASKAN FURY

KAASHIFAH

"The winds breathe foul today, mon Dhi'b." 'Aqrab's words were like a warm breath against the back of her neck, rousing Kaashifah from a dead sleep in an instant of total panic.

Though Kaashifah couldn't see the djinni, she knew he was nearby from the way the drapes seemed to waver above the bed. Over the long years of bondage to the Fourth Lander, she had trained herself to almost *see* the odd flicker of the light where he danced, half in his own land, half in hers. Some days, she was better at seeing it than others. Often, it came and went with her mood. Anger made it easier. Fear...

Well, fear made it impossible.

And there was so much to fear.

Swallowing, Kaashifah sat up and threw back on the façade that had kept her sane these last three millennia of torment. "I told you not to enter my room as I slept, 'Aqrab."

"You have told me not to enter other rooms," the djinni said, manifesting out of thin air, a seven-foot mountain of ebony flesh glaring down at her. "But not this one." He gave her a vicious smile and gestured at the small cabin that the wereverine had built for them.

"I told you not to enter my *bedroom* as I slept," Kaashifah snapped, hating the way the djinni could manage to intentionally misinterpret even the most simple commands. "What is there to mistake about that?"

'Aqrab's violet eyes narrowed on her. "Since this is to be my place of residence, and as I am *bound* to this land, and our hosts built only one dwelling for the both of us, and that dwelling only has *one* bedroom, this room is technically not *your* room, but *my* room, too, making it *our* room. You never told me to stay out of *our* bedroom, mon Dhi'b."

Oh, she *hated* the convolutions he could come up with in order to reason out his own actions. It was the very reason she had hunted him down in the first place and inadvertently begun this nightmare, three thousand years ago. His twisted, monkey-pawing, oath-breaking, selfish *rationalizing* that had destroyed the city of Ji'fah. Wiped it completely off of the map with a single wish. He had monkey-pawed a kingdom into ruin, and reveled in it. So much so that her Lord had told her to destroy him.

...and the bastard of a whoreson had bound himself to her to save his worthless hide. Soul-to-soul. Beginning a nightmare that would never end.

"'Aqrab," Kaashifah said, "Leave."

While most days, the djinni would have given her a snide look and asked her to 'leave what?' now he simply narrowed his eyes and vanished.

Too many meanings to words. Too many interpretations. Too many loopholes. Kaashifah had learned this long ago, and had been living in torment ever since.

Reluctantly, unsure if the djinni was truly gone due to her own inner turmoil—'Aqrab kept her as off-balance as possible, as often as possible, because it gave him the power to come and go at will—Kaashifah nonetheless threw the covers off and slipped, naked, off of the bed.

Her suspicions were confirmed when a voice above and behind her said, "I left, mon Dhi'b. And I returned. Perhaps now you will listen to what I had to say?"

Kaashifah fought a surge of terror, knowing the beast was directly behind her, knowing that her naked form was completely exposed to him, but she fought it down and straightened her spine, hiding it well. She could, after all, use her last wish to kill the monster, and they both knew it. And, having begun the duel of souls so long ago at the oasis of Tafilat, to take his head now was to bind his soul to hers in perpetual servitude, from which only her word could grant his release. It was probably the only reason the creature hadn't already used her body to his delights, repeatedly. After all, as he so loved to claim, he was 'bored enough to drown' being imprisoned here. And she *knew* he craved her body. She could see it, whenever he looked at her.

"Another instruction I gave you, 'Aqrab," Kaashifah said evenly, "is never to spy upon me while I am disrobed."

"I am not spying on you," 'Aqrab said. "I am standing within arm's-reach, fully within the darkness of your lands." The sneer was back, his hatred firing every word.

Kaashifah fought another spasm of terror and turned, slowly, to look up at him.

True to his word, 'Aqrab stood less than an arm's-length away, peering down at her over his huge, muscular forearms, crossed over his enormous chest. He stood like a mountain before her, his black body like a deeper shadow in the half-light. He wore a thin, gauzy sirwal to cover his waist and legs, but not much else. And, through the film of silk, she could see the hardness there, the longing. Three thousand years of longing, for he made it very plain that he held his imprisonment against her, despite the fact that *he* was the one to do it.

And three thousand years ago, the longing had been just as strong. Back then, she was pretty sure he would have done it out of violence, out of fury for what she had done to him. Now, she was sure he would *relish* in it, make it last until she screamed for death. He would despoil her in a heartbeat, if she didn't have the Fourthlander Law binding him by his own making.

The djinni, of course, made no effort to hide his desire. He knew it upset her, threw her off balance, left her terrified of what he might decide to do as a final hurrah, a last goodbye, one glorious revelry before he vanished like a lick of flame to the wind.

It was all Kaashifah could do not to simply break down right there. She'd fought him for so long, endured his torments for so many eons... It had worn at her soul, left her dreading each new day, each new ordeal he painstakingly crafted for her.

"'Aqrab," she whispered. "Please."

He gave her a malicious smile. "Please what, mon Dhi'b? Please take your tiny virgin body upon my shaft and pierce you until you scream? Please break your neck? Or please fetch you a shirt? You must be more specific."

Kaashifah closed her eyes and fought the despair that had been building for three thousand years. It now weighed on her like a mountain, making it hard to breathe, hard to think, hard to face each heartbeat. "Please leave me alone," Kaashifah said. "Just go."

"Make your wish," the djinni growled, "and I will happily do just that."

By Fourthlander Law, he was bound to her for three wishes. She had made two. The third was going to be her last, and both of them knew it.

Kaashifah looked away. "Get out of this room and let me dress."

For a long moment, it looked like the djinni would disobey her. Which, due to the way he had bound himself to her—and her background in the arcane—could mean great pain for him, when she took the shadows of the First Lands and shoved them down the cord at him. It was like throwing water onto a bonfire, and he usually screamed for hours.

She hated to do it, though. She was not, by nature, like him. She did not delight in tormenting others. It was simply something she had discovered, over the time she'd been tied to him. Which made it all the more horrible when she had to discipline him for stepping over the line.

...and all the more certain that he would make her regret every breath she had taken for the last three millennia, if he ever got free.

The djinni vanished. This time, he waited until she had slipped a shirt over her head before he returned. "Something horrible is on the winds, mon Dhi'b."

Kaashifah would have snapped at him, then, if there wasn't obvious concern in his eyes. Kaashifah hesitated, chancing a look at his groin. The hardness was still there, but muted, only half-straining against the silk. She looked away, disgusted.

"Someday, little virgin," the djinni growled. "You will moan for hours upon my shaft."

"Don't call me 'virgin,'" Kaashifah snapped.

His smiled in disdain. "You prefer 'whore', then?"

Kaashifah hurt him, then. She grabbed the nearby shadow and shoved it down the life-cord that the djinni had bound to her. Just a taste, but it was enough to throw him to his knees, gasping, big hands splayed out on the floor, head down, a low whine building in his chest. For long moments, he just stayed there on his hands and knees before her. When he looked up, his violet eyes were full of tears.

And hate.

"*You* did this," Kaashifah reminded him, though her heart was already pounding in frenzied terror under the loathing in his gaze. "You put me in this position, 'Aqrab. It wasn't me. It was your own hand that did this."

"Perhaps I missed something," the mountainous djinni whispered, "but it was *you* who just poisoned me with shadow, when all I wanted to do was tell you about the whispers on the winds."

"Because you *force my hand*!" Kaashifah screamed at him. "You threaten to break my spine. You threaten to *force* me. Every day, you make my life a living *hell* because you were too much of a *coward* to face your own death when it came!"

He slowly worked himself to one knee and wiped the tears from his face with a massive black forearm. "Little wolf," he said softly, "you obviously misunderstand my words."

Kaashifah snorted in derision. "Your words are fluid, the meanings changing with the winds, as flexible as your honor."

She watched his beautiful eyes harden. "That may be, mon Dhi'b," he said finally. "But, considering that I will be bound to a bag of *bones* if you die before you make your wish, we both know I will do what I can to keep you alive. And the winds are telling me that you're in danger." He said it with a sneer, like he was relaying information that he would rather see buried in the bottom of a latrine.

Kaashifah bit her lip, her heart skipping a beat. While he delighted in tormenting her, the djinni was also always accurate in his readings of the winds. "In danger how?" she asked softly.

But the djinni's face hardened. "Wouldn't you like to know." And then he disappeared. For good, this time.

Damn him.

Kaashifah finished dressing, taking long minutes to comb out her hair, trying to calm the trembling in her hands. As always, the djinni scared her. He scared her so much she wanted to scream for help from the nearest passerby. But there was no one who *could* help her. A djinni's magic was one of the strongest in existence. As convoluted and twisted as their minds, it was almost impossible to unravel. Only a dragon could free her of his curse, and not even a *dragon* could remove the tether he'd knotted to her soul. That would take her final wish.

Kaashifah pulled on her gloves—in North America, she had learned, men often tried to shake hands with women out of courtesy, and rather than having to choose between defiling her body or insulting the phoenix's guests, Kaashifah had begun wearing skin-tight gardening gloves under a long-sleeved turtleneck shirt. Thus, once she pulled on her baseball cap, tucked her ebony hair carefully around her ears, and laced up her boots, all that was visible of her skin was a small portion of her face.

Refusing to let 'Aqrab see her fear, she straightened her spine and walked out the front door, took the extra time to latch it and sweep a few bits of mud from the porch with a flick of her mind, then stepped down to cross the lush grounds to the Sleeping Lady Lodge. A new wave of thrill-seekers was arriving this afternoon, and the wereverine was certain to have concocted some last-minute change of plans, as he had done every time since that first highly-successful scare-fest, that spring.

The Fourth Lander already had breakfast cooking on the stove, and she smiled when Kaashifah crested the steps. "Morning, Kimber," Blaze said. The tall woman's fiery red hair was braided and wrapped around the back of her head in a Greek-style headdress. A wig, of course. Her real hair was cropped short and tucked underneath, a necessity of dealing with the public. Phoenixes, once awakened, carried sunfire in their hair and eyes. With a wig and contacts, however, none had been the wiser.

Tapping her spatula on the griddle, the phoenix looked over her shoulder with a small frown. "Where is 'Aqrab?"

They act as if he's my mate, Kaashifah thought, in agony. She hadn't yet managed to bring herself to tell them the truth, though she had the feeling the wereverine suspected. Indeed, Jack was sitting at the bar, watching her with narrowed eyes, his nose to the wind. Ares damn her body for its betrayals, but her glands gave her fears away easier than if she had written them in a book and handed it to the man.

Avoiding the wereverine's gaze, Kaashifah said, "'Aqrab is indisposed." She sat down on a stool at the kitchen's island counter, pointedly ignoring Jack. "Are there any last amendments to our plans?"

"Playing 'capture the babe' seems to be workin' pretty damn good so far," Jack said, grinning to show his fangs. "I say we just stick to that. Hell, they already got the tabloids cookin' up all sorts of stories about the 'lonely beast on the Yentna.' Why disappoint?"

The wereverine, as always, seemed to be rather short-sighted about the whole affair, but Kaashifah was being fed from the phoenix's own grounds, and the abundance of food, after starving for so many years due to 'Aqrab's handicraft, was a blessing she was not willing to give up over a 'difference of opinions,' as the wereverine so politely put it. Out of sheer desperation, she had given him her word to obey his rule whilst on his domain, and she knew the score. To break that oath was to be sent away.

...Away to starve; weak, hungry, and alone to face the djinni's torments. She had done it before, and only barely survived. To do it again, she knew, would finally shatter that tentative hold she had on sanity.

A hold that, with his every breath, the djinni was weakening.

"Very well," Kaashifah said. "Am I to take up the usual position with Blaze?"

"I'll come to grab the girl when you two are just finishing up dinner," Jack said. "Lead them on a merry goose-chase around the lodge, then boogie off into the woods to drop her in the hole."

"The last group had GPS," Blaze warned, serving Kaashifah two pie-plates full of eggs and fruit. "Remember to check her for a beacon."

"What if there are no females?" Kaashifah asked. "What is our plan in that case?"

Jack chuckled. "Oh, honey, you ain't heard?"

Kaashifah glanced at Jack, then up at Blaze. The tall woman sighed and rolled her eyes, then went back to making breakfast.

At the bar, Jack said, "They're *all* girls this time, baby. I got the whole damn *world* wantin' ta crawl up my chimney."

The djinni's daily abuse left Kaashifah loathing the crass wereverine's casual references to the physical act of union, but she managed to keep her face from twisting. After all, countless people found it an amusing enough pastime. Jack and Blaze were two of them. The scent of their pheromones was particularly strong this morning, which only made her gut clench. The djinn, as beings of the Fourth Lands, were notoriously crippled by the carnal needs of procreation. And sure enough, 'Aqrab reeked of desire, whenever he got close to her, and had spent much the last three thousand years stinking much like the little wereverine whenever he so much as looked at his mate.

Except, with the djinni, there were three thousand years of hatred behind his carnal desires. He wanted to make her suffer, wanted to desecrate her body once and for all, wanted to condemn her in the eyes of her Lord and seal her from her Fury, wanted to take her wings forever in that ruinous and sinful act that a man could do to a woman.

He wanted these things, and he spent every waking moment making sure she was aware of that fact.

"You're not eating, Kimber," Blaze said, looking at Kaashifah's plate worriedly. "Are you all right?"

Kaashifah swallowed and lowered her hand, realizing she had unconsciously lifted it to her Lord's tiny winged sword upon her neck.

"She had another spat with her slave," Jack said, wrinkling his nose.

Damn him. Kaashifah felt her fists clench with shame as she fell under the phoenix's pitying stare. "I would appreciate it, Shadowkiller," she said softly to Jack, "If you would keep your…observations…to yourself."

Jack shrugged and went back to devouring his mixing-bowl of eggs. For Kaashifah, the phoenix had served up a similar portion, size-wise, though she had made a certain effort at presentation, for which Kaashifah was deeply grateful. The curse of the wolf may force her to eat like a monster, but she tried in all ways to maintain her decorum and civility. It was one of the only things she had left of her true nature. The djinni had taken everything else.

"The kids are arriving around noon," Jack said a few minutes later, already having downed the full bowl of eggs and wiping his egg-stained fingers on the wet rag that the phoenix handed him. "We'll get them settled in, feed 'em dinner, then let the festivities start."

"No blood, no pictures," Blaze reiterated. "And no chasing them into the river." She'd had to add that one after a young man from one of the last groups had fallen into the glacial waters of the Yentna River and Jack had had to go in and rescue him, once it was clear that the boy had gone into shock. Only, of course, adding to his legend.

The Yentna River Werewolf. Kaashifah didn't know who were the bigger fools—the idiots that paid thousands of dollars to spend a week running screaming through the woods, or the wereverine and his mate, who blithely took their money and let his reputation build. As 'Aqrab had noted to her many times before, the extra attention did not seem wise, in the phoenix's case. But then, they had slaughtered the last Inquisition recovery group to come for her and had buried them—helicopter and all—in an enormous pit in the woods, so Kaashifah had grudgingly gone along with the plan.

Besides, the phoenix was the key to her next meal, and chronic hunger did something strange to one's thinking, when one thought they were about to be dumped on their ear, for raising a voice of dissent.

Afraid to open her mouth for the pain in her stomach, Kaashifah thought. *When did the Handmaiden of Ares become such a coward?*

The answer was simple: When the djinni bound himself to her, while kneeling under her blade. Surrender. The word was still bitter on her lips, an acrid taste on her tongue. The djinni had not surrendered. He had merely prolonged his life in exchange for three thousand years of torment. And a curse.

She had accepted his surrender, fool that she was. She had allowed him to get to his knees before her, present his sweaty black neck for her sword. She had lifted her blade, prepared to cut his lying head from his massive body.

And his big hand had reached out, like a snake, and he had cursed her. A blood-curse, the curse of a doomed man, the last wish of a djinni on his death bed. *May you never kill.* A Maiden of Death, follower of Ares, and she dropped her sword as if it had been afire, the very steel burning like coals in her hands, searing her fingers to the bone. And the look of victory in the djinni's violet eyes, the *triumph*...

He'd won their duel of souls. They both had known it, right then, him kneeling before her in the sands of the oasis, her standing, swordless, sun beating down on her blistered hands from above. By surrendering to her blade, he would ultimately win. Eventually, the strain would be too much. Eventually, she would crumble. Eventually, with time, he would get that third wish, and when he did, he would be free to spend his last hours in the First Realm showing her *real* torment before he killed her and returned to his homeland, her soul in tow. All it would take was time.

And, as immortals of their respective realms, both of them had all the time in the world.

After Kaashifah forced down her eggs on a queasy stomach, she spent the rest of the morning washing dishes and making beds.

'Aqrab still hadn't made an appearance, though she knew he was close. Either in his own realm, in the half-realm, or in the First Realm, he had to remain within five hundred cubits of her body. The tether only stretched thus far, one of the many Laws of the Fourth Lands. It had started as fifteen hundred cubits, but with each of Kaashifah's wishes, it had shortened by five hundred. Reminding her, of course, that if she made that last wish, there was nothing standing between the two of them, no bindings of djinni law to keep her safe.

Around eleven-thirty, while vacuuming the upstairs floors of the lodge in preparation for the guests' arrival, Kaashifah heard Jack and Blaze start up two of the 4-wheelers out back and head down the dirt path to Lake Ebony. She shut off the vacuum cleaner and tucked it away in a closet, biting her lip. 'Aqrab still had not shown himself, and, as his only 'entertainment' within five hundred cubits, the djinni usually could not resist taunting her with his presence. That he refused to appear now left the little hairs along Kaashifah's spine tingling with unease.

Forty-five minutes later, the group of girls—eight in all—arrived on the back of the 4-wheeler cart out back, giggling, asking Blaze questions about the Yentna River Werewolf. Kaashifah reluctantly went down the stairs to meet them.

When Kaashifah got down to the second story, Jack was grinning like an idiot as he carried the girls' luggage up the stairs to the guest bedrooms. The guests themselves were dressed in various states of casual attire, from a brunette in jeans and a half-buttoned flannel shirt reeking of mosquito repellant, to a blonde Nordic-looking woman in tight black leather, showing a good portion of her smooth, trim stomach. A pretty gemmed belt, its golden plates studded with large pieces of what looked like turquoise, topped the ensemble. Blaze sat them at the bar and served them iced tea while they chatted, obviously excited out of their tiny minds.

Seeing that there were no men in the group, Kaashifah stepped up and offered her hand to the blonde delicately. "My name is Kimber," she said softly. "Welcome to the Sleeping Lady." She had learned long ago that it was better to just give people a name they were familiar with than try to get them to pronounce the name of her homeland.

The blonde gave Kaashifah a dubious look down her long nose, and Kaashifah found herself caught a bit off-guard by the agelessness of her face, where she could not say, with certainty, which decade of life the woman was in. Her black leather outfit reminded Kaashifah of something she had seen on TV, a show about hunting vampires, so she guessed the woman was rather young. Possibly just out of her teens.

Yet there was something almost familiar about her steely gray eyes when the blonde woman sniffed and said, "You've got an accent. Where are you from?"

Of course. So many in this country looked at her with distrust, simply for her appearance. Like Kaashifah was going to randomly poison their tea and louse their beds because her skin was darker than theirs.

"Arabia," Kaashifah said, giving another courteous nod. "Though it's been many years."

She thought she saw the blonde's eyes sharpen, but the woman sniffed and flung her impressive, knee-length braid over a shoulder. As thick as it was, Kaashifah wondered if the woman had used hair extensions. "And what's your job here, Kimber?"

"I cook and I clean," Kaashifah said softly. It was an answer that they could hardly argue with. After all, in America, the darker the skin, the easier it was to be ignored as a servant.

Blaze, bless her, seemed at least a bit taken aback by the woman's abruptness. "Kimber got here as an exchange student," the phoenix said, smiling. "Decided to stay once she had her degree."

"Degree in what?" the blonde asked. "Bedmaking?" It was almost a sneer. Faced with such outright disdain, Kaashifah bit her lip and stepped back, deciding to let the lady of the house do the talking. After all, she was as much a guest in this place as the rest of them.

"Public relations," Blaze said. The phoenix's smile had cracked. "Would you like more lemon in your tea?"

"I'm good," the blonde said, oblivious. "So where can we find this werewolf?"

The conversation went on from there, Kaashifah thankfully forgotten. She slipped to the side, listening as they discussed potential 'lairs' and recent 'sightings' as Jack made his last trip in from outside, carrying the last set of luggage over his shoulder.

"You have an amazing place, here," the quiet brunette in the back of the group said to the phoenix, once Jack had returned from depositing their luggage in their rooms and plunked down on a seat at the bar, "Fishing lodge, yes? What made you turn to cryptid tourism?" Which launched Blaze into a pre-packaged spiel about how the Sleeping Lady Lodge was everything she'd ever wanted, come true, and how one nightmarish winter, she and Jack had been forced to defend it against forty mutant wolves.

"And you used *silver bullets.*" The brunette sounded enthralled. "Werewolves, then."

The ageless blonde in leather rolled her eyes and walked over to the bay window, glancing out at the pens of livestock out back. Oddly, it didn't seem as if the woman were rolling her eyes at the idea of *werewolves*, but rather, at the brunette herself. Some corporate power-struggle? Kaashifah idly wondered where Blaze had gotten her latest batch of clients.

"Well," Blaze said, "not according to the Alaska Department of Fish and Game." Which launched the whole group into another long discussion about werewolves, the government, cryptids in general, and the Yentna River Werewolf, who was a 'lonely survivor' of the massacre on the Sleeping Lady's back steps.

Throughout it all, Kaashifah kept her attention on the brunette, finding something strangely off about her seemingly polite nature in the face of the blonde's unabashed arrogance. The woman had an accent of the southern states, though it was tinged with something else. Mexico, perhaps? And, while her voice had the commanding tone of a businesswoman, someone used to getting her way, neither her looks nor her attire set her apart. She had a professional short-cropped haircut, as was common with the lodge's career-oriented clientele, tight blue jeans, hiking boots, and a button-up flannel shirt, the sleeves casually rolled up her arms. She had been holding her temples off and on during the conversation, as if she had a headache, and she had a gaunt look, like someone who wasn't getting enough food or sleep. And sure enough, halfway through the conversation, she popped two small white pills from a tiny prescription bottle and swallowed them down as the phoenix had regaled them of stories of heritage livestock and her ridiculously green thumb.

Eventually, after listening at length to the phoenix's ramblings about near-extinct livestock breeds and the rapidly dwindling genetic diversity of humanity's food supply, the brunette woman put her pill-bottle away and glanced up at Kaashifah with curious, glacial-blue eyes. "I heard you guys had a staff of four. Are we missing somebody? My friend said he was a real big guy. Pro wrestler or something."

Something didn't seem right about the question, and, cautiously, Kaashifah said, "He left on vacation."

"Oh," the brunette said, scratching at her forearm. "Then this is everybody? You guys are all alone out here?"

"This is it," Jack said, grinning proudly. "What you see is what you get, ladies. The Sleeping Lady. Last bastion of civilization out in werewolf territory."

The brunette reached up and fiddled with the sleeve of her shirt. "Good."

Good?

But even as Kaashifah was digesting the strange taste to that, the woman flicked something forward in a practiced gesture, and a tiny dart hit the wereverine in the man's muscular chest. His eyes widened and his mouth fell open in a wet wheeze, then he slid to the floor suddenly, his heavy body hitting the hardwood beneath his stool with a *thump* that shook the lodge, not even sprouting fangs.

Oh no, Kaashifah thought, stumbling backwards, trying to slam up a shield.

"Jack?" the phoenix asked, moving forward, frowning. She obviously hadn't seen the brunette's gesture.

Kaashifah, who had seen it, was nonetheless unable to stop it. Her shield, having gone unused and unpracticed for so long, fizzled in the face of her fear, leaving her staring at the Inquisitors in horror.

Whereas she could have ended it all with a single thought beforehand, now all she could do was turn and run.

She felt a sharp pain in her spine, then her legs collapsed out from underneath her.

"Got the bitch," the blonde woman chuckled.

Kaashifah's vision dimmed, her entire body going numb within a couple of heartbeats.

A couple of steel-toed boots stepped within sight, and the blonde woman in black leather squatted down in front of Kaashifah, a sneer on her face. She grabbed her by the hair and yanked back, so that Kaashifah was staring up into the woman's pretty Nordic face. "Guess what, beastie?" She yanked something out of Kaashifah's back and held it out where she could see. A tiny hypodermic needle, connected to a silver vial. "Basilisk venom'll put even a *wereverine's* lights out."

"I don't think that one's a wereverine," the unassuming brunette in jeans said. "My guess is a wolf, but something is off..." *Spanish*, Kaashifah realized, ridiculously placing the accent as her body failed around her. The woman was a Spaniard.

"Save your *guesses*, Imelda. Once I get her on the rack, I will tell you what she is."

Even as she heard the words, Kaashifah found herself losing the battle with her eyelids, her world blackening, swallowing her from the outside.

Suddenly a flash of light, like the fires of heaven suddenly raining down upon her, and people screamed. The last thing she saw, before she lost consciousness, was the leather-clad woman above her stand up with a cry, eyes wide, scrabbling for something on her gold-and-turquoise belt.

ABOUT THE AUTHOR

My name is Sara King and I'm going to change the world.

No, seriously. I am. And I need your help. My goal is simple. I want to champion, define, and spread character writing throughout the galaxy. (Okay, maybe we can just start with Planet Earth.) I want to take good writing out of the hands of the huge corporations who have had a stranglehold on the publishing industry for so long and reconnect it to the people (you) and what you really want. I want to democratize writing as an art form. Something that's always been controlled by an elite few who have (in my opinion) a different idea of what is 'good writing' than the rest of the world, and have been feeding the sci-fi audience over 50% crap for the last 40 years.

To assist me in my goals to take over the world (crap, did I say that out loud??), please leave a review for this book! It's the first and easiest way for you guys to chip in and assist your friendly neighborhood writer-gal. And believe me, every review helps otherwise unknown books like mine stand up against the likes of the Big Boys on an impersonal site like Amazon.

Also, I have an email! (Totally surprising, I know.) Use it! (Don't you know that fanmail keeps writers going through those dark times when we run out of chocolate???) I love posting letters on Facebook—gives me something fulfilling to do with my time. ;) Shoot me a line! kingnovel@gmail.com

You can also ask to SIGN UP FOR MY MAILING LIST! Seriously, I give away free books, ask people to beta-read scenes and novels, and give updates on all the series I'm currently working on. Stay informed! J

And, for those of you who do the Facebook thing, check me out: http://www.facebook.com/kingfiction (personal) or http://www.facebook.com/sknovel (my author page) or stay up to date on continuous new ZERO publications with The Legend of ZERO fan page: http://www.facebook.com/legendofzero